# Independence

## Cal Mackenzie

ii

For


Samuel, Elizabeth, Iain, and Emmeline

Table of Contents

# PROLOGUE

## STILL RIVER, DELAWARE
## DECEMBER 16, 1823

You could still hear some Boston in his voice though he hadn't been there for half a century. But he was there that night in '73, the night they destroyed the tea, the night impudence became rebellion, the night they sowed those first angry seeds of independence. The old men listened to this story they'd heard him tell so many times, as they would listen to a parent telling of the night they were born.

"It was so cold that December, an' that night seemed about the coldest of 'em all. When we were walkin' to the meetin', we could hear the groanin' and creakin' of the ice movin' in the tide 'long the shore. God, you could hear it half-way up the hill. My feet were frozen from standin' so long on the cold stones of the street near Old South. But torches were blazin' everywhere and thousands of people crushed together and the speakers grew louder and louder: Josiah Quincy and James Otis and Mr. Hancock--then Sam Adams, of course. 'Fore long, the passions of that night started to warm us all. I guess they still do."

The old Captain paused and gazed slowly around the room, his hands shaking slightly as they gripped the edge of the scarred oak table. The war veterans sat in a small circle in the favored place near the fire because they were old, because they were heroes. A circle of patriots, one of the young women called them. Behind them in uneven rows sat their children and grandchildren. Balfour Tavern had been the sight of most of Still River's important gatherings over the decades: marriages, elections, New Year feasts. Some of the men in front could even recall the meetings here when Henry Houghton would describe the doings of the Continental Congress or urge them to plan for invasion by the King's army. Most of them had their last drink here before they went off to join the "Blue Hen's chickens," the Delaware brigade with Washington's Continentals.

That was so long ago, and only a few survived from those days, halting in gait, hearing little, their memories still alive with sharp images of that distant time. Most of them stayed on their farms now and rarely saw each other. But this night was special, a night of resurrection, a night to celebrate that other night a half century earlier that changed the world.

"We respected the others," the Captain continued, "but Sam Adams was the one who always brought us to our feet. Nobody could rile a crowd like Sam Adams. The way he talked was so convincin', always seemed so…so true. He was just so angry at 'em that you felt guilty if you weren't just as angry."

He shifted slowly in the hard chair and took a small sip of the tea they were all drinking on this night. He never much liked tea, but he understood the sentiment and drank without complaint. As his memories gathered, he caught the eye of his son Jonathan sitting by the side wall. Jonathan would be fifty in a few years. He'd been an American all his life, never an Englishman. Could he possibly know what was going through the minds and hearts of the stooped old men in front?

"The gov'nor was s'posed to give us his answer that day: would he let 'em sail away with their cargo unloaded or would his agents seize their tea at the dock. Then word came that Hutchinson had gone off to his country home in Milton and no decision was comin' that night. Just like always, he'd paid us no heed—'spit in our eye,' Mr. Otis said. How we hated that man Hutchinson. People were shakin' their heads in disgust and bangin' the bottoms of their torches on the street. The racket kept growin' louder and louder. But then Sam Adams, he just took control. Nobody could do that like him.

"Old Sam stood at the front of the crowd with his hands at his side, lookin' straight ahead. I was outside, but the doors and windows were open and I could see him over the heads of the people in front. He just waited—it was prob'ly only a minute or so, but it seemed an eternity. Finally the shoutin' and the bangin' stopped, hushed right down, and everyone looked at him. Dead silence. Then the fury came into his face and his arms started to pump and he spoke with such fierce resolve that his words seemed to echo off every buildin' in Boston. 'Fellow countrymen,' he said–God, I remember it so clearly–'we cannot afford to give a single inch! If we retreat now, everything we have done becomes useless! If Hutchinson will not send tea back to England, perhaps we can brew a pot of it especially for him!'

"At first, I was caught up by him callin' us 'countrymen.' Not townsmen, not fellow patriots, but countrymen. What country, I wondered, is that? But then I realized he was givin' the signal. Before his words even ended, men were smilin', biddin' their kin goodnight, and quietly slidin' away from the meeting. Someone in the crowd shouted, 'Boston Harbor, a teapot tonight!' and we were off.

"I intended to join 'em, though no one had invited me. Nobody had more reason than me to be there, and nothin' would keep me ashore that night."

"Who was leading this?" a young boy asked from the back of the Tavern.

The Captain stopped and looked up, squinting for a second to focus on the questioner. "Hard to say," he responded. "You see we weren't an army or a militia or anythin' like that. There were some who were close to the Sons of Liberty; they seemed to be the most organized. Then there was a bunch of Masons, a couple dozen. They had their meetin's at the Green Dragon Tavern on Ann Street, near the wharf. One of them was a militia captain and he brought a group of them along.

"I was with some other apprentices. We were too young to be part of any of the political plannin', but most of us worked for men who were involved. We thought of ourselves as apprentice patriots just as we were apprentice gunsmiths and carpenters. We talked all the time about what was goin' on and swore ourselves to secrecy after every conversation. It was all very excitin' to us boys.

"We knew the plans for that night, and we'd collected tomahawks and pieced together what we thought a Mohawk or a Negro would wear. We left the meetin' at Old South and ran over to the Faulkner place on Milk Street and blackened our faces with coal dust from the blacksmith shed. They weren't very good disguises really, but we were all so agitated no one paid much attention to that."

The circle of old men in front listened intently now, some leaning far forward and cupping an ear to hear all the words. Familiar emotions began to rise as the story unfolded. They all knew that while the younger people could listen to the Captain describe what it looked like and what it sounded like that night, they could never know, as the old men did, what it felt like.

"When we got to Griffin's Wharf there were about a hundred of us, maybe more. Most of the apprentices followed a big man name of Pitt, who seemed to know what he was doing. I didn't recognize any of the other leaders. Remember it was dark and everyone was in disguise and we didn't want anyone to know who was there. Just patriots that's all. No names.

"I hadn't realized how scared I was goin' to be. There were British warships all around in the harbor, and we even thought the crews on the tea ships might be armed. There were three of 'em at Griffin's: the Dartmouth was the biggest and the closest in. Further down the wharf were the Beaver and the Eleanor. Pitt led us down to the Beaver and we were surprised at how quiet it was on the ships and amazed that the plank was down. Pitt walked right aboard and found only one man on watch. He seemed more frightened than we were.

"Pitt told him we'd come to get the tea. The watch wasn't a bit surprised at this and seemed happy to lead us down into the hold, even holdin' the hatch as we climbed below. None of the ships' crews resisted us at all. In fact, some of 'em seemed to be on our side. Not many friends of the King in the foc'sle of a ship.

"By the time we got to the tea, the excitement was like a ragin' fever, spreadin' through us and goin' round and round. We were shoutin' and singin' and swearin' oaths at Thomas Hutchinson and North and Dartmouth, even a few at the King. We pushed those heavy pine chests up onto the deck, steadied them on the rail, and then slashed at 'em with our tomahawks. We whooped like Indians when they opened and the tea plopped into the harbor.

"'Fore long, the water 'round those ships was one fierce brew: Darjeelin' and Canton mixed with Boston ice and the sweat of patriots. God, there were so many chests, hundreds of 'em, and it took hours to get them all on deck and opened and then emptied into the water. But we got every last one."

The boy at the back of the Tavern followed the story closely and spoke up again, "And then did you all march back to the meeting place to celebrate?"

The Captain smiled, reminded again how little the events he'd lived resembled the stories people told about them. "Sorry, son," he said, smiling faintly. "I know the legend says we were all singin' and paradin' through the streets in triumph, but t'wasn't like that at all. We'd just dumped £10,000 worth of tea into Boston Harbor. That may have been the biggest crime ever committed in Boston. And we'd directly defied Thomas Hutchinson, the colonial governor. And remember this: Boston was full of the King's soldiers, many of 'em quartered in the very houses where we lived.

"We may have been proud of what we did that night, but no one was braggin' and no one was paradin'. We were scared, and we had good reason to be. We got off those three ships and we ran. I stopped by the water when I got away from the wharf and washed all the soot off my face. I'd taken a blanket from the ship and I wrapped it around me so people wouldn't see my Indian clothes. And all of a sudden I was very cold. The torches were all burnt out, the streets were dark, and our feelin's were turnin' to fear and dread."

Fear and dread. The Captain leaned back in the chair, his face drained of all color, his eyes now unfocused. Images crowded his mind, faster than he could sort them out: the terrifying crimson waves advancing up Breed's Hill...the long, frustrating months in garrison with General Washington...a young Virginian firing with deadly aim from a treetop near Saratoga...the awful act of vengeance in a Manhattan warehouse...lying among the crying and broken bodies on a church floor near Monmouth Court House...the morning sun catching in the dark curls of the beautiful young woman in a Delaware dooryard...his aching failure at Yorktown.

History, they called it. But it was not history to him, nothing so formal and fancy as that. It was his life. Pride, courage, fear, failure, loss, love, survival—all the pieces fitting together now, a mosaic, harmony.

But the logic of it, the glory, were only there in hindsight. It made sense now when he looked back, when he described it to these children and grandchildren of his neighbors. But when he was young and the world was aflame and the horizon always seemed too close, he knew no such certainty. He only knew that he'd made choices, taken risks, ridden the furious rapids rushing through those days when his country was coming alive. He'd been born a poor man, a motherless child, subject of a tyrant. And he'd fought back. What else could he do? What else, after all, could any man do?

# Chapter 1

## Delaware
## August 1774

Down the rutted path from the only home either had known, father and son set off on the long walk to Philadelphia. They forded Still River across the narrow bend where it turned toward Delaware Bay, ascended through the last remaining copse of white oak on the far side, and crossed the largest of the cleared fields to the shire road that headed north. It was barely daylight, but already the damp air and the steady dull hum of the crickets warned of another burning, late-summer day.

Henry Houghton had never been to Philadelphia or anywhere more than a few miles to the north of home. He'd sailed to Norfolk once, in 1768, to purchase Quiet Jack and Sweetie, the two slaves who helped manage the big farm at Still River Bend. And after spring planting this year, he'd taken a small cat boat to Annapolis. That was for the meeting of middle colony leaders angry at Parliament's brutal retaliation for the Tea Party in Boston last December. Save for those two journeys, Henry had spent all of his 53 years within a few miles of the land on which his great-grandfather settled after arriving in Delaware from the southeast of England in 1683.

It was good land, and each generation of Henry's forebears had made it better. When Henry's father died in 1752, more than 400 acres of still-virgin forest stood above the 75 acres that had been cleared and cultivated. The woods produced timber for shipbuilding and bark for the tannery at Weeping Falls. And the good soil in the bottom land along the river now yielded reliable crops of grain and, more recently, of flax.

In the Delaware counties of Pennsylvania, the men of the Houghton family had grown to some prominence for their skill as cultivators of the land and their reputation as sensible traders. In a land where currency was always scarce, timber and grain were often more valuable than specie or scrip. And the Houghtons owned ample amounts of both.

As they stepped smartly along the sun-baked road, Henry and Jonathan talked little. The simple beauty of the morning and the places they passed inspired a silence that both respected. Conversation came in short bursts only when they stopped to drink or rest in the shade. In early afternoon, as they sat on a flat rock under a towering beech tree, Jonathan asked about Henry's intentions for the rest of the day.

"We seem to be making a good pace, in spite of the heat," the father replied with the thoughtful optimism that his son knew well. "Perhaps we can get to Smyrna by sundown. That's another 15 miles, but the land lays level and there's water along the way. I think it a fair goal for a pair of fine walking men like ourselves."

"What'll we find there?" Jonathan asked, laying back on the rock, his eyes closed.

"A pleasant tavern, I'm told. Mason's Ordinary. Adequate meals this time of year and clean beds." Henry answered.

"You think we'll encounter any other delegates making this journey?" The question suggested how little Jonathan knew about the trip or its purpose. He had agreed to join his father just two days earlier and hadn't had much time to think about any of it.

"Not very likely," the father responded. "Most are coming south. Those heading north will probably travel by boat. Ones coming by land are wealthier than we. They'll probably travel in their own coaches and stay in private homes. In all likelihood, we're the only ones walking. Not much choice in that, I'm afraid. Can't spare any horses on the farm this time of year."

"I guess we should be glad then that the meetings are in Philadelphia, and not New York or Boston." Jonathan laughed at his own little joke, but then began to think further about what lay ahead. "Will all the colonies send delegates?" he asked.

Henry shrugged and took another sip of water from the glass jar he carried in his pack. "No one knows. Best we can hope for is that most of them do. If anything important happens at this Congress, the others won't want to be left out. Their delegates'll come later. If nothing important happens…well, I suppose the colonies that sent no delegates will congratulate themselves on their foresight."

Jonathan looked satisfied, but Henry continued. "It's a peculiar prospect," he said turning slowly to look closely at his son. "A meeting of uncertain size for uncertain purpose in uncertain times. We barely know the other delegates from our own colonies, let alone those from others.

Word is some pretty important men will be there. Washington, from Virginia, the soldier from the frontier war. And Sam Adams, that radical firebrand from Massachusetts Bay. And Patrick Henry—he should be there, too. But how we'll all get along, and what we'll do—the Lord only knows."

Jonathan closed his eyes and swished away a fly. He tried to picture an assembly of great men, no simple task for a young man of twenty-one who'd never in his life been to a meeting of any kind. Would the delegates talk differently than men he'd known at home? Would they be brilliant minds making elegant speeches and quoting from the wise men of the ages? Would they be able to plot a course through all the dangers and confusions of these vexing times? That, of course, was the purpose of this Congress, but his father at least was uncertain that even the best men in the colonies could accomplish it.

Eager as he was to see these men and listen to their speeches, the thought of it also filled Jonathan with self-doubt. Perhaps he wouldn't be able to understand their discussions or discern their motives. These were men of the world, most of them prosperous, educated and well-traveled. He was a mere farmer, after all, and barely an adult.

Jonathan had followed Nathaniel, his older brother, to the college at Princeton. No Houghton had ever gone to a college before them, but Henry had dreams for his sons and he thought a formal education would prepare them for roles of leadership, for public lives.

Nathaniel loved the college and formed close bonds with professors and fellow students. But not Jonathan. He was bored by all the books and repelled by the pretensions of the students, many of them from the richest families in the middle colonies. He longed for the farm at Still River Bend, and stayed only one term in Princeton.

If nothing else, the time at college had convinced Jonathan that a farmer's life was what he sought. And since Nathaniel showed no interest at all in agriculture or any other practical skill, Jonathan looked forward to the time in the future when he would become the master of the place as four generations of Houghtons had before him.

But the decision to leave college haunted him at times like this, for it made him unsure of his own capacity for understanding and discussing complicated issues. He admired great men who faced hard challenges with sharp intelligence. But he doubted that he'd ever be one of them. He yearned to observe the assembly at Philadelphia, but hoped it wouldn't deplete his limited stock of self-confidence. He intended to stay on the periphery and out of discussions as much as possible, helping his father when needed but otherwise simply watching.

"Shall we move on?" Henry asked, cutting sharply through Jonathan's distant thoughts.

"Best we do," the son replied, rising slowly to his feet and fitting his pack to his shoulder. The sun had just passed its zenith and hard miles lay ahead.

Mason's Ordinary perched on a small knoll at the end of the only real road in Smyrna. Save for the ell on the south side and the small stable in back, it was not unlike the cluster of other small dwellings that composed this village. A sign nailed to the gate announced "Lodgings and Repast."

The father and son had made better time than anticipated, and some daylight remained when they passed through the gate and walked up to the only visible door on the north end of the building. The room they entered had but one small window through which only the dimmest light entered. After a long day in the sun, the darkness was powerful and gave them pause. Before they could clearly focus, a woman's voice greeted them, "Evenin'," she said. "Welcome to Mason's."

Henry said hello and inquired about lodging for the night.

"We've got six others tonight because the coach had to lay over. But there's four beds, so we're happy to have you. Others are all here, so just fit in where you can. Sleepin' room's in the back, off'n the tavern."

The room had come into clearer view as Henry's eyes adjusted to the faint light. He could see the woman's finger as she pointed over her shoulder to the left. "Thank you, ma'am," he said. "What about the possibility of some supper?"

The woman finished making a note in the large ledger before her and looked up. "Both of you eatin'?" she asked.

"We'd like to, yes," Henry replied.

"Then you come on down to the tavern in about an hour and I'll have a meal for them what's here. Garden's hung heavy this time of year, so you can fill yer plate."

Henry handed the woman two shillings, hoisted his pack, and led Jonathan through the small tavern into a modest room with four beds of different sizes. Men were asleep in two of the beds and packs on the floor by the other two indicated that the Houghtons would be sharing a bed with strangers, not each other.

9

After a dinner as ample and fresh as promised, Henry and Jonathan took seats at the end of the large rough table in the center of the tavern. Most of the other overnight customers seemed to be there, their identities taking shape as the cider was opened and the conversation unfolded. To Jonathan's left was a tall, smooth-featured man with a pleasant laugh. He said he was a lawyer, riding to Wilmington to meet with a banker about a client's confused estate.

Another man at the opposite end of the table said his name was Trevor and that he was a "cooper without a coop." His wife had died of the ague earlier in the year and he'd decided to head west into the Pennsylvania hills to make a new life for himself. His brother had preceded him on this westward trek a year earlier and his glowing reports had convinced Trevor to follow along.

After the guests finished introducing themselves to each other and exchanging the usual comments about the heat and dust, the lawyer asked Henry what had brought a farmer to Mason's Ordinary on this night.

"I'm on my way to Philadelphia," Henry responded.

"For what purpose, if I may inquire?" asked the lawyer.

Henry swallowed some cider and sat back to address all of those at the table. "There's a meeting to take place there of representatives from all of the colonies, a Congress they're calling it, a Continental Congress. The events in Boston and the reaction from London have a lot of people stirred up. Some of them thought we should all get together to talk about our mutual interests."

"Who's idea was this?" asked the cooper, looking surprised. "I've not heard of this."

"Well, the history of it is something like this. About two years ago, Sam Adams in Boston started a thing he called a committee of correspondence. At first, its only purpose was to allow the Boston leaders to tell the rest of the colonies the truth about what was actually happening there, not just what the governors or the loyalist newspapers were saying. Before long all the colonies had these committees. They became a way for us to write to each other about a lot of things. Turns out that most of the colonies were worried about the same laws that got folks so angry in Boston. Last spring, some of the correspondents suggested we have a real meeting to talk things over. So that's what's happening next month in Philadelphia."

"What takes you there?" asked the lawyer

"I'm one of the delegates from Delaware," Henry replied. "My son, Jonathan, is traveling with me and will serve as my secretary." He turned and nodded proudly toward Jonathan as he spoke.

A look of confusion came to the lawyer's face. "But Delaware isn't a colony," he said quickly.

"Not yet," said Henry, looking directly at the lawyer now. "But it will be soon, and we've functioned independent of Pennsylvania with our own legislature for some time. And we've had our own committee of correspondence from the start of all this."

A squat, broad-shouldered man with deep-set eyes and a beard flecked with gray had listened intently to all this, but said nothing. Now he spoke: "Sounds like more trouble-making to me. Pray, sir, why can't we just be good Englishmen and obey the law?"

"I agree. We should be good Englishmen and we must obey the law," said Henry, addressing the bearded man. "But some of our brethren in the other colonies, and even a few in our own, think that it's those in London who are failing in their duty to be good Englishmen. Good Englishmen don't place confiscatory taxes on their fellow citizens, they say. Good Englishmen don't massacre their own countrymen, and certainly don't use brute force to turn private homes into barracks for soldiers. We hope in Philadelphia to find a way to communicate those concerns. We want His Majesty and his Parliament to know that colonials expect to be treated with the same dignity and fairness afforded his subjects in London or Sheffield or Coventry. We may live across a broad sea, but we too are Englishmen. And, as such, we too have rights."

Jonathan watched Henry closely. He'd never seen the older man so fully engaged in public discussion, and he felt pride in his father's eloquence.

But the bearded questioner persisted, more belligerent now. "But, sir, how can we be sure that the radical elements, especially those from Boston who've already gone well beyond being law-abiding citizens, won't commandeer this assembly in Philadelphia and turn it to their own purposes? Isn't this just what they seek: a wider forum for their assaults on our King, a larger band of rogues to join them in demeaning his royal honor? A large assembly like this can make a loud noise, one heard all the way to Westminster. I fear the reaction that will cause. And the fleets that will come to unload even more soldiers to quell these radical passions."

The lawyer stood up and stretched to his full height. He walked to the small table in the corner and fetched the cider jug, filling his own mug and holding it up to see if others needed a refill. Several said "Aye," so he carried the jug to the larger table and set it down. Then he spoke to the bearded man. "Sir, I don't share your fears. This rift with the mother country has been growing for years. Its momentum can't easily be reversed. Too many people in America now think of King and Parliament as oppressors. Too many people in London have come to regard us here as impudent law-breakers. There's no turning back now. The battle for America is joined, sir. The only question is who will control the outcome."

The bearded man started to speak, but the cooper's bellowing voice cut him off. "I'm glad I'm headin' west," he said. "When the British cannons start their firin', I'll be out of range. This is poppycock. Some rich businessmen in Boston feel their wallets pinched by taxes levied by some other rich men in London. They want to turn it into a question of rights and morality. What truck do most of us have with any of this? Not much, I say.

"Let John Hancock go to the poorhouse for all I care. He never bought any barrels of me. When the British dragoons start shootin', it won't be at old John Hancock, nor at Adams nor any of the other silken men at Philadelphia. It'll be at poor tradesmen like me. We're the ones that get killed in all the wars, while the troublemakers drink their port and speak of their bloody rights.

"Liberty is what a man does between sun-up and sundown. Nothin' more'n that. If the world seems too small in one place, move west. That's my answer to all this political talk."

Henry prepared to make a plea for open-mindedness. Let the assembly in Philadelphia try to make sense of these conflicting views, he intended to say. But the woman entered the room from the door to the left and her entry stopped the conversation. Gentlemen did not usually discuss politics in the presence of women, even inn-keepers. She announced that it was getting late, that she wished to retire for the night and asked that the lodgers also turn in, so she could extinguish the candles and close the tavern.

The men drained the last of the cider from their mugs, and headed in a line for the sleeping room to the rear. Jonathan pulled off his boots and climbed into bed beside the bearded man. The narrow width of the bed and the broad gauge of the man, the warmth of the night, and the lingering passion of the conversation countered his fatigue from the day's long walk.

So he lay there quietly in the damp heat, replaying the evening's arguments, trying to imagine Philadelphia and the Continental Congress, and wondering about the new world he—and America—were about to enter.

# Chapter 2

## Philadelphia
## August-September 1774

Two more long days on the road brought Henry and Jonathan within view of Philadelphia. For Jonathan, it had been a journey of surprises. He had always felt, in the vague way that comes with little thought or information, that the quiet and isolation of Still River Bend was unique, that over the horizon there was more bustle and noise, more commerce, more people intermingling more often. But the road from Still River to Philadelphia was little traveled and their lonely days had been broken only by the occasional village or passing traveler.

On the last night they had found no tavern and had slept in the barn of accommodating farmers. Except for the rare good meal and the entertainment of evening conversation, the taverns were not much better lodging than the barn. Jonathan quickly found that sharing a bed with strangers, especially in the heat of late summer, had made him appreciate the pleasures of sleeping on a bed of soft hay in an empty stall.

But it was the broad and tender beauty of the countryside that most surprised Jonathan. Summer had begun to take its toll, and most of the flowering trees and plants no longer bloomed. But apples were ripening in the orchards they passed, and silk-topped ears pulled heavily on cornstalks in the few places where farmers had cleared the land.

Everywhere there were forests, many with trees so tall and full that no light reached the ground and there was no underbrush between the trunks. A heavy thunderstorm one afternoon soaked the ground and released the peaty fragrance of centuries of decayed leaves into the air. Some of these trees had been here longer than any Houghton, longer than any white man. Jonathan was reminded of the labor his own ancestors must have spent in clearing the land at Still River Bend.

As they neared Philadelphia, the traffic along the road increased. Wagons loaded with barrels passed them heading south and west. They passed low carts pulled by teams of oxen heading north. Most of the carts were laden with fruit and vegetables for the Philadelphia market. One carried four fat pigs, and several trailed milking cows with bursting udders. Jonathan had never seen such activity and his curiosity peaked as they entered the city and started down Arch Street.

Here the eye filled with all manner of sights, and father and son ended all conversation to attend to the panorama that lay before them. Avenues of symmetrical stone connected alleys and side streets by the score. In the distance, the spires of the State House and of Christ Church pulled their gaze into the clouds while a half dozen lesser spires competed for attention. A light breeze followed them from the south, picking up some of the scent of the river as it freshened. And everywhere were men and women moving quickly, intent on some singular purpose that pushed them steadily forward.

At every village they'd passed along the road north, their appearance seemed an event. Villagers interrupted their labors to look at, and occasionally to speak to, the two men passing through. But Philadelphia was indifferent to their presence. Men and women were absorbed in their labors, and strangers were commonplace. For the first time in his life, Jonathan felt invisible. It was the first of many unfamiliar sensations he would experience in this strange new place.

Henry and the other two Delaware delegates had determined that it would be prudent to stay at the same boarding house to facilitate private conversations they might need to have. They'd been warned that privacy was a scarce commodity in this busy place, so they agreed to get rooms together at the Widow Almy Tavern on Second Street. The arrangements had been made by post in the spring.

Henry stopped at a stable on the corner of Arch and 8th Street and interrupted a small, roughly dressed liveryman from his chores to ask for directions to the Widow Almy. The man straightened, leaned on his shovel, and looked quizzically at Henry. He responded, but in strange words that neither Henry nor Jonathan understood. Henry repeated the question and received the same indecipherable response. The man then pointed toward a door to the side of the stable and motioned for Henry to go to the door. He and Jonathan did so, and there found an older man sitting in a chair, mending a harness. Henry repeated his request for help. The man continued to maneuver the heavy needle, but said, "Don't mind the mick. Irish 'e is, but he's just got 'ere and only speaks a tongue called Gay Lick. Not gonna' be good for much but sweepin' stables 'til he learns

15

to talk. Place you want is down past the meetin' house, then go one more street and turn this way," he said, pointing to the left. "It's up a ways from there, but you'll see the sign with the widder's fat face right on it."

Henry thanked the man for his help, bid him good day, and led Jonathan back to the street. As instructed, they walked east.

The Widow Almy Tavern was squeezed between two larger structures, one a formerly elegant private home, now a mercantile office, the other a dry goods store with a long low porch in front and a half dozen horses loosely controlled by a barefoot boy in front. The street was packed hard and reverberated loudly to the rhythm of every passing wagon, ox cart, and hoof beat. It seemed like the noisiest place Jonathan had ever been. And the smell of the street began to fill their senses. Rotting garbage from the alley behind the inn, manure and urine from the horses, smoke from the cooking fires in many of the buildings--a commingling of odors that yielded no pleasure.

Their accommodations at the Widow Almy, though far from fancy were a vast improvement over what they'd encountered on the road. Henry and Jonathan had separate rooms on the second floor in back, away from the sounds of the street. Each was furnished with a clean bed, a small oak wardrobe, and a white chamber pot. Henry's room was slightly larger and had a table and chair in the corner with a brass candlestick. The curtains on the windows were too thin to block much light. But they faced north so there wasn't much light in any case, and the curtains would serve to keep the swarms of flies at bay—no small blessing in late summer. It was August 30, 1774, and two tired travelers lay down to nap in this bare abode that would be their home and refuge for the uncertain weeks that loomed before them.

Henry couldn't sleep, not with so many strands of thought weaving through his mind. How can I, so full of doubts and contradictory opinions, he wondered, contribute anything to the work of this assembly? How will the farm fare in my absence, the first time in my life I've been gone for the harvest? How will Patience and Savannah manage with all the men in the family so far away?

Men in the family. His thoughts turned to Nathaniel, his first-born son, now 26 and so resistant to life's plan. Henry had been his own father's first-born and was never permitted to doubt his lot in life: to inherit the farm and continue to build it as his father and grandfather had done before him. But Nathaniel never found comfort in that tradition. At his mother's insistence, he'd been sent to the college at Princeton in New Jersey for a

16

"fitting education." The boy was happy there, happier than he'd ever been in his life, taking special pleasure in the company of those students and teachers who loved the fine arts, as Nathaniel called them.

At Princeton, Nathaniel had taken a tutor in painting and begun to learn how to make images burst to life on a canvas. This nurtured a hunger in him and he longed to see the great works of art about which he could only hear or read at Princeton. But none of those was in America and Nathaniel, sadly in his view, was. He came home from college and spent a year working the farm with his father, younger brother, and Quiet Jack. To his credit, he'd worked hard, done his share. But his heart was never in it, and the prospect of one day taking full responsibility for managing these many acres filled him with an unyielding, but unspoken, dread.

Patience, always especially sensitive to her first-born, recognized this tension in him. They were kindred souls, and she'd always admired his affection for literature and art because they were her passions as well. She was deeply touched by the painting Nathaniel had given her when he returned from college and she encouraged him to keep painting, even convincing Henry that he should be allowed to use one of the outbuildings as a studio. Of course, there were few proper materials for a painter in Still River; but Nathaniel scavenged with great skill and came up with a few rough brushes and some oils and dyes from which he could make paints of a sort. Canvases were nowhere to be found, so he made do with smoothed boards as his principal medium.

After a year on the farm, destiny struck. Nathaniel was invited to join Henry's younger brother on one of the Edward 's regular trips to England. Edward had returned from his army service in the French and Indian Wars and joined with several other former soldiers to start a shipyard on the coast at Bogan's Beach, near the mouth of the Still River on Delaware Bay. The local timber, some of it from the farm at Still River Bend, made sturdy ships and Edward's business boomed. English merchants came to admire both the strength and design of his vessels and would buy them sight unseen. Edward often traveled to England with the delivery to finalize the sale. But these were lonely voyages and his invitation to Nathaniel stemmed as much from Edward's own desire for company as from any beneficence to his nephew.

Nathaniel was eager to go, but Henry was not eager for him to go. The farm was a challenge with all hands present, and with Nathaniel gone more work would fall to Henry, to Jonathan who was barely seventeen, and to Quiet Jack. A hired man would be essential, and expensive, if Nathaniel were to make this trip.

But Patience thought it a grand idea, and over many family dinners and a few evenings of convincing connubial conversation, she elicited Henry's consent. Her most persuasive argument was that times were changing. America was maturing. It was no longer a country of mere subsistence where everyone lived a lifelong indenture to their land and their family. Minds had to be set free if America was now to take a place among the civilized societies. That argument had worked when she persuaded Henry to permit Nathaniel to go off to college, and she hoped it would again.

Patience knew her husband well. Much as Henry loved the farm at Still River Bend and treasured the legacy of his forbears on that land, he also wanted his children to have freedoms and pleasures that he could not. Henry and Nathaniel were cut from different cloth, and they were sometimes at odds. Henry had dreams for his son, but they were not dreams that Nathaniel dreamt for himself.

Eventually Patience had her way in this because she knew how to help Henry do what his best instincts told him he should do for his children. And in late October 1772, after the harvest was in, Nathaniel Houghton sailed with his uncle Edward for Portsmouth, England to deliver the latest fine ship to come off the ways at Houghton, James, and Miller Shipyards at Bogan's Beach.

He returned a year later, but the pea had been set loose from the pod, and even Nathaniel's potent sense of duty could not overcome his longing to return to England. He felt alive in London as he never had in America, at least not in Still River. To England's ports splendid ships brought goods from all over the world. The finest brushes and paints and canvases were easily acquired. And centuries of accumulating wealth had inspired great appreciation for artists and their work. Henry could understand Nathaniel's pleasure in those things, but he had never understood the comfort that Nathaniel seemed to feel among men who had never split a log or planted a seed or drawn a scythe. Life in London seemed so distant from life in America, so deficient in simple virtue, and it troubled Henry when he contemplated the pleasure his eldest son had found there.

Around Easter in 1774, a letter arrived from a painter whose acquaintance Nathaniel had made in London, a man named Carlisle. It was an invitation to the young man to return to London to serve as

Carlisle's assistant in managing his growing business as a painter of portraits. More importantly to Nathaniel, he would be Carlisle's student and have opportunities to hone his own talent under the gently critical eye of one of Europe's best painters. And there would be a stipend on which he could live.

Henry again made his best argument about the needs of the farm and the importance of Nathaniel having a set of practical skills to ensure his ability to make a living. To these he added a strong expression of concern about the brewing political tensions between England and its American colonies and the danger they might pose for an American in London. Henry worried, too, that Nathaniel's disinterest in politics would drive a further wedge between them. Henry hated to have a cherished son so far away from home, but now he feared as well that they might be on opposite sides, not merely of an ocean, but of the most important political issue of their time. If the colonies went their own way, the father worried, would his son stay behind?

But no amount of persuasion or concern was going to work, not this time. Nathaniel was more sure of himself now than he had been two years earlier, and Patience was as loyal an ally. Henry finally deferred to a fate he could not control. He cursed that fate, but silently and with a parent's understanding that this would probably not be the last time his children would deviate from his plan for their lives.

Henry and Jonathan had walked through most of Philadelphia in the days since their arrival. The damp heat of late summer made it too uncomfortable to spend much time indoors and both were intensely curious about this city--the largest in the colonies--so unlike any place either of them had ever been.

Located at the junction of two gentle rivers and a short sail from America's great bay, the mid-point between colonies to the north and south, Philadelphia was a natural center of colonial life. The Quakers who settled there first were hard-working people and hard-driving merchants, and they were quick to reap the advantages of their geographical blessings. Old colonial towns were growing into bustling cities all along the Atlantic seacoast of America, but none could match Philadelphia in scale or activity. To new arrivals from the countryside, it seemed that movement and noise never ceased. The streets swarmed with commerce, overwhelming the narrow sidewalks on each side. Small crowds gathered easily, to play a game, listen to a bellowing salesman, or help to move a lame or dead horse. The city of Philadelphia, in the throes of its daily routines, was more entertainment than Henry or Jonathan had ever before enjoyed.

In the evenings, they took their meals at the Widow Almy or at the Indian King near the corner of 3$^{rd}$ and Market Streets. Other delegates had begun to arrive and these evenings were often spent now in awkward rituals of meeting and sizing up these strangers from north and south. These were some of the most brilliant and successful, the most eloquent and passionate men in these colonies, but here together for the first time the dominant mood was uncertainty. They were strangers to each other and amateurs all at the task, whatever it might be, that lay before them.

Jonathan was especially keen to meet the few whose names were familiar to him. Sam Adams was the Boston rebel best known to those in the southern and middle colonies. Even those who thought him a dangerous radical admired his courage in standing up to the cruel whims of a distant Parliament. At critical moments over the past half decade, it was Sam Adams who seemed to find the words that captured American disgust and anger with the royal oppressions that Adams described so vividly.

Then there was Washington, about whom Jonathan first heard as a boy. Uncle Edward had told Jonathan many stories about his service with George Washington in the French and Indian Wars. Washington had been a young man then, barely 23, when he became a colonel at the head of a regiment. He'd made plenty of mistakes, and Edward recounted them all in bloody detail. He'd been at Pittsburgh where Washington's indecisiveness had cost too many of his soldiers' lives. But Washington was a relentless warrior, and he suffered his own failings more serenely than most men. Over their time with him, the troops in his command had come to respect his judgment and his skill as a strategist.

On September 4$^{th}$, the night before the assembly was to convene, Henry and Jonathan walked along Market Street to the Indian King for their evening meal. They had come to realize in previous nights that this was the main gathering place of the delegates and each night the new arrivals were greeted here. To eat elsewhere was to miss the best show in town.

The last gleams of sunlight fell over the cobbler's shop across the street as they climbed the three steps to the oak-paneled door of the Indian King. Like most Philadelphia taverns, this one was cramped and dimly lit. The ceiling was so low that men of more than normal height had to stoop to get under the heavy beams. There were no windows, save the blackened one in front, and the brass lanterns on the walls filled the place with more shadows than light. Three small tables in the center of the room were the focus of activity . One was large and round; the dark stains and the knife marks left by a generation of whittlers showed its age. Two smaller square tables stood at the center of each of the side walls. There were mismatched chairs around the center table and benches beside the others. A low door to the rear led to the place from which food and drink emerged.

The proprietor here, Keppler, was a quiet man, said to be Dutch but that was unproven. He stayed on the fringes of the gathering, responding to gesturing and the banging of tankards on table indicating an emptiness that needed correction. The food was plain but hearty, nothing to upset the palates of men drawn from such distant cultures and cuisines.

On this night, Jonathan and Henry found seats at the center table next to a thin, balding young man. He wore the finely-cut clothes Jonathan had become accustomed to seeing at the Indian King, and he possessed the assurance of manor that seemed almost a commonplace among the diners there. They'd noticed the man's arrival two days earlier, but had yet to make his acquaintance. As they prepared to sit, Henry leaned across the table, extended his hand and said, "Henry Houghton from Delaware. Who be you, sir?"

The man looked up slowly from his plate, wiped his mouth with a silk handkerchief drawn adeptly from his pocket, and met Henry's hand. "I'm John Jay from New York," he said. "May I say, sir, that it's a pleasure to make your acquaintance."

Henry tilted his head toward Jonathan and added, "This is my son Jonathan Houghton. He's my fellow traveler and will be my secretary, should I have need for one, during this meeting."

"Let us hope," said Jay, "that words are spoken here that this lad'll find worthy of writing down." Jay was not much older than Jonathan and it seemed odd for him to be using the term "lad."

But Jonathan stepped around the table to greet Jay and said, "That, sir, is a hope we all share." The rather startled look on Jay's face caused Jonathan to wonder if his entry into the conversation might not have been presumptuous for someone so young and unofficial.

Henry addressed Jay: "Is your full delegation here, sir?"

"It is," Jay replied, "There are nine of us. Most are staying in private homes and we came separately, so we've not seen each other since our departure from New York. But I'm assured by our messenger that all are present."

At the square table behind them, a voice bellowed, "Adams, join us here." A squat man of earnest countenance came through the front door lit from the right by the sun's last rays. He had a soft mouth crowned by a large nose and a prominent double chin over the white stock that showed through the gap at the top of his brown waistcoat. But it was the man's eyes that compelled the observer's attention: dark dancing eyes, wide and alert, that seemed to speak as they moved. The man surveyed the room, adjusted to the scarce light, then ambled toward the voice that had called out to him. He quickly found a seat and Keppler brought him a dram of the rum he had been drinking in the past three evenings here.

Jay leaned toward Henry. "That's Sam Adams," he said in a low voice. "You watch. The conversation'll revolve around him from now on."

And so it did. Adams was a provocateur. He answered questions with questions, forged every discussion into a debate, led arguments along the precipice of slippery slopes. As advertised, he was a powder keg of passion, the pace and tone of his voice following the sway and swell of his thoughts. Part teacher, part lawyer, part entertainer, Adams quickly became the centrifugal force at the center of the room, the ringmaster.

Tonight, as in previous nights according to Jay's report, Adams was taking issue with those who thought that moderation was the cure for the colonial malaise. "How much longer," he asked repeatedly, "must we endure these insults to our dignity and these injuries to our lives and livelihoods? My neighbors in Boston have British soldiers living in their houses, eating their food, tramping through their yards. Why? Because of that blasted Quartering Act. Our splendid Parliament says soldiers need beds, colonists have beds; soldiers in, colonials out. Imagine what any of those earls and dukes would say to a redcoat who tried to take over his bed chamber. But they see us in a different light, not as Englishmen but as the subjects of Englishmen. And no indignity is too great if it serves the King."

A heavy-set man, roughly dressed and dragging a piece of bread through the last juices in his plate, took the bait. "Our King," he said, "has been doing only what was necessary to keep order in an unruly colony. What did you expect the King to do when your deranged friends dumped his tea into Boston Harbor? Send them a note of thanks?"

"His tea?" Adams quickly retorted. "His tea? It was our tea. We bought it and we were to drink it. But our sovereign masters in London couldn't resist the urge to make a few shillings for themselves from our commerce. It was scandalous, the tea tax, and the boys of Boston could abide no such nonsense."

"They took the law into their own hands," the bearded man replied without pause.

"Law?" said Adams. "Law? This is not law. I've practiced law my whole life. Law is what a people decide together to regulate their transactions. How can it be law when a small group of men, most of whom have never worked a day in their lives and many of whom are elected by no one, decide to squeeze as much sterling as they can from colonists they've never seen in places they've never been? Did a single Massachusetts man vote to close the port of Boston? Of course not, nary a one. But the port is closed and our ships rot at their piers. This is not law, it's thievery. And this wobbly, inconstant King of ours is the biggest thief of all."

It took but a second for Adams's last words to send a startled gasp across the room. Most had never heard such calumny spoken of their sovereign, and the sound of it found no comfortable landing place beyond their ears. But Adams didn't pause. "If we're to have the respect we deserve as Englishmen, we simply cannot stand by while unwarranted taxes rain down upon us, while the crown's governors pay no attention to our own legislatures, while ships unload more and more soldiers who commandeer our houses and abuse us in the streets.

"Think who we are. My ancestors came to this land a century and a half ago. They came to escape the very tyranny that now follows us here. Are we yet subjects of the crown, Englishmen? If so, then are we not entitled to all the rights of Englishmen? And if we are not Englishmen, then what are we? London seems happy now to draw bold lines around our rights, to send its army and navy to keep us in place. They can succeed at that only if we let them. And, gentlemen, we must not let them."

Over the next hour, some in the room poked about for holes in Sam Adams's logic. Others paid no heed to his arguments, merely noting their irrelevance. The reality, they felt, was that the colonies had a government, a British government, and enjoyed many benefits from that government. The problems were manageable if people would only be reasonable. The task was to correct the misunderstandings and misapprehensions that seemed these days to make it so difficult for King and Parliament to deal fairly with their American constituents.

At 10:30, Sam Adams departed. The rest of those present drifted away shortly thereafter. As they were walking back to the Widow Almy, Henry said to Jonathan, "Now, perhaps, you can better understand why we're here. Men like Adams have stirred up the coals, and the fire has begun to blaze.

"But don't be seduced by Adams. His logic is forceful, but he's a radical. He seems already to have passed into a new world. But we don't live in that world. We still live in the world of our fathers and their fathers. And in this world, Parliament makes the laws and the King reigns. And the army stands with them. Men like Adams have their place, I suppose. But we must be on guard to keep them in their place."

Jonathan listened, but said little. He had never heard arguments such as those Sam Adams had made, never seen logic used so effectively in forcing men to reconsider their own opinions. Jonathan had always comfortably accepted Henry's views on public affairs because he respected his father and thought him wise. But the tavern talk tonight suggested that there might be ideas he'd never heard and events he'd never seen. And these offered a different view of the world than the one he'd absorbed in Still River Bend.

Could a King really be wicked? Could men defy authority and be right? These questions, and not Henry's words of caution, filled Jonathan's mind as he walked the dark streets of Philadelphia on the eve of the First Continental Congress.

Henry had rented a horse for the day to ride to Carpenters' Hall. It would have been a simple walk, but the road was dusty, and somehow the occasion seemed to demand an approach on horseback. He cantered slowly through the streets as Jonathan walked alongside.

He was surprised as he drew closer at his own nervousness. Would he be overwhelmed by the talent and eloquence of the others gathered here? Henry was just a farmer--a successful farmer, to be sure, and in Delaware a man of some importance. But Delaware was a small place and some of the others came from the great colonies of Massachusetts Bay and New York and Virginia. Many had reputations that preceded them. But none of them would have heard of Henry Houghton. He was not a lawyer, had engaged in no acts of rebellion, had spoken no deathless fighting words, and had never been ahead of his time.

The Delaware people who had sent Henry to Philadelphia had given him no instructions. But he was sure they bore no passion for great change, certainly not for revolution. They merely wanted to live the lives they'd inherited in the middle colonies without arbitrary interference. Politics seemed out of balance to some of them; they only wanted Henry Houghton to help right it.

But Henry worried that the momentum of the times was accelerating so rapidly that his opinions would find no home here. If everyone was talking like Sam Adams, who would listen to a Delaware farmer who was proud to be an Englishman and wanted only to convince London to attend more closely to the concerns of its overseas colonies? Was this going be a rearguard action? And, if so, would Henry be alone in waging it?

It was a gloomy morning with the threat of rain. Henry and Jonathan had several times walked this way over the past few days, but Henry was still unsettled by the fine-cut symmetry of the place. When the Congress was first called, Joseph Galloway, the brilliant Pennsylvanian, had sought to hold it at the grander State House, one of the masterpieces of Philadelphia architecture. But local Tories would have none of that: this bunch of schemers and plotters was not going to defile their august State House with their bickering about the King. Galloway was turned down. So on this morning Henry approached instead the newer and much simpler Carpenters' Hall, the recently completed guild hall for the city's builders.

Carpenters' Hall was not much larger than a gentleman's house, but handsome in its way. Three tall Palladian windows topped the stone balustrades. The belt course separating its two floors was made of wood, unusual for a building like this but emblematic of the working medium of the craftsmen who built it and who thought it their home. The only ornamentation was an elongated cupola on top. Carpenters' Hall was not grand in any way, but its simplicity seemed almost comforting to Henry Houghton on this morning when nothing else seemed simple.

A Negro boy of about 12 took the reins of the mare as Henry stepped down from the saddle. "Be keepin' her over here, sir" the boy said, pointing toward a stable beyond a tall elm tree to the south. Henry nodded and began to walk hesitantly toward the hall. Clusters of men stood outside in lazy conversation, many looking past their conversation partners to see who else was present, to listen in on other conversations. Henry was impressed with the bearing of many of these men. Most were neatly turned out, some in dress that seemed much too heavy and formal for a warm summer day.

The Massachusetts delegation stood together at the edge of the street. Henry had met all of them at the Indian King and recognized Sam Adams in his bright red suit. His sullen cousin John Adams lingered off to one side looking away, while Thomas Cushing and Robert Treat Paine listened in amusement to whatever it was that Sam Adams was saying. Another man in a light gray frock stood discreetly at the edge of their group, saying little and eyeing the surroundings.

Henry knew few of the others, except for Jay whom he met the previous night; Caesar Rodney and George Read, from Delaware; and John Dickinson, a Delaware man but here as part of the Pennsylvania delegation. He looked in vain for Washington, but the Virginian had not yet arrived from his lodgings.

It was a relief when George Read exited from one of these clusters and approached Henry. A familiar face was much welcome on this anxious morning, and Henry exchanged warm greetings with Read. They'd often been opponents in the colonial legislature at New Castle, but here they suffered a similar anxiety and found some relief in sharing it.

"What do you make of all this, Houghton?" said Read.

"Who can tell?" Henry replied. "It feels like the whirlpool that forms when many rivers come together in one place. We're all American colonies and yet we're so different. I listened to Sam Adams hold forth at the Indian King last night. He was full of fire and anger. It was some show. But I never felt that he was speaking for me or the people of Delaware. We know nothing of tea parties and soldiers in our houses. Should we all be fighting that battle or is this between Massachusetts and the crown?"

As Read prepared to reply, a slender man in bright blue coat came out the door, removed his hat and called out loudly, "Gentlemen, the hall is ready for you now." The clusters dispersed and everyone moved quickly inside, happy to get the assembly underway and to be out from under the first drops of rain.

The early days passed slowly in the heavy heat. The delegates crowded each morning into a room barely large enough to accommodate the four dozen or so who normally attended. After prayer, they moved laboriously through issues large and small. Soon patterns evolved, leaders emerged, and sides took shape. Even in assemblies as grand as this, routines seep insidiously in.

And there was not much, it turned out, for a delegate's secretary to do. The sessions of Congress were full of overheated debate, but few decisions were reached and the record made by Charles Thomson, the official secretary, seemed more than adequate for future communication to the citizens of Delaware. So Jonathan spent his days exploring the city.

Philadelphia was a metropolis of 30,000 people in 1774, the largest city in the empire outside of England, and it was full of things that an intensely curious young man from a tiny place like Still River had never seen and could barely imagine. One day he explored books about unfamiliar and exotic subjects at the Library Company. On another, he investigated the docks and observed the cordwainers, the shipwrights, the stevedores, and the sailors coming and going from the Man Full of Trouble tavern. He'd seen a few ships in his visits to Uncle Edward's shipyard, but never so many nor any so large as those loading and unloading along the Philadelphia waterfront.

The days of exploration produced a cloud of impressions. Never had Jonathan imagined that there could be so many religions and so many different churches. He was familiar with the Church of England, his own church, and with the Quaker meeting houses of some of his Delaware neighbors. But of Mennonites, Presbyterians, Saturday Anabaptists, Lutherans, Roman Catholics, Zinzendorfers, and Schwenkfelders he knew nothing. Every Philadelphia block seemed to have its own church. He tried to keep them separated in his mind, but soon found the task impossible.

And never had Jonathan imagined a world of so many objects: implements for farming and building, foods of every description, men's and ladies' fashions, fine china and glassware. He soon shed his reluctance to enter shops merely to inquire about the items in the window he did not recognize. On some evenings, he felt a great fatigue from trying to absorb all the new information and fresh experiences Philadelphia presented to him.

But the evenings provided stimulation of another kind as Jonathan joined his father and other delegates for dinner and conversation in the taverns of the city. These occasions afforded the young man his clearest vantage point on the issues and personalities that were coming to dominate the Continental Congress. He never missed one.

One night in early October, father and son were taking dinner at the City Tavern at 2$^{nd}$ and Walnut Street. There were more than a hundred taverns scattered through the neighborhoods of Philadelphia; City Tavern was one of the newest and certainly the grandest of those. It had become a favorite haunt of many delegates, and soon there was little dividing line between official debate at Carpenters' Hall and unofficial debate at City Tavern.

Henry was in animated and distressed discussion on this night with Joseph Galloway. Earlier that day, a post rider from Boston, a man named Paul Revere, had shot a bolt of lightning through the Congress by delivering to Sam Adams a document that had just been voted by the leading men of Boston and surrounding towns. Adams had handed it to Peyton Randolph of Virginia, the president of the Congress, who instantly read it aloud to the hushed assembly.

The Suffolk Resolves declared all the King's Coercive Acts to be unconstitutional and, therefore, not to be obeyed. They further called for Massachusetts to form its own government, to collect its own taxes, and to pay nothing to the Crown until the Acts were repealed. Economic sanctions against the British were proposed and the Resolves called on the men of Massachusetts to gather arms and form their own militias.

No sooner had Randolph finished reading the document than the Congress exploded into shouts of affirmation and support. Delegates crowded around their colleagues from Massachusetts, clapping their backs and shaking their hands. For Patrick Henry, Sam Adams, for Big John Sullivan of New Hampshire and Dr. Shippen of Pennsylvania, for all those who hoped this Congress would mark the beginning of a new era on the American continent, this was a great day.

But not so for Henry Houghton, Joseph Galloway and a few others who had steadily urged a more moderate course, who continued to hope that the Congress could convince the government in London to come to its senses. For them, the quick approval that Congress gave to the Suffolk Resolves underscored the growing difficulty of their position.

As Henry and Galloway commiserated by a window toward the front of the tavern, Jonathan sat at the center table where Patrick Henry was holding forth. The happy events of the day had inspired a greater than normal consumption of spirits at night, and the center table was awash with toasts and singing and general boisterousness.

Patrick Henry's reputation for oratory had preceded him to Philadelphia. With expectations so high, people hung on his every word; even his most pedestrian thoughts were received with deepest respect and widely repeated. Jonathan remembered the night early in the Congress when even his father, no great admirer of the fiery Virginian, repeated verbatim Patrick Henry's words from that morning's debate over how many votes each colony should have: "The distinctions between Virginians, Pennsylvanians, New Yorkers, New Englanders are no more. I am not a Virginian, but an American!"

"Only a few of the delegates share Patrick Henry's view on this," his father had said, "but that statement will spread across the colonies and people everywhere will think that Patrick speaks for us all. No radicals anywhere ever had better propaganda than a Patrick Henry speech."

On this night in City Tavern, the indefatigable Virginian was after the King himself, filling the air with grievance after grievance, with contemptuous descriptions of the King's appetites, with pessimistic scenarios of a future in which Americans remained supine subjects of what Henry called this "gluttonous, disdainful, inconstant bore." Every cheer that Henry's words provoked inspired him to higher and higher flights of rhetoric.

After a while, Jonathan began to notice that John Adams was sitting alone at a small corner table. Adams, short and dour and wearing a perpetual look of impatience, rarely took any active part in these clamorous proceedings. He enjoyed conversation and loved a good argument, but he had not a rowdy bone in his body.

Though they disagreed on the central issues before the Congress, Henry Houghton had acquired a great respect for John Adams, for his genuine passion for justice and for his learned skills in debate. Henry worried more about John Adams as an opponent whose potent arguments would worm their way into the hearts of the delegates than about the oratorical flourishes of Patrick Henry or the incendiary spouting of Sam Adams. He knew that as the days wore on and the delegates got to know each other better, the effects of oratory would diminish and the force of rational argument would grow. And no one in this Congress, it seemed to Henry Houghton, could make a rational argument with more intensity and lasting impact than this unpleasant and irritating man from Boston.

His father's growing respect for Adams intrigued Jonathan and inspired him to move toward the table where Adams sat alone. At first, Adams did not take his gaze from the center table which he'd been watching in bemusement and faint disgust. He had little affection for Patrick Henry and none for personal insults hurled at his King. Jonathan stood uncomfortably for a moment until Adams inclined his head upward and nodded a curt hello. Jonathan thrust his hand in Adams's direction and introduced himself as the secretary to Henry Houghton of Delaware.

Though he tried to say this with as much formal flourish as he could, Adams quickly pricked any dignity in the moment by saying, "Oh yes, you're Houghton's boy. And I suppose you intend to be an Englishman for life like your father."

Jonathan was caught off guard by this familiarity and could only say, "It is an honor to meet you, Mr. Adams."

Adams invited Jonathan to join him. Jonathan retrieved his mug of cider from the center table and did so. "Still god-awfully hot," Adams said, as Jonathan settled into the only other chair at the table. "In Boston by now we'd have color rising in the trees and the relief of cool air in the evenings."

"I guess it just seems normal to me," Jonathan replied. "In Delaware we share the weather with Philadelphia. It will cool off soon enough. Always does."

Adams made a gesture with his eyebrows suggesting that he intended no further talk of the weather. He glanced again at the center table, his attention drawn by the loud response to a song that had just ended. "Mr. Adams," Jonathan interrupted, "please tell me about Boston. Is it true that the army's everywhere and people there must do whatever soldiers tell them?"

"The damned soldiers have been with us now for several years," Adams replied, "but we've never accustomed ourselves to them. As more soldiers have come, their imposition on our lives grows steadily larger and more aggravating. There aren't barracks adequate for this garrison, so they live in our houses. They can't bring sufficient of their own stores on their ships, so they eat our food. They've closed our port and cut off our commerce, so many men of Boston have little to do but sit through the day and complain of the scarlet noose around their necks.

"In Philadelphia, there's nothing like this. In this Congress, we listen to the delegates make abstract and hypothetical arguments. But there's nothing abstract or hypothetical about life in Boston now. There's but one way to describe it, young man. We're under siege."

"I hear that some of the citizens are taking up arms. Is that so?" Jonathan asked.

"Hard to say," said Adams. "There's so much rumor and exaggeration. If a tradesman comes from Malden or Menotomy where he's seen a farmer with a musket, by the time he gets to Quincy the story has grown and he's talking about companies of farmers drilling for war. On the other hand, some militia companies have been formed and some of

30

the men in Massachusetts are angry enough to make a war. We try to communicate as best we can, but it's difficult. The army intercepts our communications and punishes the messengers. And since we have no central organization of any kind, each of the towns outside of Boston seems to operate independently of the others. If there's a military organization in Massachusetts, it's one run by lieutenants, not generals.

"And that's the great fear. The King's army looks imposing and it is. But its commanders worry constantly about the secrecy of what goes on around them. They hear the same exaggerated stories we do and often take them seriously. So they're easily spooked. A minor insult hurled at a passing soldier may look to the soldier like the beginning of a skirmish. And so he reports to his officers. Boston's a powder keg. It'll only take a small spark to set it off."

"And what then?" Jonathan asked.

"No one knows, lad. That's why this Congress is so important. If Massachusetts colony goes to war with England, we'll lose badly and many of my fellow citizens will die in vain. If we all stand together, however, there's a chance that London will find the situation here impossible to manage and seek to cut its losses. But who can predict what London will do? The King is so driven by whimsy and the government so corrupt and uncertain of itself. The very knowledge that this Congress is meeting may drive the King himself to send more soldiers and ships, maybe even to begin more active repression of outspoken opponents like Sam and Dr. Warren. These are not laughing matters. All of us could have our necks stretched before it's over."

"But here's what I don't understand," said Jonathan, looking perplexed and leaning forward. "Wouldn't it be better to try to find some compromise with the government in London, to show that we're loyal subjects of the King who only want to express our concerns and have them addressed?"

"Ah, I hear the sound of Henry Houghton's boy, I think," said Adams, smiling briefly. "Your father makes those very arguments in Congress, and he makes them well. He's a sensible man. But he hasn't lived in Boston. We've been trying to get the King to address our concerns for a decade.

"Of course, we never see the King. Every man at this Congress is a subject of the glorious George III. He has been our sovereign for as long as most of us wish to remember. But not one of us has ever laid eyes on him. Our colonial governors carry no weight with our King, and we have no more influence in the choice of members of Parliament than most of our poor English brethren.

"I admire your father's faith in compromise, lad, but I know no way to accomplish it. How can two parties compromise when one believes he owns the other? How do we compromise with a government that responds to our every entreaty by sending more soldiers to repress us? If there's any hope left of coming to some accommodation with this government, you won't find much of it in Boston."

Jonathan paused before responding and Adams used the opportunity to take his leave. "The hour's late, young man, and I find it nearly impossible to sleep in this heat. So I believe I'll excuse myself now. I hope you'll try to enlighten your father about the realities we face. If a war does start, we'll need men like him as much as soldiers and firebrand orators. We'll be Englishmen forever if enough people in these colonies are satisfied with that. Don't let him be satisfied with that. And don't you be either."

# Chapter 3

## Still River, Delaware
## September 1774

"Oh, such wonderful news!" Patience Houghton exclaimed, leaping to hug her daughter. "Marrying Marinus Marshall! It's like a dream."

Savannah paid little attention, looking out the dining room window, across the garden where boughs of white and purple hydrangea caught the last nurturing rays of summer. She focused on the west corner of the barn where already Quiet Jack and the hired man were well into the day's work. Her mother's words were expected and had little impact.

"Now we'll to have to plan a grand spring wedding, grander even than Celia's. The marriage of a Marshall and a Houghton..." Patience mused aloud, "Only a grand wedding will do. Marinus Marshall is a wealthy man, from one of the best families in Delaware, and his future is full of promise. You're a very lucky young lady."

Savannah always tried to ignore these fixations her mother had with status and family name, her constant comparison of her life, her husband, her children, and the size of the Houghton farm with everyone else's she knew. She was not surprised that after nearly twenty minutes of conversation about Marinus Marshall's marriage proposal, Patience had said not a word about love or romance, and had not once asked Savannah if she were happy.

Was she happy? Savannah was unsure. The Marshall family was one of the oldest in Delaware. Albert Marshall had been one of the first European settlers on Delaware Bay and he had shrewdly collected rights to as much land as he could, living frugally to invest every penny in expanding the Marshall estates. His sons and grandsons had cleared the land more quickly than most of their neighbors and now grazed cattle and the finest horses in the Middle Atlantic colonies. Wealth was the key to prominence in colonial society and the Marshalls, by most accounts, were the wealthiest family in Delaware.

Marinus Marshall, now five generations removed from Albert, was charming, and he was handsome enough in the fashion of a gentleman. At thirty, he was seven years older than Savannah. Neither he nor his brothers worked the land. That was now done by slaves, of whom the Marshalls owned nearly eighty. This freed the Marshall boys, as they were known, to follow their own interests.

Marinus was the oldest and most ambitious of the boys. He had read the law under the guidance of Justice Marcus, his father's good friend, and now had a growing legal practice of his own in Dover. People said Marinus Marshall was the smartest young attorney in Delaware. He had carefully cultivated contacts with political leaders, Justice Marcus the most prominent among them, and it was now widely rumored that he would have a seat and probably a leadership position in the new colonial legislature when the old dispute with Pennsylvania was settled and Delaware became a colony of its own next year.

No doubt, Savannah understood, marriage to Marinus Marshall would put her at the center of Delaware social life. She would be one of the colony's most prominent ladies with an elegant house, clothes from Philadelphia and abroad, and time to do needlework, play the clavier, and attend the teas and parties that filled the days of the finer ladies of the colony.

"Your father will be so pleased," Patience said after waiting for and receiving no response from Savannah. "He so wants all of you to have opportunities in life that eluded him because he's been so tied to this land. He's worked so hard, and he's made a name for himself as an honest, a thoughtful man. Of course that's why he's in Philadelphia now. Because people in Delaware respect your father, and when he started to go to the meetings about the problems with the King they listened to what he had to say.

"But sometimes he lets it slip that he wishes we were wealthier, wishes that he didn't have to spend so much of his own time managing this farm, wishes we could afford more help and more animals. He hated that he and Jonathan had to walk to Philadelphia. Just hated it. But he knew that with the harvest coming we couldn't spare any horses. And remember how his first letter from Philadelphia was so full of descriptions of Governor Bowdoin's coach that brought the Massachusetts men and the fine clothes and refinements of some of the other gentlemen."

"Oh, mother, you're imagining things," Savannah finally responded. "Father is proud of this farm and proud of the family line that cut it out of the wilderness and passed it down to us. Think how many times you've heard him say that we have—oh, what does he call it—an 'honest life.' We work hard and we enjoy the fruits of our labor. Remember when he went to Norfolk to buy Quiet Jack and Sweetie. The argument he had with Nathaniel. Nathaniel was full of all those college ideas and argued with him about the morality of slavery. Father had doubts about buying slaves, but not about the morality of slavery. He never even gave slavery much thought. What worried him was that our 'honest life' would be spoiled by owning slaves to do work that Houghtons had always done for ourselves.

"Father knew in his heart that the farm was getting bigger and more complicated, that Nathaniel was not interested in farming and Jonathan was too young to help much. He knew something had to be done. But like all things for Father, it was a practical problem, and buying slaves was a practical solution." Savannah rose and moved to the window that looked out over the valley to the north. She tried to imagine what Philadelphia must look like, and New York where her sister lived.

"Oh how I hated that," Patience added quickly. " Those slaves cost most of the money we'd ever saved from this farm. I told your father that we could get by without them, that Jonathan would be a man soon enough and we could hire a hand in the meantime. But Henry made up his own mind in the end. He's never believed I had much notion of how things really work."

"He doesn't let on, but I think he must be beside himself with worry about us and the farm, stuck up there in Philadelphia," said Savannah. "It's the first harvest he's missed in his life. I wonder how he concentrates on all those political things." She gazed again toward the fields in the distance, thinking about the details of the harvest and what she'd been learning from her conversations with Quiet Jack.

Patience took up her napkin and began to rub at a smudge on the table top. "It would have to be a grander wedding than Celia's. After all, no one knew anything about the Carter family and they weren't from Delaware anyway. She may be our eldest daughter, but this will be a far more important social event."

Savannah was still contemplating her father and the farm and the plans for the harvest. Her mother's return to the topic of the wedding was jarring to her and beginning to irritate. "Mother," she said, "this is premature. I haven't accepted Marinus's proposal yet, and he hasn't had an opportunity to speak to Father. Frankly, I don't know what I'll do. I've known Marinus a long time. I've always liked him well enough. But I never pictured myself marrying him, and it will take some time for the prospect to settle in."

Startled, Patience looked up as she continued her rubbing, "You're a very lucky girl, Savannah," she said. "All that needs to settle in is for you to realize that. Think of your sister's life in New York. She lives in a majestic house on one of the best streets. Her social calendar is full. Godfrey's business seems to be doing so well. She seems so happy, and I long for you to be happy, as she is. "

Savannah rose and opened the door. The air was crisp this morning and rows of small purple clouds were marching on Delaware from the northwest. Savannah's thoughts turned to Silly in New York. Only Savannah ever called her that. Her real name was Celia, of course, and she was a year and a half older than Savannah. But when Savannah first started to talk, her sister's name always came out as Silly. Savannah continued to call her that because it was easier to say and, as Celia grew older, she thought the name often seemed apt.

Celia had married Godfrey Carter at Christmas in 1770 when she was just twenty-one. Neither of her parents were happy about the marriage, at least not initially. Carter was a stranger to everyone when he came to Uncle Edward's shipyard in the summer of 1770 to arrange for the refitting of a large merchant ship. He settled in to oversee the project and, as an apparently prosperous visitor, he was invited to the usual round of harvest balls.

Godfrey Carter was not like the Delaware men. He had jade eyes and dark black hair, which he wore long and carefully curled. His clothes were of fine, bright silk, and he always seemed dressed to dance. He was charming and glib and polite, but he could talk at length on many subjects without leaving a trail to his true feelings about anything. The young women around Still River were quite taken with this exotic stranger. The men found him more curious than appealing.

Carter quickly took an interest in Celia and, before anyone realized what was happening, he was courting her. No one was more surprised at this than Celia herself. She had not been an especially pretty child, but as she moved into adulthood, she seemed to grow more comely each year. Most of the Houghton's had hair in dark hues of brown, but Celia's hair had a reddish cast that made it almost glow in the sunlight. With it swept back and tied in a bow, her high forehead and well-defined features made her seem almost regal.

36

The local young men had begun to take notice of the blossoming of this elder Houghton daughter, but it had happened so quickly that none had yet moved to dominate her attention. Godfrey Carter suffered no such hesitation. While others planned, he moved. And in the fall of 1770, he swept Celia Houghton off her feet.

Henry was caught by surprise on the day in October when Godfrey came to ask for his daughter's hand in marriage. He had taken no particular liking to this suitor, though Edward had told him that Carter was an astute businessman. But he hadn't imagined that Carter's courtship of Celia had proceeded this rapidly. Without a thoughtful response prepared, he answered simply, "If it's what Celia wants, you have my assent." This was very much what Celia Houghton wanted in the fall of 1770.

They decided on a Christmas wedding because Godfrey's work in Delaware would soon be done and he would be traveling to New York on the refitted ship. He wanted Celia to go with him. So, with what Patience regarded as far too little planning, the marriage took place on Christmas Eve at St. Andrew's Church in Dover. Celia and Godfrey left three days later, and Savannah had not seen her sister in the nearly four years that had passed since then.

Sweetie came in to clear the breakfast plates, and Savannah moved through the kitchen and out into the dooryard, leaving her mother in intense concentration now on the spots she was vigorously trying to rub from the table top. The dooryard was a working place. Firewood, a large flat stump, and a splitting maul dominated the corner by the kitchen door. Near the stone wall stood a rough table and bench where vegetables were prepared for the kitchen. An angled wooden door, now bleached almost colorless by the sun, marked the entrance to the root cellar. And a menagerie of hens and turkeys scuttled around in search of seeds they'd missed from Sweetie's morning feeding.

Savannah settled on the bench and tilted her head back toward the sun. Colonial ladies were supposed to avoid the sun, her mother had often told her, but Savannah loved its warm touch on her face, especially in the morning when everything felt so fresh. She'd found herself drawn to the dooryard in recent weeks with the farm so quiet. Silly was long gone, Nathaniel had left for England in the spring, Father and Jonathan had now been in Philadelphia for more than month. She was lonely, and here in the dooryard she could always find solace and comfort in the view out past the barn, over the browning fields down to the river below—the place where she had lived her entire life.

Father said this was all forest when his great grandfather, Jeremiah Houghton, first settled it. Over the years, the forest had been pushed back up the hill as it was harvested and fields of grain and flax took its place. Men still came in a heavy wagon every day to take down trees for the mill. But in the years since her childhood, the rhythm of their long saws and the intermittent punctuation of a large oak crashing to the ground had moved further away from the house. She never heard them now, and the coming of the wagon in the morning and its departure at dusk were her only reminder that timber was a principal source of the Houghtons' livelihood.

Many of the large farms in Delaware now had names: Oak Hill, Sunset Ridge, Proud Point were some of those adopted by their neighbors. Celia and Savannah had often played at inventing a name for the Houghton farm when they were little and once or twice a week they would come to Henry with a proposal. Once, when Savannah was twelve, they lobbied hard for River Valley Plantation, a name they both liked because it captured the essence of their life on the bank of a pretty river and because they thought a plantation was where dignified people lived.

Henry enjoyed their game, but had no intention of naming the farm. He thought names for plots of land were pretentious, and he especially disliked the term "plantation." It sounded too much like Virginia to him, and he had no desire for his farm, or anything else in Delaware, to emulate Virginia. Virginians, he believed, were ostentatious by birth, frustrated aristocrats who accumulated much larger landholdings than anyone could reasonably manage and then purchased scores of slaves to run the places. Each was a community of its own, and the Virginians all acted like dukes and earls with their own fiefdoms. Not an "honest life" in Henry's view and certainly not one he intended to copy, whatever his amusement at his daughters' playful attempts to convince him otherwise.

So as Savannah sat in the dooryard on this splendid September morning, it was just the Houghton farm she overlooked, not River Valley Plantation. For a few minutes, as she bathed in the warmth of the sun and surveyed the landscape sparkling in the lucid air, feelings of loneliness were pushed aside and she felt no compulsion to think about Marinus Marshall or the adult life she would soon need to contemplate.

Savannah's reverie came to an abrupt end when Sweetie dashed into the dooryard from the direction of the barn, waving an envelope in her hand. Thom Mason, the hired man, had picked up the mail that morning on the way to work and had given it to Sweetie when she brought warm bread out for Thom and Quiet Jack. "Letta' come from Mista Henry," Sweetie exulted as she pushed it toward Savannah.

Savannah walked through the kitchen and found her mother dabbing even more vigorously now at the spots on the dining room table. "We've a letter from father," she said excitedly, as she pulled up a chair next to Patience.

"Please read it, dear," Patience said. "Your eyes are so much better than mine in this light."

The letter was two pages with both sides of each covered with Henry's cramped script. Savannah read slowly, allowing her mother to absorb and occasionally comment on each sentence before she moved on. This was the third letter they'd received from Henry since his departure more than a month ago. From Jonathan, the alleged secretary, they'd heard nothing.

Henry's earlier letters had been filled with florid descriptions of Philadelphia and portraits of the famous men he'd met there. But in this letter he seemed less ebullient. He wrote of the tedium of the daily debates and the squabbles that were now almost constant between the delegates from the large colonies and those from the small ones like Delaware. He said that the great issue of relations between London and the colonies was often pushed aside by disagreements between merchants and farmers and lengthy discussions of specie and currency. The assembly was full of lawyers, he wrote, and all they wanted to do was argue about arcane legal procedures. A month into the Congress and they still hadn't decided on what basis, if any, its authority rested. Eloquent encomiums to morality and natural law and basic human rights filled the air, but these brilliant individuals seemed to Henry to have no common sense about how to handle the practical grievances that had brought them there

He reported on their approval of the Suffolk Resolves after Sam Adams's clever stunt of having a man named Revere ride in dramatically with reports of British oppression in Massachusetts—reports, Henry noted ruefully, that later turned out to be erroneous. And he talked about the growing split between those who saw no hope for reconciliation with London and those, like himself, who thought that the alternatives to reconciliation would all be worse. "It looks like we're losing this argument," Henry wrote. "The radicals have at least forced the question of a clear break with England. More and more the debate is about how to accomplish it, not whether it's the prudent course. Galloway has stood valiantly against this momentum toward a break, but he and I and our small band are plainly in the minority now.

"This week we'll consider what's being called the Continental Association. It calls on every citizen in the colonies to stop trading with the British, bans all imports later this year, and all exports to England a year from now. It will surely give Parliament all the reason it needs to send even more troops and to pass even more measures to punish us. It may well mean a shooting war. And I have the gravest fears for its impact on our commerce in Delaware. If Edward cannot sell his ships to the British, if we cannot ship our timber to London on British ships, if our flax cannot be sold in British markets, what misfortunes will the Houghtons have to endure for this false promise of liberty?"

Patience thought, as she listened, about the tenuous position the Houghton family enjoyed in Delaware society, a status sure to be destroyed by the economic shocks to which Henry alluded. The Houghtons had no reservoir of wealth, only the land on which they lived and their capacity to reap a steady living from it. But if Edward could not sell his ships nor the tannery its leather, the market for Houghton timber would soon evaporate. And when the pinch was widely felt, who would then buy the other crops and animals that the Houghtons raised for market. The prospects seemed all bad, and they filled Patience with a darkening gloom.

Savannah finished the letter and looked at her mother, sitting forlorn and pale, her hands at rest now on the table top. Patience disliked politics and rarely took an interest when Henry discussed public issues. It was all too vexing to her and too crass. But when Henry left for Philadelphia with Jonathan, she'd been forced to realize that there would be no easy escape now from the debates and arguments she so disliked. One of her daughters was in New York where British ships filled the harbor. Henry, though no radical in his own opinions, was part of what London viewed as a nest of rebels in Philadelphia. Jonathan was there with him.

How glad she was that Nathaniel had escaped from the torturous passions of these dangerous times. He was so much like her: artistic, literate, gentle, devoid of interest in public affairs. How good that he was away from this tumult and free to develop his talent in the safety and refinement of London. With so much to worry about here, Patience was glad for this: that her eldest son would not be pulled into the rapids of change that seemed such a cruel force on the rest of the Houghton family, dragging them toward a terrifying and uncertain destiny.

# Chapter 4

## *Philadelphia*
## *October 1774*

The voice was so soft Jonathan barely heard the words, "May I be of service to you, sir?"

Jonathan looked back over his left shoulder and spotted a slender man in black frock bending toward him. The man placed a gentle hand on Jonathan's arm, and repeated the question.

Jonathan rose and turned to look upward. Sitting on the steps of Christ Church, lost in his thoughts, Jonathan hadn't heard the man approach. "No, sir," he said. "I was just enjoying the morning sun on your steps. I hope I wasn't causing a problem."

"Not at all," the man responded. "I was only worried that you had tried the door and found it closed. I'm Archibald Wentworth, the rector of this church. You're more than welcome to stay and enjoy the comfort of these steps. Or perhaps you'd like to join me in back. I was just about to enjoy a pot of tea, and your company would be welcome."

"It's most comfortable here, sir, but I'd be pleased to share some tea with you. My name is Jonathan Houghton."

The rector extended his hand to Jonathan and touched him warmly on the shoulder to complete the greeting. As they walked along the east side of the church in the bright morning sun, the rector said, "I believe I've seen you on this street a good deal in recent days. May I ask what brings you here?"

"Certainly," Jonathan replied. "I'm here for the Continental Congress." Seeing the rector's look of surprise and confusion, Jonathan quickly added, "My father is a delegate from Delaware and I'm here as his secretary."

"Oh, I see," said the rector. "What does a delegate's secretary do?"

"Precious little, it seems. Occasionally father has me take notes on meetings he's had outside the hall or conversations that occur at tavern in the evening. I've also drawn up some letters to people in Delaware and I kept the minutes of a few brief meetings of the Delaware delegates. But the honest truth is that Father has had very little need for a secretary."

"So how have you filled your days?" the rector inquired.

"I've walked the length and breadth of Philadelphia and come to know it intimately from the Delaware River to the Schuylkill," Jonathan said. "I've been to the Library Company for books, I've lunched in many of the taverns, I've visited the shops. When you found me this morning, I was simply watching the people pass by on Market Street, something I do often. I see more people here in an hour than live within 50 miles of our farm in Delaware."

"But even all that must get tiresome after a while."

"Yes, of course. But with Father's reports and the evenings with other delegates at City Tavern, I've also begun to enjoy a close acquaintance with the members of the Congress and the issues that fill their days. I may not be much use to them, but they're of great use to me. No man my age ever had a better education than I've had in this month in Philadelphia."

They passed through a low door near the rear of the church into a cramped, dark room. Wentworth lit a candle and set it in the middle of a small round table that stood between two high-backed walnut chairs. Jonathan looked around, but saw nothing resembling tea. No fire was lit and there was no kettle. "Have no fear, Jonathan," the rector smiled. "Mrs. Wentworth brings a pot of tea every morning at exactly 10 o'clock."

He pulled a silver watch from his vest pocket and squinted at it in the candle light. "She'll be here in twelve minutes. That, sir, is one of life's few reliable certainties."

As his eyes adjusted to the light, Jonathan began to notice the details of the room, which was apparently used by the rector as a study. Books of brown and red leather filled shelves along one wall. A large trestle table took up most of another. The papers scattered over the top of the table indicated a work in progress. The frequency of lined out words and recopied sentences suggested that progress was slow.

"As you can see, this is where I write my sermons," said the rector. "Another of life's certainties: every Sunday a new sermon. I'm a God-fearing man, Jonathan, but not a very literary one. Somehow what I plan to say evaporates into the air whenever I dip quill to ink. God must sometimes wonder at my feeble attempts to convey His word to my flock." He laughed aloud at the thought of his weekly struggles.

"You're not alone, reverend. Every day I listen to Father and the other delegates bemoan their inability to find just the right words to convey their ideas, to express their agreements and mask their arguments. I had pictured something more stately than this, a group of great men who would reason together and come to a bold consensus. No such thing has happened.

"There are great men here, and some of them—like John Adams, Mr. Jay, and John Dickinson—seem worthy of the greatest respect. General Washington, too, although he apparently says very little. But even the best of them get caught up in petty arguments, spend hours debating the precise meaning of certain words, trying to win the most trivial points in debate. Father says that it takes forever to get anything done because there are so many disparate voices, each wanting to be heard at length on every subject."

Wentworth nodded and leaned forward attentively in a way that encouraged Jonathan to continue.

"Now they're arguing about trade with England. Some of them want to stop Americans from purchasing any British imports. The New Englanders seem to want that. Of course, everyone realizes the risk in that--a retaliatory response from London banning the import of American goods.

"The New Englanders can survive without British trade, so they're not much troubled by that risk. But we can't survive without British commerce, and others further south can't either. How will the Virginians and Carolinians fare if they can't sell their tobacco or their cotton abroad?   How will we in Delaware survive if we can't sell our timber to British ship yards and our flax to British milliners?"

Deep lines furrowed the rector's forehead as he pondered this complex issue. He wasn't much of a political man, and while some of the delegates worshipped with his parish while they were in Philadelphia, he had engaged none of them in conversation about their business. He hadn't thought a rupture with England was very likely, and he'd held out hope that reasonable men would come to an amicable settlement of the differences between the King and his colonies. Now Jonathan suggested otherwise and this distressed him. "Given what you've just told me," he said, "I shall have to stop my complaining about the burdens of writing my weekly sermon. Clearly, much bigger burdens are being borne just a few steps away."

Jonathan smiled at the rector's sudden humility. "Soon," he continued, "they'll have to vote on this proposal to prohibit British imports. If the Congress approves it, they'll form a Continental Association of the colonies and each city and town will elect a committee to enforce the ban. To some of the delegates, this seems like the beginnings of a new government--and the beginning of the end of fidelity to the King and his government. So the stakes are very high."

"Will the proposal succeed?" the rector asked.

"Father seems uncertain." Jonathan was now enjoying his role as knowledgeable insider and began to speak more rapidly. "He expects the vote to occur next week, and he fears that the delegates who want to force a confrontation with London have been growing in strength since the Congress began. It's not that Sam Adams and Patrick Henry have drawn others to their radical notions. It's the men in the middle, the ones who came here without any clear vision of the future. They're the ones who now seem frustrated at the possibility of ever reaching an accommodation with London.

"Father says that being here has forced many of them to think harder about the realities than they ever have before. And they've all listened, almost every day, to the New Englanders' descriptions of their wretched treatment by the army. Major Sullivan of New Hampshire has had a particular effect on some of those in the middle with his estimates of the army's plans and its capacity for shattering colonial hopes.

"When you think about it, Reverend, all these men just getting to know each other may be the most important thing that's happened here. In City Tavern the other night, I overheard Mr. Galloway praising Roger Sherman and Richard Henry Lee. He even hinted at some generous feelings about Sam Adams. Mr. Galloway may be the strongest loyalist at this Congress, yet here he was praising men with whom he argues every day. In the end, I think, it'll be much easier for the doubters to go along with the majority if they respect the men with whose plans they disagree."

The rector thought about the men in his congregation, men of trade and the law, physicians and instructors at the new College of Philadelphia—many of them loyal and worried Tories. So often he had heard them criticize these delegates and their rabble rousing, wishing they would just pack up and go home. Then he realized Jonathan had fallen silent and asked, "Where does your father stand?"

This was Jonathan's first conversation about the Congress with anyone who was not a delegate. He suddenly realized how much he was enjoying his moment as an expert, and he was struck by the force of his own opinions, by the sharpness of observations he'd never before had occasion to articulate. "My father is a quiet man," Jonathan continued, "and he's especially quiet about his own thoughts. He came here as a confirmed loyalist. Our family is English through and through. My grandfather was a deacon in the Anglican Church in Kent County. And much of the timber we cut on our land goes to England on British ships for spars and planks on other British ships. The rule of the Crown has always fallen gently on us, and until a month ago, I had never laid eyes on a British soldier. There was no reason for Father to think that some better life would come to us if we rejected our King, especially if it required a bloody war to do so. "

"And is he still so inclined?" the rector wondered.

"On the whole, I think so," said Jonathan hesitantly. "He still believes that negotiation and compromise are the safest way out of our current troubles with London. But he's said some things that make me think he's less sure of his opinions than he used to be. I know he's found no justification for the way the army has treated the people of Boston. And he worries about the inability of King George to comprehend what life is like in the colonies and what concerns his subjects here. The other night at the tavern, Father said to Mr. Paine, 'George is an unfortunate king for these trying times.'"

"How does he feel about this Continental Association, if that's what it's called, this prohibition on British imports?"

"Terribly, of course. Nothing could be more frightening to him, the uncertainty of being able to sell the crops we harvest, the potential loss of the income it brings us. Our entire colony would be in grave danger if this comes to pass.

"But Father also sees the longer view. Eventually the British will have to trade with us because they've become so reliant on the products we send them. Perhaps an importation ban will force them to take us seriously, to meet our demands, to repair the rifts in our relationship. One can never tell. And sometimes you have to take risks—even great risks— to find out. That's what Father said when we had breakfast yesterday. I think he's right."

"So he'll vote to approve this Association?"

"I don't know," said Jonathan. "His heart's not in it. It's certainly not in the best interests of the Houghton family or most of the citizens of Delaware, at least not in its immediate consequences. But if he senses that a large majority of the delegates want to take this step, I think he'll be inclined to go along. Not because he thinks this particular action is right, but because he thinks acting is right and acting in unison is especially right.

"Father's greatest fear is that the Congress will end up locked in squabbling with no resolutions of any kind. That's precisely what the British are hoping. And it will only encourage them to continue to treat us as petulant and ill-behaved children. Father's fondest hope is that the Congress…"

The creak of the door shot a bright arrow of daylight into the small room, interrupting Jonathan's answer. Wentworth stood up quickly to help his wife with the heavy pewter tray. The rector was tall and angular. He had a thin face with close-set green eyes and a small shock of black hair that stood alone at the front of an otherwise bald pate. His wife, on the other hand, was short and plump with masses of gray curls tumbling out from under the cotton lappet that covered most of her head. She wore a blue and white calico dress with full skirt that made a whispering sound as she moved to the table.

The rector pointed toward Jonathan and introduced the visitor to his wife. She smiled slightly and said, "Good morning, sir, and welcome."

Jonathan nodded in response. Before he could say more, she was gone.

"My wife is a shy woman," the rector said, "an unusual characteristic in a preacher's wife. Please don't be offended by the dearth of conversation."

"Not at all, sir. I seem to be more than compensating with my own wordiness this morning."

The rector poured tea from a blue china pot into two matching cups, then passed one to Jonathan. He slowly stirred sugar into his own cup and returned to the conversation. "What are your plans when the Congress ends? "

"Well, Father and I'll return to the farm. We hope to get back in time for the end of the harvest, but certainly for the busy logging time after the leaves are off the trees. My plans are simple. I'll be working the land as my ancestors have done.

"As we clear more acreage of timber each year, we pull the stumps and put it into other crops. It's hard, endless work and the more hands we put to it the quicker it gets done. But it's challenging, too. We've been trying some new techniques of crop rotation and crop variation in the past few years. We've got wonderful bottom land along the Still River with deep dark soil. But any land gets worked out if you ask it to produce the same crops every year. So we've been experimenting with moving the crops around, planting corn one year followed by flax the next, then rye the third. So far, we're pleased with the yields."

"You seem quite scientific about all this," the rector said as he tried to picture Jonathan's scheme. "Is this the way all Delaware farmers manage their land?"

"Oh, not at all," Jonathan laughed. "Farmers are creatures of habit and they tend to grow the same crops in the same fields every year. Some believe that it's better that way because the pests you destroy one year won't be back the next. But I think they overlook the importance of the soil and the benefits that come from rotating crops so that you're not always drawing on the same natural elements in the ground."

The discussion had become too technical for the rector and the unfinished sermon on the writing table was tugging more heavily on his attention. Jonathan felt the change and realized it was time to leave. He thanked the churchman for the tea and conversation and wished him well with the sermon. They shook hands again at the door before Jonathan walked quickly away along the narrow path beside the church, down the wooden steps in front, and then south on 3$^{rd}$ Street toward Carpenters' Hall.

In the previous two weeks, Jonathan had acquired the routine of meeting his father when the Congress took its mid-day break for lunch. This made the son feel at least superficially like a dutiful secretary—though Henry rarely had anything that Jonathan needed to write down. But the meetings did afford Jonathan valued opportunities to meet and observe the delegates and to listen to their conversations.

The sessions of Congress were closed to the public. But Jonathan had noted that men like these didn't leave their ideas or passions in the meeting hall. Their discussions continued over lunch, through dinner, and into the amber glow of the tavern at night. And Jonathan had become quietly adept at finding vantage points to observe and listen. As time passed, his familiarity as "Houghton's boy" made him almost invisible and few of the delegates censored their words in his constant presence.

From time to time, certain delegates would seek Jonathan's assistance on some matter of immediacy to them. Happy to have something to do, Jonathan was a willing aide. As the Congress neared its end in mid-October, many of its members sought Jonathan's help with last-minute tasks. He carried drafts of documents to the printer, served as a go-between in late-night exchanges between groups of delegates refining the language of the proposal for a Continental Association, and on one occasion he was sent to Brimley, the candlemaker on Race Street, to order an extra week's worth of beeswax candles for the Congress. So it was not remarkable that Jonathan came to play a role in organizing the big farewell dinner at City Tavern on October 20th.

A steady autumn rain had been falling on Philadelphia for nearly a week, and this posed a problem for the planners of the event. The delegates lived in taverns and private residences all over the city. The farewell dinner would be a formal occasion to which they would be wearing their finest clothes. A great feast would be served and ladies would be in attendance as well. So it was decided that coaches would be rented for the day to transport those delegates who lived furthest from City Tavern. Charles Thomson, the secretary to the Congress and a man possessed of great fondness for detail, had asked Jonathan to oversee the procurement and deployment of the coaches.

For several days, Jonathan worked on nothing else. He visited every livery stable in the city, examined their finest coaches and negotiated the rental of those he thought suitable. But his efforts still produced too few coaches of sufficient quality, so he began to walk along Chestnut Street, out to Bush Hill, and past the Georgian and Palladian mansions set back in graceful symmetry along the Schuylkill. Here one could observe some of the largest and finest houses in America. But Jonathan was less interested in the homes, which he'd often studied before, than in their stables and carriage houses. He stopped at each large home and peered intensely at its outbuildings, looking for privately-owned coaches that might be suitable for the attendees at the farewell dinner. Upon spying such a vehicle, he'd approach the front door, present himself to the servant who answered as a representative of the Continental Congress, and ask to see the master of the house.

This usually produced the hasty appearance of a startled gentleman wondering what possible business the Congress could have with him. Jonathan would then explain that there was to be a grand celebration of the success of the Congress and "invite" his host to participate by allowing his "exceptionally fine" coach to be a part of this great and historic occasion. To one reluctant coach owner, Jonathan promised that "artists will render this event for years to come. How magnificent it will be for your children's children to see the family coach at the center of the picture bearing George Washington in his finest uniform." Jonathan had much success with this approach and used it wherever he encountered resistance. He began to fear that arguments would later break out all over the city among gentlemen claiming that it was their coach in which the great soldier had ridden.

Even those who had no use for the "rebel rabble of Carpenters' Hall," as one called them, were often willing to set aside their politics for a place in history. Only at one stately home on Spruce Street did Jonathan fail to secure the use of the coach. This was a special disappointment because here the carriage house stood at the edge of the street, not behind the main house as was more common. Jonathan had been able to view the coach, and it was the finest he had seen anywhere. When he entered to speak to the owner, he was confronted by a stern woman of upright bearing who began their conversation with a gruff scolding. "Gentlemen do not come calling at this hour without advance notice, young man," she said.

Jonathan apologized for his unannounced and uninvited appearance, then went on to explain his purpose in the usual way. The woman cut him off before he finished. "Don't waste any more of your time," she said. "I haven't any disposition to aid that group of mangy radicals in any way. They've infected our city with their presence for weeks, stirring up trouble, insulting our King, inspiring antipathies that will lead us who knows where. I wish they'd never come, and I look forward with the greatest anticipation to the day they depart. I'd rather my coach were used to carry all their proclamations and resolves to the docks and dump them into the river than to have it used in a celebration by any of them."

Jonathan was caught off guard by the woman's contempt, but sought to recover. "I understand how you feel, ma'am," he said, "but your coach is too grand for use by one of the radicals. I was hoping you might make it available for George Washington personally. He asked me himself if we might be able to borrow your coach for his use."

There was no truth in any of this. Jonathan had come to know many of the delegates, but Washington had eluded him. He and the soldier had never had a conversation of any kind, and certainly not one about preference in coaches.

The woman was not persuaded, even by Jonathan's resolute lie. "Geoooorge Waaaashington," she said, stretching the words in mock solemnity. "What has become of that man? I so admired his bravery in the frontier war, and he has always been a man of such honorable bearing. Yet here he is carousing with this army of hooligans who want to defile the very things for which Colonel Washington fought so valiantly in the west. He's too young to be senile, so I can only assume he's a turncoat. I wouldn't have him as a footman on my coach now."

Jonathan stammered briefly, looking for another line of advance, "But ma'am…" he started.

She cut him off. "I think I've made myself clear, young man. This conversation is at an end." She glowered at him, raised her eyes toward the door, then pivoted sharply and exited the room. The doorman appeared immediately and escorted Jonathan out. He seemed well-practiced at the maneuver.

The encounter had only lasted a few minutes, but Jonathan spent many more replaying it in his mind, wondering what other strategy he might have used, but contemplating as well the woman's anger toward the Congress and even toward Washington. He knew that there were plenty of doubts in Philadelphia and elsewhere about the course the Congress was following, but he was surprised that even Washington, the military hero so well and favorably known throughout the colonies, had become tainted in her mind. Where, he wondered, would all this lead?

As he walked away, Jonathan glanced back toward the carriage house. One of its double doors was open, and he could see the woman's magnificent coach, its brass fittings gleaming proudly in the half-light. What a pity, he thought, as he moved on to his next target.

Philadelphia had rarely seen a grander evening than October 20, 1774. Since its establishment a few years earlier by subscription of the leading gentlemen of the community, City Tavern had often been the site of gay parties and important meetings. The delegates had flocked to it during their stay for that very reason. So it was only fitting that City Tavern would host the farewell dinner for the Congress.

On this night the place was decked out as never before. The rain had stopped the previous day, but the streets were still rutted in mud. Boards had been nailed into small platforms to greet the arriving carriages and men had been hired to stand by to push those carriages that needed help in getting under way. Tall torches marked the entrance and the corners of the building at 2nd and Walnut Streets and illuminated the surrounding block. Garlands of flowers criss-crossed the entry hall, and overstuffed vases adorned every surface. Decorative lanterns gave every room a burnished yellow glow.

The delegates arrived in small groups from the taverns where they resided, often sharing one of Jonathan's coaches. Sam Adams wore the blazing claret suit the Sons of Liberty had purchased for him just before his departure from Boston. His cousin John, normally not a man much tormented by fashion, wore a fine suit of canary and blue and a new wig that hid his disappearing hairline. Washington, arriving last as always, drew gasps from the ladies and nods of awe from several of the men as he entered the large room upstairs in his blue and gold dress uniform, medals sparkling in the light and polished sword hanging gracefully at his side. At forty-two, taller than any other man present, graying hair arranged in curled tiers around his large head, broad shoulders and powerful chest accentuated by his erect bearing, Washington was magnetic under any circumstances. On this evening, in his finest uniform, he seemed to be the very center of the universe.

A meal of many courses, the work of a team of the city's finest chefs, lasted almost three hours. Then the music began, and the dancing. And what dancing it was. The members of this happy crowd, released now from their weeks of arduous negotiation and fueled by the premium stock of many a Philadelphia wine cellar, set aside their differences and gamboled with an unprecedented unity of purpose. Even John Adams danced, a frightening quadrille with Mrs. Lynch who would later brag to her grandchildren about the dangers she endured this night for the cause of liberty.

Only long after midnight did the throng of tired delegates and guests begin to melt away. Jonathan had marshaled his carriages in a staging area along Front Street two blocks away, and recruited runners to fetch a coach when the party assigned to it was ready to leave. The system worked well until the very end when Walnut Street in front of City Tavern had become so churned by the heavy traffic that horses could get little footing and carriage wheels were quickly swallowed by the mud. Only the brute strength of Jonathan's team of pushers and pullers made it possible for the guests to take their leave.

The last to leave was George Washington himself. He had planned to depart sooner, but guests detained him with their usual questions about his war exploits and their endless toasts to his honor. He escaped finally and appeared on the steps of the tavern, beckoning for his coach. He traveled alone.

52

Jonathan had but one carriage left and when the runner came, he sent it to collect Washington and whisk him home. But the street was by now a gooey brown sea, and the best efforts of Jonathan's men could not move the team nor budge the coach. Jonathan himself removed his frock and waded in to help. He urged one final magnificent surge which his men delivered. Its only effect was to snap the left rear wheel on this heavy carriage, disabling it and bringing a deeply troubled grimace to the face of its lone occupant.

The night was very late, George Washington was a proud but very tired man, and no other carriage remained to take him home. Jonathan, thinking quickly, pulled himself up on the axle, leaned in, and said to Washington, "I'm very sorry, sir. The wheel has broken." He realized then that he had not introduced himself to Washington and that this was their first conversation. "Begging your pardon, sir," he continued, "I'm Jonathan Houghton, and I'm responsible for these carriages. If you'd be so kind as to wait here for a moment, I will return quickly with another one."

Jonathan had no idea where he would find such a coach and vaguely hoped that one of those dispatched earlier might return in his moment of great need. Washington offered only a frown and indicated with a resigned shrug of his shoulders that he would do as Jonathan had asked.

Jonathan pulled himself out of the mud, moved to the side of the street, and had a sudden flash of inspiration. He quickly shouted to two of his men to release the team of horses from the disabled carriage and lead them to where he stood on firm ground. Happy themselves to be free of the mud, the team of four moved smartly. Jonathan climbed the traces between the wheel horses, grabbed the reins in his hand, and drove them quickly the three blocks to Spruce Street where sat the magnificent coach that had been denied to him three days earlier.

No time now to worry about permission and courtesy, he thought to himself, when the leading citizen of the colonies is stuck in the mud of a Philadelphia street. The door to the carriage house was unlocked and Jonathan quickly turned the team so that it faced the street. He dismounted, backed the four horses slowly until he was able to hitch the end of their box to the carriage. That done, he bounded to the driver's seat, released the brake and snapped the reins. The team jolted forward and three minutes later, Jonathan pulled the carriage to a halt on 2$^{nd}$ Street, a few doors above City Tavern and out of the mud. He ordered two of his men to wade to the disabled coach and carry Washington to the dry sidewalk. This they did, struggling with the weight of the large man and the uncertain footing.

Washington remained undirtied and quickly pulled himself to his full height, seeking to retain a modicum of dignity and pleased only that none of the delegates or guests was here to view this sorry scene. Jonathan jumped down off the seat, landing but two feet in front of Washington. Without thought and with much subsequent embarrassment, Jonathan snapped off a salute and said, "Sir, your coach awaits."

The last half hour of Washington's life had been one of the worst, but he could not suppress a smile at the antics of this young man. Unsure how else to respond, Washington returned his salute and stepped around Jonathan to enter the coach. Jonathan remounted the carriage and drove the team and his now bemused passenger the length of 3rd Street to the handsome Harp and Crown where Washington took his lodging.

When they stopped in front, Jonathan pulled the brake, tied the reins, and dropped down to the street. He turned the handle and held the door while Washington stepped out, acting all the while as if this were an entirely normal routine. Washington looked at him and spoke to Jonathan for the first time, "Did you say your name was Houghton?"

"Yes, sir, Jonathan Houghton."

"You're Henry Houghton's boy?"

"Yes, sir, I am," Jonathan said, trying to look as if that were an honor he wore proudly.

"Mr. Houghton, I'm grateful for your efforts tonight. I'd be even more grateful if you would join me for tea, here in my quarters, tomorrow afternoon at three. There is a matter I would like to discuss with you."

Greatly surprised by this invitation, Jonathan only managed to nod in affirmation and say, "Certainly, sir." Before he could think of more to say, Washington turned and proceeded through the gate and up the walk to the front door. Jonathan stood in stunned silence for a moment, then turned to close the door to the carriage. "The carriage!" Jonathan suddenly realized. "Oh my God, I'm a carriage thief."

He leapt quickly back up to the driver's seat, and turned the team around in the street. Not wanting to make any unnecessary noise when he arrived back at Spruce Street, he released the team at the corner, and using more strength than he thought he possessed pushed the coach slowly back into the carriage house. No light had come on in the house, to Jonathan's great relief, so he silently pushed the door closed, tiptoed to the street, then ran at top speed back to the waiting team. He mounted the traces again, snapped the reins, and rode off into the night that--unknown to him at that moment--had changed his life forever.

His "rescue" of Washington and then the invitation to the meeting today set Jonathan's mind on a roiling course that sleep could not calm. So as he turned west outside the Widow Almy and headed down Arch Street to meet with the great man, he felt a peculiar mixture of anxiety and excitement. What did Washington want? Merely to thank him for his exertions? To dress him down for allowing his carriage to get stuck in the first place? To ask Jonathan to run some kind of errand for him? If he'd known Washington better, Jonathan might have had a keener sense of what to expect. In reality, he couldn't even make an informed guess.

Though Washington had lived during the Congress at the Harp and Crown Tavern, he often held appointments at the home of Josephus Maynard on Chestnut Street. Maynard, a friend from the campaigns on the frontier, was now in Europe on business but was happy to let his old commander use his house, one of the finest in Philadelphia. William Lee, Washington's dignified manservant, met Jonathan at the door, led him into the large front parlor, and announced that the Colonel would be along in ten minutes. Jonathan took a seat and looked around the most imposing dwelling he had ever entered.

The room was at least thirty feet long and almost as wide. Intricately patterned red Persian rugs lay at each end, covering most of the polished oak floors. Arrangements of furniture were grouped around the room, all in fine brocade but each with its own color scheme. Fan carvings splayed out above the tall windows on three sides of the room. Rich blue curtains, which to Jonathan's nervous touch seemed to be made of pure silk, were tied to the side of each window allowing bright afternoon sun to stream in from the west. Massive oil paintings filled the open spaces on the walls between the windows. The scenes were unfamiliar to Jonathan, mostly romanticized views of countryside that did not look like any place Jonathan had ever been. One painting especially caught his eye, a dark and shadowy scene of heavy clouds forming over the sharp rocky peaks of a mountain range. The clouds seemed powerful and threatening, but it was the mountains that commanded Jonathan's attention. He had never seen mountains.

Standing alone with these paintings, Jonathan thought warmly of his brother. When he came home from college in New Jersey, Nathaniel had set up a studio in one of the outbuildings on the farm. From time to time, Jonathan would drop in when Nathaniel was painting. There was never much time for this—certainly far less than Nathaniel would have preferred—so it took a long time for him to finish a painting. And he was always complaining about not having the right materials: brushes, paints, or canvasses.

But Nathaniel's few paintings were nothing like these. Mostly they were small scenes of flowers in an earthen jar or a pair of hands or once, Jonathan remembered, of the face of a fierce-looking man. When Jonathan asked Nathaniel who's face it was, his brother only said, "No one real."

The family had received only two letters from Nathaniel since he left for England nearly six months earlier. He wondered what his brother's life was like there now, whether he was able to paint as he'd hoped, whether he was painting any more horrible imaginary men.

His thoughts were interrupted by Washington's entrance. "Good afternoon, Mr. Houghton," he said, striding briskly toward the young man. "So good of you to come."

Jonathan turned quickly and looked directly at Washington, "I'm honored to be here, sir, and to be of service to you."

Washington motioned toward a cluster of green and white chairs at the end of the parlor furthest from the door. He and Jonathan moved toward them and sat down.

"That was a fine bit of horse work last night," Washington said. "I know how hard it is to manage a team of four from a wagon seat. To maneuver them as you did while standing on the traces was quite remarkable. You obviously know how to handle horses."

Jonathan tried to appear humble despite the pride exploding inside him. "Thank you, sir," he managed to say. "I've lived with horses my whole life on our farm in Delaware. We harvest a lot of timber and I spend most of every day on horseback in the woods. Sometimes I ride on a large log, twitching a team as they drag it from the woods. Horses just feel like part of me."

So this was it, Jonathan thought to himself. He asked me here just to thank me for last night.

Washington brushed some lint from his stocking then looked up at Jonathan, signaling a change of subject. "In the weeks I've been in Philadelphia," he said, "I've been worshipping at Christ Church. I'll be leaving for Virginia tomorrow and I wanted to invite the rector there to tea before I left. Reverend Wentworth. He was here on Tuesday and we had a good talk. His sermons are sometimes a little hard to follow, but he's a caring soul and much beloved by his parish.

"While he was here, he mentioned a conversation he'd had with you about farming. Told me of your ideas about crop rotation and variation. Wentworth obviously has never been a farmer and he confused some of the details, but he did a good job of conveying your enthusiasm for these new ideas."

Washington bent forward now and looked intently at his guest. "When I go back to Mount Vernon, Jonathan, I have to face up to the hard fact that our harvest this year will be another disappointment. I have nearly 3000 acres in cultivation now, mostly in grain. We get plenty of rain, but the soil is poor. It's a bigger struggle every year to get a good yield.

"I've been hearing about this crop rotation and variety planting, even been experimenting with some of it myself. But I don't know enough about it. I was hoping you might tell me what you know." Washington smoothed a wrinkle on the sleeve of his gray frock, then looked away from Jonathan, indicating that he was ready to receive the young man's answer.

Jonathan sat stunned. Of all the topics he'd imagined they might discuss, farming was not one. Washington was perhaps the best known farmer in America. His plantation at Mount Vernon was legendary. Yet here he sat in a Philadelphia parlor asking a man half his age for advice on farming. Of a stranger turn in conversation Jonathan could not conceive.

"Well," he started, collecting his thoughts "we've been experimenting with crop rotation in our fields along the river. Began three years ago, so this will be our third harvest." Then for nearly twenty minutes Jonathan explained in detail how he and Henry had studied crop rotation, how they'd planned their plantings, and how their yields had increased. As the details unfolded, Washington listened closely, interrupting occasionally to probe a detail or pose a question. When tea arrived, Washington motioned for it to be set on a side table, but neither man took a cup and no tea was consumed.

As the sun began to fade, Jonathan was running out of things to say. But he so enjoyed this unusual audience that he kept adding details as they came to mind. Washington's absorption never waned.

Nearly an hour and a half after Jonathan's arrival, William Lee interrupted the conversation to remind Washington that another guest would be arriving for an appointment in a few minutes. Jonathan assumed that the conversation was over, but Washington had several more questions before letting him go.

As they walked to the door, Washington thanked the young man for all the information he'd provided and said, "I wonder if you might be amenable to a visit to Mount Vernon in the spring. I'd love to continue this conversation and I'd like very much to show you our fields and hear what you have to say about them. Perhaps we could ride Mt. Vernon together and you could give me your opinion on how we might implement some of these ideas. I'd be deeply indebted if you could make the trip-- and very pleased, of course, to have you as our guest."

It later occurred to Jonathan that spring was the busiest time at Still River Bend and a trip to Mount Vernon would take up several weeks under the best of conditions. But when he immediately accepted Washington's invitation, none of that crossed his mind. The two men parted with a vigorous handshake and an agreement to see each other again in April.

Walking back to the Widow Almy, Jonathan paid no attention to the houses and people he passed. All of his thoughts were on the meeting that had just ended. Perhaps I'll never make it to Mount Vernon, he thought; maybe Washington was just being polite. But at least I'll have this time with the man to remember in the years ahead, perhaps to tell my children about. Washington's renown will probably have faded by then; they may not even know his name. But I can tell them that for a few minutes in October of 1774, I sat in personal conversation with the most famous man in the colonies.

"Mr. Houghton!" The shout broke Jonathan's preoccupation. He looked to his left and saw Reverend Wentworth, standing on the steps of Christ Church. "How are you today?"

"Fine, thank you, sir," Jonathan replied. "Father and I are heading home tomorrow. There's much to be done in Delaware when we get back." Jonathan was thinking of the farm and the busy month ahead.

"I expect so," said Wentworth. "Now that the Congress has created this Association, I imagine your father will have a big job explaining it to the people there."

"Oh yes, that too," Jonathan said.

"Say," Wentworth continued, "I never heard. Did your father vote to approve the Association? I know you told me he had serious doubts about the direction the Congress was taking."

"He did, sir. He voted for it."

"And what about Galloway? Wasn't he dead set against it?

"He was, sir. Made a long speech criticizing it. But in the end he voted for it, too."

"How do you account for that?" asked Wentworth, looking puzzled.

"Galloway said we all had to be in this together, even if we didn't always agree about how to proceed. Said he couldn't get comfortable with the idea of separating England and her colonies, but he also knew we couldn't tolerate the treatment we'd been getting. Said he'd vote with the majority so we didn't send the wrong message to London."

"Well, Jonathan, this is going to spoil Christmas in London."

Yes, sir, I expect it will."

# Chapter 5

## *London*
## *Christmas 1774 - January 1775*

The singing around the spinet stopped for a few minutes and
Nathaniel Houghton moved toward the small fireplace to take in some of
its warmth. In the months since his arrival in London, he had found the
climate peculiar in every way. Far cooler than Delaware in summer,
similar in temperature in winter, but with a damp and relentless chill.
Even in the warmth of this room packed with Christmas celebrants, the
tepid coal flame did little to soothe Nathaniel's cold limbs.

Christmas was still nine days away, but this was the fourth of the
holiday parties Nathaniel had attended and two more lay ahead. Though
the guest lists changed some from party to party, the evenings were
remarkably similar. Guest arrived by coach or cab around seven, glasses
of punch and small talk until eight, then a tinkling bell that started a quick
shuffling to dinner around a long broad table in a heavily-paneled room
laden with green boughs of holly, bows of red ribbon, and scores of
flickering white candles.

The dinners had begun to run together in Nathaniel's mind. Heavy
silver platters of boar, mutton, fowl, salmon, and loin of beef. Goblets of
port and Madeira lined up like soldiers in front of every plate. Sterling
bowls heaped with potatoes and yams. Gravies and sauces and fruit
preserves scattered randomly where space allowed. All this followed by
trays of steaming puddings. Elegantly dressed servants moving silently
among the diners offering dish upon dish in an endless parade from the
serving pantry.

By ten, the overfed guests had migrated to a large reception room-
-oval in the finer houses, rectangular in those less grand. Here the
decorations would be even more fanciful: yellow angels with silver-tinted
wings, bright green wreaths on the windows, woven boughs of holly
strung everywhere. Someone designated by the host would begin to play

at the spinet or harpsichord, and soon all would join in the caroling. Servants would move silently among the guests with warm toddy and platters of sweet pastries.

Nathaniel only knew the simpler Christmas celebrations of Delaware, a few days of anticipation topped by some carol singing on Christmas eve and a hearty family meal on Christmas day. These London gatherings were utterly different, and they dazed him at first with their opulence and excess. Why have one meat when six were available? Why only one wine when the cellar yielded a dozen?

The town houses that held these parties were larger and far more elegant than any he had ever seen in America, even during his stops in Philadelphia on the way to Princeton. They were close to the cobbled street so that carriages could leave their guests at the entrance. Tall paneled doors with fierce brass knockers defined each entry as unique. Through the doorways, one passed into high and hospitable front hallways, painted in light hues, with glittering chandeliers and sedate oil paintings centering the walls.

Then it was into the reception rooms and parlors, the dining rooms and, for the men, the library. Most of the houses had been in the same family for generations and each succeeding earl or duke had added a layer of ornament to the inheritance.

Nathaniel was especially alert to the art work that adorned these old houses. A family whose ancestry boasted a Navy man would have a disproportionate share of seascapes on the walls and on every table top and mantle piece a collection of scrimshaw or baubles gathered from exotic ports of call. Most families seemed to have had their share of horsemen and hunters, so romanticized equestrian scenes and "the hunt," as the British called it, were common themes of household art as well.

But Nathaniel quickly noticed that the dominant art form in these fine London houses was portraiture. In the home of the sixth Earl of Lansdowne, one was sure to find large, gilt-framed portraits of each of the five previous Earls plus their wives and children and the siblings who had the misfortune not to be born first and thus to inherit no titles.

Nathaniel had been in London only a few days when he came to realize that portraiture was by far the most common genre in all London painting because there was no other reliable way to know how someone had looked or how fashionably they had dressed once they died. Every person of means had his or her portrait painted. Many Londoners sat for portraits every year or so to record changes in appearance, a new position or title, the growth of a family, or merely to mark the purchase of a new dress.

Royalty aside, of no class of men were portraits painted more often than of political leaders and military figures. History relied on portraits to fill in the details of how leaders appeared, how battle scenes took shape, how famous speeches were delivered. Most citizens knew their leaders and their military heroes only through these portraits. Propaganda relied on portraits, especially in times of war or succession crises in the royal line. Admirals strode boldly on the decks of sturdy ships as cannonballs whizzed through the mizzens overhead. Generals sat easily in the saddles of chargers rearing on their haunches while scores of bloody soldiers lay impaled on swords and pikes all around them. Politicians looked up to rapt galleries leaning over balustrades to hear their every word or stood proudly by tables adorned with some treaty or resolve they had helped to author. At least in their portraits.

One of the ironies of the time, Nathaniel quickly noted, was that portraits had become the great cliché of 18th century painting, an art form upon which even its most successful practitioners often looked with disdain. And yet it was a primary source of income for many of the important painters of the period. So, much as they belittled the form, they lived well from the commissions it generated.

Even Thomas Gainsborough, whose landscapes were so touching in their use of color and contrasting moods that Nathaniel could happily stand before them for hours, had attained greatest renown for his portraits. When he was but twenty-one, Gainsborough's rendering of his neighbor Mr. Andrews, flintlock slack on his arm, leaning insouciantly next to Mrs. Andrews in blue dress and simple bonnet, had captivated the London art world and created a market for his portraits that remained robust almost 30 years later. And though he stood above the rest, Gainsborough was not alone. George Romney, Allan Ramsay, and Joshua Reynolds, the great English portraitists of the time, were all kept busy—and wealthy—by the insatiable demand for renderings of the famous and the rich in the bustling British capital.

One of those drawn to portraiture more by its financial than its artistic appeal was Benton Brooke Carlisle. When Nathaniel first met Carlisle in 1771, the artist was 63 years old. He had built a favorable reputation in his early years for his paintings of landscapes and still lifes. He was especially well-regarded for his depictions of clouds and the changing moods of the weather. Some even thought him the equal of John

Constable in this vein. But Carlisle's work, though always in favor with the connoisseurs, had never reached the level of renown that produced easy sales or high prices for his paintings. Only when he began to accept a few commissions for portraits in the late 1750s had his fame grown, and his income with it.

Nathaniel's first encounter with Carlisle came at the end of the young man's tour of the European art centers—Florence, Rome, Paris, and Madrid. He'd come back to London for his scheduled return to Delaware with Uncle Edward. In the two weeks before they were to sail, Nathaniel spent as much time as possible along the Thames and in Grosvenor and St. James Squares sketching scenes that he hoped to paint later when he could get the brushes and paints he would need to execute them. One afternoon, while he was sketching a garden on the Brook Street side of Grosvenor Square, an older man who'd watched him from a short distance for some time—to Nathaniel's discomfort, in fact—stepped up and complimented him on his images. Nathaniel had now done enough sketching to know that an artist with a pad and pen in a public place often received uninvited reviews of his work and paid little attention to the man or his comments.

But then the older man offered Nathaniel some suggestions that indicated he was knowledgeable about the difficulties of capturing shadows and light tones in an ink sketch. A conversation evolved that went on for more than an hour. The older man took the pen on several occasions and showed Nathaniel how to place human figures in drawings of grand scale, how to keep the shadows of trees to appropriate length for the season or time of day, how to make clouds look realistic even in a single dimension and color.

They spoke little in complete sentences, only in brief phrases and exclamations accompanied by gestures, turns of hand, or simple strokes of pen on paper. But Nathaniel thought it one of the richest conversations he'd ever had. As the older man prepared to leave, Nathaniel rose to his feet and thanked him sincerely for his criticism and his suggestions. The older man bowed respectfully and began to step away. Then Nathaniel realized he had not introduced himself or learned the older man's name, so he thrust out his hand and said "I'm Nathaniel Houghton."

Nathaniel hoped the older man would respond with a similar introduction, but he merely said, "A pleasure to meet you, young man."

So Nathaniel was more blunt, "Beg your pardon, sir. Might I ask your name?"

The older man smiled gently and said, "Of course, I should have offered it. Benton Carlisle."

"Benton Brooke Carlisle?" Nathaniel responded with surprise. He'd seen two of Carlisle's landscapes in museums in Italy and a delicate still life that Carlisle had painted nearly twenty years earlier hung prominently at the Museo del Prado in Madrid.

"Correct," Carlisle said. "Do you know the name?"

Nathaniel told then of his trip through Europe, of the paintings he'd seen by Carlisle, and of his profound admiration for the older man's work.

Carlisle listened silently, not wanting to interrupt the flow of kind words. When Nathaniel stopped, the older man said simply, "Why don't you come by my studio tomorrow afternoon and we can talk further about some of the problems we've discussed here. I would like especially to show you how paint can do things with the sky that pen and ink cannot begin to capture."

Nathaniel readily agreed. To be invited to a private tutorial from one of England's finest painters—Nathaniel thought he must be dreaming. Carlisle indicated his address on Bloomsbury Square, of which Nathaniel made indelible mental note.

That chance meeting had occurred more than two years ago in the summer of 1772. Now Nathaniel was attending a Christmas party at one of the finest homes in London's Marylebone with Benton Carlisle, whose fame and growing network of connections among the powerful and the wealthy of London were Nathaniel's ticket of admission to all such gatherings. A year after his return to Delaware with Uncle Edward, Nathaniel had received a letter from Benton Carlisle, inviting him to return to London to work as the painter's assistant and—so the letter seemed to imply—to be Carlisle's only student.

Nathaniel had seen Carlisle only one more time on that first trip to London, the visit to his studio. But the older man and the younger, the teacher and the student, the mentor and protégé so enjoyed each other's company that the afternoon together had remained fixed in Carlisle's memory. So, too, had the talent he'd seen in Nathaniel, a talent much in need of tutoring and shaping, to be sure, but full of promise for work of great merit.

When demand for Carlisle's portraits began to grow and his commissions to swell, he found himself in dire need of an assistant, someone to help set up the sittings, manage the consistency of light, and

64

complete work on the backgrounds and solid areas after Carlisle had finished with the detail of the subjects. Nathaniel was a natural candidate for this work as a way of earning his keep while he studied with Carlisle in the finer arts of landscape and still life.

Carlisle's letter brought great joy to Nathaniel, but it also brought days of turmoil to the Houghton home. To Nathaniel, this was an unimaginable opportunity: to go to live in one of the art capitals of the world, to work and study with one of the important painters of the age, to have the time and the means to nurture his own talent. And, it need be said, to escape the life of a Delaware farmer that Nathaniel had never wanted and only barely tolerated.

At home, only his mother found any pleasure in Carlisle's invitation to Nathaniel. Patience had always seen and loved the artistic side of her eldest child. He was the one, more than any of her other children, who would let her read him stories, who would study with her the flowers she cultivated in the garden on the south side of the Houghton house, who, as he grew older, devoured books and talked about the characters he liked and those he despised. Henry had seen these traits in Nathaniel but regarded them as impediments to the role he was destined to play as the next steward of the Houghton farm at Still River Bend. He was tolerant of Nathaniel's interests and understanding of Patience's affection for them. But there was work to be done and as Nathaniel grew old enough to contribute to that work, Henry often felt that the boy's head and his heart were elsewhere.

When Carlisle's invitation came, Henry complimented Nathaniel on it, but assumed that reason would prevail and his son would see the impossibility of gallivanting off to England. When it became clear that Nathaniel intended to entertain seriously the idea of going and, in so doing, of abandoning his birthright on the farm, Henry was heartsore. Patience later said that it was a measure of Henry's humanity that he didn't resist more overtly when Nathaniel announced his intention to return to England.

It's hard for a father to admit that a son, especially his first son, has fallen short of his hopes. And Henry never did say such a thing out loud. But Patience knew, and his other children strongly sensed, that Henry felt the deepest disappointment in Nathaniel, disappointment that he would repudiate the tradition and opportunity he inherited in Delaware for something so ephemeral as picture painting, and disappointment that he would leave America for England at precisely the time when the two were poised for a defining struggle across the ocean that separated them.

Nathaniel, too, sensed all of this, though his father never put his disappointments to words. Sons always know when they've failed to live up to paternal expectations. No words are needed. Communication is by downcast glance, by rolled eye, mostly by silence. But sons know. They always know.

So it was a measure of Nathaniel's passion, of his certainty about what he wanted from life—and what he didn't want—that he would leave for England in the spring of 1774 in the face of the painful disappointment his departure caused in Henry Houghton. Nathaniel loved Henry, and he loved Henry's feelings for his land and the family history and hard work it represented. There were nights while he was wrestling with this decision that Nathaniel wished he were a different person, wished he could toe comfortably the long line of tradition his ancestors had plotted for him. But he knew he could not, though the knowledge of that did little to diminish his own sadness at the effect his departure would have on his father.

It was an awkward scene on that day in late May. Nathaniel's two bags had been tied atop a pile of logs in the back of the heavy wagon, the team was hitched, and Quiet Jack sat stoically at the reins. Journeys at sea were always dangerous, but no one said, or thought, much about that. Thoughts were of the past, of moments and hopes now passing into history, not of the details or risks of the days ahead.

The morning mist still clung to the hillside as the family lined up at the edge of the damp path to say their good-byes. Savannah, the most reticent and careful of the Houghton children, was first. She held her composure, kissing her brother lightly on the cheek, looking him in the eye, and wishing him great good luck.

Jonathan bore this departure with a heart almost as heavy as his father's. His brother had always been his best friend and primary playmate. And he knew that Nathaniel's going would have a greater impact on his own life than any other Houghton's. He would now be expected to take over the farm and, because one son had already failed to meet that expectation, the pressure on Jonathan would surely intensify. Just as Nathaniel was escaping from a destiny in which he'd had no hand, the grip of that hand on Jonathan's future was tightening.

Tears swelled in Patience's eyes as she hugged Nathaniel tightly. She was so very proud of him, of what he was becoming, of what he would be. She could not say that in Henry's presence, but she did not need to. Nathaniel knew, and it mattered to him greatly that she felt that way. He often wondered what his life would have been had Patience not been his mother. On no day did that question weigh more heavily than on this one of deep and dissecting emotions.

Finally Nathaniel turned to Henry who had been giving directions for delivery of the logs to Quiet Jack. Father and son faced each other. Everyone noticed how alike they were: not tall, but lean and strong. Both had full heads of hair, drawn back on top and curled on the side in the style of the time. Henry's nose was slightly longer than Nathaniel's, his eyebrows fuller, his hair darker. But both were handsome in the strong and clean lines of their countenances. Their resemblance, in this setting especially, was powerful.

Henry shook his son's hand. The Houghton men did not embrace. He fumbled briefly with words, but wished his son good fortune and safe journey and, pointedly, swift return. And then, though it seemed there was one more thing he wished to say, Henry stepped back so Nathaniel could mount the wagon.

Nathaniel stood quietly, focusing briefly on Henry's damp eyes. Then he tipped his gray hat to the entire family, bounded up to the seat beside Quiet Jack, and looked ahead as the team started at the whip, and the wagon began to roll slowly down the path, away from the house where Houghtons had lived for nearly a hundred years.

That seemed such a long time ago to Nathaniel as he stood now at the edge of a large London drawing room. His life in London had been even fuller and more stimulating than he'd hoped on that May day. Carlisle was an exacting, but a caring and gentle teacher. He and Nathaniel often worked hard to stay abreast of their portrait business, but Carlisle never failed to make time to tutor the young man as he worked his way through a variety of increasingly vibrant still lifes. There had been too little time for ventures into the countryside to paint landscapes, but Carlisle continued to insist that they would get to that when Nathaniel's studio techniques reached a higher level of proficiency.

They worked together nearly every day, and their affection for each other grew. Nathaniel was an eager student, often staying up until dawn to work on his own paintings. And he was utterly reliable about carrying out Carlisle's instructions in finishing off the broad strokes in the portraits. London artists of the time were known for flights of temper and excesses of ego. Gainsborough's battles with the Royal Academy, leading ultimately to his angry resignation, were juicy gossip at the parties and dinners Nathaniel attended.

But Carlisle was no prima donna, and Nathaniel counted himself blessed for that. As Carlisle moved into old age, without children of his own, and as Nathaniel struggled with the guilt of abandoning his father and his family, the two formed a strong bond based on the eternal male search for a father or a son.

Nathaniel's reflections were interrupted by a tinkling bell signaling the time in all of these evenings when the men and women separated. Most often, the women would go to a parlor or drawing room to discus fashion, the "season," or upcoming marriages and births. The men would retire to a study or library, someplace more suitable to serious talk, where their conversations would range over politics or business dealings or new scientific discoveries.

Nathaniel had never found a comfortable place at these male gatherings. He was usually one of the youngest people there and was unknown to most of the others, save for a formal introduction earlier in the evening. No one asked Nathaniel's opinion about anything and he volunteered none. So he sat near a wall, watching and listening, but not participating in the talk. He began to realize after a while, that the other men present did not know or did not recall that he was from America. They engaged in conversation much more critical of Americans and more insulting to American behavior and character than would have been likely had they been more cognizant of the presence in their midst of a member of this species they found so worthy of invective and contempt.

The discussion on this night turned quickly to the First Continental Congress. Mr. Pettibone, the barrister who first broached the topic, said the words as if they were some evil taste he was trying to expectorate. News had just reached London of the final actions of the Congress and copies of its petition to the king had been printed and circulated. Dr. Sudworth, the host, walked around a table at the end of the room and drew a copy of the document from a drawer. The ink marks in its margin suggested that he'd read the document with some care.

"What impudence," Sudworth stated loudly, holding the petition aloft. "They act as if citizens have the right to tell their King how he should treat them and how his government should be organized to serve their interests. Look here where they complain, as a violation of their rights for God's sake, that the King has sent the army to America. These are the same brigands who dress up as savages and pour tea into the ocean in the middle of the night, who burn the houses of the King's magistrates, who tar and feather those who disagree with them. Can they not imagine why a prudent sovereign would think the army was very much needed to curb their law-breaking excesses?"

"Frankly, I must tell you that I'm worried about all this," Pettibone interrupted. "We're not talking here about some scruffy peasants from Lancashire, unhappy that their earl expects them to work on the Sabbath to get in the harvest. These Americans have a society of their own, one that in many ways mirrors ours. The radicals are not from the lower orders, but the higher. In fact, many of those without means, tradesmen and simple farmers, have no more affection for these seditious diatribes than we do. But it's the wealthy traders, the lawyers, clergy, and the gentlemen who seem to be at the forefront of this movement.

"Have you seen the list of delegates at this Congress? I've been to New York. I know about some of these men. I don't know all of the names, but I certainly know George Washington, who fought with us in the Seven Year's War, and the Adams cousins from Boston. Troublemakers, the both of them, but the best lawyers in the city. Joseph Galloway of Pennsylvania, for God's sake, I thought him a reliable voice of reason. And Richard Henry Lee is from one of the finest families in the Virginia colony. These are men whose participation in this scheming should give us pause. They know how to organize, they're masters of propaganda, and they have wealth. If they truly represent colonial sentiment, then we're moving rapidly toward a crisis beyond our imagination."

John Fay, whom Nathaniel had seen at several of these parties, rose, poured himself more brandy, and moved to the fire. "They've taken leave of their senses, gentlemen," he said. "Their actions are inflammatory and all they'll accomplish is the arrival of more ships of the Royal Navy loaded with more of the King's grenadiers who will in very short order put the trouble makers in their place—or, better yet, put them in the best brig in Boston."

Glasses were lifted in reaction to Fay's remarks and several men said "Hear, hear." Smiles passed around the room.

But Pettibone was having nothing of this. "How many ships, how many soldiers are we prepared to send, gentlemen?" he asked. "How much of our treasure will we put to this task? How long are we willing to endure the loss of British lives and the draining of the British treasury while the Americans wait us out. This will not be like fighting the

Prussians on some European battlefield. This will be a different kind of warfare, entirely.

"In America, citizens have muskets of their own. They use them to hunt for their table and to protect their families from the dangers of the wilderness. How can a few thousand soldiers occupy and control a continent where more than two million persons, most of them armed, are scattered over more than a thousand miles? While it's true that our army is the equal of any in the world, can it conquer a group of our own citizens who will be wise enough to avoid direct engagements with superior forces?

"And remember, too," Pettibone continued. "These are men whose families have been in America for more than a century. We may think of them as His Majesty's subjects, and they may even describe themselves that way. Look at the petition that Dr. Sudworth holds in his hand. It's addressed, very politely and very formally to 'the King's most excellent majesty.' But when you scrape their skin, you find not English blood, but American. More and more of them, like that young fellow Henry from Virginia, are calling themselves Americans. As they start to think of themselves that way, they'll start to act that way. And they'll find reason after reason to sever the bonds with us when those bonds seem to them not of affection but of oppression."

Nathaniel listened to the discussion in stunned silence. What would they think, he wondered, if they knew my father's name was on the very list of delegates they were discussing? Were they right about colonials coming to think of themselves as Americans and not Englishmen? He hadn't been very interested in these discussions when he was in Delaware, but he knew that there were people in both camps and that the situation was fluid. Just as some people were growing more frustrated with British rule and were calling for an American rebellion, others were digging in their heels in loyalty to the crown. He doubted that these gentlemen, over brandy in their fine houses, could possibly comprehend the complexity and diversity of views in their American colonies.

Lord Wickersham, the oldest man present and a member of the House of Lords now after years of service in His Majesty's government, tried to summarize the discussion. "Gentlemen," he said, "we're a very old country and we've endured every imaginable threat to our survival and sovereignty over the past millennium. Be assured that these complaints and dissents emanating from our American colonies will not be the end of us. We'll manage them as we have managed other challenges in the past. We in Parliament have sought to get the Americans to pay a larger share of the cost of their own defense. They've resisted that policy. We'll continue to legislate until we find an American policy that's effective.

"The Americans are not a government, not a foreign power, not even one people. Most of the trouble is in Massachusetts, and we're dealing with that. But this petition is pitifully weak, a plea from those who, however bold their language, realize that they can't consolidate their interests effectively to resist the government and thus must plead with their King to treat them more gently.

"These leading Americans, these men of the higher classes, as Pettibone called them, will not instigate a rebellion because they know, first, that they could never combine their own interests in an effective government to manage a rebellion and, second, because the cost'll be too high. They talk boldly, but when their fortunes and their farms and their lives are at stake, this talk of rebellion will quickly vanish into the air. Then the normal processes of government will resolve the crisis."

This argument seemed to find broad support in the room, though Pettibone frowned at Wickersham's conclusion. But the hour was late and the discussion had reached a natural end. Men began to bid their host goodnight and to call for their wraps and carriages.

Nathaniel and Carlisle had sat on opposite sides of the room during the discussion and had made little eye contact. Though Carlisle was gifted at conversation, he rarely spoke on political matters. Partly that was lack of interest in affairs of state, partly prudence on the part of one who derived income from painting the portraits of leading politicians.

But in the carriage on their way home, Carlisle asked Nathaniel for his impressions of the evening. Though the two men had become very close, Carlisle knew little of Nathaniel's political views and little as well about Nathaniel's family.

"I don't know what to make of it," said Nathaniel. "While I was at college, and from time to time at home, I would listen in on similar conversations full of highly philosophical discussions about rights and obligations. The only difference here is that many of these men seemed to believe that ultimately relations between the King and his colonies will be decided, not by what is right or proper, but by brute force. I certainly hope they're wrong about that."

"Well," Carlisle said with a laugh, "you can be sure of one thing. No matter how much blood is spilled in America, not a single drop of brandy will be spilled in the drawing rooms of London."

During a sitting the next day, Carlisle grew frustrated with his subject. Viscount Barrington would sit patiently for few minutes while Carlisle painted, then he'd jump up to speak to an aide or turn his head to engage in conversation with some junior minister or messenger. Portraits of politicians were essential to Carlisle's income, but the more important the politician, the longer and more difficult the sittings. The business of state had to go on, even as its leaders were being recorded for posterity.

Barrington, the state secretary at war, was proving an especially difficult subject. Carlisle had begun the portrait two weeks earlier, before the holidays. But the social demands of the season had forced the minister to suspend the sittings until after the new year. So here on January 4, 1775, Carlisle was hoping to complete the sitting part of the work.

But things were not going well. There was much activity on this day as the government got back to business after the holidays. The American crisis seemed to be the primary issue on Barrington's agenda that day and other officials repeatedly entered and departed his quarters at Whitehall.

Nathaniel's principal task during these sittings was to manage the lighting. That required the exercise of control over the natural lighting entering through Whitehall's large windows and the addition or movement of lanterns to add candlelight. No portrait painter could hope to be effective if the light on his subject varied with each sitting. So Nathaniel had to recall how the light had fallen on the subject in previous sittings and try to recreate it for each new one. The longer it took to complete the sitting and the more of each day it consumed, the more demanding was his task.

During the course of a sitting, Nathaniel would often be in motion, opening and closing curtains, lighting or extinguishing candles, moving lanterns to change the light they shed on the subject. After the first several portraits on which he worked with Carlisle, he was surprised to notice how the subjects came to regard him as simply part of the mechanics of production. Later, he came to understand that this was the treatment afforded servants who were regarded as invisible, deaf to the details of any conversation in their presence, and never permitted to speak unless first spoken to. So Nathaniel's presence never affected the conversations that transpired during these sittings and he rarely muttered a word, not even in response to direction from Carlisle. The subjects would engage in conversations about intimate family matters, business dealings, or serious matters of state, as if Nathaniel and Carlisle were not there.

Late in this morning of their work on Barrington's portrait, they were again interrupted by his need to read an apparently important paper that had been handed him by a tall, upright junior minister from the Admiralty. Barrington read through it carefully, thought for a moment, and asked, "Is this, then, the Admiralty's recommendation?"

"It is sir," the junior minister replied. "We've calculated the availability of ships from the current fleet, then estimated when those under construction will come on line, and concluded that we can spare another sixteen ships to support General Gage in Boston. The army will soon have its estimates on how many soldiers it will provide for the campaign there, but now they will know our transport capacity for soldiers and their kit."

The junior minister seemed confident of his knowledge and Barrington asked him no further questions. "Fine then," the Viscount said. "Tell the First Lord that he has my approval to proceed." Barrington pulled on a wide ribbon behind his desk and a small, bald clerk appeared almost instantly carrying a heavy metal seal. Barrington handed him the paper he'd been given by the junior minister and the clerk quickly and proficiently affixed the seal.

The clerk departed with the seal in hand and the junior minister close behind. Nathaniel checked the light as Barrington returned to his chair, saying not a word to either Carlisle or his assistant about the fateful policy decision that had just been made in their presence.

Work on Barrington's portrait had been completed in the studio in late afternoon, and Carlisle was pleased with Nathaniel's finishing touches on the curtains and walls in the background. He mentioned especially the way Nathaniel had used the lighter hues of crimson to capture the folds in the curtains. He had even taken one of Nathaniel's brushes and showed him how to roll it as he drew the line of the shadow to soften it to look more natural.

They'd celebrated the completion of this difficult work over a fine dinner in the basement supper rooms at The Pantheon in Oxford Street. Carlisle's wife, Lydie, had joined them and the three were in high spirits.

Lydie Dernier had married Benton fifteen years ago when she was twenty and he fifty-one. Benton had been painting landscapes in Rouen in France where he was the guest of Jean-Louis Dernier, Lydie's father. Dernier was a gentleman of great inherited wealth and a passionate collector of 18th century art. He had discovered Carlisle's work many years earlier on a visit to London and had invited Carlisle to dinner. He later came to Carlisle's studio and purchased several of his paintings including one, intended to be a study of a willow tree overhanging a stream in Ealing, that Carlisle had just begun. Over the years, Dernier had bought more of Carlisle's paintings, some of which he had strategically given to friends and museums to help enhance Carlisle's reputation.

Dernier had frequently invited Carlisle to visit his estate in Rouen and to stay as long as he wished to paint the landscape of the surrounding Normandy countryside. Carlisle had finally done so in 1758, making his first trip to France. He stayed for 14 months, one of the happiest and most productive times of his life.

Contributing to the happiness was his encounter and blooming relationship with Dernier's daughter, Lydie. At first, their age difference kept their encounters formal and brief. But Lydie was being tutored in English and she enjoyed coming to Carlisle's studio when he returned in the afternoons to engage him in conversation. As Lydie's English improved, the conversations lengthened. Sometimes they would even communicate in English over dinner which created something of a secret society between them because neither Dernier nor anyone else in the household spoke English with any degree of skill. Carlisle and Lydie began to have little secrets which they would discuss openly in English in the presence of others, knowing their secrets were safe behind the barrier of the strange language they shared.

One day it occurred to Carlisle that their secret sharing and their daily meetings for English conversation were, in fact, a form of flirting and that this was not language training so much as mating ritual. What alerted him to this? He wasn't sure, but he reasoned that Lydie would not be spending so much time with him if her only interest was instructional. That, and his admission to himself that he was deeply in love with her.

This situation—a much older man falling in love with the daughter of his host—was unprecedented to Carlisle and the proprieties were unclear. Should he cut off the conversations with Lydie to prevent any expression of his feelings for her? Should he confess those feelings to her and apologize for them? Should he speak to Jean-Louis and ask his counsel? Or should he simply return to England, leaving these torturous options behind?

One morning, as Carlisle was collecting his materials for the daily trek into the countryside, Jean-Louis entered the studio and asked a minute of the painter's time. He was a stout man of ruddy complexion, and he pushed his plumed hat back on his head and leaned against a post near the middle of the studio. "Monsieur, mon ami," he began, then went on to speak of the special bond that parents have with their children and how a father could perceive feelings and emotions in a child that required no articulation. He said it had become clear to him over the past several months that his daughter was in love. He thought there might be some young man she had fallen for, but their estate was isolated and few young men crossed her path. Then he had begun to realize that it was Carlisle with whom she was in love. This did not worry him, but he wanted Benton to know that if his daughter's girlish affections were a distraction from his painting, Jean-Louis would speak to her and prohibit her from coming to the studio.

Surprised and uncertain how to proceed, Carlisle decided to be direct. "Jean-Louis," he said in French, looking resignedly at his host, "I, too, am in love." He then went on to explain how their attraction had grown steadily but innocently over the previous months. Neither had intended a love to bloom, but one surely had. Benton recognized the awkwardness of their age difference and said he would understand if Jean-Louis thought he should cut off contact with Lydie.

Jean-Louis appeared surprised at this but uncertain about what to say. For a moment he simply looked confused, then he shrugged his shoulders, pulled his cap back down into place, and started for the door. He stopped suddenly, turned back toward Benton and apologized for taking too much of the painter's valuable time. And then he smiled broadly and added, "If you wish to court my daughter, you are welcome to do so; and I will be honored if you succeed."

Court he had, and in July of 1759 Benton and Lydie were married in the great cathedral at Rouen. The local gentry, especially the ladies, raised eyebrows at this marriage between Jean-Louis Dernier's eldest daughter and an Englishman more than twice her age. Some even questioned the propriety of this marriage when France and England were at war. But France and England were often at war, and affairs of art--and of the heart--were rarely interrupted by affairs of state.

The new couple traveled to Italy for several months after their wedding, then returned to London where Carlisle had used the proceeds from the sale of many of his paintings in France, and his wife's dowry, to purchase an elegant townhouse for them on Bloomsbury Square. They had lived there ever since.

As the threesome dined in the dimly lit room on a large joint of beef, plates of oysters, brown bread, and butter the color of old gold, Nathaniel closely observed the way Lydie and Benton interacted. He had seen Lydie from time to time while at the studio, but the studio was in the mews behind the house and Lydie came there only infrequently because ladies did not go to the mews. Lydie managed the household, though the couple had no children, and she played a growing role as an agent for Benton, advising him on prices for his work and drafting the correspondence about commissions for his portraits. Once in a while Benton would invite Nathaniel to dinner in the house, but those occasions were infrequent. So this evening afforded Nathaniel a rare glimpse of Lydie and Benton together.

He noticed that they never touched, though they sat adjacent to each other under a homely mural depicting a pastoral scene. Their conversation was formal and often dealt with upcoming portraits or a show of Carlisle's English landscapes that was being discussed for the gallery at Cambridge. There was warmth and respect and comfort, but Nathaniel, who had no special experience in the realm of romance, could not quite envision what it was that had drawn these two people together over the generation that separated them.

Often on nights they worked late, Carlisle would have his driver take Nathaniel home to the room he rented near Clerkenwell. On this night, he made the same offer as the carriage pulled up before the Carlisle house. But Nathaniel had eaten heartily, as they all had, and had drunk more wine than was normal for him. He decided to walk, and he bade Lydie and Carlisle good-night, thanking Benton generously for the fine dinner.

The night was cold and damp, and the chill soon penetrated Nathaniel's cape and waistcoat. But he found the brisk walk energizing and he warmed eventually from his own exertions. From the Carlisle house on Bloomsbury Square, Nathaniel turned onto Hart Street and then south to High Holbourn. This took him through the fish market, quiet now in the middle of the night, but reeking of the day's ripe and rotting remains. The new gas lamps along High Holbourn lit the way to Hatton Garden, where he would normally have turned left up to St. Cross Street, then to the massive gray stone building on the corner of Great Kirby Street where his room took up a small corner of the third floor.

But he was enjoying the walk in spite of the cold, and his mind was full of unfinished thoughts about his life in England and the brewing troubles in America. Something else was stirring him tonight, as well; something he did not want to admit, but could not seem to control: thoughts of Lydie Carlisle.

So instead of the normal turn to the left off High Holbourn, Nathaniel turned right into Fleet Market and stepped through the detritus of stalls and the previous day's garbage as he walked past Fleet Prison toward Ludgate Hill. He'd never turned this way before, having once been told by another resident of the building on Great Kirby Street that civilization ended at High Holbourn.

What Nathaniel encountered as he passed through the narrow, twisting streets and alleys below Ludgate Hill was not the end of civilization. But it was a place so densely packed, so noisy even in the middle of the night, and so putrid with smoke and sewage and stale cooked foods that it bore no resemblance to any place Nathaniel had ever been. Here, just a few blocks from the elegance and charm of Bloomsbury Square, was London's wretched and revolting dark side.

On several of the cramped streets through which Nathaniel passed, people huddled in doorways and in corners, seeking warmth; some were asleep, others merely seemed in a trance. Nearly all had too little clothing for the chill air. Along one street, a fire had been lit in a pile of refuse and a half dozen dazed men leaned silently toward it. An emaciated milk cow with an open wound on her left hip stood forlornly behind them. At the corner of Shoemaker's Row and Creed Lane, Jonathan spotted a public house, The Fiddler's Bow, that seemed to be open. He stepped through the creaking door, seeking relief from the cold and some brandy to warm his insides.

The place was dimly lit and clamorous. To get to the serving bar in the back of the room, Nathaniel had to navigate around several tables of men playing cards and cursing loudly. In a corner to the left, several women, neither sober nor fully dressed, sat playfully in the laps of men who, Nathaniel noticed, had not removed their hats. On the floor, just to the side of the bar, was a fat man prostrate on his back, either dead or drunk. It was too dark for Nathaniel to tell.

At the bar at last, Nathaniel caught the attention of the publican and asked for a brandy. He received instead a look combining bemusement and disgust. "Brandy, sir?" said the thin man with a wispy beard and a right eye that did not seem to focus. "This look of the sorta place what would be sarvin' brandy? Rum and ale is what we ha' here, sir. And no' much rum."

"I'll have an ale, then," Nathaniel said quickly. He looked again at the large body on the floor to his right. When the publican returned with a warm mug and passed it across the bar, Nathaniel took a long swig then asked, pointing toward the floor "Is this man alright?"

"Drunk he is, dead drunk," the publican responded. "Been like that fer near a month since his boy died. Wife ga' him four sons, now they's all dead. Smallpox got the first two on the same day 'bout a year ago. Third died, age eight he was, when he was unloadin' barrels of flour and a wagon rolled o'er him. Last 'un burned up 'n a stable where he 'uz sleepin'. Ain't much left for the bloke to live fer now."

"What about his wife?" Nathaniel asked.

"Nothin' more'n a common whore, she is. 'At's her there." He pointed toward the side wall where the women sat in the laps of the men. "Loud one's her."

Nathaniel saw a stout woman, her gray bodice unlaced about half way down, seated on the lap of an equally corpulent man. The man had his hand under her dress and she made short squealing noises, apparently in response to whatever was happening under the dress. Both were very drunk.

"She's not concerned about her husband on the floor?" Nathaniel asked.

"Can't stand the bloke. Never could."

"Yet they had four sons?"

"Reckon so. Needed 'em to bring money in, she says. 'ad 'em workin' when they 'uz six, but they didn't live long enough to bring much. Most a what she's got now, she gets from what ya see 'ap'nin' there. Husband's a good man. Worked fer years in Brick Lane peddlin'. Ev'ry marnin' be there early. Stay the whole day. 'Ard worker he was. But never made 'nough ta put food on the table or get a reg'lar roof o'erhead. They slept in cellars and stables most 'a the time. When the last boy died, 'e just give up. Drunk all the time, 'e is now."

Nathaniel looked again at the sad body on the floor and then at all the desperate vignettes around him. The images seemed to call for some profound comment, but Nathaniel was too confounded to offer one. He simply sat there, slowly sipping the warm ale, scanning the sordid scene, thinking how close this was to the drawing rooms of London's fine houses, thinking how far this was from the self-satisfied lives of elegance and ease that were lived there.

# Chapter 6

## *Still River, Delaware*
## *April 1775*

It was the first important ball of the spring and the Marshall plantation had never looked lovelier. The early crops had all been planted; and for more than a week the Marshall slaves had busily worked the grounds around the house, planting pansies and petunias and impatiens, trimming the shrubbery, smoothing the dirt pathways and scrubbing the brick walks. Fences had been whitewashed and the pillars lining the portico had been scraped and freshly painted. When the guests began to arrive, all remarked on how handsome the plantation looked and what an asset it was for Kent County.

This would be the first ball in anyone's memory without Geoffrey Marshall as the jovial host. He'd never recovered from a dreadful fall from his horse the previous summer and had succumbed in early autumn. The ball was the official end of the mourning period for the Marshall family. It also marked the emergence of Marinus Marshall as the head of the family.

And Marinus was ready. Now thirty years old, tall and aristocratic with lean body, pale skin, and straight blond hair swept back from his lank face, he walked with a confident grace through the guests, chatting briefly but earnestly with each. Marinus had climbed quickly to the top of the legal profession in Kent County—in all of Delaware really—and people already spoke of him as a legal and political power. When the counties came together this year and resolved their border dispute with Pennsylvania, people assumed that Marinus Marshall would be elected to the new Delaware colonial legislature and soon emerge as one of its leaders. He was prepared, he was hungry for this, and he certainly looked the part.

The Marshall ball had been planned and timed by Marinus to serve this precise purpose. The guest list included all of the most important political leaders in Kent County, and a few who made the journey from Sussex and New Castle counties as well. Marinus circulated through the guests, making and cementing the kinds of contacts that could only accelerate his own emergence as a man of prominence and power. He had hoped to add the *coup de grace* of announcing his engagement to Savannah Houghton on this night, but Savannah had not yet responded to his proposal of marriage and, to Marinus's unspoken irritation, had failed to appreciate the benefits of making the announcement at the first ball of the spring season.

When the Houghtons arrived, people gathered to greet them. Many had not seen Henry or Jonathan since their return in the fall from the Continental Congress. With Jonathan's assistance, Henry had written a report to the county legislatures, but he'd been so busy catching up on the work at Still River Bend that he'd had far less opportunity to talk with his neighbors than he would have liked. He was looking forward to this evening as a chance to compensate for that.

Savannah was the subject of much whispered comment as she ascended the portico steps and entered the center hallway through the large mahogany double doors. She wore the rose and cream gown on which she and Patience had worked for weeks. The bodice was adorned with a fine patterned lace that Henry had purchased in Philadelphia and the skirt was of silk that Edward had brought back from London. These were materials rarely seen at Delaware balls and during the evening nearly all the women made their way to Savannah for a closer look and a complimentary remark.

Rumors had spread as well about Marinus's marriage proposal to Savannah Houghton and some speculation had circulated that there would be an announcement of their engagement tonight. If so, their wedding would be the most important social event in many a year.

The Houghton family was not nearly as wealthy nor as socially prominent as the Marshalls. But the Houghtons had been in Kent County since its founding—Henry's great grandfather, Jeremiah Houghton, had been one of the founders, in fact—and they had always played an important role in the political life of the county and of Delaware. Like Henry, the earlier generations of Houghton men had a reputation for probity, caution, and courage. Houghtons were never foolish or rash. You could count on a Houghton, and citizens of Delaware had been counting on them for almost a century.

So a marriage between the wealthy and socially prominent Marshalls and the proud, trustworthy, and politically prominent

Houghtons would be an event of note. And nearly all of those present hoped it would come to pass. None more than Marinus Marshall himself whose affection for Savannah was genuine and nearly equaled his desire to join their families for his own political benefit.

Henry Houghton favored the match as well, though he spoke to no one about it because Marinus had not yet come to ask him for Savannah's hand. That wouldn't occur until Savannah accepted his proposal, and she hadn't yet done so. He only knew that she'd been asked because Patience had revealed that to him within minutes of his arrival home from Philadelphia.

But Henry harbored his own hopes for the Houghton family. Events were moving rapidly in America. Though he lacked enthusiasm for much of that momentum, it seemed increasingly likely that Americans would take on a larger share of responsibility for their own governance, that the Crown would be forced to compromise and to grant the colonial legislatures more power, probably even to permit each colony to elect its own governor. He hoped that one of his sons might one day become such a governor, though he thought now that Jonathan was the more likely candidate.

A marriage of his daughter to a member of the Marshall family would give the Houghtons some of the social status they had always lacked, despite their success as farmers and their constant prominence in politics. Henry had said nothing to Savannah about the marriage proposal, but he hoped she would have the good sense to accept it—because it would lead to a life of comfort and happiness for her, but also because it would have salutary consequences for her brothers and their progeny.

The dancing had gone on for almost two hours, a dizzying and exhausting swirl of jigs and reels and formal minuets. When some of the older men retired to what had been Geoffrey Marshall's library upstairs, it was as much to rest from their exertions as to engage in the ritual discussion of public affairs. Marinus joined them in this and called a black houseman who arrived quickly and passed a silver tray with glasses and silver-edged decanters of brandy and port. This was the first time Marinus had been in one of these sessions in his own house and it marked his passage from the young men to the old. He seemed at ease with the transition and began the talk by asking Henry to share some thoughts about the Congress.

Henry described the delegates, finding favorable things to say even about those like Sam Adams and Patrick Henry with whom he felt little sympathy. He described the difficulties in getting men from so many different colonies with such different experiences to come to consensus on how to proceed. He concluded by indicating his feeling that the most important outcome of the Congress was that it set a precedent and established a framework for future mutual consultation and joint action by the colonies. "The greatest thing we have to fear," he said "is one colony, like Massachusetts, going off in some deranged direction that causes the British to clamp down on us all. I think this Congress has reduced the chance of that happening."

Abraham MacDonald, who owned the mill to which the Houghtons took their logs for sawing, asked the first question. "But won't this Continental Association strike terror in many hearts in London? Won't they see it as us Americans forming our own government outside of the constitutional structure?"

Henry paused before responding and looked around the room at the concerned and attentive faces of his neighbors. "I've worried a lot about that, Abraham, as you know. Several of us spoke strongly against a formal association at this time, hoping we could rely on good faith to enforce the boycott of British goods. But we were greatly outnumbered and when we realized our arguments would never prevail, we talked among ourselves and decided it best to sign on to the Association lest the government in London think us Americans hopelessly divided. The end was more important ultimately than the means."

"But what if the Association doesn't work," MacDonald persisted. "What if some colonies observe the boycott and other disregard it? Won't those who participate be at a great commercial disadvantage as against those who don't? If I have to manufacture my own saw blades, I'll be hard put to compete with a mill in South Carolina that is buying blades from Birmingham."

"True enough," Henry replied. "This will be a test of heart for all of us. The worst, in fact, probably lies ahead. If the British respond by cutting off imports from America or by blockading our harbors, we'll all pay a high price. You won't get your blades, but it won't matter much because we won't be able to sell our timber either. And my brother won't be able to sell the ships he builds because no one can profit from sailing them. Everyone needs to be aware that the risks are very high, and all of us stand to suffer economically if we're to stand our ground politically."

"And for what?" Marinus Marshall asked pointedly, coming to his feet by the bow window at the end of the library. "Haven't we been caught up in events that have little to do with Delaware and that can only lead to tragedy? Isn't independence the only likely outcome of all this? Your Congress has raised the ante, Henry. Now the British will call our bluff. They'll send more ships and more soldiers. Some hothead will start shooting and we'll be at war. Then we'll realize we can't be at war with our own countrymen and we'll call an end to British rule and try to form our own government."

Marinus had their attention now and felt the familiar rhythm of a jury swaying to the force of his arguments. "But what faith can we have that we can form a better government than the one we now have, for all its faults? Government is never perfect, gentlemen, and it's a far better thing to try to fix what we have and know, to repair the government that we've lived under in some of these colonies for a century and a half, than to cast it off and replace it with who knows what. Would you want to live under a government devised by Sam Adams? By Patrick Henry? I would not.

"Abraham, you saw logs. Henry, you're a farmer. Your brother builds ships. I practice law. Does it really make any difference whether we do so under the flag of England or the flag of some new government stitched together here? I say it does not matter one whit. I say let's accept the known evil and try to correct it. To me, the unknown evil is far more worrisome."

Marinus returned to his chair and took a slow sip of his brandy. Like a barrister completing his case, he looked for agreement in the jurors' eyes. But he found only the vexed look of men who found merit in his argument but were not certain it should prevail.

The room was silent for a moment and then Henry responded. "Marinus, I find much to agree with in what you've said. But you assume that independence is inevitable and I do not. We're not at war with the British. They have sent troops to Boston to maintain order; they would argue that they've done so to protect us. Surely we can imagine how the tea party and the actions of the boys of Boston have looked to the ministry in London.

"But there was little talk of independence at Philadelphia. We sent the king a petition, asking respectfully for a response to some particular grievances. We expect a response which, if not perfectly conciliatory, will help us to find compromise and to move ahead as prosperous colonies. The effort at Philadelphia was, I believe, a valuable beginning in our

84

efforts to get these colonies to speak with one voice in clarifying how the crown will govern us. It's premature to see it as anything more than that, and I can assure you that most of the delegates share this view."

Marinus thought to rebut Henry's rejoinder, but decided against it. His duties as host and a rational desire not to anger his future father-in-law prevailed over his instincts as a lawyer, and he said instead, "Well, gentlemen, perhaps enough of politics for tonight. How did the planting go for all of you this Spring?"

Savannah danced with nearly all the gentlemen at the ball, but not with Marinus. Marinus, in fact, danced little, preferring instead to mingle with the guests and make conversation. Only later in the evening, after the men had returned from their sojourn in the library did Marinus encounter Savannah taking some of the fresh spring air on the portico.

"Dear Savannah," he said with a faint smile, "fancy meeting you here."

She turned her head and looked at Marinus over her shoulder, returning his smile. "It's been a wonderful party, Marinus, the equal to anything your father ever managed, You should feel very proud."

"I would have felt even prouder if only I could have announced the engagement of Savannah Houghton and Marinus Marshall. Then this would have been the finest ball ever."

Savannah turned back toward the fields and the river, silhouetted on this night by the lucid half moon hanging in the eastern sky. For a moment, she said nothing, then she turned fully toward Marinus and reached to touch him gently on the arm. "Marinus, you will have to bear with me. I so want to make the right decision for us both. And everything seems too confusing right now. The colonies are in an uproar about the King. Father and Jonathan were away in Philadelphia for two months, and Mother and I had to hire men and make so many decisions about the harvest. Now, it seems, they'll be off again after spring planting for another Congress in Philadelphia. Celia is in New York and we hear so little from her."

She stepped back and leaned on one of the pillars, looking along the front of the portico, her face now only an outline in the moonlight. Marinus noticed the grace of her profile seeing it more clearly now than ever before. Savannah was one of those women whom no one ever called beautiful, but whom men found powerfully attractive. It was the strength of her face and figure, the confidence with which she carried herself and spoke her mind, her intelligence. She was always holding something back, a woman of rich emotions well-masked. Savannah was a challenge to men and, because she did not overpower with her beauty, she was a challenge that men were eager to accept.

"Then there's Nathaniel," she continued. "Mother and Father say little about him, but I know they're both worried. We've only had two letters from him, but they were full of detail. He's assisting a painter while he studies and works on his own painting. Mostly they do portraits of famous people. Many of them are in government, and Nathaniel has access to the salons and offices of some of the most powerful people in England. Not because of himself, but simply because he's regarded as the portrait painter's assistant or servant. No one ever speaks to him, nor him to them. They look right through him, Nathaniel says. They don't know he's an American.

"But he does say that most of them speak of Americans with the greatest disdain. They talk like extensions of the King and speak of us, not as fellow Englishmen, but as 'our subjects in America.' Nathaniel has always been the least political of all the Houghtons, even less interested in politics than Mother. But his last letter revealed some real anger at the cruel feelings toward the colonies that seem to prevail in London. We all noticed it, perhaps because anger is so rarely visible in Nathaniel.

"Now Father and Mother are very worried that people will learn he's an American and try to punish him in some way for actions that have occurred here. There are so few Americans in London these days that a single one would probably stand out. Father doesn't think that Nathaniel would be strong enough to handle that, and it troubles them.

"So our lives are so full of worry and uncertainty, Marinus, that it's hard to make decisions about the future. This doesn't mean that I am not deeply gratified by your proposal, touched by it really. It only means that you'll have to be patient with me in this peculiar time." She could see the growing look of disappointment in his face and tried to find the right words to check it. "Marriage to you and the life it offers would be attractive to any woman. It is to me. I only need time to be certain that I'm ready for it--ready to leave my family in this worrisome time, ready to be the kind of extraordinary wife you deserve."

"I admire your sensitivity to your family's needs, Savannah," Marinus replied. "That sensitivity is one of the many traits I find so appealing in you. I only wish you would see that our marriage wouldn't change the political situation in the colonies or the lives of your sister or brothers. You would be safe here. I'm not involved in this incipient rebellion, nor am I going to be. I will not be drawn off to congresses in Philadelphia or battles in the north, should war break out. This is not my fight. I think we've already pushed things too far and that the prudent course is to tend to business and to mend our differences with the Crown through proper discussions, not petitions or resolves or boycotts or tea parties. If the wrath of the King does fall on these colonies, it will not fall on me. For a wife and future mother, that's no small consideration."

"But Marinus, how can we just stand and watch when there is so much at stake. If we bow and scrape every time the King's government imposes a new tax on us or sends more soldiers to live among us, are we then any better off than our own slaves?"

Marinus smiled paternally. "You've been paying far too much attention to the news from far away, darling. There are no soldiers here. Our bay is not closed by the Royal Navy. If Boston has made a nest of troubles for itself, that isn't our problem. The King's taxes and colonial policies touch only the very wealthy here, and none of them has been impoverished. We need to keep a sense of proportion about all this. It's just politics, the good and the bad. A new election in England, a new government, some day a new king, and all will change. But breaking our bonds with our mother country, fighting our own countrymen: these are responses grossly disproportionate to the dangers we face."

Savannah began to respond when she saw Jonathan in the doorway behind Marinus and sought relief from the conversation by calling to him, "Jonathan, do join us."

Jonathan looked her way, then moved quickly in their direction. "Here you are," he said, "I should have known you and Marinus would find a place to be alone. I'm sorry to interrupt, but Mother is very tired and she's anxious to head home while there's moonlight to light the way."

"Of course. It's been a full evening." She turned to Marinus, "It's been a wonderful party, really it has, but we must be on our way. Thank you for being so gracious and generous a host." She kissed him lightly on the cheek and started toward the door. Jonathan shook Marinus's hand, extended his own thanks, and turned to follow his sister. Marinus said nothing, watching blankly as Savannah left him, yet again, in an unusual and uncomfortable state of uncertainty.

The scheduled date for the new Congress arrived all too soon for Patience and, as it drew nearer, she began to plead with Henry to leave

Jonathan at home. "We need him here," Patience said in exasperation. "This farm is too big, too overwhelming for two women to run in your absence. Jonathan has a knack for this. He sinks his mind so easily into the details of growing things and tending to animals. And you know better than anyone that the experience now will be invaluable to him when we're gone and this farm is his sole responsibility."

"I agree with all you've said, dear Patience," Henry replied. "And I know what strain it's placed on you and Savannah to make so many of the decisions that men have always made on this land." He'd noticed the effects of that strain when he and Jonathan returned near the end of the previous October. Patience had seemed weary and she was thinner than when he'd left. Even her eyes seemed tired with worry.

Patience had never been much interested in any of the details of how things worked, and had never in her life borne sole responsibility for any decision. So the sudden burden of managing the farm had fallen heavily upon her last August. The happy, plump girl Henry married, the girl who so loved to read and to talk of finer things, the girl with those magnificent black curls beneath her bonnet, had little sparkle these days. And Henry knew that his absences, and her new responsibilities because of them, were the principal cause of the unhappy changes he saw in her. He understood the dread with which she anticipated another long absence by her husband and son.

But Henry also had a growing sense of the imminence of events, and of the inevitability of their impact on the lives of his children. "These are unusual times," he said to Patience. "Perhaps I should leave Jonathan here. But we must also be alert to what's best for him. Perhaps he'll not be merely a farmer who dabbles in public life as I and other Houghton men have been. Perhaps we're at a turning point and we colonists will be taking on much greater responsibilities for managing our own affairs. Then we'll need the very best men among us to come forward and take that responsibility. I fondly hope the Houghton men will be among them, Nathaniel and Jonathan."

Patience listened stolidly. She'd heard this argument before and didn't really want to hear it again. Nor did she want to admit that there were uncontrollable forces beyond their farm, beyond Delaware, perhaps even beyond America that were pulling her family apart. Yet she betrayed no impatience because she trusted Henry's judgment in these matters, a habit she'd acquired long ago.

"Nathaniel, of course, may never get involved," Henry continued. "For all I know now, he may choose to become an English gentlemen and never return to Delaware. But Jonathan has the mark of a future leader. I wish you could have seen him in Philadelphia, dear—how he held his own in discussions at the tavern, how he began to catch the attention and command the respect of some of the most important delegates. The way he rescued Washington's carriage on that last night was a remarkable piece of quick thinking. George told me so when we said our good-byes. He's not a boy any more. I know that makes him especially suitable to stay here and run things while I'm away. But it also means there is so much for him to learn from being at the very center of these difficult and fateful times. No father would want his son to miss that."

Patience pulled back the quilt and climbed into bed while Henry banked the fire. They were both tired from the ball and the long ride home over muddy roads. Patience felt even wearier now as she contemplated the months ahead with Henry and Jonathan gone. The planting was done, but there were always battles to fight in the growing season: too much rain, too little rain, locusts, weevils, weeds, sick animals, broken wagons, hired men gone missing…. A sad sleep slowly consumed her, a brief but blessed escape from the troubles she saw piling up in the path ahead.

After two windy days crossing Chesapeake Bay, Jonathan was pleased to be on the firm bank of the Potomac. His horse seemed even more pleased and drank greedily from the trough at the bottom of King Street.

Jonathan stretched his legs and looked about, noting that Alexandria was quieter than he'd anticipated. Uncle Edward had said it was one of the busiest ports in America but, while barrels were piled as high as gravity would allow and stood on every available piece of ground or dock, no one seemed to be moving any of them. A dozen or so large ships stood at anchor in the river, but only two, both of them small bay sloops, were unloading at the dock. There were plenty of men about, but few seemed engaged in any activity resembling commerce.

Jonathan tied his horse to a post in the shade by the trough, and meandered toward Gadsby's Tavern on Royal Street. Several men sat in chairs on the planked porch in front, one whittling vigorously, but the others in subdued conversation. Jonathan stepped inside. The heat of the day had begun to accumulate in the tavern's main room and only a few men sat at the tables eating or drinking. Jonathan caught the attention of the tavern keeper and asked for a mug of ale to quench his thirst.

"Don't know ya', do I?" the tavern keeper asked.

"No, sir," Jonathan replied, "I've never been here before. Just came over on the boat from Delaware."

The tavern keeper was lining up mugs on a small table to the left and didn't look up. "Windy ride, warn't it?" he asked.

"Yes, sir. Not very comfortable. My horse was scared half to death."

"Horses ain't made for boats, I reckon. What brings you here?"

"I'm headed for Mt. Vernon," Jonathan replied. "Been invited to visit Mr. Washington."

"You an' half the people in these colonies. Ain't a night goes by that some'un isn' visitin' with the Colonel. He's always invitin' some 'un or other to come up to Mt. Vernon. He likes to show the place off, ya' know. Also likes to put on a feed. Folks aroun' here think it's because he ain't ever had any chillun. They got Martha's young 'uns up 'ere now, and he treats 'em like his own. But he seems the sort what wanted a large fam'ly of his own and never got 'un. So he keeps the place lively by invitin' folks to visit."

"All the time there's someone there?" Jonathan asked.

"Without fail. Jus' like you, they get off the boat here or ride into town and ask directions to Mt. Vernon. Some's common folk, but some is soldiers in fancy uniforms or gentlemen in fancy clothes. Of'n the women come with 'em. Sometimes they stay a couple weeks. More of'n, they's there a few nights then go on their way and some 'un else arrives. Any idea why he invited you?" The tavern keeper finished with the mugs and now leaned on the bar and looked directly at Jonathan in the faint light seeping in from the door and the two small windows on each side.

"I met him in Philadelphia last fall. We got to talking about farming techniques and he invited me to come and give him advice on how he might use some of them here."

The tavern keeper took a long look at Jonathan, trying to guess his age in the dim light. "You a farmer are ya'?" he asked.

"My family has a large place at Still River Bend, above Delaware Bay. We harvest a lot of timber, and then over the years we've built up the cleared fields to grow corn and flax and some grains. It's good land and we usually get good yields when the weather's decent."

90

The tavern keeper listened intently but still had trouble believing that a man this young would have much to teach George Washington about farming. On the other hand, Washington's reputation as a soldier, surveyor, and statesman greatly exceeded what the locals knew about his skills as a farmer. "Maybe you can he'p the Colonel," the tavern keeper said. "Mt. Vernon's a grand place, and he's got a herd o' slaves to help him work it. Got their own little village up there, you'll see. But the soil ain't so great, and the Colonel's always strugglin', like his uncle did, to make it pay."

"Maybe I can help," Jonathan said, placing his empty mug on the bar and dropping four pence beside it. "Thanks for the ale, and the information." He turned to leave, then stopped abruptly and turned back toward the tavern keeper. "Say, what's the reason for all these barrel's piled up here and so few of them being loaded on the boats?"

"Politics," the tavern keeper replied. "Embargo they made up there to Phil'delphia stopped things dead, 'ceptin' the coastwise trade. Everyone here's takin' it serious, mostly outta respect for the Colonel. No British goods comin' in, after we turned two ships away in January real angry-like. And now no British ships want to carry our goods t'other way. Most of them barrels holds tobacco. Been dryin' since last summer and it's ready to go. But ain't no one to take it. Tit fer tat is what they're sayin'. Folks here startin' to get a little itchy 'bout all this."

The long broad path meandered up from the road along the river to the high plain where Mt. Vernon sat on a broad point above the Potomac River. The tavern keeper had warned Jonathan that "they's much abuildin' up there," and indeed they were. Teams of horses winched beams into place. A stout man in a brown coat, but bareheaded in the morning sun, walked along the construction on the north side of the house, looking up and shouting orders. Everywhere were black men and boys carrying tools, swinging long boards, measuring and marking: syncopated players in a saw-and-hammer band.

Jonathan turned his horse toward the main house and stopped to survey the scene. Even in the midst of so much construction the place had a compelling presence. The main house, its center two and a half stories high, all white with gray shingled roof, was now flanked by two incipient additions that would broaden the building both north and south. As Jonathan rode around the north side of the bell-shaped and neatly tended lawn in front, he could see gardens in bloom with an array of vegetables and flowers. Two older black men were hard at work with hoes and weed baskets. To the south of the building were several smaller structures, all white and neat and behind one of them Jonathan spotted a long brick edifice that appeared to be a stable.

This was no grand mansion. In fact, in its current state of unfinished construction, the house at least was not very grand at all. Overall, he judged the main building was smaller than the Marshall house in Delaware. But as Jonathan drew closer to the main building, he began to get a sense of the magnificent and graceful symmetry of Mt. Vernon. And as he approached the house and could see beyond it to the north and south, he was struck as well by the glory of its location, high above the river with bold views all around of a broad virgin landscape, dappled in pine green and slate blue and aquamarine. Could there be a vista anywhere in America more exquisite than this?

Jonathan's absorption in the surroundings was interrupted by a black man in morning coat standing before him, holding the reins of his horse. "Mornin', suh," the man said. "Is you Missah Houghton?"

"I am," Jonathan replied as he shifted his weight to the left and dismounted.

"Massah's expectin' you, suh. He's down in the souf field s'mornin' and hopes you'd join him dere. I'll be showin' you your room firs."

Jonathan followed the slave toward the front door of the house. A boy of about eight came and took the horse by the reins, leading it confidently away toward the stable. Summer always came early along the lower Potomac and even now in late April the heat was asserting itself. Jonathan ascended the four stone steps to the front door where the man who'd greeted him banged twice on the tall wooden door. Another black man appeared almost instantly and held the door while Jonathan entered the broad main hallway. Because of the warm morning, the double doors at the far end of the "passage," as the houseman called it, were both open wide and once his eyes adjusted to the light, Jonathan could see out over the front porch, down the long sweep of lawn and over the copse of trees along the shore to the full width of the river and the dark forest on the opposite shore. The morning light poured into the space and the two ornamental lions over the double doors looked down in contentment on this splendid lair.

The houseman made no effort to show Jonathan the other rooms, knowing that the master himself always took pleasure in that. He simply led Jonathan up the genteel staircase that wound to the left along the front of the house and led him to a small bedroom on the north side of the second floor. The racket from the construction made conversation difficult, which seemed a relief to the houseman. In a quick glance, Jonathan inventoried the room: small bed with simple white canopy, a single brown Windsor chair beside a plain stand on which was a brass candlestick, fireplace in the corner, mahogany credenza by the window topped with an ivory colored bowl and pitcher. A familiar room, not unlike those at home in Still River Bend.

Jonathan set his kit bag by the chair and followed the houseman back down the stairs and out the front door. The stable boy brought Jonathan's horse and another black man on horseback came around the salt shed and invited Jonathan to follow him to the south field where his host was spending the morning. If Mt. Vernon the house was more ordinary than Jonathan expected, Mt. Vernon the estate exceeded his every imagination. The black man and the white man rode for nearly a half hour, past small herds of grazing cattle and sheep, through the gates of long white board fences, into small orchards of peach and cherry trees filled with squabbling robins until finally they came upon the master of the estate locked in intense conversation with one of his field overseers. Around them were more than a dozen slaves with picks and hoes breaking ground that to Jonathan's trained eye had never before been planted.

As they approached, Washington looked up and smiled toward Jonathan. He stood beside his large gray stallion in brown breeches and dusty black riding boots. He had removed his frock coat in the heat and wore only a white shirt with ruffled collar. An old wool hat shielded the upper half of his long face from the sun. Jonathan had never seen Washington look so informal in Philadelphia, hadn't ever imagined him without his coat fully buttoned.

Washington welcomed his young visitor and chatted animatedly about the morning's activities. He seemed transformed--from the serious and reticent delegate at Philadelphia to the happy lord of this great estate. It reminded Jonathan of his own father, at home in the fields he had tended all his life. After his own years of working the farm at Still River Bend, Jonathan was beginning himself to know some of the emotional attachment of men to their land, the comfort that comes from knowing the familiar swell and sway of a place, the deep satisfaction of looking about and saying to oneself, "I built that wall," or "I planted those trees," or "I broke that soil and turned that stubbly hillside into a green garden of corn."

A man feels the pride in his land, knows the connection to it, absorbs the energy from it. When you came of age in a place, ran and rode over it as a boy, worked it from sun-up to sundown as a man, grew to know its seasons and its shades, its treasures and its torments, then the land takes possession of you. If you're lucky, and the land is generous, then you are blessed by this possession and it becomes the true and solid center of your life, the sane and safe place to which you return from all the travails of that world beyond the gate you and your father built together so many years ago.

So it was with Washington and Mt. Vernon. The older man's mind was at full race as he rode with Jonathan along the edges of the fields, describing his problems and the experiments he was undertaking to address them. Tobacco was the staple crop of Virginia, but tobacco had never grown well at Mt. Vernon and Washington had abandoned it entirely in 1767. He told Jonathan what was already obvious to the young man's eye: that wheat was now the estate's most important crop. But there were fields of maize and other grains and orchards in varying states of maturity.

They discussed different strategies for crop rotation, the proper depth for plowing, the use of natural fertilizers, the advantages of oxen over mules and horses. Jonathan was taken by Washington's scientific approach to all this and by the passion that fueled his hunger to understand what made a crop of a particular kind grow successfully in soil of a particular kind in climate of a particular kind.

Though he suspected they had only seen a small portion of Mt. Vernon, Jonathan noticed a hollow ache in his stomach and realized that the two men had been riding like this for many hours. They reached the end of a path at the top of a knoll and Jonathan saw the house looming ahead. He should have known that even so deeply engaged in conversation and thought, Washington knew exactly where he was going. They rode slowly toward the house, around the greensward in front, with Washington proudly describing the plantings and the functions of each of the buildings. The construction had ended for the day and the cacophony that accompanied Jonathan's arrival was now gone. They dismounted and passed their horses to the stable boy.

Jonathan asked Washington how he had procured such fine white stone for the building in this part of the country where building stone was

94

rare. Washington laughed and drew Jonathan to the front face of the house. "Feel this," he said, and lifted Jonathan's arm to touch the surface. It felt sandy and coarse like stone. The beveling at equal intervals was also characteristic of stone. So Jonathan asked again, "Where is it from?"

Washington turned and pointed toward the trees that lined the paths leading to the house. Jonathan was now completely confused and turned his palms upward and raised his shoulders in a gesture of ignorance.

"It's wood, Jonathan, not stone at all," Washington said. "Rusticated boards we call it. We cut the timber to equal widths, then bevel it to look like the placement of stone. Then we mix sand with the paint to create the appearance and feel of stone. You're quite right that stones such as these appear to be would have to be imported from a great distance. So we made our own." Washington smiled proudly and waited for all this to sink in. "Had a man here to visit after I returned from the Congress in November. He wanted to write a piece for the Alexandria paper about what happened there. In the first paragraph, he wrote about coming to Mt. Vernon and said it was one of the finest stone houses in Virginia. Happily his reporting about the Congress was somewhat more accurate."

Washington turned and led Jonathan from one side of the house to the other, stopping to draw a diagram in the dirt with his riding crop of the exterior façade and the internal plan. They walked around to the front and in the soft light of late afternoon, Washington indicated where the grand Palladian window would go and shared his thoughts for the placement of a center cupola on the roof. His frustration at the slow progress of construction was patent. "I'd hoped we could have this completed before I left for Philadelphia in a few weeks, but that is now out of the question. When I'm away, everything seems to move more slowly here. When I returned from the Continental Congress last fall, it looked much as it had when I left. I'm not sure why. When I return from the Congress later this summer," he said with feigned authority, "I shall come here every morning with a great long whip and oversee the work myself!"

After dinner that evening—a fine meal of planked shad from the spring run and wild rice and brown bread with currant jam--Washington and Jonathan moved to the piazza along the front of the house overlooking the river. They smoked clay pipes and talked more about farming and house building. Washington inquired about the farm at Still River Bend, asking detailed questions about crop selection and rotation, about harvesting practices for the timber, about market prices. As if calculating how many people were necessary to run such a farm, he then asked if Jonathan would be accompanying his father to the new session of Congress as he had to the last.

"It's not completely decided, but it seems I will," Jonathan replied. "Mother wants me to stay to run the farm, but Father thinks that events are about to take a fateful turn and that I would learn much from being in Philadelphia. The planting is done and if the Congress goes on longer than the last one, I can always leave before it's over to return to the farm. So it appears I'll be there."

"Good," Washington said with a twinkle. "You never know when I may need an emergency carriage rescue in the middle of the night!"

Jonathan smiled at the reference, then asked, "How long do you think this session will last?"

Washington rose and stepped to the edge of the porch to knock the burnt tobacco from the bowl of his pipe. "Hard to say," he replied. "Things are moving so fast. There has been no good response from London to our petition. The embargo appears to be working well in some places, but not others. I had a letter from Robert Paine last week indicating that tensions are rising in Boston as more soldiers arrive and the quartering of them grates more heavily on the people there. People are leaving Boston in droves, except those loyal to the King. Paine said most of the towns now have militias in training and they're actively seeking arms and powder, even stealing it in some cases. I suspect the Congress will focus on that situation most immediately and have to decide whether all the colonies have a stake in Massachusetts and what to do about it."

"Do you see a war coming?" Jonathan asked.

"By God I hope not," Washington replied, leaning now against one of the pillars and looking off to the north, toward the trouble. "You may know that I spent five years with the British army as General Braddock's aide and then commander of the Virginia militia. I have the greatest respect for its soldiers and its generals. It is easy to dismiss an army on campaign, especially one thousands of miles from home. But the British Army has been campaigning for centuries, and the British Navy has been delivering the supplies and disrupting the enemy supply flow through all that time. It has defeated some of history's greatest forces and on foreign soil.

"Here we have no army. We don't even have a country. We have some farmers playing at being soldiers, carrying the family musket and spending an hour each night marching in a cow field with their neighbors. They're brave and honorable men, I'm sure. But their bravery may quickly flee when they see before them that long line of redcoats, backed by the King's cannon, and holding the finest weapons in the world. I've seen that long line and I've seen how it causes the courage of very brave men to melt.

"But that's only part of the problem we would face. An army is not just men and guns. It's transport and uniforms and two meals a day. It's horses and powder and ball. It's places to sleep and be safe. It's officers who know the order of battle and have themselves been tested under fire. Such officers exist here and there, blooded as I was on the way to Fort Duquesne. But it's not even clear which side they would take were such a war to break out.

"No, Jonathan, war is not a happy prospect. We have much to settle with our friends in London. But I hope the Congress can accomplish that with words and diplomacy, not by sending fine young men like you charging into a maelstrom of burning lead and slashing swords and bloody bayonets. I know war well, Jonathan, too well, and it is not for the faint of heart."

# *Chapter 7*

## *New York City*
## *April 1775*

"But it's excellent quality, and worth every shilling." Godfrey Carter stood his ground unshakably, as he always did in negotiations like this. No soldier was going to get the best of a businessman like him, not even one dressed up in the clothes of a gentleman as Colonel Wilberforce was. "We purchased the beef from the best farmers in New Jersey and then supervised the salting process ourselves. Then we had it stored in the strongest barrels made by the best coopers in the city. This'll stand all the extremes of weather, it'll travel safely, and it'll last for a year or more. Your men will praise the day you came here to buy it, Colonel."

"Please, sir, we agreed that we'd use no real names. I'm not questioning the quality of the product. I've been in the quartermaster corps for almost 20 years and I've inspected it myself. But your price is too high. We can transport our own salt beef from London at about the same price."

"Well, then," Carter replied, "that's what you should do. I can't make a profit if I sell it for a farthing less than the price we discussed. If my beef is too expensive, bring your own across the Atlantic, endure the gales and confront the pirates, if you will; months of its useful life already spent before a soldier ever dines on any. Or find some other American supplier who'll meet your needs. Hah! Fat chance of that. All the American suppliers turned tail when they passed this embargo in Philadelphia and some of the local committees began bringing 'em up on charges for violating it.

"What it comes down to, Col-," he stopped himself before saying the name. "What it comes down to Mr. Black," he said, using the code names to which they'd agreed, "is that you buy from me at my price or your men have to depend on an unreliable supply of an inferior product. You're the one responsible for feeding the Army. You decide."

It was an old business ploy, and Carter had used it for years. Know your opponent's options, then condemn them. Make him feel that you're his only real choice. Make it a moral question for him and put yourself on the side of God. All the old tricks. And they were working here. The Colonel was pondering.

Carter knew that it was best to give a man a few minutes alone when he was trying to calculate how to pay for something more expensive than he'd anticipated. So he rose from his chair and walked out of his office to the small anteroom where Drouin, his Irish clerk, was at work over a large ledger. Carter stepped toward the window and looked out over the harbor. From here, on the fourth story of this Queen Street warehouse above Lyon's Slip, he could look up and down the waterfront at dozens of docked ships, their bowsprits stuck out over the pier like swords at a military wedding.

Beyond them in the harbor were scores of others. Many had been nowhere for months--victims, Carter thought, of this wretched and irrational embargo. Sailors lay drunk in the taverns for weeks on end because there was no work. Merchants along the waterfront were stuck with bulging warehouses and no way to ship their goods to the European markets. With so little coming in from abroad, the importers spent their days in card games and wagering for a day's pay on cockfights. All of this so a few self-righteous politicians could make a point with the King.

At times like this, Carter knew, a man had to be creative, had to use his mind to stay ahead of his competitors. In the marketplace, there are winners and losers. Often the winners are the ones who take advantage of the plight of the losers. Carter applied that calculus to the American market and came up with this. If he couldn't sell to Europeans in Europe, perhaps he could sell to them in America. There were thousands of British soldiers and sailors in America now—hell, their presence was the reason for the embargo. Armies always try to develop local sources of supply, especially when they're so far from their base of operations. In a war, if they're lucky, they can live off the land, off the produce from local farms and stores. But this was not a war and the Army was under strict orders not to upset the locals by plundering their homes and shops.

So Carter had passed word through his own network of contacts to General Gage himself that supplies for the troops and sailors in Boston could be readily procured in New York if the General was interested in a sound business arrangement. That's what brought this pitiful Wilberforce to New York. Carter had spotted him quickly as an easy mark, no business man at all, but a career soldier whose only real talent was for counting blankets and sorting them in piles.

It was getting late in the day and, though the sunlight lasted longer now, Carter was rarely home before dark. Too much to do, too many new opportunities to cultivate. But tonight he'd promised Celia he be home for dinner at eight because she'd been complaining about seeing so little of him lately. He hoped he'd have time for a short stop in the alley off Maiden Lane on the way home, but that looked increasingly improbable as the British officer dithered in the next room. Time, Carter thought, to force the action.

He pulled his watch from his pocket and, catching Drouin's attention, tapped it twice. This was their well-rehearsed signal for Drouin to leave. Because of the hour, the clerk closed his book, took his hat and cape and headed out the door, done for the day. Carter then stepped back into the office where the Colonel paced the floor in deep contemplation. He was a stout man, not surprising for a supply officer. The civilian clothes had obviously been hastily borrowed for the trip to New York. They were too small and showed the wear of the road. The bursting calves of his stockings were caked in mud and in the wrinkles of his waistcoat one could count the nights spent at taverns in Rhode Island and Connecticut.

"I need a decision," Carter said. "If you don't want to buy these barrels at my price, I'll sell them to someone who does."

The Colonel smiled, sensing an opportunity. "Who else is going to buy barrels of salt beef?" he asked. "You can't ship them to England and there's no other army in America."

Carter was ready and he sprung. "No embargo on shipments to France," he said. "There's a big army there. Be happy to have good American salt beef, even what's already been in the barrel for three or four months. I can sell it to sailors. There's still ships moving and their crews need all the salt beef they can store." He paused until the Colonel looked at him, then he lowered his voice conspiratorially. "And, from what I hear, there may be another army in the field here real soon and they'll be needing to build supply sources from scratch. It's a damned competitive market right now, Mr. Black."

Carter was lying, of course. He knew nothing about the French army nor did he have any information about an incipient colonial army. And certainly there were far too few ships departing New York to create a significant market for his goods. This was another ploy. Lure your

100

opponent into thinking he's found a weakness in your position then quickly turn the weakness into a strength, overwhelming him with the impregnability of your bargaining position. If you had to lie to do that, lie.

The Colonel looked dejected and finally said, "All right, I'll accept your offer."

Instead of smiling or showing any sign of gratification, Carter pressed his advantage. "But you understand, Mr. Black, I have to convince my own suppliers that you're a reliable customer. In these uncertain times, everyone's fearful of producing on speculation. If we're to refill the warehouse after these barrels go to Boston, I'll have to have a commitment from you for future orders."

The discussion continued for another half hour. The British colonel sat in the chair trying to deflect each new demand from Carter. Carter, realizing that the Colonel had no options, circled slowly about him, trying to load more and more future commitments onto the deal. Finally, Carter took his long quill, dipped it methodically in the silver inkwell that was one of the few adornments on his desk and quickly drew up two copies of a contract that specified in exact detail all of the arrangements to which the Colonel had committed the Quartermaster Corps of His Majesty's Army and the sterling of His Majesty's Treasury. As agreed in advance, the actual parties to the contract were both disguised: the Honorable Mr. Brown made his deal with the Honorable Mr. Black.

Wilberforce left without handshake or acknowledgement of gratitude. Indeed, he felt none. It had been a bruising negotiation and he felt like a wounded officer leading a defeated army from the field. Virtually all of the terms of the agreement were exactly as Carter had laid them out when their discussion began several hours earlier. Instead of improving the terms, the Colonel had only ended up making a larger and longer commitment on Carter's terms. He would review this negotiation over and over on the long ride back to Boston, never relieving his perplexity.

After Wilberforce left, Carter closed the window facing the East River, looking one last time at the idle ships along the waterfront. He congratulated himself for not giving in to the fates that so many other businessmen were cursing these days. There's always an opportunity for profit, he thought, if only you have the imagination to find it.

He looked again at his watch and thought of Celia waiting at home. It was late. But perhaps if he hurried, a quick stop in Maiden Lane was not out of the question. What could Celia do anyway, but complain?

The ladies loved coming to tea at Celia's. And she loved entertaining them. The grand house on Beekman Street was one of the finest in New York in the new Georgian style. Three stories high and nearly seventy-five feet across the front, it was imposing for its mere bulk. But Godfrey had managed somehow to lure the best craftsmen in the city to build the fence along the street, decorate the cornices and lay the thousands of bricks that such a house required. The four chimneys had been designed by the masons for appearance as well as function and they invited frequent comment for the way they widened near the top as if they were bumping up against the sky. The weathervane was a square rigger under full sail. "Like us," Godfrey had said to Celia when first she saw it.

Tea was always on Thursday, and always in the larger of the two parlors. Eleven women were always invited, making an even dozen with Celia. This permitted them to play whist if they chose, and twelve was the number of teacups in the gorgeous gold-embossed set that Godfrey had brought home one day to Celia's delight. When Celia asked where he got it, he simply responded, "God works in mysterious ways." He said that in answer to many of her queries about the sources of their largesse. She was never sure whether it was a religious proclamation or whether "God" was a shorthand for Godfrey.

Today's tea had been an especially happy one for Celia. She'd received a letter from her mother in the morning's post and it was full of information she shared with the ladies. Her mother had written at length about the Marshall ball, opening the local social season. Celia had attended several Marshall balls when Geoffrey Marshall was still alive and master of the estate. But as she read her mother's description now, she snickered and rolled her eyes.

When she finished that part of the letter, she rested her hands in her lap and smiled broadly. "Now, you can see," she said, "how the rest of the country finds its merriment. Before I came to New York, I couldn't imagine anything more elegant than the Marshall ball. We'd look forward to it all through the winter months—to the grandeur of the place, the beauty of the music, dancing with all the handsome men. How pitifully simple it would seem now. All those farmers in clothes they rarely wore, stumbling through dance steps they barely knew, anxious only to get off with the men to talk about the spring planting. Ten of those Marshall balls in Delaware would not equal one of our ordinary balls here. Thank God for New York," she said. "It gives me hope that we may yet become a civilized society."

The ladies nodded in agreement, twitching their fans and sipping from the gold-embossed tea cups. They asked questions about the Marshall ball, trying to imagine the homely scene. With each answer, Celia became more and more theatrical in her portraits of farm life in Delaware. She alone among the women at her teas had moved to New York as an adult. All the rest had been born and raised in the city and knew nothing of life in the countryside.

Godfrey's growing wealth was the reason he and Celia had been invited into the city's rarefied social circle. And Celia loved it. The fine clothes, the shopping for furniture and carpets and exquisite objects for the house, the constant round of parties and balls: she couldn't imagine a happier life than this. It troubled her that Godfrey seemed to be home less and less, but he told her that his business was so much more difficult since "your father's embargo" that he needed to spend more time at it. Things would get back to normal, he said, when everyone cooled down and we went back to trading again with London.

When Celia queried further about what it was Godfrey traded and with whom, he would always change the subject, muttering that she was well cared for and there was no need for her to trouble her pretty head about men's work. Since none of the other ladies seemed to know much about their husband's business affairs, Celia saw no need to inquire further about Godfrey's.

"Now listen to this," Celia said, inviting the ladies to lean forward for what promised to be some especially delicious gossip. "My sister is getting married." A crescendo of "oohs" and "ahs" rose from the circle. "Well, it's not definite yet. She hasn't accepted the proposal. But mother is sure she will. It's too good to resist."

"Who is the lucky man?" one of the ladies asked.

"Marinus Marshall," she replied. "He's the head of the Marshall family since his father died and an important lawyer in Delaware. If you have to live your life in Delaware, he's as good a catch as she'll find. Mother thinks Savannah's very lucky he proposed."

"Why hasn't she accepted his proposal?" one of the ladies sitting across from Celia asked.

"You have to know my sister. Sometimes I think she wishes she'd been born one of the boys. She's never been very fussy about clothes. When we were little girls, I liked to play with my rag doll. I'd sometimes go out in the kitchen with Sweetie and we'd talk about food the dolly liked. Savannah had a doll, too, but didn't play with it much. She preferred to sit in the dooryard reading or go down by the barn and watch the boys working with Father and Quiet Jack. She liked to ride a horse when they'd let her, although the boys kidded her all the time about that. I always dreamed of marrying a handsome and rich man. She never wanted to think about the future, said she just wanted to find something interesting to do that day.

"Mother says that Savannah likes Marinus but doesn't want to respond to his proposal until she's ready. Just like her, not wanting to think about the future. But Mother has faith that Savannah'll come to her senses. She usually does. Then she'll realize that a marriage to Marinus Marshall is about the most a Delaware girl could hope for in life."

The ladies sat silently, most trying to imagine the life of a Delaware girl living in near isolation on a family farm. In most of their minds, the picture would not form.

The ladies left at five o'clock, as they always did. Celia went to the kitchen to speak with the housekeeper about dinner and then returned to the smaller parlor where she worked on her needlepoint. She thought about Savannah's life and hers. How lucky she'd been, Celia thought, to escape her life in Delaware. In New York, she was in the middle of things. There were always people to visit, and there was always entertainment. She could buy fine things here that never made it to Delaware. And she had the beautiful home, more than twice as large as the one at Still River Bend and fancier by far than any of her family could imagine. She hoped that some of them would visit soon so she could show it off.

She sometimes heard Godfrey talking with the men about the awful things that were happening in Boston, and her mother's letters always included descriptions of what her father had been doing in Philadelphia. She wasn't interested in politics, so she never read those parts very closely. She just hoped all these troubles would get settled soon, so the ships would all be sailing again, bringing the silks and wines and furniture from London that they all so loved. She could think of no good reason to be angry at the English. We're all English, after all, she thought, and we should be proud of that. I must write that in my next letter to Mother and ask her to tell Father the way I feel, the way all of my friends here feel.

The eight sharp pings of the silver clock on the mantel jarred Celia from her thoughts. Darkness had fallen, but Godfrey was not yet home. She had specifically asked him to be home tonight for dinner at eight; and she was sad, even a little angry, that he was not. But she upbraided herself for her feelings, knowing that her husband worked very hard to provide her with fine things and she shouldn't be upset with him if his work kept him at the waterfront. She rang for the houseman and instructed him to tell the cook that dinner would be delayed.

Godfrey's carriage pulled up to the curb at nine-thirty. Celia watched from the parlor window as he spoke some brief instructions to the driver, then stepped through the gate and up the brick walk. She greeted him affectionately at the door. As always, Godfrey made no apology for the hour of his arrival.

Within minutes, they were seated at the new walnut table in the dining room. Plates of ham and sweet potatoes were placed before them, bearing only slight evidence of the extra hours they had been kept warm. Godfrey ate heartily and gulped his wine. Celia's efforts to start a conversation barely penetrated his eating ritual.

"It must be terribly busy at the wharf right now, dear," she said.

"Wharf's not busy at all," Godfrey replied between swallows. "I'm busy trying to make a living when most of the ships aren't sailing. Not easy."

"Do you expect this will be over soon and trade'll return to normal?"

"Not if those bast…" — he caught himself before his real thoughts emerged — "not if the Congress in Philadelphia has anything to do with it," Godfrey responded. He wiped at his mouth and finished the wine in the bottom of the glass. The houseman stepped in silently to refill the glass. "They've already put half the seacoast out of work with their follies last year. They're about to meet again, and now that they've had some practice one can only imagine the destruction they'll wreak on our businesses."

"Please don't speak of the Congress that way, Godfrey. I'm sure my father and the rest of them think they're doing the right thing for the welfare of the colonies."

Godfrey ran some bread around the edge of his plate and bit off a large chunk. "Yes, darling," he said diplomatically, "I'm sure they're trying to do what's right. But they ought to come and spend an evening at The Bosun's Mate. Talk to all the seamen there who haven't had work for four months. Measure up their 'welfare.' Or walk along Queen Street and peer into all the warehouses bulging with the goods that have no place to go or no way to move. If the…if they thought this was going to make us all band together against 'our British oppressors,' as they keep calling them, they've badly misjudged. There's more support for the King here in New York right now than there was last summer. Give them another few months in Philadelphia and we'll be inviting old George to build a summer palace on Harlem Heights."

"Oh, Godfrey, you're much too harsh. I had a letter from Mother today. Let me read some of it to you about what Father thinks." As Celia rose and left the room to retrieve the letter, Godfrey sat back and rolled his eyes. He had nothing in particular against Henry Houghton. But the man was hopelessly naïve. Thought that managing a farm was running a business. Three days working at my warehouse, Godfrey thought, and Henry Houghton's head would be spinning. That's the trouble with these politicians. Most of them are lawyers or gentleman farmers. They have too much time on their hands, so they sit around and read their philosophy and get together with their other lazy friends and draw up schemes to fix the world. The world would be just fine if they'd stick to their parlor games and their hunts.

Celia hurried back in with the opened letter in her hand. She picked up a candlestick from the sideboard and placed it next to Godfrey. The houseman stepped over quickly and lit it. "Here," Celia said, "this is the part."

"'Father is anxious about the upcoming meeting of the Congress in Philadelphia," Celia read aloud. "The King has not responded to their petition as they'd hoped and the reports from up north are that more soldiers and ships keep arriving in Boston harbor. Now he's worried that the delegates who thought last fall's actions were too timid will want to try to do even more at this Congress, maybe even to initiate some kind of continental government and then ask the Crown to recognize it as legitimate.

"But he's also worried about all those soldiers gathering in Massachusetts. If they kill any citizens there, even by accident or miscalculation, it might set off a reaction that will get out of control very

106

quickly. He remembers how the radicals gained the upper hand in the last Congress. If soldiers start shooting at colonials, he's afraid that the moderate delegates won't stand a chance.

"What do you think?" Celia asked when she finished reading.

Godfrey was lost in thought. He was calculating how many ships and soldiers might actually be in Boston and whether the beginning of a real conflict might quickly bring thousands more. Would he have warehouse space enough for the supplies such an army would need? Could he get those supplies to Massachusetts? And where could he get powder and lead to sell the army for its guns? To hell with salt beef, he thought, the real profits were in gunpowder and shot and cannon balls. If a man could get access to a supply of those, he could make a fortune selling them to an army at war thousands of miles from its own factories.

"Godfrey," Celia pleaded, "what do you think? What should the Congress do?" But Godfrey's mind was racing and he barely heard her. She wanted him to talk to her about all the dandified maneuvering at Philadelphia, all those words and petitions and resolves. But he was too busy for that. Mr. Brown was getting ready for war.

# Chapter 8

## Philadelphia
## May-June 1775

"Welcome back, boys" Keppler shouted heartily. "We've missed you. Business has been slow since you left." He laughed and pointed Henry and Jonathan toward the center table where there were two empty chairs among the four men engaged in intense conversation

The Second Continental Congress wasn't scheduled to convene for another week, but Henry and Jonathan came by boat this time and couldn't get passage any later than the first of May. Henry regretted the few extra days away from the farm. But he also knew that conversations with the delegates before the opening of the Congress might help the moderates to plot a more effective strategy than they'd mustered the previous fall.

Patience had continued to pleaded with Henry to leave Jonathan behind to help with the farm. But Henry reiterated his view that future leaders need an apprenticeship in the art of politics and Philadelphia was the best training ground in the colonies. Since his visit to Mt. Vernon, Jonathan was more anxious to return as well. He and Mr. Washington had spent two glorious days together, observing the fields full of Washington's experiments, riding over the countryside, and talking late into the evening about warfare and politics. When he started to ride away from Mt. Vernon, Washington had called to him, "See you in Philadelphia." Now Jonathan wanted to go more than ever.

Surprisingly, it was Savannah who helped most to resolve the family conflict. She urged her mother to let Jonathan go with Henry, promising to take on more responsibilities herself and then negotiating with Marinus for the loan of two of the Marshall slaves to help with the harvest of the early crops.

So Jonathan was back, this time as secretary to the entire Delaware delegation. It was a role not likely to be more demanding than the one he filled the previous summer for Henry only. But he would again have a keen vantage point as the struggle escalated between the American colonies and the King of England.

They had arrived in Philadelphia that morning and walked up from the docks to the Widow Almy on Second Street where they had again secured rooms for the duration of the Congress. They'd hurried through dinner that first night in order to catch up on the news and sample the mood of those delegates who had already begun to arrive.

"I'm tellin' ya," Henry heard one of the men at the center table say, "he been there and he seen it with his own eyes. Every bloody shot."

"Where's he now?" one of the others asked.

"He's been talkin' to some New York gents, but he said he'd come over here when he was done. Trouble is, everyone he talks to wants to pump the details outta 'im and it slows 'im up. But it's war, sure enough."

Henry took a quick drink from his mug and asked, "Pray, sir, what are you talking about?"

"Near Boston, some of the local boys started shootin' at the redcoats. Brave as hell, they were. Killed a lot of them and drove them off." The man's excitement rose as he spoke and his words tumbled together in a rush that defied comprehension. "Soldiers turnin' tail and runnin' off every which way. Our men just standin' there, calmly shootin' straight and hittin' them soldiers, one by one."

"You were told this by someone who was actually there and saw it?" Henry asked.

"Well, I ain't spoke to the man, but word's gettin' around Philadelphia like lightnin'. I heard about it at the stable a few hours ago."

"Who is this man telling the story?" Henry inquired, looking around the table.

One of the other men spoke. "I hear it's someone Sam Adams sent as a messenger."

"Where's he now?" asked Henry.

"Comin' over here soon's he can," the first man replied.

"Will this mean war?" Jonathan asked to no one in particular.

"Shouldn't last long with the lickin' those redcoats took," one of the others added, to general agreement. "They shoulda knowed better than to take on Massachusetts boys protectin' their homes."

After several more minutes of this hearty bravado, a broad-shouldered man in gray frock, flop hat, and dusty riding boots came through the door and stepped into the boisterous gathering. One of those at

Henry's table spotted him and said, "There's your messenger." He rose and hurried to the door, took the messenger by the arm and pulled him to the center table. Another man pulled up a chair and someone quickly fetched him a mug of ale.

Henry spoke first, "I understand you've come from Massachusetts, that Sam Adams sent you, and that you have news about some events there."

The man took a long drink, then looked from right to left. Every man in the tavern had now gathered around the center table to hear the messenger's report, their faces incandescent in the glow of the two candles on the table. "Sam Adams didn't send me. Don't know Sam Adams. Mr. Paine thought I should come 'cause I saw what happened at Lexington and I'd been to Philadelphia before."

"Lexington?" Henry quizzed.

"It's a town, sir, on the road west from Boston. Not very large. Mostly farmers. My brother lives there and I was helpin' him get his plantin' done."

"Planting now?" said Jonathan quietly, then he quickly remembered the much shorter growing seasons in New England.

"Men in Lexington have a small militia. Have had for a while now. They drill on the green in the center of town, coupla nights a week. Got a captain named Parker who organized 'em and leads the drills. Fought with Rogers Rangers; he's a good man. They been storin' powder and ball at a secret place in Concord, the next town west. Even got some sixteen pound cannon hidden in barns, under hay. Lot of the town militias been doin' that. With so many British soldiers around, they all want to be able to protect their homes.

"In Boston, we've got this group that keeps an eye on the army. We call ourselves spies, but we're really just men watchin' closely and passin' information along to the likes of Dr. Warren and Sam Adams. Soldiers get drunk and start blabbin', we listen up. Our boys heard some soldiers talkin' about marchin' to the west to destroy some of these places where the militias hide their powder. We wanted to warn the folk, but we weren't sure where they were goin'.

"One of the boys worked out this plan that we'd post sentries. If the soldiers marched up the neck and headed that way, we'd signal a rider that they were comin' on land. If they took boats across the harbor to Lechmere Point, we'd signal they was comin' by water. The easiest thing to see from the other side is the steeple of North Church, so we hung lanterns there for the signal.

"They started movin' across the bay in boats at night on April 18[th,] and when we figured out their plan, we signalled to Paul Revere who was the rider that night and he rode out along the road to the west to warn the militia that the army was marchin' their way. Another fella', Dawes, he talked his way right past the sentries on Boston neck, then high-tailed it west, warnin' the minute men that the soldiers were movin'. The redcoats formed up 'round two o'clock and marched through Menotomy and got to Lexington just at daylight. The road forks around the green there and Cap'n Parker had the militia waiting for them in two lines on the green. My brother's in the militia, and I went down to watch. I didn't have no musket of my own or I woulda' joined 'em."

Every man in the place now hung over the table, listening in rapt silence to the messenger's report.

"I have to tell you," he continued, "it was some sight. We could hear them big kettle drums before we saw anything, 'Dum-de-dum-dum...,' keepin' the cadence as they marched. All you could hear was them drums and the sounda their boots all hittin' the ground at the same time. There's a bend in the road just before the green and when the first soldiers came into sight, they pivoted around that bend like they was born to walk that way. They all looked like giants, not a runt in the litter, and their bayonets was sparklin' up there on top of their long rifles. You could see some of the militia men looking down at their own muskets and comparin' them to those long British guns. They kept coming till there were hundreds of them. Then their officer called a halt and they all stopped at exactly the same time, almost as if they were sharin' the same brain.

"Then the drummers drummed something different, the sergeants shouted things I couldn't make out, and the British formed up in straight lines in front of the militia on the other side of the green. They had a major on a horse to the left. He shouted at the minute men real angry like to lay down their arms and disperse. I think a bunch of them thought that a capital idea since they was outnumbered badly and standin' there in front of them reg'lars was feelin' a lot like suicide."

"How big a green is it?" one of the men asked.

"Not very large, just a small field really. With those redcoats on one side and the militia on the other, there wasn't much room between 'em. The redcoats, well it was almost like they were goin' about their business, hardly payin' any attention to the militia. They loaded their weapons and maneuvered around and the drums was bangin'. The militia men mostly stood still, but you could see some of them twitchin' a little, lookin' at each other.

"That militia was some strange lot facin' these real soldiers. There was grandfathers and young 'uns. Some sons was standin' next to their fathers. Mostly men whose families'd lived in Lexington for years. I was pretty scared just watchin' from behind a tree, so you can imagine the fear that musta been in some of them. A lot of them redcoats was young, probably never been shot at before. Same with most of the militia, 'cept a few of the officers.

"Then it got powerful quiet. There's houses all around the green and you could see people peerin' out the windows. Some of the soldiers was yellin' at the minute men to git out. Then Cap'n Parker shouted for the militia to disperse, but to take their weapons with 'em. Then the shootin' started."

"Who fired first?" Jonathan asked.

"No one could figger that. I didn't see any smoke on the green. But then the reg'lars all started shootin', like they was crazy. Even the officers couldn't git 'em to stop until they'd fired a buncha volleys.

"Pretty soon the whole place was full of smoke so's you couldn't really see anything, except every few minutes the smoke would clear a little and you could see them redcoats standin' there, firin' away.

"There was some redcoats lyin' on the ground, but they'd just step over them and keep on shootin'. The militia broke up pretty fast when some of 'em started to fall. No way they could stand there and face them soldiers and not get slaughtered. Saw one boy kneel down over his father, both of them covered in blood. Wailin' he was. Pretty soon the militia was runnin' off, 'cept for a few stayed to drag off bodies. Eight of the militia was dead, 'bout the same number wounded. Seen more blood than I've ever seen 'fore that.

"Then the soldiers regrouped on the road with those damn drums bangin' the whole time. They left a couple behind to gather up wagons for the wounded, then they marched off down the road to the west, still looking for the store of ammunition, headin' to Concord."

The messenger stopped and took two long gulps of ale. An impatient listener asked, "What happened next?"

"Well, I didn't follow them to Concord. My brother'd been nicked in the leg and I helped get him home. But later in the day, the soldiers

112

came marchin' through again, headin' back toward Boston. Some of the militia boys was followin' 'em and takin' shots from behind trees and rocks as they marched. One of the Concord boys stopped at Edward's house—that's my brother—for water and said there'd been more shooting on the wooden bridge over the river where the local boys had picked off a few of the soldiers and done alright themselves.

"Word was gettin' around real fast and minute men come runnin' from Lincoln and Bedford and other places too. By the time the redcoats got back to Merriam's Corner easta' Concord, there musta' been a thousand minute men in Merriam's fields. Some of them followed the marchers all the way to Menotomy and kept shootin' at 'em, but the redcoats was draggin' their wounded in carts and didn't form up for any more shootin' themselves 'cept for a few of the light infantry they had flankin' the column."

"So we've got them on the run," one of the men standing behind Henry said with pride. He raised his mug and called for three cheers for the boys of Lexington.

When the cheers ended, the messenger put down his own mug and grew more grim. "Twas an awful sight there in Lexington," he said. "All the noise and the bullets ricocheting off rocks and striking houses in the distance. Men fallin' with blood squirting out of them. Watchin' my own brother get shot and fall to the ground.

"Couldn't really tell who won or lost. Dead and wounded on both sides. But those redcoats was a frightenin' sight. So big they were and so smooth the way they maneuvered. And their boys didn't flinch. Took their shots, reloaded, and took more. Someone'd fall next to 'em, they'd hardly look down. And then watchin' them march back to Boston, drums bangin' loud as ever, them swingin' their arms in cadence. They didn't look like no losers that day, only like men who had a job to do and had gone out to Lexington and done it."


The news from Massachusetts energized and excited some of the delegates as they arrived. Others it mortified. But when the delegates held their first session on May 10th, it was the primary topic of every discussion. The agenda of the Second Continental Congress formed around this singular new reality: American colonials and British regulars had begun to shoot at each other.

For Henry Houghton, April 19th was a black day. The war he dreaded was at hand; the fissure lines between England and America were deepening. How could he make a case for caution and moderation when musket balls were flying across Lexington green.

At the end of the second day of the new Congress, Henry walked alone down Locust Street to the Brother-in-Arms, a sad little tavern that none of the delegates frequented. It had been chosen for that very reason by the handful of Henry's colleagues who wished to caucus away from the watchful eyes of the others. It was almost 10 o'clock when Henry arrived, a time chosen to ensure that darkness would reduce the likelihood of their being spotted.

Henry was the last to arrive and he joined the other five at a square table in a small room they had to themselves. Two candles sat on the table, the only lights in the room, and cast a dim glow on their faces as they talked. These were the men who were not yet ready to admit defeat in their efforts to find a compromise that would restore good relations between London and the colonies.

John Dickinson, their acknowledged leader, reminded them of the larger issues. "The shooting at Lexington," he said, "seems to have produced the sentiment that a war has begun. In reality it was a minor incident involving a rogue militia that has little to do with the rest of us. We must make that argument repeatedly: that this was a regrettable event but not an act of war. The King didn't order any shooting, nor did the Congress."

"No one's going to buy that, John," said James Duane, a delegate from New York. "The word's spread through the colonies like smallpox. Everyone's heard of it and everyone now believes that a war's begun. Instead of arguing about strategies for resolving the difficulties between us, most men are taking sides. Some have even begun to take up arms, as many, it seems, *for* the King as against. At least in New York."

Henry leaned forward and set his mug on the table. The others looked toward him. "Our primary task now," he said, "is to remain a force in this debate. We're slipping into the minority here. If the radicals get control of the Congress and catch the fever of sentiment against the King, we might as well pack up and go home for all the good we'll do. We have to work with the other delegates, even those who'd have us manning cannon tomorrow. The question, I believe, is what steps can we now take to slow the momentum toward war?"

"Houghton's right, as usual," Dickinson said. "One suggestion we might make is that the Congress should study the facts surrounding the incident in Lexington. We could offer the argument that a legislative body should not act without gathering the facts and, at this moment, all we have is the rushed recounting of a few messengers, only one of whom says he was present.

"Remember how the Congress jumped into action last fall when Sam Adams's messenger arrived with news of the troubles in Boston. Only later did we learn that Adams had tricked us and things weren't as dire as we'd been told. Let's not be burned again by acting in advance of the facts. Perhaps we could recommend that the Congress send a delegation to Massachusetts to meet with the militia leaders in Lexington and survey the situation in Boston. Send delegates who are not Massachusetts men to give us a more objective view of conditions."

"Good idea," several of them said at once, inspiring Dickinson to continue.

"Look, we know there are already moves underway here to discuss the formation of a continental army and to send out feelers to France and Spain seeking their support. I even overheard two delegates last night at City Tavern talking about establishing an espionage network. Fascinating, isn't it, how peaceful men love to play at war.

"These moves'll be hard to blunt. There's just too much enthusiasm for preparing to fight. I think we'll be more effective if we support those efforts, but argue that we must prepare for war in order to give Parliament evidence of our seriousness. That'll improve our bargaining position when we seek a compromise that'll avoid war. Why should Parliament bend in our direction if they don't fear us, if they doubt our commitment to stand our ground? Surely we're more likely to be heard, if their generals report back that we're preparing to put an army in the field."

James Wilson stood up from the table and walked around to the other side so he could face Dickinson directly. "I see your point, John," he said, 'but we've got to be aware that events have a life of their own. When we have an army, how can we be sure that we can control it? Soldiers fight; and a continental army may invite attacks from the regulars. That'll simply raise more cries for war. This is not chess, sir, and creating an army is not feinting with king's rook. We must be extremely careful."

"Granted, James," Henry interjected. "But John is right. We probably can't stop those who want an army. They are too many and too unified. We must surrender on that point and try to get the others to see it as only one part of a broader strategy. As we prepare to fight the British on the battlefield, we must also reach out to them with further efforts at compromise. If we're lucky, the former will abet our efforts at the latter.

"This is no time for us to lose sight of reality. Everything has changed since the first time we met here last September. We petitioned the crown and were rejected. We established an embargo and formed an association to enforce it. Both have worked reasonably well, and we've more confidence in our ability to work together. Arms have been raised, and now arms have been used. Things are changing fast, gentleman, and we must not lock ourselves into wishful thinking about a time that is quickly passing away.

"It was one thing to be for peace and negotiation and all-out effort to preserve our bonds with England when there was still hope of returning to the relationship that existed 20 years ago." Henry warmed to his argument and questions began to tumble out. "But what hope is there of that now with Lord North and his henchmen barely reading the solemn documents we send them? With Edmund Burke's hopeful effort at conciliation soundly rejected by Parliament? With the King declaring that Massachusetts is in open rebellion and ordering his troops to use force to subject the people there? With our countrymen here in a louder and louder uproar? With dead Americans lying in the grass on Lexington green?" He paused and looked slowly at each man. "We must not let events consign us to irrelevance."

"Henry, by God man, you sound like Sam Adams," said Dickinson.

"I suspect that's an insult to Adams," Henry said, forcing a small smile. "I just don't want history to say that a new dawn broke over us and we couldn't see the light."

Jonathan walked the length of the fifth livery stable he had visited that day. His disappointment was evolving into genuine frustration. City horses, he had concluded, were a different species from those in the country. And a far inferior one. That's when he spotted the brown stallion.

In a stall near the end of the stable was a horse as magnificent as any he had ever seen—many hands high, a beautiful strong head, a light wispy mane, and heavily muscled legs. Jonathan walked toward him and touched the side of the horse's face. The horse briefly cast a suspicious eye toward Jonathan then looked away, as if he had better things to do than consort with humans in this miserable stable.

116

Jonathan inquired of the livery man about the brown stallion. "Brought here from the mountains to the west," the man answered. "Some feller that was takin' a boat to the Indies. About two weeks ago. Feller wasn't sure he was ever comin' back, so sold 'im to me for a song. Course I'd expect to make a good profit on a fine critter like that."

Jonathan had been granted an allowance from the Congress for his trip and offered the man a good chunk of it for the horse. No use looking any further, Jonathan thought; this may have been the finest horse he'd ever seen. They haggled briefly and agreed on a price which Jonathan paid in silver on the spot. A handsome leather saddle had come in with the horse and the livery man sold that as well for one quid more. A half hour later, after some getting-acquainted time in the stable, Jonathan and his new horse road slowly up Chestnut Street headed for the Widow Almy.

The group of moderates who'd met at the Brother-in-Arms found little interest among the other delegates in their proposal to send a committee of delegates to Boston to study the situation there. So they decided to act on their own and recruited three respected local men who were willing to make the trip and report their findings when they returned. The Congress did finally consent to their trip and made a small appropriation for it.

Because access to Boston harbor was closed, they would make the trip over land. They had asked for an aide to accompany them and Dickinson had suggested Jonathan Houghton. Henry was reluctant at first, not anxious to have his son roaming through the dangerous uncertainties of Massachusetts. But, since he was one of the principal supporters of the fact-finding trip, Henry could not offer much objection. He discussed the assignment with Jonathan who was delighted at the prospect. Philadelphia held far fewer charms for him on this second visit, and his imagination had been fired by the tales he'd heard of this eventful spring in Massachusetts.

So he found himself a horse, saw to the arrangements for his three official companions, collected maps and writing supplies, and on the damp morning of the 19th of May, Jonathan and the others rode out of Philadelphia heading northeast.

Henry had seen enough of him to know there were few forces in nature as powerful as John Adams with an idea. All morning he had been cornering delegates, proposing they follow up on their decision the previous day to form a Continental Army by electing George Washington to be its commander. Hardly a man had escaped Adams's relentless pursuit. And as he approached the group of delegates standing in the shade by one of the wings of the State House where the new Congress was meeting, he bore the most determined look Henry had ever seen.

In the weeks since Jonathan left with the committee, the moderates came to realize that no mere facts were going to alleviate the pressure for war that was building in Philadelphia. The committee's report, whatever its content, would fall on ears that were not deaf, just uninterested. When Peyton Randolph, who had presided so fairly over the first Congress and had been elected again to preside over this one, left abruptly to return home for a meeting of the Virginia Assembly, John Hancock had been elected in his place. Hancock commanded wide respect, but he was a Massachusetts man and his election as president of the Congress was a powerful signal of the direction in which things were turning.

The decision to create a Continental Army sparked surprisingly little debate, its success being a foregone conclusion. Even some of the moderates supported the notion with enthusiasm, preferring an army under the control of Congress to bands of roving militia that seemed to be under little control. But the value of having an army depended heavily on how it was run, and now the question was who should command this new, and as yet entirely imaginary, fighting force.

Adams was the shortest among them, a funny-looking man really-pear-shaped and pale, though the flame came rapidly to his cheeks when he was excited. The delegates had come to revel in stories of his hypochondria. Adams was a walking encyclopedia of information about ailments and diseases, nearly all of which he believed to afflict him in one way or another. But his mind was unmatched among those at the Congress, and debating him was the most exhausting mental exercise any of them ever experienced.

When he stepped into the group of delegates standing in the shade, they knew why Adams was there. His methodical solicitation of support for Washington's appointment was already well-known even though it was only a few hours old. "Good morning, gentlemen," he said in a rare effort at social grace. "I hope you have given some thought, as I have, to the very important matter of electing a commander for our new army. And I hope you'll agree with me that there is only one possible choice here. That, of course, is Washington."

118

"I'm not sure he'll do it, John," one of the men said. "He maintains that he's retired from military service and simply wants to get back to Virginia as soon as this Congress is over."

"I'm not sure he's the right man, even if he were willing," said another. "When he commanded the Virginia militia in the last war, there were many who thought him lacking in decisiveness, too quick to take his troops from the field. He failed to press his advantage and let the enemy slip away too often. Some of his mistakes cost an unnecessary loss of lives. There are some who marched with Washington who think his reputation greatly exceeds his prowess as a commander."

"My brother was in that war," said Henry. "He didn't serve under Washington directly, being from Delaware. But he was often in engagements where Washington was commanding one of the regiments. He admires the man and thinks he's a good soldier. He made some mistakes, but we should remember that he was colonel of that Virginia regiment at the age of twenty-two, his military training was limited, and the regular army officers disdained him as they disdained all the colonial commanders. They left him on the field of fire without support more than a few times."

Adams impatiently cut off this unsolicited offering of opinions and made his own points, succinctly and forcefully. "Gentlemen," he said, launching a carefully prepared argument, "Washington's appointment would accomplish several things. First, he's the most experienced military commander in the colonies. He knows the order of battle and he knows how to drill troops into readiness to fight a professional army.

"Second, he's widely known and admired and his appointment will instill public confidence in this new army. Our brethren will believe that this is a serious undertaking, with real prospects for success, if Washington commands it.

"Third, he's a Virginian. Politically, this is very important. If we're to get the other colonies to line up behind a continental army in Massachusetts, the army must have a leader who's not himself from Massachusetts or even from the northern colonies. With Washington at its head, this truly would be a continental army.

"Finally, George is one of us. We know him and trust him, and he knows us. There'll be difficult times ahead in providing proper financial support for this army. But the Congress is much more likely to do so if we have faith in the necessity of the requisition requests we get from the commander in the field."

As Adams finished, the others stood silent. Some of them had serious doubts about Washington's soldiering skills or his desire to resume his military career. But Adams's argument had deduced to so forceful a logic that it seemed hopeless to raise those doubts further. Henry then offered the only question that any of them was willing to broach: "Will George accept the command if it's offered?"

"I haven't spoken with him directly," said Adams. "I'm certain that he wouldn't be willing to be considered if there were other candidates, that his ego would not submit to the possibility of being rejected. Nor do I believe that he actually prefers such a position. I think him entirely genuine in his expressed affection for returning to the life of farmer and esteemed first citizen of Virginia. If you've seen the light that comes to his eyes when he talks of Mt. Vernon, you know what it means to him.

"But Washington remembers well the way he was treated by the older regular army officers in the west. He has no love for England or its King. He speaks rarely here and he's not the most eloquent among us, but his faith in the future of these colonies as self-governing entities always emerges clearly. I can't but believe that if we came to him in unison, playing upon his deep sense of duty, and asked him to take on this command as a matter of the most sacred honor, that he would not be deeply moved to accept. If we're united in this, he'll humbly demur. But ultimately he will not resist."

The following night at City Tavern, as the delegates in two's and three's stopped at Washington's table to congratulate him on his new command, Henry saw John Adams sitting quietly at his accustomed table in the corner. How odd, he thought, the league of these two men. Washington the beloved hero and optimistic planter, comfortable with his fate, soldier of arms. Adams, the crabbed Boston lawyer, perpetually restless, soldier of words. One to make the battle, one to fight it. One the object of affection at the center table where the light was brightest. The other barely noticed in the shadowy corner, comforted briefly by a momentary sense of satisfaction.

On every street corner of Philadelphia, in every tavern, around the hearth of every home, at every school and church, the talk was of war. But everywhere there was the same struggle to find the right words. War with whom? War for what?

120

The long days in Congress and the long nights at tavern were filled with talk of armies and militias, logistics and supplies, allies and spies: the details of making war. Less thought was spent on the rationale for war, on clarification of a war's objectives, on where such a war would take the relationship between King and colonies.

Near the top of nearly everyone's list of things to do was the opening of diplomatic channels to France and Spain. One night, while walking back to the Widow Almy with Henry, Caesar Rodney said, "We can never hope to drive back the British army, so long as the British navy bottles up all of our ports. We'll push the redcoats to the sea, but their ships'll just pick them up and move them somewhere else."

"But we can never hope to build a colonial navy to fight the King's navy. And where would we find the captains and crews to sail our ships even if we could build them?" Henry responded.

"The answer is not here, Houghton, it's in France or Spain. They have the navies we need, and they have no love for the British. If we can convince them that our rebellion is serious and likely to endure, they may agree to ally with us and to occupy the British navy away from our ports. Without them, we'll be outgunned and constantly outmaneuvered.

"There's talk now of sending Jay to Spain to begin negotiations. I saw John this morning and he's anxious to go. We need a man in Paris as well. Whatever it takes, Houghton. We can't lick the British alone."

"Aren't we getting ahead of ourselves, Caesar?" Henry replied. "Do we truly want a war? Think of the death and destruction that will bring. Think of our own sons, Caesar. And what is our objective even if we go to war? To force Parliament to grant us a measure of self-government? To get them to acquiesce in letting us send our own representatives to London? To break the bond completely and become an independent country?"

Henry surprised himself with his questions. He'd been in politics a long time, but never before had he suffered such uncertainty about where he stood. With the stakes so high and the issues so complex, he found himself engaging in debates like this, not so much to permit his opinion to triumph as simply to allow it to form.

"And what would that mean?" he continued. "An American King instead of a British King? A Parliament in Philadelphia instead of London? Would we be truly better off? We've seen how these colonies have struggled to agree on even the simple resolutions we've made here. How would we ever manage a war, raising the money and building the system of support that would require? And, my God, Caesar, how would we ever run our own country as thirteen fiefdoms forced into union? I hope, at least, that we won't yet give up in our efforts to find a peaceful way out of this dreary mess."

Rodney was about to respond when they turned the corner onto 2$^{nd}$ Street and ran into a small crowd gathered by the stable on the corner. A large gray horse stood at the center of the group and sitting sternly upon it was George Washington. Another horse and rider sat alongside, with a third horse bearing their belongings. Washington was in uniform and for the first time he wore the stars of a general.

Henry and Caesar Rodney worked their way through the small crowd and moved toward Washington. "Good afternoon, General," Rodney shouted, heavily emphasizing the last word.

Washington turned their way and allowed himself a small smile. He had accepted the command of the Continental Army reluctantly and without apparent pleasure. He longed only to return to Mt. Vernon and the wife he called "his beloved Patcy." Instead, duty called him hundreds of miles in the opposite direction for an assignment of no certain duration.

But his grim aspect stemmed not just from personal concerns. More than any other man in Philadelphia, Washington knew what a war with England would mean, how difficult such a war would be, how dear would be the cost of victory—or failure. He had noted with sad amusement the feverish planning, the bold pronouncements, the fearless predictions of his fellow delegates. Few of them had ever been to war and fewer still had the slightest knowledge of its cruel realities. How easy for them to talk so confidently of making war, thought Washington, when they are such strangers to it. What hard lessons lie ahead.

"Thank you for coming," Washington said. "I shall miss my friends in Philadelphia."

"And we you, General," said Henry. "Our prayers will be with you."

"I'm grateful for your prayers, Henry. But the Continental Army will be even more grateful for whatever funds and supplies you can persuade the Congress to send us."

Washington pulled the reins to the left and turned his horse toward the north. As he rode away from them, the small crowd dancing along beside him, Henry said, "He will make us proud. I'm certain of that."

Rodney turned to leave, saying only, "He better."

A few days after Washington's departure, the Congress voted to issue two million dollars in paper money, with each of the colonies agreeing to assume a portion of the debt. This first issue of American money had passed quite easily and at City Tavern several of the delegates at the center table were toasting their genius in making money out of thin air. As the toasts accumulated, their schemes for financing the war grew more creative--and more ribald.

At one of the side tables, Henry sat with Caesar Rodney, James Wilson, Edward Rutledge, and John Dickinson, discussing the prospects for war. "Our army has no officers, save Washington, no cannon, no uniforms. It has no stated objective," said Rutledge. "And it has no eyes and ears. How can an army survive without those things? We can appoint officers and buy uniforms. Washington will collect cannon where he can. And he'll have no trouble finding spies in the colonies. The poor Redcoats won't be able to sneeze without Washington getting a detailed report.

"But the British command is impregnable. Not a word of their tactics or plans will leak from the generals here. They're professionals, and they know how to keep secrets. And in London we are blind and deaf. If Washington had some way to know London's intentions, to discover the orders that are coming to the British commanders here, the enemy would be stripped of much of its capacity for surprise. I'm told that it takes ten weeks on average for the British army to get its orders from the ministry. If we could learn their plans in London and send them back here through a spy trail of our own—why, with some luck, Washington might know what the British were planning before their own commanders knew, or at least soon enough to prepare a response."

"We have no spies in London now?" Rodney asked.

"Apparently not. We've had no need. We're Englishmen, you know," Wilson said with a sardonic laugh.

"And one can imagine the difficulty of sending spies there when it's hard enough to book American passage on any ship to England right now with the embargo in place," added Dickinson. "Our only hope may be in getting some Englishman to turn. With enough money, these things can be made to happen. But even finding and encouraging someone to penetrate their wall of secrecy will be difficult when we have so little presence there."

Rodney turned to Henry, "What do you think, Houghton? Jonathan told me about your boy Nathaniel getting to meet all the bigwigs in Parliament. Maybe he could help us find a turncoat?"

"Sorry, gentlemen. I'm afraid that's the least likely thing to happen in this struggle," Henry replied, amused at the thought of his son the painter trolling the drawing rooms of London is search of potential spies.

# Chapter 9

## Boston
## June 1775

"One hundred and fourteen, sir," Aubrey Armistead announced as each of the officers responded to General Gage's request for a count of men available for duty. The march to Lexington and Concord had decimated several of the companies involved and one of Major Armistead's had suffered the worst. That had been nearly two months ago. More fresh troops had arrived in recent weeks, but no replacements had yet been assigned to Armistead's battalion and the strength of each of his companies was still limited by the effects of those two days.

"And what is that company at full strength, Major?" Gage inquired.

"Two hundred and ten, sir, according to the table. But as you know, we've never had a full complement in any of our companies. This one had four men killed at Lexington, eleven men at Concord, and two more on the return march. That's seventeen dead. Twenty-two more are still wounded too badly to report for duty, sir. And we have eight men sick. We have forty-seven men off the line in this company alone, sir. One hundred and fourteen effectives." He had given essentially the same report each week for the past two months, but it was one of the unquestioned rituals of army life, the morning report.

Gage nodded and continued around the room gathering status reports from his other commanders. Armistead had always hated these morning reports, where all the agony of war was reduced to an accounting. Here real men—men with wives and children, men with histories and hopes, brave men—were reduced to mere numbers. What was death here but a vertical line on a piece of paper with a slash drawn through it. A man with a musket ball in his lung became just a number struck off a chart. Armistead had been in the army for fourteen years. He'd been through this drill many times. He understood its importance in running an army. But still he hated everything about it.

Gage seemed to have no blood in his veins when it came to these exercises. He was not a field general, not a man who led troops, though as a younger officer he had done so. Now he was content to sit at headquarters and deal with what he called "the larger problems."

"Granny Gage," some of the men called him. Of medium height and bland countenance, nondescript even in the uniform of a Lieutenant General, he seemed to have little passion for battle and little aptitude for the necessities of running an efficient campaign. The officers in the Boston garrison waited for his plan to put down the rebellious militias around them, but Gage never truly settled on one.

The engagements in Lexington and Concord had embarrassed Gage, and scuttlebutt among the younger officers was that his command might be in jeopardy when word got back to London. No one expected His Majesty's forces to be shot at by a rabble of colonials, certainly not to be routed as they had been at the bridge in Concord. Gage would have to answer for that, and answers would not be easy.

Armistead had seen a lot of war in his life, but nothing like the march back to Boston after the withdrawal from Concord. As his company stepped along the road, small groups of what the colonials were calling "minute men" kept appearing behind fences and rocks, firing their muskets at his troops. Fortunately, most of their weapons were crude and they were firing from too great a distance. Probably not one shot in a hundred hit close to its target. But a few of his men fell and this caused fear to ripple through the ranks.

Like their commanding officer, none of the men in his company had ever before been fired upon while marching away from a battle. Armies formed up and faced each other and did their shooting in that gentlemanly way. Battles took place on the field of fire. When one army withdrew, the engagement usually ended. But the troops coming back from Concord felt as if they were marching though an American carnival. It was a shooting gallery and they were the targets. The minute men shouted at them derisively as they fired. Then as soon as their balls had flown, they ran away.

It was a most peculiar kind of warfare, and it caused Armistead to worry about what lay ahead. The British army had often campaigned great distances from England. That was not the problem. The campaigns in Canada and India were every bit as challenging as this one. The navy would deliver supplies and bring fresh troops. But warfare in the homeland of an enemy was never easy. Every local was a potential spy or saboteur. And when armies went scavenging, as they always did, they turned even friendly locals into angry enemies. They'd already seen that in Boston, in the reaction of the citizens here to the Quartering Act. Many British soldiers went to bed in Boston houses at night wondering whether they'd find whale oil in their boots or sand in their gun barrels in the morning.

Armistead and the other officers also worried about the ministry's intention to rely on loyalist units in the colonies to carry much of the battle if war came. No regular likes to rely on militia, especially when the loyalty of the militia is so uncertain. Perhaps these loyalist companies were dead set against this rebellion today, but how would they feel a few months from now when they realized they'd be shooting at their neighbors and maybe even their brothers or cousins? And what stomach would they have for a fight after they discovered how frightening a fight could be? No, Armistead thought, give me ten regulars to a hundred irregulars any time.

Armistead's mind continued to wander into canyons of frustrating speculation as the meeting droned on. He was not the kind of officer who whined about the failures of his commanders. But he harbored grave doubts about this campaign. Gage showed no interest in attacking the colonial militias, nor did the militias seem anxious for a direct engagement with the army. Armistead worried about what that meant.

The specter that haunted his thoughts was the worst of all possible military situations: an army in garrison subject to relentless sniping attacks from a more mobile enemy. Death by a thousand little cuts, one of the other officers called it. If Lexington and Concord were such cuts, how many more would follow? How many more staff meetings where his morning reports would toll up the casualties of a campaign that seemed, to his knowing eye, to be disintegrating into chaos?

Jonathan and the three members of his fact-finding mission lost contact with the Congress as soon as they left Philadelphia. The thrust of debate had made their mission irrelevant almost as soon as it began, but they had no way of knowing that and had carried out their assignment with dead seriousness.

In Lexington and Concord they visited the scenes of battle and interviewed participants. The Massachusetts Committee of Safety was especially helpful in finding observers with blood-curdling stories to tell of British atrocities. Jonathan found a local artist who drew diagrams and scenes of the battles and sketched in the principal areas of contact on the British retreat to Charlestown.

At the end of more than a week, the committee felt it had accumulated information that would help the fact-finders understand exactly what had transpired in these towns west of Boston nearly two months ago. But the committee had a second charge, and that was to observe and assess the state of the colonial forces in Massachusetts. To this purpose they rode toward Cambridge to visit the headquarters of Artemas Ward, the commanding general of the several militias that had surrounded Boston after the engagements at Lexington and Concord.

Riding along Mt. Auburn Street toward Ward's headquarters, Jonathan hardly felt himself in the middle of an armed camp. Cambridge was a compact town of fine wooden homes and narrow stone streets lined with brick shops. Large elm trees crowned the streets with their branches and morning glories hung lightly on the picket fences like strings of gleaming amethyst. The buildings of Harvard College took up most of one side of Cambridge Common, and the town seemed filled not with the spirit of war so much as the excitement of the end of the academic year. It reminded Jonathan of the brief time he had spent at college in Princeton and how easy it was to be carefree when Homer and Euclid, not cannons and Kings, dominated your thoughts.

As they turned down Brattle Street, military activity grew more apparent. Horses came and went, sentries in unmatched uniforms were posted by the gate, and muskets were much in evidence. The four men pulled up and dismounted in front of an elegant three-story house with four square pillars in front and a long veranda on the left side. Over the porch hung a flag of white linen fringed in gold with black bars across the top and bottom and a squat green tree in the center. It bore the words "Liberty Tree: An Appeal To God."

Jonathan stepped toward the sentry and presented their credentials, a letter of introduction from the secretary of the Congress. The sentry carried it to a dour man standing on the porch who looked it over, nodded, and handed it back. The sentry returned and instructed the four to enter the house where an officer would take them to General Ward.

Jonathan knew little of Artemas Ward and had never heard his name until a week ago. As they'd learned in Lexington, this wasn't much of an army, not in the normal sense. A shadowy Committee of Safety appeared to run things, but its principal task seemed to be negotiating assignments among the various militias. Many of the eastern

Massachusetts towns had sent men to participate in the siege of Boston after word got around of the shooting in Lexington and Concord. Militia had come as well from New Hampshire and Connecticut. A few men had even ridden up from New York, not as part of any formal unit but simply anxious to get into a fight with the British, against whom they had some personal grievance.

Some of the militia men had uniforms, some did not. Even within individual units, the quality and color of uniforms varied. There was a distinctive home-made look to many of them. Most of the militia companies were headed by local men who'd fought in the French and Indian Wars. Some, Jonathan had learned, were excellent soldiers and leaders. But several people had told the committee that Artemas Ward had little control over the individual units and was himself a cautious and uncertain leader.

Jonathan had expected someone who resembled George Washington: tall, erect, dignified, and heroic. Ward was none of those things and seemed too busy to spend much time with the committee in any case. He explained that more ships had been arriving in recent weeks with reinforcements for Gage's army of occupation. Most of the citizens of Boston had been driven out by the British takeover, but a few patriots remained and they were a steady source of information. Ward had learned that three major generals had arrived to assist Gage: Henry Clinton, William Howe and Gentleman Johnny Burgoyne. And the talkative Burgoyne had described, within earshot of one of Ward's spies, the plans the British were making to attack at Dorchester and circle behind the colonial positions, rolling up the militias from their flanks and forcing a quick surrender.

Ward told the committee that the militias believed that the longer they waited the stronger the British would get and, as the glow of Lexington and Concord began to dim, colonial enthusiasm would diminish as well. They could not wait for the British to choose where and when and how an engagement would occur. So it had been decided to force the action by moving troops and guns close enough to fire on the British ships in Boston harbor.

He unfolded a wrinkled map on the table in the center of his office and showed them the situation around Boston. Though the colonials held positions in the heights of Dorchester and Roxbury, south of Boston neck, they'd decided to move on Charlestown to the north because it overlooked the narrow passage through which ships had to sail into the Back Bay. The smaller of the two Bunker Hills above Charlestown, Breed's Hill, was close enough to the water for the American guns to reach their targets. By fortifying Breed's Hill and firing from there, the militias would force the redcoats to engage; they couldn't simply sit in Boston while colonials picked off their ships and patrols. It was June 16th, and the militias would be moving as soon as darkness fell that night.

Jonathan now understood the reason for the comings and goings from Ward's headquarters. It was clear as well why there were so few soldiers in the garrison. Most were staging for the forced march into Charlestown that night. If the committee was truly to assess the state of the colonial forces here, they would have a very good chance to do so in Charlestown.

But the committee members were reluctant to get in harm's way. They had not come to join a battle, they agreed, nor to take any chances. Their duty was to gather information and to get it back to Philadelphia. They had especially noted on Ward's map that the narrow entrance to the Charlestown Peninsula afforded little cover and could easily be closed down by an enemy circling from the rear. The three members chatted among themselves for a few minutes and decided that they would spend the night in Cambridge and follow reports of the engagement, if there was one, from there.

"Suppose then," Jonathan suggested, "that I ride to Charlestown with some of these soldiers, make my own observations, and draft a report for the committee."

The three looked at each other and quickly nodded their assent to Jonathan's proposal. "Excellent idea, Houghton," one of them said. "You're a reliable draftsman in any case and your maps and drawings should be very helpful to all of us. We would just be in your way." With that they retreated to their horses and rode off in search of lodging for the night.

Jonathan had other plans. He asked one of the sentries where he might find militia men heading toward the main force that was moving on Charlestown. The sentry gave him a blank look suggesting he knew nothing of Charlestown, and Jonathan was reminded that he must be more careful of what he said. But the sentry pointed to his left at three men in breeches and open-necked shirts who were loading picks and axes on a small cart. He led his horse in their direction.

The men were showing the effects of the warm day and one stopped for a moment to refresh himself from a wooden canteen. He was a compact, muscular man of medium height, perhaps a year or two older than Jonathan. The blond streaks through his brown hair sparkled in the sunlight, and a broad smile, more bemused than friendly, came to his face as he spotted Jonathan. "Morning" he said. "A great day for killin' redcoats, don't you think?"

Startled by the man's macabre and cavalier tone, Jonathan fished for the right response. It was indeed a beautiful morning, but he hadn't regarded its amenability for killing anyone as part of the day's charm. He answered simply, "Hello, what are you doing?"

The man smiled mischievously. "Gettin' ready to dig some deep graves. Wanna' bury those redcoats so deep their bones'll never be found."

Jonathan could not suppress a laugh and thrust his hand toward the man. "I'm Jonathan Houghton from Delaware."

The man's head turned slowly from side to side and he smiled and let out a loud whistle. "Delaware, boys," he said to the others. "We're gettin' reinforcements from everywhere. Before you know it, the whole damn state of South Carolina will be here."

He stepped toward Jonathan and received his hand. "Well, it's a pleasure to meet you, Mr. Delaware. My name is Ezekial Isaac Flint. People just call me Flint. You should, too."

Jonathan laughed at this engaging man with the odd name. "Which militia company are you with?" he asked.

Flint smiled and whistled again, "Now there you got yourself a good question, Mr. Delaware. I guess you'd have to say that they move me around where I can cause the least trouble. I'm a Boston boy, but I'm not a reg'lar member of any militia. No real militia in Boston since the redcoats took over the town. I've been itchin' to get at these redcoat bastards and, after the battle at Lexington it seemed like we was finally ready for a fight. I reported here to headquarters, but they didn't quite know what to do with me or a few other boys who rode in from south of here. There ain't no real army, just these militia companies. So we went around and tried to find someone who'd fit us in. Most was happy to have us, but some is pretty closed up, all kinfolk you know. I been marchin' with the Connecticut boys under Colonel Putnam. Israel Putnam, you heard of him?"

Jonathan had not, and so indicated with a slow shake of the head.

"A good man. Was a ranger in the French and Indian War. Knows how to fight and treats the troops decent. He's been hankerin' to get at these redcoats, 'stead of sittin' around just watchin' 'em drill. Buildin' this fort in Charlestown was his idea. Gen'l Ward was dubious, but old lead ass is dubious about everythin'. We'd die of old age before we'd ever fire a shot, if he had his way."

"So what's happening here now," Jonathan asked.

"You ask a lot of questions, Mr. Delaware. You plannin' to get into this fight?"

Jonathan explained that he was accompanying a committee sent by the Continental Congress to assess the situation here, that he had not come to join the hostilities, only to observe.

"Big wig, huh?" Flint said and whistled again. "Well, Mr. Congress, you'll be havin' plenty to observe in Charlestown."

The early morning light sparkled in the east-facing windows of the wooden houses on Gibb's Lane as Aubrey Armistead walked with several other officers toward the long wharf in the northeastern cove of Boston neck. Flowers of every kind and color were blooming in Boston on this beautiful June morning and the scents wafted on the light breeze that had just begun to blow off the harbor. As the officers approached the docks, Armistead and a captain named Pound separated from the others. No staff meeting for them this morning for they'd drawn reconnaissance duty along the Charlestown shore. Boston had been under siege for more than a month now, and there had been some reports that colonial troops might move on to the heights above the town across the bay. They were going to have a look for themselves.

A longboat with ten oarsmen from the HMS Lively awaited them at the end of the pier. Pound took a seat in the bow and Armistead moved to the stern. On a day such as this, duty of this sort brought no complaint from any of the men in the boat as the ten oars pulled them steadily along the east shore of Boston neck around the point toward the thin channel that separated the two peninsulas.

As they neared the point, Armistead noticed something on the smaller of the two hills above Charlestown, something he hadn't seen in earlier reconnaissance missions, not even when he scanned this sector yesterday from atop Beacon Hill. He took his spyglass from its sheath and braced his arm against the gunwale. The slight chop on the water made a steady sighting difficult, but he acclimated and began to move with the boat. Slowly he surveyed the crest of the hill above Charlestown.

Now Armistead noticed that the front of the hill was lined with heavy wooden breastworks, what appeared to be trenches, and several firing positions suitable for cannon. It was a kind of fort, with walls strengthened by what appeared to be hogsheads, probably filled with dirt, and the bundles of sticks that engineers called fascines—hazards that infantry men hated. He took a piece of paper from his goatskin knapsack and drew some crude diagrams of what he saw, trying to count accurately the rows of fortifications.

When he looked at what he had drawn, Armistead was stunned by the elaborateness of the structures, but more by how quickly they'd been put in place. Nothing had been on the hillside yesterday morning; today there were fortifications from which several hundred men could fire their weapons without exposing themselves to return fire from below. To a veteran soldier like Armistead, the speed of construction and the complexity of the fortifications were unimaginable. It looked like the work of several companies of engineers, but Armistead knew that these colonial militias never gave a thought to separate companies of engineers. He passed the spyglass down to Pound and commanded him to make his own observations. After a minute of adjustment and several minutes of peering through the glass, Pound turned to Armistead and said, "My God, sir, what have they done?"

Armistead ordered the boat to come about and head back to Boston. As the oarsmen stroked vigorously, Aubrey Armistead looked back over his shoulder at the long black lines snaking across the top of Breed's Hill, feeling the awful terror that soldiers always suffer when their enemy has taken the high ground.

Jonathan, Flint, and the other two men with the cart had caught up with their Connecticut regiment on the crest of Breed's Hill near midnight. Jonathan had never seen such a sight. Several hundred men spread out over two hundred yards building a fort in the darkness. Colonel Gridley, the engineer, hurried along behind them, shouting instructions and answering questions. The furious activity continued through the night, and when the first shafts of light rose from behind Noodles Island at dawn, most of the exhausted men were sleeping in their new fortification.

It was morning now and, despite his fatigue, Jonathan had no time for sleep. He walked along behind the breastworks with paper and pencil in hand, sketching the position and making notes on the strength and equipment of the units in place there. When he found a man awake and unoccupied, he'd stop to ask a few questions. He noted the rag-tag look of these units, but he also found them ready for a fight. Over and over, they mentioned Lexington Green and how they had to stop these redcoats here before they poured into every town and shot up the locals as they had there.

Jonathan also took note of the bravado of some of the militia men, especially those who'd yet to see their first battle. They talked of slaughtering the redcoats and piling up the corpses and sending the survivors running and yelping back to London. It reminded him of something Colonel Washington had said in one of their chats at Mt. Vernon, "The thrill of war is quickly exorcised by the terror of battle."

When Jonathan returned to the hole that he and Flint had dug during the night, the Boston man seemed to be in deep sleep. But when Jonathan stepped toward the hole, Flint sat up quickly and grabbed his musket. This startled Jonathan, but when Flint recognized him, he set the musket aside and laughed his mischievous laugh. "Lucky, you weren't no redcoat," he said, "or we'd be buryin' you in this hole."

Jonathan expressed his gratitude that Flint knew the difference between redcoats and civilians and slid down into the hole. He wiggled around until he found a comfortable position, then sat for a moment watching Flint arrange his ammunition. "Why are you here?" he asked after a few moments of silence.

Flint seemed confused by the question and answered, "Because the captain told me to be here."

"No, I'm sorry," Jonathan responded. "I meant why have you chosen to join the militia and get into this fight? No one forced you to."

"Oh that," Flint said, easing into a corner and sitting back. "I guess I got some scores to settle."

"What scores? What do you mean?"

Flint pointed toward Boston across the river. "See that hill over there. The one with the big houses."

Jonathan peered into the distance and found the hill that dominated the end of the neck. "I see it," he said.

"I grew up there, down on the south side. Weren't no other children in my family. My mother died right after I was born. Jes' my father and me. He was a printer. No real education, but he worked hard, had a pretty good business. I started workin' with him when I was about eight. Never went to school any after that. When Otis and Sam Adams and Dr. Warren, some of them, started stirrin' people up 'bout all the new laws the Parliament was makin', they'd come to my father to print up their notices and bills."

Flint pushed his hat back above his forehead and wiped the sweat from his face with his sleeve, then he continued. "In 1768, the governor decided to bring a halt to all the radical noise makin' and sent some soldiers out to tell the leaders to stop. They paid 'em no mind. Then the soldiers started comin' round to the printers and tellin' them not to be printin' anythin' critical of the King or Parliament, that it weren't right."

Jonathan listened carefully, as Flint's story unfolded. "I remember the day they first come to my father's shop. There was four of 'em, and to a boy like me they looked huge and mighty scary. Filled that place right up. Warned my father he'd be in big trouble if he was involved in any of this sedition. I didn't know what that meant, but he 'splained it to me after they left. Said they didn't want him printin' nothin' that criticized the gov'ment."

"So did he stop?" Jonathan asked.

"Ha! Not my father. Just made him angry, English soldiers tellin' him what to do. No, he kept right at it. Even started goin' to Sons of Liberty meetin's. Before long, he was doin' more of their printin' than just about anythin' else. Sometimes we'd print late at night when we was doin' secret bills 'bout meetin's and things."

"Then one mornin', soldiers came again with an officer. The officer read somethin' said my father was bein' charged with sedition and they were takin' him off. He said he weren't goin' nowhere, so they tried to grab him. He snatched up a tray a print and whacked one of the soldiers with it. But the officer drew his sword and stuck it right under my father's chin and said he was goin' or they'd run him through. Then they started pushin' him out the door. Two of the soldiers stayed behind and smashed up the press."

"What did you do?" Jonathan asked.

"I thrashed at 'em some, but I was still only a boy, jes fifteen. They pushed me into a closet and blocked the door."

"What happened to your father?"

Flint gazed off into the distance toward Boston and sat silently for a moment. Then he focused directly at Jonathan with a look that was all steel. "Don't know," he said. "I never saw him again."

Jonathan gasped unintentionally, then said "My God, man, they did that?"

Flint nodded. "Dr. Warren told me once he thinks some of the soldiers hung him, then the officers wanted to hush it up because they didn't follow no legal procedures. But I never found out for sure."

"What did you do after that?"

"Apprenticed a while with a gunsmith. Then did manual labor for folks when I could get it. But mostly I became a trouble maker. Joined up with the Sons of Liberty. Spent a lot of nights harassin' soldiers, carryin' messages for Adams and Otis. Spent one beautiful December night turnin' Boston harbor into the world's biggest teapot. Made a fine lookin' savage, if I do say so."

Flint leaned forward and made a fierce face, showing Jonathan the look he'd worn on December 16, 1773, and asked, "You still wonderin' now why I'm here?" Then he leaned back and smiled broadly.

Jonathan's question had been answered and he said no more.

In mid-morning, the men on the hilltop saw a longboat from one of the British warships rowing along the shore. It stopped for a few minutes while a man in the stern appeared to study the new fortifications through a spyglass. This sent a wave of apprehension through the ranks, reminding the three hundred or so dug-in colonials that a real enemy lay before them and was beginning to take their measure.

Flint said that the officers expected it would take the British a few days to plan and mount an attack. He was glad for the additional time this would provide to build up their position and to bring in more ammunition and supplies over the neck from Cambridge. He left in the early afternoon to patrol with a small platoon of Connecticut men. Jonathan put his notes in his pack and lay back to catch some sleep until dark came and he could ride back to Cambridge and report what he'd seen to the members of the committee.

Armistead and Pound jumped from the boat and ran up Long Wharf through the rough stone streets to Gage's headquarters. Burgoyne and Clinton sat outside in the shade seeking relief from the rising heat and engaged in excited debate. Burgoyne, as always, was doing most of the debating. He was a member of Parliament and, Armistead thought, he acted like one.

The two officers asked for an immediate audience with their commander and he received them in the plush library of his quarters. They reported what they'd seen on Breed's Hill and after a few questions, Gage called his generals together to hear their report. "What do you think they're doing up there, Major?" Howe asked.

"Provoking us, I would say, sir," Armistead replied. "We wondered why they would fortify the lower of the two hills, then we looked at our maps and realized that their guns could not reach ships in the narrows from the higher hill. They must feel they can draw us out of Boston if they can pick off our ships from that vantage point. I suppose they might also be fortifying in preparation for launching an assault on Boston from there, but that seems less likely. They'd need a lot of boats, and they'd never get the boats launched with our ships firing on them from close range. I don't think it's preparations for an assault, sir. I believe it's an effort to break the siege by forcing us to engage them."

"And we'd be crazy to take the bait," said Clinton. "Rowing our troops across the harbor where they could see us coming, then assaulting a fortified position uphill--even colonials know what an advantage that'd give them. We've been working on a good plan to attack Dorchester and pivot behind their emplacements. That makes a lot of tactical sense, and I think we should stick to it. Especially now that they've got a force tied up in Charlestown." Burgoyne nodded in agreement.

But Howe suggested an alternative. "Why not take the Dorchester attack plan," he proposed, "and simply reverse it." He walked to the large map on the wall and, using his crop as a pointer, showed them how the infantry could land at the small beach below Moulton's Hill and advance behind Breed's Hill to get at the colonials from the rear. "Bombardment from the navy would keep the front of the fortification engaged," he said, "and once the beachhead was secure, a column could be sent to cut off the peninsula from the rear. The colonials would be overwhelmed by the strength of the infantry and with their supply lines and route of withdrawal cut, would have no alternative but surrender."

Howe had more experience than the others at amphibious landings and they listened in earnest to his suggestions. Clinton remained doubtful. "It's a good plan, William, from a tactical sense, but it depends on too many contingencies, especially effective support from the navy. And we know little about the strength of the infidels on that hill. Perhaps this is a feint intended to shock us into acting precipitously while they mount an assault elsewhere or march down the neck. Or perhaps they have all their troops up there and we'll run into a rain of fire. I think we should wait until we know more. Our ships can keep a respectful distance from their guns in the meantime."

Gage listened to his generals and weighed his own options. He knew there were complaints in London about his indifferent command. He knew they'd given him the additional title of Royal Governor to encourage his boldness. He knew these three generals had been sent here to prod him to act more vigorously. He also knew that these were ambitious men and each of them would replace him in a minute if offered the chance. He had to act here and he had to act decisively or someone other than Thomas Gage would soon be the commanding general of British forces in North America. "Gentlemen," he said, "prepare to attack Charlestown. Let us destroy them here and end this rebellion now. Howe, you will lead the assault."

Armistead looked at Pound and began the ritual he had followed before every engagement. "Are the men ready, Captain?" he asked.

"They are, sir" Pound replied.

"Then may God look proudly on our service to his King."

With that Armistead ordered his battalion of Light Infantry, the 22$^{nd}$ Foot, into formation at the base of Breed's Hill where they awaited his orders to attack. But then word passed down the line that Howe's flanking maneuver had already failed, and Armistead felt a first trace of terror at what now lay ahead. The landing below Moulton's Hill ran into unexpected colonial resistance and Howe's artillery got stuck in the marsh and produced no supporting fire. So there would be no diversion, no closure from the rear. But instead of pulling back, Howe was throwing two regiments under Brigadier General Pigott into a frontal assault on the freshly constructed fort atop Breed's Hill.

Armistead worried about Howe. Soldiers respect a commander who can make decisions, who inspires in his troops the confidence that he knows what he's doing. But veterans like Armistead also knew that brash gamblers like Howe too often forget that they're wagering men's lives. They force the action, trumping prudence. Howe had said in their briefing that morning that the colonials' will to fight wouldn't survive the first sight of a British bayonet at their throats. He'd told his officers that their troops would run the rebels back to Cambridge and sleep that night in Harvard Yard.

Armistead wasn't so sure. He'd been in some battles with inexperienced troops. He knew that when the smoke cleared from the first few volleys some of them were long gone. Dropped their weapons and fled into the woods. But he'd also seen the opposite, young soldiers standing their ground and finding courage—even anger—when musket balls flew their way for the first time. Perhaps these colonials would flee when they faced the waves of British regulars coming up the hill at them. But they hadn't fled at Lexington and Concord, at least most of them had not. And they did have the powerful advantage here of a fortified position on high ground. Armistead was worried.

His soldiers formed up, as always, in three lines. They would be the first wave in the advance up the hill. His men looked beautiful in the mid-afternoon sun—that he had to admit. Because they expected to bivouac in Cambridge they were carrying their full packs and extra ammunition. The temperature was nearing ninety, so most carried two heavy tin canteens as well. But even weighted down, the men stood erect in a long scarlet line stretching before him. At his command, they fixed rifles in the fighting position, bayonets gleaming in the sun, and stepped off smartly to assault the breastworks above them.

Armistead marched at their side. It worried him that there was no firing from the breastworks. Untrained troops usually fired sporadically and often before their targets were in range. But, save for an occasional cannon shot, there was no firing coming from the fort above them. Could the colonials have retreated? That seemed unlikely. Surely a retreat would have been spotted and reported. The closer the $22^{nd}$ Foot got to its objective, the stranger the silence became. Sweat poured from under Armistead's hat and soaked his shirt and breeches. The heat was awful, but with no resistance his men were moving faster than expected up the long gentle slope of the hill. Armistead noticed the look of bewilderment in some of his own officers. Where were the sounds of engagement?

Suddenly he had his answer.

"So much for goin' back to Cambridge tonight, eh Mr. Congress. Guess that committee of yours will have to get its report after we kill ourselves a mess of these redcoats. Be a more excitin' report anyway." Flint had dug himself into a corner of the hole he shared with Jonathan. Powder and balls were carefully placed on small dirt shelves he'd dug out of the side of the hole. Whenever the breeze stilled, mosquitoes swarmed from the Mystick marshes to feast on their new targets on Breed's Hill.

Israel Putnam had ordered that no man place his musket in a firing position until so ordered. And even then, he said, he didn't want anyone firing until the redcoats came into range and they could see the whites in their eyes. So Flint kept his weapon at his side, even as he saw the infantry form up and begin their steady march up the hill. He had to admit, though he hated every one of them for what they'd done to his father, those straight ruby lines moving in even cadence were something to see.

Jonathan peered through a small hole in the breastworks, trying to stay out of sight but also trying to see what was happening so that he could faithfully record the events of this day. He was worried about having no musket of his own, but Flint assured him that he'd do enough firing for two men. In the few hours since they'd met, Jonathan had begun to find comfort as well as amusement in Flint's bravado, but he was anxious nevertheless about being so defenseless in this moment of maximum danger. He knew that the sweat that now bathed him was the result of more than just the God-awful heat.

"Did you see them?" Jonathan said to Flint. "They look ten feet tall and those bayonets are the most ferocious-looking weapons I ever saw."

"They are ten feet tall," Flint said in mock solemnity. "It's a law. No redcoats under ten feet tall. And those bayonets—they put diamonds in 'em so they sparkle in the sun. They been scarin' colonials like that for centuries. Half the time the enemy just surrenders without firin' a shot. I hope Colonel Putnam's got his white flag ready to go up." Then he laughed and slid his weapon along the edge of the hole into firing position and began to sight on one of the ten-foot men in front of him.

The single sharp word "Fire!" came tumbling down the line, followed quickly by an burgeoning roar and a heavy, dense cloud of smoke. Jonathan could barely see Flint beside him and he could hear nothing. Flint quickly reloaded and fired again. A smile burned into his face, half pleasure, half ferocious intensity. Jonathan would later come to recognize this as the look of Ezekial Isaac Flint honoring his father.

A small zephyr blew off the bay and pushed the smoke away for just a moment. Flint let out a loud yelp. "Look at 'em, Delaware. They can hardly climb over the stack of their own corpses to get at us."

Jonathan leaned forward and peered through the hole in the breastworks. The sight he saw at that moment stayed with him for the rest of his life and recurred every time he ever heard men who'd never seen battle talking about it. Scores of redcoats covered the ground, their bodies twisted and contorted and broken. Hats and canteens and packs were scattered everywhere; rifles and swords pointed toward the sky, as if from a giant pin cushion; and from each of the writhing, moaning bodies came tributaries of blood quickly forming a vast red sea. Here and there

140

Jonathan could see a disjointed foot or an arm or even a dismembered head where colonial cannon balls had found their target.

The slaughter was gargantuan and revolting and Jonathan felt not pride, not satisfaction, not any sense of victory, only nausea. He was embarrassed when he vomited up the remains of his dinner, embarrassed at what Flint would think of him. But Flint had more important concerns, and he began firing again as the waves of tall men from the 22$^{nd}$ Foot kept coming and coming.

More than anything, Armistead hated the smoke. How could an officer make sensible judgments when the field of battle disappeared from view. When the colonials did finally start to shoot, they rained squalls of lead on his troops. He had seen many of them fall before the line disappeared in the smoke. It was impossible to communicate in the noise and impossible to reorganize in the dense white fog. He had no choice but to continue the assault. They were moving up the hill and if they could only get close enough to put their bayonets to work, the colonials' advantage in defending a fortified position on high ground would be overcome. This much he knew about the men he had trained: no one was their equal in hand-to-hand combat.

Armistead tried to see Pound to signal the order for a final assault. A waft of breeze briefly cleared the smoke, and he thought this would allow him to spot his junior officer. But what he saw was a sight he had never imagined. There across the slope of the hill to his left were his troops, piled on each other, bent and broken in every possible way, crying out their agony. The few who still stood had stopped in bewilderment, unsure what to do, simply shocked into immobility by the sight before them.

Armistead knew he should think, knew he should act. But he felt his capacity for reason swimming against a torrent of emotion. His instinct was to retreat, but his mind was clear enough for him to know the impossibility of that. Waves of men were coming behind him and there was no escape route. On the field of battle there are only two strategies: advance or retreat. Unable to do the latter, he shouted the only order he could: "Advance men! Advance!"

Then Armistead reloaded his own weapon and moved toward his troops to form them up into a single rank. He looked for Pound but could not spot him. He began to run now, stepping over corpses and the writhing wounded as he ran. "Major," he heard one shout and, as he looked down, he saw the bars of a captain whose arm lay limp beside him on the ground and whose uniform was soaked in blood. It was Pound. His eyes blinked to focus, but could not. He started to say something and Armistead stopped briefly and squatted low beside him to listen. But no sound emerged, and Pound's body twitched violently then was still.

Another heavy barrage from the top of the hill brought Armistead back to his task. As he reached the small body of survivors, he began to rally them into line and establish an order of fire. They started back toward the top when a deep searing pain shot through Armistead's right leg. He looked down at it and saw a dark circle of blood quickly staining the front of his breeches. Then he felt an even sharper pain in his right shoulder. He looked toward the top of the hill and took a half step forward before a soft white cloud enveloped his mind and he fell unconscious to the ground.

Flint's carefully arranged store of powder and balls was shrinking rapidly. He was handy with a gun, as Jonathan had quickly noted, and he could reload as fast as any man on that hillside. But the redcoats kept coming, and he was worried now about his dwindling ammunition. Had the British delayed their attack a few days, more supplies could have been brought to Charlestown. But Howe's attack had come before the new fort was adequately stocked for this kind of intense battle.

Jonathan began to notice that some of the colonial troops were beginning to run down the back side of Breed's Hill. Perhaps they were out of ammunition. Perhaps they'd seen something so horrifying they could no longer fight. Perhaps they were just scared and were running away. Who could tell? Strange things happen to men in the face of live fire. Some are inspired to unimaginable bravery; some cower in fear. Neither is a reaction from reason. Spontaneous instinct takes over. Brave men no more order up their own bravery than frightened men order up their fear. It just happens, and no man knows until the bullets start to fly what his own reaction will be.

Flint was clearly one of the brave men, shooting and shouting as furiously an hour into the battle as he had at the beginning. Jonathan was not so sure about himself. The wave of nausea had passed and he felt more in control of himself than he had been when the firing started. But he still had no weapon and the relentless surge of the British troops was pushing closer to the hilltop, and he was afraid.

"Here comes trouble," Flint muttered, and Jonathan quickly understood what he meant when several rounds tore into the wooden fortification above their hole showering them with splinters and dirt. A fragment of something found its way into Jonathan's left eye and he rubbed vigorously to get it out. Another round of fire tore away most of the remaining logs and suddenly Jonathan could see that the battle was at their doorstep. The soldiers were hurtling over the breastworks, often using the bodies of their own dead comrades as steps.

The order to retreat passed quickly down the line, and Flint told Jonathan to leave the hole from the rear, run to the left and head for the stone wall on the north side of Breed's Hill. Flint kept firing to cover Jonathan's exit, though he was down now to his last few balls.

Squatting behind a stump about a hundred feet down the hill, Jonathan looked back and saw Flint coming out the back of the hole toward him. Jonathan felt relief that they'd both gotten away before they'd been overrun. Perhaps Flint could have defended himself against a bayonet assault, but Jonathan had no faith in his own ability to do so, especially without a weapon.

Jonathan stopped to wait for Flint, but Flint waved him on and shouted, "Get outta' here, Delaware. Run like hell." As he started to turn, Jonathan saw a spray of blood fly from the front of Flint's left thigh. Flint took one more step then tumbled to the ground, his weapon falling a few feet in front of him.

Seeing this, Jonathan crouched down and duck-walked quickly back toward the fallen man. Flint was in horrible pain, but still conscious when Jonathan reached him. He grabbed Flint's shirt and started to drag him down the back side of the hill. Flint shouted through clenched teeth for Jonathan to retrieve his weapon as well. Jonathan did this and was now holding the musket in one hand and dragging Flint with the other, pulling backward as hard as he knew how.

They moved fitfully downhill through the high grass toward the stone wall where other retreating colonials had taken up defensive positions. Jonathan suddenly sensed that bullets were flying up the hill barely over his head and when the report of the weapons followed, he realized that redcoats had reached the top of the hill and the colonials behind the stone wall were firing at them. Jonathan was in the center of the field of fire with shots now coming from both directions.

After a minute or two, the shots stopped coming up the hill and he saw that the colonials were retreating further back. Jonathan reached the stone wall, but no one else was there. Flint was conscious but mumbling incoherently. When Jonathan looked back over the wall toward the top of Breed's Hill he saw only confusion. Some of the redcoats had stopped and seemed to be looking for officers to direct their movement. A few had fanned down the back side of the hill in pursuit of the retreating colonials. Two of those were approaching the wall, about 20 yards in front of him.

Jonathan picked up Flint's weapon and was overjoyed to see that it was loaded and primed. Like most American farmers, he'd used a musket for hunting, so he knew how to cock the hammer in the firelock and take aim. He laid the weapon on top of the wall and pointed it at one of the advancing redcoats. They had apparently been unaware that anyone was behind the wall and both stopped and began to load their weapons. Jonathan fired at the one on the left and the soldier jerked backwards and fell hard to ground almost as soon as Jonathan felt the musket thump against his shoulder.

Seeing what was happening and realizing Jonathan would need to reload, the other soldier lowered his rifle to waist height and began to fly toward the wall. He was now just a few yards away and Jonathan froze momentarily at the sight of that long luminous bayonet careening toward his throat. Some provident instinct seemed to take over in that moment and as the soldier reached the wall, Jonathan pushed the top stones over in his direction. They caught him at the knees and caused him to fall forward, cursing and driving the bayonet into the ground. Jonathan jumped to his feet, took Flint's gun by the barrel and swung as hard as he could at the soldier's head.

The force of the blow scattered red hat and scalp and brain matter in every direction. The soldier's large body writhed briefly, then lay motionless. Jonathan stood over him, the barrel of the weapon in his hand, the stock covered with blood and small pieces of the dead soldier's head. Jonathan felt nothing, absolutely nothing in that moment; then a feeling of sheer exhilaration swept over him. His legs were shaking and streams of sweat flowed down his face. But the bayonet was gone and he was still alive. He looked toward the man he had just killed, thinking he should feel something: revulsion, pity, sadness. He felt none of those, only relief— and, surprisingly, a sense of strength. This was the biggest test of his life, and he had endured it.

This flow of emotion was interrupted by Flint's tortured voice saying, "Nice imitation of a soldier, Delaware. Now get me the hell outta here."

144

William Howe looked splendid in his clean uniform as he stood over the bed where Aubrey Armistead lay. Two other wounded officers filled cots on either side. "Glad to see you're doing better," Howe said, sounding more formal than sympathetic. "You showed a lot of courage, Major, and I'm proud of you. We set the rebels to flight and we couldn't have done it without the bravery of the men in the 22nd Foot. Your men will be mentioned specifically in my report on the battle of Charlestown."

It had been more than week since Armistead was wounded and the pain in his shoulder was subsiding. The surgeons had told him that the broken bone would heel, that the musket ball had passed clean through him, and there would be no permanent damage. The leg would take a little longer, but that would heal as well. But Armistead's relief at the nature of his own wounds brought little relief from his suffering over the fate of his men. Four hundred and ten men had marched up Breed's Hill under his command. Fewer than a hundred had returned unscathed. One hundred and nineteen of his men had been killed, including Pound and three other officers. Nearly two hundred had been wounded, some so grievously that they would never fight again. More than two dozen of the wounded had had lost one leg, or both.

It was a slaughter, the worst he had ever known. The sight he had seen in that brief moment when the breeze cleared the smoke of battle, the awful picture of his infantrymen piled in death and pain before him, had prevented his sleep and tortured every waking hour since he recovered consciousness after the battle. The generals were saying now that it had been a great victory, that the colonials had been driven from their fortification; that one of their heroes, Dr. Warren, had been killed; and that they had learned how hard it would be to stand up to the relentless assault of a seasoned army.

Perhaps. But the other wounded officers were saying something quite different. Only generals and politicians could call this a victory, they said. We'd thrown 1500 soldiers into this battle, half again as many as the Americans; and more than a thousand had been killed or wounded. Nineteen officers and more than 200 men were dead. If this was a victory, one wounded captain had said, "God save us from too many more of these "victories."

The officers also whispered what no general could say: that when the bodies were falling in front of them, some of their own troops had turned and run. All the talk about professionals on one side and untrained militia on the other, all the predictions about how the battlefield would drain of colonials once the bullets started to fly—that talk had quieted now. Some of the colonials had fled, but most had not. And some of the King's soldiers had fled as well. In his quiet moments, Armistead wished that some of his own men had possessed the sense to flee rather than to follow his orders and march to their deaths.

Cambridge was quiet, a typically drowsy Sunday. A few men and boys stood patiently along the curb while an even smaller number of women waited behind the fences. A heavy rain had fallen all morning and, though it had now begun to clear, General Ward had decided earlier to cancel the ceremony welcoming George Washington, who was riding in from Watertown that morning to complete his journey from Philadelphia. Jonathan waited on the porch of Wadsworth House with a few militia leaders and the members of the fact-finding committee. They'd intended to return to Philadelphia a week ago, but the battle at Breed's Hill and the word of Washington's arrival had caused them to postpone their departure. Surely, they thought, when Washington assumed command of these forces, he'd want to hear personally from them.

Jonathan had run over that morning from a house along Cambridge Common that had been commandeered as a hospital after the battle. He'd been there every day to see Flint and was pleased that his leg was healing and he was hopping around cursing everything. He'd be walking normally in another week or two and would be able to return to the Connecticut militia. Many of the Connecticut boys had been in to see him. They told Jonathan that Flint was a fine soldier, and they were anxious to get him back.

Israel Putnam himself had been by to see Flint one morning and as he was leaving, he ran into Jonathan in front of the house. He shook Jonathan's hand vigorously and told the young man that he wished he'd consider joining up with the Connecticut militia. "There's a lot of fighting ahead," he said, "and you, sir, are a brave man. We would love to have you fighting at our side."

Every day, it seemed, someone said the same thing to Jonathan. Many of the retreating colonials had observed his bravery at the stone wall and the story of it spread widely. He'd faced down and killed two attacking soldiers, protected a wounded comrade and slowed the British advance. It was the sort of story that soldiers loved to tell, and the impact was magnified whenever it was mentioned that Jonathan was just a civilian who happened to be caught up in the battle, an innocent who didn't even have a weapon of his own.

Despite the recruitment efforts and the praise in which they were often encased, and despite his growing admiration, affection even, for the men he'd come to know since arriving here, the thought of becoming a soldier held little appeal for Jonathan. He had to get back to Philadelphia and then home to Still River Bend. He would gladly leave the soldiering to others.

The clip-clop of hooves on the cobblestone now brought a hush to the small gathering as every eye turned toward the street. A tall man in a deep blue uniform rode at the head of half a dozen soldiers trailed by a small herd of boys skipping behind. The sentries instinctively straightened as the horses approached and Jonathan felt himself catching the rhythm and doing the same. They stopped at the gate, where the riders dismounted and the sentries took their reins and moved them away. The gate opened and the tall man stepped through. He stopped and looked around him. Men began to clap and cheer. General George Washington had come to take command of the Continental Army.

As he ascended the steps, the General received salutes and then shook hands with the militia leaders. When he reached the members of the fact-finding committee, he greeted each. For Jonathan he had an especially warm smile, and said, "Good morning, Mr. Houghton. You do turn up in the strangest places." Jonathan returned the smile and the iron handshake.

At ten o'clock the next morning, Washington had scheduled a fifteen-minute meeting with the fact-finding committee. The members arrived promptly with Jonathan and were ushered into the room that Ward had been using as his headquarters. Washington rose from the large, dull Chippendale chair in which he'd been reading papers. He greeted them all briefly and asked them to sit in the chairs arrayed in a semi-circle around his.

"As you can imagine, gentlemen, there are a great many things I need to do over the next few days, so I cannot afford to give you all the time I would like. The service you are doing here is invaluable and I'm sure will make an important contribution to the deliberations in Philadelphia. Tell me please what you've observed here and what you've learned about Lexington and Concord."

The committee members all offered their observations, with Washington frequently interrupting to ask questions or seek further details. It seemed to Jonathan that the General was especially interested in their assessment of the morale of the troops and their courage under fire. He seemed pleased at what they told him and took special pleasure in their descriptions of Breed's Hill and the way the colonials had held their ground as the waves of British infantry mounted their up-hill assault. And he nodded knowingly at their report of colonials who abandoned their posts or failed to fire their weapons—a reaction to battle that he remembered well from his days on the frontier.

As the committee's report came to an end, Washington thanked them. "Our task now," he said, "will be to turn all these separate militias into a real army. It won't be simple, especially since I'm a Virginian and the militia units here are mostly New Englanders. Will their stomach for a fight be as large in harvest season or in the cold of winter as it is now? That will be the real test of this rebellion, gentlemen. I'm sure General Gage sits across the river thinking he can wait us out. I suspect I would do the same."

The committee members rose to leave, and Washington walked with them to the door, shaking hands with each one. Jonathan was last and when he faced the General to say good-bye, Washington said. "Mr. Houghton, would you stay one moment longer? There is a matter about which I would like a word."

Jonathan turned toward the committee members, with a look of surprise and uncertainty. They shuffled away, and the General and the young man stepped back into the room and closed the door. Washington walked behind the large oak table and stood in the brilliant morning light by the long window on the east side of the house. "Jonathan," he said, motioning the younger man to retake his chair, "on the ride from Philadelphia I did a great deal of thinking about this command I've just assumed and how best to manage it. There are no precedents, of course; no one has ever commanded a Continental Army in America before. No one has ever commanded an army that serves thirteen separate colonies. Few generals, in fact, have ever commanded an army against their own King. So there is no history that tells me how to do this.

"I did come to the realization that my political flanks will be as vulnerable in this post as my military flanks, that there'll always be people who would rather have someone else in command, who'll be watching me closely for the slightest sign of indecision, of weakness, of failure. Some of them, no doubt, will be my own generals."

Jonathan caught Washington's meaning. He'd already heard whispers of criticism from Massachusetts men dubious about a commander from Virginia. He nodded this understanding as Washington continued. "I'll need to have a few men, good men, outside of the chain of command whose loyalty is unimpeachable. I'll need them to take on special assignments, to be my eyes and ears, to warn me when trouble is brewing in the ranks, to help me form independent assessments of the other generals, to observe the armies that are not under my immediate command. I learned on the frontier that a commander can't rely solely on the official reports for an objective assessment of the performance of his troops. The need for other sources of assessment and information will be especially keen in this new situation where we're trying to make one army from so many independent militias."

Washington turned away from the window and walked back toward Jonathan. He grabbed one of the chairs and pulled it close, sitting just a few feet in front of the younger man, their eyes level. "Jonathan, I'd like you to join me here. I'll secure you an appointment as a captain in the Continental Army. You'll report directly to me and be one of my aides. You'll have no command responsibilities, but will be given special assignments by me. Sometimes you'll be with me; other times I'll send you to be with other generals or on other business. I'll rely heavily on your observations and advice."

Jonathan was dumbfounded. He'd not expected the private audience with the General and certainly not the offer that now lay before him. His head was spinning. What about Father in Philadelphia? What about the farm? Why him? He tried to rescue his feelings from the torrent of questions. He looked at Washington, back by the window now, wisely giving Jonathan a moment to collect his thoughts.

"I'm deeply flattered by this, General, please be assured of that," Jonathan said, as the words began to form in his mind. "But why me? I'm no soldier and I have no experience as a judge of men. I seriously doubt that I'm the right person for this assignment."

"Then let me explain," Washington replied. "That you are not a soldier is one of the things that qualifies you—though I must say, I heard some stories last night about your exploits in Charlestown that suggest you may be more of a soldier than you think. Israel Putnam said he'd never seen bravery like yours, facing down two grenadiers at point blank range to save a comrade. But any soldier I might assign to these tasks would be suspected by others of being a loyalist for his own militia company or region. I want an aide whose only obligation is to me.

"I also need a pair of eyes unclouded by poor training or misguided military doctrine. This so-called army is full of soldiers who have a lot of un-learning to do. But you're not one of them, Jonathan.

"What I really need here is a brave man, a resourceful man, an intelligent man, and—more than anything else--a loyal man. I've seen your resourcefulness on one muddy night in Philadelphia. Our conversations at Mt. Vernon certainly revealed your intelligence. Your bravery, I'm told by some men who've seen a lot of war, is beyond reproach. Of your loyalty to me, Jonathan, I have only faith—faith that I can earn it and faith that you'll come to possess it."

Jonathan had never seen such effective salesmanship. Washington had clearly thought about his pitch to the younger man and it was note perfect when he made it. Jonathan's objections melted away—save, that is, for his concern about his father and their farm.

"General," he said, "It's hard to resist your offer. It'd be a great honor to serve with you in this way. But I'm concerned, of course, about the effect my absence will have on our farm in Delaware and on my father."

Washington returned to his chair, facing Jonathan. "I understand that concern completely," he said. "A little more than two weeks ago, John Adams came to me in Philadelphia and said the Congress wanted me to command this army. I'd no intention of doing this, only of returning to Mt. Vernon at the end of the session and experimenting with some of the techniques you and I discussed in April, of overseeing the work on the enlargement of the house. I thought myself a retired soldier. My first thoughts, like yours, were of home and family.

"But, Jonathan," he said, leaning forward again, "we don't always control our own destinies. If you believe, as I do, that the Almighty put us here for a purpose, then you must be prepared to act when that purpose is revealed. The time has come, Jonathan, when all of us must make choices. There are powerful forces descending on our land and they will sweep us all up in one way or another. There's no place to hide. Men will take sides. Some men'll fight for the side they choose. Others will seek to avoid the battle, but it will find them--or its effects will.

"I'm no radical, Jonathan, as you've observed. In many ways, I share your father's doubts about much that's happening in Philadelphia. But I can feel the weight of destiny falling upon us. If we're to be free

150

men, we may have no choice but to fight those who would steal our freedom. We may think of them as our countrymen and honor the ancestry and the traditions we share. But that only adds to the tragedy and the agony of what we face. It might be easier for us to take arms against a Frenchman or a Spaniard or a savage, but that's not the destiny that's come to us. Our oppressors are English, and so we must take arms against Englishmen.

"I've made the choice to do that, Jonathan, because I think it's the right course. Whether we'll succeed or fail, I can't be certain. But I can be certain that failure in the right is always better than success in the wrong. I hope you'll see it that way, too.

"You're a young man, Jonathan. The conflict that we're in now may well determine the kind of life you'll be able to live, the kind of life your children and grandchildren will be able to live.

"I can offer you no guarantees of what the months ahead will bring, if you join me here--only that you'll be able to say to your children that you saw a moment of destiny, a moment of great choices, and you seized it. There'll be danger and hardship and sadness and many lonely times for us all—the tariff that men must always pay when they seek to shape the future with their own hands."

Washington rose again and paced back toward the window, letting his homily sink in. Playing on men's honor and sense of destiny had worked well for him in the past, especially on those occasions when he'd had to convince troops to stay in the field after their enlistments were up. He felt confident that Jonathan would be affected by it as well.

And he was right. Jonathan stood up, moved toward the General and extended his hand. "I'd be honored to accept your offer, General." Washington smiled and the two men shook hands enthusiastically.

"I'll return with the committee to Philadelphia and inform my father of this change in plans. I'll rejoin you at the end of the Congress."

Washington shot Jonathan a skeptical look. "There's no time for that. I need you now. You'll have to send the committee off without you. You can write to your father, and the committee can carry your letter to him. We have ten thousand British troops sitting in the city of Boston with a large group of citizens who are loyal to the King. Some day very soon, they'll come at us with blistering force. We don't have an hour to waste in preparing for that.

"I'll have your commission papers drawn up immediately. You can see the quartermaster, if there is such a thing here, about a uniform and kit. And I think it'll be wise for you to select an aide of your own. You'll often be traveling on official business and it's much safer for two than one. One man can always remain awake in protection of the other. So find a good man, a good soldier if you can. Make it a man you can trust completely. I'll commission him a lieutenant and he'll report only to you."

Washington had clearly thought of everything. Jonathan really did want to return to Philadelphia. He knew that Henry would be deeply unsettled by this extraordinary change in plans. It was the sort of thing that a son should tell his father in person. But that was impossible now. Washington had made that clear. So Jonathan left for his lodgings, his head full of thoughts of the letter he would write to his father--and the strange days ahead as a soldier in a rag-tag army engaged in a war with enemy soldiers ten feet tall.

# Chapter 10

## London
## Late Summer 1775

"Mrs. Macauley has arrived to see you, sir." Dartmouth nodded at Carlisle, then looked over his right shoulder toward the porter standing silent and erect by the door.

"Bring her in, Edward, but first inform her that I'm sitting for a portrait and won't be able to rise when she enters."

"Of course, sir," the porter said, inclining his head deferentially and backing out.

The subject turned back and faced Benton Carlisle, who was standing behind an easel bearing a large and nearly completed portrait of William Legge, the Second Earl of Dartmouth. Carlisle and Nathaniel had been coming to Dartmouth's large Whitehall office every day for nearly two weeks, arriving promptly at eight forty-five each morning and departing shortly before noon. The office faced east, overlooking the busy river below. In the late summer, the light was only good during these morning hours.

This was the second portrait Carlisle had painted of Dartmouth. The task had been much easier the first time, in 1773, when Dartmouth was serving at the Board of Trade and their sittings were rarely interrupted by any official business. This commission was much different. Dartmouth was now Secretary of State for the American Colonies and the sittings were regularly interrupted by the comings and goings of officials and other visitors with news or papers to review or advice to offer.

When he assumed this position at the request of Lord North, Dartmouth knew it would be a challenge. But he liked Americans and was supportive of their efforts to establish a more reliable relationship with Parliament. As one sympathetic to the colonists, he thought, he could help negotiate a resolution of their grievances with Lord North and the King.

But it hadn't gone well. The King had become angrier and angrier at his American subjects, and had told North to order General Gage to take hard action against the rebels in Massachusetts. Dartmouth had questioned the wisdom of this to North, but North had said there was no reasoning with the King when it came to America. He was determined to root out the trouble-makers by whatever means necessary. Gage had sent a regiment out into the countryside to destroy a few barrels of powder and his best troops had been brutally assaulted by some colonial irregulars who then had sent word to London claiming a great victory. Gage had been characteristically slow in submitting his own official report and, when it arrived two weeks later, it seemed incomplete and pitifully defensive.

As if that weren't enough to vex the Earl of Dartmouth, the group of colonials who called themselves the Continental Congress, after all their protestations last fall, had sent a very strange document that arrived in London at the end of August. They called it the Olive Branch Petition. Now, perhaps having lost their stomach for a fight, they were seeking a peaceful resolution of the troubles. This outraged the King even more, coming as it did just a few weeks after the news of their militias slaughtering so many of his soldiers at Charlestown. The arrival of the petition just confirmed his own view of the wisdom of the Proclamation he'd issued the day before, declaring that his American colonies were in a state of rebellion. Dartmouth's ministry had become the focus of the King's fury and the quiet Earl found new reason every day to wonder if this expanding conflict could ever be resolved.

"Good day, William. It's so good to see you again." The words entered almost before the woman. Short and slender, with upswept brown hair, wearing a thin dress of light blue silk, Catherine Macauley moved brusquely toward the three men, but seemed not to notice two of them. She addressed all of her conversation to Dartmouth and never acknowledged or addressed Carlisle or Nathaniel as they worked on the portrait.

Nathaniel had come to recognize this behavior as typical. Though the best portrait painters of the time—Carlisle, Gainsborough, Ramsay, Romney, and one or two others—were much in demand and well-paid, and though they were treated as minor celebrities at social events, when they were at work they quickly came to be regarded as if they were servants or furniture. In the tightly regimented social structure that Nathaniel was beginning to recognize in London, people in a room merely providing services were rarely acknowledged by those who lived or worked there.

Occasionally a visitor would say a few words to Carlisle, having met the painter at a social gathering or perhaps having sat for one of his portraits. But Nathaniel found that he himself was totally invisible. The position of painter's assistant ranked very low on the social scale, probably in the vicinity of stable boy or chambermaid, and in all the sittings he and Carlisle had conducted together, Nathaniel had not once been addressed by anyone other than the painter nor had he spoken a word. He doubted that anyone they had painted even knew he was an American.

So it was not unusual this September morning that Catherine Macauley, the historian whose Whig opinions so irritated most of Lord North's government, should pay no attention to anyone other than Dartmouth. She and Dartmouth had known each other for years, and she had come to plead for caution and moderation in the government's policy toward America. For twenty minutes she talked without interruption about the justice in the Americans' claims and the government's failure to treat the colonials with the respect due to English citizens. Dartmouth sat facing Carlisle during this monologue while Mrs. Macauley sat in a straight chair to his left, away from the light.

"I've some sympathy for your views," Dartmouth said finally, without facing his visitor, "but you must remember, Mrs. Macauley, that we've now passed beyond simple arguments about principles and philosophies. The King's soldiers have been viciously attacked and murdered by the rebels. This is no longer a mere war of words, not simply citizens irritated by a policy with which they disagree. These are acts of war, and the King and his government are determined to respond in kind until the rebellion has been put down." She listened, unimpressed, to his remarks, hoping they represented a party line he felt obligated to espouse and not his own opinions.

"No doubt," he continued, "there needs to be some reconsideration of how the colonies should be governed, but that's not possible while our garrison in Boston is under siege as it is now. First the Americans must lay down their arms; then we can talk about the niceties of colonial government. If they will not lay down their arms voluntarily, then His Majesty's Army shall have to disarm them in its own way.

"We're already raising more troops for this purpose, Mrs. Macauley, and the negotiations with the German princes have gotten us fifteen thousand of their best troops. Soon it will not be just royal grenadiers and infantry facing them across the battlefield, but Hessians as well. Let's hope they come to their senses before there is a terrible slaughter."

The visitor continued her arguments for a few minutes more with little apparent effect on the minister. The porter then entered and indicated that the time for the appointment was at an end. Now Dartmouth rose and smiled at the woman, thanking her for coming and assuring her that he would give her words the most serious consideration. She returned the smile and nodded graciously, then turned and stepped out of the room ahead of the porter.

Though he looked relieved at the departure of his visitor, Dartmouth said nothing to Carlisle as he returned to his chair while the painter carefully contemplated his subject. Dartmouth's thin face bore a constant worried look. The top of his head was all smooth skin surrounded on the sides by thick bands of curls. It was always a challenge to paint bald men, to capture, without exaggerating it, the spot of light that reflected from their shiny pates. Carlisle enjoyed the challenge and had discussed it with Nathaniel that very morning on their way to Whitehall.

Some minutes later, the door opened again and the porter announced the arrival of the First Lord of the Admiralty. The Earl of Sandwich and the Earl of Dartmouth had known each other for many years, and Nathaniel had noticed that Sandwich visited almost every day. Often they had important matters to discuss, but frequently their discussions trespassed across the border of government business into the land of gossip.

"I see it was your turn to receive the harpy historian, William," Sandwich said with a snicker. "I trust she convinced you that our policies are utterly without merit and that you'll be going to Commons this afternoon to announce that we've capitulated to all the American demands."

Dartmouth continued to face Carlisle, but he laughed heartily. "I always try to be respectful to people who are writing the history of our ministry, John. It never hurts to be in their good graces, even if they are colossal ear aches. I wish she'd just go to America and leave us alone."

"So do I, William. But, as you know, nothing about America ever yields so simple a solution. I've received a communication from Gage in this morning's pouch. He's asking for many more troops, saying now that it'll take ten thousand more soldiers to quell the rebellion. My God, what is that man thinking? That America is our only concern? We've fewer than fifty thousand soldiers in all of His Majesty's army. We can't keep compensating for his timidity and indolence by sending more troops. Some days I think he believes that we'll end this conflict with a mere show of force. Fill Boston harbor with enough ships and cover Boston neck with enough red coats, and the Americans'll fold their cards and slither back to their farms. This is your department, William, but I pray you'll think about replacing him with Howe or some other commander who's ready to fight."

Sandwich stepped around behind Carlisle now so that he could look directly at Dartmouth. "I know Gage was chosen for this command because of his experience fighting in America. But we're learning that fighting against Americans is not at all like fighting beside them. And Gage seems incapable of adjusting. He has an American wife, for God's sake. Surely that should help explain his apparent disinclination to engage the rebels. They're almost like family to him"

Nathaniel noticed the look of discomfort that began to shadow Dartmouth's countenance as he listened to Sandwich. He'd heard these men in discussion before and knew the candor of their conversations. They were old political comrades who trusted each other completely and happily criticized and abused the subjects of these conversations, knowing that neither would ever violate the confidence of the other.

"I know, I know," Dartmouth confessed. "He is a frustration. We sent three generals to buck him up, even Johnny Burgoyne who could buck anybody up. But it doesn't seem to have had much effect. North and I have talked about this. Unless there's a quick jolt of energy through this command, we'll have to contemplate sacking poor old Tom Gage and replacing him with one of the others.

"We can't give him ten thousand regular troops, of course. Not now. But we've got to raise more men here, and I do think we're making some progress in Europe. The Russians turned us down, but we'll have Hessians from some of the smaller German states who are desperate for our money."

Well," Sandwich interrupted, "any thought that the Americans would simply crumble in front of our fire is gone now. Their Congress has voted to create an army and they've picked as their commander that Virginian, Washington, who fought with us—with Gage, believe it or not—in the Seven Years' War. They're not crumbling. They're fixing for a fight. And we must as well." Dartmouth nodded, silently and sadly, in response.

As the sun rose near its apex, the light faded in the room. Carlisle signaled to Nathaniel that their work was done for the day, and to Dartmouth he merely said "Thank you, sir," indicating the end of their session. Dartmouth rose and continued his conversation with Sandwich, paying no further attention to Carlisle and Nathaniel. The painters placed their materials in a box in the corner, moved the easel toward the wall and covered it, and slipped quietly out the door of the minister's office.

Leaving Whitehall in the bright mid-day sun, Carlisle and Nathaniel turned north past Scotland Yard toward Charing Cross. "Doesn't it amaze you," Nathaniel said, "how they seem so oblivious to us?"

Carlisle shrugged and then smiled. "I guess I've just gotten used to it," he said. "They praise me to the heavens when they seek to engage me to paint them. At parties, they often treat me as if I were one of them because I've acquired some modest renown as a painter and they all want to appear to be patrons of the arts. But when we come to do our work, it's as if we're a different species, one several notches below human."

Nathaniel started to reply, but Carlisle cut him off. "And if they ever knew you were an American, knew that your father is one of the rebels of whom they speak so contemptuously, that'd be a laugh, would it not? But they never will know that, because none of them'll ever deign to address you nor tolerate any conversation initiated by you. You might as well be deaf and mute.

"I keep asking myself why I do this, I hate it so. The work is so empty of challenge and excitement, painting the fat pale faces of pompous asses and the fat pale faces of their arrogant wives, being ever so quiet so's not to interrupt their corrupt schemes. Why do I submit to this? I know why, of course. Because, damn them, they're making me wealthy. With their money, I can do the work I really want to do. And with the fame that's come from painting them, there are more patrons for my real paintings. Art, Nathaniel, what a strange, strange business it is. We enslave ourselves so that we may be free."

Nathaniel had never heard Carlisle speak so critically of his subjects nor of his own work in painting their portraits. "These are the leaders of your country, Benton," he said. "Don't you admire them at all?"

"I suppose I did once. In Bath, where I was raised, the gentry often came to take the waters and socialize in winter. It became the business of the town, catering to the gentry and there were gay times. My older brother ingratiated himself with them as best he could and acquired several sponsors who sent him to university and encouraged him to read law. I felt good about that. He returned to Bath and was elected to Parliament. Bath is one of the rare places in this corrupt island where the people actually chose their own Member. Most places, as you know, the local baron has the place in his pocket and just buys the votes necessary to win. But folks are more independent-minded in Bath.

"When Amos—that's my brother—arrived in London, most of the party leaders wanted nothing to do with him. They were suspicious of anyone from what they called 'radical Bath'; and, despite his university degree, he had none of the social credentials that'd admit him to their clubs and parties. Amos became more critical of the government and the King. They tried to shut him up, but he felt he had a duty to his electors to speak his mind. One day a constable came to his door and placed him under arrest. Said the government was charging him with libel. They rushed him through a sham trial and had him in Fleet Prison before we even heard about it at home. Three years they kept him there; and when they finally turned him out, he was a broken man. He couldn't stand being here any more and took passage to the West Indies. But his ship went missing, and we never heard from him again.

"It's not easy, Nathaniel, sitting there every day trying to make handsome pictures of the bastards who ruined my brother. The only comfort is that I'm taking their money away from Gainsborough or Ramsay or one of the others who think that they can be accepted as gentlemen by painting gentlemen. It's a cruel rot that infects them all."

The sunlight was fading and Nathaniel gathered the pedestals around the easel and began to light the candles. He wanted to finish his work on the Dartmouth portrait today, even if it required another late night. Carlisle had been in the studio for a while in the morning to give final instructions and to help Nathaniel repaint a table leg at the edge of the portrait, a piece of the work that had not gone well the first time through. In the afternoon, the older man had taken a coach to Windsor Castle. He had a commission to paint one of the King's children and, since it was his first commission to paint a member of the royal family, he wanted to spend a day searching out a proper place for the sitting.

So Nathaniel worked alone, as he did more often now that his skills, and Carlisle's confidence in them, were growing. Nathaniel had always had intense powers of concentration, even as a child. But work absorbed him now as never before. He found that he could paint for hours without recognizing the passage of time. He'd look up from what he thought was a few minutes at the easel to find that whole mornings or afternoons had slid by. The unobserved flight of time occurred even more regularly at night when there were no changes in the light coming through the north windows to alert him to the hour. So he wasn't quite sure what time it was when the opening of the studio door startled him from the trance of his work.

"I thought you'd be hungry." Lydie smiled as she swished through the door toward him. "The cook roasted a duck tonight and with Benton gone, there was much I couldn't eat. But I know how hungry painters can get when they're lost in their work."

Lydie placed a copper tray on the table behind the easel, then walked around and stared at the portrait. "Another stuffy lord," she said. "They all start to look alike after a while. I don't know how Benton can make them all seem unique. To me, they're like slices off the same stale loaf." She frowned excessively, feigning disgust.

Lydie wore a light blue dress with scooped bodice and long full skirt. It accentuated the narrow waist and firm bust that formed her sharp silhouette, the good proportions that the artist in Nathaniel had always thought so nearly perfect. The natural dark tint of her skin seemed to set her face aglow, especially when she smiled, which she did often. Her lips were thin and wide, her nose small and slightly upturned, and her bright green eyes dazzled with bemusement and generosity. Her light brown hair was pulled back in a commodious twist of long curls, natural and ingenuous, like the woman herself.

Lydie and Nathaniel had enjoyed only a few brief conversations in the time he'd worked with her husband. She rarely came to the studio, never attended a sitting or joined them on a sketching trip to the countryside, and stayed away from most of the social events that Carlisle felt compelled for business reasons to attend. Nathaniel had thought he might see her from time to time at one of the parties; in fact, he rather longed to have someone to talk to during those long evenings when no one was the least interested in him. But Lydie found no pleasure at all in London society and had Benton tell the hosts that she did not come because she spoke so little English.

Nathaniel had a good laugh the first time he heard Benton telling that lie to a prim London hostess. Lydie, he knew, spoke excellent

English. He'd never heard her converse in French and only occasionally detected a random inflection indicating an accent. She had a gift for language, Carlisle once told him, and absorbed English as if born to it. Language barriers were a convenient excuse, but utterly mendacious--the sort of playful amorality in which Lydie seemed to delight.

Lydie pulled over one of the old chairs that were scattered around the studio. Like everything else in the room, it was splattered with drops of paint. She ran her hand over it before sitting to be sure that the paint was all dry. "Please sit and eat," she said, "and we shall have a proper talk."

Nathaniel placed his brush on the small stand beside the easel, then found a rag and wiped his hands. He poured some water into a large bowl by the closet where the clean canvasses were stored and used it to scrub his hands. He was shaking the last drops of water off as he pulled a chair up to face Lydie and set the copper tray on his lap. There he confronted, not only a beautiful woman, but the most delicious meal he'd tasted in weeks. He lifted a cut-glass goblet filled with sauterne and held it toward the light. He was admiring the shape of the goblet, but Lydie misunderstood the gesture and said, "It's French, from Loire. We only drink fine French wines in this house."

Nathaniel laughed. "I wouldn't have imagined otherwise," he said sticking his fork into a slice of the dark pink meat of the duck.

"Are you happy in London, Nathaniel?"

Nathaniel looked up as he chewed and nodded his head to indicate that he was. He swallowed quickly, took a sip of the wine, and said, "This is the best time in my life. Benton is extraordinarily patient with me and I've learned more from him than I could have imagined there was to know. In America, we have too little time for art and culture. There's always so much to do. Americans are busy building things right now, houses and churches and roads and canals, building a society, building an economy. It's demanding work and most of them are consumed by it. They don't stop to seek out the refinements of life. Perhaps they will some day, but not now."

"Here society is much older and people have progressed beyond mere practical things. There are grand houses and museums and orchestras. People know about art and some people have a passion for it. I do miss my family, Lydie, and I even miss the openness and quiet of the countryside. But here I can tell people that I'm a painter and I don't feel embarrassment at that."

"But what about the English people? Do you like them? Do you like their ways? Are they like Americans?" Lydie asked, leaning forward, trying to focus the conversation.

Nathaniel took another piece of the duck and twisted it slowly on his fork as he pondered her questions. "No," he said, "they're not like Americans. We look much the same, and we speak the same language-- with some variation in the way it comes out. But everything else is so different. You have to remember that, while all of us are subjects of His Majesty George III, neither of my parents and none of my brothers and sisters has ever set foot in England. Neither did my grandfather or his father. What it means to be English in America is very different from what it means to be English in England." Feeling good about his answer, Nathaniel smiled slightly and took another drink of the wine.

"How do you mean?" Lydie asked, looking a little nonplussed.

Nathaniel thought for a few seconds. Then he stood up and walked to the side table where he placed the tray, retrieving the half-empty goblet and carrying it back to the chair with him. He sat and leaned toward Lydie. "Think about this." he said. "Here on Bloomsbury Square are some lovely homes. Further west, in Mayfair and Fitzrovia, are homes even larger and more opulent. The people who live in those homes rarely do any real work. Most call themselves gentlemen and ladies and they fill their days attending each other's teas and parties. At three-thirty every afternoon, I hear the horses and carriages leaving the mews and rolling around to the front of the houses to pick up the finely dressed ladies who'll be taken to some other part of the city where they'll disembark to have tea and cakes. Then two hours later the carriages'll return to pick them up again and bring them home. Every day. Those are the English of London.

"Yet less than a mile away, south of Fleet Street by the river, live another group of people. They own no fine houses; in fact, they own no houses at all. No carriages come to transport them. They wear no beautiful clothes; most are fortunate if they've enough clothes to stay warm in the winter. They're crowded together in the smallest, filthiest, noisiest, most frightening quarters one could imagine. Many of the gentlemen I overhear at the parties I attend with Benton love to criticize Americans for the practice of slavery. I share their concerns about the morality of slavery. But most slaves in America live in better conditions than tens of thousands of poor wretches in the East End of London. I never hear the gentlemen raising a word of concern about them. In fact, they're always talking about amending the poor laws to rigidly confine the wretches to their own parishes so they never even have to see them. There are few places in America, Lydie, where the rich live as well as they do in London. But there are also few places where the poor live in such inescapable misery."

Lydie watched Nathaniel closely as he spoke, trying to picture the images he invoked. She felt much discomfort of her own with London and the rigid structure of its social life, but she had not framed her concerns in the stark way that Nathaniel had, and she'd never seen the sections of the city of which he spoke. She asked more questions and she was an eager audience for his answers. Well into the night they sat in the dimly lit studio, their faces just inches apart, as Lydie asked questions, probed for details, twisted her face in horror as Nathaniel described, with an artist's keen eye for color and detail, all that he had seen on his visits to the dark and fetid neighborhoods of the London the gentry never knew.

In the post one morning a few days after his evening with Lydie, Nathaniel received an envelope that contained only a piece of stiff leather. There were no markings on the envelope except for the address. The leather was about eight inches long and four inches wide and the center had been cut out in the shape of a keyhole.

For several days, Nathaniel was haunted by the strange arrival. He rarely received mail of any sort in London and he had no friends or acquaintances who would send him such a thing, even as a joke. He wondered if this was some instructional device that Carlisle was trying on him. Once before, the teacher had given him a pointed piece of metal and told Nathaniel to draw three animate objects that resembled its shape. But there'd been no mystery about that as there was about this strange delivery in the post.

Nathaniel even wondered if this was some secret message from Lydie. Though he felt guilty admitting it to himself, he still felt the warmth of the evening they'd spent in such intense conversation—and concentration upon each other—in the studio. Perhaps, he imagined, she is signaling that I unlocked some vision for her or gave her entreé to some place she had never been. Men's minds know few limits when imagining romantic possibilities, and Nathaniel found this explanation unexpectedly titillating.

But no explanation emerged and, while the leather piece continued to sit on a shelf in Nathaniel's room, his interest in it began to

wane as he fell into the daily routine of walking to the studio on
Bloomsbury Square to finish work on the Dartmouth portrait and then
spending most afternoons painting the late-summer flowers along the river
bank under Carlisle's watchful eye. They would later return to the studio
so that Nathaniel could clean up their materials. He would often stay on
into the night to work on a painting after Carlisle had gone into the house
to dine with Lydie.

Nathaniel walked home alone after just such an evening in mid-
September. The chill night had the benefit of a clear sky and a waxing
moon as Nathaniel walked along High Holbourn heading east. He stopped
for a few minutes at The Hounds and Fox public house on the corner of
Furnivals Inn Court where he often stopped on the way home for an ale
and some sausage. The place was quiet, save for a few casually dressed
men playing cards at a table in the corner, and an unusually small man in a
dark cloak standing alone at the end of the bar.

Nathaniel finished and paid his bill, pulled up the collar on his
coat and stepped back out into the chill. Unnoticed by Nathaniel, the man
in the cloak followed him out the door a half minute later and proceeded
in the same direction. As he passed Fetler Lane the streets became very
quiet, except for the footsteps Nathaniel could hear behind him keeping
pace with his own. The syncopated cadence began to trouble him and he
cast a glance over his shoulder, seeing only a single small man in the
shadows behind him. Nathaniel decided to step into a small alley and let
the man pass. He did so, clinging to the wall out of the moonlight.

Suddenly the sound of the man's footsteps stopped, and Nathaniel
stood still and anxious, waiting to hear if he would start again and move
off. He looked around and realized that the alley was small and closed,
that it offered no escape. The quieter he tried to be, the heavier became the
sound of his own breathing and the more frightening the thoughts that
filled his mind. Where had that man gone? Why was he following me so
closely? Was he going to rob me?

A minute or two passed, though it seemed much longer to
Nathaniel. Perhaps the man had gone. Maybe he lived nearby and had
entered his house. Maybe there was no man, and I just imagined it.
Nathaniel's mind searched feverishly for some logic.

Suddenly the man spun around the corner and stepped into the
alley just a few feet from Nathaniel. Instinctively Nathaniel crouched and
clenched his fists, waiting for the stranger to pounce. But the man stayed a
few feet away and said only, "Mr. Houghton?"

Stunned that the man had called him by name, Nathaniel didn't know whether to remain silent, to respond, or to run. The man spoke again. "Nathaniel Houghton? Is that you, sir?" He spoke not with the butchered inflections of the East End but in the rhapsody of a gentleman, almost as if he had come to offer Nathaniel tea or brandy.

Nathaniel relaxed slightly and responded, "Yes, what is it?"

"Are you Nathaniel Houghton, sir?"

"Why do you want to know? And who are you? And why have you followed me into this alley?"

"I wish to discuss an important matter with you, sir."

"Who are you?"

"That doesn't matter, Mr. Houghton. It's best you not know who I am or see my face. That is why it was necessary to approach you in the dark. I apologize for any fright that may have caused, but it was unavoidable."

"What, then, do you want?"

"I want your help, Mr. Houghton. Your help with the most important business of our time. I'm an American agent, one of a network of agents in London. Most of us are citizens of London, but we abhor our government's policy toward the American colonies and we're doing what we can to ensure its failure."

Caught off guard, Nathaniel tried to make sense of all this. "What do you mean? What does this have to do with me?"

The man paused to let Nathaniel's thoughts collect. Then he continued with his explanation. "We're trying to help the Americans, and for most of us that means passing information through our channels to America. Sometimes we learn things which can have great strategic importance to the American commanders and politicians. A few of us hold positions in the government and have access to information through those. But none of us has access to the most powerful ministers, so some information—very important information—eludes us.

"Here's where you come in. We have reason to believe that you may have access to that information, Mr. Houghton, and we want to enlist your help in our efforts."

"Me? What access to information do I have? I'm not in the government. I'm an American, a painter. Politics is not for me." In truth, Nathaniel had often thought how easy it would be to purloin state secrets that he heard almost every day. But the thoughts were always hypothetical, a fantasy of a more adventurous life than the one he had chosen for himself.

"But you spend much of your time in the offices of Whitehall painting portraits of government officials," the smaller man reminded him. "We know that those men do not cut off the flow of business when they're being painted. And we know that you must overhear conversations and have access to documents full of information that would be very helpful to your countrymen in the struggle in America."

Nathaniel no longer feared this man and leaned back now against the wall, much relieved that he was not being robbed—or worse. He realized that his shirt was almost completely damp with the evidence of the fear he had felt. He knew not what to make of this conversation. "Well, what are you asking me to do?" he said after a minute.

"We're asking you to listen and to look. When you hear something that may reveal the military plans or tactics of the government, when you spot a document that may contain such information, we'd like you to make notes and then pass those along to a contact we'll establish for you. We'll then speed the information to America. In this struggle, Mr. Houghton, speed is everything. It often takes two months for the admiralty or the colonial office to get instructions to their generals in America. If we can intercept those instructions and get them there sooner, the American commanders can make their own plans knowing their enemy's intentions.

"Frankly, nothing could contribute more to the success of the American cause. It's a risky business and, I don't want to mislead you, it's a very dangerous business. Killing spies is a treasured pastime in this country. But we believe the benefits justify the risks, Mr. Houghton, and we believe you will, too, when you think about it. I'd like you to take a couple days to think this over. Then I'll contact you again, and you can give me your answer. I hope you'll help us. I hope you'll help your own people."

"Wait a minute," Nathaniel blurted. "How do I know you're not just setting me up, luring me into a trap that'll get me sent out of the country or killed?"

"I can't prove otherwise, Mr. Houghton. But perhaps this letter will help." The man reached beneath his cloak into a cloth pouch hanging just above his waist. He retrieved an envelope. Nathaniel could read none of the writing on it, but he could feel the wax seal on the back.

"What is this? Who is this from?" Nathaniel persisted.

"Hide it now, please. Take it with you. Read it. Perhaps it will help you decide. And when you read it, Mr. Houghton, I suggest you'll find it most enlightening if you examine it through the keyhole." The man pulled his cloak to cover his small chest, pivoted quickly, and was gone. In the shadows, as he left, Nathaniel recognized the slight figure of the man he'd seen earlier at The Hounds and Fox.

Back in his room, Nathaniel lit a candle and placed a globe over it to magnify the light. He sat down and examined the envelope in his hand. There was no writing on it at all, only a scarlet seal on the back bearing the overlapped letters W and G. Nathaniel studied it for a moment longer, then broke the seal and opened the envelope.

Inside were two pages of handwriting that he immediately recognized as that of his brother, Jonathan. He hadn't received any correspondence from Jonathan in all the time he'd been in London and so was pleased, excited even, to hear from him now. But then he contemplated the peculiarity of the delivery of a letter from Jonathan by a man asking Nathaniel to join a ring of spies. What a strange night this is, he thought.

He held the letter near the light and began to read. It was a peculiar, stilted letter, sounding little like his exuberant and informal brother. The Jonathan he knew would never waste his time writing things like, "The weather here is full of lightning bringing danger to the crops." Nor would he ever say "George Washington is a general now and Father has a new aide who is going to Cambridge after the seige of business in Philadelphia." What? It made little sense to Nathaniel. Had his brother lost his mind?

Nathaniel read though the entire letter of homilies and faulty syntax and strange phasing. He put it down and rose to change his still damp shirt. Then he spied the piece of leather on the shelf by the bed and recalled the words of the man who'd approached him in the alley: "…you'll find it most enlightening if you examine it through the keyhole."

Nathaniel grabbed the piece of leather and carried it to the table. He picked up the first page of the letter and flattened the crease with his hand. Then he laid the piece of leather over the letter, aligning it along the top. The leather was exactly the same length as the stationery, and when placed over it like this, it formed a keyhole shape around some of the words. Nathaniel moved the lantern closer and saw that the words that appeared in the keyhole formed sentences of their own, and he began to read them. He hurried through all four sides of the stationery, realizing that each contained a continuation of the sentences that appeared in the keyhole section of the previous page.

He went back to the first page and covered it with the leather keyhole. Then he began to read, discerning a voice that sounded much more like Jonathan Houghton:

> *Much has changed here. A war is raging and I've joined it. General Washington has taken command of the army combining all of our forces. I am his aide and we are in Cambridge. We made a lightning strike near Boston and did well. Now we have surrounded the city and have it under siege. But we will need all the help we can get, Information is very important to us, and I hoped you could assist us, based on what you've told Mother in your letters. A man will approach you and ask for your help. He will be your contact. Please do this. Our future is uncertain, but it is ours to make. If you need further confirmation of the genuine nature of this correspondence, notice that it is Washington's seal on the envelope.*
>
> > *Your loving brother,*
> > *J*

Nathaniel set the letter down and picked up the envelope again, closing it to reconnect the split pieces of the seal. W and G? No, G and W, he thought: George Washington. He leaned back and closed his eyes, reviewing the events of this most extraordinary evening. His brother was a soldier. Boston was under siege. He was being asked to be a spy.

What an odd turn this is, he thought. I, who abhor politics, spend most of my days sitting in the office chamber of politicians. I, who escaped America, am called to her service from across the sea. I, who revel in the life of culture and art, am invited into the life of war and intrigue.

He had much to sort out. His growing distaste for the inequalities and injustices of London had heightened his sympathies for the spirit and purposes of the American rebels. He knew that the government here would never grant the colonies the freedoms they sought. Even the lowliest minister talked like a puppeteer, trying to manipulate the marionnettes in America. And he knew now that this was more than just

168

an argument, more than just a philosophical debate. His brother had taken up arms. His father had signed his name to documents and petitions that made him a traitor in the eyes of the Crown, and his life was in jeopardy. And Nathaniel knew from discussions he'd overheard that soldiers and ships would soon be on their way to the middle colonies, placing the farm at Still River Bend and his family in harm's way.

Nathaniel thought of the arguments for accepting this invitation to espionage, and there were many. He thought about the arguments against accepting it, and could conjure up none—except concern for his own safety. He stared at the glimmering light for a few moments, then he rose and walked to the table where he kept a small decanter of port. He poured himself a glass, then found his sketch pad and pen. He returned to his chair, dipped the pen in the small jar of ink, and began to make notes from the store of official conversations once overheard and now clearly lodged in his memory.

# Chapter 11

## Philadelphia
## Still River, Delaware
## Fall-Winter 1775

John Hancock called on the round-faced man with the spectacles and bald pate, and every eye in the room turned his way. Delegates rose to their feet when they spoke--all but one. Some paced the floor, hurling their words at an often inattentive audience. Others stood by their chairs and looked upward, as if seeking divine inspiration. A few, like Dickinson, walked to the front of the room to be better seen and heard.

But not the old man. He rarely rose from his chair. And when he spoke, others leaned closer to hear him or get a better view of his shining, expressive face. Ben Franklin was not one of them. To the younger delegates, Franklin was a treasure surviving from another time, the *eminence grise*, the sage, the grandfather. Franklin was nearly seventy on this November morning when the King of England told the Second Continental Congress to go to hell.

They listened because of all the men there, only Franklin knew George III. He had spent twenty years in London, knew its streets and parks, played chess with the wife of Black Dick Howe, the famous admiral, dined at the homes of the leaders of Parliament, exchanged scientific observations with James Watt and Joseph Priestly, and matched wits with Samuel Johnson. In this Congress of farmers and merchants and lawyers, Franklin stood alone, the one genuine cosmopolitan American.

Franklin's sympathies were well known by this point. Despite the pleasant years he'd spent in London and his affection for some of its people, in his final year he'd come to believe that there were no options left for the colonies, no options save a clean break from the King and his Parliament. The delegates had all heard Franklin's recounting of the brutal abuse he received when he went before a special hearing in Parliament to seek the removal of Thomas Hutchinson as Royal Governor of

170

Massachusetts. He didn't need to retell that tale now, though Franklin was never above retelling a good story.

This afternoon he spoke simply, like a lawyer summing up his case. He recounted the progression of affairs, the careful efforts the Congress had made to form a consensus, to state its case, respectfully to petition the King. Even after hostilities had broken out in the spring, hostilities that most of the men in the room thought the result of provocation by the ministerial army, the Congress had sought a peaceful solution. The Olive Branch Petition in which they'd placed so many of their hopes proposed an end to the fighting and a rejoining of their bonds, albeit on different terms than before.

1775 was nearing an end, and during the months that Congress had waited for the King's response, everything had begun to fall apart. Most of the colonies were operating their own governments. Congress created a post office and began to debate other ways to form the elements of a continental government. In every colony, neighbors were fighting neighbors as militia men rooted out and confronted loyalists. The skies were darkening and Americans were taking sides, the remaining islands of neutrality sinking into an angry sea of animosity. Many Americans wanted only to avoid the storm they saw looming ahead, but they could find no safe harbor.

Now, Franklin told them, the King's outright rejection of the Olive Branch Petition was the final blow they should endure from that quarter. What further hope could there be? The King had no intention of changing the ways the colonies were treated. The colonies had no intention of continuing under the old ways. It was a classic impasse, and they must force their own escape. Henry sat in his accustomed place along the west wall and listened earnestly as Franklin powerfully renewed his plea for an independent league of colonies.

Walking back to the Widow Almy later, Henry caught up with Franklin near Elfreth's Alley off 2$^{nd}$ Street. "Congratulations, Doctor," he said "That was an eloquent and moving statement you gave us this morning?"

Franklin eyed him sharply, with the small twinkle that always betrayed his sense of mischief. "So then, you're now prepared to vote for independence are you, Henry?"

"Independence is not before us, as you know, my friend. We have buttons yet to sew before we throw out the pants." In his conversations with Franklin, Henry always found himself trying to talk the way the older man talked, but never quite succeeding.

Franklin winced at his colleague's homely metaphor and laughed. "But you know it will come to that, Henry. You know we're just finishing off the preliminary moves before we must put the King in checkmate."

Henry was ready to concede the argument and the test of wits. He clapped the older man on the back and they turned and walked along together in the descending dusk.

"I expect you're right, Doctor," Henry said. "But, my God, I hate the thought of it. What have we done here? One of my sons is in London facing who knows what danger. My other son is in the army with Washington. We sit here each day and argue and draft language and vent our opinions. But it's our sons who may yet pay the highest price for our idealism. I must tell you, Doctor, heavy feelings of guilt and fear hang over me."

"And I," said Franklin. "My own son, William, no longer speaks to me. The King has made him Governor of New Jersey, and he thinks we are mad. He thinks me the maddest of all, seeking to cut off the very hand from which he feeds. I tell myself that my only brief is for liberty, and I try to act on that. But my son despises me for it. And every time I make a speech, as I did this morning, or write my thoughts in a letter or address, a piece of my heart aches for the price I must pay in the lost affections of my own child."

Henry felt a special kinship with the Pennsylvanian because they shared the special torment of parents forced to make public decisions that affect the private lives of their families. When Henry came to Philadelphia for the first Congress, it had been to engage in a conversation with other colonists about some mutual problems. Henry had not imagined that a year and a half later, he would be voting on the creation of armies and navies and the requisitioning of troops. When he and Jonathan walked the length of Delaware to get here, it seemed an adventure. Now the sense of adventure was long gone. And so was Jonathan.

When Henry learned of the return of the fact-finding committee in July, he'd run out of the State House to greet them. He had not imagined how happy he would be to have his son back safely. But his son was not back safely. His son was not back at all. He listened in stunned surprise as the committee members described how Jonathan had been caught up in what they now called the Battle of Bunker Hill, how he'd acquitted himself so bravely, and how he had decided to stay on at Washington's invitation. In the letter they gave him, Henry read all this in Jonathan's words, especially his final sentence: "So now, Father, you must do your part to give this war a purpose, and I must do my part to win it."

War. He'd called it a war. That was a term rarely heard in Philadelphia where most of the delegates still chose to view the activities in Massachusetts as a localized conflict, one that many still hoped to resolve through an exchange of communications with London. But a war—and his son a soldier in that war—these were notions that tore at Henry's heart, that freighted his conscience, whenever he contemplated them. Had he sent his son to war? My God, he thought, how could I have done that?

As tensions escalated with London, Henry worried too about Nathaniel. It had been a year and a half since his older boy left. They'd had only a few letters from him, and now private communication was almost impossible with the mutual embargoes in effect. For all Henry knew, the King might have rounded up Americans in London and clapped them in prison or shipped them off to Australia. Or perhaps Nathaniel had fallen in with the English lords and ladies, perhaps he felt more at home there than here and had become one of the very people against whom his brother had taken up arms.

And though he tried to think about it as little as possible, the fate of the farm weighed heavily on Henry, too. He'd been kept in Philadelphia much longer than anticipated. He knew the toll his absence was taking on Patience as she and Savannah tried to manage without any of the Houghton men. Nathaniel would never be the master of the place, and only a miracle would get Jonathan back to Delaware before spring. What had happened to all those dreams Henry'd once had for his sons, for the good life he'd be passing on to them, for the proud tradition they'd be joining?

Now all that seemed ruined by a train of events that was lurching out of control and crushing all those dreams in its path. And yet here he sat, among these good men, forging the very actions that were scattering his family and shattering their future. Like Ben Franklin, he was coming to realize what a cruel calling duty could be.

Daylight departed early now as the month of December descended on the Congress. The candlelight was feeble in the State House, so their sessions often ended in mid-afternoon, allowing the delegates to return to their lodgings before darkness fell. Now the nights at City Tavern had become as much a part of the routine of the Continental Congress as the days at the State House. In the daytime, the delegates all sat in one room and followed rules of order imposed by the stern hand of John Hancock. In the evenings, especially later in the evenings, they sat in separate rooms, usually with those of like mind, and their conversations, like the ale, flowed more freely.

Henry's friend, Joseph Galloway, had not returned to the second Congress, to the delight of the radicals. This left Henry, and a handful of others, to try to slow the tide that was moving inexorably toward a break with England. The louder voices each night came from the room upstairs where Richard Henry Lee and Franklin usually held court. Some nights their disquisitions on the splendors of liberty and the evils of their King— their jaunty songs of happy freemen and vicious tyrants--shook the walls and echoed through the tavern.

Downstairs, where Henry could usually be found with men like John Dickinson, John Jay, and Edward Rutledge, the tone was quieter and more solemn. It wasn't that the men in this room were defenders of the King or opponents of liberty. Their doubt, their hesitance, was more practical. Was it worth a war to call ourselves Americans rather than Englishmen? What would a war do to our people and our land and our fortunes?

The men upstairs saw independence as an end, a logical conclusion to a century and a half of colonial evolution. The men downstairs saw it as a beginning, a beginning to uncertainty and intercolonial strife and great vulnerability. How could these colonies, so varied in size and interests, so prickly in protecting their own perquisites, meld into a single coherent unit? Wouldn't the larger colonies quickly come to dominate the smaller? Wouldn't the great empires come to prey on them without their British protectors? Some of the delegates were passionate in their desire to abolish the practice of slavery; others were equally ardent in their will to preserve it. If the English king were thrown off, would there be an American king crowned in his stead? Upstairs they had answers; downstairs they had questions. Upstairs was hope; downstairs was fear.

More and more, as the days passed and the passion of events came to challenge the reason of debate, Henry found himself slowly cutting loose from his doubts. It was not that the doubts were shrinking; if anything, they were swelling. But his convictions were fortifying against them, as he found it harder to defend the alternatives to independence. He

174

admired John Dickinson, always had. A good man, a wise man, a powerful advocate. When Henry first read Dickinson's pamphlet, *Letters From A Farmer In Pennsylvania*, eight years ago, it was as if he was hearing the sound of his own voice, so closely had Dickinson's views matched his own.

But Dickinson had a fatal weakness: his mind was hard to open. Having once taken a position he would stick to it tenaciously even as rivers of opposition rose around him. And, for all his admiration of Dickinson, Henry found himself drawing away from the turf they and Galloway had earlier defended together. This Congress punished its members that way: forcing them too often to take sides against men they deeply admired. Henry felt himself coming to that now.

"If we vote for this motion tomorrow," John Dickinson said to Henry and the four other men sharing their table, "we will have effectively declared our independence. How can we disavow our allegiance to Parliament and have it mean anything else? Will anyone really believe that we can remain loyal to the King when we've sworn off the edicts of his Parliament. Come, come, gentlemen. This slicing of syntax will be lost on those outside this assembly. They'll see this motion for what it is: a final and utter parting of the ways."

"You read this too closely, John," said Rutledge. "We're raising the ante, that's all. They rejected our petition. Now we must say that we can no longer tolerate their rule under current conditions. It doesn't say that we can never tolerate their rule, only that the conditions must change if they want us to accept their actions."

"And what do we hope to get from this?" Dickinson responded, slowly looking into the eyes of the each of the others.

There was no response for a moment, the Jay replied. "Only a fool would predict, but let us hope that they'll see more clearly the need to engage us in a dialogue, a dialogue in which we can find a way to hold the empire together."

"Perhaps you're right, John," Henry added, looking at Dickinson. "Perhaps they'll see it as a statement of independence. Would that be terrible? How could things be worse? Their ships close our ports. Their army kills our sons. What more can they do to afflict us?"

Dickinson turned sharply, his intense eyes flashing as he looked down the crease of his sharp nose at Henry. "Houghton," he said, "I wouldn't have expected such nonsense from you. You know the pain that independence'll cause. You've always spoken with keen insight about the uncertainties we'll face should we try to stand alone without a government, without allies, without a real army or navy, with so many in the colonies against us. Surely you've not forgotten all that."

"I've forgotten none of it, John," Henry replied. "But we must all keep our eyes open to the changes that are swirling about us. I was against independence when I came here last year because I thought there were many less risky alternatives we could try. But, John, we've tried those, and what have they gotten us? More British ships, more British soldiers, and more brutal rejection from King and Parliament. Our options are narrowing, John. Perhaps now there are only two left: independence or capitulation."

"Will you then vote tomorrow to disavow allegiance to Parliament, Henry? Is that what you're saying?" Dickinson asked, as he leaned forward, placed his mug on the table, and stared directly at Henry Houghton. The other men all followed suit. Henry turned his head slowly, taking them all into his gaze and forming his words carefully, and then he said simply, "I believe it is the proper thing to do, and I shall do it."

It was in the candlelight after supper, when Patience was doing needlework, that Henry's attention was drawn to the protruding bones in her wrists and her cheeks. How different she looked from the picture he carried in his mind during the long months in Philadelphia. The happy, plump Wheelock girl he'd married was gone now, transformed into this unfamiliar matron: gaunt, fretting, burdened by a sad and incurable fatigue.

Tomorrow would be Christmas, but a visitor would have been surprised by that. The family was rent by events: Nathaniel in London, Jonathan in winter camp in Cambridge, Celia in New York. No songs filled the parlor. The tree that Quiet Jack had set in the corner bore no candles nor ribbons, and the gifts that Henry had brought from Philadelphia for his wife and daughter made only a small pile beneath it. Savannah had suggested they all walk to the little church in Still River where they always gathered with their neighbors on Christmas Eve to pray and sing. But Patience said she didn't feel up to it, that she had nothing to sing about, and Henry had chosen to stay with her. Savannah had gone instead with her old friend Primmy Hartnett.

Henry watched his wife for a while in silence, then rose and moved behind her. He placed a hand on her shoulder and began gently to caress it. Patience stopped the steady movement of her hands and leaned back into Henry's touch. She loved this man, but she also hated him.

Henry Houghton was everything a young Delaware girl could want when they married 32 years earlier. He was intelligent and conscientious. He came from a respected family, a family that had made a fine farm and could ride comfortably over the ancient cycles of weather and crops and fickle economies. And, though never the handsomest of men, he cut a fine figure. Little of that had changed, and she still loved the things about him that she had always loved.

But he was not hers anymore, and she hated him for that. It was not a mistress to which she had lost Henry Houghton, not some alluring other woman. It was his insatiable craving to do right, to perform his duty, to meet his obligations that now pulled him away from her. First it was the few weeks when he went alone to Annapolis, then the two months last year with Jonathan in Philadelphia, then the much longer time he spent there this year. It kept getting worse and worse.

She tried to fill his long absences by attending to her own duty to manage the farm, to make the decisions that he used to make. But he did it so easily and for her it was such dreadful toil. Fortunately Savannah had stepped in to take control of the farm. Now Patience could spend her days doing her needlepoint or just sitting by the window, thinking back on the days when her family was all here and nothing interfered with their good life together.

Some nights now she woke up in a piercing fright from dreams about Nathaniel being taken off in chains by soldiers in armor or of Jonathan left alone on an open field confronting long lines of red-coated men rushing at him with bayonets. She hated the war that was stirring all around them, the war that was gobbling up her children, the war that her husband had failed to stop. When Henry walked off to Philadelphia that first time, she was happy he was going. He is such a sensible man, she thought then, surely the others will listen to him and find a way to resolve our disagreements with the King.

But now Henry was telling her, not only that war was unavoidable, but that it was probably essential. This man she loved, this man she trusted—oh, how she hated what he was becoming. How could he let these things happen to their family? How could he let her world come apart?

Patience brushed Henry's hand away and continued with the steady push and pull of the needle in her hand. She didn't look up at him or acknowledge his gesture. Sometimes it was just easier for her to get through the day if she denied to herself that he even existed.

Some of Henry's earliest memories were of the New Year's Day feasts at Balfour's Tavern at the end of the mill pond in Still River. Michael Balfour was a Scotsman who'd emigrated to Delaware in the 1720s. He'd worked in the sawmill, often taking his pay in timber ends. When he accumulated enough of those, he'd built a small tavern and quit the mill to run it. Michael died the year that Nathaniel was born, but his son James had taken it over and in the intervening years he'd expanded the tavern several times, just fast enough to provide space every year to accommodate the New Year's Day feasts of the slowly expanding population of Still River.

Usually people gathered in late morning with their baskets of ham and venison and guinea hen, their large loaves of bread and dense sweet jams to spread on them, the carrots and yams and potatoes that survived in their root cellars. Certain women were renowned for their pies and cakes, and by some universally recognized but silent dictum, they, and they alone, brought samples of their oven artistry.

If the cold had burrowed in, as it did some winters, people skated on the pond. When daylight faded, fiddles and flutes came out and the dancing began. Later food covered every surface in the place, and James Balfour, a marvel of perpetual movement at the bar, supplied the neighbors with drink.

Patience had never missed one of the New Year's feasts, but that morning she said she felt too tuckered to attend. Henry and Savannah tried to persuade her that she would be missed by all her friends, that she'd be energized by their company, even that she had a duty to go. But Patience was unmoved and unmovable. It was not that she was defiant, just withdrawn and unresponsive and listless. Henry worried about her, but felt compelled to go, indeed he wanted to go, and Savannah did as well. They gave instructions to Sweetie to keep a close watch on Patience and to make sure that she took her meals and stayed warm on this cold morning.

At Balfour Tavern, Henry was surprised and pleased to see Marinus Marshall. The Marshalls had never come to these celebrations before. They lived too far away and were not part of the Still River community. But Marinus had invited Savannah to dine with his family that day and she'd declined, citing her desire to attend this annual event with her family. So he'd asked if he could come to the feast and she could think of no reason why not. He was there, in deep conversation with some of the men—voters, Henry was certain—when they arrived.

Marinus left his conversation and quickly approached their wagon when he saw it draw up beside the tavern. He greeted Henry warmly and they shook hands. Then he reached up to help Savannah down from the wagon seat. She needed no help, but recognized the futility of a protest and accepted his arm. Marinus lent Henry a hand in carrying the two large baskets they'd brought, one containing a roasted rump of beef, the other three of Sweetie's squash and cinnamon pies. After they'd found a place inside for the baskets, Henry was handed a mug of cider by Thom Mason, and Marinus returned to the yard where Savannah was waiting by the wagon. The mid-day sun had eased the chill and they began to walk the path that encircled the pond. A few children skated close to the shore where the ice was thick enough to hold them but, save for the scraping of their blades on the frozen surface, quiet encompassed the two figures ambling slowly along the shore.

They hadn't seen each other for several weeks, so Marinus reported on some of his successes in court, and Savannah filled him in on Henry's return and the decision of the Congress before adjourning to disavow allegiance to Parliament. "I heard about it," Marinus said with thinly veiled disgust. "The clubs in Dover are full of talk about what it will mean for us. Everyone is certain that war will surely come now, that the King and Lord North will see this as the provocative act of infidels and send their army into the field."

"My brother is in our army now, " Savannah said, "so I hope you're wrong."

"Our army? Jonathan is not in our army, dear Savannah. We are Englishmen. Our army wears red coats and is here to protect us from men who would take the law into their own hands. I have great affection for Jonathan, as you know, but I rue his decision to join up with the rebels. If a real war does start, then our army, our real army, is sure to prevail. I pray that Jonathan is spared, that all of the colonials are spared, but I'm deeply worried for him, for all of them. There's no reason, no cause, important enough to justify the sacrifice of a single one of them."

"Perhaps you'd feel differently, Marinus, if you lived in Boston. Father says the Boston men tell terrible tales of their treatment by the British, that on the road back from Concord and Lexington, they burned houses at random and shot at women and children. He hates the prospect of war, but he seems to be losing faith that it can be avoided, or even that it should be."

"But, darling, we're not in Boston. Let them make a separate peace, if they must, or fight a separate war. But here in Delaware we can live happily as Englishmen. We don't need this war. It's not our fight."

They'd reached the end of the pond and begun to walk along the far shore. Savannah stepped quietly now and Marinus said, "Perhaps we should talk about other things. I was hoping that on New Year's Day, you might see fit to agree to marry me. It was such fond anticipation that brought me here."

Savannah continued along, saying nothing, holding formally onto his arm. "You are patient with me, Marinus, and I'm grateful for that. You must continue to be. I can't leave home now. The boys are both gone. Father is kept away by the interminable sessions of the Congress. And Mother suffers her dark spells more and more frequently. She barely eats and some days she sits and rocks by the fire, gazing out the window, saying nothing. I worry constantly about her, but nothing seems to help. She seems to have no disease, just a deep, incurable sadness."

Marinus listened in silence, paying little attention to her words. He was growing impatient with Savannah's reluctance to respond to his marriage proposal, but he knew that any effort to speed her decision would be counter-productive. She remained the best match for him, he was certain, and irritated though he was by her procrastination, he would wait a little longer.

"So I'm running the farm now," Savannah continued. "No one really says that, not Mother, not Father. No one wants to say aloud what we all know: that Mother cannot perform her duty. When there are decisions to make, I tell her about them, seek her advice. But she merely says, 'Whatever you think,' and continues staring out the window. I can't leave her now, Marinus. I can't leave the farm. I have responsibilities there."

"But Savannah, you must live your own life, too," Marinus replied, deciding to nudge her just a little. "Surely you mustn't sacrifice everything, mustn't surrender the life we could have together. No one could expect that of you. You may feel you have important obligations on the farm, but you also have a life of your own. Shouldn't that be your paramount concern?"

Savannah looked away as they walked, deep in her own thoughts. "I don't know, Marinus. I simply don't know. Do any of us

really have a life of our own any more?   My brothers are in harm's way.
My Father is taken up in the most important work. My mother is sinking
into a state of desperation. How can I say that none of that matters. Could
I have a happy life of my own, even if I did walk away from all that?
Perhaps that seems possible to you, Marinus. It doesn't seem possible to
me."

Henry took a long drink of cider as the round of singing ended.
He looked across the room at all the people gathered there, realizing that
he could name every one of them. The ritual had not changed much in
nearly fifty years, and the memories of all those New Year's feasts at
Balfour Tavern were a sturdy, unbroken chain through Henry Houghton's
life, linking the years together, connecting them to this land and the
people with whom he shared it. The old died, the young were born.
Children grew up and married their neighbors, as he had, and had children
of their own. Tragedies happened. Fire and disease and extremes of
weather were constants in all their lives. But they pulled together in such
times, rebuilding a ravaged barn, bucking up the shattered parents of a
child lost to typhoid, banding together to harvest the crops of a neighbor
injured by a runaway wagon. These were the frames of a man's life, the
turns of fortune, the blessings of family and friends, the bounty and
heartbreak of the land. The cycle of simple lives in a simple time,
punctuated reliably and happily by the New Year's Feast.
No year ever looked bad when glimpsed from the vantage point of
its first day. Hope always triumphed in these moments of celebration
when Henry and his neighbors looked ahead. Surely the weather would be
benign, the pests would go elsewhere, prudence would protect us from
fire, disease would pass our children by. We'd have food on the table and
money enough to meet our needs. Danger would not darken our doors.
Not in our faithful anticipation, not on New Year's Day. So the toasts
sang. So the happy neighbors prayed.
But few of them truly believed the words they spoke to each other
on January 1, 1776, and Henry least of all. Had any year ever loomed so
ominously ahead, Henry wondered. Two great armies were drilling
anxiously and drawing a bead on one another. Commerce had stalled to a
standstill. Neighbors looked suspiciously upon one another, as men kept
their muskets ready and hoarded powder and ball.
It was hard to feel the old feelings at this New Year's feast, even
if they all managed to say the old words and sing the old songs.  It may

have looked like the New Year's feasts of Henry's memory; it may have sounded like them. But Henry Houghton knew that nothing was really the same, nor would it ever be again.

## Chapter 12

## *Boston*
## *Winter 1776*

Had there ever been a column in military history more bedraggled than this one, Jonathan wondered, as Henry Knox led his rag-tag parade of oxen teams and mismatched soldiers down the frozen dirt road past Cambridge Common. Local folk came out of their houses and watched in confusion and wonderment, not quite sure what they were seeing. The teams and their heavy loads circled up on the common and came to a full stop. Despite the freezing weather, men flopped on the ground in utter exhaustion, experiencing the peculiar mix of exhaustion and exhilaration that comes at the end of a devastating but successful effort.

Jonathan was still very new at this soldiering business in the fall when Washington asked him to accompany Knox on this fateful campaign. Washington liked Henry Knox; but, as with most of the officers he'd inherited upon assuming this campaign, he'd had no opportunity to measure the man's talents or loyalty. Knox owned a bookstore, and he'd read a great deal about warfare. He was especially interested in artillery and as a colonel under Artemas Ward he'd been very helpful in organizing the siege of Boston. He seemed intelligent and enthusiastic, but he was only twenty-five and, as soldiers liked to say, he hadn't yet been blooded under fire. So Washington was full of doubts about his capacity to do the important job for which Knox had volunteered. Sending Jonathan along gave Washington confidence that Knox would have a constant reminder of the General's—and the army's—interests.

As they plotted it on the large map in Washington's headquarters, their task had seemed straightforward enough. In May, Benedict Arnold and Ethan Allen had captured Fort Ticonderoga and Crown Point on the southern end of Lake Champlain. Part of the booty they captured were many large pieces of artillery, bigger and better guns than any that Washington could deploy in the emplacements around Boston. The guns he had there now could barely reach the city; none could disrupt the movement of ships in the harbor. And since Ticonderoga sat in the wilderness of New York, hundreds of miles from any known British force, those great guns were of no effective military use. Henry Knox's mission was to go to Ticonderoga and bring those guns to Boston.

As Jonathan dismounted and stood with the other exhausted men of Knox's troop, he wondered if anyone could ever imagine what they'd been through, if they could tell the story vividly enough to capture even a tenth of the ardor and agony they'd endured. There were too many guns at Ticonderoga for the force that Knox commanded. So he'd carefully selected fifty-nine of the best weapons. Then they'd scoured the countryside to find teams of oxen. Snow covered the ground, so they decided to mount the guns on heavy sleds rather than carts. It took many days to get the equipment mounted for travel. Some of the mortars weighed more than a ton, and Knox also thought it necessary to transport thousands of pounds of lead to make shot when they returned to Boston.

They'd lined up their forty-two sleds just as a devastating snowstorm struck. But waiting only meant they'd have to dig out their transports, so they set off across more than three hundred miles of hilly, wooded, and icy New England countryside. Day after day, the exhausted men in Knox's command pushed the sleds up hills and over frozen streams, through thickets of heavy brush and around ravines. Each hill they surmounted seemed only to lead to a higher hill. There was little to eat and no place to get warm. Men fell under sliding carts or tangled legs in the heavy ropes they used to slow the carts' descent down steep inclines. The sleds only got heavier as they became transport not just for guns but for the growing corps of weary and injured troops.

Then came the cruel thaw of early January when the rains turned their path into an oozing compound of slush and mud. The whole column would have to stop for hours at a time as the liquid earth swallowed up a single sled or disabled a team. Progress slowed to a few hard miles a day as Knox's men labored against the iron grasp of nature and the iron laws of physics.

As Colonel Knox and Captain Houghton trotted off to report their return to Washington, Jonathan looked back on the large circle of artillery and the haggard bodies flopped on the ground beside it. The worn-out men on Cambridge Common had not seen a single redcoat on this long journey through the wilderness, but they felt like they had fought the fiercest battle in the history of warfare. Victory was theirs at last on this cold January morning, a more important victory than any of them could then know. But none of them had an ounce of energy to celebrate it.

His thin wool cape wrapped tightly around him, Aubrey Armistead leaned into the damp wind slanting across the continent from the northwest. The damn wind never stopped blowing, or so it had seemed to him through this long, cruel winter. At the corner of Marlborough Street, Armistead turned left onto School Street and entered the square brick house that General Howe had used as headquarters since taking command after Gage's departure. These morning staff meetings were part of the routine of garrison life, but they held little meaning these days. As long as the fierce weather held, the army was stuck in Boston. There were not enough men or supplies to launch a major assault on the Continental headquarters in Cambridge and too few ships to pull out.

Howe gathered his senior commanders in the library upstairs away from any spies who might be walking past the windows at ground level. Boston was a nest of spies. Though most of the civilians who remained in the city were indeed loyal to the King, some of the professed loyalists were not loyal at all. And even in loyalist families there were sons or brothers or cousins who hated the soldiers and were happy to steal what information they could and pass it to their contacts on the other side of the neck. Armistead had learned in his months here that an army of occupation rarely enjoys the affection of the people whose city it controls.

After the standard report on the condition of the forces, Howe described plans for the evacuation of Boston. He reminded his officers that he'd wanted to evacuate in the fall, but that weather had prevented that and stuck their army in Boston for this long and dreadful winter. The bark that arrived the day before, the first ship from London in nearly a month, carried information from Lord Germain, Dartmouth's replacement as minister for the American colonies, that more ships and stores would be arriving as soon as there was safe passage. So, Howe said, plans for the evacuation should move forward. It was important, he reminded them, to get out of the city before the Continental Army got stronger.

Howe had learned from his own spies that many of the militia troops had gone home when the cold weather set in and that Washington's forces around the city were weaker than they'd been in late summer. But the spies also reported that most of the Continental officers assumed that fresh troops would arrive in the spring. Howe knew that Washington was using this time to organize the militia companies into a real army with a centralized chain of command, reliable supply procedures, separate artillery units, and all the other details of war that allow an army to fight effectively. Howe had studied Washington, picking constantly at the recollections of men who had served with him under General Braddock in the Seven Years' War. Few of them had great admiration for Washington's battlefield leadership, but most said that the Virginian inspired loyalty in his men and could organize disparate troops into a unified fighting force.

The other officers watched Howe closely for clues to the kind of leader he would be. He was not yet fifty, but looked older. The years in the sun, the heavy weight of command, and the rigors of the Boston winter painted deep lines across his forehead and around his sad mouth. As his face had grown thinner from the short rations, his slightly cock-eyed look had become more salient. He was, Armistead had to admit, an almost comical figure as he paced the end of the room, his hands chopping sharply at the air.

Howe paced constantly at these staff meetings. He'd spent his career leading light infantry troops and, like them, seemed always on the move. A major command like this was new to him, and some of his officers worried that he would treat the entire army as if it were a light infantry unit, overlooking other important elements in the order of battle. But there were no hints to any of that this morning. Howe had little new to say, and while all feigned intense interest, few listened closely. It was hard to hear, in any case, above the rumbling of so many empty stomachs.

When the staff meeting ended, Armistead started back to the house where he was quartered on Essex Street. At the bleak corner where Hog Alley diverted from Newbury Street, he heard the sounds of men shouting and laughing. Sounds of joy were so rare in Boston that he quickened his step to get to the group of soldiers standing in a circle near the doorway of a squat stone shop. When he approached, one of them noticed his colonel's insignia and called for the others to make way. Armistead nodded his gratitude and looked through the opening in the circle to a dead milk cow lying on its side in the street and two men with knives removing its brown and white hide.

"What's happening here?" Armistead said to one of the men who was tearing away at the animal. "Took a foragin' party last night, sir. Got us a couple cows, we did. One of 'em we already et. Another's gone to a company on the Common. This one we're gonna eat right 'ere. Would the officers be likin' any, sir?"

Armistead smiled and politely declined. "Carry on, men," he said as backed out of the circle and walked away.

The siege of Boston was the worst that Aubrey Armistead had ever seen. After the bloody skirmish in Charlestown—his lingering limp seemed to shoot pain every time he thought about that awful day—it had seemed that the rebellion might end quickly. Despite the terrible loss of men in the assault on those hills, the King's forces had prevailed and taken control of the redoubt at the top of Breed's Hill. Some of the other officers assumed that the militia would disperse after that and that Gage would lead them through a clean-up sweep around the towns surrounding Boston.

But Gage never seized the advantage that Charlestown seemed to give them. There'd been a few patrols into the countryside and some foraging parties for food and stores. But not once since that bloody June day had His Majesty's forces launched a major attack on any of the Continental troops surrounding them. As the summer of 1775 wore on, the officers mumbled more and more about "Granny" Gage.

So on that night in September when Gage was recalled to London, many toasts were drunk, but more in relief than admiration. He spoke to the officers that afternoon, wishing them well in his absence and saying he looked forward to a speedy return. He hadn't returned, however, and it was clear now that he never would. Word filtered back in the few arriving ships that Lord North and George Germain had had their fill of Gage's lethargy and wanted this rebellion crushed as quickly as possible.

As he walked through the bleak and quiet streets of Boston, Armistead wondered what the politicians in London thought about their army in America. If they could see what I see, he told himself, perhaps they wouldn't allow their eager imaginations to play quite so easily at war. After he recovered from his wounds, Armistead had been promoted to lieutenant colonel. The loss of officers on Breed's Hill had required a number of promotions to fill the vacant ranks above him. As a colonel, he now commanded a regiment, the Third Battalion of Light Infantry. All his adult life, he'd pointed to this: becoming a colonel and commanding a battalion. It was as high in the army as a man like him could hope to rise, with no titles of nobility in his family or no seat in Parliament.

But his days now did not fit his youthful image of himself as a colonel in His Majesty's Army. Instead of riding a sturdy stallion at the head of a column of finely-trained soldiers, he walked the streets of Boston every morning, surveying the condition of his starving and frozen men. Winter came early in November of 1775, and it had held the city in a tight icy vise ever since. Only a handful of Navy ships with supplies from England had arrived during the winter; the weather had kept most others away. Or perhaps, London had never sent them. Back Bay had frozen over early and now his troops had to be on the alert to the possibility of an infantry attack across the ice. Food had run out as the new year began and only a few foraging parties provided any sustenance for the hungry soldiers. They and the small sloops that arrived on moonless nights from New York with salt beef and other victuals from a mysterious supplier in New York whom Wilberforce referred to only as "Mr. Brown."

A few thousand loyalists remained in Boston, in garrison with the Army. But their lot was as bad as the soldiers'. Armistead admired their commitment to their King and their courage in facing up to the horrible conditions solely for a principle in which they believed. It was odd, he sometimes thought, to be fighting an enemy that doesn't feel like an enemy at all. The rebels were making great sacrifices because of something they believed in deeply. The loyalists were making sacrifices just as great because of something, however different, in which they believed. He admired both groups for that.

And why was he fighting? To defend a principle? Perhaps. But what principle? That men should obey their King? That colonies should remain subservient to a distant government in which they had no say?

No. It wasn't that. He was there because he was a soldier, and soldiers followed orders. It was part of the structure of life, the way civilized societies worked. Soldiers were the enforcers of law and the instruments of authority. Take away soldiers and you'd have chaos, anarchy even. Soldiers didn't always love the monarchs in whose name they fought. They didn't always agree with the laws they were enforcing. They didn't always hate their enemy. But none of that mattered. Soldiers are the sentries of order and civilization. They do their jobs unquestioningly, whatever the hardships, to ensure that legitimate authority prevails. These American rebels may be admirable in some ways—in the principles they hold and their willingness to die for them— but they represent no legitimate authority, and civilized societies cannot stand by while any self-appointed group takes arms against a rightful government.

Armistead had thought all this through many times, for he was a man who always needed to explain things to himself. But none of it gave him much comfort this morning as he leaned into the chill wind. The

188

wooden houses of Boston were nearly all gone now, victims of freezing soldiers and loyalist families needing fuel for their fires. Dogs had begun to vanish as well. The supply of candles had run out weeks ago and when the sun set in late afternoon, Boston melded into the dark sea around it. It was the beginning of March, and the winter showed no signs yet of abating. As he walked along Boston's desolate streets, Aubrey Armistead prayed that Spring would beat the Grim Reaper to town.

Henry Knox was now a celebrity at Washington's headquarters. Civilians and politicians are always impressed by unique acts of bravery under fire or brilliant tactics on the field of battle. But real soldiers know that wars are won and lost by the men who get the goods to the fight. And Henry Knox had gotten the goods to the fight.

In the weeks that followed his return from Ticonderoga, the new commander of the Continental Artillery began to get his big guns ready for use on the besieged city of Boston. The councils of war at Washington's headquarters grew more intense as the longer days brought the promise of better weather. Boston in winter, Washington said one morning, was the perfect place to conduct a siege. Stuck out on Boston neck, surrounded by water, connected only by a narrow causeway, overlooked by hills on all sides, impossible to re-supply in the fierce cold, Boston was a military nightmare. Washington wondered how soldiers as experienced as Gage and Howe could have allowed themselves to get penned up there. But he also knew that when the weather broke, the British ships would fill the harbor with sails, bringing food and guns and fresh troops. If his new army was to end this war quickly, it would have to strike soon, before British reinforcements arrived.

It was one of the peculiarities of Jonathan's position that he could attend these councils, even though he commanded no unit and was far younger than most of the senior officers present. They'd accepted him as Washington's aide, and they took his constant presence for granted. Some of the officers had even come to regard him as Washington's third ear. If they wanted to convey a message to the General, some of them believed, communicating with Captain Jonathan Houghton was the most effective way to do it.

Jonathan never spoke at these councils, unless asked by Washington for a piece of information. So he merely sat in one of the oak chairs against the wall and watched and studied and learned. What he saw was an odd lot, these perpetrators of rebellion. Henry Knox, whom he now knew well after their days together in Hell: jowly, bookish, precise, a face like a pillow but a backbone of iron. Israel Putnam--"Old Put" his Connecticut men called him--crusty and wrinkled with a round face and neck so thick that he could rarely connect the top buttons on his shirt. He'd gotten rich in his life from land speculation and at his age, nearly sixty, he hardly needed to be here. But men close to him knew that he was a man made for war, that his heart only found its true rhythm when there was an enemy to out-fox or out-fight.

Artemas Ward, descendant of Pilgrims and scion of Boston, was second in command now. Washington treated him with deference, but Ward said little in these councils. Aging and rheumy, terminally disappointed at his loss of command, he seemed to sense that a new generation was running things now. The others listened to his opinions, praised them and thanked him politely for them, then moved on to do things their way. That ritual had become his only contribution to the preparations that were now under way.

Slowly as well, Jonathan began to form opinions of the others. Nathanael Greene, the sharp-witted Rhode Islander; John Sullivan, audacious commander of New Hampshire militia who'd driven the British from Fort William and Mary in Portsmouth; Horatio Gates, veteran of the British army and now Washington's adjutant. The one man upon whom Jonathan had not yet gotten a fix was Major General Charles Lee, also a veteran of the British army and third in command after Washington and Ward. Lee kept his own counsel, but Jonathan often noted a flicker of disgust at the corner of his mouth or the roll of an eye when Washington suggested plans of action. Lee rarely spoke in disagreement, but Jonathan noticed that he kept his enthusiasm for Washington's leadership well under control.

A few days earlier Washington had proposed an assault on Boston over the ice across Back Bay. To him, this seemed to be the most vulnerable facet of the diamond-shaped neck and, while the bay offered his troops no cover, neither did it present any obstacles to the kind of swift assault Washington favored. He calculated that his Continentals and militia outnumbered the British troops about three to one and a frontal assault would quickly overwhelm the defenders of the garrison.

But some of the others worried that Washington's estimates of troop strength were overly optimistic. As their enlistments ended, men had been leaving camp all winter. The Continental army in February was much smaller than it had been in October. And while spies poured information into Washington's headquarters, no one had an accurate estimate of the effective strength of British forces. The troops were scattered all over the city and never massed in a single formation where anyone could count them. Estimates from the spies varied by thousands.

Several of the officers suggested an alternative plan, to fortify Dorchester Heights and put Knox's big guns up there overlooking the city. The Ticonderoga guns had greater range than anything else in the American arsenal and would give the Continentals control of the harbor which they'd never had. This would force the British to attack across Boston neck where they could easily be flanked by Continental troops. Once a fight began on the neck, a force held in reserve could move across Back Bay and attack the British from their rear.

Washington agreed that the Dorchester Heights plan made better use of Continental assets, and during the last few days of February, the council of war worked feverishly to implement it. All agreed that the key to success was a speedy fortification of the Heights and emplacement of Knox's guns so that the British did not counter-attack before the position was defensible and the guns could be trained on the garrison.

On the night of March fourth, Washington decided to stay at his headquarters so as not to alert the spies who watched his every move. He sent Jonathan to accompany General John Thomas, twenty-five hundred men from the Massachusetts regiments, a long train of supply wagons filled with prefabricated fortifications, and a parade of caissons bearing the guns that had already traveled hundreds of hard miles to get to the hilltop in Dorchester.

The moon was full that night, but the wind was still and a haze on the ground gave the Continental troops almost perfect cover for the work that lay before them. A steady bombardment of the city from the Lechmere Point artillery, on the other side of Boston, masked the noise on Dorchester Heights. It's never easy to fortify frozen ground and the Continental engineers had worked around the clock for weeks to plan the construction of two small forts above ground. As Jonathan walked through the Massachusetts men building those forts, he thought back to harvest days on the farm. How hard the work seemed to him then. But that was a holiday compared to the sawing and hammering, the grunting and sweating he saw that night on Dorchester Heights. One after another, fortifications and reinforced gun positions sprung up around him in the moonlight.

Washington once told Jonathan that war was mostly about survival, about keeping troops together and warm and fed and shod and safe from boredom and disease. It was drudgery and discomfort and hardship. But then, he said, men endured all this because war had its magic moments when soldiers performed acts of super-human courage, overcame insuperable odds, accomplished impossible tasks. Such moments were few, Washington had said, but they were very precious. Jonathan wished the General had ridden with the troops that night to see the magic moment unfolding on the hillside overlooking the tired city of Boston.

On even-numbered days, Aubrey Armistead commanded the watch along Boston's eastern shore, from South Battery down to the neck. Gage had left night watch duties to junior officers, but Howe believed that the Continentals might launch a surprise attack across the frozen surface of Back Bay and he wanted the state of alert that he knew only senior officers could impose. So each night, one colonel commanded the neck watch, another the west shore, and a third the eastern shore. Normally, it was a night of sleep with an occasional interruption for a status report from the watch posts.

But last night was different. The Continental batteries in Cambridge were firing all night. Their balls rarely hit anything in the city and they couldn't reach as far as the eastern shore, but the noise made sleep nearly impossible and raised in the minds of all the watch officers the fear that the cannons were softening up the city for an attack. Armistead had not slept at all when his relief came at seven o'clock on the clear morning of March fifth.

It felt warmer this morning, Armistead thought, as he walked toward the neck to meet Colonel Clark for breakfast. The outer harbor had never frozen and it looked glassy in the still air. Little wisps of haze evaporated before his eyes revealing the outline of the headland to the southeast. Armistead saw Clark approaching along the road and greeted him with a nod of recognition. The men were old friends and since they always had watch command on the same nights, they had been meeting for breakfast like this for weeks now.

As they walked toward the officers' mess, they always talked about what they planned to eat. Clark: "Perhaps I'll start with the fruit, the melon especially. I just love the melon in winter. Then I'll have biscuits and blackcurrant jam. Then lean ham and beans. Then tea and a cake with

192

the tea." Armistead: "That's no breakfast, Colonel. A real Englishman would have venison sausage and new potatoes, roasted tomato and squash, Dorset stilton on fresh bread. And the tea, of course, Darjeeling tea. You were right about that part."

It was all a game, of course. For weeks, their breakfast had been stale hardtack and tiny portions of salt beef. The tea had long since run out and wood was too scarce to waste it in cooking. They all would have starved weeks ago, except for the coastal sloop that snuck in at night from time to time with supplies that Wilberforce had procured from New York. The politicians in England might be having fine breakfasts, but they weren't sending any of them to Boston, where even the officers ate well only in their imaginations.

Suddenly a loud cascading roar caught up with the two officers, and a few seconds later a nearby crash sent bricks flying over their heads and filled the air with splinters and dust. Uncertain what was happening, they dropped to the ground and looked around apprehensively. "Sounds like a magazine blowing up," Clark said.

"But there's no magazine near the shore here," Armistead replied.

"Then what the hell could it be?" shouted Clark as an even louder noise clamored around them.

"It's got to be the bloody colonials," shouted Armistead.

"Can't be." said Clark. "They haven't got any guns that can reach this shore. You know that."

"Damned if I know then, but we better find some cover." They started to run along Belchers Lane toward South Battery when another blast exploded in front of them sending missiles of stone and wood in every direction. Now they ran at full speed, seeking the shelter of the South Battery fortifications and some relief from their confusion about what was happening.

They shouted the password and ran past the sentry into the main bunker from which a very frazzled colonel was trying to respond to an assault he couldn't identify. He surveyed the harbor with a telescope, thinking the firing must be coming from ships. But his hands shook so badly he couldn't focus on anything. When he saw Armistead and Clark coming toward him, he handed the spyglass to Clark who quickly adjusted it to his eye. His gaze swept from north to south along the waterfront, but he saw nothing unusual. In the windless harbor, the ships at anchor all had different headings. Certainly there was no sign of any warship broadside to the town with gunports open.

He swung the telescope further south toward the Dorchester shore. And then he saw what had to be a mirage. He adjusted the focus on the glass and looked again. "Bloody hell," he shouted. "What is that?"

He peered intensely into the lens and the other men looked out in the same direction with naked eyes. When they began to realize what they were seeing, disbelief changed to utter amazement. Along the breast of Dorchester Heights, where yesterday there had been only grass and a few patches of snow, where signs of life rarely appeared save for an occasional Continental patrol, today there were six dark forts reaching from one end of the Heights to the other. And from behind those forts came bright flashes of artillery fire launching deadly masses of lead hell-bent for Boston town.

The watch officer dispatched a runner to General Howe's headquarters to report what they'd seen, and Armistead and Clark soon followed. Knowing Howe, he'd call them together right away so they might as well head there now. Clark, the master of gallows humor, turned to Armistead as they scrambled through the streets and said, "Damn, another fine English breakfast spoiled by the call of duty."

Howe was already pacing when they got there. A few of his officers were present, but they waited impatiently for the others. One could almost see Howe's mind racing as he paced. Soon the others arrived, and Howe called them to order. They listened to a situation report from the watch commander, and Howe then turned to his chief engineer and asked him to explain what might have happened on Dorchester Heights.

"Something utterly impossible," came the reply. "It's simply not possible to construct so elaborate a fortification and then to put so many guns in place in one night. They must have had twenty thousand men working on that hill last night. There can't be any other explanation."

Howe turned to the others and looked slowly around the table at some of the most experienced officers in the British army. "Now what?" he asked.

Pigot spoke first. "From what we've seen, they have bigger guns up there than any they've had before. And they're in a position from those heights to command the harbor. It appears those guns can reach most of the ships across to Governor's Island. I ordered the South Battery to return fire on them this morning, but our guns could not elevate adequately to hit any of their fortifications. They now appear able to control the harbor and to do so without any discomfort from our own guns."

Howe looked around at the other downcast faces. He rubbed his thumb and forefinger above his dark eyebrows as if trying to force a good idea into his head. Then he pivoted and faced his officers. "Fine, then," he said, "we shall attack."

You had to concede this, Armistead thought, Howe never wasted time on second thoughts. At Breed's Hill, it was Howe who kept sending waves of infantry up into the Continental breastworks. A lot of men had been slaughtered that day, but Howe had pressed the attack. And now he was going to confront danger again by taking the offensive. Armistead understood that mentality, but he also knew its risks. Commanders like Howe won wars because you had to fight to win. But they also walked into ambushes and put troops at needless risk and spent their assets at a furious pace. Maybe with a fresh army on a more promising field, Howe could pull this off. But the thin and desperate ranks in Boston, on open land surrounded by an entrenched enemy, were hardly a recipe for salvation here.

But Howe was in command, not Armistead, and the General began to unfold a map on the table in front of him. The others stood and walked to Howe's side to get a better view. By their best count, the British could muster seventy-five hundred effectives in Boston. Howe proposed that General Daniel Jones lead three thousand across the neck and in direct assault on Dorchester. Howe himself would lead another four thousand across the ice of Back Bay and then in a loop through Roxbury and down toward Dorchester to catch the Continentals from behind. That would leave only a few hundred men to defend the city. Howe knew the risk in that, but he was nothing if not a risk-taker.

As Armistead calculated in his own mind how many days it would take to mount these assaults, Howe looked up and said, "Get to work, gentlemen. We attack in the morning."

So it had come to this. After nearly nine months, eyeballing each other across the water, the two armies would now engage. If Howe's forces prevailed, their victory would be a devastating blow to American morale. Washington's reputation would not recover from this failure to take advantage of his army's superior position and greater numbers. The militia would wander off. In London, the doubters would be quashed and those who supported the King's desire to stomp the rebels would be newly energized.

If the Continentals succeeded, especially if they could force Howe's surrender, the war might end here. Leaders in London would realize the futility of trying to beat the Americans on their own soil and would accede to their political demands. The fledgling army would have done its job, Washington would be a great hero, and much bloodshed and heartbreak would be spared. Those were the stakes in the battle that Howe intended to instigate on the sixth of March.

There were no secrets in Boston. What Washington's forces couldn't see from their observation posts on the hills around the bay, their spies learned from inside the garrison. The main body of British troops camped on the Common, an open field in plain sight from the Cambridge side of Back Bay. The furious activity there throughout March fifth made it clear to Washington that the engagement he sought was imminent. He ordered his own troops into place and tried to anticipate Howe's plan of battle.

In late afternoon, he rode down to Dorchester, to view the new fortifications there and to buck up the men for what lay ahead. Some of them were veterans of the slaughter on Breed's Hill, and he knew they would need all the inspiration he could muster for this next fight.

Washington rode along the line, stopping at one fighting position after another, shouting encouragement to the men from his saddle. The men seemed in fine spirits despite the lack of sleep during the construction the night before. "We're ready for 'em now, General," they called back, and "They'll be deadcoats soon, sir." Washington felt heartened as he rode back to Cambridge at dusk. They're good troops, he thought, and they're as ready as we can make them. He went to bed shortly after dinner, anticipating an early rise in the morning. But sleep was elusive as his head filled with anxiety on the eve of his first great battle in command of the Continental Army, and the rising wind slapped branches against the side of the house outside his bedroom window.

When Howe stepped out into the street to mount his horse and ride to the staging point for his troops, the fierce wind and freezing rain pounded his head and quickly soaked through his wool uniform. Shingles tore off the rooftops of houses and blew at vicious angles across streets and into alleys. Visibility was but a few yards in the furious compound of snow and rain and sleet. Soon a blast took Howe's hat to join the shingles flying past him. After riding a few blocks, Howe turned back and returned

196

to headquarters. He shook his cape and told his orderly to get him an engineer.

Soon several officers appeared and Howe quickly engaged them in a discussion of the weather. Weather tormented soldiers, as it did farmers. Most men who lived in a place for a while could read the signs. High heat and dense humidity often preceded a violent thunderstorm. Puffy purple clouds from the west brought days of clear sunshine. A day of stillness and overcast was often followed by a day of fury. But Boston weather was hard to predict, and the British officers possessed neither the years of necessary experience nor any scientific system for knowing with certainty what the next day would bring. No one had suggested to Howe that March sixth might be a bad day for a battle.

But it was, and his engineers pleaded with him to call off the assault. Bad weather favors defensive forces because it slows an attack and makes communication almost impossible. The attackers have to move their supplies while fortified defenders do not. And sending thousands of troops across a frozen bay in driving rain and a howling gale was not likely to be effective preparation for an engagement on the other side.

Howe listened for a while and then relented. He ordered the troops to stand down and called off the attack for that day. The officers left and he was alone for a few minutes. He understood the feeling of relief that washed over him. He hadn't really believed that an attack made sense. His troops were outnumbered, the enemy held the high ground, and the long winter had taken its toll on morale and readiness. He wished they'd abandoned this God-forsaken city when he'd wanted to last fall.

He'd called for the assault as a matter of honor to show the damn Continentals that they couldn't fire at will on British troops. And he knew he had the ghost of Old Tom Gage to live down. If he didn't pursue the battle, if he merely twiddled his thumbs in garrison, then soon he'd be called back to London and Henry Clinton or Johnny Burgoyne—Johnny Burgoyne, for God's sake—would be commanding His Majesty's forces in America.

So maybe the weather saved him from the biggest mistake he'd have ever made. If he'd launched this battle and lost, if he'd had to surrender his army here, it would be one of the blackest days in the history of the British army. His career would be over, his country would lose control of its most important colonies, and his family of generals and admirals would be tainted forever by the infamy he caused. So, as his officers gathered in the next room, William Howe took a deep breath and said a prayer to Aeolis, the wind god who'd blown in that day to save him from his own impetuous sense of honor.

"Some pretty sight, ain't it Cap'n," Flint said as he pushed his cap back on his head and surveyed the sight before them.

In July, Washington had encouraged Jonathan to choose an aide. Jonathan knew right away who he wanted and had gone to see Flint in the hospital where he recovered from the wounds he'd received at Breed's Hill. Jonathan offered the job and a commission as a lieutenant to the man whose life he'd saved. Flint was reluctant at first. He liked the novice soldier from Delaware but said, "I don't want to be no one's boot black."

Jonathan assured him that they would have important work to do and that their time in the field would greatly exceed their time in headquarters. Though unconvinced, Flint felt compelled by their growing friendship to accept this offer from the man who'd saved his life.

After their mission with Henry Know to retrieve the guns from Ticonderoga, Jonathan heard no more complaints from Flint about headquarters duty. Flint had suffered as much as anyone from the long, terrible trek--from hunger and frostbite and sheer exhaustion. But he'd been a great source of strength as well: unfailing in his duty, constantly encouraging the troops, finding humor in every desperate situation. Once when a heavy gun sled broke loose from its restraining rope, Flint had hopped aboard and ridden it at break-neck speed down an icy hillside until it came to a gentle stop in a field below. When the rest of the party caught up to him, he was sitting atop the gun, legs casually crossed, smoking a clay pipe. He turned to the troops, as if startled by their arrival, and said, "Fancy meeting you here."

Because they had suffered together the miserable burden of getting those guns to Boston, Jonathan and Flint were feeling especially proud on this March morning. The two men sat on their horses behind a long line of shouting troops on Dorchester Heights. Below them the harbor was full of ships under full sail, carrying away thousands of British troops and hundreds of loyalists. They sat low in the water because Howe had filled them with everything they could carry.

Some of Washington's officers were dumbfounded that no smoke rose from the city. Military doctrine required Howe to burn the city as he left, destroying the supplies he couldn't carry away. But Boston wasn't burning, and they wondered why.

Jonathan and Flint knew why.

198

When spies told him that the British had decided to evacuate and were scurrying to leave before they were attacked, Washington sent word to Howe that their emissaries should meet. Howe was reluctant, thinking Washington would ask for his surrender and then launch a furious assault if Howe declined. But Washington sent assurance that he was not seeking a surrender.

So on March tenth, Lieutenant Colonel Aubrey Armistead of His Majesty's Army rode past the blockhouse on Boston neck to the large white barn on Jeremiah Phillips's farm in Roxbury. A Continental sentry signaled him forward and opened the door to the barn. There waiting for him were Captain Jonathan Houghton of the Continental Army and his aide, Lieutenant Ezekial Isaac Flint.

Jonathan saluted the higher-ranking British officer and Armistead returned the salute. Jonathan had never had so important an assignment and he was plainly nervous. He said to Armistead that Washington knew of the British evacuation plans and had sent him with a message that he would read. He turned to Flint who handed him a single sheet of paper which Jonathan unfolded and started to read. It said simply: "We propose this. If you do not burn Boston as you leave, we will not impede your departure."

Armistead waited for more, then realized there was none. He reached out to secure the piece of paper from Jonathan, but the American withdrew it and quickly handed it back to Flint. "I'm sorry, sir," he said. "My orders were to deliver the statement orally, not in writing. You have my word that it comes directly from General Washington. But no one is to know about this, except us and our principals."

Armistead began to understand. He nodded, offered his own salute, and remounted. The door opened again and Armistead rode quickly back to Boston.

Now it was March seventeenth and Jonathan and Flint watched from the heights as the last ship slipped down over the horizon. They rode back to Cambridge that afternoon to tell Washington that Howe had kept to their bargain.

Washington had never been in Boston before, and many of the officers wanted to join him in a ceremonial entry. But Washington decided that the Massachusetts officers should be the first to enter the city and it was around them that the beleaguered citizens marched in joy and relief.

The next morning, Washington's small party rode quietly across Boston neck into town. Two boys were playing along Orange Street as they passed and they looked up at Washington in his splendid blue uniform. "Good morning, boys," Washington called down to them, "How are you this morning."

"Wonderful, sir, just wonderful," they replied. "Have you heard the news?"

"What news is that?" Washington responded with a smile.

"The lobsters, sir. The lobsters have all left the harbor."

# Chapter 13

## London
## March-April 1776

    Nathaniel's task had rarely been easier. The long broad windows of the state apartments on the north side of Windsor castle cast the sort of light that painters adore: diffuse and even and soft. Neither the subject nor the easel needed to move in the entire morning. So Nathaniel sat on a chair behind Carlisle and watched him paint.

    Not an ordinary chair either, for nothing in Windsor Castle was ordinary. With a heavily cushioned seat covered in red velvet and gilded arms and broad carved legs, it was surely the finest chair in which Nathaniel had ever sat, perhaps the finest in which he would sit.

    Windsor Castle had loomed above the Thames for almost seven hundred years, its broad round tower overlooking the little village of Windsor out over the realm and all the possessions of all the kings and queens of England. Nathaniel thought of all those monarchs—Henrys and Elizabeth and the Georges—walking its endless passageways and staircases, climbing its turrets, praying in its chapels, playing in its courtyards, and dancing in its great halls. Surely they must have thought they owned the world, or at least held powerful entitlement to it.

    This was the largest portrait Carlisle had ever done, the first for the royal family, and probably his most important. If the King liked it, there could be more royal commissions ahead, with attendant consequences for Carlisle's wealth and fame. Nathaniel could tell that Carlisle was concentrating especially hard on his work. For five days, Nathaniel, Carlisle, and Prince Frederick Hanover had sat in this room in almost total silence while the Prince posed, Carlisle painted and repainted, and Nathaniel watched.

    Carlisle said this morning as they walked in the garden that this would be the last day of sittings, and Nathaniel hoped he was right. Though both enjoyed living at the Castle during this time, the days dragged on for Nathaniel and there were matters that needed his attention in London, where they would return this afternoon. The enormous portrait would come in one of the King's large wagons a few days later, once the paint had sufficiently set. After finishing it in Carlisle's studio, another wagon would take it back to Windsor where the King would view it. There were a dozen or more royal portraits painted every year, and this was the standard procedure.

So it was a great surprise to the painter, his assistant, and Prince Frederick when at noon on the last Saturday of March, a herald appeared at the door and announced the arrival of His Majesty, King George III. Though Benton Carlisle had been a subject of this king and his grandfather and great-grandfather, he had never laid eyes on any of them. And as the King burst brusquely into the room, Carlisle and his assistant stood mute.

Nathaniel had seen many renderings of the king--some wicked caricatures in America, others romanticized, larger-than-life images in London. None of them resembled this man who now stood before the unfinished portrait of his son. The real George III was slender and quick on his feet. His forehead sloped down to his nose in a straight line; his eyes were set wide apart beneath brows that raced in a line across the top of his face. He was not a handsome man, Nathaniel thought, but his manner exuded energy, as he rushed about from one momentous purpose to another.

"What a handsome prince you are," the King said proudly, looking tenderly at his son, still immobile as if posing. He walked to the boy, placed a hand softly on his shoulder and kissed his cheek. Then he stepped back in front of the portrait, peered closely at the details of the face, and looked back again at his son to compare the image with the real thing. He continued this way for several minutes, looking back and forth between the boy and the picture of the boy. Then he pivoted sharply and strode toward the door, which the herald closed behind him with a loud thump that echoed around the vast room.

The King had said nothing to the painter and his assistant, had not even acknowledged their presence. Nor had he given even slight indication of approval or disapproval of their work. It was a moment of such stunning abruptness that neither man mentioned it during the final hour of the sitting or in the following hours as they packed up paints and brushes and gathered their bags for the coach ride back to London. Even on the return trip they said nothing about the King, deterred by the presence of royal footmen hanging on the back of the coach a few feet away.

But as soon as they arrived back in Bloomsbury Square, they skipped up the steps into Carlisle's house and asked Bartholomew, the house man, to find Lydie and bring her and some fine brandy to the drawing room. There for several hours, they replayed their meeting—no, they couldn't really call it a meeting—their opportunity to observe the King of England. They recounted every aspect of his dress and manner and interaction with his son, arguing, to Lydie's delight, over the slightest details. Painters are acute observers of detail, and these two painters described every last one.

Nathaniel was especially struck by the King's failure to make even the slightest effort to greet the two painters. He said that it fit the widespread American perception of him as a man who held his subjects in utter contempt. Carlisle was more generous, noting the tenderness of his brief interaction with his son. "Perhaps," he said, "his visit had nothing to do with seeing or judging our work. It was just a way to make contact with the Prince. And observing our portrait was just an excuse for a few minutes with his son."

Nathaniel was caught up by Carlisle's use of the word "our" in describing the portrait. It was the first time he'd ever suggested that work on which Nathaniel assisted was anything but his own.

"That's a kindly view," Nathaniel said, "but I still think basic human decency requires an acknowledgement of people in the same room. He acted as if we were furnishings not persons."

"Well," Carlisle said with a laugh, "you can't expect too much from this king. He's a very odd sort. You know his story. He became king when he was barely twenty-two and hardly ready for the burdens of his reign. He's always seemed a little off, or so people around him say.

"You Americans think he has a particular dislike for you. An incapacity to deal competently with any of his subjects may be closer to the truth. He rants about the smallest things, loses faith in his ministers for matters of minor consequence, forces people in and out of government almost constantly. He thought Lord Dartmouth was too weak and conciliatory toward the Americans so he got North to sack him. Now you have George Germain running your affairs and he's a much harder sort. More to the King's taste. At least for this week. But who knows what he'll want next week, surely something different."

"Well, he must have some charms," Lydie said with a sly smile. "He does have eleven children."

"Ah, darling, even lunatics have passions," said Carlisle, cringing slightly at the word he'd chosen to describe his sovereign. "Apparently it's only his mind that's afflicted."

At that, they all laughed. For several hours they continued this conversation about the King of England, recalling in ever more vivid exactitude their brief meeting with him, sharing ribald imaginations of what his life must be like.

At ten-thirty, Carlisle's exhaustion overcame him and he said goodnight to his wife and his assistant before ascending the stairs to his bedroom. He was a man of remarkable vitality, but Nathaniel had begun to notice in the past year that he tired more easily and had stopped apologizing for the brief naps he took in the studio in the afternoon or the way his eyes closed after a meal or his earlier departures for bed. He was nearing seventy, but most of the time he bore the years easily, a characteristic of men who've spent their lives doing what they love. Only the easier onset of fatigue and the hitch in his step belied the change that was slowly overtaking him.

"You know," Lydie said, "he thinks of you now like a son. A few days ago he came in from the studio carrying the small painting you did of the row of forsythia in St. James Park with all its bold yellows. He wanted to show me how good it was, and he was alight with pride. He said he hoped that you'd start doing some portraits of your own soon, so that you can take over some of the commissions when he can't paint any more. Then he laughed at that and said, and I remember this so clearly, 'No, Nathaniel will be too good. He won't need to paint portraits at all. He'll live well from the sales of the pictures he wants to paint. He'll be a free man, not a slave to the rich.'" She laughed in delight at her clear recollection.

Nathaniel was touched by what Lydie reported. He'd sensed this growing affection in Carlisle's relations with him. To Nathaniel it seemed more like the feelings of a proud teacher toward a prize student than a father toward a son. But now, as Lydie described it, the image took form in his mind. Some of his own feelings toward Carlisle were similar. Nathaniel had a father and he loved his father, respected him. He knew that Henry Houghton loved him, and that Henry was the best father he knew how to be.

But a father's capacities and a son's needs are rarely a perfect fit. And what Nathaniel desperately needed from Henry--pride in the person Nathaniel really was, not the image of a son he might some day fit; delight in Nathaniel's passions; genuine and enthusiastic encouragement of Nathaniel's chosen life course—these things were beyond Henry's capacities. Nathaniel's bond with his father would always be deep and strong, but it would be a bond of familiarity and shared experience and mutual respect, a bond painstakingly constructed across a chasm of differences, not one forged forever in the alloy of shared enthusiasms. The painter in Nathaniel knew that brilliance sometimes comes from contrasting shape and color, sometimes from blending them. So it has to be in the affections between fathers and sons.

But in Carlisle he found what was missing from his relationship with his own father. They were kindred spirits, and they shared a passion for perfection in their work, for the honest beauty they could sometimes render from tints and hues of color, for the freedom that all artists crave. Carlisle would never be his father, of course, nor ever diminish his love for his father. But he could be for Nathaniel what Henry Houghton could not. And that was more than reason enough for the feelings of affection that were growing stronger between them.

But this complicated all the more the sentiment that stirred strongly within him when he was with Lydie, especially, as now, when he was alone with her. More often lately, he'd been invited to dine with the Carlisles or simply to come in at the end of the day for tea and some conversation. He was becoming part of their small family. And more often, Benton would leave them alone, usually by calling an early end to his evening. Nathaniel and Lydie developed an easy familiarity that flowed comfortably through their hours and hours of conversation. They laughed and they argued and they mocked their favorite target: the pretensions of the British gentry. And there was no shortage of other targets for their humor in this peculiar country where both felt like aliens. Nathaniel didn't know what these times alone together meant to Lydie, but he knew quite well the excitement they were stirring in him.

And this terrified him, for it was an awful mistake to be falling in love with Benton Carlisle's wife.


The meetings always occurred in a different place. When Nathaniel had information, he would leave the curtains on the one window in his room closed all day. George would see the sign and contact

Nathaniel about the meeting place. Or maybe someone else spotted it and told George; Nathaniel never knew how many people worked with George. Sometimes an envelope under his door would identify the meeting place, in the cipher they now used in all their communications. More often, when Nathaniel was walking a crowded street or through a busy park, someone would brush up against him and place a note in his hand.

Nathaniel would arrive at the designated time and often wait ten minutes or more before George showed up. George was not his real name, of course, and the choice of it was the one sign of irony or humor he'd detected in this small and angry man. All their meetings occurred at night, usually in a park or other open place where anyone watching them could be easily detected and their conversations could not be overheard. George would often approach the bench where Nathaniel sat and say nothing for a few minutes. Then Nathaniel would say, "Are you Charles?" And George would say, "No, I'm George."

Then Nathaniel would report the information he'd gleaned since their last meeting. Sometimes, especially in their first few meetings, this had been quite general and often too vague to be of much use. When he reported Dartmouth's indications to Mrs. Macauley that the ministry was recruiting more soldiers to send to America and negotiating for Hessian mercenaries, George said he needed more detail. How many men? Which units? How many ships? When would they leave? What was their destination? Slowly Nathaniel got the hang of it, and his reports became more plush with detail. Yet another new trade; his education as a spy paralleled his education as a painter.

Tonight Nathaniel had only some tidbits to report from a conversation he'd overheard at a dinner party in Marylebone the previous week. "Howe has been complaining about the lack of supplies and reinforcements, and Germain is committed to getting Howe's army in shape. Now that the weather has abated, they'll be sending a fleet soon with more regiments and guns. Since I overheard this at a dinner, I couldn't get more details."

"It's consistent with other things we've heard," said George, "but we don't know where they're going. Are they going to Boston to strengthen the garrison there, or will Howe pull out and go to New York or Philadelphia or somewhere else? And we still need to know more about Canada. That's the great danger now--that a British force will come down from Quebec, probably along the Hudson, and try to cut the

206

colonies in half. It's hard enough for Washington to run a war with one army. It would be unimaginably difficult to do it with two, with the enemy dividing them.

"We had some information that the King was angered by the loss of Ticonderoga and has ordered his ministers to get it back. But that may be one of those orders that they conveniently forget to carry out.

"In any case, if you can find out anything about where Howe might go if he leaves Boston or what's happening in Canada, report it instantly. Boats will be going more often now that winter is ending, and we can move our information faster."

A wind eddied around them as they sat under a dark sky. Good weather for spies, Nathaniel thought, hard to be seen, hard to be heard. He looked at George, barely taller than a boy and usually dressed in the sort of hooded cloak a woman would wear. George usually ended their conversations and left as soon as the information exchange had finished, but he lingered briefly on this night, providing Nathaniel an opportunity to pose a question that had been on his mind since their first meeting in the alley. "Why do you do this?" he asked.

George laughed, a little too sardonically Nathaniel thought, and carefully formed an answer. "Have you ever heard of John Wilkes?" George said.

"Perhaps, in passing. A troublemaker, wasn't he?"

"Yes, exactly," said George. "Of the very best kind. Wilkes was the most honest man I ever knew. And he could smell the stink of corruption more acutely than anyone in Britain. He set out to try to fix things. Got himself elected to Parliament and started to introduce reform bills. Started a newspaper that really got under the skin of the fat arses with the big wigs. They'd been running this cesspool of a government for years, winning so-called elections by piling up the rotten boroughs. You know what that means?"

"No, I don't think so," Nathaniel replied.

"Most of the members of Parliament don't really represent people. They represent some earl or duke. Maybe a couple hundred years ago, they gave a seat in Parliament to some town because it was isolated from the rest of the shire. Now the town's only got six people in it, but it's still got a seat. So the local gentleman goes around to the other five people and pays them a shilling each—more like a farthing probably—and they all vote for the person he tells them. Most of them can't vote anyway because regular folks have no right to vote. All over England there are seats like that—rotten boroughs and pocket boroughs they call them--where the King and the ministers control the seat. There's some honest places, too, where the elections are pretty straight, but there's enough of the bad ones to get a majority most of the time. Then the King pays them off to vote his way.

"Well, John Wilkes wanted to change all that. Had some support, too. But when it looked like he had a chance, they came and took him away, trumped up some sedition charges against him and declared him an outlaw. Eventually clapped him in the Tower of London."

Nathaniel listened closely, noting the resemblance between this story and the one that Benton had told him about the fate of his brother in Parliament. "I was one of those who supported John Wilkes," George continued. "I loved the man. And after what they did to him, I knew we had to find ways to get rid of this government, but we'd have to do it on the sly. The rebellion in America is a chance to do that. If the army fails in America, people in Parliament are going to be humiliated. They'll be looking to blame someone. That could be the end of Lord North. It might even lead to putting more curbs on the King. But if the army wins and the rebellion is put down, the King'll be stronger than ever. We can't let that happen."

George paused a moment, studying Nathaniel's reaction, then he looked around and continued in his conspiratorial hoarse whisper. "You asked how I got into this. I got into this because I love this country, but I hate the way it's being governed. My ancestors go back to before Edward the Confessor. They're probably turning over in their graves at the mess that's been made here. There's a few good men around, and they're trying to carry on the work that John Wilkes started. We call ourselves the Freedom Alliance. This is what we do."

"So, then, it's really not sympathy for the American cause that drives you?" Nathaniel said after a moment.

"Sure it is. Americans want what we want. Freedom, equality, chance to vote in good men and vote out bad ones. If they get it, there'll be more pressure for change here. America's a long way off, but everybody's watching. They're watching in Spain. They're watching in Holland. They're watching in France. And we're watching here. If the rebellion succeeds in America, it'll light a fuse that'll set off fireworks in a lot of countries. I've never been to America. Doubt I'll ever go there. But the outcome there means everything to me.

208

"Don't fool yourself, Nathaniel. What we're doing here is not a boy's game. It's dangerous. There are people trying to find out who we are and stop us. They catch you passing secrets and they'll have a hanging party before morning. That's why we're so careful. It's very risky, what we do. If your heart's not in this, you better get the rest of your body out of here as fast as you can."

The studio had but one decent chair, though even it was daubed in years of paint residues. Carlisle sat there, occasionally looking up from his reading at the finishing work Nathaniel was doing on the portrait of Prince Frederick. The portrait was so large and its success so important that Carlisle was exhausted from the weeks he'd spent trying to get it just right. Rarely in history, he estimated, had so much labor been dedicated to the likeness of a pudgy twelve-year-old boy. Now Carlisle was happy to sit as Nathaniel completed the background painting.

"I'm quite surprised at you," Nathaniel said. These were the first words that had passed between them in nearly and hour, and they seemed to startle Carlisle.

"I'm sorry. What did you say?"

"I said I'm quite surprised at you. I thought with the importance of this piece that you'd be hovering behind me, advising on every brush stroke."

Carlisle leaned back, removed his spectacles, and fixed his gaze on Nathaniel standing a few yards away. "I should be, I know. You're wholly untrustworthy when I leave you unsupervised." He added a mocking laugh at his own words.

"Actually, I'm captivated by this pamphlet. It may be the most powerful argument I've ever read for anything. I think America has found its voice—though, oddly, the voice seems to be English."

Nathaniel kept his eyes on his work, but asked, "What are you reading?"

"I was at a dinner last knight at Lord Darby's. When we were upstairs after the meal, he gave us all a copy of something called *Common Sense*, by an Englishman in America named Tom Paine. It was published there in January, but copies just arrived here a few days ago, and Darby had it reprinted at one of his print shops. Most of us had never heard of it, but he called it the worst piece of vile slander he'd ever read."

"Is it an attack on the King?" Nathaniel asked.

"I still have a few pages to read, but one could hardly call it that. Certainly not merely that. What he seems to be suggesting is not so much that the King is evil as that the time for kings has passed in America. I think Lord Darby has missed the point. This isn't a slander on the king, our sovereign and--I might add, to keep you focused on your work--our patron. It's a manifesto for rebellion, a justification for Americans to break free from their attachment to the King. Here, listen:

> *There is something exceedingly ridiculous in the composition of monarchy; it first excludes a man from the means of information, yet empowers him to act in cases where the highest judgment is required. The state of a king shuts him from the world, yet the business of a king requires him to know it thoroughly; wherefore the different parts, by unnaturally opposing and destroying each other, prove the whole character to be absurd and useless.*

"I guess we've seen our share of that in the past few weeks at Windsor," Carlisle said with laugh. He turned a few pages, "Now here's another one:

> *In England a king hath little more to do than to make war and give away places; which in plain terms, is to impoverish the nation and set it together by the ears. A pretty business indeed for a man to be allowed eight hundred thousand sterling a year for, and worshipped into the bargain! Of more worth is one honest man to society and in the sight of God, than all the crowned ruffians that ever lived.*

"Then he really swings the axe:

> *Every thing that is right or natural pleads for separation. The blood of the slain, the weeping voice of nature cries, 'TIS TIME TO PART. Even the distance at which the Almighty hath placed England and America, is a strong and natural proof, that the authority of the one, over the other, was never the design of Heaven."*

Carlisle set the pamphlet down, removed his spectacles and looked at his assistant. "How will that argument set with your father, Nathaniel?"

Nathaniel searched for a simple answer and found none. "I'm simply not sure. When I sailed to England two years ago, Father was dead set against rebellion. He wanted the colonies to negotiate with the King and Parliament, to settle their differences so life could go on as it always had. But I've sensed a change in him. Not from anything he's written. He's not much of a writer. The few letters I've gotten from him have mostly been factual reports about the men he's come to know in Congress. He never talks about his own opinions."

Benton listened intently for this was one of the few times Nathaniel had talked about his father's politics. "But I had a letter a few weeks ago from my sister, Savannah. She said that Father seems to be giving up hope that negotiation will ever succeed, that he seems to be sliding into the camp of those who are starting to believe that independence may ultimately be the only course. He's apparently still working with the group in Congress who want to keep trying to find a peaceful resolution, but Savannah says that group is shrinking.

"What was most unusual about this letter was Savannah's anger. She was always my little sister and the girls never got into the discussions about politics. I guess I never did much either, for that matter. But in this letter, my Lord, Savannah seemed almost fervent about what's happening in America. She raged at the evils perpetrated by British soldiers in Boston. She praised my brother, Jonathan, who's now an officer in the Continental Army. She even said that she'd been arguing with Father about the need for the Congress to take a firmer stand against the King. My little sister talking about politics. What a change. A very powerful wind must be blowing across America."

Carlisle slowly rose to his feet and walked toward Nathaniel to look at the portrait. He tossed the pamphlet on the bench behind him and said, "Read this, Nathaniel, and you'll feel some of that wind."

After looking over the canvas for a few minutes, Carlisle picked up one of Nathaniel's brushes and darkened one of the folds in the drape to the Prince's left. He then stepped back, surveyed the entire work and said with mock formality, "I declare this royal portrait complete."

Lydie entered the studio as the two men stood in front of the portrait admiring their work. "Benton," she announced, "the man is here to take you to the ministry."

Carlisle put down the brush, removed his smock, and said simply, " I should be back in a few hours."

When he'd left the room, Nathaniel turned to Lydie who was now standing beside him looking at the portrait and said, "What is that all about?"

Lydie gazed at him in surprise, "He didn't tell you?"

"Tell me what?"

"About the portrait of Lord North."

"What portrait of Lord North?"

"At Lord Darby's last night, a man approached Benton and asked if he would be available to paint a new portrait of Lord North. I forget the man's name, but I think Benton said he was secretary to North. He told Benton that there was an informal policy that a first minister had a new portrait painted every year. Then he made some joke about how that was necessary to trace their slide into disgrace. But he said North admired Benton's portrait of Lord Dartmouth and would like to commission him to do his own. So Benton agreed that if North sent a man to get him, he'd go to Whitehall today to discuss the possibility of a commission."

"God that's wonderful news, extraordinary," Nathaniel responded, thinking to himself about his recent conversations with George. "I can't wait to start. This is the best news I can imagine. I never dreamed we'd get to paint North."

Lydie was surprised at Nathaniel's enthusiasm, knowing he shared Benton's distaste for portraiture as little more than a way to subsidize what they called their "real painting." "Why are you so happy about this?" she asked.

Nathaniel caught himself and gathered up his brushes, then carried them over to the bench where the cleaning took place. "Oh, it's nothing really. I was just pleased at this sign that Benton's reputation is spreading."

"But you sounded like you really wanted to paint Lord North."

"Oh, no, no," Nathaniel quickly replied, trying to hide any further show of excitement. "You misunderstood. He's just another politician. I was only happy that we were getting another prominent commission."

Lydie still looked perplexed, but she turned again to look at the portrait of Prince Frederick. It was the largest portrait she'd ever seen in the studio and she stepped back to take it all in. As she did, her skirts bumped against the bench where Benton had tossed the pamphlet and, remembering that paint was everywhere in the studio, Lydie pulled quickly away, losing her balance in the process.

Nathaniel saw this and leapt to break her fall. Only his instant reaction kept her from tumbling into the portrait and sending his royal highness crashing to the floor. With Lydie held stiffly in his arms, Nathaniel dropped to his knees.

For a few seconds they balanced there precariously, neither knowing what to do next. Suddenly and simultaneously, Lydie began to laugh. She looked down to see that her rescuer's paint-splattered hands were wrapped around the sleeves of her manteau and had added several hues to its pale yellow. "What an oaf you must think me," she said. "You've saved the portrait, Nathaniel. I hope the King gives you a medal for this!"

Nathaniel searched for a jaunty response, but words would not form. He was overcome by the light and delicate feel of Lydie in his arms, by the sweet lavender scent of her perfume, by the tingle that raced through him when her curls touched his cheek. He'd never held a woman in his arms before, never felt such tenderness nestled against him, never imagined how quickly every other perception could melt away from a touch so soft and warm.

For a long moment neither of them moved nor said a word. It was an awkward pose, this tangling of bodies on the studio floor, but both of them let it endure slightly longer than decency allowed. Nathaniel shifted his weight and lifted Lydie in one motion to her feet. Then he laughed a small, uncertain laugh and tried to lighten the moment, "No medals, my lady. But perhaps some solvent to take the paints from your dress." Then he busied himself searching for a clean rag.

Lydie watched him silently, awash in embarrassment, chagrin, and another sentiment not quite so identifiable but more powerful, she thought, than anything she'd ever felt before.

# Chapter 14

## New York
## June 1776

It was the big battle for which all the men had been waiting and on which they'd placed their heaviest wagers. The Jamaican's bird, Samson, had never been beaten and had made his owner a wealthy man. But the local bird, now called Liberty, though a survivor of fewer fights, had a reputation for unremitting ferocity. A cockfight is always a battle of undefeateds, but rarely had two birds combined such a long string of successes.

More than a dozen fights had preceded this one, some lasting twenty minutes or more. It was now nearly four-thirty and the sun would soon be up. He should have been tired, but Godfrey Carter was on a winning streak and he eagerly anticipated the battle between Samson and Liberty. He'd seen both birds in earlier fights and was sure that the Jamaican bird could take the local favorite. But he'd talked up the local bird to encourage more betting and now had total wagers of more than a hundred quid on the large-breasted, blue-combed Samson.

It had been years since any rope had been walked in the old rope walk on Peck's Slip. No houses or other buildings were nearby, so it was an ideal place for cockfighting, and that had been its principal use since Black Bart Tappan came across it more than 6 months ago. Bartlett Tappan worked in Godfrey Carter's warehouse, at least officially. In reality, he spent most of his time on what Carter liked to call "special assignments." Finding a place for the cockfights was one of those.

Carter loved cockfighting, loved the anticipation, loved the faces peering intently over the fighting pen, loved the psychology of one owner trying to convince another to set their birds against each other. He loved the ferocious way the birds went after each other, both looking for the quick kill. But most of all he loved the money. Cockfighting was the ultimate gambler's game, and Godfrey Carter fancied himself a gambling man.

On this night, June twenty-eighth, he'd already lost what most men would call a small fortune. So he'd wagered heavily on this last fight, the big one, hoping to reverse his fortunes and make the night a success. He knew that faith was an unreliable habit in a gambler, but he had faith in the Jamaican bird. He'd won on it before and felt confident he would tonight.

The fight master, a short stocky man with a fur hat and a wisp of brown beard, called the birds to the rail. The owner of the Jamaican smiled serenely as the bird nestled in his hands, hardly stirring, looking— if this can be said of a bird—serenely confident. The local bird wiggled constantly across the pen, seemingly unglued by the 40 of so men crowded together there. For a few seconds everything was still in the heavy air, then the fight master gave the signal and both birds dropped quickly to the dirt floor. Samson rushed in for the kill, the feathers on the back of his neck at full attention, his beak a stiletto, his head moving back and forth like a hammer. Liberty moved to the side, avoiding the first rush and circling clockwise around the pen, his eyes unflinching.

This local bird is scared to death, Carter thought. He won't last a second after the Jamaican catches up with him. Samson continued the pursuit, his head moving faster than ever as if building momentum for one quick and deadly thrust at the throat of his scurrying opponent. Faster and faster they circled, with Liberty moving sideways and Samson trying to find a direct angle of assault. The moment of closure appeared at hand when Samson jumped into the air, furiously flapped his wings and dove hard at the neck of his opponent. Liberty suffered a few seconds of stricken horror as the light flared off the large Jamaican's murderous beak. The kill was about to occur when the local bird stepped quickly aside and delivered a death blow of his own to his descending opponent. With his feet off the ground, Samson couldn't change direction quickly enough to respond to the local bird's sidestep, and he fell to the dirt in a writhing flurry of feathers, blood spurting from the large and fatal wound on the side of his neck. Liberty moved in for a few finishing thrusts, but the outcome was determined by that first hard strike and Samson could only lay there helplessly as the local bird finished him off with savage efficiency.

The brief fury of the fight was followed by near total silence while the men tried to sort out what they'd just seen. The end had come so quickly and with such a reversal of forecast outcomes that surprise was the dominant emotion. Only after a few seconds did some begin to calculate the meaning of winning and losing, of life and death. Carter was one of those who calculated most quickly, and it was not a happy arithmetic. He'd wagered heavily and lost heavily on this fight. In fact, he'd lost heavily all night. He could endure the financial loss. He was not much troubled by that. There'd be more fights, and he'd win back some of what he'd lost tonight. So it went for a gambling man.

It was the blow to his reputation that bothered him more. He'd talked up the Jamaican bird to encourage more betting. He'd bet heavily on the bird himself. And now the quick death of the favorite made it less likely that men would trust his recommendations in the future. Gamblers like to win, but they like even more to bear the aura of a winner. Among gambling men, nothing is more prized than a reputation for knowing the odds, for judging chances, for keeping boldness and prudence in their proper places. Every gambler loses some. A reputation only suffers when a gambler loses big against the odds. That's what Carter had done tonight and it bothered him so much that he could hardly look at the other men as they finished their drinks and started to leave in the first light of dawn. Godfrey Carter knew that he'd slipped down a few notches in the hierarchy of smart gambling men.

Eben Gray knew it, too, and came over to say a few comforting words as they were departing. "We all have a bad night, now and then, Godfrey. You'll beat us all next time, as you usually do." Gray clapped Carter on the back, trying to cheer him up, as they stepped out onto the pier.

But Carter remained glum and quiet as they walked south along Queen Street. A few wisps of clouds stretched high across the sky as the sun asserted its presence. A fresh southerly breeze kept the normal morning stench of Manhattan at bay as the two men strolled toward Fort George.

When Gray saw the sight looming before them, he started to draw Carter's attention to it. But Carter was already focused on the scores of tall ships that filled New York harbor that morning as it had never been filled before. Carter drew his gaze slowly from east to west. Ships under sail, ships in formation, great ships of the line filled every inch between. "My God, what is this?" Gray shouted.

Carter knew by simple process of deduction. It could only be one thing. His Majesty's Navy had arrived in New York.

Suddenly his gloom was gone and his heart was racing. Godfrey Carter was not a man to linger on his losses when new possibilities loomed. Already his mind was calculating how many men the crews contained, how much they'd need to eat and drink, how much canvas and rope and pine tar the ships would require. Where would he get the materials he'd need to supply them? How could he get them to New York sooner than any of his competitors and sell them for less?

The tragedy of Samson, the Jamaican bird, was gone completely from his mind now as it hurtled forward through the profits he saw lining the horizon before him this June morning.

Carter remembered Gray standing there and tried to recall his question. Oh yes, now he remembered. "It looks like the Navy has arrived in our harbor," he said. "And what welcome visitors they are."

"I thought, after the humiliation in Boston, they might just have sailed back to London." said Gray.

"Why would they have done that?" Carter responded.

"Given up. Cut their losses. Saved their men and ships for a fight with one of the European powers. Not wanting to squander them further in a fight they can't win. They confronted Washington's Continentals and he drove them out."

Carter laughed sarcastically. "Don't be fooled by the Yankee propaganda, Eben. Everyone's praising Washington for winning a great victory in Boston, but that was no victory. After Bunker Hill, there was hardly a British soldier killed by Continental fire. When the weather allowed, Howe got his men on their ships and they sailed merrily away. Washington didn't defeat them. He didn't cripple them. He didn't even scare them. The British army was in an untenable position in Boston and it escaped unharmed, ready to fight another day.

"They didn't sail to London at all. They went to Nova Scotia, where they waited for reinforcements. The reinforcements have arrived and now they're here. Off in the distance there, take a look." Carter pointed toward Staten Island. "I'll bet you Howe's troops will be setting up camp there tonight. And nobody will be surrounding them here like Washington did in Boston."

"How do you know all this, Godfrey?" Gray asked in amazement.

"Got my sources," Carter replied, recovering some of the feeling of mastery that he'd lost at the cockfight. "Got my sources."

In the chaise on the way home, Carter thought about the changes that were sweeping over New York. When the shooting started last year in Boston, a firestorm had swept through the colonies. Outraged supporters of the Boston men had begun to create or enlarge militia units. They began to call themselves patriots and to take sides against those who remained loyal to the King. Loyalists and patriots. It seemed to Carter now that the world he knew was divided into those two camps. Patriot families were no longer invited to the parties of loyalist families. Loyalist parents forbade their children to play games with the children of patriot parents. Neighbors watched each other closely to see who might be hoarding food or acquiring a musket. All certainty was gone, and few people ever spoke much about the future except in terms of anxiety and fear.

After news arrived of Bunker Hill, loyalist families began to leave the city, worried about a militia uprising there against the small British garrison at Fort George on the tip of the island. Houses were vacated and some farms were divided up for lots by those who stayed behind. Soldiers seemed quieter and more alert as they walked the streets. It was not the same New York it had been a year ago. Celia complained almost constantly about the dreariness of this social season compared to the one previous.

To Godfrey the changes were a mixed blessing. No businessman likes uncertainty, and he had his share of worries about the future. He'd found a thriving market supplying British forces. With the siege of Boston, his sloops were often the only ships provisioning the garrison there and he could charge what he liked to call a "King's ransom" for his goods. He'd profited handsomely until the evacuation. He'd joined in ventures with other wholesalers in Canada and the south to supply British troops there as well. Now with the arrival of the enormous force he'd seen this morning, profits could only grow.

But trading in war is dangerous business. He wore no uniform and saluted no flag, but to the Continentals he was as much an enemy as any redcoat. So he had to be very careful. He worked with secret contacts. He disguised his identity with code names and ciphers. He worked through middle men. So far, he felt confident, no one in the Continental Army and none of the patriots in New York had any idea that the large Carter warehouse on Queen Street was usually stuffed with supplies for the Kings' army.

Carter was lucky, and he knew it. That was the gambler in him. He knew that you could study a situation trying to master the possibilities.

You could do things to improve your odds of winning. But some things had to be left to chance. He studied and decided that the British army would pay more for supplies than the unreliable Continentals, that the pound sterling was as good as gold while the Continentals' paper was the currency of fools.

Marrying Celia had turned out to be a smarter move than he could have imagined. Her father was a member of Congress and now her brother was an officer with George Washington. Who would ever expect the son-in-law of Congressman Henry Houghton or the brother-in-law of Captain Jonathan Houghton to be trading with the enemy. The fortuitous side-effects of his marriage even allowed him to retain his loyalist friends and business associates without inspiring suspicion among the patriots. And if the time should come when the British abandoned their American colonies, he'd have these good contacts to help him drum up business on the patriot side.

As the chaise came to the fork on Crown Street, Godfrey stuck his head out to the side and looked back up to the driver. "Turn down here," he called, pointing toward Maiden Lane. The driver did so, and they approached a tawdry wooden building covered with cracked amber shingles with nearly a dozen horses hitched to a post in front. Godfrey motioned to the driver to stop. Though it was now nearly seven in the morning, the sounds of frolicking men and giggling women still poured out into the street. At Godfrey's instructions, the driver pulled the carriage around the corner to wait while his employer climbed the familiar steps into the house the sailors called simply "The Yellow Palace."

Celia paced the front parlor, glancing every minute or so through the window that looked out on the street. She'd not eaten breakfast, even though she'd been up for several hours. She'd always loved breakfast on the farm--the apples and grains, fresh cream, eggs, sizzling rashers of smoked bacon, and Sweetie's warm bread. She'd retained the habit of a hearty breakfast in New York, even though they never measured up to those of her childhood. But now the nausea took away her appetite, and she wondered if she could ever enjoy breakfast again.

When they were first married, she and Godfrey had always enjoyed breakfast together. He was so lively in the morning, bursting with plans and ideas, all of which he hoped to squeeze into the day. He shared those generously with his wife. But lately, they rarely dined together in the morning. In fact, they rarely dined together at all. Celia's appetite took unpredictable turns because of her pregnancy and Godfrey always seemed to have some business demanding his immediate attention. Some nights he got home so late that he didn't rise in time for breakfast. Other nights he never came home at all, sleeping at the warehouse where there was an important order to get out or some critical bid he had to prepare.

Celia felt sorry for Godfrey; he seemed so preoccupied with his work. She assumed that it was concerns about his work and her swelling body that accounted for his recent lack of interest in intimacy with her. She hoped that things would go back to normal after the baby was born and the war ended.

She hated this war. Hated the demands that it made on her husband. Hated that her younger brother was in the army and had nearly been killed at Bunker Hill. Hated that her friends were all taking sides and the social season was being ruined by this constant bickering between loyalists and patriots. Most of the women had little interest in any of this, but seemed drawn into the sniping and bickering because their husbands were either joining militia units or signing up to fight in the loyalist companies that were starting to form all over Manhattan. It was hard to plan a ball when the potential guest list included so many people making plans to shoot each other.

The saving grace was the baby, and Celia looked forward to its arrival. Then she would have something to fill the long days. Then Godfrey would start to pay more attention to her again and to be home more often to play with his child. And Savannah would come to visit. She'd promised she would when Celia wrote to tell the family that she was with child. Savannah wrote back right away, saying how much they all missed her and pledging to come to New York for a visit as soon as she could get away after the baby arrived. Celia knew that would probably be in the fall after the crops were in because Savannah seemed to be taking a large role in managing the farm now that Father was in Philadelphia so often, the boys were away, and Mother's dark spells were coming more often. She worried about the sister and mother she hadn't seen for six years, and it made her look forward all the more to the promised visit.

She hoped that she might see Jonathan before long, too. Father had written that Jonathan had bypassed New York on the way to Boston because he was with a committee that was in a hurry. But maybe he'd be coming south again soon. Perhaps when the British withdrew, or when the army moved south now that Boston seemed to be secure. How she'd love to see him. She knew it might be dangerous for a Continental soldier to come to New York. It was still occupied by redcoats. But there weren't many of them in the city and Celia knew of other patriot soldiers who'd slipped in and out without detection. She would write to Jonathan and tell him that. With Godfrey away so much and the social season so disappointing, Celia missed her family more than she had in all the years since she'd left Still River.

A noise in the street caught her attention, and Celia looked out to see Godfrey's carriage pulling up to the gate. He walked slowly up to the door, looking tired, unshaven, and wrinkled. Celia greeted him affectionately when he came into the parlor and Godfrey gave her a quick peck on the forehead and touched her stomach with his right hand.

"You must be exhausted, darling," Celia said, as Godfrey removed his brown striped coat.

"Things have changed quite suddenly," he said, "and now there is more work than ever. I don't know how I shall keep up with it. With so many families leaving the city, it's getting hard to hire more help."

"What do you mean, Godfrey, 'things have changed quite suddenly.' What things?"

"Come with me, dear Celia, and you can see for yourself. He took her arm and led her to the large curving stairway in the front hall. Together they climbed to the second floor, then walked around past the bedrooms to the stairway at the end of the hall and climbed to the third floor. Then Godfrey led her into the unused room on the south side and pointed toward the window. Celia walked over and looked out. She looked back after a few seconds and said "What is it, Godfrey, what am I supposed to see from here?"

"Look in the distance, dear. Look out into the harbor," he instructed. Celia looked up and focused on the horizon. Then she saw the ships strung out across the full width of the harbor, some now at anchor, others still maneuvering under sail.

"Oh my God, oh my God," she said, holding her hands to her cheeks. "What is it?"

"It's the beginning fo the end of this nonsense, dear Celia. It won't be long now before the rebels will be paying the high cost of making our King angry."

# Chapter 15

## *Philadelphia*
## *Summer 1776*

"He may not realize it now, but Rutledge has given us a great gift." John Adams slowly moved his head from left to right, pausing briefly to look into the eyes of each man. The single candle in the center of the table cast a shadow that magnified his gesture. Richard Henry Lee, the sprightly Virginia aristocrat; John Hancock, probably the richest man in America, whose great house in Boston had only recently been liberated from the King's army; Benjamin Franklin, the passionate sage; Charles Carroll, scion of Maryland's leading family; Henry Houghton, Delaware farmer.

What an odd lot of revolutionaries are these, Henry thought. At the State House every day, they spoke of their oppression, of the denial of their liberties. But had there ever been in human history a group of people less oppressed, more blessed with liberty than these? Revolutions, Henry thought, are made by the have-nots against the haves, to realign the order of things and bring about broader access to a society's wealth and benefits. What a peculiar twist then to have John Hancock presiding over this Congress of revolutionaries, to have lawyers like Adams and children of privilege like Lee and large landowners like Carroll seeking the kinds of changes that this Congress now debated every day.

Franklin had said a few days ago that revolution was a rare phenomenon in human history, but if the Americans could make a successful revolution, no tyrant would ever again sit easily on his throne. Perhaps he was right, Henry thought, perhaps the stakes here were higher than the simple question of who owned America. But it was hard to think of any other society in the world where the richest men, the possessors of the land, the barons of the bar would lead a revolution against the established authority. Usually such people are the beneficiaries of established authority, its protectors—not its enemies.

Henry had been thinking a great deal about larger questions in recent days, as the Congress moved toward what seemed to be a defining moment. Words like "independence" and "revolution" were now on everyone's lips; a year ago they were rarely spoken. The daily debates were a mixture of grand philosophy and the pettiest of politics. One moment the delegates engaged in moving colloquies about human liberty; the next they struggled to agree on the proper placement of a comma in the middle of a sentence. It was the twin dilemma that politicians face everywhere: getting consensus not only on principle but on the specific words that implement the principle.

As the Congress moved toward a decision on the question of independence, Henry was not alone among the delegates in seeking an intellectual escape route from his own tortured uncertainty. For so long he'd stood with the doubters, the men who saw great risks in independence and held out hope for a reconciliation with London. That seemed like the prudent course to Henry in the spring of 1774 and through most of the subsequent two years.

Now he was not so sure. Every respectful approach to the King had been rebuffed. More soldiers and ships kept arriving. The opinions of colonists everywhere were hardening and, after Lexington, most had hardened into ardent opposition to the King and his army. Henry understood the risks of war and the uncertain dangers of independence. But he found it harder and harder now to justify the alternatives. How could he explain to his friends in Delaware that we needed to be more patient with a King whose ships had blocked their commerce and whose soldiers were massing to invade their coasts? How could he explain to his son that he was siding with the very enemy that had nearly taken his life on a bloody hill above Charlestown?

The circle was closing for Henry Houghton and more often in the evenings now, he found himself in the company of the men who wanted independence and not those like John Dickinson and John Jay—men he deeply admired but with whom he could no longer agree. He knew their disappointment in him. It was one of the painful things he'd learned here: that on the rocky shoals of principle, friendships often founder.

"What do you mean, John?" said Lee. "What is the gift?"

"We're close to our goal, but if we'd taken the final vote today, we'd have lost. New York is incompetent to make a decision. Delaware is split. South Carolina and Pennsylvania are still against us. We need yet more time to win them over, and that is the gift that Rutledge gave us today when he moved to postpone the vote for three weeks. That will bring us to the beginning of July and we'll need all of that time to bring the wandering sheep into the flock."

"And what do you propose we do in these weeks, John?" asked Hancock.

Adams was nearly trembling now from the rush of ideas through his mind. "All of us, and all who agree with us, need to talk to the doubters. Every day, every minute, we have to find them and fill them with reasons to support independence. Many of them are ready to turn, but we mustn't let Dickinson hold them back. If they hear from enough of us and hear the full range of our arguments, and hear them constantly, we shall undermine their will to resist any further.

"Then we need to communicate with our supporters in the legislatures, especially in Maryland and Pennsylvania and New York to get them to instruct their delegates on the proper course here. Dickinson still seems to control Pennsylvania against us, but the others are more promising.

"Finally, we need to attack the lingering opposition with a powerful indictment of the King. It will be hard to vote against independence if we can make the King sound like the tyrant he's been. We've all found words to repudiate him in our debates, but now we must bring those together in one place and lay it on the table, forcing the delegates to vote up or down. Are they for this tyrant or against him?"

"How do you propose to do that, John?" Lee asked.

"You gave us a brilliant start, my good friend, when you brought us the Virginia resolution. It was precisely the kind of clear and direct statement we needed. And it forced some of the waverers to sit back a little and take a second thought on how they might vote when actually confronted with a clear written proposal.

"But we need more than the Virginia resolution, gentleman. We need a document that offers a full and specific indictment of the King. Then we can ask the delegates to vote, not just on the philosophical issue of independence, but on the specifics of the King's actions. It's a lot easier to be against independence in theory than it is to be for the King in reality." Adams was breathing heavily now, struggling to keep up with the torrent of his own thoughts. "This all needs to be properly done, putting the King's actions in a historical context and probably a philosophical context as well. We must leave no doubt that the King has acted so badly that he has left us no choice but to reject his sovereignty."

224

Adams rose from his seat, as he sometimes did when he wanted to focus the attention of an audience or a jury. He took out his silk handkerchief and dabbed the sweat from his cheek. The he sat down again and leaned forward. "Today the Congress appointed a committee to draft a statement of independence. That must now be the focus of our most intense efforts. If we can state our cause with telling force, some of those still on the fence will find it hard to stay there. If only we can frame the argument for independence convincingly, arrange it with the force of a powerful logic, then we can help them justify their vote to their legislatures and to their consciences."

The next two weeks passed in a blur. Most of the delegates found it odd to be in Philadelphia with no sessions of the Congress to structure their days. Some had ridden home to seek instructions from their legislatures on the independence vote that loomed ahead. But most spent their days outdoors, usually in parks or gardens where they could find shade and an occasional breeze to mitigate the heat. All over the city there was talk, furious talk, among men coming to realize that they were at center stage for the most important performance of their lives. Those among them who were avid readers of history reminded the others that they could find no precedent for what the Congress was about to do, that nowhere else in recorded history had a democratic assembly voted to sever its bonds with a sovereign. Democracies of any kind were rare flowers in the garden of human history. Democracies born of revolution against a sovereign—a precedent for that eluded even the most scholarly among them.

In the midst of all this talk was a tireless and cantankerous dervish from Massachusetts. If John Adams had any capacity for charm—and none of the delegates had observed such capacity in him—it would not have emerged during these days in any case. Adams was not out to charm those who opposed him; he intended to wear them down, to beat them into submission, with the sheer force of the case he had built for independence. Over and over, day after day, he repeated the arguments to one delegate after another. From morning to night he sought out anyone who would listen, even those who had heard the litany many times before. So it was no surprise, when Henry encountered him one afternoon walking along Market Street, that John Adams began again to offer up a splendid vision of an independent America in full control of its own destiny.

Henry sought to change the subject. "Where are you headed, John?" he asked.

"To Seventh Street, Henry, to check in with Jefferson."

"Ah, poor Tom," Henry said. "Is he hard at work, even in this heat?"

"I hope so," Adams replied. "I stop by every day to encourage him. He's such a perfectionist that he's never satisfied that he's got a thing done right. So he tinkers and tinkers. You should see him. His hands are stained black from the ink, and his writing table is in utter disarray, with scraps of paper everywhere. I know he'll finish, because he's a most reliable soul. But he may expire the moment he's done. Come with me, Henry. Tom admires you, and your presence might cheer him up."

"All right," said Henry. "But I thought the committee was going to write this document. How did Tom get roped into it?"

"Politics, of course," muttered Adams. "Someone needed to write a draft, since no group can do that together. Livingston couldn't do it, of course, because he doesn't even believe in independence. Franklin was the logical choice, but he's very sensitive about his son, the Kings' governor in New Jersey. The patriots there have just declared William Franklin an enemy of liberty and Ben did not want to make his loyalty to the King seem any more flagrant by drafting a document that states the very reasons why his own son is all wrong. Sherman was out because the poor man can hardly write a coherent sentence."

"So that left you and Tom," said Henry. "Why not you, John."

"Well, I could have done it, but it made no sense. I'm the most hated man at this Congress. And there are still some here who think that the New England delegates have always had independence as their sole agenda. We needed a draftsman who wasn't despised and who didn't represent the most radical faction in the convention. That ruled me out."

"And poor Tom in," said Henry.

"Well yes," Adams quickly retorted, turning now to look at Henry as they walked. "But as you know he has qualifications beyond the mere fact that he was the last one standing. Anyone who has read his "Summary View of the Rights of British America," anyone who watched the splendid way he captured our feelings in his draft of "On the Necessity of Taking Up Arms" last year knows well that there is not a more felicitous pen in these colonies than the one Tom Jefferson wields. He would be the right man for this job," Adams said with a rare twinkle, "even if he were not the only man for the job."

They approached the simple brick house at the corner of Seventh and Market Streets where Jefferson took a room. The open shutters on the second floor indicated his presence and Adams called up to him, "Tom, may we come up?"

A few seconds later, an angular young man in a damp shirt leaned from the window and looked down. His red hair was matted in dark curls around his head and he looked tired. "Of course," he said, expressing the pleasure at interruption common to writers seeking relief from the tyranny of unruly words. Seeing Henry, he added "And you too, Henry." They entered through the large black door and ascended the narrow staircase in the hallway. Adams knew the way well.

Jefferson's room resembled a torture chamber. The bed was unmade. Clothes were heaped upon it. The open window brought no relief from the heat but only an army of flies and all the sounds and smells of the busy intersection outside. Jefferson seemed a prisoner, happy to realize it was visiting day.

Adams pulled up a chair, removed his hat, and placed it in his lap. "How goes it, Tom?" he asked solicitously and with more tenderness than Henry had ever before heard from the stern lawyer.

"It is a devil of a thing," Jefferson responded. "One moment I think I should be searching for a new philosophical principle to mark the uniqueness of what we seek to do here. But then I think the more important task is the political one, to find the words that capture the feelings of our countrymen so that when they read this they'll exclaim, 'Of course, that's just what I feel!' I struggle every minute to find the right balance. I don't know if I'll be able to do it, John. Honestly I don't."

"There's no one but you who can do it, Tom. No one but you has so sure a feel for the experience of injustice and the tonic of liberty that we must convey. You've written against privilege and injustice for years. Your pen has the power of lightning, Tom. And when you bring its full electric force to these issues, the opposition will melt away. I have the greatest faith in you. God could not have given us a more inspired architect of His will."

Henry watched in awe as Adams elevated Jefferson's spirits. It was an artful performance by a man gifted with a talent for burrowing into the minds of others. Adams, Henry knew, harbored real doubts about whether anyone could pull off the task that Jefferson had been assigned. But he'd be damned if he was going to admit those doubts to the

Virginian. If he lacked absolute confidence himself, he was a paragon of confidence here at Jefferson's writing table.

"Would you like to look at what I have?" asked Jefferson, picking two sheets of paper off the table and thrusting them in Adams's direction.

Adams looked toward the pages for a second, then pulled back, and placed his hat on his head. "I would not, sir," he said with dramatic effect. "There is not one word, not one comma, I could add that would improve upon the prose of Thomas Jefferson. I would not presume to try. It is your document, Tom, and I'm sanguine that we shall all rejoice that none but you has penned it."

With that Adams rose, smiled formally, bowed to the seated Virginian and signaled to an astonished Henry Houghton that it was time to leave.

Despite the heavy heat and the bad news that had come in a steady stream over the previous week, most of the delegates were pleased to be back at work. The invasion of Canada, which Sam Adams had convinced the Congress was the key to a victory against the British, had failed. Of the thirteen thousand men Benedict Arnold had led into the wilderness, only five thousand could still report for duty when the bedraggled army retreated to Crown Point on Lake Champlain. The British force in Canada was stronger than ever, and an American army stood in ruins.

Word had come as well that a British fleet and a force of two thousand infantry were preparing an assault on Charleston, South Carolina, spreading the war now throughout the colonies. And a messenger had just arrived with the report that Howe's fleet, whose evacuation from Boston had brought such joy to this Congress a few months earlier, had finally been found—in New York Harbor with 150 ships and countless troops who'd landed on Staten Island without resistance.

It was a black backdrop indeed for the debate that was about to begin. But to most of the delegates almost anything was an improvement on the waiting and politicking of the previous three weeks.

John Dickinson spoke first, painting a bleak future if the colonies declared their independence now. Young men slaughtered by British soldiers. Ports ruined by a rain of naval bombardment. Indian tribes moving east to rape colonial women and scalp their husbands. Spain and France muscling in to reclaim a piece of the great American bounty. America would be a young country with no proven government,

228

immobilized by its own internal divisions. "Premature" is what Dickinson called independence, over and over through the hours he spoke.

Henry listened intently, as all the delegates did. This was important business and there were no wandering minds in spite of the suffocating heat on this first of July. During Dickinson's speech, a messenger entered the chamber and handed a piece of paper to John Adams. Adams looked at it and smiled, then refolded it and tucked it into a pocket of his brocade waistcoat. Henry wondered what was going through the Boston man's mind on this day toward which all his formidable energies had so long pointed.

When Dickinson finished, Henry could tell from the nods around the room that many of the delegates had been impressed by his remarks. After all these months, Henry had come to believe that Dickinson was wrong about independence, but his admiration for his good friend, for his tenacious defense of the old order, had never stopped growing. How wrong it seemed to Henry that only the men who supported independence were called "patriots." He could not imagine a more patriotic soul than John Dickinson's. He loved his America as much as any man; he just loved the America that was dying and he could not bear its death.

None but John Adams could lead the arguments for independence. Adams began by drawing from his pocket the note that had been handed him earlier. It was from Samuel Chase, a Maryland delegate, who had returned home during the recess to seek the support of the Maryland legislature for independence. Slowly and clearly Adams read the outcome: a unanimous vote for independence in Maryland.

Then Adams replayed all of the arguments for independence he'd been thrusting at the delegates for months. He paced in front of the circled chairs, his short frame pumping as if extracting each argument from some deep well of rectitude. He swabbed the sweat from his forehead with a linen handkerchief and paused occasionally for a sip of water. But the words never stopped flowing. In mid-speech the skies began to darken and a wind started to swirl through 5th Street outside. Windows were lowered and candles lit. But still John Adams talked. A furious storm crackled through the humid Philadelphia afternoon. But still John Adams talked. The thunder bellowed from the west; John Adams bellowed louder. By late afternoon, most of the delegates had made up their minds. But still John Adams talked.

When finally Adams sat down, depleted by his labors, the room was silent for a long time. Then delegates rose from their chairs and came to him, touching his shoulder and congratulating him on the power and passion of his argument. Benjamin Harrison of Virginia, presiding now so that Hancock could sit with the New Englanders, asked for a test vote on independence, and the clerk called the roll of the colonies. Everyone listened closely, even the exhausted warrior, John Adams.

Nine colonies voted for independence, but four did not. Delaware split, with Henry voting yes and George Reade voting no. Caesar Rodney had gone home to deal with a clash between loyalists and pro-independence groups, and did not vote. New York's delegates refused to act until they had instructions from their legislature. Pennsylvania and South Carolina, by narrow margins, voted against independence.

John Adams's colleagues were deeply dismayed as they caucused after the vote. Henry expected that Adams would be as well, but when he looked across the room what he saw was Adams back on his feet, talking furiously to two delegates from South Carolina. A few minutes later, Adams walked over to Henry. Henry looked the shorter man in the eye and began to offer his condolences on the outcome of the vote. But Adams cut him off. "No time for that now, Houghton. We have too much to do before the final vote tomorrow. New York is hopeless, but they won't vote against us. I think we may be able to get somewhere with Rutledge. Jefferson and Franklin will talk to him tonight. If he turns, South Carolina will come with us.

"Pennsylvania and Delaware are the real challenges. I will try to get with Dickinson later, though for the life of me I don't know what's left to say. Perhaps we can persuade him that Pennsylvania will be standing alone and he'll have to bear responsibility for the failure of something so widely desired by his countrymen. He's a good man in spite of his obstinacy. I yet hope that he can be reasoned with."

Then he turned and looked at Henry squarely. "Now, Henry, you must do something of the greatest importance. We agree that there's little likelihood that George Reade is going to vote for independence. So we must have Caesar Rodney here to vote. He is with us on independence and his vote will put Delaware on our side. You have to get him here."

"I agree, John." Henry said, shrugging his shoulders in frustration. "But he's eighty miles away. How can I possibly get him here in time for the final vote tomorrow?"

"I don't know how, Henry. I just know that you must." That was all Adams said. Without further words or any expression of emotion, he pivoted and went to look for John Dickinson.

Henry moved from the chamber to the lobby where he located Franklin wrapping himself in his cloak as he prepared to step out into the driving wind and rain. "Ben," Henry called to him. "A word if I may."

Franklin turned slowly. He'd put his spectacles in his pocket and it took a second for him to recognize Henry. "Ah yes, Henry," he said. "I was on my way to the church of lost causes to pray for a miracle."

Henry had little time for humor and barely smiled at Franklin's attempt. "Ben, I need to find the best rider I can, someone who can get to Delaware tonight and find Caesar Rodney. Do you know such a person?"

"Delaware? Tonight?" said a disbelieving Franklin. "You don't need a Philadelphia rider, Henry, you need Pegasus."

Franklin's capacity for amusement never abandoned him, even in the darkest moments. But Henry was in a hurry. "Absent that," said Henry, "might there be a human who could help?"

Franklin paused to think for a moment, then a smile came to his face. I've heard of a man who is a genius with horses and has a very fast one of his own. He's an Irishman who works at a stable at Arch and 8<sup>th</sup> Street. Come with me, I'll take you there."

Henry quickly put on his own cloak and the two men hurried off into the storm. A few minutes later they were pounding on the stable door. It creaked loudly as a man holding a lantern pulled it open from the inside. Franklin and Henry stepped in. The door closed and all three men stepped into the light. Speaking in an Irish brogue, the livery man asked what they needed. Henry had a brief flash of recognition, but couldn't place the man. He explained as quickly as he could that they needed a rider to go to Delaware that very night to get a message to a man named Caesar Rodney telling him that he must return to Philadelphia by tomorrow.

The man whistled when he heard Henry's plan, indicating its impossibility. "Never been ta Del'ware," the man said, "but I've haard 'tis a mighty long wiy. Don't b'lieve can be done."

"But," Henry responded, seeking inspiration, "it has to be done. If Caesar Rodney is not here tomorrow, the Congress will not vote for independence and we will all remain subjects of an English King. I know that is not an appealing prospect to a good Irishman like yourself."

"Tis surely not. I took a long boat ride to get 'ere, to be getting' awiy from the bloody English kings. No one wants ind'pendence more'n me. You tell me where to find this Julius Caesar, and I'll be gettin' him for ye t'night if'n I have to run there meself."

While the livery man saddled his tall horse, Henry quickly described the way to Delaware and the most promising place to look for Caesar Rodney. "Is that your best horse?" Henry asked.

"Best harse in Philadelphia," the man answered. "Everyone calls 'im 'Miracle.'"

"A proper name for this task," said Franklin, reaching in his pocket to offer the rider a few shillings.

But the man held his hand up firmly and said, "To help kiss that bastard George goo'bye 'tis all the piyment I'll be needin'." Henry pulled open the stable door, and the rider and horse sped off though the wind and the rain, heading south into the surly night.

Henry leaned back in his chair, casting his hundredth glance toward the chamber door. Adams had done his work. Robert Morris and John Dickinson, the fire-eating anti-independence men from Pennsylvania, were not there. A night of frantic negotiating had convinced them that they did not represent the sentiments of most Pennsylvanians, and they had agreed to stay home. With their absence, the Pennsylvania delegation would swing to independence. Across the room, Henry could see Adams and Jefferson talking warmly with Edward Rutledge. His vote for independence now also seemed secure, bringing South Carolina along. New York would abstain again today, still awaiting instructions from its assembly.

So only Delaware remained an uncertainty, and there was no sign of Caesar Rodney. Harrison had delayed the opening of the chamber as long as possible and finally called the men to their chairs so the voting could begin. Every session of the Congress began with a prayer, and Harrison called upon Reverend Duché, whose prayer in September 1774 had opened the first session of the Continental Congress, to open the session on this fateful day. Adams, noting Rodney's absence, had caught the minister in the lobby beforehand and indicated to him that a very long prayer might be especially appropriate on this day. Reverend Duché complied happily with Adams's suggestion.

The prayer finally ended, and the delegates leaned back in their seats. Harrison asked the secretary to call the roll.

"Connecticut," he called. Henry was growing more worried with each passing moment now. He and Reade had agreed that Henry would respond for Delaware when it was called. But without Romney, he could not cast the vote for independence.

"Aye," shouted Roger Sherman. Henry looked toward the door one last time. No Rodney.

"Delaware."

Henry paused as long as courtesy allowed then rose slowly to his feet. "Delaware seeks to pass," he said quietly.

The room came alive as men started to breathe again, a sign of relief.

"Georgia," the secretary called.

Henry was a God-fearing man, but he rarely looked to prayer to solve his immediate problems. Farmers knew better than that. Men had to count on their own wits and energies in times of trial. But here there was nothing he could do but wait—and pray.

He heard "New York," followed by "The delegates from New York enthusiastically support the cause of independence, but in the absence of instructions from our assembly, New York abstains."

All at once the door to the chamber burst open and boomed as it slammed against the wall. A lone man stepped in, his coat and breeches spotted with mud, a relieved smile on his face. He briefly looked around, trying to determine what was happening, when Henry caught his eye and signaled him to the empty chair reserved for Caesar Rodney--here at last, found by an Irish Pegasus and borne to Philadelphia on a horse named Miracle.

Henry was surprised that John Adams was not at City Tavern to join in the celebration that went late into the night on July fourth. Perhaps he was just exhausted, Henry thought, from the struggle to round up wayward votes over the previous three weeks, and then the last two days of defending Jefferson's draft of the Declaration from the quibbles and nibbles of the delegates. Perhaps there was a limit to the energy of even the tireless John Adams.

But his absence worried Henry. So, after joining the others in raising a few mugs of ale to their spanking new United States of America and even, with no small undercurrent of derision, to their former King, Henry took his hat and left the noisy celebration behind.

It was not much quieter outside. Torches lit the city and long lines of happy people—husbands and wives, coopers and smiths, shopkeepers and sailors, Philadelphians of every description and size—snaked through the streets singing "Yankee Doodle Dandy" and a quickly-learned parody called "Farewell Britannia." Henry headed for John Adams's lodgings, but his journey was slowed on this night of nights by newly minted Americans wanting to toast him and swing him around in their merry dance.

Henry finally reached the wooden frame house where Adams had resided for much of the past two years, torn, as Henry was, from his wife and children. A lone light in the west window on the second floor fueled Henry's suspicion that while Philadelphia celebrated, John Adams was alone in his room. The window was open on this warm night, so Henry called up. "John, it's Henry Houghton. May I come up, sir."

A few seconds passed, then Adams's bare head appeared in the window. "You should be celebrating, Houghton, not wasting your time with me."

"Time with you is never wasted, John," Henry called back.

"Come up then, sir, if you're so allergic to fun."

Henry entered and found his way by the stairs to Adams large room. It was lit only by a single candle under a globe. A quill and ink and an open book--a diary apparently--stood on the otherwise bare pine table. Adams was dressed only in breeches and linen shirt, the first time Henry had ever seen him looking like anything other than a lawyer headed to court. Adams's vanity leaked out slightly when he apologized that he was not dressed to receive visitors.

Henry pulled up the extra chair and the two men sat facing each other in the small bubble of light in the center of the dark room. "You must feel extraordinarily happy tonight, John. You've worked so long for this. It wouldn't have happened without you."

Adams rubbed his left ear in pursuit of some small pain. He looked drained, almost anemic. The razor edge of his words seemed strangely absent, and he struggled more than Henry had ever seen him to form his sentences. "I'm gratified, of course," he said. "We've done the right thing. And I know how hard it's been for men like you, full of reasonable fears and doubts, to come to the decision we made today. We're all renegades now, Henry. The King should be sending out the hanging parties any moment."

Adams rarely attempted humor and neither man found much in this feeble effort. "I wrote to my wife earlier," Adams continued, "and I was surprised how much more joy there was in the words that stretched across the page than I've been able to feel here. I suppose we all must hide our doubts when we talk to our families and friends about the work we've done in this Congress. We've asked them to sacrifice so much; we can't have them thinking that our enterprise is unworthy."

"But surely, you don't think any of this is unworthy, John?"

"No, perhaps not. But, Henry, I must tell you that the joy of the moment passed very quickly for me after the vote for independence two days ago. I thought we would then introduce Jefferson's Declaration and it would be adopted by unanimous consent. It was such a splendid statement of our purposes. And no prosecutor ever drafted a more telling bill of indictment than Jefferson's points against the King. I weep very infrequently, Henry, but I wept when I first read it.

"But then the southerners raged against the paragraph that blamed the King for the plague of slavery and, when that happened, everyone found something to change. My copy had so many lines through sections and scribbles in the margin that I could hardly read it when we finally voted on it today."

"But isn't that just politics, John? Shouldn't we have imagined that two score self-important men would all have some tinkering to do before they would sign their names to something so vital and so visible as this declaration of independence?"

Adams continued with his thought, not responding to Henry. "It worries me terribly, Henry. Now that we're no longer English, we must become something else. Will we be able to do that, or will we squabble our way into oblivion and irrelevance? We've been through a long struggle to get to this point. The ardor of it makes some of us feel it's the hardest thing we've ever done. But we'll soon learn otherwise. Declaring independence is the easy part. Being independent will be much more difficult.

"Now we have to construct a government of our own and conquer our passions and self-interests to make it work. Will it? I don't know. Will New York learn to live with Virginia, will slave-owners and slavery haters find common ground, will exporters in Delaware be willing to live by the same laws as importers in Massachusetts? The answers are up to us, Henry, but are we up to the task of finding them? I swear I don't know."

Adams rose now and walked to the window, searching for a few wisps of night air. He stood there for a second facing the street, listening to the explosions in the distance. The he turned back to his visitor. "My children are young, Henry, but yours are not. You and I have voted this week for independence, but in so doing we've also voted for war. How long will that war last? How will it end? How many of our children will die?

"I know I should feel the sheerest joy tonight. A man stopped me in the street on my way home and thanked me for giving us all independence. Ha! Would that we had. But all we've done is to impose a sentence on the people of these colonies, a sentence to years of hard labor in pursuit of a government that can manage our differences. A sentence of death to many brave men fighting to win the very independence for which we have merely cast our votes. What we have written in words, other men must now write in their toil. And their blood."

## Chapter 16

## New York
## August-November 1776

"Ready, sir." The aide handed the reins to the Colonel, saluted, and stepped away. Armistead's clean red uniform was resplendent in the August sun, the polished brass buttons gleaming as he turned to face the assembled troops behind him. He turned his headed slowly from left to right taking them all in: his own regiments in scarlet, the Scotsmen of the Black Watch in their kilts and bearskin grenadier hats, the Hessians in blue and orange—a rainbow of soldiers stretched to the horizon.

How far this seems, Armistead thought, from those dark March days in Boston. When General Howe landed his forces on Staten island in June, no one opposed them even though Washington's army was already in New York. When Howe sent him to invade Nassau Island, Armistead was certain there'd be opposition there. The island was full of farms, of cattle and produce that his troops could live off through the Fall; surely the Continentals would try to keep them away from such a bounty. There was nothing a Continental general liked more than having redcoats eat salt beef and dry hardtack.

But only a few militia tried to stop their landing on the long island. Perhaps the Americans are ready to give up the fight, Armistead thought. Even he had to admit that the sight of four hundred British ships in New York harbor and of the thousands of British and Hessian troops ready for battle would throw a shiver up the spine of any general. Never before in history, Howe had told them, had so many British ships and soldiers gone to war abroad. The Georges—King George and George Germain--meant business.

But soldiers are always suspicious when things happen too easily. Why hadn't Washington resisted? The spies had made it clear that he had a large army of his own and he'd been fortifying Manhattan Island all summer. Perhaps it was too risky to try to keep us from Staten Island, but why not throw a force against us on Nassau Island? Some of Howe's generals thought little of Washington, thought him a plodder. They figured he'd try to repeat the success of Bunker Hill, as commanders often did. If one battle plan works, keep using it over and over. They'd made us attack a heavy fortification in Charlestown and we'd paid dearly. We captured the hill finally, but they'd probably be happy to sell us a lot of hills at that price.

The consensus was that Washington now hoped that Howe would throw his troops at another fortified hill, that this was why Washington had not tried to meet them on open ground, why he seemed to be waiting now for the invaders to make the first move. Well, Armistead thought, he'll get his wish. We will make the first move. But damned if Howe will make the same mistake again. We'll attack them all right, but not uphill from the front. They'll have to turn around if they want to see us coming.

Armistead gathered the battalion commanders around and explained the assault plan. Spies were everywhere in this war and Howe had learned the importance of keeping tactics quiet until the very last minute, even from his senior officers. "We believe Washington has about ten thousand men, most of them regulars, in fortifications on Brooklyn Heights," Armistead said, dismounting and using his sword to draw a diagram in the dirt. "He expects us to meet his army in the field in front of those fortifications, then to retreat there and kill us off as we attack.

"But he's in for a surprise. We'll attack all right, but from his rear and his flank. We'll use our flat-bottomed boats to move the troops to his east, then circle behind him from there, trying to get between his armies and their fortifications." Armistead dug more and more deeply into the ground as he spoke, so that by now his diagram had become an angry mass of piles and holes. He asked his adjutant to go over the order of battle while he remounted his horse and rode off to review the troops before they moved off to the boats.

It felt good after the humiliating evacuation of Boston and the months of uncertainty in Canada to be back at the business for which he was trained. It had been more than a year since Bunker Hill. He still bore a slight limp from his own wound that day. But that mattered little. It was the dreams, the infernal dreams that came to him night after night filled with severed limbs and smashed faces and red uniforms soaked with dark, damp blood. He was haunted by the good men he'd lost on Bunker Hill. He couldn't bring them back. You never could. But in a war you sought redemption through revenge. Hallow the brave memory of those dead men by killing the enemy on some other ground, by settling the score. He'd waited a long time for this August day when the settling would begin.

Drouin knocked on Carter's door. "Just come in, goddamn it!" Carter yelled. Every hour or so, Godfrey Carter sent his clerk up to Trinity Church to climb the steeple and focus a spyglass on the troop movements across the East River. Then Drouin would scurry back to report what he'd seen.

Carter waited anxiously for each report. He was a civilian in a war zone, and he was worried about his warehouse and his home. Washington's army had been digging trenches and making forts all over Manhattan for the previous two months. When they needed a house, they simply took it. When they needed to block a street, they just blocked it. The citizens of the city resented all this, of course, especially the thousands who remained loyal to the King. But the soldiers had no time to listen to their protests.

That was bad enough, but if the fighting actually came to the city, nothing would be safe. He'd wanted to get Celia out of the city, for many reasons; but she was very pregnant now and after so many miscarriages, she did not want to travel and risk the baby. Her brother, Jonathan, was living with them while the army occupied the city. Carter didn't like Jonathan much and especially didn't want him snooping around. But he was a major now and his closeness to Washington meant that no other troops would be quartered in their house. And Celia complained less about Godfrey's absences with her brother around to provide her some company.

The warehouse on the waterfront was Carter's major concern. When the Continentals came to the city, they inspected all the warehouses. When they found his was full of the kinds of supplies that armies could use—blankets, mess kits, tents, salt beef, and bandages—they negotiated with him to buy the contents. What a boondoggle this was. He'd already sold those supplies to the British before they evacuated Boston. But then he couldn't ship them, since the British were nowhere to be found. Now the Continentals were buying the same goods.

What fools these soldiers are, he thought. Not only had he negotiated a better price from the Americans than he had from the British, no one had asked why he had a warehouse full of such supplies. He'd told the inspectors that he'd bought everything on speculation, hoping to sell it to the Americans. Then when he showed them around, no one asked if there was a basement to the warehouse. He couldn't believe his good fortune. Not only was there a basement, but at that very minute it was piled to the ceiling with barrels of gunpowder, canisters of grape shot, and blocks of lead for musket balls. It had taken him most of a year to collect all that ordnance, most of it purchased from pirates in Jamaica who stole it from Spanish ships heading to Florida. He hoped to find a lucrative market with the British, but had not yet been able to negotiate with them. If the Americans had found those stores, they probably would have just commandeered them, costing Carter a fortune. But now there was still a chance that he could sell to the British, especially if they captured Manhattan, as he assumed they eventually would.

Carter had never felt so vulnerable. He was in harm's way, and at any moment a British attack on lower Manhattan could send his warehouse up in flames. In fact, a wayward cannonball making its way to the basement of the warehouse, and the gunpowder hidden there, could send most of lower Manhattan up in flames. He was playing for high stakes here, he knew. If things went his way, it would be the biggest score of his life and he would be a very wealthy man. If things went wrong, he could be very dead. But Godfrey Carter was a gambler, and he knew that only the high-stakes players ever won the big pots.

Drouin had reported earlier in the day that a lot of British ships seemed to have loaded troops and moved them up the shore east of Flatbush. He couldn't see their movements that far away, but the noise coming from that direction was loud and steady, and there was smoke everywhere. Carter listened to the report, then traced it with his finger on the large map on his office wall. Double good news, he thought. The engagement has begun and it didn't happen on Manhattan.

Captain Flint jumped from his horse and rushed to Washington's tent. The General had decided to stay at the fort on Brooklyn Heights to oversee the action that he expected to unfold in front of him. To his great dismay, Howe's men did not engage his own head-on as he'd thought they would. That, after all, was the way Howe fought at Bunker Hill, and Washington assumed he would again—hit the enemy in his middle then overcome him with superior force, the classic British battle plan.

Flint rushed in, glanced quickly at Jonathan, then saluted Washington. "What have you seen?" the General asked.

"Big trouble, Gen'ral," Flint responded. "Appears they moved their men in boats and landed 'em to the east of our lines. Then one column attacked our flank while another one looped 'round to the rear. Now they're rollin' us up on the east, and they slid in behind us, cuttin' off the retreat back up here to the forts. It's an ugly sight down there, Gen'ral. Lotta' shootin'. But mostly confusion. Nobody seems to know where they're comin' from."

Washington kept his eyes on the map, trying to fit Flint's report to the terrain depicted before him. He said nothing. Howe had fooled him. He'd abandoned the kind of frontal assault he'd used on Breed's Hill, probably anticipating that we'd prepare to fight from fortified positions as we had there. Now my troops will start to run because no one can hold troops in place when they're being attacked by superior force from the flank and the rear.

Sure enough, fleeing Continentals were already starting to arrive back at the fort, reporting chaos and slaughter down below the Heights. "No place to hide," one soldier reported. "There's one brave group of Marylanders tryin' to hold back the redcoats at the mouth of the creek, but everyone else is fleein' fast as they can. There's redcoats everywhere and some soldiers in blue coats, too, some Russians or somethin'. I saw 'em capture two of our boys and then just stuck 'em fierce with their bayonets. Our boys were pleadin' for mercy, but it didn't even seem like they could understand what they was sayin'. They just kep' stickin' 'em. Blood squirtin' out everywhere. We see that and just started runnin' faster."

Through the long afternoon, things got worse and worse. Retreating troops, most without the weapons or packs they'd discarded so they could flee faster, poured into the fortifications on Brooklyn Heights. Washington rode along the lines, directing a strengthening of the defenses, expecting a momentary attack from Howe's forces. Darkness fell and the Americans dug in, peering into the blackness for signs of enemy movement, a long and grisly day behind them, a long and terrifying night ahead.

Armistead's battalion was sprawled across a cornfield within sight of the American forts. The men were exhausted and hot, but feeling the rush of energy that always follows success on the battlefield. Their plan had been faultless, their execution superb. His Majesty's Army had rarely fought with greater skill. Armistead told the officers that he was proud of them, that their King would be proud of them as well. "But," he said, "we have only begun. They're on the run and they're scared. Now we'll have to attack their fortifications before they get reinforced and recover their order from the beating we gave them today. Tell your men to rest now, but to prepare to attack again soon."

No orders had come down to Armistead, but he assumed that Howe would want to press his advantage and chase the rebels back across the river to Manhattan. He'd go after them quickly, Armistead was sure, before Washington had a chance to regroup and plot his defenses or make an effective withdrawal. So Armistead found shade under a tree, but pitched no tent.

The day passed and the sunlight faded, but no orders came. Armistead sent a rider to General Clinton who was commanding this attack. An hour later the rider returned and reported that no further attack was planned for that day. "Clinton and Vaughan seem anxious to have a go, sir," the rider said, "but Howe told them to stay put. Clinton says Howe wants to lay siege to the heights, not risk losing a lot of men in an assault."

Armistead couldn't believe what he was hearing. To no one in particular he said aloud, "An enemy on the run, and he won't pursue? Has General Gage returned to take command? Where's the Howe who sent us up Breed's Hill over and over. Now we need some of that boldness. We can end this war today if we capture Washington's army on Brooklyn Heights. This is no time for a siege. It's time to attack."

But night came and then the sunrise and then another day. And there was no attack. Aubrey Armistead cursed silently as the opportunity of a lifetime slipped slowly away.

The days passed into weeks and the Continental defense of New York grew more and more shaky. Washington realized that Brooklyn Heights was no place for his outmanned army to make a stand against the British and the Hessians. So on a foggy night Washington loaded his men into every boat they could collect along the East River shore—the mosquito fleet, one soldier called it—and withdrew to Manhattan.

The British fleet in New York harbor grew larger almost daily as Admiral Richard Howe, the General's brother, received a steady arrival of new ships from London. The Howes did not press the battle in New York, Washington finally learned, because they thought the time was right to sue for peace. They'd even gotten Germain and North to appoint them commissioners to negotiate for peace--an odd role, Washington thought, for military men. But the terms they offered to the Congress closely resembled a demand for surrender, and they found no American takers.

242

As the cooler days signaled the approach of autumn, Washington grew increasingly perplexed in his efforts to anticipate the British plans. He sat at breakfast one morning in his fine stone headquarters at Number One Broadway with Jonathan and Flint. There would be a staff meeting with the generals later that morning and Washington was weighing his own plans.

"Captain Flint made an observation last night that may be worth contemplating, General," Jonathan said, as they finished their tea.

Washington had seemed lost in thought, but he perked up and turned to Flint who sat at Jonathan's side. "What was that?" he said.

Flint leaned forward intently, struggling as always to keep his perpetually moving body in the chair. "I was thinkin', Gen'ral, that if I commanded Brooklyn Heights, and I had my big guns over there, I'd be lobbin' cannonballs over here every day. It'd shake up the troops and interfere with us strengthnin' our fortifications. But not once since they been up there has a single ball come this way. Makes me wonder if they don't see Manhattan as a perfect spot for a winter camp and they're holdin' their fire to keep the buildin's intact."

Washington smiled. "You know, I've had the same thought. The British hate to campaign in winter, and after spending last winter holed up on Boston neck, Howe may see New York as a much more promising winter camp. I assume that he'll attack some time soon to try to drive us out. Then, if he succeeds, he won't pursue. He'll simply hold his army here until spring. This harbor won't freeze and the ships can keep coming with fresh supplies."

"That won't work, if we hold Manhattan," Jonathan interjected.

"Perhaps we need to plan for both possibilities," Washington said, seeming to think aloud. "We can put our best efforts into the defenses at Fort Washington and into our positions on Harlem Heights. At the same time, we can make Manhattan a much less desirable winter camp."

"But how we gonna' do that, Gen'ral?" Flint asked. "We could burn the damn place, but the Congress already told you not to do that."

"Which shows what my friends in Philadelphia know about fighting a war," Washington quickly added. "Every chapter of military doctrine I know says you should destroy anything your enemy might want before he can get his hands on it. Destroy your guns. Blow up your ammunition. Burn your crops. Whatever it takes to keep anything valuable out of the enemy's hands. If Howe wants Manhattan for a winter camp, we should burn it down. But the Congress wants to save the city and to

243

hell with winning the war. I have to obey directives like those, of course," Washington said, rising and walking to the window where he looked up Broadway at the long row of handsome houses, "but I sure wouldn't rush out the fire brigades if I should smell smoke some night."

It was nearly midnight and Godfrey Carter was ecstatic. This was the life, he thought. Big gambles, big payoffs. Three nights earlier, a Loyalist boatman from Ten Eyck Wharf had rowed him out through the dark mist to the flagship of the admiral of the fleet. There he'd met personally with Black Dick Howe to discuss the sale of a large store of powder and ordnance which he said he could "procure quite quickly from a reliable supplier." Howe had demanded the personal meeting because he didn't trust Americans, even though his quartermaster said he'd dealt with Carter before and he always delivered the goods.

After an hour or so of negotiation and a bottle of port, Howe and Carter closed the deal. The British would take possession of the contents of his warehouse basement as soon as they drove Washington's army from the island. It was the biggest sale Carter had ever made and he was about to become richer than he'd ever dreamed. The contract was now ready and, as he and Howe had agreed, Drouin, his clerk, would go to the steeple of Trinity Church and light a lantern to signal that Carter was ready to return to Howe's ship the following night with documents ready for signing.

Drouin had been drawing up the contracts all day. Carter perused them closely, made a few minor changes and then instructed Drouin to carry out the plan at Trinity Church. Carter called down to his driver to prepare his chaise as the clerk departed. Time enough yet, Carter thought for a stop at the house off Maiden Lane.

Drouin moved carefully through the night. A stiff breeze from the south was blowing through the dark streets and it felt unusually warm for mid-September. Continental soldiers and sentries were everywhere. He wasn't carrying any papers this night, but he still practiced caution. You never knew what a drunken soldier would do if he caught a civilian sneaking through the streets late at night, especially one with an Irish accent.

As Drouin crossed into the shadows of Broadway, he noticed something strange. There was a large wagon in front of Trinity Church and three men dressed in plain clothes were carrying something inside. He slid closer along the line of houses to the left and could see that the wagon was full of hay and the men were carrying armloads of it inside, then returning for more. They made barely a sound, moving very efficiently, as if carrying out some well-rehearsed performance.

It made no sense to Drouin. So many Loyalists had abandoned New York when Washington came last spring that some of the churches were now being used to house soldiers. A few had even been transformed into stables. But not Trinity Church, the greatest of all Manhattan's churches and the symbol of the Anglican faith. Even Washington worshipped here. So why were these men bringing hay inside now? And why in the middle of the night?

The clerk stood still and watched until the wagon was emptied of all its hay. Then the three men came out and closed the door behind them. One of them said to the man at the reins, loud enough for Drouin to hear, "The deed is done, Cap'n!" The man at the reins laughed loudly and responded "Praise be to the Lord, boys!" Then the others climbed into the wagon and it drew quickly away. Confused, but anxious to accomplish his own purpose, Drouin moved quietly toward the church door. He stopped to look around and saw no one. Then he slowly pushed the heavy oak door open and slipped inside.

If he ever made his way to Hell, thought Drouin, it would look like this. Hay was strewn the full length of the church aisle and it was burning rapidly. Several of the pews were also blazing and the robes around the altar were all afire. The linen drapes along the walls were seething with flame and the vault of the church was filled with dense, black smoke. It felt like an oven and Drouin could feel his own flesh start to sear. He looked at the horrible sight for no more than a few seconds, then pulled open the door and dashed out into the street.

He ran along Broadway looking back over his shoulder to see that the flames had broken through the roof where the strong southerly breeze was pulling them down toward the row of houses to the north. The steeple would soon be gone, he was sure. As he turned onto Broad Street, racing now, having abandoned any thought of stealth, he saw that three houses at the south end of the street were also burning and the flames were consuming all the others in their northward path.

A few more minutes in search of an escape route and Drouin came to realize that much of Manhattan was caught up in one massive conflagration. It was as bright as noon from the combined luminescence of all the separate flames. Here and there as well, Drouin saw groups of three or four men, standing by, watching the swirling fires, making no attempt to douse the flames. He was by now utterly confused and very terrified. Then the worst terror of all struck him. The warehouse!

If these flames got to the warehouse, they'd set off the gunpowder there with who-could-imagine-what effect. All of Manhattan might blow up. Ships in the harbor might be knocked out of the water. Drouin himself might be killed.

He decided that the most important thing in the world right now was to find Godfrey Carter and figure out what to do. Mr. Carter always seemed to have an answer for everything, an escape from every trap. He'd figure something out, Drouin was sure.

The years of working for Carter equipped Drouin with full knowledge of his employer's habits. He knew Carter was an indifferent husband who rarely mentioned his wife except as a problem needing a solution; and, while he knew that Celia was expecting a baby soon, he'd only once heard Carter mention it when he was telling an acquaintance why he couldn't get her to leave the city. He knew that Carter's real affection was for a mysterious and disreputable woman who ran an illicit trade in a place called the Yellow Palace. Drouin had been sent there a few times to bring her gifts on Carter's behalf because Carter did not want to be seen on that street in daylight. Drouin thought it likely that Carter was there now, and headed for Maiden Lane.

Most of the fires, Drouin now determined, were burning along the west side of lower Manhattan. Maiden Lane was far enough away that he could neither see the flames or hear any commotion when he reached the steps of the notorious Number 14. Drouin was not a man who frequented prostitutes and the thought of it filled him with dread. Sexual relations with his wife, who disliked them, were burden enough; he couldn't imagine performing with a woman who enjoyed the act. So when a stout matron in heavy rouge came to the door and let him in, he spoke with great economy. "I need to see Mr. Carter. It's very important."

"No one 'ere by the name o' Carter," the woman replied, giving the standard response.

"I know he's here. Get him now." Drouin screeched in growing impatience.

The woman pivoted and waddled away, leaving Drouin enveloped in a cloud of cheap perfume.

No more than two minutes later, Godfrey Carter came rushing down the stairs, pulling on his clothes as he moved, aflame with anger.

"What are you doing here, Drouin? What's the meaning of this?"

"Sorry, sir. But there's a fire sweeping over the island and I was worried about the warehouse. I thought you should know."

"A fire? What fire?"

"Trinity Church, sir. And houses. Dozens of houses."

"My house, Drouin? What about my house?"

"Don't know, sir. Haven't been up that far. But everything's aroastin' on the west side."

A stricken look came over Carter. Should he go to the warehouse or to his home? Celia and was at home and their baby was due any day now. But his fortune was in the warehouse. Suddenly the image of a massive explosion formed in his mind, and his decision was made. "Call the driver around from back. Let's get to the warehouse."

"Faster if we go on foot, sir. Fire everywhere. It'll terrify the horse."

Carter finished tucking in his shirt, and the two men sped out the door and down Maiden Lane toward Smith Street. As they ran, Drouin thought again about the devastation and loss of life that would happen if the fire reached the warehouse. That thought never crossed Godfrey Carter's mind.


Celia sat gingerly in the chair by the bedroom window. It was the first time she'd been out of bed since the birth of Godfrey Houghton Carter two days ago. She was beginning to recover from the long ordeal and it felt good to be free from the prison of her bed.

The wet nurse brought the baby into the room and placed him in Celia's arms. He was barely awake after nursing and he seemed so peaceful as Celia gazed down now on his rosy forehead. What a time to bring a baby into the world, she thought. When he was born on the afternoon of September twenty-first, the city was still smoldering from the horrible fire of the night before. Nearly a third of the houses in Manhattan had burned to the ground, including those of some of her best friends, houses where she and Godfrey had attended balls and gay dinners. It filled her with such sadness.

Her labor had started in the middle of the night, shortly after Captain Flint came and said something to Jonathan about the bright flame of liberty. She'd had trouble sleeping and had overheard their conversation in the hall. Captain Flint came here often and they were always talking about liberty and independence. Jonathan left after that and had not come back for hours. When he did, Celia had begun her long labor. Jonathan fetched the midwife, who lived nearby. Godfrey had not come home that night and Jonathan went to find him. But he never did. Nor has he since. She filled with dread. A new baby in the world and his father nowhere to be found. And the awful fire. She didn't want to try to connect those things in her mind.

She just thought about the precious little body in her arms. After six years, after three miscarriages, after Godfrey's cruel accusations that she was incapable of bearing them a child, now she had. And what a fine child it was. The first Houghton grandchild. She couldn't wait for her mother to see him, though she knew that would not happen for a while with this terrible war. But Savannah had promised she would come if there was any way possible to get to New York. Celia knew she would. When her little sister made a promise, she kept it.

Having Jonathan with them for the past few months had made her long for her family. Jonathan stood so erect in his uniform and seemed so competent about everything. Men came to see him here all day long and they all saluted when they saw him. How much he reminded her of Father.

She thought often of Father. What trials he's enduring, she thought. Stuck so much of the time in Philadelphia with everyone squabbling now about starting a new government. Mother sick at home and Savannah trying to manage the farm. Nathaniel away for years in England; what dangers must he face there? And Jonathan a soldier.

Celia remembered the last holidays the family spent together before she met Godfrey. It was 1769. It had been such a good year on the farm with plenty of rain and no pests. Timber prices were up, and everything they could cut was sawed at the mill or put on ships for London. They'd just come back from the New Year's feast at Balfour's and they were all sitting by the fire getting warm before retiring. Celia had asked them all to say what they'd like to be doing in ten years. She'd forgotten what the others had said, even forgotten what she'd said. But she would never forget what Father said: "Exactly what I'm doing at this minute. Sitting by a warm fire on this blessed old farm with all my wonderful sons and daughters."

Celia reached down with the sleeve of her dress and dried the tear that had fallen on the face of her wonderful son.

# Chapter 17

## London
## October 1776

"So, Benton, I imagine this war with the colonies has been an unexpected boon to your business." Lord Twickenham had been one of Carlisle's first subjects when he began painting portraits and they'd been friends ever since. Not tell-me-all-your-troubles friends, but more never-a-serious-word-between-us friends. Men friends. Twickenham only talked to Carlisle about the business side of painting, never about the artistic side. He never let Carlisle forget that, for all his protests about the agony of portrait painting compared to the satisfactions of landscapes and still lifes, it was the former that was making him rich and famous.

"Really," Twickenham continued, "when we're at war, the bastards at Whitehall feel they have to get their portraits painted every few months just so the rest of us will picture them hard at work. And the King's patience is so thin, he keeps rolling them in and out of office. So every time there's a sacking and a new appointment, the cry goes out: 'Painter! Painter!'" He put down his glass and laughed heartily at his own images. "I guess that makes you a war profiteer, Benton."

As always at these dinners of the gentry, Nathaniel hung at the edge of the conversation, silent and unaddressed. He was always amused by Twickenham, and he had to admit that the man had a point. Since the news arrived in August of the American Declaration of Independence, London had changed. In a sense, London was always at war. With colonies so far-flung and a Navy that was the mightiest military force on earth, England was always contesting with someone for something. Every street corner in the realm, every church vestry, every quayside, every cemetery, every village square bore a marker or monument that told the tale of Britons at war in some distant and exotic place: Culloden or Zierenberg or Mainz or Gibraltar.

But the war with America was different--so Nathaniel perceived and so the older men at these dinners said. America was the crown jewel of the British empire, they said. Lose America and the trouble will really start. One-by-one all the colonies will push for independence. Then what will we be? A third-rate power confined to a tiny island in a chilly ocean. No tea, no rum, no timber, no cotton, no tobacco. All those goods that we import from our colonies will fall out of our control and probably out of our reach.

No, they all said. Can't let that happen. We must fight the American rebels as we've never fought before. It won't be easy because they're not savages or darkies or heathens. They're like us in so many ways, and it's harder to kill those who speak your language and practice your religion and share your ancestry. But, damn their souls, we simply can't let them get away with their insolence and their disrespect for our King and our authority. There's too much at stake.

So London was at war in a way it had not been for a long time. And one of the effects of that, as Twickenham clearly noted, was strong demand in the portrait business. There were more generals and admirals, more junior lords of the admiralty, more members of Parliament seeking commissions. All needed a handsome portrait as testimony to their fitness for these positions of honor and note. And, of course, in Windsor Castle sat—or perhaps, Nathaniel thought with a sly smile, one should say lay— the most fertile monarch in royal history. George III and his dear wife Charlotte had already produced eleven children and they continued to come, like the seasons, every year or so.

So the roads to Windsor were worn to dust by the carriages of portrait painters coming and going. All of the little princes and princesses—George, Frederick, William, Charlotte, Edward, Augusta, Elizabeth and on and on--needed to be painted at every birthday and every celebration of a new title. And then the King seemed compelled to have a family portrait painted in every room of the castle.

So, yes, Twickenham was right. The portrait business had never been healthier. And Benton Carlisle had been one of its principal beneficiaries. Tomorrow, they would start on Lord North himself, the first minister. After that, seven commissions were queued up, waiting for Benton's brush. Though the steady flow of work tired him now and though he still professed his disdain for portraits as an art form, Carlisle kept at it. No man is immune to the lusty charms of Dame Fame, not even one so emotionally secure as Benton Carlisle.

250

The boom in the portrait business was a boon to Nathaniel, as well. In two ways. As Carlisle grew less patient with the details of painting portraits, he was shifting more and more of the brush work to Nathaniel. In the early days, Carlisle would paint the face and body of the subjects and Nathaniel would simply fill in the broad colors of rugs and draperies and other background elements. Then Carlisle began to let Nathaniel work on hands and clothing details. Now, more and more, Carlisle would sketch as well as paint during the sittings, then back at the studio Nathaniel would work on all but the most complicated details of eyes or mouth or hair. Nathaniel took this show of confidence seriously and felt his own skills steadily growing.

But there was more. With Carlisle securing so many commissions to paint members of the royal family, senior officials in government, and high-ranking military officers, Nathaniel had more access to valuable intelligence about the war effort than he could have ever imagined. Ministers and officers were busier than ever. They couldn't shut down the flow of affairs for hours on end while they sat for their portraits. So it was business as usual while Benton and Nathaniel went about their work in silence. State papers were left openly on desks before them. Maps on large tables showed the location of the fleet or the movement of armies. Nathaniel was already familiar with the names of many of the crack regiments of the British Army—the King's 8th Regiment, the 43rd Highlanders, the 37th Foot—and he'd heard so much third-party discussion about their strengths and foibles that he felt himself an intimate acquaintance of the Howe brothers and Lord Cornwallis and Johnny Burgoyne and Henry Clinton.

George, Nathaniel's contact in the Alliance, showed him great respect and for good reason. Nathaniel was a gold mine. He was smart and clever. He had steady and reliable access to important information. He was almost immune from suspicion—who would have ever thought of a painter's assistant as a spy. And now that the sides had become so clearly drawn, now that his father had taken the side of independence, now that his brother was an officer in the Continental Army, now that his sister was in the center of the field of fire in New York, now that all justification for neutrality or indifference had evaporated, Nathaniel's commitment to their cause was growing stronger every day. When Benton's portrait business boomed, the espionage business did as well.

"Have you heard what the Earl of Rochford is saying about the fighting in New York?" Twickenham's voice interrupted Nathaniel's thoughts, and he looked up to see the tall, shambling bear of a man with his arm around Carlisle, pointing his glass toward the wigged figure standing by the marble fireplace at the end of the library. They moved in that direction and Nathaniel followed along.

The Earl was then Secretary of State for the Southern Division and he was sharing news that had just arrived by boat that afternoon. "It shows what amateurs they really are," Rochford was saying as the three moved into the range of his voice. "Howe had taken several weeks to get his troops ready for an assault. Washington apparently believed that Howe only knew one strategy, the one he'd used in Charlestown to attack that bloody hill by the bay, and that he'd use that again as soon as he determined where the colonials were entrenched. So Washington fortified a place called Brooklyn Heights, across the river from the town, and just waited there for Howe's attack.

"Of course, New York is crawling with good citizens loyal to their king and Howe's spies gave him the details of everything Washington was up to. When he'd determined where Washington had his regiments placed, Howe sent his men upriver to flank the colonials and caught them from the side and the rear. What do you suppose happened then?" The Earl of Rochford was clearly enjoying his role as The-One-With-The-Information, and he paused to allow a moment of speculation. Men looked at each other in delicious anticipation.

"The colonials saw what was coming, took a terrible fright, threw down their weapons and ran. Howe's report said his own men could hardly pursue because of all the discarded guns and packs along the pathways. They chased them all the way back to their fort on the Heights. Howe was sure Washington was waiting to lure him into another attack on a fortified position on a hilltop, but he avoided their trap. He put them under siege and a few days later, Washington withdrew in a fright under cover of darkness. Howe says it was quite a sight to see those terrified colonials rowing across the river in every scow and tub they could commandeer." He took a sip of his brandy, then smiled a broad and satisfied smile.

"What now, my lord? Has Washington's so-called army scattered back to their farms?" Everyone laughed at the image of terrified colonials running full-tilt across the land to avoid the specter of waves of trained infantry in steady pursuit.

"Not quite." Rochford said. "Washington did manage to regroup some of them on Manhattan where he has a small fort and some defensive works. But Howe has a plan to drive him off the main island of the city and occupy it. In fact, he hopes to make winter camp there. With so many houses and so good a harbor, he thinks it a capital place to prepare for the final attack in the spring."

"Much better than Boston last winter, I'm sure," said one of the others, to knowing laughter.

"But won't Washington try to burn the city before he leaves," asked Twickenham. "Isn't that what any sensible commander would do?"

"Not very likely," responded Rochford. Howe was wise enough not to burn Boston when he left, and he thinks that now stands as a rule of engagement: Englishmen are fighting each other and they will not burn English cities. He also doubts that Washington would have leave from his Congress to burn so large a city, and they control the finances that keep his army alive. In any case, he hopes to catch Washington by surprise before a fire can be started.

"It's not out of the question gentlemen that this rebellion could end before the year is out. If Howe can destroy Washington's army in the field, or crush the morale of his troops, there'll be no one left to pursue the rebellion. They'll have to tear up their ridiculous Declaration of Independence before the ink has even dried. They will have learned a very hard lesson—that the sword is a damn sight mightier than the pen!"

"Now," Twickenham said, to the hearty agreement of those around him, "there's a truth that is self-evident."

Nathaniel liked to walk on these splendid autumn mornings, but Carlisle protested that the distance was too great for his "ancient legs." So they had fallen into this habit. Carlisle would hire a sedan chair carried by two strong boys, while Nathaniel walked along beside him. This way one could walk, one could ride, and they could converse the entire way.

They were on their way to paint Frederick, Lord North, a very important commission indeed. North was a stickler for punctuality and they had left early enough to arrive in plenty of time to set up for the sitting that was scheduled to begin at nine o'clock. But there was a loud commotion just ahead of them as they came upon Charing Cross. A handful of soldiers stood in tentative command of a much larger group of scruffy and ill-tempered men.

The soldiers had long rifles with bayonets and were attempting to herd the men into some kind of line or rank. But the men clearly lacked enthusiasm for whatever it was they were being encouraged to do. The road was blocked while the soldiers continued to try to impose some order on their sorry charges, so the boys lowered Carlisle's sedan chair to the ground and waited. Carlisle beckoned to the boy in front, "Is this a prison detail?" The boy gave him a blank look.

"Run and see if you can find out what's happening here," Carlisle instructed the boy, who ran off toward the crowd that had gathered to watch. A few minutes later he returned and said to Carlisle, "Man in the crowd says it's an impressment gang, that this is what they rounded up from public houses around Smithfield Market and at Newgate Prison."

Nathaniel was listening in on this, and asked Carlisle, "What's an impressment gang, Benton? It looks more like the soldiers have captured some prisoners."

Carlisle laughed. "Well, in a sense they have. Impressment gangs are sent out whenever recruitment for the Army falls too low. They have a quota, and nobody asks many questions about where they get the men to fill it. Tradition is they go to the dramshops and round up the drunks. They're in the Army before they even sober up. And then they go to the prisons and offer the prisoners a commutation of their sentences in exchange for joining the Army. So that's what's happening here. These soldiers are an impressment gang and this is what they swept up."

Nathaniel looked on in amazement as the bedraggled and dirty men began to line up and struggled to stand at attention, a posture with which most seemed decidedly unfamiliar.

"I hope this hasn't spoiled your impression of the elite soldiers of His Majesty's Army," Carlisle said with a broad smile. The soldiers and their recruits began to march off, after a fashion, and the way cleared for Carlisle and Nathaniel to move on to their appointment.

Soon they were in the largest and richest of all the offices they'd seen in Whitehall, a relic of the time when this fine old palace had been the home of the Kings of England. Heavy drapes of green silk bordered the tall windows. A Persian carpet, more than thirty feet long and nearly as wide, covered the center of the marble floor. Fireplaces decorated in intricate mosaic patterns stood at each end of the room, casting some small warmth on this unusually cool October morning. Three tables, apparent victors in some ancient contest of classical wood carvers, filled the center of the room. Each was covered with a map or account books or neat stacks of paper and parchment. Quills and inkstands stood at the ready.

In the rare moments when he sat still for the artist, Lord North posed on a low-backed, dark oak chair cushioned in rich red brocade. But he rarely sat for more than a few moments at a time, popping up frequently to meet with his busy schedule of appointments or to stand before the largest of the maps, the one of the Middle Colonies in America on which the positions and movements of his armies had been traced.

Yesterday a visitor whom neither Carlisle nor Nathaniel recognized had complimented the first minister on the detail of his maps. North had cursed and said it was comforting to ministers to look at maps like these but they were all useless. The information they had was never less than six weeks old, and it took about the same amount of time to get orders to his commanders in the field and at sea. There was only so much London could do in running a campaign, he'd said, because the flow of information was so damned slow. "Germain and I are trying to give the Howes their instructions now that they have a foothold in New York. But, for all we know, Washington may have already surrendered. Or perhaps he escaped and he's on his way back to Boston. It's a constant frustration to wait so long for news."

Today North seemed more placid than normal and Carlisle was deep in concentration, taking advantage of the extended sitting. North was a challenge of the sort that portrait artists often faced. He was a homely man, well past whatever physical prime he might once have had. He had puffy lips and several chins and bulging eyes that gave him a perpetually frightened appearance. Yet, as always, the subject saw himself differently and expected a portrait that would be both a keen and recognizable likeness and yet also a glorification of a famous man. Painting portraits of politicians, Carlisle had once said, was like trying to lie and tell the truth in the same sentence. That was the challenge they faced this morning.

Carlisle seemed to be struggling especially with Lord North's eyes, the feature that dominated his appearance yet also destroyed any sense of symmetry and order in his face. Nathaniel had noticed in other recent portraits he'd done that Carlisle seemed to be losing some of his confidence about capturing the eyes and mouths of his subjects. He'd begun to ask Nathaniel to do some sketching himself during the sittings and back at the studio he'd sometimes make changes based on Nathaniel's sketches. He even had Nathaniel take the brush to do the eyes of Georgiana, the Duchess of Devonshire, and had applauded what he'd called a "perfect capture."

So he was working very slowly on Lord North's eyes this morning and looking grim as he did. Nathaniel sat quietly behind Carlisle, sketching with a pen. Just then, the porter entered and announced the arrival of George Germain. North started to stand, but Carlisle pleaded for "Two more minutes, sir?" and North granted it.

When Germain entered, North was still seated so the visitor walked around behind the artist and looked first at North then at the emerging portrait. Carlisle hated this viewing of a work in progress and usually banned it. But in the office of the First Minister of His Majesty's Government, in the great Palace of Whitehall, he felt more restrained than normal and said nothing. Germain looked back and forth between the portrait and the subject for nearly a minute. Then to the evident delight of Lord North, he said, "Our wise King has certainly placed our fate in the hands of a very fine looking man, Frederick. He may well want this portrait himself to hang in the great chamber at Windsor."

North was unsure whether Germain was joking or merely being his usual patronizing self. "Thank you for those words, George," he said. "But I'm sure it's not art criticism that brought you here this morning."

"No, Frederick, it's criticism of generals and admirals instead."

"Ah, the usual then, is it?" said North.

"General Howe's report indicates his intention to drive Washington from New York, then make camp there for the winter. Damned Howe has always believed that the armies of civilized countries don't campaign in winter. But the winter in the Middle Colonies is rarely very severe and it would be a terrible mistake to let Washington regroup his forces after he's been so badly beaten in New York. We have to order Howe to chase Washington until he's caught him and beaten him."

North nodded at Carlisle and rose from the chair. He tugged briefly on his stocking and smoothed his breeches, then took Germain's arm, leading him to the center table. There North picked up a long round stick and began to point at the map. Nathaniel could not see the map from where he sat but quickly realized it was the one of the Middle Colonies.

"I don't disagree with that," said North. "Defeating Washington's army must be the prime objective. But we also must remember that we're in a political struggle there, as well. Look here."

North moved his stick toward the southern end of New Jersey. "If Washington retreats into New Jersey, as our spies indicate he's likely to do, he will be moving toward Philadelphia. I think that capturing Philadelphia should be an objective for Howe second only to defeating

Washington. If he can do that, we will have driven the colonial government from its seat, taken the largest city in America, and struck a terrible blow to colonial morale. With their army on the run and in disarray, with New York and Philadelphia occupied by our army, and with their Congress who knows where, most of the colonials are going to begin to see how hopeless their cause has become."

Germain studied the map closely as North spoke. Nathaniel leaned back in his chair, listening carefully and no longer sketching. Yet his pen still moved as he made cryptic notes on the conversation he was overhearing at the map table.

"I think you're right, Frederick," said Germain after considering North's words. "That's an excellent thought, in fact. Philadelphia is well within Howe's sights, and if our intelligence is accurate, he should be able to capture the city while simultaneously pursuing Washington. If Washington still has an army to lead away from New York."

"If we're in agreement on this, we must secure the King's enthusiasm. That will weigh heavily with Howe, as you know. And we can't let him take his army into winter camp. Not now, there's too much at stake. The opportunities are too ripe. So we have to get word to him as quickly as possible before he's settled into New York society for the winter."

Germain left with instructions from North to draw up orders for the Howes. North said he would make an appointment to see the King as soon as the papers were ready. And he told Germain as he left to secure a fast ship to get those orders to New York before the winter storms took control of the shipping lanes. Then, as if the fates of thousands of men had not just been sealed here in this opulent London room, North returned to his chair and the business of his glorification.

Carlisle's fatigue got the best of him, as it usually did, around ten o'clock in the evening. Nathaniel, still working on the last few broad strokes of the Duchess of Devonshire, sat on a bench in front of the large portrait wearing a smock with sleeves rolled up. Lydie was reading in the chair by the fire that she now occupied almost nightly when her husband and his assistant were working in the studio. Carlisle scrubbed the last daubs of paint from his hands, walked to his wife and kissed her gently on the cheek, then said goodnight to them both.

"He seems to tire much more easily now than he used to," Lydie said, pulling her chair closer to Nathaniel's bench. He seemed ageless for so long, but now time seems to be catching up with him."

"I've noticed that a little as well," said Nathaniel, "but he's still such a masterful craftsman that his work is as good as ever. Look at this portrait. Here's one of the most beautiful and admired women of our time, the object of every gentleman's desire. It is so hard to paint a legendary beauty because everyone already has a romanticized image of her. But Benton has created a likeness that is entirely accurate, yet makes her look even more beautiful than most people will have imagined. I daresay this may survive as his most famous portrait. Of course, that depends in part of what becomes of the Duchess."

"Yes," said Lydie, moving her face close to Nathaniel's to get a better look at the portrait. "I hear that she is—oh how shall I put this?— exceedingly generous with her affections." They both laughed.

These times with Lydie, after Carlisle had retired for the night, had become the highlights of Nathaniel's days. He was regularly in the company of members of the royal family and famous people now, his talents were improving steadily and he'd begun to sell some of his small paintings. He had a secret life of danger and excitement. But nothing compared with the minutes he spent with Lydie. The way her eyes turned to emerald when she smiled, the melodic rhythm that pulsed through him when she laughed, the electric sensation he felt when her swishing skirts brushed against him: this was the magic in his days, not the proximity to princes and ministers and harlequins.

Each night it seemed their conversation became more intimate, their bodies more proximate. Nathaniel had no doubt about what he was feeling. He sensed that Lydie felt the same. Yet they were separated by a curtain of commitment to Benton Carlisle who loomed so large and so treasured in both their lives. And as their attraction grew, so too did the guilt that accompanied it. The unspoken covenant between them was this: only by avoiding corporal expression of their feelings for each other could they cage the monstrous guilt it would bring.

Yet even that covenant looked fragile as their attraction grew stronger and more resistant to denial. Lydie would have to strike the first blow—both sensed that—and she did. As they sat, nearly side-by-side, admiring the portrait of the beautiful Georgiana, drawn in to its libertine sensuality, Lydie gently placed her hand on Nathaniel's. He felt the warmth like a jolt, but did not move. Slowly Lydie began to stroke the back of his hand and then his uncovered forearm. Then she moved her fingers to his face and softly moved them across his cheek.

Nathaniel could sit calmly no longer. He turned to face her, and without conscious direction their lips met in a sweet, pliant moment of exploration. Soon their bodies were locked in a deep embrace that seemed eternal--until the pendulum clock by the studio door began to chime the hour of ten o'clock and Nathaniel was transported jarringly back to earth and England and London and the war of rebellion. He withdrew from his entwinement and rose to his feet, somewhat embarrassed at the obvious evidence of his passion.

He looked down at Lydie, placed his hand lightly on her shoulder and said, "Please forgive me. I've nearly forgotten something very important and I must go now."

Lydie was startled by the sudden change of direction and stammered briefly. "I don't understand," she said. "It's ten o'clock. Why must you leave so quickly now?"

"I'm sorry," Nathaniel said, buttoning his linen waistcoat and reaching for his cape. "I can't tell you more than that. But I must go. I shall see you tomorrow night." With that, Nathaniel strode across the studio and exited quickly through the door to the street behind the mews.

Lydie sat, startlingly alone, overcome by the strangely shifting emotions of the previous moments. First, she had found herself in Nathaniel's strong embrace, surrendering blissfully to the passion that had been building in her for months. Then, in an instant, Nathaniel was gone and the bliss was shattered. She started to cry.

Perhaps this is a terrible thing, she thought. We can't do this to Benton. But it's more than that. We can't do it to ourselves. Maybe that's what happened to Nathaniel. He experienced, as I did, the full heat of our erupted emotions and he realized how quickly all restraint could melt away. At least he had the sense, which I lacked, to stop in time, before we did something we would have truly regretted. He's right, of course. This flirtation has gone too far. Now we must stop. Before we destroy a man we both love. Before we destroy each other.

Nathaniel ran down Southampton Street to the wash house on High Holbourn. There he lit a match and held it above the hinge to the second door. Freshly carved in the gray wood was the number 3. So he ran to the east and made several more turns until he entered Rose Alley off Eagle Street and slid along the dark west wall, counting the doorways as he went. At the fifth door, he knocked twice, paused for three seconds, then knocked twice again. The door opened into a dark room and Nathaniel stepped quickly inside.

"Are you Charles?" Nathaniel asked softly.

"No, I'm George," a disembodied voice responded. "The curtain was closed in your window. What is it?"

"North and Germain are sending orders to Howe to capture Philadelphia before winter, whether they defeat Washington or not. They think it will have a devastating effect on American morale if Philadelphia falls. Howe wants to go into camp in New York as soon as the city is secure. But they want him to pursue Washington and try to get into Philadelphia before the end of the year."

"When will the orders go?"

"As soon as possible. North told Germain to draw up the papers and get a fast ship ready. But he has to see the King first to get him to acquiesce. It'll probably all take a couple of days."

"Good. Then we have a chance to beat them. Pray for fair winds. Now go."

The door was opened by an unseen hand and Nathaniel slipped back into the alley. He retraced his steps to Eagle Street, then turned right and started to walk slowly to his lodging. Only then did he begin to review in his mind the precious moments with Lydie that were now seared so vividly into his memory.

# Chapter 18

## New York
## New Jersey
## Autumn 1776

Celia was learning that in war one had to find solace in little things. So as her carriage passed along Nassau Street then up John Street and along Broadway, she found herself enjoying the silence. It wasn't a perfect silence, of course. The Continentals had left the city, but the sharp echoes of exploding artillery occasionally swept down from skirmishing to the north. The British troops drilling in the streets and squares could also fill the air with their crisp cadences. But most of the time Manhattan was quieter than it had been since the Continentals arrived in the spring.

So there was one thing at least to be happy about. But only one. Everything else, Celia thought, seemed terrible. The awful fire had destroyed so much that New York would never look the same. Everywhere she passed charred ugly hulks of what had once been fine houses or lovely shops. Many of her friends had lost their homes and been forced to move in with neighbors or leave the city entirely. Today was the first in more than a month that a group of women had been able to get together for tea and whist. But she barely knew some of them.

When the carriage stopped in front of the Kyper house, things looked much the same there as they always had, and Celia was pleased. The fire had missed this part of the city and the Americans had not quartered here. But as she stepped down from the carriage and approached the house on foot, Celia quickly noticed three British soldiers in their flashing red uniforms leaving the large stone house next door. They gave her a brief admiring look then moved off. It pleased Celia when men looked at her that way, especially now after so many months of being pregnant and feeling frumpy. My looks must be coming back, she thought happily.

The houseman took her wool wrap and led her into the Kyper's parlor, one of her favorite New York rooms with curved indigo walls, deep blue rugs, and a gleaming silver chandelier. She was pleased to see it untouched by the war. She greeted the other women and sat in one of the rosewood Hepplewhite chairs near the fire. Anna Kyper apologized for the low fire, telling the familiar tale of her difficulties in getting any firewood in these times.

Tea was served and quickly the talk turned to all the dreadful changes taking place in the city. A large woman with flaming red hair, someone Celia had never met, described the burning of her house. "The soldiers were devils," she said. "They smashed our windows and threw torches through them. Then they stood back, whooping and hollering, admiring their work. I stood in the street with all four children crying, and they paid no attention. I shouted at them that we were on their side, that we were patriots, but they looked at us with hatred in their eyes. 'Everyone's the enemy now,' one of them said to me. Then they lit more torches and went off to burn the Flemming house across the street. It was just a terrible, terrible nightmare. Now we're all living with my sister, crowded into her little house on Warren street."

The women all murmured in sympathy and looked compassionately on the red-haired woman. Then Henrietta Astor, one of Celia's best friends, spoke. "We were more fortunate. The men with the torches came up Church Street, burning all the houses as they came. The wind was whipping the flames into the air, and it was terrifying. James and I and the older children were trying to carry our most valuable things into the street, but we could only carry a few things out and the children were too scared to be much help. Then, as the fires started three houses down, some British sailors came into the street with guns and stopped the men with torches. Until this point, we'd thought it was the British doing the burning. Then we realized it was Continentals.

"The sailors surrounded the Continentals and began poking at them with their long rifles. Then, with hardly a word, they threw a rope over a big tree by the corner of Barclay Street. The sailor in charge placed a loop over the head of one of the men who'd been burning houses and the another sailor yanked on the rope. Suddenly, the man was several feet off the ground and he was writhing in a frenzy at the end of the rope. Finally, he just stopped and drooped. They lowered him down, and did exactly the same to the other two."

"Oh my God, Henrietta," one of the others interrupted. "How could you bear to watch?"

"It all happened so fast, it took a minute to recognize what I was seeing. Then I realized our house had probably been saved and—oh, I'm ashamed to say this—I cheered and hugged James. It didn't seem like humans they were hanging from that tree. We certainly didn't have any sense of who was a soldier or sailor of the king and who was fighting for independence. It was just some men intent on burning down my house and some other men who stopped them from doing it. Politics just evaporates when your home and family are threatened like that."

The women all sat silently for a few minutes as they tried to absorb the horror of the scene Henrietta Astor had just described. The houseman brought more tea, and then Celia thought to ask Anna Kypers about the soldiers she'd seen next door.

"Oh," Anna replied, "they've been coming around surveying all our houses. Walking through all the floors, counting the rooms, and looking closely at the pantries and kitchens. We think they intend to quarter soldiers here and they're trying to see how many can fit in each house."

"It's already happening," one of the others, another stranger to Celia, added angrily. "They came last week and six soldiers moved into my house. They made all my children move into one room and threw the servants from their quarters. We're prisoners now in our own house. They come and go at all hours. Some nights they come home terribly drunk. They play loud, crude card games in the parlor where the children can hear them and they eat when they want with no concern at all about us. Words are rarely exchanged, and mostly we glare at each other. It's the most dreadful thing you can imagine. I've been loyal to the King through all this, even when the Continentals were roaming the city. But these soldiers in my house, I hate them." The last few words barely passed her lips before she started to cry. Several of the others gathered around to comfort her. Tears fell from their eyes as well.

Several of the other women told their own stories of the travails of quartering British troops. More than half the women there had soldiers living in their houses and others expected they would soon. It reminded Celia of the terrible summer of her youth when the termites got into their house in Delaware and nearly ate away its underpinnings before winter came and disaster was averted. Soldiers were not termites, of course, but their takeover of so many New York houses felt like an infestation nonetheless.

Winter was coming in New York, and things would only get worse. All of the women believed that the British would make their winter camp in Manhattan and that all the houses would be filled with soldiers in garrison. And a soldier in garrison, they'd all come to learn from their experience with the Continentals, was loud, frustrated, hungry, crude, thieving, drunken, and filthy. The prospect filled them with a dread that was not relieved by Celia's attempt to lighten the mood: "Let's pray for an early spring."

Every day the sadness came. Celia could do nothing to curb it. From the moment her eyes opened in the morning, she awaited the knock on the door. Every night, her dreams were populated with men in red coats climbing all over her beautiful house. She couldn't bear to look out the window for fear she'd see them coming up the walk.

Yet, it was almost mid-November now and none had come. She was sure they would, that they had just missed her in some soon-to-be-corrected oversight. When they did come, she felt certain, they'd make up for lost time. When Godfrey was home, he always assured her that they would be spared, that soldiers would not be quartered at their house. She inquired about the source of his confidence, and he would answer only with his enigmatic "God works in mysterious ways." But she didn't believe that. Everyone she knew now had British soldiers living in their houses. Surely, any day now, they would come storming in here.

So the knock on the door gave her a terrible fright early one evening as she sat by the fire. She had kept the house dark, hoping to avoid any notice, and no lantern was lit in front. She walked trembling to the door. She knew it wasn't Godfrey because he would never knock. Friends didn't visit at this hour, especially not now with the curfew. And no one she knew would send a messenger at night. So it must be the men looking for sleeping quarters for the soldiers.

It took a second for the relief to set in when she opened the door and saw before her, not a British quartermaster, but the smiling sweet face of Jonathan Houghton. She threw herself into his arms and hugged him hard, surprising Jonathan with the intensity of her delight at his arrival. He had, after all, been living with Celia and Godfrey for months until the withdrawal of most Continental troops from Manhattan in late September. "What was that all about?" asked Jonathan.

"Oh, I was so sure you were one of the British coming to tell me that soldiers were going to start living in my house. I live in deadly fear that any moment now they'll come marching in," Celia answered.

"I watched your house from the hedge across the street for several hours before I came to the door. I assumed you would have soldiers quartered here and I didn't want to confront any of them. I thought if I waited they would go out to the tavern, and I could visit you. I saw them leave the other houses, but none departed this one. So I figured that they had duty and had not come home or had left earlier. Do you mean to tell me that all the other houses on this street are quartering soldiers and you and Godfrey are not?"

"Yes, Jonathan, they've just overlooked us I'm sure. That's why I assume that any time now they'll recognize the oversight and the soldiers will arrive here. I sometimes just wish they would so I won't be living in such terror every time there's a sound at the door."

"Celia, the British army has its faults, but disorganization is not one of them. You can be sure that the absence of soldiers from this house is entirely intentional. Even if it were an oversight, soldiers in the other houses nearby would have noticed it and pointed it out to their commanders. No, dear sister, there is a reason why troops are not quartered here. I wonder what it is."

"But we didn't have Continental troops here either when they occupied the city as most other houses did."

"But I arranged that with the adjutant. I told him that I would quarter here and that I would be having meetings here that would be inhibited by the presence of other soldiers. He agreed not to quarter any other troops here. So the simple explanation is that I used my influence to keep any of our men out of here. But I wonder what explains the British decision." Jonathan walked toward the small fire to warm himself as he pondered this.

"Is Godfrey home?" Jonathan asked, quite certain what the answer would be.

"No. He said he's been working on a big order all week and he's barely been home at all. It's terrible that he's so busy right now. You'd think he'd want to be home spending time with his new son. Little Godfrey looks so much like him, it almost makes me cry to think how the business keeps him away."

"What kind of an order?" Jonathan asked, still facing the fire with his back to his sister.

"What do you mean?"

"What kind of a big order is Godfrey working on? Who are his customers?"

"Oh dear, I don't know. We never talk about the details of his business. These days, he's so tied up in his work that we rarely have much time to talk at all."

"So you don't know what he buys or sells, or whom he deals with?"

"Oh no. Why would I care about that?"

Jonathan shrugged and walked back toward Celia, who was seated on the petit-point settee where she usually did needlepoint on these lonely evenings. He kneeled next to her, bringing their faces to the same level. "I can't stay, Celia. Most of the army is in New Jersey now, except for the men at Fort Washington. It's too dangerous to come back into the city with so many British soldiers everywhere. I had to slip in tonight in the back of a wagon loaded with potatoes. I just wanted to make sure you were safe.

"Everyone is worried about your being here with so much of the war all around you and so far from home. I had a letter from Savannah a few days ago. She says Mother is in a terrible way and rarely leaves the house. She's especially fearful for you, and she's always crying that she hasn't seen you for almost seven years. I think the arrival of the baby has stirred up something very powerful and very painful in her. Savannah wanted me to tell you that she won't be able to come for a visit this fall. Father thinks it's much too dangerous for her to travel through the paths of the armies, and he's right about that. But she also thinks she shouldn't leave Mother."

A heavy melancholy fell over Celia when she heard these words. She had so looked forward to Savannah's visit. The anticipation of it was an island of comfort in the rough seas upon which she spent her days. Now even that had disappeared. She started to speak, but produced only tears. Jonathan put his hand on her knee, trying to comfort her.

After a few moments Celia's crying stopped and she dabbed at her eyes with a small handkerchief. "I have to leave now," Jonathan said softly. "Please take care of yourself."

Celia dried her eyes and looked at her brother. "Where will you go now?" she asked.

"We'll try to hold the forts we have here, Fort Washington on Manhattan and Fort Lee across the river on the heights in New Jersey. If that fails, then I suspect we'll try to draw Howe into New Jersey. With winter almost here, it's hard to predict if he has the stomach for a general action. But we have to take a stand somewhere soon, If we don't, the militia will all go home and General Washington may be relieved."

"Relieved," Celia said. "What does that mean?"

"Removed from his command. Replaced by someone else."

"But how could that happen? He's the commander."

"There are men plotting now to have him removed. They point to the string of failures here in New York and say he's not up to the task of beating the British army. One of our other generals, Charles Lee, seems to be positioning himself for just such a move. He's Washington's second in command, but he treats the General with disdain, only carries out those orders that please him. Some days it seems like he's running his own war. We've even had reports that he's sending letters to politicians complaining about Washington and suggesting himself as a replacement.

"So, it's a difficult time in our headquarters and Washington is showing the strain. Some days he's very sullen, sometimes his temper seems to get the best of him. But he knows that time is running out if we're to make anyone believe that an independent United States can stand up to a wrathful English King. There are dark days ahead, Celia."

"Jonathan, don't be foolhardy." Celia leaned forward now and tenderly ran her hand along the side of her brother's head. "You have so much to live for. Don't risk all that for a cause that can't be won. It's not worth it."

Jonathan stiffened slightly and jerked his head away from her hand. "I don't agree, Celia. Now's our time. If we don't fight now with every ounce of courage we can muster, we'll lose all that we've fought for so far, all that Father has argued for, all that those men died for in Boston and here in New York."

He rose and stepped across the room, agitated by this reminder of the selfishness he'd never admired in her. "If we lose this fight now," he said firmly, "we may never again have the chance to be our own people, to control our own destiny. That seems worth it to me."

"I understand how you feel, Jonathan," replied Celia, abashed by the fervor of his conviction. "But look around you. It isn't just men like you who are affected by this war. So many others are drawn into this, so many innocent people who don't want to fight, who don't want a war, who just want to live their lives quietly. Look at these streets. A year ago, this was a vibrant place full of happy people. Now most of them are gone, their houses torched or just overcome by their fears. Those who remain are prisoners in their houses, starving, freezing, stripped of all the dignity in their lives.

"I pray for you, Jonathan. You're my brother and I love you." Her voice grew steely now and she locked on his eyes as she spoke. "But never forget that while some men play at war, death and desperation follow everywhere in their wake. It isn't just your war. It doesn't just kill soldiers. The war kills and maims us all. It doesn't discriminate between those who love the fighting and those who hate it."

The cannon roar made it hard for Jonathan to hear the conversation between Washington and Nathanael Greene. Greene commanded Fort Washington on Manhattan and Fort Lee on the New Jersey shore where the men now sat on horseback. Washington had made the decision, on Greene's recommendation, to leave a few thousand men at Fort Washington. But now the fort was under siege and the two generals could see from the flatboats in the river, the cannon fire booming from neighboring hilltops, and the steady advance of assault troops from several directions that there was little hope for a successful repulse of Howe's brilliant attack plan. It would be impossible to send a messenger now with the fort surrounded by British and Hessian troops. Washington hoped that Colonel Magaw, who commanded the garrison, would have the good sense to surrender before there was terrible loss of life.

Another fort lost, Washington thought, another dark chapter in this New York campaign. He looked back over the past four months and found little cause for cheer. It had been one long withdrawal, starting on Brooklyn Heights and coming to a conclusion here, probably in the next few hours. Some of his generals had tried to put a good face on things. We saved most of our army, they'd said. Faced a superior force and escaped without the one big defeat that would have ended the war. We held them off for months and now, with winter coming on, we'll have time to regroup and rebuild our army. Could have been worse.

Could have been worse. The words that every commander hates. You lost a lot of big guns, sir. Many of your men were killed or wounded. Your troops are walking off the battle field and going home. Morale shrinks steadily. The Congress is in a fret. But: could have been worse.

It was hard for Washington to imagine how. Lee had been after him to withdraw from Manhattan sooner. Said it was undefendable, that any men left there couldn't be reinforced and would be surrounded. Now the proof of his wisdom is right before my eyes. He'll be telling his politician friends that I've failed again, that I didn't listen to him even though he was right. And, dammit, he was right. Maybe it's time for someone else to command this army. I've given them plenty of reasons to lose confidence in me.

"There it is, sir," Nathanael Greene said, pointing to the white flag slowly moving up the flag pole over the south end of Fort Washington. "They've surrendered."

"Call a council of war," Washington replied, his commander's instincts now re-engaged. "We have to determine what Howe will do next."

The generals rode off with their aides in tow. Jonathan hung back, knowing that Washington would have little to say and that this was a good time to leave him to his own thoughts. He'd come to know the General well in the year and a half they'd been together. He knew there were times when Washington needed a sounding board and times when he needed silence. Brooding was part of his nature and Jonathan was sure that this was a brooding time.

Besides, he had sent Flint to Manhattan last night on a reconnaissance mission and he expected him back as soon as darkness fell and he could row undetected across the river. He rode on now past Fort Lee and south along the shore to the point where they had agreed to meet. He took Flint's horse with him.

It was a perfect night for Flint's mission, Jonathan noted as he sat waiting in a copse of pine trees near the hook just east of Bergen. Heavy clouds covered the moon and a slight breeze would blow the sound of his oarlocks away from the Navy vessels anchored to the south. A little after ten o'clock, a small canoe slid onto the slender beach and Flint jumped out and hauled it quickly up into the trees. He and Jonathan exchanged passwords, then mounted their horses and rode up the narrow path to the top of the bank. It was too late to try to make it back to Fort Lee that night, so they fetched up a small lean-to of pine boughs and wrapped themselves in blankets. The wind from the south made it feel warmer than normal for mid-November.

When they were in their beds, such as they were, Jonathan asked Flint to tell him what he'd found in Manhattan.

"Well you guessed right about the activity there," Flint reported. "They musta had every soldier in the city in on the attack on Fort Washington. I only saw a few sentries round the waterfront. There were a lot of sailors around, but I carried a caulking hammer everywhere and they took me for a shipwright. No one even stopped me once to ask who I was. So I was able to do a lot of pokin' around.

"Down on Queen Street, I noticed wagons kept coming and going from the loading doors of the big brick warehouse. Wouldn't have thought much of it, 'cept they was Army wagons and soldiers was drivin'. I couldn't get close enough to the wagons to see what they was puttin' in 'em, and they had 'em covered when they pulled out. Got my curiosity up that they was tryin' to be so secret about this. So I followed one of the wagons for a few blocks. As I 'spected, they stopped by the tavern there on Golden Hill and the soldiers all ran in to get a grog 'fore headin' back toward all the noise to the north. Good spy tip, Major Delaware: never underestimate the desire of a soldier to hide out in a tavern when there's a fight goin' on.

"Anyway, this give me a chance to sidle over and take a look at what was under the canvas. Quite amazin' really. They had barrels o' gunpowder and big wicker baskets full o' musket balls. Interesting thing is there was no markings on any of the barrels or the baskets. Damn redcoats have markin's on everythin', so this seemed strange."

Flint charged on with his report, needing no encouragement from Jonathan who listened with intense curiosity. "Then I got to thinkin'—if this is ammunition, why was it comin' from a warehouse and not from the ships. Brits always store stuff on their own ships 'til they need it. Then they can sail away with it if they get overrun. Remember in Boston. Even in the winter, they kept gunpowder on ships, 'cept what they needed near the guns to repulse a surprise attack."

Jonathan lay back in thought, staring at the damp pine boughs over his head. "What do you make of that?" he said.

"Don't know fer sure. But it 'curred to me rowin' back that maybe they's gittin' powder from some local source, not from London. Maybe that warehouse was full of powder that some supplier here got for 'em, so's they didn't have to haul it across the goddamn ocean. Can put a lot more soldiers in them ships, if they don't hafta carry powder and lead along with 'em."

Jonathan thought about the implications of this. People had been saying since the start of the fighting that the British Army was better trained and more professional than any army the Americans could put in the field. But the Continental Army would have the advantage of fighting on home ground where local folks would provide them with supplies and

270

disrupt the invaders. But then he'd heard Celia tell him that many of her friends had come to hate the Continentals for burning so much of Manhattan and cheered the British sailors who hung the men with the torches. And now he was hearing from Flint that it seemed likely that even local merchants were supplying the British. There goes any advantage we were supposed to have, he thought.

"Somethin' else." Flint said.

"What?" Jonathan asked.

"I figgered a little grog wouldn't hurt no spy either. So when the soldiers drove the wagon off, I went into the tavern myself. Was just havin' a mug of warm ale, sittin' in the corner tryin' not to be noticed. I hear this conversation 'tween two fancy dressed men sittin' just far enough away so I could hear 'em and they didn't think I could. They wuz talkin' about Lee."

"Lee?"

"Gen'ral Lee. Said he was the only one that Howe really worried about. Didn't think Washington had the heart for a real fight, but that Lee was ruthless and smart, That he'd proved that the way he drove Clinton outta' South Carolina."

"Well," Jonathan said, "I'm sure they're always judging our generals just as we're always judging theirs."

"Wait a minute. I ain't done. One of these gents says he had a relative, cousin I think he said, was in Congress. And his cousin told him that Lee has been writin' 'em letters saying Washington weren't the right one to lead the army, that if they'd let Lee run it and give him total control for a little while, he'd have the British hightailin' it before winter."

"Really?" Jonathan said. "Well, I guess we better tell the General about that. He won't like hearing it, but I don't think he'll be surprised. There aren't many surprises left in this war."

Fort Lee fell to the British four days later and now the British controlled New York, from the Hudson to Long Island. Only a delayed pursuit by General Cornwallis allowed Washington to withdraw his bedraggled army to Hackensack, New Jersey. There he called yet another sad council of war.

Jonathan sat in his accustomed place at the edge of the circle and watched as the tired and defeated officers of Washington's command tried to make sense of what was happening to them. "Where is Lee?" Nathanael Greene asked.

"I frankly don't know." Washington replied. "I left him with five thousand troops to hold New Castle in case Howe decided to attack there. I've since ordered him to join us. He pays attention to my orders only when they please him."

"But we need him now," Greene said. "Our own strength is down to around three thousand—fewer men than we left behind in the cemeteries and prison camps of New York."

"I'm well aware of that," Washington snapped back.

The General looked exhausted, Jonathan thought. Few men saw Washington as often as his young aide, and few knew as well as Jonathan the agony he endured when men under his command were captured or killed. Soldiers were precious in this war where battles were won by superior numbers as often as by smart tactics. Every man lost made the next day's task more difficult. And replacement of lost troops by recruitment grew more difficult with every defeat.

Years ago, when they'd first talked at Mount Vernon, Washington had warned Jonathan about the dark side of war, about the terrible pain and suffering. Every day now Jonathan saw that and was sickened by it. He could only imagine the terrible burden, the inner sadness of those who ordered men to their deaths in battle, who had to watch as they pulled back, torn and bloody and tormented from battles lost. Washington had been doing that for months now, and Jonathan was sure it was the source of the deep silence that inhabited the commander in his private moments.

"What should we now expect from Howe?"

The question came from a man Jonathan didn't recognize, someone new to these councils. Normally Washington introduced new men at the councils of war, but nothing was normal in these hard times. He was a man about Jonathan's age, handsome and erect, wearing the uniform of the New York Artillery and bearing the rank of captain. Captains did not normally attend the war councils unless, like Jonathan, they were members of Washington's staff.

"Following his normal pattern, I would expect him to hold back in New York, to make winter camp there, and fortify the city. Presumably he would build up supply caches for a general action in the spring when the weather allowed. But we've just received intelligence from London indicating that Germain has ordered him to capture Philadelphia before going to camp for the winter. That indicates that he will try to dash across New Jersey, chasing us as fast as he can."

Washington stood firmly in the front of the room. His cares seemed to evaporate when he was engaged like this in the meticulous labor of war planning. Planning for battle is the great tonic for all the maladies of war. Strategy and tactics, constant scrutiny of intelligence reports, reviewing troops, seeing to the hundreds of details that make the difference between victory and defeat—all of this focuses the mind and keeps it from contemplating the wretched reality of what war really is: the brutal impact of hot metal on soft flesh.

Washington continued now. "That doesn't sound like Howe, but he has his own political problems in London. We know they sacked Gage because they didn't think he was pursuing the fight with enough vigor. I suspect Howe spends every day contemplating a similar fate."

"Is the intelligence reliable, General?" Colonel Mercer asked.

"Yes." Washington replied quickly. "We now have a network in London that seems to be getting us very good information. Not everyone there is a fat country gentlemen who disdains Americans. When we can get our intelligence on a fast boat, we know what Howe's orders will be before Howe gets them. We can be quite sure that he won't go into camp until he's at least made an effort to grab Philadelphia."

"Will it then be our objective to protect Philadelphia?" asked Mercer again.

"I think not," Washington quickly responded, suggesting that he had thought this through carefully. "I hope we can hold Philadelphia, but it's not sound military strategy now to try to protect so large a city with so small and tired a force as we have here." He went to the map and pointed out the difficulty Philadelphia presented for a besieged army. Many of the officers were taken by the geographical resemblance between Philadelphia and New York. None wanted a repeat of what they'd just been through.

"I think it better that we should take our army in that direction, as if we were intending to protect Philadelphia, but stay out of the city. We can lead Howe on a chase through New Jersey, staying just far enough ahead to make him think he can catch us, but slowing his approach. When opportunities arise, we can strike at his flanks or his outposts, but we certainly can't afford a general action now. My surmise is that he'll try this for a while, then tire of the chase, and go into camp, perhaps all the way back in New York."

"What if he fails to take our lead, and simply marches his army to Philadelphia?" the New York captain asked.

"Excellent question," said Washington admiringly. "That's a risk we must take. We can make a blocking action if we must, but I don't think we could succeed. I've warned the Congress of our intelligence and its members are making plans to abandon Philadelphia as soon as the necessity arises. Given the state of our army, I think it would be better to leave Philadelphia to Howe, if we must, than to lose the war in a symbolic gesture. We can probably survive the loss of Philadelphia. But I can't survive the loss of my army."

"Captain Alexander Hamilton, this is Captain Ezekial Isaac Flint," Jonathan said to the New York officer, smiling as he always did when he pronounced Flint's full name. "But if you call him 'Captain Flint' he'll probably think you're talking to someone else and he won't respond. He's been an officer for a year and a half, but he still thinks like a private. That, in fact, is his only charm."

The two men shook hands. "Hamilton's on the General's staff now, Flint, and he asked if he could go with us tonight."

"Better get him out of them fancy britches or every loose lip in New Jersey'll be reportin' our movements," Flint said with little emotion. "You from Manhattan Island?"

"I am," Hamilton replied, "though I was not born there. I did graduate Kings' College and New York is my home now."

"Another college man, Major," Flint said to Jonathan, flashing his giddiest smile. "We may not outfight these redcoats, but we sure oughtta outsmart 'em." Flint laughed and clapped Hamilton on the back.

"Flint's right, Hamilton. You don't want to be wearing a uniform tonight. This is a part of warfare you've probably never seen before."

Hamilton left to change his clothes while Jonathan and Flint and the small group of volunteers going with them, prepared for their mission. They packed several horses with long skeins of rope, then checked their own saddles. They'd decided that muskets would only encumber them, so they carried no long rifles. Hamilton soon returned, still looking a little too dandified for Flint but no longer wearing the uniform of a captain of artillery. They all mounted at Jonathan's command and rode to the south.

When Washington talked Jonathan into joining the army in their conversation in Cambridge so long ago, he said nothing about real soldiering. Jonathan pictured himself at meetings and riding at Washington's side and carrying messages. But in the months since, Washington had come to rely on Jonathan more and more for special missions of great importance and high danger: reconnaissance behind enemy lines, blowing up supply depots and powder magazines, tracking down British spies. But on this cold early December night, they set off on a mission unlike anything they'd done previously.

Washington had been right about Howe. He sent the main force of his army under General Cornwallis in pursuit of Washington across rainy, muddy New Jersey. It was a typically laggard British pursuit, however; and Washington, tearing up roads and sawing down bridges behind him, had little difficulty staying just ahead of the chase. Washington had reached Trenton a few days earlier and had decided his next move would be south across the Delaware River. He hoped to delay Cornwallis there, twenty-five miles north of Philadelphia, and convince him that he couldn't get to Philadelphia before the worst of winter struck.

Jonathan's mission was to secure every boat for miles along the east bank of the Delaware River. Washington would use these to ferry his own army across, then destroy them so that Cornwallis would be stuck with no way to transport his own army across. When they got to the shore after dark, Jonathan dispersed his volunteers to designated sectors along the river with orders to collect every boat, every form of flotation they could find and tow them to a point just outside of Trenton.

Flint, Jonathan, Hamilton and two other men rode south more than a mile to a place where their map showed the location of a ferry. They found several smaller sloops and bateaux along the way and the volunteers were left to move them upstream to the collection point. The three officers rode on to the ferry.

At a small peninsula near a turn in the river, they came across a simple wooden house in front of which was a long flatboat large enough to hold a wagon and team. Smoke came from the stone chimney of the house, but there was no light in its single window. "This must be the ferry," Jonathan whispered as they pulled up and dismounted.

"It's as good as we'll find for floating artillery pieces," added Hamilton.

Flint took a long coil of rope and walked along the shore toward the boat. He boarded it quietly and tied the rope to a post at one end of the flat, featureless vessel. Then he walked quickly back toward Jonathan and Hamilton, unwinding the rope as he went. He tied the other end to the pack horse and they began to walk along the shore path to Trenton. They'd have to walk the whole way because they were headed upstream and they'd need to work the vessel along the shore. Little pockets of surface ice along the edge of the river groaned as the boat began to follow them.

No more than thirty yards further on, they all heard the sharp crack of a musket and the awful, familiar sound of a musket ball whizzing through the bushes beside them. They fell quickly to the ground and, following all their instincts, sought to determine the source of the shot. The mystery ended almost immediately when a large man stepped from behind a tree, musket in hand, and yelled, "Get up, ya goddamn thieves."

Hamilton and Jonathan rose to their feet, but Flint who was a few yards away stayed still on the ground, hoping the darkness would have prevented the man from counting them.

"Don't shoot us, sir," Jonathan said. "We're soldiers in General Washington's army, not thieves."

"In a pig's eye," the man said. "You're thieves and you're stealin' my boat."

"We're not stealing it, sir," Jonathan protested. "We simply need to use it to transport soldiers across the river. The British army is coming this way and we want to get to the other side of the river ahead of them. We'll keep your boat over there to keep it out of enemy hands."

"Enemy, hah!" the man bellowed. "The only enemy I got is the ones what try to steal my boat. This here's my livelihood. I'm a ferry man. You steal my boat and I ain't got nothin'. You're my enemy. I ain't got no interest in soldiers."

Flint realized now that the man had not seen that there were three of them. He started to crawl very slowly and quietly behind the man, glad for once for the damp ground that made less noise than dry leaves would have.

Hamilton tried his hand at convincing the man. "We'd be happy to pay you rent for a few day's use of your boat. What might that cost?"

"Rent?" the man said. "Thieves don't pay no rent. Don't try no tricks on me. This boat stays here, and I'll kill anyone tries to move it."

"Sir," Jonathan tried again, "you're a citizen of New Jersey. Your state has delegates to the Congress in Philadelphia. The Congress has authorized General Washington to do whatever is necessary to defeat the British invaders. Nothing is more necessary now than a means of transporting our army across the Delaware River. I'm afraid I must order you to step aside, so that we may proceed to use this boat for the purposes of the Continental Army."

"Go to hell!" the man shouted and he raised his musket again and aimed it directly at Jonathan's head. Hamilton froze at the sight. Just as the man pulled the trigger, a rock the size of a cannonball crashed fiercely into the back of his head. He slumped forward causing the musket to fire into the ground, sending mud all over the clothes of Jonathan and Hamilton. Flint leapt quickly to his feet and jumped on the man's back.

But there was no response. When they collected their wits and rolled the man over, the back of his skull was crushed and blood gushed from his left eye out of which stuck a large twig. Flint touched his neck for a minute and said simply, "Bastard's dead."

No one spoke for several minutes as the three Continental officers stood over the dead man in the darkness. Finally Jonathan said, "We can't bury him, we have no tools. Let's just drag him to the cabin and cover him with a blanket. Someone will find him when they come for the ferry."

Hamilton stood motionless. "We've killed an innocent man," he said to no one in particular. "My God, it's awful."

"It's war, Cap'n," Flint said. "Everyone of us woulda fought just as hard as he did to protect our livelihood. Gotta' admire the man for that. But he wouldn't listen to reason. We need that boat to save an army. If we don't take boats and cattle and corn when we need 'em, we'll all be singin' 'God Save the King' the rest of our lives. Didn't intend to kill him, but he was fixin' to shoot the two of you. Nothin' innocent about that. Anyone with a gun aimed at American soldiers, that's the enemy to me. No quarter, Cap'n. No quarter."

Howe had joined Cornwallis a few days earlier and taken command. His first decision was to choose the Third Battalion of light infantry to lead the march on Philadelphia. Colonel Armistead had his men trained to high efficiency and their bravery at Brooklyn Heights and then in White Plains was a model for the entire Army. Armistead was a fine officer. One of the best. A true professional. He'd be an excellent general, Cornwallis had once said to Howe, if only he had the right connections.

Washington was on the run now. He got out of Princeton just in time, but he could be caught north of Philadelphia or put in siege there, Howe believed. He won't survive long if he makes it to Philadelphia because it'll be an impossible city for him to defend. Too wide, too many approaches, no forts. Howe was sure he had Washington—and glory—in his sights. And Aubrey Armistead was the man he wanted commanding the lead troops.

So on December eighth, to the heavy beat of the kettle drums and the whistle of a dozen fifes, the Third Battalion stepped off toward Trenton and the Delaware River. At mid-morning, Armistead rode at the head of his column to the Trenton shore and surveyed the river bank on the other side, a third of a mile away. He saw no soldiers anywhere and nothing that resembled a gun emplacement. It would not be an easy shoreline to defend in any case, he felt. Washington must have just kept on marching when he got to the other side. All his military intuition told him it was safe to cross.

He called his officers together and they all sat on their horses in a circle. He directed them to take their men up and down the river bank and collect every boat they could find. He especially reminded them to be on the alert for large flat ferry boats that they could use to transport their large artillery pieces and horses.

Armistead was a little surprised to find no boats here where the road led to the river's edge. He had never been to Trenton and so assumed that there must be a basin nearby where boats were kept. He could see many masts on the other side, but saw none nearby on the east shore. While his soldiers collected boats for the crossing, he rode back to report a short delay to General Cornwallis, who was riding ahead of Howe in the column.

Two hours later, Armistead arrived back at the river bank, surprised to find all of his officers mingling there and not a boat in sight. "They got them all, Colonel," one of the officers reported. "We've been up and down the river for miles. There are scores of boats, but every single one of them is tied up on the other side. What Washington couldn't use, he burned. Folks along here said they'd never seen anything like it. Soldiers snuck in during the night and towed all the boats up here, loaded their troops and supplies, and got across in a few hours. Then they destroyed most of the boats on the other side, except the larger ones that they sank in the mud. That must be all the masts we see.

"A woman downstream said they stole her husband's ferry and murdered him when he tried to stop them. Crushed his head and left him to die in front of their fire while she hid in bed. They seem to have put a terrible fright into everyone."

Armistead sat for a moment in stunned silence. He was coming to hate this frustrating, mocking enemy. Always so close to defeat, always

278

finding some way to escape the trap. But he had to admire what they'd done here. It was brilliant soldiering. It would take days, he knew, to build rafts enough to ferry Howe's army across the river. Winter was settling in and that would make the work so much harder. Meanwhile, Washington was who knew where, resting his troops and planning his next move. We nearly had him at Princeton, Armistead thought; we could have defeated him on the road between here and Philadelphia. Now, damn it all, we'll have to spend a week as boat builders. And then another winter in camp.

He turned and issued an order to one of his officers. "Put the men at ease. We're not going anywhere today."

# Chapter 19

## Still River, Delaware
## December 1776

"Missuh Houghton, you'se home, suh. We wuzn't 'spectin' you yet. I'll run an git' da missus." Quiet Jack slipped down off the pile of oak logs atop the wagon, and skipped off toward the house. Henry set his bag on the frozen ground and looked around at the farm he had missed so much over the past three years.

It looks surprisingly good, he thought. The fences are all intact. The barn and the house must have been painted since I left. And, from the looks of things, the timber cutting goes on even in this cold weather. He was relieved, for the care of the farm weighed heavily on him when he was away.

"Father!" came the cry from the direction of the house, and Henry turned to see Savannah throwing a shawl around her shoulders and running toward him. She reached him quickly and hugged him hard. Henry pulled back slightly and looked at his younger daughter. "You look like you're surviving this war quite well, young lady," he said with a smile.

"Still River seems to be the only place in America that the war has not really touched, Father. More people would be surviving it well if they could just spend their days here as I do. You're home earlier than we expected."

Henry gathered up his bag and he and Savannah walked toward the house. A fire burned in every fireplace and the house was warm, or so it felt after Henry's cold journey by sloop from Philadelphia, then the long wagon ride from Bogan's Beach to Still River. He hadn't felt warm for days. He hung his long wool coat in the kitchen, then asked. "Where's Mother?"

Savannah hesitated, then walked toward him and put a hand on her father's arm. "She's in the parlor, Father, but I have to warn you: she doesn't look good. We weren't expecting you this early and you'll see her now as she is most days. The war's been very hard on Mother. You'll see that."

Henry entered the parlor and saw his wife sitting in the small pine rocker close to the gray stone fireplace. A white cotton bonnet enveloped her small face which looked eerie in the orange glow of the fire. She was heavily wrapped despite the warmth of the room, and when she looked toward Henry, all she could offer was a small, wan smile. She didn't speak.

Henry crossed the room and kneeled down beside the chair in which Patience sat swaddled in dark blankets. He kissed her sunken cheek and said, "Hello, Mother. I'm home early. How are you?"

Patience looked blankly at Henry. For a moment she was silent, then said simply, "Why are you here now?"

Savannah stepped over and pulled one of the blankets up around her mother's shoulders. "Would you like some tea, Mother?" she asked. Patience nodded and Savannah went to the kitchen to find Sweetie.

"I've been worried about you, and I wanted to get home to you as soon as I could," Henry said. "I do hate being away from you and the farm. Look at me, Patience."

She slowly turned her head toward his, and Henry could see the ravages wrought by her anxieties. Her skin had no color at all, a rheumy glaze masked her eyes and the beautiful curls that had captivated him decades ago were just a memory now. She seemed an empty shell. He touched her cheek, which was cold and almost brittle, then slowly stroked the side of her face. Patience closed her eyes and said nothing for a moment. Then her eyes suddenly opened and she said to Henry, "Will the war end soon?"

Savannah re-entered the parlor followed by Sweetie carrying a tray with teapot and cups. Sweetie nodded a silent greeting to Henry, then placed the tray on a table beside Patience and backed away toward the door.

Henry rose, poured himself a cup of tea and stood in front of his wife. "I'm afraid not, dear," he said.

"Afraid not what, Father?" Savannah asked.

"Mother asked if the war will end soon. I'm afraid that it won't. Washington's army escaped the British in New York and is outside of Philadelphia now. It appears that the armies are about to go into winter camp, so there won't be any more fighting for a while. But the optimism we all felt after the British were driven from Boston seems to have evaporated. The war will go on for a while longer."

"If the army is outside Philadelphia, it's not far from here. Are we in danger now?" Savannah asked.

"I hope not," Henry responded after taking a long sip from his warm tea. "But I'm concerned. I left the Congress before the session was over because I wanted to get home to see Mother." He looked fondly toward the silent woman heavily wrapped before the fire. "But I also wanted to meet with the neighbors to prepare a defense plan of some kind in case the war moves any closer. It's hard to predict what will happen in the spring."

"Will Jonathan be here soon?" Patience whispered from her chair.

"I hope we'll see him soon, Mother. If the army makes winter camp near Philadelphia, perhaps he can get home for awhile. I sent a letter to him in the pouch to Washington telling him that we all missed him and expressing the hope especially that he might get home to see you. He's a major now, you know. Washington sent me a note a few months ago saying what an invaluable soldier he'd become and how proud I should be of him."

"How long has it been since I've seen him?" Patience asked.

"Almost three years, Mother," Savannah quickly responded. "I've seen none of my brothers or sisters in that time."

"I hate the war, Henry," Patience said feebly, showing some emotion at last. "It's taken away my husband and my children. Soon it will take away our home. Why did you ever let us come to this? You were in Congress, Henry. You could have stopped the war from coming." Her voice was quaking in anger and tears began to appear in the corners of her eyes. "When you left for that first Congress, you said you were sure reasonable men would find a way to end the crisis. All those so-called reasonable men did was to start a fight."

One of Patience's blankets fell to the floor, freeing a spindly arm which she pointed at her husband. "Now look at us, Henry. One son in London, maybe even in jail. Another one in the middle of every battle. Celia's in New York with our grandchild and they're burning houses all around her. And now you say the armies may be coming here to chase us out. You failed us, Henry. You failed your family and soon we'll all be dead."

Patience fell back in the chair and her head leaned heavily to the left, her energy spent. "I don't think that's fair, Mother. Father hasn't failed us. He's tried to do what's right," Savannah said, looking at her mother.

Henry set his cup on the table and returned to kneel beside Patience. He put a hand on her arm. "Things changed, Mother. The hopes I bore when Jonathan and I walked off to Philadelphia that first time were all dashed. The King wouldn't listen to reason. The government wouldn't compromise. We were in a vise and it kept getting tighter. Our liberties were disappearing and finally we had no choice but to fight for their preservation.

"There isn't a man in Philadelphia who enjoys this war. We all hope it will end soon. But most of us now believe that it's our only hope if our families are to have the kind of future we want for them.

"I know how hard this is for you, Mother," Henry continued. "It is for me, too. Every time I vote a requisition for the army, I think about Jonathan. Every time we talk about diplomatic approaches to London, I think about Nathaniel and wonder if he's safe." Patience's brow furrowed deeply at the mention of Nathaniel, but she remained silent. "The happiest vote I cast in the past year was the one on instructions to Washington not to burn New York. I thought: at last, I've done something that will keep my children from risk. Then some hotheads in Washington's army went and burned a third of the city anyway. Every day, I pray for a speedy end to the war."

Patience's eyes were tightly closed now and Henry realized she was asleep. He pulled the fallen blanket over her arm. Then he rose and put a heavy log on the fire. He and Savannah moved quietly from the parlor to the kitchen.

"She just fell asleep," Henry said in wonderment.

"She does that all the time now," Savannah said. "Especially when the conversation turns to something she doesn't want to hear. It seems to be her way of avoiding things she finds too painful."

"I'm worried about her, Savannah. She looks so weak and frail."

"She's been like this for months, Father. Just a few weeks after you left last time, she seemed to just give up, to surrender to all her burdens. Now she seems simply to endure each day, barely moving from her chair, saying almost nothing, showing no emotion. The little bit of anger she aimed at you in there was the first sign of any emotion I've seen in weeks. It's as if Mother has departed and only some soul-less specter of her remains behind."

Most people thought there wouldn't be a New Year's feast on the first day of 1777. The war was very close by, and somehow a celebration seemed out of place. One of Henry's neighbors had lost a son in the battle on Harlem Heights in New York, and that had thrown the whole community into mourning. The New Year's feasts had always been about happy anticipation, toasts to the year ahead, cheerful optimism that the next year would be better even than the last.

But no one in Still River, Delaware felt that way now, and no New Year's feast was planned. So it seemed odd to Henry to be standing by the fire in Balfour Tavern in the winter, just a few weeks before the first day of the new year, and to feel none of the cheer that had always infused the annual gathering of his neighbors. Men came through the door this night, men he'd known his whole life, men he loved as if they were cousins and brothers, not simply neighbors. But they were not here to celebrate. They were here to plan to defend Still River against the greatest threat it had ever faced.

Henry called the men to order, and they pulled their benches toward the back of the room where Henry stood facing them. None of them, even the oldest, could remember a time when there wasn't a Houghton to lead meetings like this. There had never been an election really, it was just that everyone trusted Henry as they'd trusted his father and grandfather. The Houghtons were fair men and honest, and that was all anybody required in a leader.

Henry began by telling them what he knew about the war, about Washington's escape across the Delaware and Howe's delayed pursuit. He reported that as he left to come home, members of Congress were preparing to move their meetings to Baltimore, having concluded that Philadelphia was no longer safe with the British army so close at hand.

"Will Howe attack Philadelphia now?" one of the neighbors, John Wicklow, asked.

"Don't know," Henry said. "British don't seem to like to fight in cold weather, so he may go into camp and wait 'til spring."

"Will he make camp in Trenton?"

"Don't know that either, John," Henry said. "Washington thinks he may take the army back to New York and just leave outposts in New Jersey."

"So, then we wouldn't have the whole British army breathin' down our necks all winter?"

"Well, probably not," said Henry. "But we can't really be sure of anything and we need to prepare for the worst."

"Yes," shouted Edward Markham whose family owned the farm next to Henry's on the bend and had been in Delaware almost as long. "And don't forget we got as much threat from Washington's army as from the redcoats. If the Continentals come down here, they'll be takin' our horses and cattle and stickin' men in our houses and barns. An army's like a pack of locusts. They come through town, nothin' much left standin' when they leave."

"I'm sure Washington's army wouldn't plunder us the way the British will if they come here," said Wicklow.

"The devil they won't," Markham replied. "My nephew in New Jersey wrote to us and said the Continentals came through his place, took all his animals and most of his corn. Roasted his pig right outside the barn and lined up to eat 'im there. He said they were starvin' and most of 'em didn't have any warm clothes or blankets. Wiped him out. Then they left and a few days later the redcoats came. He didn't have anythin' left for them to take, so they stuck a bayonet at his throat and accused him of hidin' all his animals. His wife screamed for them to leave my nephew alone, they just whacked him in the stomach with a rifle butt and rode off."

Henry tried to focus the discussion on planning. "It's true that any army coming through here will want our animals and the grain and corn we've got stored. There's not much we can do to stop them, but we can move some of our animals to the farms that are off the main roads. They may still find them, but if they're in a hurry they won't be searching as thoroughly as they would in camp. We all need to make some provision for our valuables, too. Find a safe place on your land, and bury the things you don't want stolen."

"But the ground's frozen, Henry," said a voice in the back of the room.

"Build a damn fire on the ground, then dig through the thawed ground under it," said another.

For the next half hour or so, men offered suggestions and asked questions. Several had stories to tell of horrors visited on relatives in the path of one of the armies now abroad in the land to the north. Then Martin Abelson, the oldest man in Still River, spoke for the first time. "When will it end, Henry? Can we beat these British boys?"

The room quieted and everyone looked to Henry Houghton. When Henry was a small boy, Martin Abelson used to come to the farm to buy logs from his father. He didn't buy them really, not with money. The Abelsons had the biggest wagon Henry had ever seen and it would come filled with lambs or chickens and go away filled with large bolts of oak. Henry had always called him Mr. Abelson in those days, and he still did. "I honestly don't know, Mr. Abelson. We're doing our best. Washington is an able commander and our boys always fight like the dickens. But the British are better equipped and their soldiers are better trained. Right now, they have more men in the field than we do. If Washington can hold them off for awhile, take advantage of opportunities when they arise, perhaps we can hold things together until our army gets stronger or London gets tired of the cost and gives up the fight."

Abelson rose slowly to his feet now. "But is it worth it, Henry?" he asked in a voice barely above a whisper. "Our sons are getting killed. We're trying to do business with paper currency that's almost worthless. Two big armies are beating down on us, and now we're worried about the ruination of our land. I'm trying to remember what was so bad about just being Englishmen."

Several heads around the room seemed to nod, and there was a murmur of agreement as everyone turned to Henry, awaiting his answer.

He stepped into the center of the half-circle and looked from side to side. In that moment it struck him that these men in Delaware, these simple farmers he'd known his whole life, were not very different really from the lawyers and merchants and plantation owners at the State House in Philadelphia. They harbored the same passions, the same concerns for family and home, the same goals for children and grandchildren. Their words were plainer and they had no interest in legal debating points. But the issues—and the qualms—were the same in Still River as they were in Philadelphia.

"Think about our ancestors, Mr. Abelson. Think about the dangers they endured. They left England and got on small ships and crossed a dark and dangerous ocean to come to a place none of them had ever seen and about which they knew almost nothing. They arrived with a few tools and some clothes and not much more. And when they stepped ashore on Delaware Bay, nothing greeted them but wilderness and savages. There were no shops, no doctors, no relatives ready to help out if tragedy struck. They used their hands and labored exhaustingly for years to clear the land

and turn it into a decent place to live. Many of them died and their little children died and some of them couldn't endure the trials and went mad."

Henry winced at these last words as he spoke them, thinking of Patience. But he believed in his argument and continued without pause. "Why did they do this? Surely it would have been much easier to stay in England. Things may not have been perfect there, but were they bad enough to justify the danger and tribulations of coming to America? They must have thought so because now we have a thriving community here. Now we have a place we all love, a place where we can raise our families and have our churches and organize our own schools. We wouldn't have those things if our ancestors had been afraid of danger, if they'd shrunk from risk, if they'd taken the path of least resistance."

Henry paused and moved toward Martin Abelson, stopping just a few feet in front of him, as he'd often seen John Adams do when questioned in debate. "I think that's about what's happening now, Mr. Abelson. It'd be easier, for sure, to quit the fight, to send the soldiers home and tell the King that we've decided that being Englishmen isn't so bad after all. But what then of the life we'd leave for our children and grandchildren? Will they be told what they can and can't do by a government thousands of miles away, a government that calls itself a democracy but gives them no say? Will they be forced to bow down every time a soldier in a red coat comes by and takes a nap in their bed or makes a meal of their cattle? Will they pay confiscatory taxes to support a corrupt government across the ocean?

"None of us likes the burdens we have to bear now, Mr. Abelson. I know those burdens personally, and I hate them. But if we can stay the course, I think we'll prevail. And if we do that, we'll have an opportunity that no other nation has ever had—to make our own government and to do so with our own hands. That won't be easy, and we probably won't get it perfectly right. But, by God, I think the chance to do it is worth fighting for."

Henry looked around the room. Some men were sitting silent. A few seemed deep in thought. Others nodded agreement. No one said a word. After a long moment, Henry broke the silence. "Now," he said, 'we should talk about organizing our own militia."

"Where are all these logs going?" Henry asked, as he and

Savannah finished breakfast. He rose and walked to the window where Quiet Jack, Thom Mason, and another man he didn't recognize were hoisting heavy saw-logs into three large and unfamiliar wagons.

"To Annapolis," Savannah replied.

"Annapolis?" Henry said. "We don't sell logs to Annapolis. I wouldn't even know how to get them there."

"We take them on the wagons to Cambridge on the Maryland shore," Savannah said softly," then we put them on a schooner that takes them across the bay. There's a shipyard, Backson and Brace, that's building ships for the American navy. They buy all the clear oak we can get them."

Henry returned to his chair and looked his daughter in the eye. "What is this, Savannah? I don't know about any of this."

"Uncle Edward's yard has been very quiet for months. They've lost all their British business and they couldn't get enough local business to keep busy. Uncle was very kind and kept buying our logs, piling them up in his yard, even though he couldn't use them. Finally he couldn't afford to do that any more, and he rode up here to tell Mother. He didn't know about her condition, so I intercepted him. He still thinks of me as his little niece and he was uncomfortable talking about business. But I think I impressed him enough with what I knew about the farm that he explained everything to me. He said his yard was in big trouble and that they hadn't gotten any of the contracts for the new Navy ships. Backson and Brace got them."

Savannah looked directly at her father who was sitting back in his chair and listening intently. "I thought about this for while and it occurred to me that maybe Backson and Brace would buy our logs. So I got Thom Mason cleaned up and got him some of Jonathan's good waistcoats and breeches and shoes. Then he and I rode to Cambridge."

"You went on horseback?"

"Had to," Savannah said. "Couldn't risk leaving the wagon at the wharf. Remember Father I've been riding with the boys since I was a little girl.

"Anyway, we got to Cambridge and caught the boat to Annapolis. Told them that Thom was going there on business and I was his sister. When we got to Annapolis, we found our way to Backson and Brace, and Thom asked if he could see one of the owners about selling some oak. They were happy to see us because they'd been having trouble getting thick bolts for the heavy planking on these warships. I'd told Thom what

288

to say, but he did the talking because I knew they'd never pay any attention to a woman. They offered us a deal, but Thom followed my instructions and told them to write up a contract that we could look over. We got rooms in town and took the contract back there and I looked it all over. I made a few changes, then signed it. I kind of blotted my signature so they really couldn't tell whether it said Savannah or Samuel, which was the name I told Thom to use.

"So we've been selling our logs to them ever since, about 4 months now, and they're buying more than Uncle ever did. That's why I hired another man to help with the cutting. Even with the cost of shipping them across the Chesapeake, we're making more per running foot than we ever did before. The only trouble is that they pay us in paper, so we sometimes end up with a lot less then we would if we were using sterling."

Henry's jaw dropped. Literally. He had no idea that Savannah was this involved in running the farm, no hint that Edward was no longer buying their logs. And he couldn't imagine his daughter—or any woman for that matter—crossing Chesapeake Bay and negotiating a business deal with one of the biggest shipyards in America. And talking about the relative benefits of different currencies on top of that.

"My God, Savannah," he finally said. "You seem to have a hand in everything."

"There hasn't been much choice, Father. With you gone and Mother not well, who else was there?"

"Well I wonder if Marinus Marshall knows what a competent wife he's getting himself. Perhaps next he'll have you running the Marshall plantation."

Savannah rose from her chair, walked to the stove where she checked the fire, then turned to face her father. "I won't be marrying Marinus. I turned down his proposal."

"What?" Henry said. "Mother told me nothing about that."

"She doesn't know."

"She doesn't know?"

"I couldn't bear to tell her. She is so beaten down by her worries for Nathaniel and Celia and Jonathan—by her worries for you, too, Father—I couldn't bear to take away the one thing that made her happy. I should have turned Marinus down sooner; in fact, he was a dear to wait so long for me. But I just couldn't bear to think what it would do to Mother. Now that Mother doesn't leave the house, I thought she wouldn't hear from anyone else. And it was only fair to let Marinus know so that he can look elsewhere for a wife."

"But Savannah, everyone thought you two were the perfect match."

"Everyone but me, Father. Marinus Marshall is a fine man. But if I married him, I would always be just the wife of Marinus and the lady of the plantation. Every day would be arranged for me. And when he gets into politics, as he surely will, then I would just be the little woman at home.

"For a time, that almost appealed to me. And I know how much it meant to you and especially to Mother. But these last few months have been wonderful for me, even with all the concern about mother and the rest of our family. I love this farm, Father. I always have. I love to sit in the dooryard and look down the meadow to the river. I love the pungent smell of the woods in the spring when the winter is coming out of the ground. I love riding along the fences, looking for breaks. And in the past few months, I've felt, not like a little girl who just happened to be born here, but like the person most responsible for the care of this place."

As she continued, Henry noticed the glow in her eyes and a confidence he'd never heard before in her speech. "I've listened so many times, Father, as you've expressed your own feeling for this land and how it passed down to you like a family treasure from your great-grandfather and on through each successive generation. That was always just father-talk to me, and all of us used to even imitate you when you weren't around, especially Nathaniel. But now I have many of those same feelings. A few days ago, I went out to get some water. As I was standing by the well, I remembered the story you told us once about watching your father and grandfather dig that well. I think you said it was in the hottest summer in the history of the world, or so it had seemed to you when you were seven years old. There I was standing by that same well, and it was almost as if I could hear their shovels biting into the ground. I just can't walk away from this now."

"But, Savannah," Henry said, "you need to have your own life. I've been thinking about resigning from Congress and staying home to be with Mother and resuming my responsibilities on the farm. I think the price of my being away so much has been far too high."

"You can't resign now, Father," Savannah nearly screamed. "The work you're doing is too important. The Congress has to make us a new government and you should be involved in that. And, besides, Mother

290

won't miraculously improve if you're here. Her dark spells seem resistant to everything I try. You've been home for almost ten days now and she hasn't changed at all. I can manage this farm, Father. Trust me. I can. And I want to continue as long as it's necessary.

"Everything is different now. Who could have imagined the fate of our family, even five years ago? It's a terrible time. But we don't all have to surrender to it, as Mother has. Jonathan hasn't. I'm not going to. And you shouldn't either."

Henry looked out the window, letting his glance roam slowly toward the top of the hill where large logs sat piled on the ground, beyond the barns he'd always known, over the fields he'd cleared, past the well he watched his grandfather and his father dig in a distant time when the whole world seemed to stop at the edge of the Still River.

# Chapter 20

## New Jersey
## December 1776 – January 1777

Another Christmas away from home, Jonathan thought sadly, realizing that he'd not seen the farm or his parents for more than a year and a half. The New Year's feasts at Balfour Tavern, the shining moment of every winter, were dimming now in memory. He always tried to avoid these thoughts, they pained him so. So he focused instead on this discussion in the parlor of the little house in New Town, Pennsylvania where Washington had met with his generals each morning since their escape across the Delaware.

He watched the General in admiration. The last few months had been the worst part of Washington's life. The demoralizing defeats in New York. The hair's breadth escape across New Jersey. Intercepting the terrible letter that General Lee wrote to the Adjutant General fiercely criticizing Washington's leadership. Then the capture of Lee, the second-ranking general in the American army, by the British ten days ago.

Jonathan could only begin to imagine the pressures that Washington felt. Yet here he was, pacing the floor, leading his commanders through a sprightly discussion of their options. Some thought it a prudent time to go into camp. The men were exhausted. On the flight across New Jersey, they'd had to burn their tents and blankets and supplies for lack of transport. They were cold and hungry and many lacked coats or shoes. And the deadly grip of winter was around them. Certainly it made sense to avoid contact with the enemy and rebuild the army for a spring offensive.

But another pressure weighed most heavily on Washington, and Jonathan could see that he had no intention of going to camp now. The General listened patiently to those who pushed for winter camp, then he stopped abruptly before the calendar on the wall. "This," he said, "is a our great enemy now." And he pointed to the last day of December 1776.

On January first the enlistments of nearly all the New England troops would come to an end and they'd march home. Washington knew that if his army did not engage now, he would soon have no army to lead. So he had to develop a plan and execute it quickly before the enlistment crisis was upon him.

The meeting ended just before noon with consensus that there would be a surprise attack on the other side of the Delaware as soon as possible, probably at Trenton. Tomorrow, Washington said, as the officers departed, we will work on the plan itself. Jonathan was a little surprised by all this, for usually Washington's staff meetings went an hour or two longer, and he hated to delay planning, even for a day. The General seemed to have something on his mind. "Let's take some air," he said to Jonathan and Hamilton as the two staff officers watched the others leave.

Outside on the veranda in front of the house, Washington stood looking across the cold countryside. Patches of snow still dotted the ground after the melting rains of the previous days. The northerly wind had returned last night and frozen everything solid again. And as the three of them stood there saying little—Washington's capacity for small talk was utterly depleted these days, Jonathan had noticed—two Continental soldiers rode up pulling a disheveled man wearing a blindfold with his hands bound behind his back. They dismounted and pushed the man toward the veranda where they saluted Washington. "What is it?" the General asked?

"We got a prisoner, sir," said the taller of the two men, a sergeant. "Caught him spyin'. He was carryin' a map of this here town with all the supply barns marked on it. Wonderin' where we should take 'im."

"Right here!" Washington snapped. "Spies have been crawling all over us. Perhaps it's time I interrogated one myself. Take him there into the parlor. Then you men wait out here."

The soldiers dragged the spy into the room where the meeting had just ended and pushed him roughly into a chair. Then they saluted and left. Washington instructed Hamilton to close the door, then the three officers pulled up chairs in front of the spy, a New Jersey man who'd refused to tell his name to his captors.

Washington leaned forward and said softly, "How are you, Honeyman? Have you been harmed?" Jonathan and Hamilton exchanged confused glances.

"No, sir, not badly. It's a rough game," the spy replied.

"Tell us what you've learned. This is Major Houghton and Captain Hamilton. They won't betray you."

"I got into Trenton for about a week. Got some cattle up river and went there looking like I was trying to sell them. They bought the story and were happy to have me around because I told them I could get more cattle any time. Even had dinner with Colonel Rall a few times. They're all Hessians over there and he's in charge. Colonel likes his ale, so it wasn't hard to get him to talk, especially after I convinced him that I loved the King and hated the Continentals. Got a good look around, and I can draw you a map of the town and how the troops are laid out."

"Untie him please, Hamilton." Washington ordered. Still thoroughly confused by the unfolding scene, Hamilton walked behind the spy's chair and stood him up, then loosened the rope and pulled his arms free. Honeyman walked to the table and began to draw a detailed picture of the street plan of Trenton, the quarters of the Hessian troops, Rall's own headquarters, and the location of their ammunition magazine and supplies. He then spent the next half hour describing in detail the daily routines of the Trenton garrison.

"You also might want to know," Honeyman said, "that Rall thinks the Delaware River is the best line of defense he could have right now with all the ice that's in it. He's even planned a big celebration Christmas night with light guard. Doesn't think the Continentals would dare risk crossing the river till the ice gets out."

When he was done, Washington thanked him for his service and went over the details of their plan. Honeyman would be charged with spying for the enemy and ordered by Washington to be hanged in the morning. He'd spend the night in the stockade, but during the night the guard would fall asleep and the gate would be left unlocked so that Honeyman could escape. The guard would awaken and fire at him, but aim high and miss. Honeyman nodded his understanding of all this, then Hamilton retied the rope around his arms. The waiting soldiers were called in and ordered by Washington to take the notorious turncoat to the stockade and prepare for his hanging in the morning.

When the door closed, Washington pulled himself to his full height and looked at his two utterly confused staff officers. "A little lesson in warfare, gentlemen," he said. "Know thy enemy." Then he smiled that glorious clever smile that Jonathan had not seen for months and said simply, "Best we start planning our Christmas party."

294

Flint sat with a newspaper by the fire in the small room he and Jonathan shared. It had once been servants' quarters for the larger house that Washington now used as his headquarters. The room had a single window, but in these short winter days little light ever entered. So Flint leaned forward trying to catch what illumination he could from the fire.

"Where'd you get a newspaper?" Jonathan asked as he pulled off his boots.

"Some men of the 16th caught a spy today and he was carryin' it," Flint replied. "It's from Trenton, but it ain't a loyalist paper."

"What's the news? I hear there's a war on somewhere," Jonathan joked.

Flint was slow to respond. "Oh, don't have much news 'cept about weddin's and such. But there's this long writin' by that Paine, the same English fella' that wrote that pamphlet everyone was readin' last year. It's mighty good."

"Paine? Tom Paine? What's he writing about now?"

"Let me read the first bit of it. You'll see what he's sayin'. It's titled 'The Crisis' and he says:

*'These are the times that try men's souls.*
*The summer soldier and the sunshine patriot will, in*
*this crisis, shrink from the service of his country; but*
*he that stands it now deserves the love and thanks of*
*man and woman. Tyranny, like Hell, is not easily*
*conquered; yet we have this consolation with us, the*
*harder the conflict, the more glorious the triumph.*
*What we obtain too cheap, we esteem too lightly; it*
*is dearness only that gives everything it's value.'"*

"I hope some of the short-timers get to this read this," Jonathan said. "We've got an awful lot of summer soldiers planning to head home in two weeks."

It's the soldiers and the junior officers who win the wars, Washington had told Jonathan at least a dozen times. And John Glover and his Marblehead men had proven him right at least as many times. They'd been with Washington since Boston, and every time Washington needed to move men or supplies by water, he knew where to turn. Glover's men had grown up in boats. No high wind, no fierce tide, no cascading falls were too daunting a challenge for these practical New Englanders.

But on this night, Christmas 1776, they faced their greatest challenge. Washington's plan was to cross the Delaware nine miles above Trenton, then march twenty-four hundred men in two columns to catch the celebrating Hessian garrison in a crossfire. It would be challenge enough to move so many men so far on a freezing night when the northeast wind drove sleet and snow at the thinly covered backs of the soldiers. But the wide river clogged with large chunks of ice made the plan especially bold—or foolish.

The Marblehead boys had rounded up forty of the square Durham boats that local folk used to carry grain on the river. Glover said he'd be laughed out of Marblehead harbor if he ever showed up in anything so homely. And they were hard to handle even on smooth water; trying to maneuver them in the heavy flow of Delaware River ice would test good men who'd learned their trade on a fierce ocean.

Jonathan surveyed the battalions shivering in the snow at McKonkey's Ferry as he rode over to John Glover busily giving orders along the shore. "General wants to know if you're ready for the men to board, John. He wants to go with the first group," Jonathan said, melted sleet dripping off the end of his nose.

"You tell General Washington that it's a splendid night for swamp Yankees, and we'll take him all the way to London if that's what he wants," Glover replied with a tight grin.

"I'll tell him that," Jonathan replied, "but I think Trenton will do just fine."

A few minutes later Washington rode to the head of the column and watched from his horse as the troops began boarding the fleet of Durham boats. He then climbed into one of the boats and John Glover saluted him. "Long way from that warm day at Breed's Hill," he said to Washington as both leaned hard into the wind and the river filled with black shapes moving cautiously through the rough ice.

Once across, it was nine miles to Trenton over narrow, glazed roads. Many of Washington's men had only the remnants of boots; some had no shoes at all. And yet, because the crossing had taken so long, Washington now knew that that it would take a forced march to get his army into place before dawn. Soon both columns were moving at a trot, one led by General Sullivan along the river, the other by Nathanael Greene traveling inland.

Tired and wet, most of their weapons unable to fire because of the drenching, the Continentals arrived at the outskirts of Trenton just as the first light of dawn began to illuminate the clouds in the eastern sky. "Thank God, we've finally gotten bayonets for these troops," Washington said to Jonathan as his battalions took their places for the attack. "We'll certainly need them today."

They sat on their horses near the artillery battery that Hamilton still commanded and looked over the sleeping town below. As Honeyman had reported, Christmas celebrations had taken their toll and no one stirred. Even the pickets were nowhere in sight. Washington gave the order, a moment passed, then Hamilton's cannons roared.

Soon there was firing and smoke all around the town. The pickets came to life and fired as they fell back into Trenton's streets. They shouted in German. None of the Continentals could comprehend them, but panic needs no translation. Dazed Hessians were soon in the streets unable to organize a defense. Colonel Rall, showing every sign of a night of heavy celebration, appeared at his door. But he was struck by a musket ball before he could establish command. The two Continental forces closed quickly and forty-five minutes after it started, the firing ceased. Rall lived only long enough to surrender.

Jonathan and Flint had left Washington's side early in the fight to carry an order to Greene. When they rode into Trenton after the ceasefire, they were both stunned by the scene before them. Hessians were lined up in the streets, many of them barely dressed, their hands up over their heads. Bodies were everywhere on the ground, some motionless, some writhing in spasms of pain and death. Dark blood soaked the white snow. Many of the prisoners were crying in fear.

"They think we're gonna' eat 'em," Flint said, laughing. "That's what their officers tell 'em to keep 'em from surrenderin' and runnin' off. Tell 'em Continentals eat their prisoners. Course maybe after a few months of freezin' on short rations in our prison camps, they'll wish we had eaten 'em. But, I gotta tell ya', they don't look that tasty to me."

By noon, the prisoners had all been rounded up. Some were led off to remove the Hessian dead and wounded. Jonathan kept the accounts as the commanders surrounded Washington and gave their reports in the house that Rall had used as his headquarters. After some quick addition, Jonathan gave his summary. "More than a hundred Hessians killed or wounded," he said. "Approximately eight hundred and fifty officers and men taken prisoner. Four wounded on our side, no one killed."

Greene turned to Washington and said, "Did you see the ones who ran off, General? Some of the best troops they got and they were running for their lives toward the creek. Must have been a couple hundred of them."

Washington was always subdued after a defeat and equally subdued after a victory. He showed little emotion in the midst of his happy commanders and only said. "It was a pleasure to see that the men running from the battle this time were on the other side. I hope they run all the way to New York and tell Howe about this day."

Then he glanced slowly around the room, congratulating his officers. He stopped at the ruddy countenance of John Glover who stood quietly at the edge of the group. Their eyes met and Glover smiled his thin smile and mouthed the words, "Merry Christmas, General."

Jonathan hadn't been to Philadelphia for a year and a half. He was shocked by the change. The new year would begin in three days, but there was no sign of celebration. In fact, there was little sign of anything. Shops and taverns were closed, and some were boarded up. In many of the larger houses along Spruce Street, the draperies were pulled shut and gates bolted. Streets that used to be full of people were quiet and empty. And when he rode past the State House to show Flint where the Congress met, there was no indication a Congress had ever been there. Philadelphia was bracing for war.

This was not a social call and the two officers rode quickly to the Glorious Independence Tavern. Jonathan recognized it as the old Royal Arms, but as with so many things in America now, names suggestive of an English past had been changed to reflect a new order. The two men arrived at five o'clock and walked their horses around to the back of the tavern. There a tall young man waited for them and they exchanged passwords. He led the horses away, while Jonathan and Flint ascended a back stairway to the second floor of the tavern.

They entered a room lit only by a single candle, where a well-dressed man sat waiting for them. "Good evening, "Mr. Morris," Jonathan said, "It's good to see you again." He shook the older man's hand, then took a seat at the table while Flint remained by the door.

"Well, young Houghton is it? And it's Major Houghton now I understand," the older man said.

"Yes, sir," Jonathan replied, remembering how recently he had run petty errands for this man.

"What brings you here?" Robert Morris asked.

"General Washington has desperate need for your help, sir," Jonathan replied.

"What kind of help does the General need?"

"He needs you to help him hold his army together. In three days, the enlistments of most of the New England soldiers will be up and they're intending to return home. We've won a smashing victory at Trenton and the General now wants to chase the British out of New Jersey. But if those soldiers all leave, he'll have no army to do so.

"His plan is to offer them a bonus to re-enlist for another month or two. He'd like to pay each man ten dollars in Continental currency. But he has no money to pay a bonus like that."

Morris leaned back in his chair as the picture formed in his mind, smiled knowingly, and said, "I suspect this is where I come in."

"It is, sir. General Washington believes he'd be very well served if you could raise fifty thousand dollars for him."

Morris whistled slightly under his breath. "And I suppose he needs the money right now?"

"On no, sir," Jonathan laughed. "Tomorrow morning would be soon enough!"

"I understand the importance of this, Major. The victory at Trenton has electrified everyone here. As you can imagine, in Philadelphia we're all terribly worried about the threat of British occupation. I'm sure I can find men here who'll be willing to support Washington's effort to keep the British as far away from us as he can. I will meet you here at ten o'clock tomorrow morning."

"Thank you, sir. The General wanted me to convey his good wishes to you."

"And mine to him, Major." The older man took his gray hat and started to go.

"Oh, one more thing, Mr. Morris. The General also has a special need for some sterling, a hundred and fifty pounds to be exact."

"One hundred and fifty pounds in sterling? I don't know where I can possibly get such a sum in sterling by morning. What does he need it for?"

Jonathan hesitated, then looked the older man in the eye. "I can only tell you, sir, that it's terribly important. In war, there are expenses that cannot be discussed, but which are often critical to the outcome of the battle. This is one of those."

Morris nodded soberly, then turned and left.

Jonathan and Flint waited for ten minutes then stepped through the inside door and walked along the hallway to the room that had been set aside for them. "What was that all about?" Flint asked as he started to pull off his boots.

"That was Robert Morris, probably the richest man in Philadelphia. The General thought it would be easier to get money from him than from Congress. Congress has hightailed it to Baltimore, and they've pretty much left the General on his own to run things the way he wants. About time, if you ask me."

"Does that mean he has to raise all his own money?" Flint asked.

"Not really. But he doesn't have to get anyone's approval to do something like this."

"You think this is gonna' work? Them boys whose enlistments is up are itchin' to get home. They're damned tired of freezin' and starvin'. Don't seem likely to me that ten dollars is gonna keep 'em here."

Jonathan sat on his bed and looked at Flint. "I don't know either. I know the General's in a terrific fret about it. If those men all go home now, and we lose the chance to strike another blow or two while the redcoats are confused, the people in New Jersey may decide it's best for them to stick with the King since his soldiers are all over their state threatening them if they don't. Then if New Jersey drops out of the union, it cuts the country in half. It seems to me that keeping those boys here a while longer could be the most important thing that's happened in this war." Jonathan leaned back and then—in an odd turn, it seemed to Flint––started to chuckle.

"What's so funny?"

"Oh nothing. Just sometimes I start thinking about how strange all this is. Six months ago, when the Congress was debating independence, two men from Philadelphia stood in the way. John Dickinson and Robert Morris. My father admired them both, but neither one was ready to vote for independence. And without Pennsylvania, it didn't matter much what the other colonies did. They had to all be in it, or there wasn't anything to be in. On the night before the vote, July first, my father and a few of the others persuaded Dickinson and Morris to stay home the next day so that the Pennsylvania delegation would have a majority for independence.

Those two men had every right to leave the Congress, even to turn their backs on this whole new country that they opposed. But here's Morris financing the war to get rid of the King he didn't want to get rid of. And what do you suppose John Dickinson did?

"What?"

"He joined up in the Pennsylvania militia to fight the redcoats."

"Did you get it?" Washington asked anxiously, as soon as he was alone with his aide.

"Morris said to tell you that the mission is accomplished, General." Jonathan laid a large pouch on the table and opened it.

Washington peered inside and observed the stacks of currency. "What about the sterling?" he asked.

"He gave me a hundred and twenty-five pounds, sir. Flint is sitting with it outside."

"Does he know what to do with it?"

"He does, sir. I repeated all your instructions. He'll ride toward Princeton now to meet the spy where you indicated."

"Fine. Now I want you to send a message to all the battalion commanders that I want every man in this army paraded here at nine o'clock tomorrow morning."

Jonathan sent off runners to each of the battalion camps. At nine the next morning each battalion marched to its place in line along the street in front of Washington's headquarters. Washington sat on his horse in full dress uniform with his aides standing nearby. The colors were raised and the band struck up a vigorous march as the troops formed up. When all were in place and standing at attention, the drums rolled in long and loud anticipation.

Washington nudged his horse forward so that he was alone in front of his army. Jonathan watched closely and worried. Washington was many things, but a powerful orator he was not. He inspired men by his courage, his integrity, his bearing, but rarely by his words. Now, however, the pursuit of the British at Princeton, the safety of Philadelphia, perhaps the outcome of the war and the survival of the new United States would depend on the effect of Washington's words in this street.

"Gentlemen," he began. "Your countrymen could expect no more from you than what you have already given them. You have served with great bravery and extraordinary persistence through some very hard times. I know many of you are anxious to go home to your families. I understand that. Indeed, I often feel that same desire myself."

Washington looked from side to side as he spoke, trying to project his words to the very last man in line on this still morning. He knew what a risk this was. If he failed, it would be taken as a measure of his leadership. If his army walked away at its moment of greatest promise, who would regard him seriously as a commander? Yet there he sat, vulnerable and alone, all his chips in the pot, playing his last card.

"But we are on the precipice of a great opportunity. And if you go home now, that opportunity will be lost. And with it may well go the very things for which you have fought so valiantly and which we all cherish. I ask every man here, in the name of his country and the cause for which we fight, to stay with me for six more weeks. I will pay a bonus of ten dollars to every man who agrees to do so. The future of our country may depend on this. If you will stay with me and continue to serve our cause, step forward now."

As instructed, the drums rolled, rising to a loud crescendo. No one moved. Some men looked at other men. Still no one moved. Some men looked at Washington. Some simply closed their eyes. Yet still no one moved. Washington sat before them, silent now--in prayer, Jonathan guessed.

One more swelling of drumbeats. Still no one moved. Then off to the left, two men from Connecticut stepped forward. Jonathan could see a small smile begin to form at the corner of the General's mouth. A few more men down the line also stepped forward. And then, as if synchronized, whole companies stepped forward. The band broke into "Yankee Doodle Dandy" and Jonathan felt his feet twitching, wanting to dance. Washington smiled broadly now as he looked slowly from left to right, watching with great relief as most of his army stepped across the line. They would fight another day.

Aubrey Armistead was working with his junior officers on the plans for Howe's winter camp in New York when the messenger came from Cornwallis. Armistead had always liked Charles Cornwallis. He was a soldier's general: aggressive, tireless, concerned about the welfare of the men under him. He may have been Lord Cornwallis, but he never let his peerage prevent him from thinking about the foot soldiers. They were not just cannon fodder to him.

But Cornwallis was clearly upset when Armistead went to see him. He had been on board a packet preparing to sail to London for some leave, when Howe ordered him to New Jersey to take command there after Washington's surprise attack on the outpost at Trenton. The whole British command had been caught off guard by Washington's bold move. No one thought an army could cross the ice-choked Delaware River, and certainly no one expected Washington to do so on Christmas night. Now Howe was worried that Washington had other plans, and he wanted Cornwallis to hurry to Princeton, then lead a force to Trenton to check Washington who was now back on the Pennsylvania side of the river.

Cornwallis had marched his seven thousand men to Trenton at top speed, but when they arrived as darkness fell on January first, they found that Washington had crossed the Delaware to New Jersey yet again and had his army camped along Assunpink Creek, just outside of Trenton. At a brief meeting following their arrival, Armistead and several others had recommended an immediate attack on Washington. But Cornwallis thought his men were too tired after their hard march and postponed the attack until morning. "Don't worry," Cornwallis, had said, "Washington likes to dig in and wait for us to come at him. We can tell from the fires and the digging noises across the creek that he's got his men building breastworks, just as he did in Boston and New York. Rest the men tonight. Tomorrow will be soon enough to attack. Washington will be there waiting for us"

The old Washington maybe, but not the new one. Not the Washington recharged by the victory at Trenton and invigorated by the re-enlistment of his troops. "He seems like a different man," Jonathan said to Hamilton, as the latter supervised the movement of his heavy artillery down the back road to Princeton. "I think he's come to believe that he can rely only on himself, that he can't trust Congress to support him or Lee to follow his orders or even some of his generals to perform effectively. He seems more prepared to take risks than I've ever seen him. Perhaps because he realizes that so much is against him, he has to do the thing least expected."

Calling it a road may have been stretching a point. There were still stumps along the path and in places the puddles were more than a foot deep and frozen solid. The old farm path had only begun to be turned into a road in the past year, and the job was a long way from completion. It didn't even show up on many of the maps, and Washington had learned about it only from the spy who had been paid with the sterling that came from Morris. That same spy had provided the General with detailed plans of the British garrison at Princeton, and Washington was leading his army there now for another surprise strike.

Cornwallis had played perfectly into Washington's hands by marching to Trenton on the main road and leaving only a few companies behind to protect Princeton. And Washington was not about to signal his intentions to the enemy. He'd left his own small force on the hilltop across Assunpink Creek, and he ordered the men there to build enormous fires and to spend the night hitting axes and shovels on the frozen ground, creating the illusion of furious construction. Meanwhile Washington was moving most of his army down the back road for an attack on Princeton while Cornwallis was in Trenton. When dawn arrived, the small garrison at Princeton was surprised by the appearance of the American army behind a fence at the edge of town and mounted a valiant, but brief, defense.

"General's enjoyin' this," Flint said as he and Jonathan rode along at the edge of the firing line. Washington was in front of his troops now with sword drawn riding the line and urging them on. "Stay with your officers men! Halt and fire! Use bayonets!" Jonathan had seen many drawings of Washington in the past year and a half. Most of them pictured him heroically, sword drawn, large steed up on hind legs, flags waving, leading his men in battle. That wasn't the Washington he knew, who was cooler and more calculating. But on this third day of 1777, life, for once, followed art.

"Damn it," Cornwallis cursed. "He's gone." Armistead looked across the creek to where Cornwallis was pointing. There were no breastworks there, no fortifications of any kind. The remains of a dozen fires smoldered, but there was no sign of an enemy. Washington had fled the field.

"He must have gone back across the river when he saw us here," one of Cornwallis's aides suggested.

Cornwallis grimaced and rejected the suggestion. "No, we had the river under observation. That would have been too dangerous any way. We could have destroyed him from the rear. No he's gone to Princeton, you can be sure. I don't know how in hell he got there, but these bloody colonials seem to know about roads that our mapmakers have never seen."

Just then a rider came dashing toward them and dismounted. He handed a piece of paper to Cornwallis who read it quickly and swore again under his breath. Then the angry commander looked up and shared the news. "Washington attacked Princeton this morning and overran the town. He took three hundred prisoners, nearly everyone else fled, including apparently our column of reinforcements. He came so quickly that nothing could be burned or blown up. He got all the powder and the artillery pieces. Damn him."

Armistead watched as Cornwallis considered his options. A minute or two later, the General looked at his officers and said. "Back to Princeton, gentlemen at double time. We have to catch him before he gets to New Brunswick."

Armistead rode quickly back to his regiment. His men were exhausted from the hard march over frozen ground yesterday. Now he had to tell them that they were going to do the same again today, in reverse. He knew how unhappy they'd be. He shared their sentiments. Washington was a frustration. Every time he seemed beaten, he slipped away. He commanded a terrible defense of New York. He had no right even to be commanding the army now. Yet here we are running all over the countryside trying to find him. God, Armistead prayed, please hasten the spring time when we can finish him off forever.

# Chapter 21

## London
## February 1777

The news of Washington's victories at Trenton and Princeton added to the chill of the cold London winter. After word had arrived near Christmas of Howe's splendid success in driving Washington from New York, London was ablaze with light, and the air filled with ringing bells and cheering crowds in St. James Square. Surely it would be over soon and the colonies would be secured. All that was needed was a full display of the might of the British Army and the Royal Navy.

But now the mood, like the London weather, had turned gray and somber. The optimists saw Washington's surprise victories as the death throes of a defeated army trying to salvage an ounce or two of honor before the end. But the realists knew that the Americans would never capitulate easily and that many more months and many more men would be necessary to put an end to this independence business.

But tonight all gloom was set aside, for this was to be one of the highlights of the social season: the unveiling of Benton Carlisle's portrait of Lord North. The word had already circulated that North was delighted with the portrait, and all of his friends and all of those who sought to curry his favor were here tonight at North's official residence in Downing Street.

The portrait of Lord North would soon hang in Whitehall, at the first landing of the grand hallway in the spot normally reserved for portraits of the first minister. But the formal unveiling would occur here, and most of the leading members of Parliament were present with their ladies. Dukes and earls and lords, resplendent in finely cut silk, stood in small pockets of conversation throughout the reception rooms on the first floor. Footmen in bright red coats and matching cravats circulated with glasses of port and large silver trays of caviar and smoked eel.

Benton Carlisle was the center of attention, though he clearly realized that most of those who lavishly praised his work were probably hoping to arrange with him a commission for a portrait of themselves. These were politicians, after all, and not above copious palaver when it served their purposes.

Nathaniel, as usual, stood at the edge of the crowd, observing the rituals of the political class, saying nothing. For several months he had been keeping a notebook of his impressions of these men. When a dozen or so pages accumulated, he would pass them on to George, thinking they might be of interest to those in America who had to try to anticipate their moves and reactions.

The unveiling was scheduled for nine-thirty, and a few minutes before that, Nathaniel found the butler and, indicating that he was feeling unwell, inquired if there might be a place where he could rest for a few minutes. The butler asked if a doctor should be called, but Nathaniel said, "No, no. That's not necessary. I've just been suffering from dizzy spells lately and I'll be fine after a few minutes off my feet."

The butler nodded and led Nathaniel upstairs to a small, pale blue room on the second floor. He struck a match and lit a candle, then covered it with a cut-glass globe that projected the light into every corner. The room was apparently little-used because it contained only the candle stand and a large settee. "This should be comfortable, sir," the butler said. "Is there anything else you wish?"

"No thank you," Nathaniel replied. "I'll be fine in a few moments, and I'll find my way back down. Please go now. You don't want to miss the unveiling of the portrait." The butler bowed and left.

Nathaniel laid motionless for a few minutes until he heard the ringing of the brass bell that invited the guests to gather in the largest of the first floor rooms where the portrait stood under a velvet canopy. At that moment, he rose quickly to his feet and moved to the door. He opened it slowly and looked up and down the broad open hallway. Seeing no one, and assuming that the attention of everyone in the house was concentrated on the ceremony unfolding downstairs, Nathaniel slipped along the north wall, opening each door as he went and peering into the rooms. Most had fires laid and glowing, and this afforded enough light for him to make a quick decision.

At the third door, Nathaniel found the book-lined room for which he'd been searching. When he and Benton were painting North's portrait, Nathaniel had often heard the minister ask clerks to put documents in his pouch for night reading in his library at home. That pouch sat on a small oval Pembroke table beside the ponderous desk that filled most of the corner of the room. Nathaniel closed the door quietly behind him and moved quickly in that direction. He carefully noted the position of the pouch on the table, then lifted it and kneeled by the fire where he could better see it contents. He shuffled through the papers looking for documents of interest. What he found was disappointing. Reports of the waterworks in South London. Estimates of the value of last year's corn crop. Several letters from cousins of the king complaining about slights from members of Parliament. Only a brief report on the recruiting efforts of the Royal Navy even touched on the war effort.

Nathaniel quickly returned the documents to the pouch, taking care to keep them in their original order. Then he placed the pouch as he had found it on the small table. It was unlikely he would ever get into the first minister's library again, and Nathaniel was annoyed to have found nothing there of value. He turned to leave, glancing around quickly as he did. Then something caught his eye.

On the Sheraton chair behind the desk was a single piece of paper. Nathaniel stepped around in that direction and picked it up, again carefully noting the way it laid before moving it. He took it to the fire and held it low until it caught the light. His disappointment evaporated as he began to read. He read it through several times more, committing the precise wording to memory. Then he replaced the paper on the chair in its exact original position, moved quickly across the room and through the door. He arrived downstairs just as North was removing the canopy from the portrait. There were a few seconds of silence, then applause and loud cheering.

George Germain stepped forward when the noise diminished and raised his glass. "Three cheers for our excellent—and very handsome—First Minister." And three rounds of cheers broke out. In response, Lord North raised his own glass toward Benton and said, "And certainly a cheer is due this most imaginative and creative artist who can make even the dullest weed look like a spring flower." A broad wave of laughter was followed by cheers for Benton as well.

Nathaniel looked to his left and saw the butler standing there. "Good to see you're feeling better, sir," he said.

Indeed I am, thought Nathaniel. Indeed I am.

When the two painters returned from the festivities at Lord

North's, Lydie was waiting for them in the small drawing room at the back of the first floor of the house in Bloomsbury Square. She was anxious to hear about the evening, but she was also anxious to see Nathaniel. Benton poured brandy, then provided his usual mocking and self-deprecatory description of another London social event. This had become a happy ritual for all of them, and it was as close as Lydie chose to get to London society.

Benton tired after an hour or so of this conversation and excused himself, leaving his wife and his assistant alone by the fire. This was the time Lydie had patiently awaited all evening. But Nathaniel seemed anxious and preoccupied and, after a few minutes of conversation, he apologized to Lydie and said he, too, was very tired and should be getting home. Lydie's disappointment must have been patent, so Nathaniel apologized again, and said that perhaps they could spend some time together in the studio tomorrow afternoon.

As he was putting on his long wool coat at the door, he asked Lydie if he might have several pieces of paper and a quill and ink to take with him. "I have to write my father a letter," he said, "and my supplies have all dwindled." Lydie walked off and returned a minute later with a small wooden box containing the items Nathaniel had requested. They said goodnight and Nathaniel, feeling both hurried and guilty, reached up instinctively and touched Lydie's cheek. She looked at him with a mixture of affection and sadness, but he was gone out the door without responding.

Lydie shut the door and leaned back against the wall. The man is a mystery to me, she thought. Sometimes I think he is deeply drawn to me, as I am to him. Then at other times, he seems miles distant. And where does he go when he hurries off like this. He didn't seem tired to me. Many nights I've seen him come back from these parties and work in the studio for several hours.

She didn't want to admit the dark possibility that had begun to creep into her mind. Perhaps there was another woman. Perhaps Nathaniel had once been drawn to her, but he had pulled away out of guilt or respect for Benton and then he'd met another woman who now commanded his affections. Lydie had never known jealousy before. She'd married the only man she'd ever loved, and he was unwaveringly faithful to her. But Nathaniel sparked something in her that she'd never felt before, not even in those days in France when she and Benton realized where their flirtation was leading. Now she felt the sharp stiletto of jealousy whenever Nathaniel left her company abruptly as he did tonight.

Lydie walked into the drawing room and extinguished the candles, thinking as she did that the time had come for her to find out what powerful attraction it was that kept pulling Nathaniel away from her.

After leaving the Carlisle house, Nathaniel walked to St. Cross Street as quickly as he could. The rapid movement warmed him against the damp chill, and though his room was cold when he got there, he wasted no time building a fire. Instead, he lit a candle, covered it with a globe, and sat down at his small table. He opened the box Lydie had given him and began to write the words he had memorized earlier, exactly as George Germain had written them.

> I wish to inform you sir that the orders have been prepared for General Howe. They inform him of our decision, to which His Majesty assents, that we must launch an aggressive attack from our Canadian bases on the Continental armies in New York. General Burgoyne will command this mission and move his forces down the lakes and into the Hudson Valley as soon as the weather allows.  When he is successful, the colonies will be divided in half and Burgoyne will undertake the rapid recapture of New England while our southern forces pursue Washington in New Jersey.
>
> Howe will be informed that arrangements have been made with our friend, Mr. Brown, to supply Burgoyne's army with powder and ball and ample stores of food to get him through the summer. Those materials will be shipped from New York by boat and ox cart and will be available to him at the southern end of Lake Champlain. This will free him from slowing his advance by the necessity of transporting all of his stores from Canada.
>
> With the blessing of a divine Providence, the King's colonies will be secure in his sovereignty by autumn.
>
> Your obedient servant,
> Germain

Then Nathaniel spent the next two hours translating these words into the cumbersome code in which George had instructed him. When he was done, he placed the coded paper in the false bottom of the middle drawer of his mahogany commode. He then built a fire into which he dropped his notes. He watched until they turned to powdered ash, then fell exhausted on his bed. In the morning he would have to remember to leave the curtain drawn on his window.

In the studio the following afternoon, Nathaniel worked on a painting of the mist over Ranelagh Gardens that he'd begun in the fall. The portrait work had kept him so busy lately that he'd had little time for his own painting. It felt good to see the strokes flow from his own imagination, to watch the brush dance freely across the canvas. The dull discipline of finish work on Benton's portraits gave him none of the satisfaction he derived from these hours he spent transforming the picture in his mind to an image on canvas.

He was so engaged in his efforts to capture the white translucence of the mist that he hadn't heard Lydie enter the studio. He jumped when he heard her voice behind him saying "More red. You can't capture the sunlight without red."

He laughed. Lydie was always giving him instructions when he painted, but they were done in jest and had nothing to do with the task before him. They reveled in these little rituals where he often did quite the opposite of what she suggested as he praised her good judgment. It was one of the many secret forms of communication they'd developed over the past year, each one designed to create a private space that only they inhabited. It was the only intimacy that seemed proper in the awkward circumstances of their growing affection for each other.

"I didn't hear you come in," Nathaniel said. "You are a spirit, aren't you."

"Of course I'm not a spirit. An elephant could walk in here without you noticing when you're at the easel."

Lydie pulled up the old chair in her accustomed position next to the painter's stool.

"Where is Benton?" Nathaniel asked. "I desperately need his advice on this mist. He'd have the answer in a flash."

"He's gone to tea at the Royal Academy. George Romney specifically asked him to come. Something about some impetuous demand from Gainsborough. I wish he were not so busy, Nathaniel. I do fear that it's wearing him down. He waited so long to be famous and, now that he is, he worries that he won't have enough years left to enjoy it."

"But don't you think he's very happy. He complains constantly about the burdens of painting portraits, but I think he's come to realize that his portraits and not what he calls his 'real paintings' will be his artistic legacy. People will be looking at his portraits and judging his talent by them long after his other paintings have disappeared from public view."

"How sad that is," Lydie said, smoothing the peach silk of her skirts, "to be remembered for something you did unwillingly."

"Not really so unwillingly, I think. He pours his full energies into his portraits, and he's certainly wealthy enough now to turn down every commission if he really wanted to. My own observation is that he has come to think of himself as a portraitist who does other things on the side. When I first came here, it was the other way around. There is nothing wrong with that. We should all be lucky enough to find our true calling before we die."

Nathaniel went back to his brush work and Lydie sat quietly beside him. When Nathaniel seemed ready to stop for the day, she rose slowly and stood behind him, first resting her hands gently on his shoulders, then softly rubbing his neck. Nathaniel said nothing but leaned back comfortably into the delicate circular movement of her hands. Neither spoke for several minutes. Then Lydie leaned down, tenderly laying her face against Nathaniel's brown curls, sweetly kissing the top of his head. Nathaniel sat still, savoring her touch. Then he leaned his head as far back as he could and his lips met Lydie's.

"Oh Nathaniel," Lydie whispered, "you are so dear to me."

Nathaniel rose and quickly wiped his hands on his smock then dropped it to the floor. He wrapped Lydie in his arms and pulled her tightly against him. They said nothing, simply held the embrace for many minutes. Nathaniel opened his eyes to look at Lydie and was jarred by the darkness in the room. My God, he thought, it must be after 5 o'clock. He kissed Lydie tenderly just above the thin line of her eyebrows, then pulled slowly back, disentangling himself from her arms. "Dear Lydie," he said, "I'd forgotten how late it was. I have an appointment and I must be going."

Lydie pulled abruptly away and gave him a sharp look. "I don't understand you," she said. "If you think we must end this infatuation, then admit that. But please don't make excuses to depart every time I want to

312

hold you. I'm as aware as you are of the awkwardness of our situation. I hope we can be honest with each other about it."

Nathaniel gave her a sad uncertain look. "No, no. It's not that. I truly must go. But I agree that we must navigate here with total honesty." He went to the bench and began hurriedly to clean the brushes and cover the paints. Lydie said nothing and quickly withdrew.

A few minutes later, the clean-up completed, Jonathan pulled on his wool coat and gloves and left through the studio door into the mews. He walked quickly away along Southampton Street. In his hurry, he failed to see the figure moving behind him in a heavy dark hat and long overcoat.

Benton stepped down from his coach in front of the house. He righted himself on the slippery stones as the coach pulled away. Then he turned north and walked half way down to the corner to glance at his watch under the gaslight. The tea had gone on much longer than he'd anticipated. Nothing like squabbles among artists to eat up an afternoon, he thought.

He turned back toward his house just as the front door opened. Lydie dashed down the walk into the street wearing one of his long coats. She turned south and hurried off, covering her head with one of his large hats as she did. Benton stopped for a moment in the street to ponder this. He'd seen several odd actions from his wife in the last few weeks, but none that matched her trundling off before dinner dressed like a man.

She seemed different lately, and it perplexed him. They'd always had such an easy affinity with each other, perhaps because their age difference added layers to their marriage that many other couples lacked. But now there seemed to be a brittleness between them that was new and very uncomfortable.

Perhaps I'm the cause of this, Benton thought. Perhaps I'm growing old and don't see myself clearly any more. I encounter very few men who are older than I, and most of them seem doddering old fools. Maybe I am as well, but I don't know it. Maybe Lydie is just humoring me when, in reality, I'm an old bore. He could come up with no other explanation.

But why was she going out on a cold night dressed like a man?

Lydie caught sight of Nathaniel as he stepped up to the wash house in High Holbourn. He didn't enter or even remove his gloves. He simply walked slowly past the south door, stopped and looked at it for a minute, then turned around and headed south. She followed him to St. Martin's Lane where he quickly entered the darkened church yard.

Lydie stood silently in the shadow of a dark shop, across the street from where Nathaniel sat next to a small figure on the recessed rear steps of the church. So this is it, she thought, he meets a woman here. She silently crossed the street never leaving the shadows until she could feel the barren hedge against her arm. Then she slid quietly along the hedge, moving toward the steps where Nathaniel and the woman now sat. She could see that Nathaniel was doing most of the talking and that he was moving his hands very rapidly the way he did when he described some beautiful scene he'd sketched.

She came to the end of the hedge and realized there was no more cover between her and the steps. She wanted to get closer, perhaps to overhear their conversation, but it was too risky. So she stayed hidden behind the hedge and watched. It was all she could do to muffle the staccato click-click of her shivering.

A few minutes later, Nathaniel and the woman ended their conversation. Nathaniel got up to leave, making no effort to embrace the woman. Lydie realized that he might walk toward her, so she turned quickly and trotted silently along the hedge, then back into the shadow and across St. Martin's Lane. When she was around the corner, she started to walk as fast as she could without drawing notice and a few minutes later, winded and now warm, she turned into the gate of the house on Bloomsbury Square.

She twisted the door handle as quietly as she could, opened it slowly and looked into the parlor. Seeing no sign of Benton, she slipped through the door quickly, pulling it silently behind her. She started to shed her coat, when a voice from the darkened parlor called out. "Hello, darling. Have you been to a costume party?"

Lydie's breath caught in her throat and only the darkness prevented Benton from seeing the look of panic that fell over her. But she righted herself quickly and said, "Oh my goodness, you scared me, Benton. I didn't know you were here." Then, her thoughts rushing, she said, "You've caught me sneaking a walk on a cold night. I've been trapped here all day with visitors and I felt a powerful need to take some air. I'm sure I looked a fright, but your wool coat is so much warmer than anything I have and with your hat pulled down over my hair, I thought no one would recognize me. Can you ever forgive me, dear Benton, for being such a silly child?"

Benton laughed in relief, then struck a match to find a candle, remembering again the coltish charms of the whimsical French maiden he'd loved for so long.

*Chapter 22*

*New York*
*New Jersey*
*April 1777*


On any number of days when they were little girls growing up, Savannah would have been happy never to see her older sister again. Silly was often simply irritating. She constantly pestered Savannah to come inside and play with the dollhouse Father had painstakingly built for them. But Savannah never liked the dollhouse and was happy just sitting in the dooryard with a book or helping mother snap beans. And whenever Savannah talked the boys into letting her ride with them, Silly called her names: "Horsey Man" and "Brother Number Three." And in the dead of winter, when it was too cold to sit in the dooryard or ride, when they were forced to spend hours together by the fire, Silly often drove her crazy with the made-up songs she sang loudly and out of tune. No, there were many times when Savannah would have preferred life with no sister at all.

But not now. She hadn't seen her sister since Celia and Godfrey left as newlyweds right after the New Year's feast in 1771. So when the carriage pulled up that afternoon in front of Celia's wide beautiful house, Savannah was nearly overcome with excitement. She'd come this long way to visit even though the trip worried Father. New York was occupied by Howe's army and who knew when the fighting would start again. Washington had gone into winter camp in Morristown in the New Jersey foothills, wisely deciding that a strike at New Brunswick was stretching his luck and his men beyond the breaking point. Howe had pulled back from the posts he'd stretched across New Jersey early in the winter, but he'd be back when the weather warmed and the ground dried.

Savannah calculated that between the end of the planting at Still River and the ripening of New Jersey for war, she would have a few weeks in which she could make a short visit to see her sister and nephew. Celia's letters of late carried an edge of desperation and Father had grown

316

more concerned about her. And while he'd urged Savannah not to make the trip, once she'd made up her own mind to go, he was secretly pleased that Celia would have her company.

So was Celia, and she cried and laughed irrepressibly when she greeted Savannah in front of the house on Beekman Street. She hadn't been this happy for a very long time. The first few hours of their visit were consumed with Savannah holding young Godfrey and Celia telling her story after story about the sweet habits her son had acquired. At seven o'clock, the nurse came and took young Godfrey to his bed for the night. Celia kept looking toward the street, and finally Savannah asked "What's wrong, Silly? Is it all the soldiers going by?"

"No, no," she said, "I'm used to that. I was just hoping Godfrey would be home by now. I know how excited he is to see you."

His absence had seemed odd to Savannah as well. She'd assumed, after so many years apart, that both of them would be home to greet her when she arrived. Celia had apologized earlier saying that Godfrey was terribly busy at work, but that she knew he'd be home any minute. Now it was dinner time and his absence was becoming an embarrassment to Celia.

"Perhaps we should start dinner," she said. "He can join us when he arrives."

So they moved to the grand dining room where Savannah admired the three-pedestal walnut table and walked around the side board admiring a handsome oval tray with silver gadroon and the gold Regency bread basket. She asked about each item, and Celia told her how Godfrey had imported this one from Ireland and that one from Manchester. Savannah had never seen such lovely pieces of silver and gold and bone china. A servant arrived to announce the service, and the two sisters sat together at one end of the long table enjoying a meal of ham and fowl and biscuits with wonderful apple butter. Savannah had heard that food was very scarce in the British winter camp, but Celia's table was not wanting.

The women finished their meal, still without Godfrey, and retired to the small parlor for tea and cakes. They talked for another hour, then the days on the road began to catch up with Savannah and she asked if it would be rude for her to go to bed now, before Godfrey arrived.

"Not at all. If anyone has been rude, it's Godfrey, and I shall scold him mightily when he gets home," Celia said with a forced laugh.

The warehouse hummed loudly from the combined sounds of all

the activity. Wagons came and unloaded goods. Wagons came and took goods away. Stevedores loaded their carts and pushed them along the slip to the boats that would carry them up the Hudson River to Lake Champlain. Some men rolled barrels along the heavy oak floors; others hammered together crates and sealed them with pine tar to keep water from seeping through to the powder. Drouin ran in and out from the floor with problems for Carter to solve, decisions to make, papers to sign. Carter had worried last November that the war would come to a quick end. Washington had led his army so incompetently that it seemed Howe would overrun him before Christmas; but Howe, bless him, had pulled back and Washington was still in the field. In fact, with the surprise successes of the Continentals in New Jersey, some of the British officers now said, it might take all year to win the war.

And during that time, Carter thought, the British army would need food and horses and gunpowder that he could supply them at wartime prices—and wartime profits. It was hard work, he had to admit that, but the money was rolling in. Enough to keep Celia happy. Enough to pay off the quartermaster to keep soldiers out of his house. Enough to keep even with his growing gambling debts. Enough to buy all the pleasures that the house in the alley off Maiden Lane could provide. When he found a minute to reflect, Godfrey had to admit that these were good times for a man who knew how to seize his opportunities.

When the chaise came to take him home, Godfrey was very tired. He knew he was supposed to have been there earlier in the afternoon to greet his wife's sister from Delaware. But things just got too busy and, if he walked in now, Celia would be upset and he'd have an awkward scene in front of Savannah. So it made sense to have the driver stop on Bridge Street so he could sit in on the last few hands of loo. Some of the British generals came by for these Wednesday night card games, and Carter hated to miss them. The generals were awful at cards, but they had family fortunes a mile deep. What more could a gambling man want?

Savannah sat alone with her breakfast at the large table when Godfrey came down. He was smartly dressed in breeches, leather vest and high-cut justacorps topped by a green silk cravat. A silver watch hung from his belt. Godfrey looked older and much heavier than the young man her sister had married seven years ago. He seemed to Savannah the very picture of prosperity. She rose when he entered, and he bowed in her direction.

318

"How good to see you, Savannah. I hope you'll forgive my absence yesterday. It was inexcusable. I tried to escape the trap at work, but simply could not."

"Please don't feel badly, Godfrey," Savannah said brightly. "I'm so happy to be here and uncontrollable disruptions seem a part of all our lives these days."

"Indeed they are," Godfrey said as he gestured for Savannah to sit down then did the same. The houseman quickly appeared with a plate of eggs and ham and beans and warm pudding. Godfrey began to eat as soon as the plate hit the table.

"You have given me such a handsome nephew," Savannah said. "You must be very proud of him."

"Oh, I am," Godfrey said. "Indeed."

"When does the nurse bring him down in the morning?" Savannah asked.

Godfrey looked flustered by the question and didn't pause from his eating. "Oh," he said, "You know it's usually after I've left in the morning, so I'm not sure exactly." Then he wiped his face broadly with his napkin and apologized to Savannah that his chaise was waiting and he had to go.

In the hour before Celia appeared, Savannah sat by the window in the large parlor watching the activity on Beekman Street. She noticed that no men seemed to emerge from the other houses to go off to work as Godfrey had from this one. But she also noticed that British soldiers in their bright scarlet uniforms seemed to flow steadily from every other house on the street. She marveled at how large and fierce they looked in their cocked hats, black splatterdashes, and regimental breastplates all gleaming in the burnished morning light.

From one house the size of the Carter's, Savannah counted eight soldiers emerging. Her other observations suggested a similar proportion for other houses. She then roughly calculated three soldiers per bedroom. After he came back from the first Continental Congress, she'd heard her father talking with neighbors about the evils of the Quartering Act and how it was turning the people of Boston against the King. But most of them had found it as difficult as she had to picture soldiers living uninvited and unwanted in their houses. Now as she sat here in Celia's parlor, she could begin to imagine British soldiers living in the house at Still River Bend and the dreadful imposition that would be.

"Good morning, Savannah." She turned and saw Celia standing in the doorway, dressed in blue and white calico. "Good morning," Savannah called back. "There's a lot of activity here in New York this morning."

Celia glanced outside for a minute, seemed briefly relieved, then responded, "Yes, I'm afraid there's a lot of activity every morning. Always soldiers coming and going. We're all hoping that with the weather improving they'll soon go off somewhere and leave New York to the New Yorkers."

"But that, of course, would mean they'd be going where Jonathan is."

"I try not even to think about that. It was terrible the last few weeks he was here in the fall. He'd be gone for a few days for some battle in Brooklyn Heights or somewhere, then he'd be back here for a few days. It was just like Godfrey, except Jonathan's 'office' was a war. God, I hope this is over soon."

"Silly, I did have breakfast with Godfrey this morning. He seems very well. Quite different from the last time I saw him. Very prosperous looking."

"Yes, well he is very prosperous. Many of the neighbors had to leave New York, some because they were patriots, but others because the war ruined their businesses. Others stayed, but are having trouble earning a living here now. We're very lucky that Godfrey has managed to keep his business going in spite of the war. I know it hasn't been easy. That's why he has to work so hard and be away so much."

"What is his business anyway, Silly? I asked him about it, but he was in a hurry and didn't say much."

"Oh it's importing something or selling something. We never talk much about it. He's so tired when he gets home that he never wants to talk about business when he's here."

"Have you ever been to his office?" Savannah asked.

"Oh no. He says it's no place for a woman."

"Where is his office?"

"Oh, it's near the waterfront somewhere. I'm not sure where. Godfrey says the waterfront is dangerous, so I don't go there."

Celia moved toward the matched walnut arm chairs by the front window and joined Savannah there. She picked up her needlepoint and began to stitch nervously as they talked.

320

"It seemed to me from what I saw this morning that there are soldiers quartered at just about every house on Beekman Street," Savannah said.

"Really?" Celia responded without looking up. "Yes, perhaps you're right. I haven't paid too much attention, but there do seem to be a lot of soldiers on the street here."

"Have you ever wondered why you haven't been made to quarter any here? This is a big house. I'd think the British would find it a very appealing place to put soldiers."

"I don't think about it very much. I believe Godfrey said something once about talking them out of it. But I don't know. Maybe some day they'll come and make us take some in. We've just been lucky, I guess. So many of my friends had their houses burned when the Continentals left. And many families we know have had to leave or live below their class because they have so little money now. So far we've been spared from the imposition of soldiers. So I'm counting my blessings."

Savannah pondered all this for a few minutes while Celia continued to concentrate on her needlepoint. Then she cleared her throat and said, "Silly, I think you're not seeing the reality of things very clearly."

Celia, startled, said, "What? What do you mean?"

"I mean you have a wonderful home and a beautiful child. But do you really have a life with your husband? Wouldn't you think he'd want to be home more often now that he has a son. He doesn't even seem to know anything about the boy's routine." Savannah paused for a moment, wanting to proceed gingerly. In the old days, she never would have been so direct with her sister, but in the last few years on the farm she'd developed a habit of plain speaking.

"Godfrey works just a short distance away, but he leaves early and arrives home late or not at all. You don't know how he earns his living but he's prospering in the middle of a war. Everyone you know has been harmed by the war in some way, but not you. Everyone on your street has been forced to quarter British troops, except you. It doesn't add up, Silly. It certainly can't just be luck. Don't you think you need to find out more about Godfrey's work—and maybe about his other activities, too?"

Celia stitched quietly, as if contemplating what her sister had said. It wasn't the first time such thoughts had occurred to her, but she'd never spoken about them with anyone. "Oh, sometimes I do wonder," she finally responded. "And I don't know why so often he comes home late. I ask him about it, but he never really answers. Says I shouldn't bother him with questions like that, that he's taking good care of us and that's all I need to know. I wish I were stronger with him, Savannah. I know I should be. But he always acts like I'm just a woman and that anything serious is his responsibility, not mine. And I suppose he's right; at least that's the way we are. He handles the business and I handle our home."

"What I see worries me, Silly. I hope Godfrey's not involved in some war activities that'll get him in trouble. If he's helping the British army, the Continentals will throw him in jail when they win the war."

"Oh I'm sure he's not doing that. Godfrey's really a good man at heart. He wouldn't do anything like that, especially not with Jonathan in the Army. He's not like that at all. Don't be worried, Savannah. Our life is different from yours, but it's a good life, and I'm happy here. Especially with the new baby to fill so much of my time."

The stage coach had crossed the river at Dobb's Ferry two days earlier and begun the long trek across New Jersey. The hours of riding had given Savannah time to reflect on the week she'd spent with her sister. On the surface, Celia seemed happy enough and she certainly had a life that most women would envy: a fine, large house; a wealthy husband; a beautiful baby. But scratch beneath the surface, Savannah thought, and everything was wrong. The fine house was in the center of an occupied military garrison dominated by foreign soldiers. The wealthy husband was a mysterious character, absent most of the time. The beautiful baby was growing up in a family that seemed to have no center, no moral code, no great purpose.

As she'd come to take on a larger measure of responsibility for the farm in Still River, Savannah found that much of what had only been background in her life was moving to the fore. The land was more than just land, more than just a resource, more than just a way to make a living. It was a bond that tied her to all the generations of Houghtons that preceded her and to all their labors and trials. It tied her as well to all those generations that would follow, children and their children and their children who would one day think of Henry Houghton, maybe even of Savannah Houghton, as an important and honorable ancestor. No, the farm at Still River Bend was not just the family's land, it was the core of the family's being, the center to which all the activities of the Houghtons—all the honest labors, the public services, all the personal tragedies—were anchored like planets to the sun.

But when she thought of Celia's life now, the bond seemed very thin. How would Godfrey Houghton Carter ever know the meaning of his middle name, the land that bore it, the proud tradition that gave it weight? Wasn't it more likely that he'd grow up a Carter, tied to no land or place, bonded to no long tradition, learning from a father he barely knew, taught to play in the shadows of life? Oh Silly, she thought, this is no life for the only grandchild of Henry Houghton, no life for you, no life for any woman.

How different now were the lives she and her sister lived. Three or four times since the beginning of her travel back to Delaware, men riding in her carriage had remarked on how rare it was to see a woman traveling alone. She knew that, of course, and it was one of the reasons why Father had tried to convince her not to go. But it was also one of the reasons she felt she had to go. Why shouldn't a woman travel alone? Men do. I can ride a horse. I can negotiate a contract. I can tell the slaves and the hired men how to use their time. Why should I shrink from traveling alone?

When we ask him why he has changed his mind and become a strong supporter of independence, Father always says that we have to realize that the world is changing very quickly now. Perhaps it's not changing quickly enough. The words those men at Congress use—freedom, equality, liberty—why don't they think of women when they say these words? Why is it still such a struggle to get even a very good man like my father to find any propriety in a woman traveling alone when he never suffers a second thought about my brothers traveling the world alone?

"Craaaack!" Savannah's thoughts were suddenly interrupted by a loud noise like the familiar sound of a branch breaking sharply from a falling oak. Then she quickly realized that the left rear end of the carriage was angling toward the ground and the stout man formerly seated to her right was now crowded heavily against her. She extricated herself from the tangle of bodies inside the coach, the coachman managed to open the door on what was now the lower side, and all four of the passengers wriggled out. They stood together in the muddy road surveying the damage: a broken axle and a wheel now tilted outward on top of which the body of the coach rested precariously.

The coachman examined the damage to his vehicle and announced that there was no way the axle could be fixed on the roadside. After a few moments' discussion, it was decided that he would unhitch one of the two horses and ride ahead to Kingstown to see if he could find a wagon to retrieve the passengers. He was especially solicitous of Savannah, the only woman among them, and told her he would ride as fast as he could to "rescue the damsel".

"I require no rescuing," Savannah said. "Do what you must for all of your passengers. I'll wait here patiently with them."

It was a warm, comfortable day, and Savannah and the other three found shade under a wide copper beech. The muddy roads were common this time of year and coaches often suffered difficulties of one kind or another. At other times it was the swirling dust, lame horses, washouts from sudden thundershowers, snowdrifts blocking passage through valleys, or bridges in disrepair and too dangerous to cross. Travel through America in 1777 was an adventure in any season and those experienced at it quickly learned to take such breakdowns in stride.

A few hours later, the coachmen returned with a farm wagon and the four passengers climbed in back and sat on the hay that the coachman had thoughtfully spread there to afford them some minimal comfort as they rode the very bumpy six miles into Kingstown. There they were fortunate to find rooms for the night at Hammersmith's Tavern, a small but clean place on the Pennsylvania road. Savannah asked the angular woman who seemed to be the wife of Hammersmith if she could get a basin of water. The woman, it was quickly clear, spoke no English, and she went to find her husband. When he appeared, he apologized for his wife. "She's Dutch," he said. "Got off the stagecoach one day from Albany and never left. But never learned no English either."

Savannah repeated her request for a basin of water, and Hammersmith appeared at her door a few minutes later with a large pot full of cold water. He left quickly and Savannah was able to remove her road-worn clothing and bathe standing up with a soft cotton cloth and the pot of water. It was the first opportunity she'd had for any kind of cleaning in the three days since she'd left Manhattan, and it felt surprisingly refreshing despite the primitiveness of the circumstances. She changed into the only other clothes she'd saved out for the trip, a simple blue cotton dress with shawl collar, and primped her long chestnut brown hair in the broken shard of mirror that stood on the chair in the corner of this very spartan room.

Savannah was hungry and she headed downstairs in search of some supper. She noticed as she moved through the tavern that it had almost no furniture nor any rugs nor curtains. In the main room, two of her fellow passengers stood looking forlorn and very thirsty. They were talking to Hammersmith, and Savannah moved in their direction.

"Nothing," she heard him say, "not a single thing they could use. They came in here and took all the furniture, nearly all the plates and mugs and silverware, all the food in the larder, the barrels of ale and all of the rum. They took my cow and all of the chickens, and they backed a wagon up and piled it high with hay, which they also took."

"Why would they want your furniture?" asked one of the passengers, a stoop-shouldered man from Poughkeepsie in New York. Surely soldiers don't sit around on furniture.

"It was November, "Hammersmith said, "and they were freezin'. They took everythin' they could carry that was made of wood. Same with all the other places along the road. They cleaned 'em out of everythin' wood, even fine chairs some folks had had in their families for generations. Same with animals. Ain't a cow left 'tween here and Trenton. Every single one's been 'et by soldiers. We was lucky to get through the winter alive. But this war is goin' to kill us all I'm afeared."

"All the more reason why we've got to drive these British out as quickly as we can," Savannah said. "They just have no respect for decent Americans if they'll come along here and do the kinds of things you just described. It's no wonder that so many loyalists are changing sides."

Hammersmith looked at her in confusion. He'd never had a political discussion with a woman before and he seemed to be wondering if the rules were different with women. Deciding they were not, he said simply, "Beggin' your pardon, ma'am, but it wasn't the British that did all this to us, it was General Washington's boys. They mowed us down like a scythe goin' through the first cuttin' of hay. Never even apologized for what they was doin'. Folks here don't care much about whether we have a king or not. But we sure do hate soldiers."

There hadn't been much to eat at Hammersmith Tavern that night, just some johnnycake that Hammersmith's Dutch wife had made from corn meal that had been hidden from the soldier's and some very weak tea. The male passengers spoke fondly of how very excellent an ale would have tasted, but they had to satisfy themselves with their imaginations for there was no ale to be had.

The evening was warm and soft and noisy with the twilight sounds of spring. There being no furniture of any kind on the porch, Savannah sat on the front steps enjoying the last glimmer of sunlight. She was joined after a few minutes by a young man who had ridden in alone an hour or so after the passengers from the wounded coach arrived. Savannah had seen him only briefly before he disappeared to his room and, unlike the others, he'd not appeared for johnnycake and tea.

"Evenin', ma'am," the young man said, as he stepped through the front door and eyed Savannah. She looked back over her shoulder and saw a powerful man with thick shoulders and narrow waist. He wore a beige linen waistcoat over a white cotton shirt open at the collar. His long streaked brown hair was pulled straight back and tied behind his head. And he had an open, well-proportioned face, the color of the outdoors. His smile, which was nearly perpetual, was wide and very handsome. "Mind if I set here with you. There don't seem to be a whole lot of sittin' places." The broad smile filled his face as he swept his hands toward both ends of the porch.

"Not at all," said Savannah, sliding to the left to make room on the step. "You're quite right about the seating choices."

"Fine ev'nin'," the man said as he sat a few feet away from her. Savannah nodded in agreement, a gesture the man could barely discern in the fading light.

For a few minutes neither said anything as they peered into the hastening darkness and listened attentively to the echoing chirps of a thousand crickets, the dull snap of fireflies, and the sounds of birds adjusting to their sleeping perches for the night. When the man finally spoke, his voice seemed like the sound of thunder against the serenity. "Hear you had a bad breakdown today."

"Yes," Savannah said, "That's pretty common when traveling by coach along these roads."

"Wouldn't know nothin' about that," the man said. "Never rode in a coach myself. Always walked or rode a horse."

"I think you're wise," Savannah said. "Much less to go wrong when you're walking or riding. And frankly a horse with a good saddle is a lot more comfortable than bumping and bouncing along in these coaches."

"I never run into a woman at one of these taverns before. You travel a lot by coach, do ya'?" the man asked. Then before Savannah could answer he said, "Course I ain't stayed much at taverns. Usually just sleep in a barn or by the road if the weather ain't bad."

"No," Savannah said, "This is my first trip. I have a sister in New York who had a baby not long ago, and I traveled there to see her."

"Kinda dangerous travelin' like this with a war goin' on, don't' ya' think?" The man seemed intrigued now, and solicitous. He moved a little closer to be able to make out Savannah's face in the darkness.

"Yes, I'm sure it is," she said sadly. "Everything is hard with the war going on. The poor man who owns this tavern was telling us earlier about how the Continentals came through here and stole everything he had. The war affects us all I'm afraid, only in different ways." She could see the man's face clearly now that he was closer to her, and she was struck by the intent look in his eye and the strong lines of his chin and his well-shaped nose.

"What brings you here," she asked.

"Oh, just travelin'," he replied.

"No one is just traveling," she said sharply, "certainly not now in the middle of this war. What's your business?"

"Well," he said, sliding closer to her and looking around as if wanting to speak confidentially, "Can you keep a secret?"

Something about this man appealed to Savannah. His impish smile perhaps. Or the handsome cut of his face. Maybe the way his body seemed always to be moving. The intensity of his words, even if his grammar was unschooled. Who knew what attraction was—some combination of those things and a hundred more. "Sure," she said, laughing conspiratorially, "tell me your secret."

"Wellll" he dragged the word out, "no one knows this, but General Howe and General Washington are both chess players, and they've been havin' this game since the two of 'em was in Boston in the summer of '75. But they ain't ever in the same place. So one of 'em makes a move, then sends it by messenger to th'other. Then he makes a move and sends it back. Been goin' on now for nearly two years. Washington may not be winnin' the war, but he's beating all heck out of old Lord Howe in chess."

The man's smile grew wider as he told this story and Savannah was infected by it. She found herself smiling almost as broadly as she listened. "I see," she said. "But you didn't answer my question. What do you do?"

"Oh, didn't mean to leave that out." The man was close to her now and grinning more broadly than ever. "I'm the go-between. I carry Washington's moves to Howe and Howe's moves to Washington. Got to know the passwords on both sides, so's I can get by the sentries. Dangerous work, but they pay me well. And if I ever get caught by pickets on either side, I got a secret code word. All I gotta do is say that word and they let me go."

Savannah was laughing now at the preposterousness of his tale and at the relish with which he told it. Every question she asked yielded a deeper layer of funny fabrication. Finally, the image of the two great generals more concerned about beating each other at chess than on the battlefield was more than she could bear and she broke into an unstoppable cascade of laughter.

"You are a strange man," she said to him when she finally regained control. "I would love to hear more about this unique profession of yours, but I must go to bed now. Our coach is repaired and we're leaving at daylight. But thank you so much for sharing your secret with me."

"Just remember," the man said. "Don't say a word to anyone. Could spoil the chess game and make two generals awful angry at me."

"Your secret is safe with me," Savannah said as she stood to leave. She looked one more time at the man's face, forming an image that she hoped would endure in memory.

"By the way," she said as she started toward the door, then stopped and turned back. "What's your name, sir?"

"Oh," he said, as if thinking up a name, "Ezekial. Ezekial Isaac."

Savannah laughed heartily. "I should have expected that," she said. "The perfect name for a go-between. Well, give my regards to both your generals."

"I will ma'am, especially to General Howe."

Savannah laughed one last time, then turned and walked through the door.

# Chapter 23

## New Jersey
## New York
## *Summer and Fall 1777*

The General was a comical sight with his hat and coat off as he sat in his tent in the late July heat. Since May and the departure from winter camp in Morristown, the warm summer sun had touched only the parts of his face that his hat didn't cover. Those and the backs of his hands. So when he sat here informally in his shirtsleeves as he did now with Jonathan, Hamilton and the young Frenchman, Lafayette, who'd joined the army in early summer, Jonathan thought he looked like a man who'd been painted by savages. A white body with dark brown hands and cheeks and neck. Like nearly all the generals Jonathan had come to know in this war, Washington was a man of some vanity. He would have been embarrassed to know how amusing he looked to the others.

Over the months since the terrible defeats in New York, Washington had changed in many ways. He no longer deferred, as he once had, to independent generals like Charles Lee or Thomas Conway. He'd formed firm opinions about the capabilities of others like the loyal but limited Nathanael Greene and Israel Putnam. And he no longer waited for Congress to come to his rescue with reinforcements and supplies. In Congress, in fact, he now had no faith at all. So he spent days traveling the countryside and visiting with state officials trying to recruit his own troops. And every day, he spent hours writing letters, formal letters of request to Congress, but also scores of letters to influential friends seeking their aid in convincing the Congress to requisition men and funds for his army.

In the year since declaring independence, the Congress had been slow to support the army, slow to negotiate favorable relations with France and Spain, slow to create a workable government. The drafting of some articles of confederation had been under discussion for months with little progress. The states were holding out for their own sovereignty and prerogatives, and there seemed little likelihood that a strong national government would ever emerge from this morass of self-interest.

Washington was a frustrated man, and he was not oblivious to the whispers and rumors circulating through the states about the inadequacies of his command. Nor was he unaware that the sources of many of those whispers and rumors were his own generals, especially Conway and Horatio Gates. Had it not been for the redeeming successes at Trenton and Princeton, Washington had said the other day, he might be back at Mt. Vernon right now enjoying the harvest as a private citizen.

But Jonathan had been with the General long enough to know the man's pride and his ego, to realize that he would be crushed by such an outcome. He hated criticism and he burned easily in its flame, but he had great faith in himself, and he possessed the patience to withstand both defeat and attack so long as he retained the means to navigate his own course. And, so far at least, despite the swirling rumors, he remained commander-in-chief of the Continental Army.

Washington had also learned to trust no one in making command decisions. When he'd deferred to Greene about the feasibility of defending Fort Washington and Fort Lee, it had cost him dearly. He would not make that mistake again. The young men around him this morning were there not because they were experts in warfare. Nor were they with him because they commanded large forces. No, Washington used these men as his sounding board, as his confidantes, some days even as his confessors. They were loyal to him and ferocious in their willingness to defend him. That counted more to him now than any expertise they might possess. That they were barely half his age mattered little.

Jonathan knew the frustrations that plagued Washington and he was glad the army was on the move again, despite the uncertain value of their current objective. The army under Washington had nearly disappeared during the winter. At one point total strength was down to no more than 3,000. Jonathan marveled at the way Washington had hidden this from the enemy. The General was a genius at deception. By spreading his few troops into many camps around Morristown, he'd made them hard for enemy spies to count and created the impression that there were many more under his command than there ever were. And he'd fed disinformation to known British spies, falsely and grossly inflating the strength of his forces.

Now that more men had enlisted and new militia units had arrived, Washington's army began to regain strength. And he was again ready to engage the enemy. The war had dragged on through the spring and early summer with no major action between the combatants. In June, Howe had moved the body of his force out of New York and into New Jersey, looking as if he were planning a sweep across that small state toward Philadelphia. But then he'd stopped without confronting Washington and withdrawn to New York. Now there were rumors that he was loading his army on ships. But for what? To sail up the Hudson? To sail south to make a sea landing and attack Philadelphia? Washington was utterly confused by his enemy.

"Do you all still agree that our intelligence from London is right, that Howe's going to come up from Manhattan to meet the army that's marching south from Canada and set up a solid British line along the Hudson and cut off New England?" It was often hard for the younger men to tell when Washington truly sought their counsel or when he was merely using them as an audience while waxing rhetorical. The difficulty was greater when, as now, Washington studied the papers in front of him without looking directly their way. "Wouldn't it be smarter for Howe to engage us somewhere in New Jersey and let the units coming from Canada have a crack at our northern army without worrying about our forces coming to reinforce them?"

"Howe will not engage until he has isolated you, General," Lafayette volunteered in the formal unaccented English he had learned as a child. "He is not stupid sir. He will try to eliminate the second army before he attempts the killer blow at the main force. This is good strategy."

Jonathan looked at the Frenchman who had won over Washington after arriving in his camp a few weeks earlier. Tall and aristocratic with red hair and light complexion, he was barely twenty. Yet he bore himself with the dignity and seemed to possess the wisdom of a much older man. Some had said that Lafayette's role here was simply political, that Congress had fondly hoped that the presence of a French gentleman in Washington's high command would help Benjamin Franklin's efforts in Paris to induce the French government to enter the war on the side of the Americans. But Jonathan knew better. Washington genuinely admired and respected the Frenchman, and every day he came to rely more comfortably on his judgments.

"I agree with that," Hamilton added. "Howe won't come after us right now because he has other priorities. It seems very clear that our intelligence has been exactly right about this. Howe has been ordered to cut the country in half. Then he can drive on us from the north and probably launch a sea landing south of us, so he'll have us in a squeeze knowing we have no navy to evacuate by sea if we're trapped. I think there is every reason to believe that Howe is moving or getting ready to move now, but toward his army in Canada, not toward us. Cornwallis will stay close enough to us to be a worry, but the main engagement will not be in New Jersey or Pennsylvania. Not now."

Washington rose from his chair, moving more slowly than he had two years ago when Jonathan visited with him after he first took command of the army in Cambridge. The days spent in the saddle and the nights of sleeping in strange cramped beds had begun to take their toll on this large man. He moved to the map and stood for a minute or two in contemplation. He placed the index finger of his brown right hand on Montreal, then slowly moved it down the length of Lake Champlain to Fort Ticonderoga. Then he placed the index finger of his left hand on Manhattan and slowly dragged it up the Hudson River toward Ticonderoga.

Washington turned to his aides, his two fingers now touching near Albany and said, "Will the armies join here?"

"It seems likely, General, that the fight will come somewhere between the Mohawk River and Ticonderoga." Lafayette suggested, reminding Jonathan again of the Frenchman's uncanny ability to cut to the heart of a military problem. "If you control Champlain and the Hudson, then you have cut America in two."

"Can Gates stop them?" the General asked, almost visibly bristling when he had to mention Horatio Gates, whom Congress had recently appointed commander of the northern division of the Continental Army without consulting Washington. "I've heard so little from him and now he may be at the pivot point of this war."

Hamilton answered first. "If he knows what they're attempting, he may be able to engage one army or the other before they join together, perhaps by surprise, and thus have an opportunity to blunt their strategy. But who knows what Gates is thinking. The great risk with him now may be that he's auditioning for your part, General, and may do something foolhardy to win a spectacular victory, not only defeating the British but also winning the hearts of members of Congress so that they'll turn to him to command all their armies."

Hamilton then laughed the shrewd laugh of a man who always looked for the political motive behind every action or decision. It was this keen political sensitivity rather than his ample skills as a soldier that most drew Washington to Hamilton and had led to his invitation to become the General's aide. Hamilton had eyes where Washington didn't and saw things that were invisible to most men. He may have known little about the workings of Horatio Gates's military mind, but Hamilton had a keen perception of the machinations of his political mind. And Washington was grateful for that.

Washington moved back to his chair and held his left hand to his temple, stroking slowly in the way he commonly did when he was pondering his options. He looked up after a minute and said, "It seems most important now that Gates hear directly from me. I want him to know all the intelligence we've received, and I want him to understand how important it is that he act prudently but decisively to prevent the implementation of the British plan. He seems to pay little attention when I send him a letter by courier, so Jonathan I want you to ride directly to Gates and deliver my message personally. He'll see your arrival as evidence of my direct concern, and I know you'll convey my message to him with the greatest force."

Jonathan touched his right hand to his forehead, indicating his acquiescence to the General's command, but his mind quickly filled with worries about the logistics of this assignment. "We don't know exactly where Gates has his army and we don't know exactly where the Canadian force is or where Howe is or what Howe is planning," Washington continued. "So I think you should leave today and ride as fast as you can to get to Gates before an engagement occurs. Take your man Flint and leave your uniforms and identification here to avoid capture. Gates knows who you are, and he'll know that you speak for me."

Jonathan nodded, but before he could ask any of the dozen or so questions this assignment raised in his mind, Hamilton interrupted, "Who's commanding the Canadian forces, do we know?"

"All the signs point to Burgoyne," Washington answered.

Hamilton tilted his head back and laughed the shrewd laugh again. "Ah, Gentleman Johnny," he said. "Now there's a man with more political motives than even I can sort out. Is he seeking Howe's job or Lord North's?" Hamilton smiled widely, his mind racing. "Perhaps if he wins a great victory in the north, his sights will rise even higher. King George himself might not rest easy if Gentleman Johnny Burgoyne becomes a military hero in the woods of New York."

Two days after Jonathan and Flint rode north toward New York dressed as civilians, Washington received word that the British fleet had been spotted off the coast of New Jersey headed south. Howe had made his choice: he would attack Philadelphia from the sea. But neither of Washington's messengers knew this, and the orders they carried to Horatio Gates were still premised on the assumption that Howe would move up the Hudson to join forces with Burgoyne.

The two riders had only their own horses and what supplies they could carry. They stopped at taverns when they could, but were soon travelling through woods where they encountered little evidence of civilization and had to travel carefully because of the presence of Iroquois and Mohawks whose sympathies had largely been purchased by British agents. At Meriwether's Tavern in Kingston, New York, they heard a rumor that Burgoyne had moved his army to Ticonderoga and had offered the local Indian tribes a bounty for any American scalps they could deliver. Neither of the two men had ever encountered an Indian in the wilderness, nor did either wish to have the experience now. So they moved as cautiously as they could. When they had to spend a night in the woods, one slept while the other kept watch, the necessity of which Washington himself had predicted when he recruited Jonathan into the army.

One afternoon while riding along a ridge on the west side of the Hudson north of Albany, Flint spotted three figures moving along the river bank below them. He signaled to Jonathan and they dismounted as quietly as they could, pulling their horses back from the edge of the ridge and out of sight to anyone looking up from below, then they crawled on their stomachs to the edge of the ridge and peered down. What they saw gave a turn to both their stomachs. Three Mohawk Indians had killed a deer and were slicing strips of meat from its flank. One of them chewed off pieces of the raw venison as he worked. All three of the men had the distinctive single row of hair down the center of their heads and they were heavily-muscled, dark-skinned and ferocious in appearance. Their long knives gleamed in the afternoon sun and they seemed masterful in the way they reduced the deer to a pelt and a supply of meat. When they were finished with their butchering, they washed the pelt in the river water, then wrapped the meat in it. They tied this package up with strips they had cut from the hide, then hung it over a maple sapling. Two of them hoisted the ends of the sapling and they moved down the river.

The activity of the Mohawks had been so quick, economical and sure-handed that Flint whistled softly under his breath when he was sure they were out of earshot. "Imagine what fast work they'd make of some human's scalp," he said. Then he smiled and grabbed the curl above Jonathan's left ear and said. "I tell ya', Major White Man, them savages can only grow hair on the top. They'd probably be mighty pleased to make a hairpiece out of yours."

This encounter inspired even more caution as Jonathan and Flint moved further north toward the spot on their map where they expected to encounter soldiers of what they hoped would be the Continental army. On September fifteenth, Jonathan awoke to the sound of Flint's voice. As he pulled the blanket off his head, he noted that it was covered in a white film of frost. The nights had been getting cooler as they traveled further north and into September, but this was the first frost they'd seen.

Jonathan rose to his feet and peered toward the edge of the hilltop where they'd chosen to spend the night. There Flint was in conversation with a soldier in a ragged Continental uniform. Jonathan joined the conversation and learned that the man was heading south, one of several scouts that Gates had sent along the river to look for any sign of Howe advancing to the north. Flint had stopped him with his pistol as the man passed their campsite unaware of their presence. When he saw the uniform and exchanged information, he convinced the picket that he and Jonathan were soldiers, too, despite their appearance.

"What is happening to the north?" Jonathan asked.

"Well, it's a confusion, Major. I guess it always is. Burgoyne was moving his army along the east side of the river, heading south. We thought he might be headed directly to Albany. Then a few days ago, he went back to Saratoga and crossed them all to this side."

"Is there a bridge at Saratoga?" Flint asked.

"No. Bridges is pretty scarce up here. But they made one out of their bateaux and moved the soldiers across on that. Took 'em about two days."

"Where are they now?" Jonathan asked.

"Don't rightly know. But there's a lot of 'em and they're out there somewhere."

"Where's Gates?"

The man pointed to Jonathan's canteen and asked if he might have a drink of water. Jonathan handed it to him and the soldier took a long swig, the water running over his face as he drank. "Decided to dig in. Granny's got this Polish engineer here, name of Kocusko or somethin', and they're buildin' fortifications all along the top of the ridge above Bemis Tavern. I guess they're figgerin' now that Burgoyne will come after us and we'll defend the high ground."

"Granny?" said Flint.

"Granny Gates. General Gates—that's what the soldiers call him. You ever see him?

Neither Jonathan nor Flint had ever seen Gates nor an image of him and they so indicated with a simultaneous shrug of their shoulders.

"Well, he looks like your granny. Got gray hair and a long nose and wears glasses that's always slidin' down the nose as he talks. Also got no real experience in a fight, so that's another reason why he seems like a granny. We got some great soldiers in this army like Colonel Morgan and Benedict Arnold. Most of the men feel they oughta be doin' the leadin' here, not Granny."

"Has there been any engagement with Burgoyne," Jonathan prodded.

"No, not Burgoyne. But we whupped some of his Germans real bad over to Bennington in Vermont. Burgoyne sent out a regiment looking for horses and supplies. They was headin' east when they ran into a bunch of militia comin' west to join up with us. But these weren't no regular militia. They was from New Hampshire under Colonel Stark and they knew how to fight."

"John Stark?" asked Jonathan in surprise.

"Yeah, that's the one. Some fellas said he'd been at Bunker Hill."

"He sure was," said Flint. "About as good a leader of troops as I ever saw."

"Well his boys started shootin' up them Germans real bad. They musta sent back to Burgoyne for reinforcements 'cause a couple hundred more arrived pretty soon. But Colonel Stark's boys gave 'em about all they could handle, then Colonel Breymann arrived and came at 'em from one side and some Continentals and a coupla' hundred Green Mountain Boys came at 'em from another. They got a bullet into the German colonel and pretty soon them Germans was throwin' down their guns and runnin' everywhere shoutin' stuff no one could understand. Ended up we killed and captured 'bout a thousand men at Bennington. Burgoyne's still out there, but we showed 'em that militia can fight, too."

"What will Gates do if Burgoyne doesn't attack his fort?"

"Can't tell with Granny. Arnold wants to go after Burgoyne before Howe arrives, but Granny don't seem in no hurry. Boys say Arnold lost a battle in Canada two years ago and he's been smartin' ever since, itchin' fer revenge. General Arnold and Granny don't much like each other, ya know. Wouldn't surprise me that Old Benedict would go find Burgoyne on his own, even if Granny was still frettin'. Say, you boys seen any savages down south a here?"

Flint and Jonathan looked at each other and smiled. "Yes, we saw some Mohawks skinning out a deer a couple of days ago. Why?" Jonathan replied.

"Don't want to run into none myself," the soldier said. "Ever since hearin' about Jane McCrea, everybody's been thinkin' about them savages."

"Who's Jane McCrea?" Jonathan asked.

"Local girl, preacher's daughter. One day a coupla savages attacked her house and found her hidin' in the root cellar. Grabbed her long hair and scalped her. Figgered they'd get a bounty from Burgoyne for her scalp. Now everyone's talking about it and boys is joinin' up to come fight before the redcoats and the savages get their own women."

Flint smiled and again eyed Jonathan's curls mischievously, but Jonathan could only draw a deep breath and contemplate the grotesque picture of Indian braves bartering a scalp attached to a woman's long tresses with the English Lord, Gentleman Johnny Burgoyne.

The wild turkey call was the most penetrating sound Jonathan had ever heard. And it worked. Amid the heavy smoke and the din of musket fire and grapeshot, Colonel Morgan's Rifleman heard the call and brought their frenzied flight to a halt. They began to find their way quickly back to Morgan at the top of the ravine looking down on the small clearing surrounding the farm of a loyalist named Freeman who'd had the good sense to flee before the shooting started.

Every man in the Continental Army knew about the legendary Daniel Morgan of Virginia, one of the most renowned soldiers of the war. A giant of a man, over six feet tall, weighing more than two hundred pounds, and dressed in buckskins, Morgan was all warrior. He was blunt and tough, and the story was still told of the five hundred lashes he'd once received for punching a British officer with whom he served in the French and Indian War. When Jonathan and Flint learned he was here with Gates and Arnold, they asked Morgan's permission to go with his Riflemen on this probe of Burgoyne's front. They might have thought better of this had they known that one of Burgoyne's generals, Simon Fraser, would be leading an attack column in their direction on that very afternoon.

Fraser's regulars outnumbered Morgan's Rifleman by three or four to one and, though the Virginians acquitted themselves well for a short time, Fraser's troops had begun to overrun Morgan's positions and set his troops to flight. Morgan was near tears at the sight of this and Jonathan felt his embarrassment for this show of emotion in front of Washington's own emissaries. But then Morgan yelled his turkey call and his men quickly recovered and began to return fire on Fraser's column.

Soon Benedict Arnold was in sight leading reinforcements and the very appearance of this much-admired officer stiffened the resolve of the Continentals. Flint and Jonathan had been through Bunker Hill and the battles around New York. They'd been at Washington's side at Trenton and Princeton, but they'd never seen a sustained fight like this. Nor had they ever seen the likes of Benedict Arnold.

Back and forth through the afternoon, the two armies threw their best at each other. One would advance, then fall back as the other charged forward. The noise and the smoke lasted for hours and nearby farmers must have thought that Judgment Day had arrived for surely no similar sound had ever before been heard in the ancient Hudson Valley.

Flint and Jonathan picked up muskets and powder horns from fallen soldiers and joined in the fire alongside Morgan's Riflemen. Before them, Arnold flew from side to side shouting at his men, impervious to the grapeshot coming from the British artillery and the bullets fired by Morgan's own men behind him. Even when his own aide was shot from his horse, Arnold continued unfazed in his efforts to drive his men forward to capture the British guns. "That man has no nerves," said Flint in awe. "Did you ever see anyone face down fire the way he does."

The battle went first one way, then the other, through the long afternoon and into the dusk. Then Arnold disappeared from the field and soon thereafter the shooting stopped. When it seemed clear that there would be no more fighting that day, September nineteenth, Jonathan and Flint offered their compliments to Colonel Morgan and trotted back to Gates's headquarters in the fort on Bemis Heights. They had intended to share their impressions with Horatio Gates, but walked in instead on an angry exchange between Gates and Arnold.

"With reinforcements this afternoon, I could have driven Burgoyne from the field, General. Why were there no more men for the fight?" Arnold asked angrily, the veins in his temple swelling as he spoke. His uniform was still filthy from his own sweat, the dust of the battlefield and the blood of his fallen aide. He stood hovering over Gates who was seated behind a map of the adjacent countryside.

Gates looked up slowly and pushed the glasses up his thin nose to better focus on Arnold. "I had no wish to leave this fort unprotected, General, nor did I feel it prudent to place all of our troops in an engagement with only one of Burgoyne's columns. He had St. Leger to his right and the Germans to his left. With all our forces concentrated in the center, they might have easily collapsed on us."

Arnold pulled back and let a look of disgust spread across his face. "We had their center in a death grip. With more men to force them back, neither of the other columns could have flanked us and we would have greatly reduced their force with kills and captures. It was a terrible lost opportunity. Tomorrow I shall take a large enough force to finish what we left undone today."

Gates stood now and turned slowly toward the exasperated Arnold. He said, with all the authority he could muster, "You'll do no such thing, General. Your orders are to remain within this fort until I give some further command."

The stunned General Arnold said nothing, but gave Gates a fierce and revolted look, then pivoted and walked out.

No one spoke for a few moments and Gates returned to his map table. Then he looked up and addressed Jonathan. "I apologize that you gentlemen had to see that scene. Unfortunately it occurs here with some regularity. Benedict Arnold has great difficulty understanding that I am the commander of this army, and he requires frequent reminders like the one you just observed. I hope you'll report to General Washington the nature of the difficulties of this command."

Jonathan nodded, trying to hide his disdain for Gates. He and Flint saluted and left, happy to escape the decided chill that had fallen over these headquarters. "Somethin' don't seem right to me," said Flint. "We saw about the bravest bit of commandin' we ever saw this afternoon. And then tonight we see that same commander get slapped down by Gates.

Dammit, Arnold was right. If he'd had reinforcements he'd be runnin' Burgoyne back to Canada right now."

"I agree," said Jonathan. "I'd heard from some of the junior officers that there was bad blood between Arnold and Gates, now I know what they mean. Arnold is a hothead, sure, but he's also a hell of a soldier. A good general's got to know how to get the most out of his best leaders, even when they're temperamental, even when they're insubordinate. Gates ought to realize that it'll be a lot easier to win this fight up here if Arnold's out with the men, not cooped up here."

"If we're ever gonna win this war," Flint added, "the generals better spend more time fightin' the redcoats and less time fightin' with each other."

Soldiers use ritual to mitigate anxiety, and Daniel Morgan's men were no exception. They always prepared for battle as they were on this day: cleaning their long rifles to a high gleam, filling their powder horns, arranging their lead balls in their cartridge boxes, and organizing their primers. Every soldier believes this simple thing: that only a second, only an inch separate life and death. If I can load my gun faster than my enemy, if my sights are truer, if my ammunition is handier, if my weapon is cleaner, if my aim is straighter, I will live and he will die.

The riflemen in Daniel Morgan's command believed that, and now—nearly three weeks after they last engaged the enemy here--they spread out across the clearing in the trees above the Freeman Farm, silently going through the rituals. In an hour or two, pandemonium would reign. Now they did all those small things which everyone hoped would make a difference in some critical split second in the cacophony and fog of battle.

Neither Flint nor Jonathan could bear just to watch what was about to unfold. The stakes were too high, the outcome too important merely to observe. No one wanted to win this war more than they did, and damned if they were just going to sit in some distant observation post during what might well be the turning point in the war, even a milestone on the real road to American independence. They were warriors now and this was their war. So they sat near Colonel Morgan and prepared their own weapons—and minds—for battle.

Burgoyne had given them this opportunity by not pressing the fight in the days following the first engagement at the Freeman Farm. He hadn't used his columns very well that day, but an adjustment of tactics

340

might have prevailed shortly thereafter. Or he could have retreated back to Ticonderoga and regrouped. His supplies were there and so was safety.

Granny Gates had missed opportunities as well, or so his officers were whispering when he wasn't around. Continental spies had learned that General Henry Clinton, whom Howe had left in command of the British garrison in New York, was sending several thousand men up the Hudson River to reinforce Burgoyne and place the Americans between the two British forces. Benedict Arnold was telling anyone who would listen—and most of the Continental officers would rather listen to Arnold than Gates—that the Continentals should go after Burgoyne now before Clinton arrived. But Granny did not go after Burgoyne, and no one now knew where Clinton was.

Then this morning, October seventh, Burgoyne struck, moving his cannon and several thousand men back to the wheatfields of the Freeman Farm. Any minute now, Morgan would sound his turkey call and his riflemen and thousands of other Continental regulars and militia would engage the redcoats and the Germans here on the parched ground of this old farm, still broken and blood-soaked from the slaughter of the fighting here a few weeks earlier.

The Continental forces had been swelling with the daily arrival of more regulars and more militia. There were even some Iroquois fighting on the American side now. No one knew for sure, but some of Gates's officers thought the advantage in numbers may have swung their way. But Morgan was less concerned about numbers than about tactics and leadership. He didn't much like the battle plan here, which was largely defensive, and he knew that the absence of Benedict Arnold from the battlefield had lowered morale and, more importantly, reduced the leadership quality on his side of the line of fire.

Granny Gates had had his fill of Arnold's criticism, his complaints that Gates had not even mentioned Arnold's name in his report on the earlier fighting at Freeman Farm, and his constant badgering to go after Burgoyne before Clinton arrived. So he relieved Arnold of his command and ordered him to go to Philadelphia. Morgan had been a soldier long enough to know all about the bickering among generals, but he admitted to Jonathan that he thought Gates was a crazy man. If Arnold was on the field, the chance of winning the battle would be much greater. And if the Continentals won here, Horatio Gates would be a national hero.

All these thoughts swirled through Jonathan's head as he sat with his back to a large beech tree, running a rag up and down the barrel of the

341

Committee of Safety musket he had removed from the clutches of a dead New Hampshire man after the last battle here. Flint had already finished with his cleaning and was sighting down the barrel of the weapon he'd acquired in similar fashion, bracing his thumb and testing windage.

"Kind of a shame to spoil such a beautiful day with a fight," Flint said.

Jonathan looked up and around and quickly agreed. The hardwoods had come into the full flush of their fall colors, from the fiery red of the swamp maples to the soft gold of the birches to the kaleidoscopic sumac and oaks and beeches. The sky was clear and, as it passed overhead, the warm sun kept finding new and spectacular ways to light the sea of color that flooded the land.

Jonathan thought that it would have been so very sweet simply to lie back and let his eyes float across that vivid vista for a whole afternoon, to banish all consciousness of this war and of the dangerous hours ahead. He'd been at war for so long now that it was hard to remember the opposite, the feeling of lying peacefully on one's back, absorbed only in the simple splendor of nature, not giving a second of worry to what the enemy was doing or planning. But, recognizing he had no such luxury, Jonathan rose to his feet and walked over to Daniel Morgan who was intently watching as the redcoats began to form their battle lines along the ridge that lay west of Bemis Heights.

A messenger arrived with orders for Morgan's Rifleman to circle to the right and attack Burgoyne's flank. Other Continental units would simultaneously hammer at his center. Around two-thirty, as the sun began its descent toward the horizon, musket volleys and cannon fire filled the wheatfields with a deadly roar. Morgan sounded his turkey call and his men charged out of the woods at the German troops and British light infantry on Burgoyne's right flank. Continental forces attacked from other quarters, but British cannon held them at bay, firing canisters of grapeshot into American lines. When the Americans moved near the guns, the light infantry came at them in bayonet charges and drove them back.

After a half hour or so of this, Morgan cursed in exasperation. "It looks like the last battle here all over again, back and forth, back and forth, until darkness, or the last man, falls. We may have a numerical advantage here, but Gates sits up in his cozy fort while Gentlemen Johnny is out there inspirin' his men. Look at 'im over yonder. Balls are whizzin' all around him, and he's just laughin' at 'em. He's goin' to keep his boys fightin' forever."

342

"Looks like the Germans are goin' to hold onto the center all afternoon," Flint said after climbing a tree and looking through Morgan's telescope. "And the British are holdin' their own on this side, too. Looks like the redcoat general, Simon Fraser, right out there with his infantry."

Morgan listened to Flint's report then turned back to face the situation before him. A messenger appeared and shouted down from his horse. 'General Arnold says to move your men forward fast. He's going to charge up the hill against the Germans."

"General Arnold?" Morgan said in stunned surprise. "You must mean someone else."

"Nope," the messenger replied. "Benedict Arnold's down there now and he's taken charge."

Morgan's look of surprise was soon replaced by a satisfied smile and the turkey call echoed up and down the line. Soon Morgan's riflemen and a fresh Continental brigade were running uphill into the face of heavy German musket fire and the pizzing sound of grapeshot flying over their heads. Something hit Jonathan's hat and popped it off his head. Then he felt a short, sharp pain just above his right knee. He looked down just long enough to see the trickle of blood coming through his breeches, but also to realize that his leg was still functioning. So he continued to run toward the German lines.

But the German fire was too much and the Americans pulled back. Then Jonathan looked to his left and saw the sight that may have transformed the day. There was Benedict Arnold, sitting atop his horse, holding his hat high in the air, shouting at his men to form up and charge again. Form up and charge they did, with Arnold at the front, cursing and bellowing at the enemy, riding his own lines, impelling his men forward. He sent orders to Morgan to move his men to the left and soon they were surrounding the Germans.

In a few moments, Jonathan could see the blue backs of the Germans' coats as they dropped their weapons and packs and took flight, retreating as fast as they could from the invigorated force in front of them. The rout was on, and Benedict Arnold was not going to let this chance get away. This act of glorious insubordination would be his last; if the British survived to fight another day, Benedict Arnold would be hearing about it in the stockade. "After them now, boys," he shouted. "The chase is on. Don't let it end until we get to Canada. Victory or death. Victory or death. Victory or death."

With the Germans in rapid retreat, Morgan's men stopped to reload and catch their breaths. Morgan sent Flint back up a tree with the spyglass to survey the field. Flint was up and down like a monkey. "This side has collapsed. Looks like Burgoyne has lost his horse and he's runnin' around tryin' to rally his troops in the center, but he ain't got many troops left. Fraser's in front of us now and he seems to be standin' firm."

Morgan took the spyglass back and asked Flint to point in Fraser's direction. Flint did so quickly, and Morgan turned the glass that way. Then he closed it up and looked slowly from side to side. He yelled to a sergeant nearby, "Find Tim Murphy and bring him to me. Snap to it." The sergeant ran off to the east.

"Who's Murphy?" Jonathan asked.

"Best sharpshooter I ever saw," Morgan replied. "Boy can shoot the eyes out of squirrel at 200 yards. He ain't even human."

Within the minute the sergeant was back with a short, squinty-eyed boy in tow. He had blond hair and no beard and looked no older than seventeen. Bandages on his left hand and neck testified to the beating he'd already taken that day. The boy stepped in front of Morgan, straightened up, and said "I'm here, Colonel."

"Tim, I want you to find a tree over there on that small hill. You take your rifle up there and I want you to spot the general that's leadin' the redcoats in front of us. His name is Fraser, and he's ridin' a gray horse. He's givin' us a mess of trouble right now, and I want you to git up there and dispose 'a him."

Tim Murphy, smiled, saluted awkwardly, then pivoted and quickly ran off. Morgan sent orders down to his platoon leaders to array their own sharpshooters and start picking off British troops while there was a lull in the fighting. Morgan moved forward to a small copse of trees on the edge of the wheat field where the foliage provided almost perfect camouflage and watched with his spyglass while his men went about their deadly labor.

Within ten minutes, a voice behind them said. "Took care of it, Colonel. Anythin' else you want me to do." Morgan, Jonathan, and Flint turned around and there stood Tim Murphy, still smiling amiably, his long rifle at his side, looking like a boy playing war. Morgan turned back and slowly fanned his glass along the ridge across the field. He stopped and focused carefully when he spotted a cluster of men attending frenetically to a body writhing on the ground, clutching its stomach. A riderless gray horse stood nearby.

Granny Gates had fussed with his clothes for an hour. "What do you wear to a surrender?" he asked Jonathan in exasperation. "What would Washington wear?

"I'm afraid General Washington has had no occasion to make that decision, General," Jonathan replied. "You're the first American general who's ever been surrendered to."

Gates smiled proudly at the thought, then went back to worrying about his uniform. "But what do you think Washington would wear?" he asked again.

Jonathan was not accustomed to giving fashion advice to generals, but he thought for a minute about Washington and decided that the General would be inclined to understatement. "I'm no expert in these matters, General," he said to Gates, "but I think you've already upstaged Burgoyne on the field of battle; there is no reason to do so now when he lays down his arms."

Upstaged indeed. Burgoyne's gamble had turned to disaster. His army had been bloodied and broken and forced into a sad retreat. Benedict Arnold, though severely wounded in the thigh and borne from the battlefield on a litter, had led several magnificent and ultimately successful charges against the tenacious German and British troops.

Instead of pulling back quickly to the defenses of Ticonderoga, Burgoyne had hesitated. And the Americans had continued to launch guerilla attacks on his pickets and sentries, to burn his supplies, and to harass his sick and wounded troops. Colonel Stark had gotten upriver with his New Hampshire boys; they burned Burgoyne's boats and cut off his only line of retreat. Without horses, with supplies so low his men were subsisting on moldy flour, with the fall rains now pouring down and the nights getting colder, even a gambler like Gentleman Johnny Burgoyne knew when the last hand had been played.

A few days after the second defeat at Freeman Farm, Burgoyne sent a messenger to Gates seeking a parlay. The British playwright and the American fussbudget spent several days splitting rhetorical hairs before Burgoyne agreed to sign a document called a "convention" that never mentioned the words surrender or capitulation. Gates was going this morning to get Burgoyne's signature on that document. If he could ever decide what to wear.

345

Gates made a special point of having Jonathan accompany him, wanting to be sure that Washington got a complete report on the glory of this moment. Jonathan suspected as well, that Gates derived a kind of evil delight from the prospect of Washington having to contemplate this great victory in New York as he was reeling from the full force of Howe's armies around Philadelphia. If things went badly for Washington, Jonathan had no doubt that Gates would use his triumph here to press Congress to give him command of all the Continental armies. Jonathan was proud of this army, happy at its triumph, ecstatic that America would not be cut in half, joyous at the morale boost this victory would give to all Americans, but deeply saddened that it was Gates and not Washington who would reap the glory that would surely follow.

So off they rode, Gates and his party followed by most of the officers and men who had won what was already being called the Battle of Saratoga. All but Gates and a few others broke off and stood in ranks some distance from where Burgoyne waited in a field along Fishkill Creek. When they approached the large white tent that had been erected there, an American flag was flying, the new one with its circle of white stars and alternating red and white stripes. Gates dismounted slowly for he was not a small nor slender man and walked over toward Burgoyne. The British general was in full scarlet plumage. It somehow seemed right, as Jonathan had expected it would, that Gates had worn his simple blue dress uniform.

Gentleman Johnny Burgoyne stepped forward and handed his sword to Gates, saying "The fortune of war, General Gates, has made me your prisoner." Graciously, Gates replied "I shall always be ready to testify that it was not through any fault of your excellency." Jonathan could barely suppress a smile at that remark; any fool knew that Burgoyne's hubris, his tactical failures, and his consistent underestimation of his enemy were the very faults that had brought him to this moment of ignominy. How the Continental soldiers loved now to sing mocking songs echoing Burgoyne's earlier pledge to eat his Christmas dinner in Manhattan.

Burgoyne and Gates then stood solemnly and watched as the defeated troops paraded before them and stacked their arms in small piles across the meadow. Gates had decided to hold his own army back where it could not watch the ceremony, perhaps to preserve some honor for Burgoyne in this sad moment. But once the arms were surrendered and stacked, Gates's army had to take Burgoyne's army prisoner. So the

British and Germans began to file toward their captors, dreading the taunts and jeers of victor upon vanquished.

But Gates had given stern orders that his soldiers should stand in silent dignity as the defeated army passed in review. And Jonathan watched the most remarkable sight he'd ever seen. First came the British, their uniforms now in tatters, many of them emaciated by the short rations on which they'd been living for weeks, most limping or bandaged or scarred. Then came the Germans, most now realizing that the war was over for them, that they wouldn't capture the prizes and take the loot of which all mercenaries dream. The drums beat a cadence and the few surviving fifes sent out a tune of march, but this was no proud army now. And the fox pups and bear cubs and fawns and other pets of their months in the forest sauntered along beside the surrendering soldiers, lending an almost childish, dreamlike quality to the scene. The fierce red-coated giants that Jonathan had first seen before him on Breed's Hill seemed a lifetime away from these sad men setting off on their final march of this war.

Jonathan noticed how the British troops looked closely at the long rows of Americans who awaited them. More than 10,000 Continentals and militia were in the field now, their uniforms as varied as the states they represented, men of many ages and sizes. Some free black men among them drew special attention from the passing army. The vanquished had been told so much about this American army. Its generals all bickered with each other. Its men went home when their enlistments were up or their crops needed harvesting. They were amateurs with little knowledge of tactic or maneuver. Their rifles were old and rusty. They were uncertain about their cause.

Some of that was true, Jonathan knew. Except the last. He would report to Washington exactly what he'd seen in these weeks in New York. The British and their allies fought hard and bravely. Burgoyne may have failed them, but St. Leger did not and Fraser did not and their weapons did not and their training did not. They were a proud and brutal enemy. And there were gallons of American blood on the fields of Freeman Farm to prove that.

And he would also report that the American generals bickered and nearly squandered their opportunities as a result; some men left when their enlistments were up or their crops were ready for harvest, even though the promise of victory was in the air; some weapons were old and rusty. He'd tell Washington, too, that the officers here sometimes invented tactics in the heat of battle, and some of those were suicidal.

But Jonathan would also report that the men he saw here—the men in new blue Continental uniforms and the men in buckskin, the New Hampshire farmers and the New York laborers, the veterans of the French and Indian Wars and the men facing enemy fire for the first time, brave men like Benedict Arnold and Daniel Morgan and Tim Murphy—bore no uncertainties about their cause. They would march relentlessly into the enemy ranks, into the fury of grapeshot at point blank range, to see it prevail.

Washington would need to know that, for he was facing his own fiery trial to the south. The war did not end in Saratoga. But perhaps it turned here. And Jonathan hoped that through the dark days that lay ahead, Saratoga would cast a shining light of hope.

# Chapter 24

# Philadelphia
# York, Pennsylvania
# October – November 1777

This egg caught Aubrey Armistead on the right shoulder of his bright red uniform coat, just below the fringed epaulet. It splattered and dribbled down the back of his sleeve. "Damn," Armistead cursed to himself as he whirled and scanned the rooftop of the Free Man Tavern behind him. Yet again he saw nothing.

This was the second time in a week that Armistead had received what his fellow officers now called the "warm Philadelphia greeting." An egg, a soft tomato, a rotting eggplant—whatever could be thrown as a projectile and make a smelly mess upon impact—these were the gifts that the angry citizens of Philadelphia were offering their captors. Armistead was reminded again of something he'd been told by an old Welch fusilier years ago, "Don't expect any thank-you's from citizens whose city you occupy."

But Philadelphia was different. Armistead had been part of an occupying force in Boston and in New York. There'd been angry citizens there and some patriot efforts to harm or disrupt the occupiers. But in Philadelphia there was a kind of anger Armistead had not seen elsewhere and a boldness that turned that anger into daily assaults and insults, especially to those of high rank. Corporals and privates could walk the streets in relative safety, but colonels and generals on horseback had to keep their eyes on rooftops and alleyways. Last week, the highlander colonel, McVey, had been killed when a timber fell on his head as he walked through the narrow alley to his quarters. And on Arch Street, a hemp rope pulled taut across the street after curfew had knocked a lieutenant colonel from the 17th off his horse. As he entered the newly renamed Royal Arms on Spruce Street, Armistead removed his coat and thought perhaps he should be grateful that only an egg and not a timber had come his way.

The Royal Arms was full of British officers who had little to do during this occupation but criticize their commander and drink the local ales. And they did plenty of both. Armistead soon spotted Major Arthur Bramley, the tall Yorkshireman who was his executive officer, and Colonel Nigel Cornford, whom he'd known since their days together in the garrison at Gibraltar. These were his regular drinking companions, and they joked now that the table beneath the window in the small room on the north corner of the tavern was their "headquarters."

"I see the good citizens of Philadelphia have gifted you generously yet again, Aubrey," Cornford laughed as Armistead poured cold water over the egg stains on his coat. "How do you suppose they knew of your preference for eggs over vegetables?"

"Bloody bastards," Armistead muttered as he scrubbed at the stain with his silk handkerchief. "We need to catch a few of them and deliver the lash in a public square. That at least will give them pause before they launch their mortars at us."

"I don't think anything will give these people much pause," Bramley added. "They don't seem to fear us at all. I thought that seizing the American capital was supposed to strike a blow at their morale. Don't see any sign of it. Their morale seems higher than ours."

Armistead finished with his cleaning efforts and hung his coat to dry over the back of his chair. He took a long drink from the mug of ale that had been placed before him, then said, "The battlefield is a safer place now for a British officer than the streets of Philadelphia. It'll be a relief to ride out of here to engage Washington. If he was smart, he'd just let us stay in Philadelphia so that the citizens here can irritate us until we surrender."

"The battlefield might be safer, Aubrey, but if Howe has his way we may never see it again." Cornford's face twisted into half a grin, suggesting his remark was only half in jest.

"What do you mean?" Bramley asked.

"Look at this. If a general had orders to avoid engagements with the enemy as much as possible, he could hardly do a better job that Howe has done in 1777. We had Washington on the run a year ago in New York; he let him get away. We stayed in winter camp in New York until June. Then we marched into New Jersey for a few days, only to turn around again and march back to New York. There we sat for weeks—weeks of good fighting weather—before Howe decided to load us on those God damn ships and sail us out into the Atlantic where we sat and sweltered for three weeks while we ate that awful salt beef and spent every morning heaving our dead horses into the ocean.

"When he finally decided to go after Philadelphia, we disembarked in a wobegone place called Head of Elk. We were almost as far from Philadelphia as we were in New York. And we'd lost more weeks of good fighting weather and eaten salt beef when every farm in New Jersey has a garden full of fresh crops. We finally have a good row with Washington at the creek in Brandywine, but once again Howe thinks we're too tired to pursue and lets Washington get away. We had another good run at him when we snuck into the American camp at Paoli, but still no pursuit. They attacked us at Germantown and we drove them off, but again no chase. So now it's the tenth of October, and our army of more than 20,000 fine soldiers has engaged an enemy with a much weaker force on only three or four days in this year. He slammed his mug on the table top. Brilliant, gentlemen, just brilliant."

Bramley looked around the room sheepishly, hoping that no one had overheard Cornford's diatribe. Such blasphemy could get an officer called before a commander and punished. He leaned forward and spoke to his table mates in a voice just above a whisper. "Careful, Nigel. I agree with you. I think we all do. But let's not get into trouble here. What really distresses me is that they'll be dancing in the streets in London when word gets back that we've taken Philadelphia. I'm sure Howe's dispatch will make it look like a glorious victory, when we know that Washington did the wise thing by avoiding a general action to save Philadelphia. He calculated that the defense of the city was not worth the loss of his army.

"And we were so slow getting here that the government was all gone anyway by the time we arrived. I think Howe thought he was just going to walk up to John Adams and arrest him. Ha! John Adams is probably a hundred miles from here."

Armistead listened intently. He shared these feelings of frustration, but they were mixed with some growing admiration for his enemy. When he arrived in Boston almost three years ago, Armistead thought the rebellion would end quickly, that a few skirmishes would show the Americans that it was suicidal to take on the British army and navy and they'd quickly compromise with London.

But he'd been wrong. Wrong about the willingness of London to compromise. Wrong about the commitment of the rebels to their cause.

And wrong about their courage in battle. They were still an inferior force, and they sometimes made terrible tactical blunders on the battlefield. Last week in Germantown when they had us retreating, they just stopped. Instead of chasing us to capture, they concentrated on a small force of ours holding the big stone Chew house. This gave us time to regroup, and probably prevented a disastrous defeat. Who knows what they were thinking? They're still an army of amateurs. But there's plenty of fight in those boys.

"The other thing that worries me," said Cornford, "is that Burgoyne and Clinton may win a big victory in the north and they'll get all the glory. Johnny Burgoyne! My God, man, can you imagine how loud his horn will blow if he triumphs over the Continentals in the woods. If the rebels give up the fight after that, he'll be the hero of the campaign and no one will waste a thought on the years we've spent through the miserable winter in Boston, the fire in New York, the awful weeks at sea last summer. We'll go home now and our colleagues at the officers' clubs will ask us, 'Whatever did you do during those years on leave in America?' And the only honest answer will be "Not much, really. We sat around in American cities and waited for Gates and Howe to use their army--which, most of the time, they decided was inconvenient."

The thin veil of snow that covered the ground and rooftops of the little town of York was a dark promise of a hard winter to come. Or so Henry Houghton thought as he walked along the muddy street to the morning session of the Congress. Farmers never lose touch with the weather, even when they're many miles from their farm as Henry had been for most of three and a half years. Snow that comes when the leaves have just fallen is an omen, he thought, a warning of a winter that will start early and stay long and chill deeply. He pulled his hat down to shield his face and bent into the frigid wind.

It was not Philadelphia, but York was a comfortable town and most of the delegates had found good enough lodgings. The local citizens were fiercely patriotic and they were proud of their sudden importance as the new capital of the nation. So they'd gone out of their way to make room for the government when it hurried west from Philadelphia just before Howe's army arrived there in mid-September.

Henry entered the vestibule of the old two-story brick courthouse on Centre Square and hung his hat and wool coat on one of the oak pegs along the wall. The scarcity of empty pegs indicated that he was one of the

352

last to arrive. Henry prided himself on punctuality, but he had to admit that it was hard to get very excited about the daily battles in Congress over the draft of these articles of confederation. Everyone knew that there had to be some official document to define the character and purposes of the national government. In fact, many of the delegates thought it a scandal that they'd been fighting a war for this new nation for years without anyone really knowing what the "nation" was.

But the wrangling was driving him mad. Every state had a pet interest; no one wanted to compromise. Most of the delegates felt that they could not commit their states to a new government without the approval of their state legislatures. So it took forever to agree on anything. And one thing was very clear. While everyone wanted a national government, no one wanted it to have any powers that superceded their state governments. And, on top of all this, there was a war to run.

Poor George, Henry thought as his mind turned to Washington and his army. Every week we get letters from him imploring us to send more men, more supplies, more money. But Congress has no men and it has no supplies and it has no money. All we can do is requisition those things from the states. But then we have no power to back up the requisitions if they disregard them—which they usually do. Then you get the self interest again. The governor of Virginia sends clothing to Washington's camp, but specifies that it only be distributed to soldiers from Virginia. When soldiers from other states see this and get nothing for themselves, they wait out their enlistments then go home. How does George stand it?

It was freezing in the second-floor meeting room as Henry took his seat. It had been like this all winter, and many of the delegates sat with blankets wrapped around their feet. The debate was already underway, more discussion from yesterday about how legal disputes between the states would be resolved. Henry listened for a while, then realizing he was hearing nothing new, passed a note to Benjamin Rumsey of Maryland suggesting a compromise on a matter involving management of the currency. After a few minutes, a messenger brought a reply. Or so Henry thought. But when he read the note, it said only that an important visitor wished to speak with him in the vestibule. Henry could not imagine what any "important visitor" would be doing in York, Pennsylvania, but he rose from his chair and walked to the door which a small man in morning dress quickly opened to let him through.

There he saw one of the happiest sights of his life. An American officer named Jonathan Houghton. For a moment, Henry froze. The appearance of his son was such a surprise and generated such a jolt of good feeling that his mind seemed to disengage from his body. Then he recovered and moved to his son, starting to extend his right hand. But he walked through that gesture before completing it and threw his arms around Jonathan's shoulders. Jonathan couldn't remember ever being embraced by his father before, yet it was a gloriously familiar feeling.

Henry stepped back and looked at his son. They had not seen each other since that day in the spring of 1775 when Jonathan rode off to the north for his temporary assignment as secretary to the fact-finding committee. Since then, Jonathan had been through the battles at Bunker Hill and around New York. He'd described those in his letters home. And he'd been at Washington's side though most of that time. Now here he stood, thicker through the chest and shoulders, resplendent in blue and gold, almost commanding in his posture--a man now, not the boy who'd ridden off to Boston.

Something happens to a father when he sees his son in a military uniform. It changes the terms of engagement, alters the normal perspectives. Henry felt that now. The soldier standing before him looked like Jonathan and sounded like him. But it was a different Jonathan: harder, more independent, wiser, perhaps more cynical.

This was no longer the boy who followed Henry through the morning chores on the farm. It was a man who'd done things: unimaginable, unspoken, and probably horrible things—a man whose life had spun far beyond the orbit of his father's control or knowledge. Seeing Jonathan again after so long a time reminded Henry, perhaps more than anything, that his son had grown beyond that time when he needed his father, any father. He'd made the passage into his own realm of competence and confidence. Every father expects that of his son, wants it for him, then watches sadly when the passage occurs, aching quietly from the pain of being unneeded.

And Henry noticed that his son wore the rank of a colonel, though he had heard nothing about any promotions. He only knew that Washington had made him a captain in Cambridge when he convinced him to join the army. So the first words across his lips were these: "Jonathan, you're a colonel now."

Jonathan smiled and said, "Yes, I was just promoted a week ago. Washington is surrounded by young men. Alexander Hamilton from New

York is a colonel now and the Frenchmen, Lafayette, is a general. I think he felt that since I'd been with him longer than either of them, I should not be a mere major any more."

"I didn't even know you'd become a major. You never mentioned it in your letters."

"There were many things more important to mention, Father."

Henry found his hat and coat on their peg and said, "Come let's leave here and have a proper talk."

"But don't you have business here, Father?"

"There'll be no important votes today. I won't be missed. And there is no business here that matters more to me than some time with you."

"But wait one moment," Jonathan protested. "I'm actually here in an official capacity. General Washington sent me with an important message to the Congress, and I must deliver it before we go." Henry directed his son to the secretary of the Congress and stood by the door, looking on proudly as several of the delegates recognized the handsome soldier walking along the wall as the "Houghton boy" they'd first gotten to know when he was Henry's secretary at the First Continental Congress. A few even rose and shook Jonathan's hand as he walked by.

Jonathan delivered his message and returned to the vestibule. They stepped out into the cold air and walked past several low buildings to the white frame house in which Henry was lodging. Mrs. Sampson was sewing in the parlor when they entered and, upon being introduced to Jonathan, asked if she could make them tea. Father and son took seats by the fire and, after serving them tea, Mrs. Sampson left them alone.

"It is such a wonder that you're here," Henry said. "I'd despaired of ever seeing you again—or Celia or Nathaniel either. How I miss our family, Jonathan. And how I long for those days when we were all together in Still River. In retrospect now, it all seems so idyllic."

"To me as well, Father. I can't tell you how many lonely nights I've survived by dreaming of the farm and all of us there. Or in how many moments of the sheerest terror, when every instinct in me said 'Run away from this,' that I've pushed on by thinking about our farm and our family and how important it is to get this done so that we may all have the lives we choose.

"A month ago, I was with Colonel Morgan's Virginia riflemen, some of the best soldiers in the army. We were advancing up a hill against Burgoyne's best troops. They were pouring musket balls and grapeshot

355

down on us, and it was like walking into a solid wall of lead. And we were trying to shoot below their grapeshot to take out the gunners. A man's conscious thoughts cease at times like those and only his training and his beliefs carry him. I could feel the heat of the balls flying by. I was hit twice, and the pain was awful. But in my mind I could see the little copse of trees on the Bend in the spring when the leaves are first out and the color is so tender and fresh. I could smell the winter coming out of the ground just before the furry buds form on the willows. And those were more powerful impressions than the smoke or the noise or the terrible bloody tangle of bodies on the ground.

Henry listened in horror at Jonathan's descriptions of images the father had never wanted to contemplate. "If we win this war, Father, it won't be because we're better soldiers than the redcoats; they're excellent soldiers. Not because we have better guns or supplies; we don't. We'll win because every soldier in our line sees a picture in his mind like the one I saw at Saratoga. And everyone will fight like the devil to get back to that place, to make it safe, to live there freely. It is the thing more than any other that separates us from the brave men across the line. They're fighting because it's their duty and their honor. We're fighting because it's our lives and our future."

To Henry, this seemed a nearly complete reversal from the conversations they'd had when last they were together. Then Jonathan was the inquirer and Henry the explainer. Now Jonathan had insights from an experience that Henry did not possess. So he listened as Jonathan described Bunker Hill and the frustrating retreat from New York and the cold surprise attack on Trenton and the precious moment when Johnny Burgoyne passed his sword to Horatio Gates. Henry hadn't even known that Jonathan was at Saratoga, assuming he'd remained with Washington in the south. All of this new information about Jonathan and his war, the vastness and vividness of it, overwhelmed Henry's emotional capacities, and he turned to practical questions.

"How are we doing, son? We get sugar-coated reports from Washington and some of the other generals, but what do you think? Can we win this war?" Henry asked.

"I thought we were invincible after Howe evacuated Boston," Jonathan answered, his face a map of perplexity. "We'd punished him mightily on Bunker Hill and waited him out through the winter. When we retrieved the cannon for Knox from Canada, it seemed like we had them outsmarted, outnumbered, and outmuscled. When I stood beside

Washington watching their ships sail away, I honestly thought we might not have any more war.

"But that was a long time ago. Now the situation looks very different. Saratoga was a big setback to them, of course. They might have succeeded in the north if it hadn't been for some good work by our spies who gave us time to get Gates's army up there to cut off Burgoyne before he met up with Clinton. Washington says that wars turn on little things like that: a tip from a spy, a key act of bravery in the middle of a battle, a commander's moment of greatness.

"But wars are also long, tedious, grinding affairs. And, in the long run, the stronger army with the best training and the best supplies usually prevails. The British have succeeded at setting up supply networks that are driving us mad. We know they're getting arms and food and uniforms and other supplies from their ships. But we also know that there are loyalists here who sell them supplies. They should be at a disadvantage fighting on foreign soil. But they seem to have overcome that, and it's hurting us."

Henry was grateful for the information and the analysis, and he was impressed by the cool and detached way that Jonathan assessed the state of the two armies. "But with the militias, don't we actually have more men ready to fight than Howe?" he asked.

"Ready to fight?" Jonathan pondered the words. "That's the key, Father. We've had times when we've probably gone into battle with a numerical advantage. It's hard to tell, because you never see all the available troops on either side. But we still have enormous problems in our command structure. The Continental Army seems to be improving. I wasn't there, but Hamilton told me that in Germantown and Brandywine we had men from one state under the command of officers from other states. That's happened rarely in this war, and it's a positive thing.

"But our army is still rife with regional jealousies. Sometimes one regiment from North Carolina won't carry out an assignment because they think it's beneath them and ought to be given to a lesser state, like Rhode Island say. At other times, another regiment from New Hampshire is angry because they thought they deserved to be at the head of a column instead of Pennsylvania. Then you have all the in-fighting among the generals and officers for the same reasons."

"It sounds like Congress," Henry interjected with a laugh.

"But we have bigger problems than those. First, our army still lacks sufficient training and discipline. The militia are fickle and inconsistent. Sometimes they fight very effectively, but no commander can ever count on militia. And in the regular army men come and go so fast, as enlistments begin and end, that we don't ever seem to have a coordinated force in the field. Just as men become experienced in the order of battle, they leave and go home. Others replace them who've never seen the enemy and never been shot at.

Henry tried to follow closely for surely these were things he'd want to report to other delegates. "Second," Jonathan continued, "these are brave men, but it's hard to get the best out of them when they have no blankets, no warm clothes, no shoes, and no decent food. We've been routed in engagements we should have won because our men were too exhausted or sick to fight on. If we're going to win this war, the Congress has to play as large a role as the men in the field. And frankly, Father, the men in the field usually think the Congress couldn't care less about them."

"I'm sure they do. It's an embarrassment, and we all feel it." Henry could hardly look his son in the eye. "But we're powerless to do much about it. Congress can't tax anybody. Congress can't conscript a single troop. Every member of Congress I know would like to spend more money on the army. But we don't have money and we have no way of getting it. We can requisition the states; that's all we can do. But we can't make the states deliver, and often they don't."

"What about France or Spain? We hear rumors that we might be getting money, maybe even troops from one of them?"

"For that, we all fondly pray," Henry answered. "Franklin is in Paris with Silas Deane from Connecticut and Richard Henry Lee's brother, Arthur. They've been negotiating with the French, trying to get them to take our side in the war. But countries are like states, they only do what's in their own interests. The French are slow to commit because they don't want to end up on the losing side, and they don't want to spend their precious *livres* on a lost cause. Franklin reports that chances of French intervention always look better after we win a big battle and worse after we lose one. Let's hope they have time to mull over Saratoga before they hear that Philadelphia has fallen."

Jonathan rose and stood closer to the fire, rubbing his hands together for warmth. "Not much good news in all this, Father, is there? The Congress has no authority to manage a war and can't even decide on a form of government for a nation that's a year and half in existence. The enemy sits undisturbed in our capital and controls our entire coast. Our own army has not much more than the bravery and conviction of its soldiers to recommend it. It's a sad state of affairs. Do you remember

358

what you wrote to me after Congress issued the independence declaration, what John Adams said to you that night?"

Henry looked up, trying to recall the precise words. "It was something like 'Declaring independence was the easy part, now it will have to be won with our toil and our blood?'"

"Yes, that was it. Quite prophetic wasn't it? There'll be lot more toil and, I'm afraid, a lot more blood yet to come, if we're to have any chance of success."

Henry nodded in agreement. As he watched his son and thought about the years the two of them had already surrendered to this effort, and thought about the years still to be spent, melancholy enveloped him. "Oh, Jonathan," he said, rising to stand by his son at the hearth, "how I wish we could be spending these years together on the farm, clearing fields and cutting timber and conducting your experiments with seeds and fertilizers. Not embroiled in the pettiest politics. Not coping with danger and death. Not separated as we are from the ones we love."

Jonathan brightened, then touched his father's shoulder—an unfamiliar but comforting gesture. "Well then, let's stop with our war stories and talk of other things, Father. Please tell me everything you can about Mother and the others."

Henry brightened, too, and returned to his chair. "Yes, that's the idea. Well, let me see. I'll start with Nathaniel. There's not much to report. We've had few letters from him since he left, and it's unclear why. Perhaps he just hasn't written much, or perhaps he's had trouble getting letters posted to America. We all know how hard it is to communicate through this blockade. What we've heard is that he is apprenticing with a painter, a quite well-known one apparently, named Carlisle. He helps him with portraits of famous people, and he's doing some paintings of his own. Of course, as an American in London he has to be very careful to avoid any involvement in or discussion of politics. But for Nathaniel, that should be no great constraint. Never was there a soul less interested in politics. I'm grateful for your brother's safety, Jonathan, grateful he's not on the battlefield. It's one less thing for your mother to worry herself about. But I do fear that your brother will one day look back on these years, this time of turmoil and torment and opportunity, and feel that he missed something very precious."

Jonathan bit his tongue. He was tempted to tell his father what he and few others knew about Nathaniel. But the risk was too great, even with his father. How much it would mean to Henry to know that Nathaniel was playing so large and dangerous a role in the war effort. But every additional person who knew about that role, even a family member, multiplied the chances for an unmasking of Nathaniel's identity and his extraordinary success in purloining the military secrets of the British high command. So Jonathan said nothing and only nodded in solemn agreement, hoping that some day he—or, better, Nathaniel himself—could tell their father the full rich details of his older son's exploits under the very noses of the King of England and his ministers.

"You probably don't know that Savannah visited Celia in the spring. She said our grandson is precious—which makes it all the more painful that we can't see him. But she also came back worried about her sister. She said nothing of this to Mother, but she told me that Celia seems lonely and isolated, that her friends have left Manhattan or feel trapped in their houses by having so many soldiers around. She said that the houses surrounding Celia's are all used to quarter troops, but hers is not. She could find no explanation for that, but it seemed odd to her. Savannah also said that Godfrey seemed very distant and that he was home infrequently. What do you make of that? What can you tell me about Celia from your time with her?"

"Well, I haven't seen Celia now for a year, Father, but I think I share Savannah's perceptions. I'm surprised to hear that they haven't been forced to quarter troops. I was able to use my influence with the quartermaster to keep troops out of their house when we occupied the city, but I assumed she would have no such luck with the British and she'd be running a soldiers' home there. I'm surprised to hear otherwise.

"I certainly noticed the same things about Godfrey. He came and went at odd hours. He seemed very busy and preoccupied, but said nothing about his business except that it kept him busy. When I probed to find out exactly what the business was he only said something vague like 'Buying and selling, like any business.' He's a hard fellow to get a bead on. And Savannah was right about his apparent indifference to Celia. He is polite to her in a formal kind of way, but he lacks any sensitivity to her needs and shows her no affection at all. At least I perceived none. Frankly, Father, I wish there were some way to get her and the baby—and, of course, Godfrey too if he would come—out of New York and back to Delaware."

"So do I, Jonathan. So do I."

"What of Savannah and Mother? How are they? And how are things on the farm?"

Henry stiffened and, in a look that Jonathan recalled as a signal of deep concern, contorted his face. "The war has been hard on your mother," he said slowly. "She's not well, Jonathan. It doesn't seem that she has any disease, at least not one that is known to us. But she has withdrawn from everything and everyone. She spends her days in bed or sitting silently by the fire. Savannah can occasionally engage her in a brief conversation, but most of the time her eyes don't seem to focus on much and she's barely present. Savannah thinks that she's just had to confront more sadness and disappointment than she's able to bear. Having Nathaniel so far away, Celia gone for seven years, you in harm's way in the army, and me away at Congress for so long. All of that has so freighted her heart that her mind can't cope. I told Savannah that I'd resign from Congress and stay home to be with her, but Savannah was dead set against that. She didn't think it would help mother at all, and she thought there was important work for me here.

Henry stood and walked to the window. The conversation had brought all of his emotional torments to the surface and he sought to control them before saying more. After a minute, feeling more composed, he turned back to Jonathan. "I must confess that some days my guilt is almost overwhelming. I can't help but feel that Mother's deep distress is my doing. If I'd never agreed to be a delegate to Congress and stayed home in Still River, things might well have remained as they were, at least for Mother and me."

Jonathan touched his father's sleeve and looked into his sad eyes. "Don't blame yourself," he said. "All of us have been confronted with choices we never could have imagined. Perhaps if I'd declined Washington's invitation and come home to run the farm as I'd planned, Mother wouldn't have sunk into the despair you describe. Or perhaps she would have, no matter what any of us had done. Perhaps it's just her life taking its course, Father, in the same way one develops a sickness or infirmity. There 's nothing anyone can do to prevent it." He paused and sat back in his chair. "I must try to get some leave so I can get home and see her."

"Yes," Henry said. "I think that'd be good. But prepare yourself. She won't look or be like the mother you remember."

Jonathan sat silently for a moment, contemplating what Henry had told him. Then he asked, "How's Savannah dealing with all this?"

A smile returned to Henry's face. "Your sister is an absolute gem, Jonathan. I don't know what I would do without her. She has borne most of the weight of Mother's distress without complaint. She and Sweetie do everything they can to be sure that Mother eats and stays warm. They keep trying, though they rarely succeed, to engage her in conversation, to find something to fill her mind. Savannah has been an angel."

"Good for her," Jonathan cheered.

"But there's more," Henry added. "She's also stepped in and taken over nearly all the details of running the farm. I would never have guessed that a woman could do the things she's done. She's hired men. Even fired one who showed up drunk one day and caused a bolt of oak to roll off a wagon and nearly hit Quiet Jack. She developed a harvesting plan for the north hill. She started new cornfields on the land we cleared above the bend, and she's started breeding horses to sell. She even took a boat to Annapolis and made a contract with a shipyard to buy our timber directly. She dressed up old Thom Mason and made him look like he was the agent doing our negotiation. I went over the account books when I was home in the spring and it was the finest set of records we've ever had. I don't want to think what state the farm would be in now if it weren't for her. When you take over the place after the war, it'll be a thriving enterprise. You can thank your sister for that."

"Maybe I'll have to find other work," Jonathan said with a laugh. "Sounds like she's running the place just fine."

Henry scowled briefly. "No, running a farm is man's work, Jonathan. But we've been lucky that Savannah has been able to manage it while we've been occupied elsewhere."

"When do she and Marinus plan to get married. And what will happen to the farm when they do?" Jonathan asked.

Henry looked surprised. "Haven't you heard? She turned down his proposal. They're not going to be married. In fact, Marinus is betrothed to a woman in Delaware, the daughter of a judge."

Jonathan sat back sharply and whistled through his teeth. "No," he said. "No one told me any of this. Why? Why did she reject him?"

"You know, I'm not really sure," Henry said. "She said she didn't want to leave Mother in her dark spells and she didn't think it fair to Marinus to continue to wait for an answer. He was much taken with her and probably would have waited as long as necessary. But I think there was more than she was saying. He remained a loyalist much longer than most other prominent men in Delaware and I think she was frustrated with his obstinacy about independence, or maybe more that he just seemed indifferent about it. Savannah is a woman of strong passions, as you know, and I think it bothered her that Marinus could care so little about this struggle, especially with me in Congress and you fighting in the army."

"I can easily imagine that something like that would irritate her," Jonathan said, remembering the many battles he and his sister had had when he refused to see things as one-sidedly as she did.

"But, you know, I think there was something else," Henry went on. "I think she really enjoys the farm, likes living there, likes running the place. And I think she saw marriage to Marinus not as the good life of the wife of a country squire, but as some kind of imprisonment that would deny her freedom to do something she truly wanted to do. Marinus kept telling her how wonderful her life would be, with teas and balls and meeting all the famous people. And the more she heard, the more she hated the sound of it. It didn't sound like freedom to her; it sounded like the opposite. I hope she made the right decision. A good catch like Marinus Marshall doesn't come along too often in a tiny state like Delaware. I hope Savannah doesn't look back in her spinsterhood and regret that she made the wrong choice."

Jonathan rose and stepped once more to the fire. He turned and looked directly at Henry. "We've all had to make our choices, Father, and we'll all have the rest of our lives to enjoy or rue the consequences."

Jonathan had a message for Washington that had to be returned that night. So, after another hour or so of conversation at the Sampson house, he and Henry shared an affectionate farewell, and Jonathan walked quickly to the livery at the eastern edge of York, where he'd left his horse.

As he stood in the stable waiting for the boy to cinch the saddle, a voice behind him drawled. "Houghton, is that you, son?"

Jonathan turned and saw the broad smiling face of Richard Henry Lee. "Mr. Lee," he said, "how good to see you. How are you, sir?"

"Capital, son, capital. Though I wish you'd beat those bloody redcoats into a hasty retreat so we could all go home and get out of this infernal cold."

"So do I, sir," Jonathan said, "but they're a difficult and dangerous enemy."

"Nonsense, Houghton. We should have captured Howe in Boston when we had him encircled. We should have resisted his landings in New York. We should have pursued him after Trenton and Princeton. The war should be over by now and the redcoats should have been sent packing long ago. I know you men in the ranks have fought bravely, but your leaders have let you down.

"I must tell you, Houghton, that this Congress is losing its patience with Washington. We once thought he was a military genius, but he seems to miss his opportunities time and again. Even John Adams—and you'll recall that he was George's champion when the Congress made him commander-in-chief in '75—even Adams is exasperated by his failures. From here it looks like Horatio Gates deserves a chance to take command or even this General Charles Conway who distinguished himself amidst Washington's confusion at Brandywine. This war is wearying us all, Houghton, and we need to find a commander who won't keep squandering his opportunities and who'll do something more than just whine to us about needing more men and money."

"But…" Jonathan started to object.

Lee cut him off. "See if you can't get a burr in the General's breeches, Houghton. I love George like a brother, but we can't allow him to squander another American life with indecision and a lack of boldness. If something doesn't change soon, I'm afraid he'll be back in Virginia before I am."

# Chapter 25

## *Paris, France*
## *December 1777 – March 1778*

"Notice how, even now in late afternoon, the spire seems to draw its light straight from heaven. It's as if God were offering an invitation to every artist in France, 'Paint me, please, for I am so beautiful.' " Nathaniel pirouetted mischievously in front of the church of Sainte-Chapelle pretending to paint in broad strokes. He and Lydie had spent the day, as they had spent most of the previous week, walking the grand boulevards and quiet alleys, sitting in the Jardin du Luxembourg, lovely in its winter symmetry even without flowers, dining in the gay cafés of the *rive gauche*.

Benton had accompanied them on a few of these strolls, but the stiffness in his knees made walking more of a struggle now and most mornings he urged his wife and his assistant to "see Paris" without him. And see Paris they did. Nathaniel had been here for a few weeks on his tour of Europe in 1772, but he'd spent most of his time in the galleries and museums. The city remained a stranger to him. But Lydie knew Paris well. She'd been here only a few times since her marriage to Benton, but as a girl her father had brought her here often from their home in Rouen, telling her—with no small measure of accuracy—that to be a "citoyen du monde," one must first become a "citoyen de Paris."

So now Lydie delighted in leading Jonathan from one Parisien delight to another: the open greensward of the Place des Invalides, strolling in the Ile St-Louis, the gardens of the Tuileries, created two hundred years earlier by Catherine de Médicis, where now the fashionable of Paris came to preen and promenade.

They hadn't come from London merely for a holiday. Benton had a commission to paint Pierre Augustin Caron de Beaumarchais, the dashing French playwright and *bon vivant*. They'd met in London when

Beaumarchais was there on business. The Frenchman had taken a particular liking to Benton's portrait of the Duchess of Devonshire and had promised Carlisle, without negotiation, the largest sum he'd ever been offered to come to Paris and paint his portrait. As part of their arrangement, Beaumarchais paid the transportation costs of Carlisle's household and offered them the use of one of his fine homes on the Rue de Grenelle near the Champ de Mars. The size of the commission and Beaumarchais's other generosity would allow them to stay in Paris for three or four months, working some of the time on the portrait but also enjoying the opportunity to concentrate on other paintings. Sittings would not begin for another week or more and Nathaniel and Lydie had used the free time to explore the city.

Each day they walked or took their carriage to a different part of Paris. Each day they meandered along new streets, wandered through different shops, viewed the river—the magnificent river—from an even more beautiful vantage point than the day before. But only the backgrounds changed; the real meaning of these days never did. Each day they spent in thrall of each other's company, in a rushing stream of playful, dreamy, happy, intimate moments. There was much unspoken between them, but little unfelt.

It was cool on this December morning and a thin sheet of ice covered some of the puddles in the street around St Germain des Prés. They sat near the grand church facing east, bathing in the warm kiss of the morning sun, Nathaniel wrapped in his black wool coat, Lydie in a gray hooded cloak and fur muffler. They sat so close together on the small bench that each could feel the warmth of the other's body.

"Perhaps a man of science could account for it," Nathaniel said, "but the light here has no counterpart in England. In Paris, a simple nondescript stone house can look charming and elegant. In London, the same structure would look simple and nondescript."

Lydie removed her hand from the muffler and touched his arm gently. "Oh, Nathaniel, Paris has captured you, has it not? How many artists have come here and been captured in the same way. But you're right, there are emotions in the air here, a profound charm that suffuses everything, that tantalizes and quickens our senses. Paris draws out our passions, scrapes the inhibitions off them. It's not science, Nathaniel. It's beyond science. It's magic."

She pressed harder against him and leaned her head on his shoulder. They sat in silence for a few moments, absorbing the morning

366

rays and warming in them. Suddenly, impulsively, Nathaniel straightened and turned toward Lydie. He put his hand against her neck and pulled her face gently toward his. They kissed lightly, then Nathaniel drew back and looked ardently into Lydie's eyes. They kissed again, this time a long deep kiss that in the irrelevance of time might have lasted seconds or minutes or years.

Nathaniel withdrew slightly again and rubbed the back of his hand against Lydie's warm cheek. "I love you," he whispered softly. "It's not Paris that touches my passion, Lydie, it's you. You are so beautiful that everything else around you is out of focus. Paris is lovely, of course, but I can only see you and, when I look at you, it overwhelms me. Feel my hand. It quivers from the touch of you."

Lydie started to reach for his hand, then pulled back and slid away from Nathaniel on the bench, looking off in the distance. The sudden and unexpected mood change startled Nathaniel, like the way a powerful thunderstorm quickly darkened a summer afternoon in Still River. He'd sensed some hesitant shadows in Lydie's emotions in the previous few days, but he was startled nonetheless by her withdrawal.

"Lydie, what's the matter? What did I say?" Nathaniel implored, his voice rising in distress.

Lydie sat silently for a moment, then turned to him. "I must confess something," she said, choosing her words carefully. "My feelings for you are every bit as strong as those you just expressed to me. I fell in love with you many months ago Nathaniel, and it has taken all my powers of restraint to keep from burying you in some expression of that. But now I do not trust what you say. And I'm terribly afraid."

Nathaniel leaned back, confused. "I don't understand. What are you saying? Did I not just tell you how much I've come to love you?"

"I hear what you say, Nathaniel, and I'm touched by it. But so often in the past few months when it seemed we were on the verge of these professions to each other, you found some excuse to hasten away. I've come to feel that perhaps I am not the true object of your affections."

"But...but, why," Nathaniel stammered, trying to make sense of Lydie's words. "On some occasions, I know, I left abruptly, but I had obligations that were very pressing. As I told you."

"Nathaniel," Lydie said with a steely look, "I am not a fool. What obligations does an artist have at 10 o'clock at night? What could possibly pull you away from so intimate a moment? Unless it was an assignation with some other woman."

367

"Oh, Lydie, that's preposterous. There is no other woman."

Lydie's anger was rising now, flowing scarlet through her cheeks and flashing in her eyes. "Ha!" she screamed. "One night when you left Bloomsbury Square, I dressed as a man and followed you. You walked, practically ran in fact, to the churchyard in St. Martin's Lane. I hid in the shadows at the edge of the yard and watched as you sat on a bench next to a small woman in black. I couldn't hear your words, nor see clearly what passed between you, but I felt a terrible pain in my heart. You'd left me to be with another woman. I don't want even to contemplate what sort of woman one would meet in a park late at night."

It took Nathaniel a moment to recall the night Lydie described. When it came to him, he gasped, "Oh, Lydie. No, no, no. I did meet someone that night, as I told you I had to. But it was not a woman. It was a man."

Lydie now bore the look of confusion. "A man?" she said slowly. "What man?"

Nathaniel looked slowly away, trying to conjure up an effective answer. "That I can't tell you, I'm afraid. But I can assure you, Lydie, that I did not meet a woman in that park or any park. Not that night. Not any night."

Lydie seemed unconvinced. "Now you say it was a man, but I saw that it was a very small person, one who looked more like a woman than a man. And you say you can't tell me who it was? I don't know, Nathaniel. I find this hard to believe. What could be the reason for this secrecy if, in fact, it was a man whom you met in that park?"

Nathaniel's mind was racing. He stood up and walked to the barren hedge to give himself a moment to form his thoughts. He'd never spoken a word to anyone about his activities with the Alliance. His contact, George, knew, of course. He assumed his brother Jonathan knew because he'd sent the first keyhole letter. But he didn't think anyone else knew of his espionage. Could he risk telling Lydie?

Could he risk not telling Lydie? Would their affection dissolve in distrust if he persisted in hiding information from her? Never had the choice among options seemed so unclear or so risky. Let me try this, Nathaniel thought, as he moved back to the bench and sat down. He took Lydie's hand, which she surrendered to him reluctantly, and waited until she looked at him.

"You must trust me, Lydie. I've been involved in the American war in a small way. The meeting you observed was an occasion for me to discuss this with someone else who's involved. That was a man, not a woman. And the meeting was, as I told you, an obligation. I had made an appointment to see him that night and I felt obligated to keep the appointment. I haven't ever mentioned this to you because this is a very dangerous time. It's risky enough merely being an American in London. If anyone ever discovered that I was not merely a painter's assistant, my life would be in grave danger. So perhaps would the lives of those with whom I have contact. That's why I kept this from you. It's not a large role I play, but even a small role would be hard to explain to the British authorities were it to become known."

Lydie's face twisted into a map of confusion and exasperation as she listened. When Nathaniel finished his explanation, she said nothing for a few minutes as she reviewed his words. Then she said simply, "Are you a spy?"

"Oh no, no," Nathaniel quickly responded. "Nothing as exciting as that. I simply report back to America some of my impressions of the government leaders here, that's all. What they're like. Whether they have any good feelings for Americans or not. Nothing very important, really."

Lydie pondered this answer and found it reasonable, though out of character for the man she had always perceived as more romantic than political. "You don't seem like the sort of person who would enjoy this kind of business, Nathaniel. I find your story convincing, and I apologize for jumping to opposite conclusions. But you can understand why I wouldn't expect you to be engaged in secret meetings and war business."

"I can, Lydie. You're quite right. It's nothing I ever would have initiated. But my brother is an army officer, as you know, and he made the initial contact. It's very hard to turn away from a family member in a war. And again, as I said, my part in this is very minor."

Lydie warmed, feeling great relief after learning that her suspicion about Nathaniel had been groundless. But then another, more horrible, thought struck her. "Nathaniel, you're in great danger. If you get caught at this, they'll treat you as a spy no matter how minor or major your role. And they'll hang you instantly. You must stop this! I couldn't bear to have you taken away from me."

Nathaniel slid closer and put his arm around Lydie. "Please don't worry. I've been very careful. I don't think there's any risk of being caught."

Lydie's thoughts came in a rush and grew more frightening. "But your father's a member of the American Congress and your brother's an

American army officer. If you were caught, they'd make a terrible spectacle of you. What propaganda that would be. Nathaniel, you really must end this. It's too dangerous. Nothing can be worth this kind of risk."

Nathaniel grew more serious now and held Lydie's left hand in both of his. "Some things are worth high risks, Lydie. My father voted for independence. He's now a traitor in the eyes of this government. That was a great risk. My brother probably faces graver danger every day when he straps on his sword than I ever will. My older sister has stayed in New York to be at her husband's side, even as war raged all around them and a terrible fire nearly burned their house. I think what little risk I face pales next to theirs."

A tear rolled slowly down Lydie's cheek now, and there was a catch in her voice. "But Nathaniel, you must stop this. You must stop now for me. I couldn't bear to see you dragged off. I couldn't bear to be without you. Please, please, please tell me that you will completely withdraw from all these activities that expose you to such danger."

Nathaniel looked silently at Lydie, at this exquisite beauty, at the sadness that enveloped her. He'd never felt such feelings as these. He was pulled toward her as if she were the sole gravitational force in his orbit.

"You're right, dear Lydie. I must stop. I will stop. I promise you that." Then he looked away, hoping she would not see in his eyes the pain that his lie inflicted on him.

Nathaniel closed the small bronze door to the guest house and began to walk through the garden to the main house where Benton and Lydie were in residence. It was said that Beaumarchais owned nearly as many fine homes in France as the king. If the others were like this, Nathaniel thought, the rumors of his wealth must surely be true. The guest house was one of three on this estate and it was almost as large as the Carlisle's home in Bloomsbury Square. The main house was many times larger. All were arrayed around a magnificent central courtyard filled with an octagonal and very formal garden. Nathaniel could only imagine how beautiful it would be in a few months when the warmth of spring set it to bloom.

A doorman opened the courtyard entrance to the main house, and Nathaniel entered to find Benton waiting for him, studying the crystal chandelier in the high central foyer. The floor and the walls were marble with inlaid Moroccan tiles. They were exquisite. But it was the delicate, gleaming chandelier that filled the eye as one ascended the circular stairway that wound its way up the three stories of the foyer. Benton had been fascinated by it since the day they first arrived.

"It's a stunning piece, and the way it floats there seems to defy gravity," Benton said when he noticed that Nathaniel was watching him. "I'd like to hide it in my valise and take it back to London."

"That, sir, would require a much larger valise than any you brought," laughed Nathaniel.

Another servant appeared to announce that their coach was ready and the two painters walked across the pillared front portico to the Rue de Grenelle where a large coach and four awaited them. They entered through a door held for them by one of the footmen and sat back for the short ride through Montparnasse to another of Beaumarchais's houses on the Rue de Sévres.

Beaumarchais was rich, fabulously rich, but he was clearly not one of the idle rich. Benton had met the Count in London and knew his reputation as a man of vast wealth and ostentatious lifestyle, one of those men who defines taste and fashion. His parties were a main intersection of French society where courtiers, *philosophes*, men of invention, and the stylish gentry all came together. But Benton also knew Beaumarchais's creative side because he had seen performances of *The Marriage of Figaro* and *The Barber of Seville*, two of his greatest plays.

Nathaniel had never met Beaumarchais, but he knew things about the man that Benton didn't know, that few people even in France knew. Beaumarchais was one of the principal financiers of the American war effort against the British. And during his visits to London, Nathaniel knew, Beaumarchais had actually spied on his British contacts and reported to his own government what he could learn of British war plans. Beaumarchais's public flamboyance masked very effectively his secret financial machinations in behalf of the Continentals, especially his financing of the phony corporation, Hortalez et Cie, that funneled arms and supplies to Americans. Few men outside America had played so important a role in its birth, and Nathaniel was looking forward to meeting the man he heard so much about from his contacts in the Alliance.

When they arrived at the large brown stone mansion on the Rue de Sévres, the coach passed through a high ornate gate, around a cobblestone courtyard to a side entrance. They were led inside, then up a long flight of stairs past a larger-than-life-sized painting of a stallion rising on hind quarters. Benton's legs wobbled from the climb and he had to stop twice on the stairs to secure his footing. A platoon of servants carried their easel and canvas and brushes and paints.

A half hour later, after they'd set up in the north-facing music room that was to be their studio here, Caron de Beaumarchais made his entrance. He was dressed in a suit of deep green satin with cream-colored silk stockings and pebbled leather shoes with silver buckles. At his belt hung a sword of gleaming steel with gold handle and jeweled hilt. He greeted them warmly in nearly accent-less English. "It is so good of you to come," he said. "You do me great honor by your willingness to paint my portrait. I know now that my progeny will continue to hang my grim face on their walls, not because it is a pleasant sight, but because it is a work of the finest portraitist of our age."

Benton laughed, clearly enjoying the shameless flattery. "Well," he said, "we will do our best then to compel the obligation of your grandchildren."

Beaumarchais was a splendid subject. He sat patiently for long spells, having warned his servants not to interrupt him for anything, "not even a visit from the King." He carried on erudite and friendly conversation with the painters, a great change from the indifference they always received from their British commissions. And he insured that at periodic intervals, well turned-out servants arrived carrying silver trays with tea and delicate sugary cakes. The light was also wonderful in this room, consistent and diffuse, and as the portrait began to materialize before them, both Benton and Nathaniel thought it would be one of their best.

Halfway through the second day of sittings, Benton's left knee began to ache and he told Nathaniel that he was going to go find a room in which he could sit for a few minutes. He asked Nathaniel to work on the long sections of Beaumarchais's stockings while he was gone. After he'd left the room, Beaumarchais rose and said, "Mr. Houghton, is it?"

"Yes," Nathaniel said, pleased that the Count had remembered his name. He doubted that any of the dozens of Londoners they'd painted ever had the faintest recollection of his name.

"Perhaps you would step with me to the window for a moment, there is something I would like to show you."

Nathaniel nodded, and the two men walked to the far end of the room, away from the door. Nathaniel started to look through the small leaded panes of the window, but Beaumarchais put a hand on his arm and said, "No, I'm sorry, that was a ruse. I have nothing to show you; I just wanted to get away from the door." Then he looked directly at Nathaniel who seemed confused. "Are you Charles?" Beaumarchais asked.

Nathaniel now seemed totally confused. Beaumarchais repeated his question, "Are you Charles?"

Then Nathaniel grasped the coded greeting and answered, "No, I'm George."

A display of confidence then spread across Beaumarchais's face and he said to Nathaniel. "I am pleased to know you. I have heard how fortunate we were to have a man of such skill and courage in London. I didn't know your real identity until I was advised a few days ago to make contact with you."

Then Beaumarchais unbuttoned his waistcoat and removed an envelope from an inside pocket. He passed it to Nathaniel who folded it once and tucked it inside his shirt. "What should I do with this?" Nathaniel asked.

"Just wait," the Count replied. "The answer will come later." Then he smiled quickly and returned to his chair. Nathaniel picked up his brush and bent to continue his work. He finished the left stocking just as Carlisle returned.

Nathaniel stood before the fire in just his linen shirt and breeches. His boots were warming near the fire, the servants had all left, and he was having a small glass of cognac before getting into bed for the night. They had now been working on the Beaumarchais portrait for five days and he was tired. Tomorrow Beaumarchais would be away, Benton was going to spend the day with the celebrated painter Jacques-Louis David on the other side of the Seine, and Nathaniel and Lydie would have the day to themselves. He could hardly wait.

He pulled a chair up close to the fire and sat, watching the flames dance in the draft. As always at quiet times like these, he thought about Lydie. How could something cause such pleasure and such pain all at once, he wondered. It seemed that the deeper his love for Lydie grew, the more anxiety it caused him. What a curse to fall in love with the wife of the man you most admired in the world, a man who had never failed to be generous and caring and helpful. He would do anything he could to shield Benton from pain. Anything he could. But he couldn't deny his feelings for Lydie. The force of that passion was undeniable, irresistible. It couldn't be stopped. And so he could only hope that Benton would never

373

find out—that for as long as Benton lived they could keep their secret from him, contain the bounds of the love they shared, keep it chaste.

But even that was growing increasingly difficult, and Nathaniel worried that a moment would soon befall them when all restraint was crushed by a force too great for either of them to command, and then all the limits they had tried to impose on the corporal expression of their love would dissolve in one great flight of passion. What a plague, Nathaniel thought, to want something so badly and to know it is so wrong.

A soft knock on the door pulled Nathaniel abruptly from his contemplation, and he set his glass on the floor and rose to answer it. Perhaps, he thought, it's Lydie. She's never come here at night, but it's exactly the sort of thing she would do if she were sure Benton was asleep for the night. He slid the bolt to the left, and pulled the heavy door toward him expecting Lydie to fall into his arms.

But instead of Lydie, Nathaniel confronted two large men, dressed all in black and wearing large wool hats that hid their faces. Without a word, they stepped into the hallway and grabbed Nathaniel. He raised his fists to resist, but they quickly overpowered him and tied a rag over his mouth and bound his hands behind him. Then they searched his clothes until they found, still in the pocket where he'd placed it, the letter that Beaumarchais had given him. They left it there. Then they threw a blanket over his head and dragged him out the door.

Nathaniel was dazed and frightened. The kidnappers lifted him off the ground and forced him to lie on something flat. Soon it started to move and he realized he was in a wagon or carriage. The muffled sounds of the horses on the stone streets indicated that he was out of sight, probably in a covered carriage where he couldn't be seen.

After a few minutes, Nathaniel began to think more clearly. Then the frightening reality struck him. He'd been caught. Beaumarchais was not passing him important information at all; he was setting him up. Someone had revealed Nathaniel's identity and Beaumarchais had passed him a document that could be used to prove that Nathaniel was a spy. Perhaps Beaumarchais was a double agent, and the men kidnapping him now were British. Or perhaps Beaumarchais had been set up, but instead of killing him—because he was too important and his death would be an international incident—they would kill Nathaniel to warn him away from any further espionage.

In any case, Nathaniel could only conclude that he was taking his last wagon ride. His thoughts raced as he tried to think of a plan of escape

374

or an explanation he might use persuasively if he were questioned before they tried to kill him. But it was hopeless. He'd been caught. It was as simple as that. Lydie had been right. It was very dangerous. Not a game. Not for the uncautious. Spies succeeded quietly or they died. And now Nathaniel was on his way to die.

The coach came to a stop and the two men whose boots had never been more than an inch from his ribs grabbed the blanket and pulled Nathaniel to the ground. Then they quickly pushed him along what seemed from the short echo of their footsteps to be an alley. There was a staccato knock on a door, then a muffled exchange of words, then a door creaked open and Nathaniel was pulled through. He was dragged along for a few more steps, then pushed down into a chair.

The men removed the blanket from over his head and, as Nathaniel adjusted his eyes to the dim light, they untied his arms and removed the rag from over his mouth. And as things came back into focus, Nathaniel saw before him not the sword of a British officer, not the rack, not the hangman, not any instrument of torture or death. What he saw instead was a smiling round face wearing small wire spectacles beneath a bald head.

"Henry will kill me if he ever finds out about this," the man said to Nathaniel with a broad grin. Then he extended his hand to Nathaniel. "My name is Benjamin Franklin. We've never met, Mr. Houghton, but I know your father well. We served together in Congress before I came here. If he knew I had kidnapped his son, his opinion of me would no doubt diminish even further."

Nathaniel took a deep breath and tried to regain a measure of composure. Franklin continued, more serious now, before Nathaniel could speak, "I apologize for what we've just put you through. But I assure you it was necessary. I needed to be in touch with you, but Paris is alive with spies and agents of all kinds. So we must be terribly careful not to be seen with our contacts. I instructed the men who retrieved you to make it look like an abduction or a robbery, so if they were seen or caught, there would be no appearance of any espionage. It looks like they carried out their masquerade very convincingly."

"Some might argue more convincingly than necessary," Nathaniel replied, rubbing the red marks on his arms. Then he looked up at Franklin. "It's a pleasure to meet you, Dr. Franklin. You've taken Paris by storm from what I hear and I'd hoped I might get to see you if not actually speak to you. I even walked past your house in Passy a few times on the chance that I might spot you in the garden. But to no avail."

"Well, then, aren't you glad I did you the great favor of sending my coach to escort you to this rendezvous?" Franklin said with a deep laugh.

Nathaniel only smiled.

"Mr. Houghton, we haven't much time. You should have an envelope for me from the Comte de Beaumarchais."

Nathaniel reached into his shirt and retrieved the envelope which he handed to Franklin.

"The good Count has been invaluable to us," Franklin said. "Not just as a generous source of financial assistance but also as a clever businessman who's been able to shield some of our arms purchases from detection by setting up corporations that not even the best French or British accountants can penetrate."

"But I assume he has plenty of go-betweens by now. Why was I used?" Nathaniel asked.

"Ah, things are changing quickly, Mr. Houghton," Franklin said, sitting down in a chair placed behind him by one of the men who'd kidnapped Nathaniel. "We're in very delicate negotiations with the French foreign minister, the Comte de Vergennes. If we succeed and King Louis acquiesces, we shall have a military alliance with the French that may well change the course of the war. That would give us access to French arms and other supplies and the French navy to escort them through the British blockade. We hope it will also bring us French soldiers to supplement our own army.

"When I left America, things didn't look good. Howe was poised to take Philadelphia, and it looked like the British armies in the north were moving at will, perhaps to isolate the rest of the country from New England. I'm still optimistic that we can win this war on our own eventually, but it's not a certain thing. If we can bring the French in, then the odds will change quite dramatically."

Nathaniel pondered this. He'd heard some talk in London about the possibility of the French entering the war, but he hadn't contemplated the possibility very carefully. "Why would the French resist?" he asked.

"Because they're smart," Franklin replied. "They don't want to squander their treasure and their armed forces in a losing cause. If they think the American rebels are bound to lose and America is likely to remain a British dependency, they would much rather have their ships and

376

their soldiers and their arms go where their own national interests will benefit, to Africa or the West Indies, for example. Our task—and it's been a vexing one—is to convince them that we can win the war and that they'll benefit in the long run from the access we'll give them to American trade.

"We're close to getting them to see things our way, but the final stages of any negotiation are always very fragile, and we can't be sure what they're thinking. That's where you come in."

"I'm glad to hear there's some reason for my surreptitious delivery here!" Nathaniel said with a sarcastic grin toward the tall men standing in the shadows.

Franklin looked at him directly but spoke softly. "Beaumarchais is well connected with Vergennes and the other French negotiators. He's a loyal Frenchman, but he's also a great friend of America. We're counting on him to inform us about the thinking and maneuvers of the French negotiators so we can be ready for them with proposals of our own. But everyone in these negotiations is being closely watched by French agents, even Beaumarchais. He was worried about using any of his normal go-betweens. When we learned that you were going to be in Paris and in daily contact with Beaumarchais, you became the perfect candidate to act as go-between. But if we'd alerted you to this in advance, and you'd been caught or detected, our connection would have been ruined. And, oh yes," Franklin twinkled, "you'd be wearing a noose and proving that Newton was right about the forces of gravity. So keeping you ignorant until this moment was in our interest, in Beaumarchais's, and, I daresay, in yours.

"The envelope Beaumarchais gave you should be very helpful to us in the next meeting we have with our French counterparts next week," Franklin added. "We need to get this treaty agreed to and approved before the fighting starts again in the spring in America. I worry what might happen if we don't."

"So you will have no more need of me then?" Nathaniel asked. "It was only this one delivery?"

"Not quite," Franklin replied, pursing his lips. "We may have more information coming from Beaumarchais and thus further need of your splendid services as a courier. But I have a suggestion that will obviate the necessity of these midnight kidnappings. Suppose we were to hire Benton Carlisle to paint some depictions of the American delegation—of me and Silas Deane and Arthur Lee at work. Then you and he would have a good explanation for being alone with us at the same time you are working on Beaumarchais's portrait and are alone with him. It's unlikely that anyone would suspect a painter or his assistant, especially a painter as famous as Carlisle, of being involved in espionage. At least you've used that cover to great effect in London. What do you think?"

Nathaniel pondered the proposition for a moment. "It seems reasonable to me, but I don't know whether Carlisle will want to take on more assignments now. He's getting older and he tires easily, and we've convinced him to cut back."

"Can't you explain to him the real importance of this?" Franklin asked.

"Not easily. He has no idea of my other activities. I've always kept that a secret from him, though I trust him completely. There is no need for him to know, and I certainly don't want to place him in any danger."

"I understand," said Franklin. "Well, see if you can find some way to convince him to do this without getting into ulterior motives. Perhaps you can lure him with the prospect of painting the most famous man in Paris today." Franklin sat back, placed his thumbs under his lapels in a gesture of mock pride, and smiled his best self-deprecating grin."

"Yes, that would probably work," Nathaniel said. "That or the offer of a large commission…"

Franklin looked scornfully and laughed. "Mr. Houghton," he said, "we are here to enlarge the American treasury, not to squander it on romanticized images of me. Heaven knows, there are enough of those around already." Then he laughed and signaled to the tall men that it was time to return Nathaniel to his state of captivity and transport him home.

Painting the Americans, especially Franklin, the conquering hero of Paris, was an idea that appealed to Benton Carlisle. But he doubted that he had the stamina to take on that work while still painting the large portrait of Beaumarchais. He said no. But he quickly noted Nathaniel's profound disappointment and his persistence in seeking to convince the older man to change his mind.

It wasn't the first time Benton suspected that Nathaniel's interest in painting certain subjects was more than just merely artistic. He'd been ecstatic, Benton remembered, when they'd gotten the commissions to paint Lord North and George Germain. Benton was no fool and he could, without much tax on the imagination, conjure up reasons why the son of an American politician and the brother of an American officer might have a special interest in spending time in proximity to the first minister of the British government or its secretary of state for the American colonies. Why he might also be interested in the American delegation to Paris required no great powers of deduction either. Benton never asked Nathaniel about this; in fact, they rarely talked much about politics. But he admired Nathaniel's passions and his self-possession, and he had long assumed that there was more to Nathaniel's life than his art. That he knew none of the details of that other life merely gave flight to Benton's imagination.

Benton had come to love Nathaniel almost as much as he loved Lydie. He had never had children of his own, but he could not have wished for a closer, more admiring relationship with a son than the one he enjoyed with Nathaniel Houghton. He prayed now that, whatever Nathaniel's secret life might be, it would not place him in any danger. He was certain he couldn't bear the loss of the talented and spirited and loyal young man of whom he had grown so fond.

So he reconsidered and suggested to Nathaniel that they accept Franklin's offer but that Nathaniel should do most of the painting. This wouldn't be a typical sitting portrait in any case. The delegates would be working. There would be some sketching as they worked, but most of the real painting would be done later. So Benton proposed that he would accompany Nathaniel to Franklin's house in Passy where the American delegates met, he would suggest arrangements of the figures in the portrait, and he would do a few sketches. But most of the painting would be done in the studio and Nathaniel would carry it out. Nathaniel was delighted, both with the opportunity to do most of the group portrait himself—the first time Carlisle had given him so free a hand—and, of course, with the occasions this would create for Nathaniel to carry secret messages between Beaumarchais and Franklin.

One morning Nathaniel and Benton sketched, while the three delegates tried to finalize a draft of one of their proposals at the large round pedestal table in the sun-flooded dining salon where they usually spent their mornings. To their left sat Edward Bancroft, a Massachusetts man whom Franklin had chosen first as secretary to Silas Deane when he was alone in Paris, now to the full delegation. A little after ten o'clock, the houseman appeared to announce the arrival of a visitor, a Mr. Jonathan Loring Austin of Boston. Franklin recognized the name and told the others that Austin was the secretary of the Massachusetts Board of War and had probably just arrived from America.

Austin was soon announced and entered the room. Before he could say a word, Franklin walked over to him, placed a hand on his shoulder, and asked, "What is the news of Philadelphia?"

Loring's smile vanished, replaced by a grimace. "It's not good, Dr. Franklin. Philadelphia fell without a fight. Washington did not believe it was worth his army to try to defend an indefensible city. The British now control Philadelphia."

Franklin's humor rarely failed him, but he had nothing comic nor ironic to say now. He turned away and walked to the high bay window, where he sat on the blue silk cushion. Philadelphia, he thought: my daughter and her husband, my grandchildren, my house and all of my books and papers—all of those now in the hands of the enemy. What pleasure they'll take from torturing my family, from destroying my possessions, knowing I'm here trying to gain allies against them. Deane and Lee looked on in silent sympathy for their older colleague.

Then Loring said, "But wait. I have more news. Burgoyne has been defeated in New York and his entire army surrendered to Horatio Gates."

Franklin turned sharply toward the visitor and cried "Say what? Burgoyne surrendered to an American army? The redcoats failed to cut us in two?"

Loring nodded emphatically. Franklin dashed over to him and said, "Hurry, let me see the pouch. This is great news." He mind raced ahead as he began to calculate the consequences for the negotiations with the French. Surely they would see the fall of Philadelphia as a major symbolic defeat. Franklin had feared that for some time. But the surrender of Burgoyne was news of far greater importance. There was nothing the French loved more than the word "surrender" pronounced with an English accent. That might be just the tune to carry these negotiations to a happy conclusion, Franklin thought.

Nathaniel should be sketching, he knew, as he watched this moment in history. But he was too compelled by thoughts of his own. He wondered about his father. Had he gotten out of Philadelphia before the British arrived? Had members of Congress been captured and, if so, would they be tried as traitors, as people in London said they should? And what about Jonathan? He was with Washington and probably nowhere near Saratoga and Burgoyne, but would this mean the fighting would now concentrate on Washington's army and Jonathan would be in even greater danger?

But then a powerful thought struck Nathaniel from a completely different angle. Had he played a part in Gates's victory? That night in Lord North's library. The document from Germain about the plan to cut the colonies in two and the way it would be executed. The fast packet that George had used to get it to America. Had that made the difference? Suddenly Burgoyne's surrender was more than just news from afar, more than a distant image from the lives of others. For the first time since he became involved in passing information to George, he now saw a genuine connection between his secretive meetings in London and the brutal reality of the fighting in America. The fighting, and on this occasion at least, the winning.

Franklin was right. Burgoyne's surrender did change French opinion about the American cause. There were still some fetters on French optimism about America's chance of winning the war, but Gates's triumph was evidence enough that America had a fighting chance and that French intervention might well tip the scales. By early February, the treaty negotiations had come to a successful conclusion. The American delegates were going to meet with Vergennes at the Ministry of Foreign Affairs for the signing, and Franklin wanted Carlisle and Nathaniel to come along to record this moment.

The painters met Franklin at his house in Passy from which they would all proceed in a small parade of carriages through the streets of Paris. The house was full of flowers when Carlisle and Nathaniel arrived. Where did Franklin get all these flowers in February, Nathaniel wondered? Another of his scientific wonders.

Silas Deane and Arthur Lee waited in the large reception room, smiling more than Nathaniel had seen in all the time he'd been with them. Deane was taciturn and not especially friendly. He chatted quietly with Bancroft. Lee, like his brother Richard Henry, was expressive and voluble. Nathaniel never mentioned to him that his father served in Congress with Lee's brother, but he suspected that Franklin had told him, but also asked him to make no mention of it. It was never in Nathaniel's interest to have his American connections known.

Franklin greeted the servants as he entered the reception room and the men all turned in his direction and saw a startling sight. In fashionable Paris where men and women were judged by their finery, where fashion was always the primary topic of conversation, where elegance was esteemed above all other virtues, Benjamin Franklin had been a contrarian. In public, he'd always worn a plain brown suit, ordinary shoes, and a hat of marten fur. His hair was uncurled and hung to his shoulders and everywhere he carried a rough applewood staff. This was an important part of the image the French had come to love: Franklin the exemplar of American frontier values, Franklin the simple Quaker. And Franklin, ever alert to his opportunities, had played it to the hilt.

So it was jarring to those who observed him on this momentous morning to see the "simple Quaker" appear before them in a suit of fine blue Manchester velvet. The servants, in fact, were frozen in their stares, for they had never seen Franklin in clothes like this.

After a moment or two, Arthur Lee spoke. "You have overwhelmed us this morning, Dr. Franklin. To what do we owe this bow to fashion?"

"It has nothing to do with fashion, Arthur. You may remember another moment in my life, in 1774, when I was called before a special hearing of Parliament to explain the request of the people of Massachusetts to have that blackguard, Thomas Hutchinson, removed as their governor. On that day, several members of Parliament tried to make sport of me and sought not only my humiliation but the denigration of any claims our colonies might have to influence the selection of their own governors. It was one of the most painful experiences of my life, and a moment of epiphany when I realized that all hope of a happy relationship with Parliament had passed."

Franklin's small audience stood listening closely, uncertain of the relevance of this bit of history. Then Franklin added, "On that day in Westminster, I wore this suit. I've never worn it since, waiting for an appropriate occasion. Today is that occasion. Today the course of the war will begin to change. Today the path to American independence is brightened. And today," he said with a broad smile dipped in irony, "I shall give this old suit a little revenge."

Nathaniel was so pleased that Benton had assented to postponing their return to London for an extra week. Franklin's invitation to the two of them to accompany him to Versailles was, Nathaniel thought, too appealing to resist even if it meant a significant change in travel plans. As their carriage rolled along the smooth stone road that led to the magnificent palace before them, Nathaniel studied the gardens.

It was only late March and they had not yet begun to approach their summer splendor. But even now he could tell that they were the most sumptuous gardens he'd ever seen, probably that he ever would see. They stretched off into the distance in every direction and what appeared to be scores of gardeners were at work, planting and pruning. Everything was arranged in a glorious symmetry of shapes and colors: red beside yellow, tall blooms backing low ones, blue against orange, classic rectangles and circles, fantasies of swirls and tails. A painter could spend a lifetime in this garden, Nathaniel thought, and never begin to exhaust its possibilities.

Riding through them was like a dream and he felt he'd been roughly jolted awake when the carriage came to a halt in front of the sweeping entrance to the Palace of Versailles. After the signing of the treaty of alliance between the United States of America and the Kingdom of France, the American delegates had been invited here for an audience with his majesty, Louis XVI and his Queen, Marie Antoinette. Franklin, ever alert to the values of publicity, invited Carlisle and Nathaniel as his guests. They wouldn't be able to sketch at Versailles, that would be far too gauche—a French word for which Nathaniel had acquired an affection. But they could observe the court and the American delegates there and paint it later from memory.

Franklin had said this would be a private audience, but apparently that meant only that a few French citizens would be absent. The hallways of Versailles were full of men and women, finely dressed and chatting aimlessly. As the Americans were led to the large reception room where the King and Queen awaited them, the courtiers watched intently, especially Franklin who was by now a celebrity of the first order and who on this day had returned to his standard plain garb. Women covered their faces with their fans and whispered to their companions as the Americans walked past, heels echoing loudly on the marble floors.

The small party stopped abruptly at the open door to the King's reception room. Music was coming from a harpsichord and a lute, but the music stopped abruptly and the servant announced their arrival in French. The Americans entered with Franklin smiling easily and the others looking stunned and bewildered by the opulence of this room and this palace. The ceilings were finely carved and embossed in soft blues and ambrosia. Draperies that seemed to have been spun of gold hung beside the enormous vaulted windows. The woodwork was all mahogany with matching carved filigree at the same height all around the room. The floor

383

was a mosaic of delicate tiles forming images of the fruit of the land--grapes and apples and lush pears.

Before them in the center of the room, surrounded by fawning servants and equally fawning members of the court sat the twenty-four-year old King of France and his twenty-year-old Austrian Queen. Nathaniel knew he should study the King for a true rendering when he painted him later. But he could not draw his eyes away from Marie Antoinette. She was well-proportioned with pale, delicate skin that seemed to reflect the light. A mountain of curls in silvery brown covered her small head, and she wore a lavender gown with an empire waist and dazzling full skirt embroidered in mimosa lace. She spent only a second looking at the American guests and was soon deeply in conversation with several young men in silk jackets and powdered wigs who stood respectfully beside her.

The Americans were led forward and stood before the royal couple, neither of whom rose from their seats. The young King called Franklin to him and they spoke briefly. Franklin later told Nathaniel that the King had conveyed his feelings of friendship for America, but then added that he hoped the treaty would benefit both nations. The greetings were brief and the King soon turned to other conversations while the Americans mingled awkwardly with the royal court—except Franklin who never suffered an awkward moment.

After the time he'd spent painting the son of King George at Windsor, Nathaniel thought he had seen the apex of opulence. But Windsor Castle was a dark and dreary hulk of gray stone compared to Versailles. There the sun seemed to be an enemy and the castle designed to keep it at bay. Here the sun was treated like a welcome ally. Large windows welcomed it in, and the dazzling colors used it to gorgeous avail.

During his time in France, Nathaniel had heard rumors of displeasure with the royal family and the huge draw they imposed on the national treasury to sustain their opulent lifestyle. But only now, in the midst of it, did Nathaniel understand what all the rumors had been about. The artist in him was overwhelmed by the stylish sensuality of Versailles. But the democrat in him was sickened. All these people who never did any work, whose hands had never been callused, who sniggered at the slightest fault of fashion or manners. How grossly unfair it seemed that they should occupy the top rung of society while so many people who struggled through their days, who toiled honestly, had neither wealth nor esteem as their reward.

Nathaniel was sure that this day would survive and shine in memory for the rest of his life, that he would tell his grandchildren about the day he went to the glorious Palace of Versailles and met the King of France. He wanted to preserve the memory for the entertaining stories it would yield about kings and their courts. But also for what it taught him about America and the power of an ideal that kings and their courts could never understand.

# Chapter 26

## Valley Forge, Pennsylvania
## February - March, 1778

"They've turned the damn town into one big party," Flint said, looking up from the folded page on which he'd scribbled a few notes. He loved these opportunities to command the attention of all the senior officers with the weekly reports of his espionage in Philadelphia. "A lot of the patriots has left, and the loyalists are feelin' free for the first time in years. So every night there's some big levee or ball. The redcoat officers is actin' like princes. They also tore the names off all the taverns and shops that said anythin' about independence or liberty and replaced 'em with painted signs that said Duke of Manchester or some such. If a bird dropped you there now, you'd think you was in bloody Liverpool."

Washington listened silently, remembering how much he'd admired Philadelphia during his sojourn in 1774. His glance fell on Jonathan, reminding him of the celebration that marked the end of the first Continental Congress, the memorable night when a young man named Houghton rescued him from a sea of mud. Philadelphia had always seemed so very American; it was hard to imagine it now in the hands of the King's men.

"What's most amazin'," Flint continued, "is they got plenty to eat. I looked in the window at one of their parties and they had roast pig and trays full of fish and potatoes and big loaves of bread. They probably threw out more'n a company eats here in a week. The stores was all full of dry goods and plenty of food. And wagons came into the city every day, loaded down with meat and eggs and chickens. It sure made my mouth water."

Washington grimaced hard at this remark. "Damn the Congress," he said. "We've had one of the best harvests ever. There's plenty of food about in the land, but we can't get money from Congress to buy it, and our quartermaster corps can't figure out how to get it here. So in a time of plenty, the British feast and we starve."

Washington's frustration emerged at all their staff meetings now. He'd moved his army into winter camp in December, in a place along the Schuylkill about 20 miles northwest from Philadelphia. It was a ridge above a small village with a tiny iron forge. It wasn't even marked on many of the maps, but local folks called it Valley Forge. Jonathan thought back to the first days here when most of the men were living in tents. Few of them had enough clothes to keep warm. Shoes were a rare luxury. Tired men, brave men survived the freezing days by sitting close to campfires. They endured the nights by huddling together, drawing warmth from the bodies of their comrades.

Washington ordered them to build wooden huts, knowing they couldn't survive a winter under canvas. But they had few tools and no supplies. So they took to the woods in teams, dragging back sticks and fallen logs, mixing mud to hold their fragile constructions together, covering their roofs with branches. When they were done and the fields at Valley Forge were lined with these ugly huts, the men were only slightly warmer than they'd been before. Sleeping inside on dirt, without blankets or heat, with no ventilation to clear the putrid, diseased air, men soon took sick. Coughing and wheezing was the music of the camp. Without soap to clean them or medicine to treat them, sores festered and smelled. The frost bit into unshod toes and turned them black. Dysentery and vomiting made strong men weak and thin and gaunt. The stench of sick, dirty soldiers filled the camp and overpowered the senses.

Yet Philadelphia partied and feasted. And all Washington could do was rail at the failures of Congress, the inadequacies of the quartermasters the Congress had appointed. And suffer.

Hamilton was the designated optimist at these meetings, often engaged in the arduous search for some redeeming feature of life at Valley Forge. "At least," he said, "we've held our army together. That's a miracle really in face of the hardships these men have had to endure. I'm surprised more of them haven't marched off and left us."

A silence followed Hamilton's comments until Lafayette spoke up in support. "That is so very true," he said. "It is a measure of the commitment of these men that they would stay this long under these dreadful conditions. I know of no other army where that would be the case."

387

Washington smiled wistfully at these attempts to cut through the gloom with the dull knife of good cheer. But he knew that Hamilton's comment hid as much as it revealed. It was true that some of the army remained and, Washington had to admit, that probably was miraculous. Desertions were remarkably few. But most of the soldiers whose enlistments ended had left, and there had been few arrivals to replace them. Total strength of the Continental army in Valley Forge was now down to a few thousand. If Howe knew that, Washington thought, he might be tempted to call a recess in the partying and march to Valley Forge, even through snow, to put this army out of its misery.

The meeting ended with Washington's usual pleas to his officers to organize his men to scour local farms for food or clothing. He knew this would produce little; the local farms had been plundered to the last ounce of their produce weeks earlier. He asked Jonathan to stay with him a moment after the meeting, then dismissed the officers.

When the room cleared, Washington, went to a high cabinet against the south wall and retrieved some papers. He laid them on the table and beckoned Jonathan to come around and view them. They were mostly columns of numbers, but Jonathan lacked a frame of reference and could make little sense of them. "I'm confused, General," he said. "What is this?"

"These were taken from Burgoyne's supply officer after the surrender at Saratoga. When Benedict Arnold came into camp a while ago, he brought me a number of papers that had been taken from Burgoyne's people. I've been looking at them in the evenings, but most of them are the usual paraphernalia of military commands: casualty lists, maps, copies of general orders, things like that. But this group is more interesting,  It appears to be records of purchases made by Burgoyne's quartermaster from loyalist suppliers. Then there's a set of instructions to the officers who made the purchases that tells them how to contact the principal supplier without revealing any identities. A spymaster couldn't have produced a more elaborate set of layers to mask identities.

"All one can really tell from these papers is that the supplier uses the name 'Mr. Brown' and that wagons or boats are sent to Manhattan to pick up the supplies. But they reveal one more thing that is quite surprising. This 'Mr. Brown' was supplying Burgoyne not only with food and rum, but with gunpowder and lead shot and cannonballs. The bullets that wounded you in Saratoga may well have come from an American in New York supplying the British."

388

Washington fished for another piece of paper. "Then…look at this," he said. He handed Jonathan a paper on which were listed the prices of individual units of goods.

Jonathan read down through it, then whistled beneath his breath. "This 'Mr. Brown' is making a fortune," he said. "He's charging the British three or four times what we pay for these same supplies—when we can get them at all.

"True," Washington said. "And they pay his price because he's reliable, because it's cheaper and surer than bringing the goods in on ships, and—dammit—because they've got a government that supports the army."

"How long do you suppose this 'Mr. Brown' has been in business?" Jonathan asked.

"There's no way of knowing from what we have here," Washington replied looking through the papers. "But we have to make sure he doesn't stay in business much longer." Then he looked up and smiled a rare sarcastic smile. "I'm sorry to do this to you, Jonathan, because I know how much you're enjoying this lovely winter at Valley Forge. But as soon as the roads are passable again, I want you to make your way to New York and see if you can find this Mr. Brown and deal with the problem he's been creating for us."

"Do you mean take him prisoner?"

Washington set his jaw and looked straight at his trusted aide. His face hardened. "I mean deal with the problem, Colonel."

For Jonathan, the only happy day of that long winter at Valley Forge occurred on March twenty-sixth when a courier entered his tent to announce that he had a visitor waiting to see him at the guardhouse. Jonathan pulled on his cloak and walked as quickly as one could across the muddy ground to see who it was. He beamed widely when he reached the gate and saw his father, sitting atop a handsome black mare. Henry was on his way home from York to Delaware to spend some time with Patience. Savannah had said she was getting worse and a visit from Henry might bring her some small measure of cheer. Henry was making that journey now and hadn't had to go far out of his way to pay a visit with his son on Jonathan's birthday.

Henry gave Jonathan a leather purse he'd had made in York and expressed his regrets that it was the first birthday they'd spent together since 1775. Then Jonathan took Henry on a brief tour of Valley Forge and watched the disgust grow in Henry's eyes. He lobbied his father hard to carry the message to Congress that this was the product of their neglect— a sad, wretched army on the brink of collapse. Henry promised that he would report what he saw.

Then as they rode, Henry began to fill Jonathan in on some of the gossip about Congress, especially the clandestine efforts to remove Washington from command. Such rumors and whispers were the stuff or camp conversations in every army; much of what Henry described only confirmed speculation and facts that Jonathan already knew.

Washington's problems were first revealed to Jonathan one night when he visited with Daniel Morgan who had brought his Virginia riflemen to join the southern army after Burgoyne's surrender. In passing, Morgan mentioned that Horatio Gates had invited the Virginian to join him in an effort to get Washington removed from supreme command of the army—with Gates as the obvious replacement. Morgan reported that he'd told Gates he'd leave the army if Washington were replaced and that ended their conversation. But Morgan had heard that Gates was pursuing his own case for overall command with his friends in Congress.

And Gates had friends in Congress, just as Washington had enemies. Henry told Jonathan that Sam Adams and Richard Henry Lee had grave doubts about Washington's leadership abilities. John Adams, the man primarily responsible for Washington's appointment to this command, had joined the doubters' chorus as well. And after Washington's mediocre leadership during the fall engagements at Brandywine Creek and Germantown, and the spectacular victory of Gates's army over Burgoyne, it was not surprising that the chorus had swelled to a crescendo.

Jonathan thought back over the past few months. He'd come to know Washington well in their years together and saw glimpses of Washington that were rarely revealed to others. Washington remained the one genuine American hero, almost an Olympian god, a man wrapped in myths and legends that even the General himself sometimes found amusing. But the Washington that Jonathan had come to know was far more human and fragile. He bristled at criticism and, when others found him wanting, talked openly of resigning to "the better life at Mount Vernon".

Jonathan had never seen him angrier than the morning in December when Washington had been handed an intercepted letter written by General Conway to General Gates, a long scathing critique of

Washington in which Conway wrote: "Heaven has been determined to save your Country; or a weak General and bad Councellors would have ruined it."

On through the rest of the winter, while the army suffered and starved at Valley Forge, Conway and Gates and their supporters in Congress plotted to remove Washington. Henry described the plots in more detail than Jonathan knew. It sickened the younger man.

"But it's over now," Henry said.

"Over?"

"Yes, over. Washington is secure and Gates and Conway have been repudiated. The General owes a big debt of gratitude to those two young men you serve with, Hamilton and Lafayette."

"How so?" Jonathan asked.

"Well, Lafayette showed up in York one day looking very elegant and sounding very brilliant. He told the Congress that he had every faith that his country would soon enter the war on our side, but that it would do so because it trusted George Washington and esteemed his leadership. If Washington were replaced, he told us, he doubted that France would have much heart for the fight. You can imagine what kind of an effect that had. With all the effort we've been pouring into securing this alliance, no one wanted to risk it now by changing commanders."

Jonathan nodded in recognition of the exceptional boldness he'd seen often in this young Frenchman. "What about Hamilton?" he asked. "You said he was involved as well?"

Hamilton's role was a little harder to discern, but no less important. What Lafayette accomplished by facing the Congress directly, Hamilton seemed to do behind the scenes. About the time Gates and Conway came to make their case for a change in command, we began to get letters from some of the brigadier generals complaining that Conway was a self-promoter and not nearly so effective a leader as he claimed. And then we got several letters from officers who'd been at Saratoga and said the real hero there was General Arnold, not Gates. One of them even said that Gates never got within a mile of any actual fighting at Saratoga."

"True enough," said Jonathan recollecting the fierce struggles between Gates and Arnold that he'd seen with his own eyes.

"So when Gates claimed that his great victory at Saratoga and Washington's inadequacies around Philadelphia entitled him to overall command, he faced some harsh and well-informed questioning."

"Well, so what did Hamilton have to do with this?"

"It seemed more than a mere coincidence that all these letters supporting Washington and debunking his critics should arrive when they did and should be written in such glowing terms. We began to realize that someone was masterminding all this, and one of the New York delegates knew right away that it was Hamilton. He'd seen him at work in New York and knew that he was a master of manipulation. Well, he sure is. And George Washington remains commander in chief now because of him and Lafayette.

"Isn't it odd that the leadership of our army may have been determined by two men who are not yet twenty-five years old?" Henry added.

"It is indeed, Father, but it's the kind of war where many skills matter and not all of them come with age," replied his son, who had seen nearly three years of war and who turned twenty-five on this day.


"Sacrebleu!" The thick-chested drillmaster was cursing again, this time in French. He didn't speak enough English to curse effectively in the language the soldiers knew. And most of his German expletives sounded to the men like grunting hogs. But in French he could swear a streak and, even though none of them spoke French, they got the point.

Washington had ridden out on the York Pike to meet Friedrich William Augustus, Baron Von Steuben when he'd arrived in February. Benjamin Franklin had met him in Paris, been impressed by his military knowledge, and recommended him to Washington. From the grim monotony of Valley Forge days, almost any escape was worth seizing. So Washington decided to greet the Prussian himself.

That was almost a month ago, but it seemed much longer. Von Steuben was everything Washington expected in a general who served under Frederick the Great: blunt, forceful, systematic, definite, and knowledgeable. It was this last trait that had made Von Steuben so welcome an addition to the army at Valley Forge. Rumors did arise that maybe Von Steuben's career hadn't followed quite the path that he'd described. Some said that he'd been a mere captain under Frederick the Great, not a general. And to those who understood such matters, his claim to be a baron seemed a little shaky as well. But Washington cared little about such quibbles. False claims of past glory were commonplace in his army. What mattered was that Von Steuben knew how to train troops. And in the month he'd been at Valley Forge, he'd begun to turn

392

Washington's courageous but disorganized and unskilled soldiers into a coherent fighting force for the first time.

But not without copious cursing. What Von Steuben found at Valley Forge was the worst conditioned army he'd ever seen. Tall, gaunt men in tatters. Most with no shoes even though they trod on snow. Sickness was everywhere and the stench was sickening. But those were not Von Steuben's problems, not directly. What he also found was an army of soldiers who had little understanding of close-order drill or standard firing formations or how to coordinate units in battle. It was amazing to him, as he surveyed the Continental Army, that it hadn't been driven from the field years ago. He told Washington that this was a credit to the courage of his men and their commitment to the cause for which they fought.

But he also told Washington that their efforts would be suicidal if they didn't learn the proper military techniques for carrying out that fight. So day after day, Von Steuben had the officers march their men to the training ground where he drilled and drilled and drilled. He showed them how to march, how to pivot, how to rotate shooting men and reloading men in small units, how to move companies and battalions around the field of fire to keep pressure on an enemy. Some of the men who'd been with Washington since New York began to recognize the tactics that Von Steuben was teaching them as the very ones that had rolled up their flank at Brooklyn Heights or scaled the cliff at Fort Washington. They'd watched in wonder, in those days, as the British routed them by simply knowing what they were doing. Now, with Von Steuben drilling and cursing at them, they too were coming to know what they were doing.

Washington stood with the Prussian one morning as the men marched in review, demonstrating their execution of some of the quick movement drills Von Steuben had taught them. Washington clucked in delight as he watched. "They're the worst looking soldiers I've ever seen, Baron," he said, remarking on their shabby uniforms and bare feet. "But they look more like an army than any I've ever led."

Von Steuben listened to the translator, then responded. The translator turned to Washington and reported, "The Baron says 'Now you will have to find a fight worthy of your army's skills.'"

# Chapter 27

## *Still River, Delaware*
## *April 1778*

"I haven't been in this part of the county for nearly three years, Henry. I've kind of forgotten how pretty it is down here."

"This time of year, it's pretty everywhere, James. But I'm still partial to Delaware in planting season. It's hard to imagine a more splendid place on earth.

James Wolversham, the only medical doctor in Kent County had been at the farm for nearly an hour. Patience had resisted his coming, but Henry insisted that she had to be seen. Henry had crossed paths with Wolversham a few times when he'd been to Dover on government business, but no one in his family had ever been treated by the doctor. Or by any doctor, for that matter. Wolversham's visit on this April morning was the first time a doctor had ever been to the Houghton farm.

In the small bedroom at the back of the house, Patience lay in the canopied bed she hadn't left for weeks. The curtain was drawn tight over the sole window, Patience having said her eyes could no longer tolerate sunlight. A single candle provided only faint light in the small space and Dr. Wolversham sat close to her, trying to make an assessment of her skin color and the condition of her eyes. "Let's try some of this," he said, pulling a small jar of pale green powder from his medicine box. He measured out about an ounce with a sterling spoon, then mixed it with water in a small tea cup. He held it to Patience's lips, but she refused to drink. "If we're to make you well," he said to his reluctant patient, "you'll need to be more cooperative, Mrs. Houghton."

Patience said nothing and looked blankly at the unadorned wall over Wolversham's head. Henry walked around to her side, lifted her hand into his own and softly stroked her wrist. "Patience dear," he said, "you must try this. We can't simply let you slide away from us."

Wolversham again held the cup to her lips. Again Patience sat motionless. After a moment with no success, the doctor put the cup on the small table beside the bed and signaled with his eyes that he needed to talk privately with Henry. The two men crossed the hallway into the kitchen where Sweetie was making preparations for the mid-day meal. She cast a look of concern in their direction but then went about her work.

"This isn't going to work, Henry," the doctor said. "She won't, or can't, take any of the powders I try to give her. I think our only hope now is to draw off some of her blood. It'll give her some relief from the vapors that seem to be afflicting her."

"What do you think ails her, James?" Henry asked, peering closely at the doctor's face.

"I think her blood has just worn down, probably from sadness. I've seen a lot of that since the war started. People seem to just give out. Then they go off in a kind of trance like the missus, or a madness begins to come over them. Had a woman about her age in Dover. She had two boys in the militia. One died from the ague in Morristown a winter ago, the other had a leg amputated after a bayonet went through it at Paoli. Seemed like she just couldn't bear the bad news. Stopped eating and wasted away. Then she started having visions in the night. She'd wake up screaming or she'd be up walking around. Her husband found her outside one night, cold night too, in just her dressing gown and a quill pen. She was sticking the pen in her arm over and over. She'd just gone mad."

"How did you treat her?"

"Let her blood a couple times. That seemed to give her some relief. At least she wasn't up screaming in the night. Gave her some aconite to relax her. But then one night her husband heard a terrible noise from the parlor, came running out and found her standing in front of the fire with her gown all aflame. By the time he got the fire out, she was all burnt over. She died a few hours later in an awful agony. We don't know whether she set herself on fire or just stood too close to the hearth and got her gown in the coals."

"If we let her blood, will you do it now?" Henry asked.

"Yes, I'll do it right now while I'm here. If she needs it done again later, I'll come back in a few weeks."

Henry pondered for a few minutes. He knew that bloodletting was often the last resort of doctors, when medicine didn't seem to work or when a disease was hard to diagnose. Henry had heard some discussion of the merits of bloodletting in the taverns of Philadelphia. Most doctors swore by it, but he remembered John Adams once saying that it was "sorcery." Of course, Adams thought most things he disliked were sorcery.

"All right," Henry said finally. "I think we should try it. The emetic didn't work and she has a full and tense pulse. We have to do something."

Wolversham nodded, and the two men returned to the room where Patience lay silently under a thick coverlet. Wolversham rubbed her arm with white poplar gum. Then he reached into his case and removed the device he use to sanctify blood, a small spring-loaded tool of several lancets that made a series of incisions on the arm. Soon blood was flowing down Patience's arm to a jar that Wolversham had placed beneath it on the floor. The doctor seemed satisfied as he watched his therapy operate. "This should do it, Henry," he said. "Ultimately everything comes down to erratic motion in the blood. This should boil it out."

Savannah had spent the morning on horseback, riding the fences of the lower fields. Quiet Jack and the hired men had done a good job of mending the breaks, she thought, and there should be no problem with any of the horses getting out this year as they had that awful morning last July when six of their best horses disappeared into the woods. Only two had been recovered and of those that were lost, two were important brood mares.

Savannah had decided that concentrating more on raising horses was good business after studying the matter two winters ago and asking a lot of questions of some of her neighbors. Horses were reliable breeders, there was always a demand for them, and profits from selling them were not as susceptible to the whims of the weather as crops were. And, of course, with the success of the timber business, more and more of the Houghton land was being converted to good pasture every year. Some time in the distant future, there would be no more virgin timber to harvest, and the farm would need other sources of income. Breeding horses seemed a prudent step in diversifying what the farm produced.

But there was no profit in runaway horses, and now Savannah rode the fences herself every few weeks to make sure there was no repeat of last summer's setback. She was happy to be out here this morning, in any case, because Father and the doctor were treating Mother and she wanted to leave that with them. She and Mother were together so much of the time, and Mother had become such a dark cloud over everything that it was a great relief to Savannah that Father was now home for a while and had lifted the burden from her. She hoped they could find some medicine that would make Mother more comfortable, give her some respite from her pain.

But she was not optimistic. She'd never been treated by a doctor, nor had any of her brothers or sisters—except Jonathan after he was wounded at Saratoga, but that was just an army doctor. No one she knew had ever had any luck with doctors. They had their powders and salves, and when those failed, they tried to draw out the bad blood. But people seemed to get healthy or stay sick, to live or die, in spite of what doctors did—or so she'd heard. Perhaps it would relieve some of Father's worries, she thought, to have Mother treated. But Savannah had come to believe that it was her mother's mind that was in the grip of a mysterious illness and the affliction had spread to her body, not the other way around. She felt so sorry for Mother, but some days she was also just very angry at her for not simply using the force of her own will to overcome her sadness. She was the mother, after all; it didn't seem fair that Savannah had to care for her.

Savannah came to the place where the fence dropped to the river, then turned east and headed back up the hill. She halted her brown stallion there and dismounted. Then she led the horse to the water's edge and let it drink while she sat on a stump in the sun with the fresh spring flow of the river at her feet. Most of the year Still River was a good name for this gentle, quiet water. But for a few weeks every spring, the river came to life. The rain filled it to the top of its banks and accelerated its rush to the sea. And the shad made their annual trek to spawn and filled it with a silvery flow from the other direction that twisted and boiled as thousands of the small fish were driven by a destiny they couldn't begin to comprehend. The cycles of the seasons, she thought. How she adored the way their rhythms accompanied her life.

But more and more these days Savannah reflected on her life. It filled her, not with dread because she felt this was a life she had chosen, but with the gnawing discomfort of uncertainty. She found it hard to look ahead and see a clear picture of her future. She'd always been comfortable merely living in the present, but more often now she found herself trying to envision her future and seeing only a shapeless haze.

Perhaps it was her age. She'd turned twenty-seven in February. Nearly everyone she knew of that age, at least among the women, was married. The plan of their lives had been divined and now they merely had to follow it. Husband, farm, children, grandchildren, death. She knew a few spinsters, but not many. Most of them stayed with their parents or went to live with a brother or sister. Women didn't live alone, except a few widows.

Where did she fit into this? Things had crystallized once when she thought she would marry Marinus. There wouldn't be any question about what kind of life the wife of Marinus Marshall would lead. But that life, or the prospect of it, began to feel like a giant vise, squeezing the energy from her. So she'd made the hard choice not to follow that path. But now what? Was there nothing between playing second fiddle to a husband or being a spinster? She could think of nothing. At least she knew no other models.

She remembered a conversation with Nathaniel once, after he came home from the College and she was still a girl. They were talking about his future and he said that he wanted to find a passion in life. Passion. That was a strange and frightening word, she'd thought at the time. She wasn't even sure she knew what passion was. Was it the kind of love that seemed to pass between Father and Mother—affectionate, respectful, like partners in an enterprise? Was it what some of her friends had said they sometimes felt when they were dancing with handsome men at a ball—physical excitement? Or was it something else, something she'd never experienced and which eluded description?

When Nathaniel had talked about painting and how it stirred such strong feelings in him when he caught the perfect reflection of a drop of dew on a sunflower or the pink that raged through the sky at dusk, his words were so beautiful. If that was passion, she'd certainly never felt anything like that with Marinus. She always liked him and enjoyed his company. He was engaging in many ways. But she could always find words to describe those feelings.

There was that one evening, that strange and wonderful night on the porch of the tavern in New Jersey when she returned from the visit to Celia. Ezekial Isaac the man had called himself--the funny, handsome man with the wild brown hair, the powerful arms, and the heavy disinclination to take anything seriously. It was probably a name he'd made up. But the hours she'd spent talking with him, flirting with him, had passed so quickly. It was like a thousand fine moments had been

398

compressed into an instant and so much energy confined in so small a space was sure, at any moment, to explode. The anticipation of that explosion, the tingling propinquity of it, might well have been the strongest sensation Savannah had ever experienced. Was that passion?

She didn't know.

It had been five days since Dr. Wolversham's visit, and Patience's condition only worsened. She was in contact with her surroundings for only a few moments each day and even that was more a silent cognition, a fleeting focusing of her eyes or set of her jaw. She said nothing any more, even the small low groans had stopped. Henry sat for hours by her side, held her hand, spoke to his unresponsive wife with great tenderness of the days when she'd first come to the farm, of the long night when she'd suffered through Nathaniel's birth, of the Christmases when all the children were happy little English lads and lasses. He searched—in vain—for some recollection, some touching moment that would ignite a memory, a familiar feeling, a recollection of some good time.

After a few days of this, Henry began to realize that he was engaged in a deathwatch, that his wife would never be herself again, that perhaps she would never again experience a moment of pleasure or pain, that her consciousness was gone now and only the frail shell of her body remained. Sometimes, when they were alone in the dark room, his eyes misted and his lip quivered. Memory comes in waves, some small and light, others large and breaking overhead. The large ones got to him. The way she made his heart dance when they were young and she was beautiful and he was full of manly dreams. The rich moments they shared when a child was born or walked her first step and rode alone off into the woods. The moment of extraordinary sadness when Nathaniel left for London and she saw her first-born child for the last time. That was nearly six years ago now, and Patience had never been the same. Her long slow cascade into darkness had begun on that day. And Henry knew it had gone too far. Nothing could stop it now.

Sometimes during this lonely vigil, Henry's mind wandered away from the melancholy scene in front of him. He thought of Celia trapped in occupied New York with a young child, a husband absorbed in his business, and few friends and no family to give her comfort. And British soldiers all around planning ways to kill her soldier brother or hang her traitorous politician father. He thought back on his recent visit to Jonathan at Valley Forge. He never failed to fill with pride when he saw his son in uniform, observed the confident way he dealt with other officers or described the military situation of the army.

Valley Forge was a dreadful sight, enough to make him think that this sad small army was on a suicide mission. But Jonathan didn't think that, and he wouldn't either if his son did not. But where would their funds come from? Where would they get more troops? Would the French or the Spanish ever really offer much hope? The war had gone on so long and still seemed no closer to conclusion than it had in 1775.

He looked down on Patience and thought about the special affection she'd always borne for Nathaniel. Because he was first. Because they shared a kindred spirit. If only Nathaniel could be here now, he thought, that might be the one thing that would revive her. But there was no hope of that. Nathaniel was an ocean away. He'd made a life for himself there, and he might never come home again. Patience probably knew that in some undeniable way, and that might be the core of her affliction now. It was not Nathaniel's fault, and Henry did not blame him, but he couldn't help wondering how life might have been different. He tried to stop thinking about things that might have been, but it was hard to stop, hard to accept the course their life had taken as he sat in silent vigil watching the life drain out of the beautiful Wheelock girl with the sweet brown curls.

"Today, our beloved Patience joins the generations of Houghtons who inhabit this ground for eternity…." Savannah only half listened to Reverend Marlow reading the words that Henry had written about his wife. Her mind filled with so many thoughts, she couldn't concentrate on the details of the ceremony. "God now welcomes this wonderful wife, this splendid mother…"

Henry's grandfather had cleared this spot on the east ridge of the big hill when his own father was dying. He wanted him to be able to see the sunrise every morning, or so family legend had it. Since then, the plot had grown as other Houghtons had come to their final resting place here. Savannah and her brothers used to come up here sometimes and count the stones, more than 60 of them now, of their ancestors. Sometimes they'd make up stories about Wild Uncle Allen or Mean Aunt Esther. But mostly they just walked around in respectful silence, reading the names and the dates of birth and death, trying to connect children to parents and plot the family line in their minds.

Patience was the first of her generation to come to rest here. Savannah imagined a time when Henry would be laid beside her, then a few years later Nathaniel and Celia and Jonathan and herself. And how many more after us, she wondered. Would Godfrey Houghton Carter end his days here? What about her brothers' children and hers? Would they be Houghtons, too, the sort of Houghtons who'd be buried in the family plot on the east ridge watching the sunrise?

She looked up at Henry. Poor Father, she thought. He has seen this coming for months now, but no preparation could stopper his grief. Nor the guilt he feels for his frequent absences over these past years. Savannah knew that every time he left Still River to go to Congress, a silent force was pulling him back, urging him to turn around and stay home. Yet his sense of duty always won out, not his duty to his wife or his land, but his duty to the broader land, to the people of Kent County and the people of Delaware who depended on him not to manage a farm, not to lead a family, but to act wisely and honestly in their behalf.

Savannah had never questioned her father's choices as her mother had. Patience sometimes hinted that she thought Henry was being selfish, putting politics before family and farm. When the first Continental Congress went on longer than anyone anticipated, when Henry and Jonathan were away all summer and through the harvest, she hoped he would see the folly of his preoccupation with politics and realize he couldn't afford the burden it imposed on his family. Then each time he left after that, Patience took it as a personal affront, almost as if he were off to see some sultry mistress he found more attractive than her.

But Savannah thought otherwise. Father had opportunities, and he should take them. And the rest of her family should be proud that he did. The farm would go on. The family would endure. No one of them was responsible alone for all the bothers, whatever Mother thought. She had seen the agony of choice that her father confronted. But she couldn't imagine anything more rewarding, more exciting than being at the center of momentous events, than the feeling of power that had come from throwing off a king or standing up to a Parliament or holding to one's principles in the face of an invading army or marauding navy. Few men in his time—and he knew most of them—would have a legacy like this. Most would live good and quiet lives, working the land, building barrels, poling a ferry across a shallow river, driving a coach. Their lives would be worthy, but they would escape the notice of history.

Her Father's life had been blessed with different opportunities and greater good fortune and it would pass much more slowly from memory than most lives. Mother may have resented that, but Savannah didn't. It was precisely the kind of life she would wish for herself, if only she were a man and it were possible to have such dreams.

"She leaves us now, but the memory of her life and her love will remain with us always...." Slowly they lowered the pine coffin into the hole freshly dug in the black dirt. "Ashes to ashes. Dust to dust...."

They stood silently for a few minutes, then the friends—the men and women Henry had known for a lifetime—slowly walked by, touching his arm, saying a few words of condolence, sharing a fond remembrance of his wife, wishing him well. Soon only Houghtons remained on the hill and they walked slowly together back to the house, leaving Henry and Savannah alone at the graveside for a final few moments.

"Your life will be different now, Father," Savannah said.

Henry listened, but did not respond, not right away. Then he said, "It's your life that will be different, Savannah. You won't have Mother to care for now. You can think about yourself in a way you haven't since Mother became sick. It's time for you to be free of the farm, Savannah, to put your own life first. I'll resign from Congress now and come back to manage the farm. I should have done that long ago, I realize now. But you won't be trapped here any longer. You've carried this burden longer than you should have already"

Father just doesn't understand, Savannah thought. "You always seem to think that I'm trapped here, Father. That my life won't begin until I share it with someone else, until I leave here. You're just wrong about that. This is my life. I love it here. Even through these hard days, with Mother so miserable, I awoke every morning anxious for the day to begin, ready to think about the chores that needed doing, about a delivery or a new foal or whether one of the crops was ready to harvest. Every day is different and the challenges never cease. This is my life, Father. It's well under way. All that will change now is that I'll have more time to do what I enjoy because Mother has found her escape from the terrible darkness that fell over her.

"Death is not always sad, you know, even if the occasion of death is a sad time. I can't think of anything sadder than Mother's life this past year. We tried our best to make her happy, to make her comfortable. But it was beyond us. Death can't be worse than what she's endured. What we've endured."

402

She turned and faced the rows of stones on the ridge. "Look at all these Houghtons," she said, slowly moving her extended arm from left to right. "Every one of them was laid to rest here on a sad day like this. The others said their good-byes, remembered their good times together, then went on with their lives. So must we. My life is here. Your life now is with Congress. I'll manage this farm just fine. You have the much harder job of winning this war and making this new government work. I have faith in you, Father. Now you must have the same faith in me."

Henry looked one last time toward the mound of freshly-turned dirt under which his wife was now at rest. Then he turned and looked at his strong and beautiful daughter, in black dress and bonnet, their farm house and barns and fields behind her in the distance, the blue Still River beyond that, and York and Philadelphia and Valley Forge and New York and Boston off even further beyond the horizon, and he said simply "You're right."

# Chapter 28

## New York
## April 1778

"What'd you say it cost to book passage on this here hay wagon, Colonel?"

Jonathan chuckled quietly in the darkness at Flint's periodic insults. They were wrapped in blankets and buried in a wagonload of hay on its way to New York City from a farm in White Plains. This had become Jonathan's standard mode of transportation into the city, another small sacrifice of comfort to safety. "You should give thanks," he replied. "The last time I came this way, it was in a potato wagon. Took me a week to get the dirt out of my hair."

"Well, Colonel Haystack, you sure do know how to travel in style."

A few minutes later, the driver warned that they were approaching the guard house at the entrance to British-occupied New York, and the talking stopped. The guards usually let produce wagons go through without a search on the theory that no self-respecting solider or spy would hide in a load of potatoes or hay. So it was this time, and at the designated spot beyond the Powderhouse on Nassau Street, Jonathan and Flint climbed out of the hay and jumped from the back of the wagon. They oriented themselves quickly, then turned down Beekman Street and walked casually to the Carter house. Arriving in daylight, Jonathan had learned on his last trip, aroused much less suspicion than if two civilians had been spotted on the streets at night after the curfew.

It was eight-thirty in the morning when they knocked on the door, expecting Celia to answer. Instead they were greeted formally by a tall, well-groomed Negro who inquired of their identities and their business. He asked them to wait, then returned a few minutes later and invited them into the front parlor. There they found Godfrey Carter poring over some documents.

"Good morning, Jonathan," he said, trying to mask his surprise at this unanticipated visit from his brother-in-law. Then he looked toward Flint, awaiting an introduction.

"Godfrey," Jonathan said, "a pleasure to see you, as always. I apologize for arriving like this, but you know how difficult it is to get messages through now. We were passing this way, and I wanted to see my sister and my nephew." Then he quickly added, "And you, too, of course. This is my friend, Mr. Flint."

Carter and Flint exchanged the sort of glances that pass between men who are measuring each other up, then they shook hands without warmth. "Well, it's always a pleasure to have family here, Jonathan," Carter said. "We see so little of people now.

"How are you? I heard you were wounded at Saratoga?"

At this point, Celia entered the room and, after a moment of shock, gave her brother a warm hug and extended a genuine welcome to Flint.

"I was just asking Jonathan about his wounds at Saratoga, dear," Godfrey said to Celia.

"Nothing serious," Jonathan answered. "A musket ball in the thigh and another in the hand, but both missed the bone. They healed quickly."

"That was a grand victory for our young country," Carter said, smiling broadly. A little too broadly, Flint thought as he watched this exchange from the side. "The kind of courage all of you showed at Saratoga is exactly what it'll take to convince these redcoats they can never win this war. We've got a great cause to fight for, and our army seems ready to take whatever measures it must to win. I tell you, Jonathan, people here are awfully anxious to have you drive our captors out. We've had our fill of military occupation. So we're all cheering you on."

Jonathan didn't think he'd ever had a political conversation with Godfrey, even during the months he lived in this house when the Continentals occupied the city. So he was surprised to be having one now, and especially surprised at the enthusiasm Carter expressed for an American victory. "Thank you, Godfrey. If enough of our people share sentiments like those, the British will never be able keep a foothold in America, not even in New York. Soldiers alone won't win this war."

"So I understand," Carter replied. "I'm sorry I can't stay and talk longer, but I must be off to work. A busy day ahead." He nodded briefly to Flint, gave Celia a small kiss on the cheek, shook Jonathan's hand again, and was off.

"Celia, how are you?" Jonathan asked as the three of them sat down by the morning fire.

Celia paused for minute, wanting to be sure Godfrey had left the house. "It's very hard here," she said, after she heard his carriage pull away. "This is a British town now and all the social life revolves around the soldiers. And they've brought in tarts by the boatload from Liverpool to comfort the troops. That's what they say, Jonathan, 'comfort the troops.' There are thousands of them here. It's dreadful. Every house on Cortlandt street, is a whore house now. And to think I used to go to some of those houses to play whist in the afternoons."

Jonathan was stunned at his sister's language, surprised that she knew about such things, startled that she would mention them, even to her own brother. The delicate, almost prissy Celia he'd grown up with seemed to be growing coarser as the war abraded her innocence.

"They treat us like their captives, Jonathan. We have no say in anything, and everyone is afraid that some random comment in a conversation may be used against us if it's reported to the soldiers. Many of the good people have left. And you can't count on finding things at the markets any more either. It's very bleak."

"Do you have troops quartered here now?" Jonathan asked.

"No. We've been lucky about that," Celia answered. "For some reason, we've never had to quarter troops. My friends are very envious of that."

"I notice you have a houseman now. How long has he been here?"

"Arthur? Oh we've had him for 3 months. His wife, Sarah, does our cooking now, too. They worked for a patriot family that left the city and Godfrey hired them."

"So things aren't that bad here, then, are they Celia?" Jonathan asked, rising from his chair and slowly walking toward the window facing the street.

"Not as bad as for some of our friends. Godfrey's business has survived in spite of the occupation. That's more than many of our friends can say."

Jonathan stood by the French walnut cabinet, admiring as he always did its marquetry of birds and flowers. He looked over the

406

beautiful pieces displayed there: jeweled snuff boxes and cut glass inkwells and small silver cups. He picked up a handsome letter opener with a bright pearl handle and soft leather case. "How does Godfrey continue to thrive in the midst of all this?" he asked.

Celia looked out the window and paused before answering. "I don't know how he does it, Jonathan. He just has a very good head for business, I guess. You know he doesn't like to talk about business when he's home."

Jonathan turned over the letter opener in his hand and noticed that hand-painted on the bottom were the words "Farrow and James, London 1777." He wondered for a moment how Godfrey had come into possession of this handsome piece from London. "Ah yes, well he is a very clever business man. We've always known that. What a handsome piece this is," Jonathan said holding up the letter opener. "I don't think I've ever seen anything this lovely."

"Oh yes," Celia said showing little interest. "Godfrey brings things like that home all the time. Says his business acquaintances give them to him."

Jonathan moved back toward his sister and touched her shoulder. "Celia, Mr. Flint and I have to go out for a while. We'll return later. We'll have to leave tonight to get on with our journey, but I hope we can spend some time with little Godfrey before we do. I want to show my nephew off to my friend here."

"Oh, Jonathan it makes me so happy when you're here. I wish you could stay longer."

"So do I, Celia, but I'm afraid that won't be possible this time. There's a war on, as you may have heard, and Mr. Flint and I have been invited to attend."

Flint looked around as his eyes adjusted to the dim light. He saw two men sitting at a small round table on the side of the room and decided they were what he was looking for. He bought a mug of ale and approached them, "Mind if I join you gents, fer a minute. I'd like to ask yer advice on somethin'."

The older man, about forty, with scruffy black beard and the patched clothes of a laborer, looked at Flint suspiciously and said, "'Bout what?"

"'Bout findin' work around here," Flint said. "Lost my job when my boss left where I was workin' on the other side of the island.

407

Wonderin' if there's any work over here. Hear tell this man Carter might have work."

"He sure keeps busy," the other man answered. He leaned back in his chair and fingered his leather vest. "There's always ships comin' in and goin' out carrying goods to and from that big brick warehouse."

"So he might be hirin'?" Flint asked.

"Don't know, fer sure, but he's as good a bet as any," the older man said.

"What's he buy and sell ta keep a business like that goin' in the middle of a war?" Flint asked as casually as he knew how.

The two men looked at each other, then smiled knowingly. The older one replied. "Only one thing's worth anything in a war and that's what soldiers need—boots, blankets, salt beef, canteens, you name it."

Flint listened, feigning only slight interest. "Really. I guess I hadn't given it much thought. So he sells boots and blankets?"

The younger man took a long drink from his mug, then looked over the top of it at Flint with a foamy smile and said, "That and the heavy stuff."

Flint took a slow drink of his own, wiped his mouth, and said "Heavy stuff?"

"Yep," the younger man replied. "There's stuff comes outta that warehouse what would break a strong man's back. Lead and gunpowder and cannons. Had a man kilt here a coupla weeks back when the hawser parted liftin' one of them cannons and dropped it on the poor devil's back. Made quite an impression on him, if you know what I mean." The two men laughed heartily at a joke they'd told many times.

Flint let their laughter expire, then smiled, trying to be ingratiating. "Ouch," he said. "That musta been a sight. D'you ever wonder where this gent gets cannons and gunpowder in the middle of a war?"

The two men looked at each other, appearing not to have thought much about this. The younger one finally said, "Don't know. Think he's got some people making cannons right here on the island. Got a brassworks up the East River, I heard. Also got a shop somewhere whey they cut lead into musket balls. Lead comes in on ships, but they ain't British ships. Must be smugglers from somewhere that the British let through the blockade. It's all kinda secret. I'll tell you, though, when them ships come in fulla lead, a lot of men on the docks think that's a good day to get sick. Ain't nobody likes haulin' that stuff."

408

Flint brightened. "So there might be work unloadin' the lead ships?" he asked.

"Yep. For fools," the younger man replied.


Jonathan watched closely for nearly an hour from an alley across the street, trying to get a sense of the routines at the wagon entrance to the large warehouse. A wagon would arrive. The driver would set the brake, then step down and go over to a small window by the door. He'd signal somehow, then the two heavy wooden doors pulled back from inside and the wagon would enter. A man on the inside walked alongside the wagon, directing it to one of the bays on the south side of the huge area. The doors stayed open each time for three or four minutes until the man on the inside came back and closed them.

After watching a half dozen wagons arrive and timing each of them, Jonathan was sure the routine was unvarying. When the next wagon approached, a steep sided cart pulled by a team of four, Jonathan waited until the doors had opened and the wagon had been led inside. Then he dashed from the alley across the street, through the large doors and to the left where he hoped he could find some cover. He looked quickly around and saw a pile of old boards, probably discarded packing, and crouched behind them. From there, he surveyed the interior of this floor of the warehouse and saw few people: those unloading wagons on the other side of the large floor and the one man who tended the door.

He noticed two stairways leading from the first floor, one up and one down. Men occasionally came down the stairs from the second floor. They'd confer with the keeper of the door, then scurry back up the stairs. But he saw no one using the stair case that led down below ground, so when the next wagon came and commanded the attention of the door keeper, Jonathan crouched low and slid along the wall to the down staircase. He looked down and saw no one, spun around and quickly descended.

It was dark down there and quiet. The only light entered through two ventilation shafts to the outdoors. But it was enough to allow him to study the contents of the large space where no one seemed to be working this afternoon. It was a sight that only a military man could fully appreciate. Scores of large barrels of gunpowder. Rows of new brass cannons, mostly twelve and sixteen pounders. Dozens of stumpy mortars, also brand new. Cartridge boxes piled to the ceiling. And in one corner, hundreds of "Brown Bess's," the best rifles on the American continent in 1778.

There was a certain familiar look to what Jonathan saw, then he remembered that the powder barrels and cartridge boxes were exactly the same as most of those they'd discovered in Burgoyne's magazines after his surrender at Saratoga. The men had wondered how all that ammunition had been transported down from Canada. Now Jonathan realized their spies in London had been right. Most of it hadn't come from Canada at all, but upriver from Manhattan, and probably from this warehouse. Who was it, the spies had said was the supplier? The name had slipped Jonathan's mind, but now it came to him, "Mr. Brown." Who is Brown, Jonathan wondered? Maybe Godfrey has a silent partner. Maybe Brown is the one in the war business and Godfrey trades in other things. Maybe. Or maybe not.

Jonathan spent the next two hours sneaking through the warehouse. It was a large and busy place, and no great problem to evade notice. At five-thirty, the appointed time, Jonathan and Flint met on the end of the Wet Dock. They sat facing across the East River toward Brooklyn and compared notes. "Talked to a dozen men in the taverns and on the piers. Story's the same from all of them," Flint reported. "Carter's warehouse is always busy. Handles nothin' but war supplies, ever'thin' from stockin's to cannon. British officers in and outta there all the time. But none of the men he hires ever deal with Carter, always with a man named Drouin."

"Well that fits everything I saw," Jonathan said, describing the contents of warehouse. "There seems to be a lot of activity and a lot of turnover, so there's no question that the supplies coming out of here are a major source for the garrison in New York and probably for Cornwallis in Philadelphia."

Jonathan fell silent for a moment, trying to comprehend the full meaning of what he'd observed. "What now, Colonel?" asked Flint, flashing the grin that he saved for their most difficult moments together.

"Damn," Jonathan said. "It had to be my own brother-in-law."

"Listen," Flint proposed. "I know what a problem this is. Why don't you lemme' take care of it. You go back t'your sister and I'll deal with this. We can meet up later."

Jonathan chewed for a second on Flint's proposal. He was surprised at his own lack of ambivalence. They were talking about the assassination of his sister's husband, the father of his nephew. Yet he felt

410

no remorse, and not even much pity for Celia. His thoughts were dominated by the hatred he felt for Godfrey Carter: profiteer, liar, hypocrite, murderer of American soldiers. At this moment, Godfrey's marriage to his sister seemed only a cruel coincidence, not an impediment to what had to be done.

"Sorry," he said to Flint, "I've got to do this. And I want to do it alone because it won't be pretty. I also need you to tell Celia a story that explains my delay in getting back to her house. I'd told her that I wanted to see my nephew. You head back toward Beekman Street. Tell Celia that I was delayed on some business in Brooklyn and had to wait for darkness to get a boat across the river. That way she won't think I'm anywhere near the warehouse. You can hide in Celia's carriage house. I'll meet you there after I've done what has to be done here and said good-bye to her."

Flint started to protest, but Jonathan raised a hand and waved him off. "Don't you see what's happened here? This bloody bastard has been using his marriage to my sister as a shield. No one would suspect the brother-in-law of a Continental officer and the son-in-law of a member of Congress of colluding with the enemy. But he's been supplying them with the very bullets they've been using against us. The musket ball that went through my thigh at Saratoga probably came from this warehouse. Think about it."

Flint already had, and he was more than ready to take appropriate action. But he also understood the personal betrayal that Jonathan felt. "But what about your sister?" Flint asked.

Jonathan looked down and said nothing for a minute or two. "What alternative do we have?" he said rhetorically. "We not only have to deal with Godfrey. We have to make a lesson of him, a spectacle. If we just threaten him or even try to kidnap him, that won't mean anything to other loyalists here. They'll be competing tomorrow for this business. We have to make it clear that he who trades with the enemy is the enemy and will get the worst punishment we can mete out.

"Poor Celia. I know she'll be devastated. But, in the long run, she'll be better off without that bastard for a husband and my nephew will be better off without him for a father."

"This sounds like God talking," Flint said, his face mirroring the complex emotions that he knew Jonathan was trying to sort out.

"No, Captain," Jonathan said resolutely. "It's a soldier talking. That's all."

Jonathan returned to the warehouse and entered as he had earlier in the day. Then he sat back behind the pile of discarded boards and stayed still there until the last rays of sun disappeared a little after seven o'clock. In the darkness, he slowly climbed first one flight of stairs, then another to the top floor of the warehouse where Godfrey's office was located on the south corner, overlooking the harbor. The warehouse activity had stopped and everyone was gone except Godfrey and a dark-haired man whom Jonathan assumed to be Drouin.

Jonathan watched them for a few minutes from the stairwell. Then he heard Carter call Drouin into his office and instruct him to go down to the first floor and get the accounts for the wagons that had arrived and unloaded that day. Jonathan quickly slid down the stairs, then spun around and slid down another flight to the first floor. He hid behind some barrels of pine tar that were stacked near the stairway. Drouin walked slowly down the stairs behind him and, on the first floor, sauntered off toward the main door seemingly lost in thought. When he passed the barrels where Jonathan hid, Jonathan reached out, grabbed Drouin's chin and yanked him sharply backward to the floor where his head hit with a heavy thud on the wood. Jonathan quickly covered Drouin's mouth with his pulled-up coat, then drew the letter opener he'd taken earlier from Godfrey's house along the line of his throat just below his bulging Adam's apple. Blood gushed up in a torrent, quickly soaking the waistcoat and shirt of the dead Irishman.

Jonathan dragged the body behind the barrels and went back into hiding there. After a few minutes he heard Godfrey shout from the top of the stairs, "God damn it, Drouin, will you hurry man. I have to get off to the rope walk before the cockfights begin."

After a minute of silence, he shouted again. "Drouin, where in God's name have you gone?"

Jonathan held his handkerchief over his mouth and moaned as loudly as he could. "Help. Help me please."

"What?" Godfrey yelled. "What did you say?"

Jonathan said nothing, and a moment later heard Godfrey bounding down the stairs. When he landed on the first floor, he began to look around and saw Drouin's foot sticking out from behind the barrels of pine tar. Thinking Drouin had fallen, Godfrey hurried over to him.

He saw the terrible pool of blood at about the same time the piece of rope slipped over his head and tightened sharply around his throat. He tried to reach back and grab his assailant but his hands grasped only air

412

and a terrible pain spread rapidly through his head. A high-pitched whine escaped from somewhere inside him but didn't seem to pass through his mouth. Then his eyes closed against his will and his head lost all conjunction with the rest of his body. Somewhere in the distance, he could hear words. "Traitor. Turncoat. May you live in hell." Then all was black and silent.

Jonathan laid Godfrey's still body on its back. He removed Godfrey's striped coat, then turned it inside out and put it back on him. Then he looked around and spotted a stanchion and pulley used for lifting heavy boxes. He made a noose from the rope that had strangled Godfrey, then slipped the hook from the pulley over it and pulled Godfrey up until his feet dangled above the ground. From his coat pocket, Jonathan removed the blue and red Union Jack he'd taken from a fallen British standard at Saratoga. He slowly tore it into strips connected by a few threads at the end, then tied it over Godfrey's head.

Jonathan stepped back and looked at the sight before him in the dim light. Then he stripped off his own jacket and shirt, picked up the letter opener from the floor and, standing as far away as he could, slashed Godfrey's throat. Blood began to drain out and soak through Godfrey's clothes especially the coat which was now turned inside out. Jonathan moved away quickly so that none of the blood got on him. It would be hard enough to face his sister later; he didn't want his own clothes marked with her dead husband's blood.

Jonathan wiped his hands, then put his shirt and coat back on. He took one last look at the spectacle of Godfrey Carter, Turncoat, then stepped silently toward the window through which he'd planned his escape.

Behind a wagon across the floor, a disobedient Captain Flint watched in silent admiration as Colonel Jonathan Houghton displayed his keen understanding of the first rule of war: "No quarter, sir. No quarter."

Jonathan stole through the dark streets, watching closely for sentries and patrols, slipping into alleys or behind fences when soldiers appeared. He saw few, however, and most of those were drunk or on their way to one of the many whorehouses near the Bull's Head Tavern along Walter Street. Encounters with Continental officers were the last thing on their mind. He arrived at Celia's less than an hour after "taking care of the problem" of Mr. Brown.

Celia opened the door when Jonathan knocked and he immediately noticed her swollen eyes. She threw herself into his arms and began to cry uncontrollably. How could she have heard so quickly, Jonathan wondered. I came right here from the warehouse. And I didn't expect the body to be discovered until morning. Who could have found it? Who could have gotten the news to her?

He put his arms around his sister and led her into the parlor. They sat down on the settee and Jonathan held her hand and tried desperately to find something appropriate to say. "I'm terribly, terribly sorry, Celia," the words finally began to flow, "I can't imagine the grief you must feel. Life will go on, but I know how difficult it will be for a while. I want you to know that I'll do everything I can to comfort you and to make these next few weeks bearable. Perhaps Savannah would come too."

Before he could continue, Celia pulled back and looked at her brother quizzically through her tears. "You're kind to think of me first, but it's your grief, too, Jonathan. I'm sure we all feel it now. And how can Savannah come here. They've already had the funeral in Delaware, and she has so much to do around the farm. No, it's I who should try to go home to visit Father and her."

Jonathan was now utterly confused. He pulled back and looked directly at her and said bluntly, "Celia, why are you crying?"

"About Mother, Jonathan, of course. What did you think? I had a letter in the post today from Savannah telling me that mother died two weeks ago."

Jonathan was suddenly in a swirl of emotions. She didn't have news about Godfrey, and he had almost said something that would have revealed his knowledge of Godfrey's death. Mother was dead. Now Celia would be struck by two grievous blows when she learned about Godfrey. Jonathan felt sad and guilty and deeply worried about Celia.

"Why did you think I was crying?" Celia asked.

Jonathan tried to find the right answer but his mind was too cluttered for cleverness. "I don't know. I don't know," he finally stammered. "I was so struck by your sadness that I wasn't thinking clearly. This is so terrible. I knew Mother had been suffering. She has been for a long time, but I didn't think she was dying. I wish I'd taken leave to see her. I never said good-bye."

"Savannah said that Father was there when she died. I was afraid he might be at Congress." Celia reported.

"He left early when he heard she was worse. He stopped to see me at Valley Forge on the way. But he never indicated that she was this bad. Maybe he didn't know himself." Jonathan looked down to avoid Celia's eyes. It was then that he noticed that dark drops on his shoe and the small red spots on the lower part of his left stocking. Suddenly very self-conscious, he tried to tuck his legs under the settee.

"Oh, where is Godfrey?" Celia asked through another heavy flow of tears. "I need him now and he said he'd be home much earlier than this. Did you see him when you were out, Jonathan?"

"No," Jonathan lied adroitly, "my business was in Brooklyn. I was there all day."

"What was the business that brought you here?" Celia asked. "It must have been important because it's so dangerous for you to be in New York now."

"You know that I can't give you an answer, Celia. In war, there are many secrets, and it's best you not know certain things. Then you'll never have to worry about telling something that could harm anyone."

"Yes," Celia sighed, daubing her eyes with a silk handkerchief. "That's what Godfrey often says."

An hour passed in which brother and sister reminisced about the mother they'd lost and recalled vivid scenes from their childhood in which she was a prominent feature. Celia's tears came and went, and Jonathan's did as well. Celia was relieved that her brother was there to comfort her in this terrible time, but increasingly upset that her husband had not yet returned home as promised.

Finally, Jonathan said, "Mr. Flint is waiting for me in your carriage house, and he and I must leave shortly. A wagon will pick us up near the Powderhouse and lead us out through the guards."

"Oh, Jonathan, must you go tonight? I can't stand the thought of being alone. And I know how sad you must feel, too. Please stay until tomorrow at least. Then Godfrey will be home, and I won't feel so alone."

At times like this, Jonathan wondered what his father would do. The answer here was obvious. So he told Celia to wait a few minutes, while he made arrangements to stay. Then he walked out through the kitchen down the narrow connecting passage to the carriage house where he found Flint asleep on a blanket in a stall.

"Flint. Wake up. We've got to change our plan," he said, gently shaking the sleeping Captain.

"Whaddya mean?" Flint asked, sitting up.

"Celia and I just got word that our mother died two weeks ago. Celia's very upset and I don't want to walk out on her now because...." He searched for the right words. "Well, you know why. I want you to catch the wagon and leave the way we planned. I'll find my own way out in the next day or two. Wait for me at the Black Horse Tavern on the Albany Road. The owner's a good patriot. He'll keep you in a place that's safe. I'll meet you there on Wednesday, and we can ride back to Valley Forge from there."

A look of disagreement began to spread across Flint's face, but Jonathan held up his hand. "Just do it, Captain. That's an order."

"But it'll be damned risky for you now. Hell, it's risky enough already. Wait 'til they find Carter."

"I'll manage. And I'll be careful. But I can't leave Celia now. You go and wait for me."

Flint curled his upper lip in a frustrated suggestion of his displeasure with the plan, but he said he would follow orders and leave the city that night on the wagon. Jonathan started to return to the house and the awful prospect from which there was now no escape, but then stopped and turned to Flint, "Wait a minute, one more thing," he said. "Take off your stockings. Give them to me and you take mine."

"What?" Flint asked, "Why?" Then he looked down at Jonathan's left leg and saw the answer to his question.

The man came just before noon. Celia didn't know him, and he said only that he was a business associate of Godfrey's. Jonathan listened from the top of the stairs and thought it might be a soldier in civilian dress who'd had the misfortune to draw the short straw. He was quick and curt, telling Celia that there'd been a terrible accident at the warehouse the night before, that Godfrey had been supervising the loading of a ship and a heavy barrel had fallen on him and crushed him. He went on, in the tone of an official report, to say that Godfrey's body had been taken to an undertaker on Garden Street and she would probably not want to view it because of the awful impact of the barrel on his head. He expressed his condolences, then pivoted sharply and left. Celia had no time to react to the news before the man was out the door.

When the visitor was beyond the gate, Jonathan quickly descended the stairs and came to his sister. This second blow in less than a day left her in a state of stunned silence. Her eyes didn't focus and she said nothing. Jonathan led her to the settee and made her sit down. He

416

poured a glass of brandy and tried to force her to drink some. But she was too numbed even for that.

After a few minutes she began to sob, then the sobs turned to rivers of grief that flowed for an hour or more before slowly some coherence began to return. Over the next two days, Jonathan did what he could to make Celia comfortable. He'd never felt such contorted emotions: stricken with genuine grief at the death of his mother, burdened with the need to feign grief at the "loss" of his detested brother-in-law. He had to watch his own words with the greatest care to ensure they conveyed the emotions he was supposed to express at a time like this, not those he actually felt.

After the early wave of grief passed, Celia began to think about the visitors who would come to pay their respects and she consulted with Sarah about preparing tea and cakes to serve when they started to arrive. Then she and Jonathan talked about funeral plans and, here and there, about her future and how she would care for herself and her son.

But only a few people came and they arrived in small groups and stayed only briefly. Celia was sure that Godfrey must have had many friends and associates who would come by, but none did—only a few of Celia's women friends who remained in Manhattan. For most of the two days after the news of Godfrey's accident, the house stood in silent preparation for mourners who never appeared.

On Tuesday, Jonathan asked Celia about Godfrey's will. "I'm sorry to talk about practical things now," he said. "But I have to leave tomorrow, and I want to make sure that I've done everything I can for you."

"Oh, I'm sure he has a will." Celia said. "But we never talked about it. He was always so busy. We never had enough time to talk about practical things. Of course, we didn't expect he was going to die, not this young. In a few days, I'll have to find out who his attorney was. I'm surprised he hasn't contacted me. Wouldn't you think he would contact me?"

Jonathan knew little about the processes of probate, but the assumption seemed logical. "I'm sure he will, Celia."

"And you can be sure that Godfrey made ample provisions for us. He was very good at things like that," Celia said. "He may have had his faults, but he was a good business man."

"Yes," Jonathan said wryly, "I'm certain that he was."

# Chapter 29

## London
## Spring 1778

Edmund Burke greeted Carlisle and took his seat in the usual giltwood armchair in the center of the ornate drawing room. He nodded at Nathaniel, as well, but said nothing to him. This was the last sitting for Burke's portrait—none too soon in Benton's opinion for Burke was a restless subject and interruptions had been constant. As a formidable figure of the opposition at a time when government policy was under intense criticism, it seemed to the two painters that all of London politics revolved around this jowly, dark-haired man with the long nose and questioning eyes.

Edmund Burke had long been a thorn in the King's side on the matter of America. Now as the failure to achieve a quick victory in America nettled official London to ever higher levels of frustration, Burke was hard at work with others in the opposition to force a resolution of the conflict.

After an unusual hour of uninterrupted painting, the porter entered to inform Burke of the arrival of the Earl of Orford for his appointment. A flicker of disgust crossed Carlisle's face; Nathaniel detected it, but Burke did not and brightened at the news.

"Good morning, Horace," said Burke when the fourth Earl of Orford, Horace Walpole, entered the drawing room and pulled up a chair to a position that allowed him to converse without pulling Burke's gaze from Carlisle's angle of observation. Walpole was a figure familiar to Nathaniel both from observations at dinners with the gentry and from discussions with his contacts in the Alliance.

"And good morning to you, Edmund. How goes the painting?"

"Quite well, I believe," Burke responded. "Mr. Carlisle tells me I shall have to sit no more days after this one, so I am relieved that the work nears an end." Benton's tight smile suggested that he shared Burke's relief.

Walpole leaned in closer to Burke indicating that he was ready to get to serious matters. "What do you make of the news of North's effort to resign?" he asked.

"Long overdue in my opinion," said Burke, "but unlikely to occur. The Government's policy has been revealed to be threadbare by all of us in the opposition. Fox flayed them so badly in Commons the other day that not one of the government ministers could speak in defense of the policy. Even North, after all these years as the King's first minister, must be tiring of the effort to quell the unquellable."

Walpole rubbed his chin and then offered what he deemed to be a confidence. "I hear that it's not just the opposition attacks on his American policy that are getting to North. The French treaty with America was a hard blow to him, and his source in Paris tells him that the French are now preparing to send shiploads of arms to their new allies."

"Is it a reliable source?" Burke asked.

Walpole smiled now, the smile of men who know secrets and feel the power it gives them over the unenlightened. "I should say so," he said. "He's getting his information directly from Edward Bancroft, the delegation's secretary. He pays Bancroft five hundred pounds a year and knows almost everything that Franklin and his associates are up to."

Nathaniel was startled by this and listened closely. He'd met Bancroft in Paris a few months earlier and had regarded him as a model of propriety. It was disheartening now to hear that he was a British spy. But then, he supposed, there were many British politicians who would feel the same way if they knew the truth about their portraitist's assistant.

"Bancroft tipped North off that the treaty was nearing completion," Walpole continued, "and that inspired North's ill-fated effort to strike a deal with the Americans. He hoped that he could settle what he likes to call the 'American affair' before the French were involved."

"That was a laugh, now wasn't it," Burke said trying to force himself to stay in the position that Carlisle had requested. "The Americans captured Johnny Burgoyne and his army at Saratoga and North chooses the aftermath of that moment to propose that they withdraw their declaration of independence in exchange for a few bones of freedom. I would have enjoyed being at their Congress when they discussed their response to that proposal."

"North is hemmed in and he knows it. Germain wants to give the Americans no quarter and would like to send more troops. The King hates the thought of capitulation, but he doesn't want more of his best troops going off to fight thousands of miles away when the French and Spanish fleets sail freely in the Channel. And the opposition thinks it's time to abandon the effort to suppress the rebellion by arms. But even among the opposition, as you well know Edward, there are those who say withdraw and recognize America as an independent country and seek its friendship; then there are others, like Pitt, who say withdraw but don't recognize American independence. There must be many days when poor Lord North feels he's trapped on a small island surrounded by quicksand."

He turned to Burke. "So you think it's unlikely North will resign?"

"He did offer to step down. I have that on good authority. At first, the King declined to hear of it, then later he told North that he would accede to the request and asked North to stay on until the King could arrange for the formation of a new government. But then, I hear, North had second thoughts. His dark mood began to pass and he decided power wasn't such an evil thing. He was also reminded of the several sinecures that the King had provided him to insure a healthy income. Now, it seems, North has indicated that he will stay on, in spite of the acute distress he sometimes suffers from all the conflicting forces that play on him."

Nathaniel listened closely as Burke and Walpole went back and forth in the most candid discussion he'd ever heard of the emotional state of the first minister of government. He knew this would be information of great interest to his contacts and to the recipients of their intelligence in America. He wanted to report accurately what they said. He appeared to be sketching as he sat in the corner, but the margins of his sketch pad were filling rapidly with the cryptic code he used to record conversations like the one he was hearing now.

Walpole was on his feet now and he moved around to Burke's right. "I understand that North's agents in America are trying to purchase some members of their Congress." He fired the words rapidly, knowing the impact they would have on Burke.

"Purchase?" Burke responded. "Do you mean our government is trying to bribe members of the American government to act in the King's behalf?"

"Precisely."

"How low have we stooped?" asked Burke in disgust.

"It's a war, Edmund. In the view of the King, it's not just a war for America, it's a war for the empire and maybe a war for the monarchy. He's willing to do almost anything to win this war and North is his principal. If bribing members of the American Congress is what it requires to get them to vote to accept the Government's conciliation proposals, then that's what they'll do."

Walpole rose, signaling his intention to depart. He placed a hand on Burke's shoulder and looked down on him. "We shall see, my friend, how it goes. We shall see, shan't we?"

"Oh, Horace," Burke called as his friend opened the door, "what does an American Congressman cost these days?" He smiled at his own crude question.

Walpole turned back, shook his head from side to side, and answered, "Don't know. Haven't found any for sale."

There was much Nathaniel needed to encrypt and pass to George. He knew the special urgency that attached to communicating the information about Bancroft working as a British agent and North's effort to bribe some members of Congress. So he'd worked on his codes late into the night after the last sitting with Burke. And he'd left the curtain closed in his window the next morning when he departed for the studio at Bloomsbury Square.

It was early April in London and the gardens were awash in tulips and jonquils and rainbows of pansies. Nathaniel walked more slowly than usual to absorb the rare sensual pleasures of spring in London. When he arrived in Bloomsbury Square at mid-morning, he spotted Lydie sitting on a bench in the square seeking those same pleasures. He walked through the large stone gate and sat quietly beside her, not saying a word. It took a few seconds before she glanced at the gentleman to her left. When she realized it was Nathaniel, she squealed a kind of girlish delight.

"What a sneaky sort you are," she declared, intending the double meaning. Lydie had thought a great deal about Nathaniel's confession to her in Paris. She'd always admired him, indeed she'd fallen in love with him, for his gentle passion, for the clarity with which he saw things and the richness of the images in which he recorded them. She loved the way he worked with Benton, always respectful and solicitous and responsive, even as it became clearer that Benton's skills were failing while Nathaniel's were burgeoning. She'd been powerfully drawn to the sweet nature of this unusual young man.

Now she knew there was another side to Nathaniel. A side that took risks, that broached danger. A side with a much sharper edge than the one she'd first seen and come to love in him. And though she hated to admit it, she was drawn to this as well. It filled him out in ways she found powerfully appealing. The painter and the spy, resident of the netherworld of colors and shapes and textures, resident of the real world of politics and war.

When Lydie first learned of Nathaniel's clandestine activities, she'd made him promise to end them, fearing gravely for his safety. She doubted he would keep the promise, even as he made it, knowing how impossible it would be for him to abandon a cause for which his father and brother risked their lives. And, while her fears for his safety were genuine, she knew she would have thought less of him had he capitulated so easily to her demands that he abandon his dangerous secret life.

She was, she thought, more in love with him than ever. It was a tragic love in some ways, though she didn't dwell on this. The deep affection they both felt for Benton stood between them. But they rarely resented that, and they'd made their peace with it. They'd learned to love each other in the best way they could, under the circumstances. If their love was denied its complete fulfillment, they'd take the pleasures they could find in what was available to them. Flirtation had its own delights, and they were committed now to a very long and very intense flirtation.

"Good morning," Nathaniel beamed. "You look lovely here among the flowers on this fine morning."

"And you, sir, are the handsomest man in all of London. How fortunate I am that you've chosen to sit on my bench."

They bantered like this for many minutes, as they often did, using clever turns of phrase and shared secrets as their surrogates for the physical intimacy that was denied them. But time passed so quickly when they were together, and Nathaniel had a sudden attack of responsibility.

"I'm sure Benton is wondering where I am," he said. "I better get to the studio."

"I'm sure he knows exactly where you are, Nathaniel. In the park, in thrall of his charming wife!"

"Indeed," said Nathaniel. "All the more reason why I must get to the studio."

"Will I see you later?" Lydie asked.

"Perhaps if you come to the studio this afternoon. Then he thought a moment. "No, perhaps I'll come to the studio to work tonight. Around nine o'clock. If you come to the studio then, we can be together. Benton will probably have retired by then."

422

Lydie had come to recognize the look Nathaniel wore when he had to attend to other important business. She had pledged to herself never to intrude again in that part of his life, never to ask the questions that filled her mind, never to remind him that he'd promised to abandon the world of espionage. To raise such questions, she knew, would only torture him— and them. So she responded with an understanding glance and said simply, "Well, yes, tonight then. I'll be in the studio at nine o'clock."

"Good," Nathaniel said firmly as he touched Lydie's hand and rose to leave. "Until tonight."

The number by the door at the High Holbourn wash house indicated that George would meet him in the Privy Garden above Westminster Bridge. This was a change from the normal meeting places and as he walked toward the river Nathaniel reminded himself to ask George why he had chosen this new location. The night retained much of the warmth of the day, but the warm air over the river produced a thin fog that spread over the city after dark.

London had many moods and Nathaniel had grown to know them well. This was one of his favorites. The gas lamps created small gauzy bubbles of light that seemed to connect the pieces of his journey as he walked along Wardour Street. At the Garden, Nathaniel sat on top of the marble wall and dangled his legs toward the river. The wind had begun to shift, chilling the air and dissolving the last of the fog. There were no gas lamps in this section of the city, but the ambient glow of the lights along the river illuminated the area around him.

A few minutes after Nathaniel arrived, a small man moved near him and stood a few feet away, looking out over the river. "Are you Charles?" he asked. "No," Nathaniel replied, "I'm George."

They said nothing for a minute, then Nathaniel asked, "Why are we meeting here?"

"Because we're worried," the man replied. "One of our agents was nearly captured two days ago. Only his fast feet kept him out of their clutches. We don't know for certain what might have gone wrong, but we fear that there may be a double agent somewhere in the Alliance. You know what a nightmare that can be."

"How was he caught?"

"Well, he wasn't caught. Thank God. He'd been playing cards with some men from the admiralty, and he'd picked up some interesting scraps of information from their conversations. As he was walking home, he stopped under a light to make a few notes. That's when two men came up on him and one of them grabbed his coat. He managed to pull away before they had him firmly in their grasp, then he flew down an alley which fortunately had an outlet at the end and he was able lose them as he cut through the narrow streets."

"Do you think they know who he is?" Nathaniel asked.

"Hard to tell. He used a false name and identity in the card games, but probably his face is recognizable to the men from the admiralty and perhaps to the two men who grabbed him. It's hard to tell. It's not even certain they grabbed him because he was spying. Might have just been two men after his purse. But we all need to be especially careful right now."

Nathaniel nodded, as a jolt of fear passed through him. He reached into his pocket and pulled out a folded sheet of paper which he passed to George. It contained the coded information he had gleaned the day before from the conversation between Walpole and Burke. George asked simply, "Is it important?"

"I think it could well be," Nathaniel responded.

George nodded and turned to leave. He walked a few steps, then turned back to Nathaniel. "Be very careful," he whispered, then walked away into the darkness.

Nathaniel waited a few minutes, following the normal routine. Then he slid off the wall and began to walk up Cockspur, taking a different route than the one that had brought him to the river. He crossed Coventry Street, then turned into Rupert Street. He hadn't yet had any dinner, so he stopped at The Claw and Talon, a public house on the corner of Compton and Greek Streets and sat in the back where he dined on a dry kidney pie and a glass of port. He paid his bill and left a few minutes later, heading toward Bloomsbury Square.

When he got beyond the glow from the window of the pub, suddenly he was in total darkness and he slowed for a second to orient himself. It was then that he had the sense of another presence. A stirring, the shuffle of a shoe, a hint of a breath, a smell perhaps. Whatever it was some animal instinct told him that another human was nearby. So Nathaniel began to step rapidly away.

Now he heard footsteps behind him, moving as quickly as he was. So he quickened his pace and began running along Oxford Street. The noise moving behind him quickened as well, and now Nathaniel felt himself in a race for his life. He started to breathe more heavily, for he was unaccustomed to running and he sensed that his assailant was gaining on him. As he approached Bloomsbury Square, he formed in his mind the image of the garden where he and Lydie had sat that morning. He thought he might be able to duck through the stone gate and into the dense shrubbery behind it, perhaps escaping the chase long enough to make his way to the safety of the studio.

At the gate, he turned sharply to the right and once inside, he slid quickly into the rhododendron bushes, struck in the midst of this awful moment by their penetrating sugary aroma. He stepped around them as best he could, but they were thicker than he thought and he soon found, not escape, but a snare from which he could barely extricate himself. He was breathing heavily and he began to experience the first flush of panic as he heard the other figure making his way through the same bushes just a few feet away.

Suddenly there was heavy hand on Nathaniel's shoulder, and just as suddenly he was on his back on the ground with a knee planted squarely in the center of his chest. He rolled to the left and was able to get out from under his assailant's weight, but not to elude his grasp. He could see the man's face now, and even in this moment of terrible fear he mentally recorded its features: black hair pulled back, long thin nose, deep-set eyes.

The man reached toward his leg and withdrew a knife from a sheath hidden in his boot. "Here's what we have for American spies," he growled as he raised his arm. Nathaniel saw the knife at once and grabbed for it, clutching the man's large left hand. Now they were in a ferocious struggle for control of the knife which the man held firmly in the hand that Nathaniel was pushing away with all the strength he could muster.

With his left hand, Nathaniel reached up quickly and struck the man a fierce blow on the end of his nose. This forced a shout of pain and the man's grip on the knife relaxed as he reached for his wounded nose with his free hand. Blood began to drip on Nathaniel's shirt as he grabbed the knife hand with both of his own and forced it to the ground. The knife fell free.

The attacker now held his bloodied nose with both hands, giving Nathaniel an opportunity to jump to his feet and try to escape. But as he did so, the man again picked up the knife and started to strike toward Nathaniel's leg, gashing a hole through one of his stockings and into the flesh of his shin. Nathaniel kicked at the knife with his other leg and caught it squarely. It flew from the man's hand into the bottom of his throat where it protruded like a belaying pin along the rail of a ship. A sharp painful gasp escaped from the man's mouth then blood began to flow past his lips and down onto his waistcoat as his eyes rolled up in his head and he fell heavily forward.

For a moment, Nathaniel froze, trying to comprehend what had just happened. Then he looked down at the silent stiff figure on the ground in front of him and rolled it over. The knife pointed toward the sky, and the man's life drained quickly away in a dark stream of blood.

Nathaniel pulled back and began to shake as the terror of the last few minutes caught up with him. He found his way out of the bushes and sat on the bench where he and Lydie had talked so lightly a few hours earlier. Then he thought about Lydie who was waiting for him in the studio on the other side of Bloomsbury Square. He waited a few more minutes until the shaking stopped, then he rose gingerly on his wounded leg and headed toward a much different rendezvous than the one he'd anticipated.

Lydie brightened when she heard the door open from the mews. It was nearly nine-thirty and she'd been worried that Nathaniel might not come after all. She looked up with the happy smile that his arrival always brought to her face. Until she saw him.

Nathaniel had no hat and his hair was tangled and dirty. His coat was torn open and a button was missing from his waistcoat. Red blotches covered the clothes on the upper half of his body and blood was soaking the stocking on his left leg. In his eyes was a look of anxious fear.

Lydie shrieked loudly and Nathaniel came to her and held her hard. "What happened to you" she cried.

"I was attacked in the garden in Bloomsbury Square," he answered. "I think a man was trying to rob me."

Lydie pulled away and looked at him. "Was it robbery, Nathaniel? Or was it someone who knows you've been spying?"

Nathaniel tried to persist in his story. "No. I'm sure it was a robbery."

But Lydie's disbelief made Nathaniel realize that it was a time for truth. "No. You're right. It was not a robbery. I was followed after I met with my contact by the river. I stopped to eat dinner on the way here, and a man pursued me from the pub. I tried to escape him in the bushes in Bloomsbury Garden, but he caught me there and attacked me with a knife. That's how I got the cut on my leg."

Lydie looked more closely at his wound, then went to the paint bench and rooted around for some clean rags to stop the bleeding. She instructed Nathaniel to sit and hold the rags against the wound, while she poured some water from the large white pitcher on the bench into a bowl. Then she removed his shoe and pulled off the torn stocking and began to clean the wound.

"What happened to the man who attacked you?" she asked after working for a few minutes on the wound.

"He's dead." Nathaniel responded.

"Dead?" Lydie wailed. "You killed him?"

"I had no choice, Lydie. We were struggling for his dagger. He lashed out at me as I stood over him and I kicked his hand. The kick dislodged the knife which flew into his throat. Everything happened in a blur."

Nathaniel began to breathe heavily as the awful picture seeped back into his mind.

Lydie looked at the disheveled, wounded man seated in front of her. What was he becoming, she asked herself. A spy, a risk-taker, a man in danger, a killer. What had become of the passionate young romantic who'd walked into her life four years ago? What would become of him now that he was a suspected spy in a city that had no tolerance for spies?

# Chapter 30

## Still River, Delaware
## May 1778

"I have to tell ya', Colonel, I expected a little more milk and honey after all the glorious talk about Delaware I've been hearin' over the past three years." Flint's eyes slowly swept the horizon from east to west as he and Jonathan rode past the farms and through the villages of Kent County. "It looks an awful lot like Pennsylvania to me."

Jonathan laughed. But it didn't look like Pennsylvania to him, not like Philadelphia and surely not like Valley Forge. He and Flint had spent a week at Valley Forge after returning from New York. The Army there was getting ready to move soon. And it did look better than it had in the depths of winter. There were more soldiers now with the new enlistments; most of the men were healthier—those who'd survived the winter; and Baron Von Steuben had worked a miracle with his training methods. Jonathan and Flint had watched a parade drill two days ago that was snappier than anything they'd ever seen from a Continental Army. A few red coats and you would have thought you were watching the King's grenadiers.

With the army still in winter camp, there wasn't much for Jonathan to do. And Washington had been pleased to hear that they'd "solved" the problem of the American supplier to the British army. So the General hadn't hesitated to grant them two weeks of leave for Jonathan to visit his family after the news of his mother's death.

Jonathan hadn't been home for more than three years, and Delaware seemed like a glimpse of heaven on this May morning, even if two great armies were camped just a few miles beyond its border. The small cleared hills rolled majestically ahead of them carpeted with daisies and black-eyed Susans. Here and there a hawk soared in the wind currents raised by the morning sun. The forests of oak and beech were every bit as heavy and deep emerald as Jonathan remembered them.

Jonathan had almost come to believe that nothing much had happened in his life before he went off to Congress with his father and then joined the army. His experiences since then had been so vivid and unique and brutal that his memories paled in comparison. But back in Delaware now he began to recall the joy of growing up in a prosperous family, all that he learned from his father about the land and how to cultivate and care for it, the days with his brother and sisters exploring everything from snakes to grandmother's trunk in this child's paradise. There had been life before Philadelphia, Jonathan remembered now, and a rich and happy life it was.

Three days of gentle riding from Valley Forge had brought them to the top of the knoll north of the Still River where the Houghton land first came into view. They stopped when they got there, so Jonathan could point out the features of the landscape: the house and barns, the cleared fields where Jonathan saw many more horses grazing than ever before, the stands of virgin oak higher up on the southern hill than when he'd left, and, of course, the bend in the quiet river that gave the place its name. He wanted to get home now, but he could have stayed there and relished this picture for another hour.

Shreds of this halcyon image—the fragments that memory allows—had gleamed in his mind in the dark hours at Bunker Hill and on Brooklyn Heights, on that terrible Christmas night before Trenton, and in the bloody wheat fields of Saratoga. Home never seems so beautiful, so beckoning, as when it's imagined in moments of terror on the battlefield. So Jonathan was gratified, and a little surprised, to see that the real thing was even more idyllic than the image in his mind's eye.

They rode down from the ridge across the northern field and forded Still River in the shallows above the bend where Jonathan and Nathaniel and Savannah used to swim on summer afternoons. Then they ascended through the lower pasture up the path to the house. Jonathan had guessed that there would be a shabby look to the place with Father away so much and neither of the boys around to run things. But they found quite the opposite. The barn appeared freshly painted. Fences all seemed in good repair. And a sense of order and purpose prevailed in the working areas between the barn and the smaller buildings scattered around it. He had to admit the place looked in better shape than ever before.

They dismounted and led the horses into the barn. As they started toward the house, Henry emerged from the house to greet them and just behind him Sweetie stood in the doorway, looking grayer than Jonathan remembered her. Jonathan embraced his father and held onto him for a long time as silent thoughts of his mother passed between them, a human antidote to the grief they both felt. Flint stood to the side, occupying himself with a careful study of the farm.

After a few moments, Jonathan stood back and introduced his father to Captain Flint. He always avoided Flint's first names in these introductions, leaving it to him to cope with the smiles that their enunciation nearly always evoked. Flint seemed genuinely humbled and unusually quiet in the presence of Henry Houghton. He'd heard so much about Henry from Jonathan, from General Washington, from Robert Morris, and from others who'd known him that Flint expected to encounter not a Delaware farmer but an American demigod. It had been less than two years since the Congress issued its Declaration of Independence, but already in the minds of their countrymen heroic halos had begun to encircle the names of the signers of that document. Flint was honored to meet Henry Houghton, but in a way he had little capacity to express.

Jonathan had warned Flint as they rode into Still River that he and his father would probably want to take a few minutes alone to walk up to his mother's grave in the family burial ground on the hill. He'd told Flint to make himself at home while they were gone. And so a few minutes after this introduction, Jonathan and Henry trudged slowly up the hill, taking time to survey and discuss their surroundings as they did.

Sweetie offered Flint a piece of rhubarb pie, and he would have been happy to accept even if he weren't so hungry. She brought the pie on a plate and pointed him toward the dooryard where he went and sat on a bench amid the soft dense aromas of foxglove and bayberry. As he was finishing perhaps the most delicious piece of pie he'd ever eaten, the gate to the dooryard swung open and through it passed a vision that seemed to Flint to have dropped from heaven. Later Savannah would say that she was embarrassed to have been caught in her farm clothes, but to Flint none of that mattered. She wore a simple peach dress of printed cotton. Her long brown hair surrounded a handsome face with its natural adornments: a rich round mouth, strong cheekbones, and brisk blue eyes that offset her clear ivory skin.

It was only as she approached him that the spark of recognition ignited. It was the woman he'd met at the tavern in Kingstown a year ago, the woman whose name he'd neglected to ask. What was she doing here?

She noticed him at that moment also and seemed slightly startled. Then the same spark ignited in her and she, too, began to wonder how the man who called himself Ezekial Isaac—the garrulous, joshing, exciting man with whom she'd flirted so happily on that night in New Jersey and who had crept into her thoughts so often since then—how had he found his way here to her home in Delaware?

She came to a dead stop and looked at him, and he at her, and neither had the slightest idea what to say. After a moment of utter silence, she started to laugh, softly at first, a small shy giggle, then louder as Flint joined the chorus. Then, not knowing what else to do, Savannah stuck out her hand and shook his. "I don't know how in the world you found your way to Still River Bend, but welcome," she said.

Flint dropped his hand, looking a little stunned and asked, "Are YOU Colonel Houghton's sister?"

"I am," Savannah replied. "Does that disappoint you?"

"I'm 'fraid it does," Flint said, the old wry smile returning to his face. "So I guess I'll jes' be leavin' now."

"Don't you dare," Savannah replied in kind, "at least not until you tell me who's winning the chess game."

It took a second or two for Flint to catch the reference to the cockamamie story he'd told her about his job as a go-between for Washington and Howe. "Well, General Howe seemed to be havin' the upper hand for awhile but then he thought he'd try the famous divide and conquer move and it tripped him up. Now Howe's gone back to England, a fella name Henry Clinton is runnin' their army and he don't play chess. So I'm outta work."

"Well, if that's the truth," Savannah said, "and I seriously doubt it is, coming from you, we always have work for strong men around here."

"And what might you need a strong man for around here?" asked Flint.

"Cutting tall oak trees, sawing them into bolts, loading the heavy bolts on big wagons, and transporting them to the Chesapeake Bay where they're turned into fine ships for the American navy."

"Well, I'm tempted, ma'am," Flint joked, "and I sure would like to help ya out. But I'm 'fraid chess is my game."

They both laughed heartily, then sat down together on the bench. Flint looked at her, perhaps longer and more deeply than was proper and thought to ask, "So you're Savannah?"

"I am," she said.

"Colonel Houghton talks about you a lot. There ain't many people named Savannah. But I never asked you your name when we met in New Jersey. I wish now that I'd thought to. Then this might not a been such a surprise."

Savannah looked at Flint sitting a few feet away from her in the dooryard, in her favorite place on earth, and thought it had never seemed more beautiful than on this shining May morning.

They reached the nub of the knoll and Henry led Jonathan to his mother's grave. In the weeks since she'd been buried, the grass had begun to spring up in the dirt and Savannah had planted some blue and yellow pansies and pink impatiens around the stone.

Jonathan and his brother and sisters had visited here often when they were young. It was always hard for him to imagine people underground, though he'd seen several of his older relatives buried here. Nathaniel told him once that they didn't actually stay underground, that once the dirt was on top, they got out of their caskets and went to heaven. So only the wooden boxes remained behind. It was a logical explanation, Jonathan thought at the time, but he still had trouble picturing how they'd get out of the caskets with all that dirt on top and no life in their bodies. He'd chalked it up to the mysteries of life, a large category of unexplained phenomena.

Now as he stood with his father, no practical questions of that sort entertained him. He was filled instead with memories of his mother. The care she'd always taken to turn them into gentlemen and ladies, to be sure that they learned to speak precise and correct English, to be courteous to adults, to know their manners. The singing she organized on winter evenings, with parts assigned to each of them, even Celia whose singing only occasionally intersected with the tune. And special occasions she made more special—the birthdays and holidays and celebrations of childbirth and marriage—with her little skits and set pieces.

In her lifetime, Mother had never traveled more than 20 miles from this spot. But she'd enlivened the place, enriched it, and brightened the lives of those with whom she'd shared it. And the feeling that infused Jonathan most strongly now was gratitude. You never thank your mother enough in her lifetime for all the little things she does, all the acts of caring and compassion she commits, all the ways she forms and directs you. Jonathan knew he never had. But now, standing on this quiet hill overlooking the home where she'd raised him, he wished he'd had just one minute before she died to thank her for being such a blessing in his life.

After a few silent moments, Jonathan and Henry started back down to the house. "The farm looks wonderful, Father," Jonathan said. "I don't know how you've managed to keep it so well, being away as much as you have and bearing the misfortune of two useless sons."

Henry smiled. "It does look grand, but none of the credit is mine. I may have two useless sons, but I have a very useful daughter. Savannah's done all this," Henry said, sweeping his arm across the horizon. "She's worked so hard; she deserves all the credit."

"Is she unhappy being so…so…obligated here?" Jonathan asked.

"I've never seen her happier," Henry replied. "I thought that the end of her engagement to Marinus Marshall would be painful for her, but it wasn't at all. It was a choice she'd made freely because she wanted to stay here on the farm. I don't know what the future holds for her. She's getting older now, but she's certainly not too old to find a husband and have a family of her own. When the war is over, there'll be a lot of Delaware men coming home. And you'll be coming back to take over the farm, so she'll be free of that."

"I'm not so sure, from the sound of things, that she'll want to be free of that. Sounds like she's happy running the farm."

"Oh, I think she is, Jonathan. But, of course, that's men's work. War changes things, and we have to make do. But when the war is over, things will go back to normal. The men will run the farms as they always have, and the women will tend to the families. That's the way of the world. Savannah's a smart girl. She'll understand that."

"I trust then," Jonathan said, smiling at his father, "that you'll be the one who tells her how the world works."


There hadn't been a Marshall Ball since 1775. With a war on, it just didn't seem right. But this year, Marinus decided it was time to stop caving in to the war, and he scheduled the ball, even though the war was only a few leagues away to the north. The invitations called it the "In Spite of It All Spring Ball."

Savannah was a little surprised that the Houghtons were invited. After she ended the courtship with Marinus, he quickly became engaged to the oldest—and everyone said the prettiest—of the Wayland sisters from Dover. Savannah assumed that his decision to host the ball again was motivated in part by an intention to introduce his fiancée to his neighbors in Kent County. Surely he must have thought about the awkwardness of Savannah attending such an event.

But Marinus was nothing if not politically astute. Any perceived slight to Henry Houghton or his family would have been far more grievous than the consequences of their attendance. And Savannah decided she and her father should attend lest there be a suggestion of hard feelings on her part. She did not want to marry Marinus, but she bore him no ill will.

The unanticipated arrival of Jonathan and Flint occurred after the invitation had been accepted. Since the invitation had specified the "Houghton family and guests," she saw no reason why the two soldiers could not attend as well. In fact, she thought they might enjoy an evening of dancing after their dreary winter at Valley Forge. She knew that she and father were ready for a little gaiety after the dark days they had endured since his return from Congress in December.

It was not quite the ball of old. Many of the men were off with the "Blue Hen's chickens," the Delaware regiment in the Continental army, so there was a preponderance of young women in the minuets and reels. Many of the older generation had sons or other relatives at war, so that was the principal topic of conversation. And the traditional optimism of the spring planting was absent this time, a victim of the general pall that enveloped a nation starting its fourth year at war with no end in sight.

Jonathan and Flint were the center of everyone's attention because they were the only soldiers present and both looked quite splendid in the uniforms of Continental officers that Sweetie had cleaned and shined to a high gleam. When the word circulated that Jonathan was an aide to General Washington and that both men had fought at Bunker Hill, in the New York and New Jersey campaigns, and at Saratoga, they were besieged by well-wishers and neighbors wanting to hear first-hand accounts of the battles. Flint's talents for colorful—and imaginative— story-telling quickly caught the favor of the attendees.

"I'm so glad you came, Savannah. It wouldn't have seemed like a Marshall Ball without you." Savannah had been watching Flint describe the surrender of Burgoyne to a rapt and mostly female audience. She hadn't heard Marinus approaching from behind. "Jonathan and his officer friend seem to be the highlights of the evening."

She turned and looked at Marinus, smiling graciously and extending her hand which he took in both of his and held for a moment as she talked. "I hope you don't mind that we all came," she said. "We all needed an evening of music."

"Not at all," he replied. "It's a delight to see Jonathan again and to meet the character he's brought with him." Savannah winced slightly at the word "character" which sounded patronizing when Marinus said it. "And I'm sure that being here is preferable to most of the ways they normally spend their time."

"Yes," Savannah said, "I'm sure it is."

"Savannah, I am so sad about your mother's passing. She was a fine woman and much admired by the people of Kent County. I hope your grief is not unbearable." Marinus looked at her solicitously.

"We're doing as well as we can. Thank you for asking," Savannah replied. Then she quickly changed the subject. "Is your fiancée here? I'd hoped we'd all have a chance to meet her."

"Yes, she is. It takes her quite a while to prepare for an occasion like this; she always wants to look just right. But I'm sure she'll appear shortly. She loves to make an entrance." Marinus proceeded cautiously. "She is a fine lady and she's already begun to make a grand impression on Dover society as we've gone through the round of engagement parties there. She also has many plans for teas and dinners and other social events here at the farm. She will be a wonderful mistress for this place. I intend to seek election as governor this fall, and I'm certain that she'll be a fine asset for a political career."

"I'm glad to hear all that, Marinus, and I hope the two of you will find great happiness together." Before Savannah could say more, Flint approached to ask her to dance. She introduced him to Marinus, who shook his hand energetically and said, "It's an honor to meet you, Captain. We are all very grateful for your service."

Flint gave him the quizzical look he seemed to save for men of military age who were not serving in the army. "Well," he said, smiling now, "it's a great way to see the country."

"We'll all be glad when this war is over and all of us can return to normal lives. It's been terrible the way our markets have been disrupted, we can't import anything, our currency is valueless. And it seems to be taking forever to bring the thing to a conclusion."

"I ain't sure things are ever gonna' be normal again," Flint responded coldly. "I know they ain't gonna be for the families of the soldiers we buried after Bunker Hill or for the good men who left the field at Freeman Farm with some of Johnny Burgoyne's grapeshot in their behinds. Don't really know what normal is anymore after you've been eatin' soup made outta hay and pine roots at Valley Forge. Not many men in any of those places is worried about markets or imports. Most of them got no currency to spend anyway. The value of nothin' is nothin' no matter what the bankers say. They just keep fightin' because they don't want no king or no redcoat soldiers tellin' 'em what they can do or can't do. Ain't about gettin' rich to most of the men in the line. More about just bein' free."

Marinus had merely intended small talk and was surprised by Flint's forceful, if naïve, reply. "Well, yes," he said. "I suppose the men in the army would need to think in those terms to motivate themselves to fight. All the talk about ideals and liberty and such does have a purpose, in that sense, but when you strip away the veneer of idealism, everything comes down to commerce. Who can sell their goods in what market at what price. And the sooner this war ends, the sooner we can all go back to markets that are free from the interference of tactics of war. For most people in the colonies—in the states, I mean—it won't make much difference who wins or loses. But we'll all be better off when the war is over. Surely you must feel that way, Captain. You must be terribly tired of the fighting."

Savannah could see the muscles tense along the rise of Flint's jaw. For a moment she feared he might try to strike Marinus. But instead his face filled with a knowing, condescending smile. "Only thing I'm tired of is not winnin'—that and all the fat-bottomed politicians who talk a good war but won't spend a penny to feed a starvin' army. We get the American people to light a little fire under their politicians, we'll end this war soon enough. And them redcoats will be scurryin' for their ships like rats runnin' away from a fire."

Savannah took Flint by the arm and tried to end the conversation. "I think, Captain Flint, that you asked me to dance." She smiled coquettishly. Flint received her arm, nodded in mock deference to Marinus, then he and Savannah went off to join the reel that was spinning in full force behind them.

Flint's dancing, like most things about him, was more energetic than polished. Watching his interaction with Marinus helped her understand what she found so attractive about this unusual man. He may not have been heavily burdened with social graces and he was not a close observer of the rules of grammar in his speech, but there was a joyous energy in everything he did. He ate with gusto. He danced furiously. He rode a horse like a madman. He stood his ground in conversation with men much more worldly and wordy than he. And, of course, he was about the handsomest man she'd ever seen.

The Houghtons left the ball earlier than they would have in previous years and were back at the farm by eleven o'clock. Father was tired and bid them goodnight. Jonathan, sensing something—he wasn't quite sure what, but he knew it didn't involve him—followed shortly.

The night was warm and cloudless, and a nearly full moon threw bold shadows behind the farm buildings. "Let me show you something," Savannah said to Flint after the others had retired. She led him through the quiet kitchen into the dooryard behind the house. The birds were silent now, but flowers never slept and the night air was heavy with their fragrance. Savannah sat on the bench facing south and Flint joined her. She still wore her beautiful mint gown with full skirt and he was still in uniform.

"All my life, I've loved coming out here in the evening when the moon is full and watching it make its way across the sky. Even in the winter, I sometimes wrap myself in a quilt and sit here in the moonlight. It seems the most serene place on earth."

"It is a damn fine moon," Flint responded. "Seems a sight bigger than the one we have up north."

Savannah laughed. "No, it's the same moon. Maybe it only seems bigger because you're taking the time to sit and really look at it. There's a loveliness to almost everything if you look closely enough. Did you ever study the delicate inside of a flower in bloom or the wing of a fly or the feather of a hawk. Patterns and colors and a glorious symmetry. But when you hurry by, you don't notice those things."

Flint didn't pause long to think about these metaphysical questions. He said instead what seemed more logical. "I thought maybe the moon looked bigger because I was mostly lookin' at the way it caught the fire in your eyes," Flint said, trying, not quite successfully, to put together words that matched his romantic mood. He turned to Savannah and studied her profile, the delicate upward curve of her nose, the fine line around her chin, the cascades of curls along her shoulders. Instinctively he reached up and gently placed his hand on her cheek. Instinctively, she relaxed to his touch.

A long, splendid minute passed, then Savannah turned and lifted her face to his and Flint kissed her warmly. He wanted to hold the kiss forever for it seemed to compress every happy sensation he'd ever known.

Soon their passions merged and they embraced, oblivious to everything else around them, to the quiet warm air, to the florid aromas, to the click-click of the fireflies in the grass. The moon crossed the clear Delaware sky, but on this night—though it had always been her favorite sight—Savannah did not watch its slow arc.

Jonathan and Flint would be leaving in an hour. Flint and Savannah had walked to the river where Savannah had something she wanted to show him. Jonathan and Henry took a pitcher of milk and some warm strawberry pie to the dooryard where Jonathan broached the subject he'd been avoiding in the days they'd been home.

"Father, I have some sad news to share with you. I'm sorry for not doing it earlier, but there didn't seem a good time, and I didn't want to further laden this week with sadness." Henry leaned forward and set down his plate. A look of worry crossed his face. "Godfrey Carter is dead," Jonathan said quietly.

Sometimes bad news seems like good news, when it's not the worst you've imagined. Henry may have thought Jonathan was going to tell him something terrible about Nathaniel, or perhaps that his grandson was ill, or worse. That Jonathan's bad news was none of those things brought him a momentary sense of relief. Then he began to think about Celia and his grandchild and the loss of their husband and father, and a deep sadness took hold of him. "How did this happen?" he asked.

"I was in New York before we came here, on an assignment from General Washington. I stopped to see Celia on what turned out to be the day she got the news of Mother's death. I'd intended to leave that day, but I stayed the night to comfort her. Godfrey did not come home at all during the night and the next morning a man came and reported that he'd been killed while he was supervising the loading of a ship and a heavy barrel fell on him and crushed him."

"Oh, that's terrible," Henry said softly, as he contemplated the tragedy. "How is Celia?"

"Devastated, of course. The double weight of Mother's death and Godfrey's is about all a woman can bear. She has household help so the baby won't be neglected, but I didn't sense that she had many friends left in New York. Almost no one came to call in the two days after he died. She will survive this, I'm sure. But it's a terrible time for her."

"I should go to her," Henry said, speaking from the heart.

"That's out of the question, Father, as you know. New York is crawling with Clinton's troops. There is no entertainment they'd enjoy more than a hanging party for a member of the rebel Congress and a signer of the Declaration to boot. You can't go to New York. I told Celia that."

"Will she be provided for?" Henry asked, turning practical.

"I suspect so. Every sign is that Godfrey was very prosperous. Celia knew none of the details of his finances or his will, but she intended to find out as soon as she could. She may well be a very wealthy widow."

Henry sat back and thought about the implications of Jonathan's words. He'd never gotten to know Godfrey Carter very well and hadn't seen him for many years. It was hard to feel much pain about the death of one so distant and little known. But he was filled with worry for Celia, in many ways the weakest and most dependent of his children. She cast her fate with Carter and let him dominate her life. She'd always said she was happy that way. But now he was gone, and she'd have to make decisions unlike any that had ever fallen to her before. Would she stay in New York or return to Delaware? How would she raise her son? Could she manage a household on her own? Could she even get food and other necessities in a city occupied by an alien army? Would she be in any special danger because her father and brother were active enemies of that army?

Henry felt a terrible frustration. He wanted to go to his daughter, be with her, fill some of the void that Carter's death had left in her life. But circumstances prevented all of that. And so he worried.

Jonathan watched him, sensing the torment he was feeling. He hated being the bearer of bad news, but then he wondered how Henry would have reacted if he'd known the full story of Godfrey Carter's life and death. Celia's future troubled him, too. But he continued to hope that, in the long run, she'd be better off without Carter than with him. Then he remembered what Flint had asked him in New York: who had appointed him God?

Who had, indeed, he wondered as he watched his father grieve for his anguished child.

*Chapter 31*


*Philadelphia*
*New Jersey*
*May - June 1778*


      The usual men gathered for their regular morning meeting around the pine table in the front room of the gray stone house where Washington kept his headquarters at Valley Forge. The major generals sat closest to Washington, the brigadiers at the far end. Charles Lee, recently returned in an exchange of prisoners, sat on the left, closest to Washington, his sour disposition more acidic than ever after a year in British stockades. Lafayette, himself a major general now—the 'boy general" Lee called him dismissively—perched on Washington's right beside the large body of Baron Von Steuben. Hamilton and Jonathan sat against the wall near the window on the east side of the room.

      A few weeks earlier, Lafayette had burst into a similar meeting with the news of the signing of the treaty with France. He trembled with excitement and even tried to plant a kiss on the cheek of his mortified commander-in-chief, affording Jonathan and the others much amusement. It was a happy lot that morning, speculating madly about how the French navy might neutralize the British blockade, how the flow of French *livres* and French arms would provide them the resources their own Congress had failed so often to furnish, how the mere fact of French entry would undermine British morale.

      Only Hamilton declined to join in the celebration. As always, he saw a cold and cunning calculus behind the French entry. What, he asked Jonathan later, did the French care about the American cause? It simply did not make sense that the most corrupt, the most profligate of all the European kings would throw the weight of his empire behind a band of rebels intent on destroying the very notion of monarchical authority. No,

Hamilton said, the French were in this for themselves, trying to outflank the British in the global war in which the two empires had engaged off-and-on for decades and seeking to regain the foothold in America they'd lost in the French and Indian War in the 1750s. It was useful now to have them as allies, Hamilton agreed, but count the spoons after they came for dinner.

"We've known for nearly two weeks that Clinton is going to abandon Philadelphia…" It was Washington speaking now, trying to get his generals to agree on a plan of assault on the British army in Philadelphia. After the long winter at Valley Forge, he was impatient for something different. And opportunity seemed to be ripening. "The entry of the French makes it likely that they won't try to go as they came, by boats in Delaware Bay. Our spies tell us that, and they don't seem to have enough boats for a sea evacuation anyway. So if they're to march to New York, should we not prepare to attack them on the road?"

Washington's tone suggested that his mind was eighty percent made up to mount an attack, but he wanted to leave a little room for his generals to debate the options. It was a sound approach for a commander, Jonathan thought, one he'd seen Washington perfect over the past three years. It was among the many ways in which he was a better commander now than he'd been when Jonathan first joined him in Cambridge. He left no doubt who was in charge, nor that the man in charge had ideas of his own. But he also showed respect and occasional deference to the suggestions of his subordinates. When they left a meeting with a plan decided, nearly all felt that it was their plan, not something imposed arbitrarily upon them.

"No!" shouted Charles Lee, looking scornfully at Washington. "It would be suicidal to attack a British army on the march. American soldiers simply cannot stand up to seasoned British troops. In the open field we shall quickly become their captives."

Lee had no friends around the table. Some of the others, in fact, had lifted a toast at the news of his capture after the army's retreat from New York. But Lee had a reputation as a seasoned and knowledgeable soldier and his opinions, especially when expressed with such vigor, usually commanded their professional respect. No one said a word, as Washington paced across the end of the room.

After a moment, Lafayette spoke. "But they will never be more vulnerable than they are when they are stretched out in formation along

441

the narrow roads of New Jersey. If we can strike them from the rear or the flank, they cannot mass their force against us."

Washington nodded his assent, happy that Lafayette had broken the silence. Others began to join in the discussion, focusing on the details of attack plans. Then Lee made his strongest rejoinder. "This is foolhardy. We can't win this war by direct engagements. Their army is larger and stronger than ours. Their soldiers are better-trained and better-equipped. We should stay right here in Valley Forge. The longer the war goes on without engagements, the longer our army will remain unbeaten. Eventually they will come to believe they can't ever regain control of their old colonies and they'll be forced to withdraw. Let us wait them out."

Another long silence. Then Washington looked around the table and said simply, "What will it be then?"

The answer came quickly from the dark, handsome man at the very end of the table, the general who had emerged in the fighting around Philadelphia as one of Washington's most reliable officers, the one the soldiers had started to call "Mad Anthony" Wayne. "Fight, sir," he said. "We should take the fight to them."

Nathanael Greene quickly added his endorsement and so did John Cadwalader. Lee stood alone, glowering--his opinion unchanged but unpersuasive. The long winter of Valley Forge was about to end.

"It looks more like a Roman circus than a military column," the young major said to his regimental commander. "By the time they get all the loyalists lined up and all the supply wagons and all the carts bearing the luggage of the officers and their mistresses, the front end will arrive in New York about the time the back end is leaving Philadelphia."

Aubrey Armistead laughed. He liked his new second-in command, this Higginbottom. He was a real officer, like Armistead himself, not some gentleman who suffered the misfortune of having an older brother and losing out on the primogeniture. Higginbottom had joined the army at age seventeen and he'd seen plenty of action in the twelve years since then. Armistead had been lucky to pluck him away from the 16th, after losing Bramley to an awful fever before Christmas.

Higginbottom believed in drill. Armistead liked that too, and he watched with approval as the major had put the Third Battalion through their paces every day on the field north of Vine Street. For most of the army in Philadelphia that winter, the fighting edge had dulled. The soldiers and their officers played cards, they put on badly-acted plays, they filled the taverns with their drunken songs, they debauched the girls of Philadelphia. But they trained little. Except for the Third Batalion. And Armistead was proud that his command was an exception in this terrible wasted winter.

General Howe had asked to be relieved shortly after they seized the American capital in November. But he'd had to wait all winter for his answer and Henry Clinton was not appointed to replace him until May. And damned if Howe was going to lead his army into battle while he waited for rotation home. Leave that to his successor.

Some of the better officers were disgusted by this. Washington's army was encamped only 20 miles away. And though Washington was clever at planting disinformation, at making his forces seem larger and fiercer than they were, there was no hiding the sad state of the Continental Army at Valley Forge. We should have attacked them the way they attacked us at Trenton a year earlier, Armistead had heard some of the other colonels say. We'd have overrun them in an hour.

But Howe was going nowhere. He was waiting for replacement; and, the crudest of his officers hastened to add, he was too busy enjoying the charms of Mrs. Loring, the American mistress he'd brought from New York.

"Good thing we're not attempting this by ship," Higginbottom said. "The weight of all this would sink the tallest ship in the Royal Navy."

"If there is a French fleet in Delaware Bay," Armistead replied, "can you imagine their delight at the sight of British ships stuffed with seasick troops and all the paraphernalia of our ladies and loyalists?"

"Do you think, sir, that the French fleet is close by?" Higginbottom asked, turning serious.

"Hard to say, of course," Armistead thought aloud, looking off into the distance. "You never know where to find a fleet until you find it. They could be waiting for us at the mouth of the Delaware River or they could be sailing into New York waiting to greet us there. Or they might even have headed to Newport. We make a much easier target than we should. After all the time we've spent in these colonies, what can we say for ourselves...that we control Philadelphia, New York, and Newport and nothing else. It will be a simple task to find us, even for the French.

Armistead warmed to his subject, now that he had an interested and worthy audience. "This war is a damnation. How do you succeed in a campaign like this? We fight well when we engage. Often we rout them.

But we don't pursue. We let them go off and regroup. More troops come to replace the ones we've killed or wounded or scared off. All the lost opportunities. We could have pursued them after capturing the hills from them in Charlestown. We could have chased them across New Jersey after driving them from Manhattan. With proper reinforcements from the south, Gentleman Johnny might have taken them at Saratoga. We surely could have crippled them with an attack on Valley Forge. My God, we have messed this up.

"Now we've got Germain and North worried about the French. They'll be detaching some of our forces to the West Indies any day now, you mark my words. And I hear Germain thinks we should attack in the South where some of the states may be more loyal. We thought that about New Jersey, but they didn't stay very loyal, did they, after we came through and scavenged their crops and livestock?"

Higginbottom studied the face of Aubrey Armistead. He'd gotten to know this veteran Colonel well over the winter. When Armistead offered him the second-in-command, he'd asked around. "Fine soldier," other officers told him. "Takes care of his men." "Cool head in battle." "Takes no foolish risks."

In the months they'd shared quarters at the Halyard and Forecastle near the river, he'd come to know Armistead almost like a brother. The Colonel had no great passion for this fight. He didn't hate Americans. He didn't demonize Washington or any of the other generals. In fact, he often spoke with admiration of men trying to control their own destiny. He said once, in an unguarded moment, that in the Continental army you got to be a general by leading men effectively in battle; in the British army you got to be a general by being born the son of a gentleman. His preference was not in doubt.

Armistead wanted to win the war, Higginbottom had concluded, because that's the primary purpose of being a soldier: prepare the troops, plot the tactics, carry them out with courage and savagery, win the day. Let the politicians worry about causes and costs and alliances. Let the soldiers take their orders and obey them.

But this campaign was a frustration because the politicians were so far away, so blind to the realities of fighting a war across so vast a continent surrounded by so-called civilians who hated you and who all had muskets of their own. And this good army, this force of fine soldiers, was so often led by generals who cared more about their reputations in London society than their military objectives here. Real soldiers, he believed, could have won this war by now. Or they might have concluded it could never be won, and so counseled their ministers at home. If they'd been allowed.

"It looks like we're finally ready to move out," said Higginbottom. "It's hard to believe it's taken us almost three weeks to get ready. Wasn't it around June first, we were informed of the evacuation? Now it's June eighteenth."

"Yes, June eighteenth," Armistead agreed, removing his hat and wiping his brow with his handkerchief, "and bloody hot." More than the cold of winter, the soldiers of His Majesty's army hated the heat of the American summer. Their wool uniforms were reasonable protection from the cold, but they were personal prisons when the sun was bearing down and the humidity closed in. Add the heavy packs they all had to carry in an evacuation and the long distance to travel, and it was not a happy band of travelers that stretched out into the distance along the road leading north from Philadelphia.

As Armistead and Higginbottom cantered along at the front of the marching columns of the Third Battalion, the Major asked, "Do you think Washington will come at us while we're on the move?"

"I would if I were him," Armistead said after considering the possibility. "Isn't it a commander's dream to have his enemy stretched out along a narrow road where you can attack from the rear and roll him up, or attack from the flank and roll him in two directions? I'm sure he knows we're on the move. But we'll have to see what he does. There've been plenty of lost opportunities on their side as well. Washington is not rash, and he may think with the French coming in that it's best to hold back. Build up his army. Let the French fleet break the blockade, maybe even block our escape route from New York, then try to corner us again like he did in Boston.

"My best guess is that his army is still too weak to mount much of an attack, even when we're vulnerable like this. We should be able to get to New York while he waits for Frankie."

At the last minute, Washington told Jonathan and Flint to ride with Charles Lee. It was a sign of worry, Jonathan knew. His original battle plan had called for Lafayette to lead the advance force of two thousand against the British rear as their column crawled along the road to New York. But Lee protested hotly that he was the senior general and that he, not the "French boy," should lead that force. Washington distrusted

Lee, but he felt compelled to follow the etiquette of war and give command to the more senior general. Lee's disinclination to engage the enemy had been loudly expressed in their staff meetings, and Washington wanted Jonathan along to remind Lee, if necessary, of his orders.

On the sweltering morning of June twenty-eighth, they found the British Army stretched out for miles along the road near Monmouth Court House. Washington ordered Lee to attack the column from the rear, presumably its most vulnerable point. Jonathan had carried the order to Lee and watched in disgust as the thin general, still gaunt from his year as an enemy captive, read it, sniffled, then bent down to pet the black poodle that traveled everywhere with him. Lee said nothing.

After a few minutes, Jonathan walked over to him and said, "Begging your pardon, sir, would you like me to carry any orders forward to begin the attack?"

"There'll be no attack," Lee answered dismissively. "It's far too dangerous to attack British troops in the open field."

Jonathan was not accustomed to arguing with generals about their battle strategy, but Washington had instructed him to be sure that Lee followed the battle plan. "But, sir, I believe General Washington is counting on you to strike the British from the rear while he organizes a flanking movement. Failure to strike here could leave the rest of our forces in grave danger."

Lee patted his poodle one more time, then straightened and faced Jonathan. "Young man," he said, "I shall decide what is in the best interests of the men under my command." Then he appeared to suffer a moment of doubt or hesitation or second thoughts—Jonathan barely knew Lee and wasn't sure what he was seeing. "All right," he said. "Tell General Wayne to move forward with his Pennsylvanians and attack the column's rear. The rest of the men will stay with me. We'll move when we see how the British respond."

Pleased that Lee seemed ready now to do his duty, Jonathan walked to Flint who was standing in the shade about twenty yards away. He told Flint to ride to Wayne and pass on Lee's orders. "I'll stay with Lee," he said, "in case he needs further encouragement."

An hour later, as Lee sat by himself under the canopy of a tall elm tree seeking relief from the awful heat, a messenger came from Anthony Wayne. Jonathan sidled closer to hear the message. "General Wayne has engaged the redcoats, sir, and we've mowed through the formations they sent against us. But now they've brought up reinforcements and we've dug in along a swamp on the edge of town. General Wayne says it's time to dispatch our own reinforcements to drive them off."

Lee showed no emotion. "Thank you" was all he said.

"What should I tell General Wayne, sir?" the messenger asked.

"Tell him to hold his position. Now go."

The messenger looked perplexed, but when a general tells you to go, you go. And off he went.

Jonathan stepped forward again. "Will we be reinforcing General Wayne now?" he asked.

Lee looked at him impatiently. "General Wayne has dug in and should be able to defend himself. Washington wanted us to probe the British rear and we have now done that. We'll move up to stay with the column, but I see no reason to risk more of our troops in this foolish adventure."

"But, sir," Jonathan protested, "I believe General Washington intended that we would continue the assault to its conclusion, not merely conduct a probe."

Lee looked away. He removed his small, round hat and wiped the perspiration from his face. Then he replaced his hat and looked directly at Jonathan. "Be careful, young man," he said, "about making heroes of rash men." Then he turned and walked to his horse.

For the next half hour, Lee led his army slowly forward. Every half mile or so, he would dispatch a few units to take up defensive positions in the event of a British counter-attack. By the time they approached Monmouth, most of his forces had been depleted in this way. By then as well, they had begun to encounter soldiers from Wayne's command in full retreat. Jonathan stopped one of them and asked what was happening. "We had 'em on the run, sir, but we needed more help. They got themselves organized and more companies of grenadiers came up and then they had us outnumbered. Now they're punishin' us somethin' awful."

Jonathan rode over to Lee and relayed what he'd just heard. "Do you think we need to send reinforcements to Wayne now, sir?" Jonathan asked, knowing exactly what the answer should be.

"No!" said Lee without hesitation. "I shan't risk another life in this madness."

Now Jonathan didn't know what to do. Washington had told him to remind Lee of his orders. He had done that, but Lee had paid no attention. A colonel could not relieve a general of command. And he commanded no troops of his own to lead off to help Wayne in spite of Lee's orders. He thought he might ride to Washington, but he didn't know where Washington was. So he sat quietly on his horse trying to decide what to do, listening to the sounds of battle a short distance ahead where the British were decimating Anthony's Wayne's regiment. He decided he had to look for Washington and prayed that he would find him before a disaster occurred.

The retreating soldiers who'd come past them kept on running toward the rear. There they encountered the units that Lee had positioned along the road. When the commanders of those units heard from the soldiers in flight, they assumed that General Lee would want them to move forward to reinforce Wayne which they began to do, each small unit moving independent of the others. Before Long, the outskirts of Monmouth were filled with companies of Americans, marching in different directions, following no plan, under no orders, inviting the very disaster that Jonathan feared.

Washington was driving his own army forward, certain from the sounds he heard that Lee had engaged the enemy. So he was surprised when he saw Jonathan Houghton riding toward him at a gallop as he approached Monmouth.

"What is the news, Colonel?" he asked when Jonathan came to a stop at his side.

"General Lee has refused to advance on the enemy, sir. He sent Wayne and the Pennsylvanians to probe the rear. They were successful at the outset, but when Wayne called for reinforcements, Lee wouldn't send them. 'Too risky,' he said. Then when Wayne's men started to retreat, they ran past Lee and stirred up the units he'd posted along the road."

"What in the world did he do that for?" Washington asked angrily. "He's spread his army out for miles. If the British knew this, they could strike a killer blow anywhere."

"I know, sir, but he wouldn't listen to me. He doesn't think the British can be beaten by Americans and so he was making defensive preparations. But now the units he scattered are all off marching on their own, who knows where."

Washington clenched his jaw and cursed quietly. He rode back for a few minutes and consulted with his commanders. Then he gave the order for a forced march.

Soon Washington began to encounter Lee's lost units. He barked orders to their leaders and turned them around toward Monmouth. Then he began to send some of his own units around to flank the British column. All the time the army moved forward at a smart step. Shortly before noon, Washington came upon Charles Lee, standing alone by his horse in the shade. When Lee saw Washington, he mounted and rode over to his side. He saluted and started to speak, but Washington cut him off.

"My God, General Lee," he cried, "What are you about, man?"

"Protecting my force, General," Lee replied. "These men are not up to a fight with British grenadiers."

"You damned poltroon," Washington replied, "it is you who is not up to the fight. These men can fight with anyone, as I will show you."

"I will not risk their lives, sir," came Lee's brazen reply.

"You will not be making that decision, General. You are relieved, sir. I order you to the rear. Do not issue another command this day."

The soldiers in earshot, officers and men, listened in stunned silence. When Washington was done with his evisceration of Charles Lee, the only sound in the swelling heat was of British cannon a few hundred yards ahead. No one present had ever seen a military sight like this one, and none had ever heard Washington use such language in front of his troops. But he was angry in a way that Jonathan had never seen him. Angry that Lee's ineptitude had cost soldiers' lives unnecessarily, angry at Lee's duplicity and disregard for orders. But Jonathan knew that the fire in Washington's eyes had another source. The General was angry at himself for replacing Lafayette with Lee against all instinct. He would never put an army at risk that way again. If he still had an army to command after today.

The commotion and noise was exactly what Armistead had guessed it was. "They found us," he shouted to Higginbottom. "Now we're caught in the middle of this damn column with an American force at our rear and probably another coming at our flank somewhere."

Commanders hated the center of the column. It was not as vulnerable to attack as the rear, but at least in the rear you could maneuver. In the middle, there was no room to maneuver, especially on a narrow road like this one. And Armistead felt imprisoned by the long line of troops to his front and his rear and the rows of thick elms on his flanks. From the time the first shots were heard, it was nearly an hour before he was able to turn his men around and begin their march to reinforce the grenadiers under attack at the tail of the column.

Word had filtered forward that the Americans had struck a deft blow at first, but that the British column had begun to untangle itself and had taken the offensive. Now the American force was in defilade along a ravine near the court house, facing a punishing response from the grenadiers. In the time he had to think about it, Armistead was not surprised that Washington came at their rear. That was sound strategy. But leaving his strike force without reinforcements made no sense at all. Maybe it was a ploy, he thought. We'll turn this column around to defend ourselves, then another American force will strike us from the north. Then we'll have two rears, the worst possible situation for an army on the march. But why is he letting the pinned-down unit take such a beating?

As the Third Battalion came out of column and moved into position south of the court house, Armistead began to get his first glimpse of the battle. He could see the besieged unit across the road, trying desperately to hold its position, without cannon or numbers. Other Contienental companies were arrayed on the field, snappily executing their firing patterns and rotating at the orders of their commanders. Armistead was struck by the difference between this and every other similar scene he'd observed over the past three years. Most of the Americans were holding their ground, maneuvering sharply when necessary to stand up to a bayonet charge from the grenadiers. This was not like the Americans he'd seen before. They were brave men. Most of them could shoot straight. But they'd always lacked military discipline and precision. Now they seemed to know what they were doing.

"Look, sir," Higginbottom shouted, pointing toward the fields in the distance. Armistead extended his spyglass and focused it where Higginbottom had pointed. There he saw American units in rapid advance, following a tall man in blue and gold atop a large horse, his sword raised above his head and gleaming in the sun. The man was shouting at the troops and pointing his sword toward the battle in front of them. It was a brutally hot day, yet they were running at a brisk pace, closing quickly on the red-coated troops around the court house.

Armistead maneuvered his own battalion into formation, preparing to engage the rushing Americans. He assumed they'd would do what they often did in conditions like this: approach the field of fire, then lose discipline and spread out too widely or fail to get their ranks and files firing in sequence. That's when they were most susceptible to the proven tactics of British infantry: file forward, file fire, file step back, next file

450

forward, repeat, repeat, repeat. The battlefield was a raging hell; training and discipline were the keys to survival.

But to Armistead's surprise, the Americans did not follow their usual pattern. "Look at them," Higginbottom shouted over the roar. "They're forming up. And look how tight they are. If they were wearing red, I'd think I was staring at a looking glass."

As the Americans moved into their formations and began to fire, the man on the horse rode the line, shouting encouragement to his troops, driving them forward, oblivious to his own safety. Armistead wondered if it was Washington himself, but he'd never seen Washington and the images of the American General always suggested someone much older, stiffer and more stolid than this angry, animated warrior he saw before him.

Armistead's mind raced as he waited for the Americans to come within range of his own battalion. If this is the main force of the American army, he thought, they may have presented us with a splendid opportunity. This could be the general action that we've been hankering for. A victory here could overcome all the ill effects of Johnny Burgoyne's terrible embarrassment and hasten the conclusion of the war. If only Clinton will let us fight the way we should.

Through the afternoon, the two armies hammered at each other, back and forth, thrust and parry, steel against steel. It was the battle Armistead and the other professional soldiers had long sought. Give us the Americans in an open field, our best against their best, and we will take them down. None of their guerilla tactics, hit and run, shooting at us from behind trees and boulders. Let us have a real battle, face-on, formation against formation, then we'll show them what real soldiers know how to do.

But it didn't turn out as Armistead anticipated. The real battle occurred. The best the Americans could put in the field against the finest British regiments. The battle wore on through the long, terribly hot day. When finally it ended, the British army left the field and prepared to resume its march to New York. Not defeated. But not victorious either.

The Americans had stood their ground. It was a new army Armistead had seen that day. An army that knew the order of battle, that stayed in formation, that could use its bayonets with deadly skill. And it was an army led by a man possessed, riding the line through the heat and the hail of fire, inspiring his own men, and leaving a clear message in the minds of those who watched him from across the line: that whatever happened in the future, they could never again assume that the better army was the one in red.

In the morning, Washington gathered his generals to congratulate them. "Yesterday, gentlemen, you fought the fight of your lives." He looked at Baron Von Steuben and smiled. "There were two professional armies in the field yesterday and we showed that the terrible winter we endured at Valley Forge was not wasted. I'm proud of all of you. When our new country finally stands uncontested in its sovereignty, it will owe much to you and your brave men."

The generals looked exhausted and some still wore their stained battle uniforms. But they beamed at Washington's words. Jonathan spotted Anthony Wayne, whose men had held their ground even after General Lee abandoned them. When the brief meeting ended, Jonathan went to Wayne and congratulated him. Then he asked, "Where is Captain Flint, sir. He didn't return to our headquarters last night, nor have I seen him this morning."

Wayne looked at Jonathan and pursed his lips. "He fell, Colonel. He fought like the dickens through the afternoon. The hammer broke on his own weapon, but he picked up the long rifle of a dead soldier and fired round after round. When a bayonet charge came at us, he lined up a half dozen men to protect me. I saw him stick several redcoats himself. Then I fell back to reorganize my right flank and left him fielding another charge. I looked back after a minute or two to see how they were doing and I saw the red coats had pulled back, but Captain Flint was on the ground and his breeches were soaked in blood."

Jonathan sucked in his breath deeply and struggled to speak. "Did he…is he alive?" he asked.

"I don't know. My own officers reported the names of their casualties, but he wasn't part of our regiment, so his name would not have been on their lists. I never returned to that part of the field after the reinforcements arrived. I think most of the wounded were rounded up last night. Just the burial parties are out there today."

Jonathan quickly left the milling generals and ran to the make-shift corral. He found his horse, threw on a saddle, and galloped toward the ravine where Wayne's troops had been pinned down for several hours the day before.

There he found all the grim evidence of the horror of the previous day's battle. Rifles and swords and abandoned packs and canteens littered

452

the ground. Small details of silent men methodically collected the dead bodies, laid them on blood-soaked litters and carried them to the collection point where they were identified and then borne off to a nearby field for burial. The smell of burning powder lingered in the air. Flies buzzed everywhere. And Jonathan choked and coughed as he moved through the stench of bloated bodies and battlefield latrines and festering wounds.

He walked up and down the length of the ravine peering as carefully as he could bear at all the torn and bent bodies, looking for the bars of a captain and the face of a friend. But his search yielded nothing.

Jonathan asked the lieutenant who was supervising part of the burial detail where the wounded had been taken. The lieutenant pointed to a church behind the courthouse and said, "Some of 'ems gone there, sir, at least the ones that got a chance to survive. In the stable over yonder they got the ones that ain't gonna make it. Don't recommend you go there. It's an ugly sight. Men cryin' and screamin', no relief for their pain, watchin' the others die, knowin' they will too."

Jonathan turned toward the town and started to walk, holding the reins of his horse behind him. The church was closer, but a terrible dread consumed him and pointed him toward the stable. As he walked, he thought about the day on Cambridge Common when he'd met the laughing soldier from Boston and the day that soldier had slid down a Vermont hillside on the back of a Ticonderoga cannon and the night along the Delaware when a poor ferryman met his maker. And, without meaning to, he began to think of things he might say in the awful letter he would have to write to Savannah.

# Chapter 32

## *Still River, Delaware*
## *Philadelphia*
## *Summer 1778*

Savannah thought her uncle looked much older than when she'd last seen him nearly a year ago. The withering of his business under the British blockade had taken a toll, she was sure. But he seemed happy today, even though his principal reason for coming was to convey his sympathies about the death of his sister-in-law.

Edward had closed the shipyard and was making a small living now running a ferry between Bogan's Beach and the New Jersey shore. It wasn't much of a business, but he was a boatman and work was hard to find for boatmen in this war. He'd thought about joining the new American Navy, had even sent a letter to Esek Hopkins, its commander, but he'd gotten no reply. So he converted an old coastal schooner for the ferry trade.

After the expression of sympathies and Henry's now-familiar encomium to his late wife, the conversation turned to news that Edward was bursting to tell. "Two days ago, as I was making the return to the Delaware side, a light morning haze cleared from the bay and I saw the most magnificent sight. From one coast to the other, it was a long parade of two-and three-masted ships under full sail. I've seen large fleets in London and New York, of course, but never so many ships in one place at sea, all trimmed and sailing smartly. It made my heart race, Henry."

"British Navy?" Henry asked. Savannah thought she detected confusion in his voice.

"No. That's the best part," Edward smiled. "They were under French flag. They were heavily-gunned, ships of the line."

"The French fleet!" Henry exclaimed. "At last. You don't know how long we've waited for this."

"What will this mean, Father?" Savannah asked.

"It can only mean something good," Henry replied. The blockade will probably end because the British won't be able to string out their Navy. They'll be too vulnerable. The British army will lose some of its maneuverability because ships won't be able to move them around at will as they did when the army was deposited at the head of Delaware Bay last fall. And, best of all, Washington may now be able to trap the red coats in New York or on a peninsula somewhere while the French navy blocks their escape by sea. This is the most wonderful development."

"Do you think this'll force the King to reconsider, perhaps even to withdraw his army and quit the war?" Edward asked.

Henry rose and walked to the edge of the porch, looking to the north toward the river. "Wishful thinking, I'm afraid," he said, turning back toward his brother and daughter. "A rational leader might respond that way. But King George is not rational, at least not when it comes to America. And while we have information that Lord North is tiring of the war, George Germain seems more committed than ever to winning a victory here and restoring the colonies. If anything, we might expect that the French entry will renew some British enthusiasm for fighting. Now the campaign is not just to put down some impudent rebels three thousand miles away, but to stand up to an ancient enemy from across the channel.

"We should probably expect the British to declare war on the French now and to come to see America as a theater of that war, not a war unto itself. I suspect North and Germain will try to convince their colleagues at Westminster that they should pour more resources into the war to beat the French. There'll be a lot more enthusiasm for that than for beating the Americans. We still have many friends in Parliament who feel a kinship to us and would like to conclude the war here with a negotiated peace. You can be sure they feel no kinship with the French."

"But, wait," Savannah said. She paused, trying to make sense of her father's remarks. "Are you saying the war may go on longer now that the French have entered?"

"It's a hard truth, I'm afraid," Henry replied.

"Then why did we negotiate to get them in? Wouldn't it have been better to go it alone and get the war over sooner?"

"It's vexing, I know. But that's the character of foreign affairs. If we hadn't tried to get the French in on our side, they might have sided with the British. I know the two countries are rarely allies, but clever diplomats could have posed this as "kings against rebels" and convinced them they had to work together to put down our rebellion or people in colonies everywhere—English, French, Dutch, whatever—might be inspired to rise up against their kings. By negotiating an alliance with the French, we averted that possibility. But the French alliance is a mixed blessing.

"And frankly, we might not be able to win this war without the French. We still have a pitifully small navy. Save for Saratoga, our army has had few real successes. The Congress still refuses to tax properly or spend properly to support a large army in the field. The French bring ships and, I assume, they will soon bring infantry. But they also bring money— and that may be their most important contribution of all. In a short war, we probably could have gotten by with our slapdash financing schemes. But this is a short war no longer, and now the pressures on our treasury may have more impact on the outcome than anything that happens at sea or on the battlefield. And if it were left to the Congress alone to provide the resources our army needs, heaven help us."

"A toast," shouted Oliver Ellsworth, rising to his feet and lifting his mug. "To Congress, to Philadelphia, and, of course, to City Tavern. The men in the large main room, nearly all members of Congress, heartily agreed.

Henry entered the room just as the toast began. He found an empty chair near Nathaniel Scudder and ordered a mug of ale for himself.

"Henry, it's so good to have you back, sir. We have missed the leavening effect of your common sense," said Ellsworth. "I am so very sorry for your loss."

Henry took a long swallow of the ale, happy to be back in Philadelphia after the long ride from Delaware. "Thank you, Oliver," he said. "What have I missed?"

"Not a damn thing, Henry. Congress hasn't changed a particle since you left. Washington sends us letters asking for more men and supplies. We take a vote and the southern states support him wholeheartedly. The delegates from New England still think we should fight the war with militia and vote against his request. Then we squabble for weeks, finally working out a compromise. But since we have no power to tax anyone or to call up troops on our own, we send out requisitions to the states which they regard as something from a foreign government. So nothing happens. This is about the saddest government any nation ever created."

Henry nodded, recognizing the familiar pattern. "When I was home," he said, "I was surprised by how much dissatisfaction I detected. My neighbors are distraught because the war has lasted so long and the blockade is so oppressive. But the thing that most troubles them is the money. They all say that the Continental currency has become worthless. They can't get anything they can't barter for. No one wants to lend money because the paper loses value so fast that the payments don't equal what's been lent. And without the ability to borrow, farmers especially, have trouble buying seeds and supplies."

"I wouldn't say they're ready to give up on independence and go back to British rule, but it's not out of the question that our glorious revolution could fail because no one can afford it."

Joseph Reed sat back and looked around the room. "We've all heard the same things from our state legislatures, Henry. 'Do something about the damn money,' they say. But none of them wants us to have a taxing power and none of them wants to raise levies on their own citizens. Well, the arithmetic is pretty simple. If you want to spend money to fight a war, and you can't raise money from your citizens, then you have to print money. God knows, we've done that. But it's a scam, and no one is fooled. It may say fifty shillings on the note, but no one will sell you fifty shillings worth of goods in exchange for the note."

"So what do we do?" Henry asked.

"I'll tell you what I think and what some of the delegates are starting to say. We need to appoint someone to superintend the finances and give him real power. People are talking about Robert Morris as the best person to do this. He's a financial genius, and he's already bailed us out a few times with his own funds. He saved Washington's army before Trenton when he came up with enough currency to let the General bribe his troops to stay beyond the end of their enlistments.

"There's also talk that we need to do something much more effective about supplying the army. We've never had a strong quartermaster and even when there are supplies available, we often fail to get them to the army. This is one area where Washington deserves some of the criticism he's been getting. He's kept his army in the field, which has sometimes been a miracle, and people are saying that the battle at Monmouth was the best show of real soldiering they've done yet. But we're never going to win this thing until the men have warm clothes and good shoes, decent food, and good rifles. Washington has been a little slow to learn that there's more to winning wars than bravery in battle."

"In fairness, Mr. Reed," Henry said, "I think Washington learned those lessons in the French and Indian Wars. He just hasn't had the kind of support from us that he's needed. Surely you don't overlook the hundreds of letters he's sent us begging for the very supplies you just cited. It's too easy to blame Washington for our own failures."

Reed pondered briefly, then responded. "Perhaps you're right, Henry. The point is that we've got to start thinking of this as a long war, not a short one. It could go on for months yet, maybe years. The two armies march around the countryside for a few months in the warm weather, rarely engaging, then they go into hibernation for months on end. Sometimes it's a little hard to see how it's ever going to end."

A hand touched Henry's shoulder from the left and he looked up to see the prim, wigged figure of John Hancock. "Henry, my deepest sympathies on the loss of your wife. How are you bearing up?"

"Thank you, John," Henry replied. "The sadness endures, but one goes on. Please join us."

Hancock retrieved a chair and placed it between Henry and Ellsworth. "I suppose Oliver has filled you in on everything that's happened here since you left. That couldn't have taken very long." Hancock laughed. "At least we're back in Philadelphia. If we're going to accomplish nothing, we can do it so much more pleasantly here than in York."

"Philadelphia looks a lot more ragged than it did when I was here last," Henry said.

"Several of us toured the city extensively when we got back, Henry," said Ellsworth. "Most of it was unharmed by the occupation. They changed the names on things to try to recover its old royal flavor. But those have all been changed back now. What's most noticeable is the number of empty houses. A lot of loyalist families left when Clinton did. In fact, they joined his caravan to New York. Word is that they were afraid their patriot neighbors would harm them or burn their houses down after the British left, so they decided to leave with them.

"No one's quite sure what to do with the houses. They're still owned by the loyalists who left. Can't imagine they're ever going to return. But you can't just move into a house you don't own. Some of them are quite lovely. You remember that tale about your son 'borrowing' a coach from an old woman to rescue Washington from the mud out front at the end of the First Continental Congress?"

"How could I forget?" asked Henry, smiling at the memory.

"Well, the old woman who owned that house was a fierce loyalist. Hated independence. Hated us. She was one of the wealthiest widows in the city. But she high-tailed it with Clinton. Put her silver and other finery in that fancy coach and rode off with him to New York. Neighbors were happy to see her go. Now they got their servants living in that big house of hers."

Henry smiled, thinking how much fun it would be to tell Jonathan that story. Then he tried to return the conversation to more serious matters. "I must tell you," he said, "my brother spotted the French fleet off the Delaware coast two weeks ago."

"Really?" Hancock replied, his eyebrows arched in surprise. "We'd had some reports that the French were here, but nothing official. That's splendid news."

"We'll see," said Ellsworth sounding grumpy. "It's a sad state of affairs when we have to depend on the flighty Frenchmen to come to our rescue. I know all the arguments for getting them into the fight, but it remains to be seen whether they'll fight or whether this is just a show they're putting on, so they can stake some claims here when the war's over. You can be sure that to their boy King, this is a lot more about American gold and American furs and American land than it's about American ideals."

"What does it matter?" asked Hancock. "The important thing is that they're here. We now have a navy. If they stick to Franklin's treaty, we should soon have trained French soldiers and their money as well. Those things can't hurt, whatever their motives."

"I've heard that Washington has intelligence from London suggesting that Germain wants to move the war to the south. He apparently thinks that there'll be loyalist uprisings when British troops arrive," said Ellsworth.

"When you think about it," Henry added, "the south may be a better place for the British to fight. There are far fewer good roads in the south than in the north. So a land-based army like ours will find it harder to move and maneuver. The British can use their ships to move their troops around faster than we'll be able to find them."

'What do you think, Henry?" asked Hancock. "Will there be loyalist uprisings? Is sympathy for independence that thin in the south?"

Henry called for another ale and thought for a moment about the question. He leaned forward and looked at the two old friends sitting with him, veterans of the birthing ordeal of their new nation. "My honest answer is that the sympathy for independence is thin almost everywhere. We're not a people who've lived terrible lives because of our government. Most Americans lived pretty good lives before this war broke out. We had land and food and water. Plenty of all of those. We had governments that were usually reliable and didn't much interfere in our lives. What we lacked was the opportunity to chose the people who governed us and to guide their actions.

"But we weren't starving or poor, not most of us. And we didn't have an upper class that owned everything and a lower class that owned nothing, as in England and France. So this isn't a revolution of those who had nothing trying to get something. It's not a social revolution, not the peasants against the barons. Seems to me it's more complex than that. It's a political revolution. If we succeed, we'll change our form of government. We'll broaden some opportunities for men to have a say in how they're governed. But if we win the war, it won't much change people's lives. They'll be living in the same places, working in the same places, earning about what they did before."

"I don't follow your point, Henry," said Hancock.

"Well, my point is simple, John. If you're going to have a political revolution to make government better, you better make government better. You have to come up with something that delivers on the promise. We're sending our sons and brothers to die for this. But for what? For a piece of paper? For some beautiful words written by our friend from Virginia?

"No. We're sending them to fight and sometimes to die so that we're free to make our own government, a government we can trust, one that has our interests at heart. That's what worries me. Not just in the south, but everywhere. Does anyone feel very good about this government? Does anyone feel that what we're doing in Congress is really much better than being governed by the British Parliament?

"I don't think Americans have given up on us yet. But what I heard from my neighbors in Delaware also suggests that we haven't proven ourselves yet. If we don't begin to do that pretty soon—bring this war to a successful conclusion, get our finances straightened out, break the blockade and get commerce moving again—if we don't do that, then let's not be surprised if our countrymen shrug their shoulders and ask what the shooting was all about."

## Chapter 33

## *London*
## *February 1779*

Lydie heard the unmistakable sound of a carriage in the street, unusual this late at night. Benton heard it, too, and they both looked in the direction of the Square. Lydie rose from her chair by the fire and took a candle to the window. Most of the illumination from the gaslights was absorbed by the winter fog, but she could make out the shape of a horse and see the shadow of a cab behind it. Who would be stopping at this hour, she wondered.

The gate opened and through it walked a familiar figure carrying a large valise. Lydie's hand went quickly to her mouth to stifle the gasp. "Benton, it's Nathaniel," she said.

Benton rose gingerly and joined her at the door which they opened just as Nathaniel reached it, startling him. Lydie held back and let Benton make the initial greeting, even though she could see that Nathaniel's eyes were focused on her. "Nathaniel, welcome back. You have no idea how we've missed you."

"No more than I've missed the two of you, I'm sure," Nathaniel replied. "I've even missed these dreadful London fogs." They laughed together and stepped inside the door. Benton took Nathaniel's cloak and laid it across the banister and the three of them sat down by the fire where Benton poured glasses of brandy and offered a toast to Nathaniel's safe return.

"How are things in America?" Benton asked.

Nathaniel cast a darting glance at Lydie, paused for a moment to taste the brandy, then formed his answer. "I wasn't able to observe much," he said. "I was able to get a ship to Virginia and I took a coastal boat across to Maryland from there, then hitched a wagon ride home. So there wasn't much opportunity to see anything or to talk with anyone. I stayed on the farm the whole time I was home, then retraced my route to return.

"The war hasn't reached that part of America, not directly, so most things there looked pretty much as they did when I left years ago. Everyone seems hopeful about the outcome." Nathaniel hoped that Benton's questions would be few. He hated telling lies to this man he loved.

"And how is your family after your mother's death?"

Nathaniel looked down in sadness. "They're making do," he said. "But it's been a difficult time for everyone."

"I suppose you caught up with your brother and sister as well?" Benton asked.

Lydie could see Nathaniel's distress and intervened. "Benton, darling," she said, "there'll be plenty of time for questions later. Let's just enjoy having Nathaniel back with us."

"Yes," Nathaniel said, "and it is good to be back. You've probably done your best work ever in my absence, Benton."

"Quite the opposite, Nathaniel. You have no idea how much I've missed your help. It seems that my work slows to a crawl without you. I finished the portrait of Edmund Burke and completed another of Baroness Fifield, but there have been days when I've not painted at all. The stiffness in my legs seems to bother more than ever and especially now in this awful dampness and cold."

"Do we have commissions?" Nathaniel asked.

"Oh, Lord, yes," Benton answered. "There's no end to the commissions. General Howe is back in London, entertaining everyone with his tales of war in the wilderness. He's begging to be painted. And Lord Grenville, who's probably going to be the new Home Secretary, has given me a retainer. There are the usual earls and dukes as well. We'll have to sit down soon and make some plans."

"I can't wait," said Nathaniel. "I'm tired now. You know how a winter crossing can be, and the boat just arrived in Liverpool three days ago. So I think I'll take my tired bones to St. Cross Street and see you in the morning."

"That would be grand," beamed a very happy Benton Carlisle. "It's back to work now."

"I'll walk you to the door," Lydie said. "Benton, you stay by the fire and finish your brandy."

At the door, Lydie pulled Nathaniel out of Benton's line of sight and whispered, "Are you safe here?"

"I think so. Meet me at Red Lyon Square at nine tomorrow morning and I'll tell you all about it." He touched her hand tenderly and looked at the face he had tried so hard to imagine over the previous six months. "I've missed you so," he said softly.

"Oh, Nathaniel," Lydie kissed his cheek, then pushed him gently toward the door, fearing she would lose all restraint if he lingered a moment longer.

When Nathaniel was gone, Lydie returned to the chair at Benton's side. "Wasn't that a wonderful surprise?" she asked.

"Yes. Indeed. Things will be better now." Then he turned to Lydie, his face a puzzle, and asked, "Do you really think he went to America?"

For Benton, it was an unusual question. Or perhaps it was simply unusual that he'd asked it aloud. He'd long wondered about Nathaniel's life, or at least the part of it that took place when the two men were apart. Did Nathaniel have no love interests, no friends of his own, no passions beyond painting? About a year earlier, he'd begun to suspect that Nathaniel might be involved in some kind of political activity. There was no solid evidence of that, but a lot of little things that Benton noticed drew him ever more firmly toward that conclusion. It was, he supposed, none of his business what Nathaniel did on his own time. But his affection for Nathaniel made it hard for Benton to draw boundaries between legitimate and illegitimate concerns.

"What?" Lydie replied, trying to appear shocked. "What...what do you mean?"

"Oh, I don't know. You know that I love Nathaniel like a son. And I'm delighted to have him back. But he's something of a mystery to me. He's always maintained that he has no interest in politics—in fact, that he came to London to escape the turmoil of America and concentrate on his painting. But he's always encouraged me to take on commissions from political leaders and men in government. He pushes me as well to go to their parties and dinners. He always says it's good for my business, but Gainsborough and Romney rarely attend parties with politicians and they get as many commissions at Whitehall and Westminster as I do.

"And then when we're painting figures like that, Nathaniel often sits against the wall and appears to be sketching. But I looked once at his sketchbook and noticed very few images, but a lot of strange and indecipherable lettering along the edge. It was too patterned to be mere doodling, but I couldn't decipher it.

"I hadn't known what to make of all this, but when he left me that note saying he had to leave in haste for America because he'd gotten word of his mother's death, I thought it very peculiar that he didn't come to tell me that personally. Surely there was time for that. It made me wonder if he hadn't gone to America at all, but perhaps was engaged in something else that involved politics in some way."

"Oh, Benton," Lydie said, bending toward him to touch his arm, "I think you're imagining things. I'm sure Nathaniel has some interest in politics, in spite of himself. What American could not in these times? But I'm also sure he did go to America. Where else could he have spent half a year? Why would he not be here, doing the work he loves? Nathaniel is just what we've always known him to be: a simple, sweet, romantic artist. Don't you find it hard to imagine him as anything more than that?"

"Perhaps," Benton said. "But a painter often see things that are invisible to others. And, to my eye, Nathaniel's palette sometimes seems to have more colors than a casual glance might reveal."

Lydie told Benton she hadn't slept well and felt the need for some morning air. He nodded compliantly and said he would be in the studio, preparing for Nathaniel's arrival later in the day. Then Lydie slipped into the street and walked briskly along Orange Street to Red Lyon Square.

Nathaniel was already there when she arrived, the only person in the square at this hour on a February morning. When Lydie approached, he rose and embraced her eagerly. She felt small and delicate and slightly unfamiliar in his arms. Words were unnecessary and for a long moment, they simply held to each other as tightly as they could. Finally, Lydie pulled back and looked at his face. "I've been so worried about you," she said. "I was certain I would never see you again. When you appeared at the door last night, it was all I could do to suppress a cry and keep my arms from encircling you as tightly as they could."

Nathaniel led them to a bench where they sat facing each other. "After I resisted the attack in Bloomsbury Square, I knew I had to get out of sight as soon as possible. There was no way of knowing then whether the British agents knew my identity or whether one of them had been tipped to our meeting without knowing either of our identities. They told me a month ago that it was safe to return."

"Where did you go?" Lydie asked. "To America?"

"No, of course not. It would have been nearly impossible to get safe passage back had I gone there, and I couldn't be sure at that time what they knew about me. After I saw you in the studio, I took a circuitous route back to my room in St. Cross Street, making sure I wasn't being followed. I climbed to the third floor of the empty building across the street and watched for several hours to see that there was no sign that my room was being observed. Then I entered through the old servants' portal in the back and made my way to the room after dark that night. The indicator was undisturbed, so no one had entered the room."

"The indicator?"

"Yes, whenever I leave, I wedge a small brown stick on the top of the door near the hinge. Should it be opened when I'm gone, the wedge will fall out, but it's so small no one would notice. Whenever I return, I check to see if it's in place before I enter."

"Oh, Nathaniel, how do you live like this?" asked Lydie, gripping his arm.

"It's just being cautious. That's all. Anyway, I gathered a small bag of my things quickly and left the room. There is an inn in…well, there's no reason for me to tell you all the details. Some things it's best you don't know. But I stayed a night elsewhere in the city and I was contacted there, following the emergency procedure, by another man in the Alliance who secured passage for me on a coach going north.

"For the past six months, I've been living in a little village on the west coast of Scotland, near Mallaig. I had brought some paints and brushes with me, and it was easy enough to tell people in the village that I was a loyalist painter who'd left America and had come there to paint seascapes. In fact, I did paint a number of seascapes. In that way, the time was well spent.

"But Lydie, I missed you so ferociously that I came back as soon as I found that my identity had not been unmasked. I'm safe here now."

"And you're done with all this dangerous activity, right?" Lydie asked, a pleading sound in her voice.

Nathaniel made no response. He held her hand in his and looked toward the dry fountain in the center of the square. Slowly, the words came. "Lydie, I'm no hero. I don't even think I'm brave. All I've wanted to do since I finished at the College was be a good painter. I didn't volunteer for the secret work I've done here; I didn't seek it out. They came to me because I had something valuable to offer them: access to the people running the war on this side. It was just coincidence. And I had a powerful urge to say no when they asked me to help.

"But how could I? How could I just turn my back on things that mean so much to people I love? My father's left our farm and his family—the two things he cherishes above all others on this earth—for this cause, to help his neighbors enjoy a kind of freedom that the King has denied them. My brother's been in the Army since the days after Lexington and Concord. He's been wounded in battle.

"I'm not a leader like my father or a courageous soldier like my brother. But I know what they believe in, I know what inspires them. And in my own way, I believe in it, too. How could I say to those who asked my help here: 'I'm sorry, I've got more important things to do. I can't be bothered.' Of course, I couldn't do that."

He paused for a moment and watched for Lydie's reaction. She looked off into the distance, sadly, and said nothing.

"And there's something else. In the years I've been here, though I've been thousands of miles from America, I think I've come to see more clearly than I could have at home why people like my father and my brother are fighting for independence and a new kind of liberty. I'm not blind, Lydie. I see the dandies and the fops and the ladies of fashion living their lives of luxurious excess, lives to which they're entitled only by accidents of birth. Then I look close by and I see so many others who live in utter desperation with no chance, whatever their talents, whatever the strength of their character, of getting the tiniest piece of that good life. They freeze and they starve. They sleep in stables or on the streets. They stink and their clothes are nests for vermin. But no one cares for them. The government makes laws to confine them in their parishes, so the gentry don't even have to lay eyes on them."

Nathaniel paused and with his left hand turned Lydie's collar up for more warmth. "I thought perhaps it was only London…a city problem," he continued. "But in Scotland, it's just the same. The gentry own huge farms and glorious houses. Land they inherited from generations that go back for centuries. But most people own nothing and live from day to day on the meager rewards of their toil. Their bodies wear down and break. They get sick. They die young.

"America's not like that, Lydie. And it won't become like that if this war succeeds. It's a kind of statement—that Americans are going to make their own way, not follow the old ways that have dominated the world since the beginning of time. If my activities here help to accomplish that, even if only slightly, then I can't stop them now. Because nothing else I'll be able to do in my lifetime—not assist one of the great artists of

466

the age, not paint a beautiful seascape, not achieve some fame on my own—will mean more than that. Not to others. Not to my father or my family. And not to me."

This was the most Nathaniel had ever said about politics and Lydie found herself touched by his passion, despite her fears for his safety. She clung tightly to him, letting him know that she understood the fervor he felt, even if it haunted her and filled her with dread.

"I know how hard this must be for you to understand," Nathaniel continued. "I'm sorry—terribly sorry—for the worry it causes you. I wish I could say I regretted it. I wish I could say I would stop to relieve those worries. But I don't regret that I'm involved in this. And I can't stop, Lydie. Not now."

Each morning for four days, William Howe had posed beside one of the antique black cannons on the Artillery Ground off the Horse Ferry Road. It was a typical general's pose—a cliché, Benton called it—and another reason why he detested military portraits most of all. Get a soldier before a painter and he wants to be holding a sword aloft or sitting astride a reared-back horse or surrounding himself with feckless and faceless junior officers or placing his hand on a cannon.

Benton and Nathaniel had joked on their way back from one of these sittings what an amusement it would be to paint a general looking confused and indecisive or pleading with retreating soldiers in a defeat or caught under a horse that had been shot from beneath him. But there are no such pictures of generals, not portraits, because the subject pays the commission.

Howe was hoping now to fix the historical record. Most of the whispering in London was that he'd been indecisive in America and had squandered far too many opportunities. No one said that to him directly and he was received in London society as a hero of the American war, but in Whitehall and the wiser salons, a more critical view prevailed. Howe had heard some of the whispers and thought the best defense against them was to tell his own story. A handsome and commanding portrait couldn't hurt.

Howe's steady pose was interrupted in mid-morning by the arrival of a young major running across the lawn with news that couldn't wait until the end of the sitting. "General," the young officer said, "word has just arrived that we've taken the port of Savannah in a quick and decisive strike. Clinton landed with a few thousand men and overran the garrison with little resistance. Now he's moving into the countryside organizing the loyalists. The beginning of the southern campaign has been a splendid success."

The major handed Howe a dispatch with details of the engagement and Clinton's report, then saluted and left. Howe set the paper aside for later reading and resumed his position by the cannon, but Nathaniel could see the pleasure this message had brought him. If America were lost, there would be a search for scapegoats and Howe was sure to be one of those. They'd blame him for letting the chance of victory escape when the American army was still too primitive to win. The best way to prevent that kind of scapegoating was to win the war. So Howe was happy at the news of Savannah. There were a lot of loyalists in Georgia, he knew, and a good chance that the entire colony would return to the King once the Continental Army had been driven out.

But his pleasure was tempered by worry and probably, Nathaniel thought as he tried to assess the internal struggle being played out on the General's face, by jealousy. Howe wanted to win the war, but he didn't want others to get the credit. If the southern campaign succeeded, if the southern colonies broke off and stayed with the King, independence would probably fail. But it would take some important victories to accomplish that, and Clinton or Cornwallis would get the credit for turning the tide. Howe would be forgotten or, worse, castigated as the failure who had to be replaced. Both painters could see clearly the calculations spinning through William Howe's mind.

Another interruption occurred a few minutes later when another general, whom neither Benton nor Nathaniel recognized, waddled across the lawn and approached the three men by the cannon. "William, have you heard the news from America?" he called as soon as he was in earshot.

"I have, Hugh, just a moment ago. Our strategy of waiting for the right opportunity seems now to be paying off. We maneuvered Washington to distraction in the North; now we've struck a deft blow hundreds of miles from his army. This was a day I've long anticipated."

"How do you think the Americans will react?" the general asked Howe.

"Always hard to say with them. Rational response often eludes them. But I would expect that this will have a terrible effect on their morale. We already know that there's abundant fatigue with the length and cost of the war. We've seen more loyalists join our forces in the past few months even than in the early days. And the south is reported to have

468

strong loyalist sentiments. I should expect this victory will hasten their demise. Although the intervention of the French may offset that."

"Not just the French, William. We've been negotiating intensely with the Spaniards, trying to keep them out of the war. But it's not going well."

"Not going well?" asked Howe. "What possible cause does Spain have to make with America?"

"Oh, it's not about America, you know that. No more than the French intervention is about America. Everyone's trying to position themselves for advantage with us. The Spanish have guaranteed they'll not make a treaty with the Americans if we surrender Gibraltar to them. Ha! Gibraltar! The most important piece of real estate on earth. Do they really think we'd give up Gibraltar just to keep them out of the American war and to keep their ships out of the Channel? But they see this as a moment of vulnerability for us, and they're doing just what we would do in similar circumstances: trying to exploit their opportunities."

Howe leaned on the cannon as Benton ceased to paint and Nathaniel worked at his sketch pad. "I still don't understand why the Spanish would become allies of the Americans."

"Oh, I don't think they will, William. They have no taste for rebellion at all. Franklin sent his associate Arthur Lee to Spain to open negotiations a few months ago. They wouldn't even receive him. The effort went nowhere. The Spanish dislike this new American government intensely. No, the greater likelihood is that they'll make an alliance with the French against us. They won't recognize the government in Philadelphia, but they'll work with the French to tie our hands."

"How likely is this to happen?" asked Howe.

"The likelihood grows larger every day. Our efforts to negotiate with them have died on the issue of Gibraltar. It seems just a matter of weeks or months now before they ally with France."

"Then what?"

"Hard to say, but it wouldn't surprise me to see an armada in the channel under French and Spanish flag. We're very vulnerable with so much of our Navy on the other side of the ocean. And I'd expect to see them lay siege to Gibraltar. If they couldn't talk us out of it, they'll probably try now to shoot us or starve us out of it. This would not be a good time to be commanding the garrison on that rock."

Howe drew a deep breath. "It's beginning to sound like you think the outcome of the American war will be decided by the diplomats of Europe, not the armies in the field."

"I never thought otherwise, William. I never thought otherwise."

"Is George safe?" Nathaniel asked the corpulent figure standing beside him in the middle of Westminster Bridge.

"George?" He pondered the name for a minute. "Oh yes, George. I'd almost forgotten his code name. He won't be your contact any more. I will be for the time being. My code name is Arthur."

"Arthur. Fine," said Nathaniel studying the broad figure in the dim light. "Is George safe?"

The stout man, Arthur, seemed to dodge the question. "Like everything else in this endless war, the Alliance has had to evolve. We had a terrible scare when you were attacked. We knew there was a double agent in the Alliance working for the government, but we didn't know who it was. That's why you had to stay away for so long. We couldn't allow you back here until we were sure you'd be safe. It took a lot of checking and rechecking details. Who knew what about what and when? That sort of thing. But eventually we narrowed it down to two possibilities. And then we began to follow them both. Finally spotted one of them making a contact with a British agent. Then we knew who it was."

"What did you do to him?" Nathaniel asked.

"Nothing right away. In this business, you always have to consider whether it's better to eliminate a double agent or use him to your advantage with disinformation. Sometimes it's more valuable to give the double agent bad information which he dutifully reports to his British contacts and sends them on wild goose chases or casts doubt on the trustworthiness of one of their own good people. Once we know one of our own is also working for the other side, we can avoid using him for any critical assignment and can make him an unwitting courier of misleading information."

"Is that what you did with the man who uncovered me?"

"Well, first of all, he didn't uncover you. He knew that George had a good source, but he never found out the identity of the source. And we didn't use him for very long. We decided it was more important to make an example of him, a lesson for others."

"I don't understand."

"He's dead."

"Who was it?"

"You don't need to know that."

Nathaniel thought hard, trying to navigate the meaning of this conversation. "Was it George?" he asked.

Arthur said nothing for a moment, just looked out over the quiet river. Then he said in a voice barely audible, "No it wasn't George. George was captured the night you were attacked."

"He was? Is he safe?"

Arthur looked grim. "No. He's dead. Here's what happened that night, as we've pieced it together. A double agent for the government knew that George had a source who was providing very damaging information. But they didn't know who the source was because George never told anyone. That was the proper way to do things. No one should know anything they don't need to know.

"The people on the other side wanted to find out who the source was, so they could eliminate him. So they started to follow George, waiting for him to have a meeting with his source. Then after you met that night, they sent someone to get each of you. You escaped. George was caught. He had the paper you'd given him, but they couldn't break the code. So they tried to get him to reveal his source."

Arthur looked away now and paused. "They tortured him terribly, but he kept his secret. Then they killed him and left his body in the street as a warning to the rest of us of the dangers we face."

As Nathaniel tried to make sense of what he'd just learned, he grew first sad then perplexed. He'd acquired some affection for George and for his willingness, though an Englishman, to help the American cause at high risk to himself. He felt terrible that he'd been killed and that he'd suffered so to protect Nathaniel's identity. But he also wondered how all of this had been discerned.

"How do you know how George died and that he kept his secrets?" Nathaniel asked.

Arthur stood mute. "What have you got for me tonight, Charles?" he asked.

"Wait a minute," Nathaniel insisted, "I want to know how you can be certain that my identity was not revealed."

"You don't need to know," Arthur replied, obviously anxious to end this dialogue.

"I do need to know. My life nearly ended. If you want me to continue to take risks, I need to know where those risks lie. How do you know that my identity is a secret?"

Arthur thought for a moment, then said slowly, "We had a double agent of our own there when George was killed. He reported that George revealed nothing before he died."

"What?" shouted Nathaniel.

"One of our own men was in the group of government agents that questioned him."

"And tortured him and killed him, right?" Nathaniel added angrily.

"I'm afraid so. It's a hard business, Charles. Sometimes you have to do terrible things for a higher cause."

"Including standing by while one of your own comrades is tortured and murdered?"

Arthur didn't answer. "Now what have you got for us?" he asked again.

Nathaniel looked out over the river for a long moment, trying to grasp all of what he'd just learned. What was he doing here? Maybe this was all a terrible mistake. Was he in the middle of some game, played by people with a perverted sense of justice, taking risks that bordered on insanity? He didn't know what to think. All that he'd told Lydie a few days earlier about the importance of what he was doing, all the high-sounding self-justifications, was that all a delusion? Now he needed time to think, though he was far from certain that thinking would provide any escape from his mind's agony.

"Charles?" the large man again implored. "What do you have?"

Nathaniel frowned, then reached into the pocket of his waistcoat and removed a folded piece of paper. "Diplomatic information," was all he said, as he slapped the paper in the large man's hand. Then he turned, angry and disheartened, and slipped off into the quiet night.

## Chapter 34

## New York
## Autumn 1779

"We need more of those potatoes, Mrs. Carter. More potatoes. And bring another plate of the mutton as well."

Celia looked at the pots scattered across the floor of her kitchen. She found the one she sought and used a long wooden spoon to scoop the last few potatoes from it. But the heavy cast iron Dutch oven in which she'd boiled the mutton was now empty. They ate so much, she thought. And so fast.

"Here's all we have—a few more potatoes. You've finished the mutton," she said as she laid the small plate of soft potatoes on the once beautiful walnut table. How she'd loved that table when Godfrey acquired it from Liverpool. Everyone who came to her parties told her it was the handsomest table they'd ever seen, so long and clear and satiny. Now it was covered with smudges and scratches, some of them from boots dragged across it by soldiers during their drunken card games.

"Is this all, Mrs. Carter?" one of the officers shouted. "Why didn't you make more mutton, woman? Can't you do anything right?"

"You just can't hire good help these days, Captain. That's all," one of the others said and they all laughed heartily.

Celia hated these men. Some of them treated her with a modicum of respect when the others weren't around, especially the Colonel. He didn't live here, but he came around from time to time to talk about army business with them, sometimes to play cards. He was a decent sort and the others were much kinder to her when he was here.

But when the Colonel wasn't here she became just another wench in their eyes, the brunt of their crude jokes, the target of their rude language. The cruelest thing they did was to act as if she didn't exist, or at least as if she were not a human. They said things about her, knowing she could hear them, sometimes when she was in the room with them. They talked about other women, about the horrors of war, about their debaucheries in her presence. Men of their class would never have done such things with ladies present, but to them she was a much lower form of the species than a lady.

And what they'd done to her house was worse than a crime. This house had been so beautiful, one of the showplaces of Manhattan. Now, Celia thought, it was just another cheap boarding house. She could hardly bear to recall that awful morning a few weeks after Godfrey died in the accident when the Lieutenant came and told her he wanted to look over her house. She resisted, saying it was a private house and he had no right to enter. She cried. She pleaded. But he was immune to all her emotions. He pushed the door open and with pen and paper in hand walked through every room, drawing a small diagram and keeping a count.

"What is this for?" Celia had asked him.

"We'll need to use this house," he said. "Need it for soldiers. We're getting crowded everywhere."

"But why now?" Celia begged. "Why after all these months? Why haven't you used this house before."

The soldier gave her a disparaging look, almost a look of pity Celia thought, and said only "Things are different now."

"What do you mean?"

"Nothing more than that," the Lieutenant said curtly. "Things are different here now."

A few days later, four young officers had shown up at the door with all of their baggage. She asked what they wanted and one of them said simply, "To move in now." Celia's look of grief deterred them not at all and within a few minutes they'd taken possession of rooms on the third floor above where she and young Godfrey slept. The next day three more officers arrived and moved into the second floor rooms, relocating Celia and her son to the servants quarters at the back of the first floor. In the days that followed, the house was transformed into something between a barracks and a cheap men's club. Occasionally one of the officers would have the decency to ask Celia where they might store a piece of furniture they were moving out. But more often they went ahead and made their changes without any consultation at all.

On the third day after the first group arrived, a young soldier with a heavy Irish accent knocked on the door. When Celia answered, he asked

474

her where she wanted the food delivered. "I didn't order any food," she said in confusion.

"Tis from Supply," the soldier said. "Rations fer the off'cers."

Celia had him put the bags of vegetables, the side of ham, the barrels of flour and all the other food on the pantry floor. "Will someone be coming to cook for them?" she asked the young soldier.

"T'aint verr likely, ma'am," he replied with a faint smile. "Most prob'bly they'll be countin' on you fer that."

When the soldier left, Celia sat on the oak stool by the cooking fireplace and began to cry. She'd held back most of her tears through the first few days of the ordeal, but this was more than she could bear. Not only had seven British officers taken up residence in her house without her permission, not only had they rearranged everything and discarded some of her fine furniture and paintings, not only did she feel like a stranger in her own home—now they would expect her to cook their meals. She'd almost never cooked a meal in her life, certainly not since she left Delaware. Ladies did not cook.

That was months ago, and she had cooked many meals since then. Breakfast and supper every day. At first the food was so terrible and so often spoiled by her failures that one of the officers had gotten a man from the regiments who knew something about cooking to come and instruct her for a few days. Her repertoire of recipes was still pretty slender, but these were British soldiers and all they seemed to care for anyway was some meat and some potatoes or bread. The kind of meat and the manner of preparation didn't much matter to them. Neither, she learned, did the flavor.

Within a month of their arrival a total transformation had taken place. Celia was expected to cook the meals, to keep the house clean enough for their periodic inspections, and to tend to their uniforms and underclothes. The other women she knew in New York who were quartering troops all had husbands to help and many of them still had some of their servants. But when Godfrey died their income stopped and she could no longer afford Arthur and Sarah, who'd left the city a few weeks later. She pleaded with them to stay, promising there'd be plenty of money to pay them when Godfrey's estate was settled, but Arthur said one of his friends had overheard his employer say that Godfrey's estate would be tied up by creditors for a long time and so they'd decided to leave for Boston where everything seemed more stable now.

Celia didn't understand what it meant that Godfrey's estate was tied up by creditors. Her solicitor had said something like that, too. Business debts or something. So she had no income and no savings and no husband. Her house was occupied by enemy soldiers and she was forced to work as their cook and servant. She was like Sweetie now, she thought. She wasn't a slave, but she did the same work a slave did, and she had no more freedom. Soldiers ran New York and civilians did what the soldiers told them. If the soldiers said "don't be on the streets after dark," the civilians stayed in their houses after dark. If the soldiers said "we're sleeping in your bedroom," the civilians moved out of their bedrooms. If the soldiers said "we're taking your cow," you watched as they led the cow away.

No difference between this and being a slave, Celia thought. I can't even run away, at least not until the auction. When they auction off the warehouse, then I'll have some money again. It'll still be hard to go because I probably couldn't sell the house. No one's buying houses in Manhattan now. Too many of them abandoned. Too much uncertainty about the future. But when I have the money from the warehouse, then I can leave even if I have to just give up the house. It'll be worth it to escape from here, to get my son out of here. Manhattan is Hell. Anything would be better. Even returning to the farm in Delaware.

Celia caught the look of worry in John Walburton's face as he looked around the cavernous first floor of the warehouse. A table had been set up on a raised platform near the stairs and benches had been placed in several rows in front of it. But it was only five minutes until the scheduled time of the auction and there were only four men seated on the benches. Walburton knew this would be a hard sell even though it was a prime piece of commercial property. It was the largest warehouse in Manhattan and it was close to the piers. It would surely command a high price and sell quickly, under normal circumstances.

Under normal circumstances. Walburton could not imagine less normal circumstances. There was a war on. New York was occupied by the enemy. No loyalists would bid because they knew that the British might abandon New York at any time and loyalists would be hung if they stayed behind. No patriots were very likely to bid either because their currency was so worthless, and the British had closely guarded their sterling to keep it out of American hands. About the opposite of normal circumstances, Walburton thought, and he'd tried to warn Celia about that. That was his responsibility as the solicitor for Godfrey Carter's estate.

But then there were the things he couldn't tell her, whatever his professional responsibility might require. He couldn't bear to reveal the manner in which Godfrey had really died. Most people in Manhattan now knew that he'd been a principal supplier to the British Army, that he'd been brutally murdered by patriot spies, that he'd been found hanging in his own warehouse, soaked in his own blood, wearing a turncoat and a shredded Union Jack. There may have been men in Manhattan hungry enough for money to deal with the enemy, even after that, but none of them were stupid enough to buy this warehouse. To those in the know, it had become the terrifying symbol of the cost of consorting with the enemy. The vivid image of the dead Godfrey Carter was a masterpiece of deterrence.

No, Walburton thought, I can't tell her about any of that. I need to maintain the illusion that her husband died in an unfortunate shipping accident. Then there are the other things I can't tell her. About the gambling debts and all the cockfighters and card sharps who've come around to my office demanding that they be paid from his estate and covering my desk with IOU's bearing Carter's signature. And I can't tell her about the grotesque woman who runs the place called the "Yellow Palace" off Maiden Lane. About that dreadful afternoon when she came to see me and said Carter was her best customer and how in the months before his accident—she curled her lips in a kind of seething delight when she said that word—he'd run up a tab of over three hundred pounds and impregnated one of her "ladies." If the warehouse did sell, all of them would have to be paid off before any money went to Celia. It was the law. He would just have to say the money went for business debts. Celia probably wouldn't ask him to itemize; she didn't much get into the details of things.

A tall, thin man in a brown velvet suit stepped up on the platform and moved behind the table. He had a small gavel which he knocked gently on the table. The men on the front bench turned his way. Who were they, Walburton wondered. Were there yet men in Manhattan who didn't know the full, unfortunate story of this warehouse?

The auctioneer announced the opening of the bidding and looked forlornly at the men in front of them. None of them said a word. The auctioneer stared at them for a minute or two and finally said, "Come,

come gentlemen. This is the finest warehouse in Manhattan. What are your bids?"

The man on the right end of the bench said quietly, "Twenty-five pounds."

The auctioneer winced, but said, professionally, "The bidding starts at twenty-five pounds. I hear twenty-five,"

Celia watched closely, but none of this made any sense. She'd never been to the warehouse before and found it more than a little haunting. It was empty now, but in her mind she pictured a bustling place and everywhere she looked she could see Godfrey, ordering men about, wrestling heavy crates, signing bills, making deals. He seemed more present to her here than he ever had in their house after he died.

As she tried to cope with those images rushing through her mind, she followed the progress of the auction. She'd expected to see a much larger crowd and much more sprightly bidding. She had no idea what a warehouse like this was worth, but she was hopeful that it might bring a thousand pounds or more—enough to free her from imprisonment on Beekman Street, perhaps to get her and Godfrey out of Manhattan and on to a new life. But there were only a few men here and they were saying almost nothing.

"Thirty-five pounds," another bidder said quietly.

The auctioneer looked more exasperated now as he struggled to coax bids that were hundreds of pounds below where the bidding should have started. "Gentlemen, gentlemen," he said, "this is a magnificent place of commerce. Picture these floors piled to the ceiling with barrels, buyers scurrying in and out. Think of the business that could be conducted here. Think of the profit one could make. I hear thirty-five."

"Forty," the first bidder rejoined.

Bottom-feeders, Walburton thought to himself in disgust. They think the place is so contaminated by the legend of Godfrey Carter's death that they can buy it for a song, then just sit on it until the war's over. They're probably all here representing some businessman who wants the place but doesn't want to be identified with Carter. Warehouse rats, that's what they are, he thought to himself, proud of the pointed analogy.

All was silent now, as Celia watched in horror. "Forty pounds?" she whispered to Walburton. "Is that all?" He looked sadly supportive, but simply nodded his head in confirmation.

The auctioneer waited mute for a few more minutes, having exhausted his bid-drawing techniques. Finally he banged the table in anger

478

and said "Sold for forty pounds." Celia's hand flew to her mouth, as she gasped in horror. "Forty pounds?" she cried, turning to Walburton. "It's gone now for only forty pounds?" He nodded sadly.

Slowly the bidders and the auctioneer filed out. The man who'd bid forty pounds came to Walburton and handed him an envelope. Walburton asked him to come to his office the following morning to complete the transaction. Neither of them made eye contact with the other.

Celia looked slowly around the warehouse, taking in its heavy oak floors, the huge square doors facing Queen Street, the stout rafters and solid masonry. She thought she should feel some nostalgia for this place that had been the source of the good life she'd lived in New York. But that life seemed so distant now, so unreliable a memory, that she felt no warmth as she explored this building with her eyes for the first and last time. It was just a place, a pile of rock and wood, and it had no meaning to her at all, nothing good, nothing familiar. It was the way she'd come to feel about everything in Manhattan. The war had spoiled it all.

The Colonel came more often now. And—it seemed to Celia— with a different purpose. In the early days of the quartering, he'd drop buy to discuss some military preparation or training plan. Sometimes he'd stay for a few hands of pitch, their favorite card game, or some chess with Captain Petersham. Now it was different. Oh, he'd still talk about army things with whomever was there, and occasionally he'd have a go with Petersham at the chess board. But most of his visits now were spent playing with young Godfrey and talking with Celia.

She began to notice the change when she realized that his arrivals seemed to be timed to coincide with the evening hours when Godfrey was up and about. Once when Celia was ill, he took Godfrey on a long walk, with the boy riding on his broad shoulders.

Colonel Armistead wasn't like the others. He was respectful. He recognized and appreciated the fine things in her house—at least those that had survived the impact of the British officers who now lived there. He paid attention to her son, even seemed to have developed an affection for him. And when he was around, the other officers were quieter and much more polite.

But always he'd come in the evening and always when there were other soldiers in the house. The need to converse with them was always his explanation for his visits. So it seemed strange, but not at all in an unhappy way, one afternoon when Celia answered the knock at the door and found Aubrey Armistead standing there, holding a square wooden box.

She realized in that startled moment that she'd never seen him in daylight before. He was taller than most of the others and the cut of his uniform accentuated his slim waist and long legs. His hair was the color of acorns and the way it was pulled back and tied behind his head made his face seem trim and muscular. His mouth barely moved when he talked, but his green eyes flashed when they caught the light and punctuated his conversation. Though he was a slender man, there was a sense of muscularity to his bearing, a power he exuded that had affected her from the first time she met him.

"Colonel," she said. "This is such a surprise."

"I'm sorry, Mrs. Carter, I didn't mean to surprise you. I shall be happy to leave now if that's your pleasure."

"Oh no, no, Colonel. I meant it was a pleasant surprise to see you in the afternoon. Please do come in."

She hung his hat in the vestibule and they stepped into the parlor where Celia had lit a fire against the October chill. The days were much shorter now and the sun barely warmed the house, even by mid-day. "What brings you here, Colonel?" Celia asked after they'd taken seats in the only two chairs that survived from the room's days of elegance.

"Oh, nothing official. But I've brought you something," he said with the kind of shy smile that suggested he'd rehearsed this conversation many times. "I've felt so terrible for the agony we've imposed on you by quartering our officers here. I can only imagine how beautiful this house was when your husband was still alive and you were the heart of New York social life. I wanted you to know that I understand how difficult this has been. So I thought you might accept this small gift as a token of my...my...my understanding of your travail." He lifted the wooden box from his lap and pulled the cover from it. Inside was a dense packing of straw and wood shavings into which he reached and withdrew a beautiful hexagonal vase, tapered from top to bottom, each panel a different painted landscape of what she took to be the English countryside. He dusted off the residue of the packing and handed it to her.

"This is Champion porcelain," the Colonel said. "It's manufactured near where I was born and raised in Bristol. I'm sure I'm partial. Some of my ancestors used to work in the shops where it's made. It has very special meaning to me. I hope you will find it tolerable."

Celia sat silently, running her hand around the splendid vase. She had owned many beautiful porcelains in her time in New York, but nothing that gave her more pleasure than this. Perhaps it wasn't the most beautiful piece she'd ever possessed. But it shone so brightly in the drab decay into which her house had fallen. And the act of generosity it symbolized shone even more brightly across the terrible months she'd endured since Godfrey's death. "Tolerable?" she said. "Why, Colonel, it's magnificent. And your gift may be the kindest thing anyone has ever done for me. I'm so touched. And so grateful. Thank you."

Celia was unable to take her eyes from the vase which she turned slowly in her hands, without looking up. "Where is Bristol? I'm afraid my geography is terribly deficient."

"It's in the southwest of England," Aubrey answered, "on the shore across from Wales, not far from Bath. The countryside there is very precious, perhaps the most beautiful in all of England."

"It must be very hard for you to be in the Army and away from your home and family for so long," Celia said.

"I'm afraid that's a soldier's lot, Mrs. Carter. I've been in America now since early in 1775. Before that I spent many years in other posts in Europe. You're quite right. For a soldier in His Majesty's Army, home is a place you think about, dream about, but rarely visit."

"Then you don't see your family very often at all then?" Celia persisted.

Aubrey looked into the fire, watching the shadow of the flame dance along the blackened stone wall behind it. Without looking back to Celia, he answered, "I don't have much family now, Mrs. Carter. My mother died when I was very young while giving birth to one of my sisters. She died, too. My father was killed a few years later when he was helping a neighbor get a wagon from the mud and a horse kicked him in the head." He continued to stare into the fire throughout this painful recitation.

"You never married then?" Celia asked.

"No. I did marry. Just before I entered the army. A wonderful girl from a fine family in the Cotswolds. We had many dreams about the house we'd build and the large family we'd raise in it. I hadn't planned to be a soldier, but work was hard to find. I had a friend who could help me get a commission if I recruited enough men from Bristol to help him form a regiment. I didn't want to leave, but I didn't feel that I had much choice.

481

And I thought I would only stay in the army until I could afford to come home and earn a decent living there.

"Shortly after I joined, our regiment was sent to Bengal. I was gone for nearly two years. My son was born while I was gone. I never laid eyes on him until he was nearly two. When I saw him, it was the happiest day of my life. I was only home for a few months, but the three of us did everything together in that time." Aubrey turned to Celia now and looked at her with sad eyes. "The regiment was heading for Canada and I'd just been promoted. So I agreed to go for one more campaign, then I intended to resign and stay home for good.

"But while I was in Canada, a terrible fever swept over the south of England. Mary—that's my wife—and my son couldn't avoid it. It killed them both. I didn't even know there'd been a fever, until the letter came from my brother telling me that I'd lost them." Aubrey looked back to the fire and slowly rubbed his neck with his left hand. All was silent for a few moments.

"I'm so sorry," Celia said softly. "That must have been terrible for you."

Aubrey nodded. "But you've had your own experience with grief, so you know the feelings well, Mrs. Carter."

"Yes, I guess I do. But I can't imagine that anything quite compares with losing your only child. I don't know how anyone could bear a grief like that."

"Somehow people get by," Aubrey said. "It's not an easy world, Mrs. Carter. Few people escape it without pain."

He rose and put a log on the fire, then took the poker and stirred the coals. After retaking his seat, he asked. "What of your family? Are they all from New York?"

Celia tried to hide the panic that Aubrey's question evoked. This was not a mere conversation between friends, she was reminded. She was talking to an officer in the British army, an enemy of her father and brother. But she enjoyed this man's company and she was learning that he was not just a soldier, not just a man of a certain rank who wore the enemy's uniform. He was warm and caring; he had a history; he'd had dreams; he'd suffered. One of the horrible things about war, she thought, is that it seeks to simplify everything. You're for us or against us. You're a patriot or a loyalist. You're a soldier or a civilian.

But she was coming to realize that most people were too complex for the categories into which the war tried to squeeze them. Patriots often had some feelings of loyalty to the Crown. Loyalists often found much to admire in the ideals of the patriots. Civilians sometimes played as large a role in the war as soldiers. There were not just two positions on the question of independence, but many.

She looked at the Colonel. He was not much older than she. They'd both suffered a tragic loss. They'd come to enjoy each other's company. She was supposed to hate this man because he was the enemy. Soldiers of his army had taken over her house and abused her. But she could not hate him nor distrust him. Beneath the uniform and the epaulet of rank was another person, struggling with a difficult life, trying to find his way though an awful time. She knew she couldn't tell him the truth about her family, but she hated all of the rules that required her to lie.

"No," she said, "not from New York. My family has a farm in Delaware. They're all farmers. I met Godfrey when he was there doing some business. After we married, we moved to New York and we've been here ever since. Or I have…or whatever I'm supposed to say now that he's not here any more…." Her words stopped as she started to cry.

Aubrey wanted to comfort her in some way, to touch her shoulder or her hand, but thought any such effort might be deemed inappropriately intimate. So he said simply, "I'm sorry, Mrs. Carter. I shouldn't have probed. I know that it's still hard for you to cope with all the memories."

She took a handkerchief from the pocket in her skirt and tried to dry her eyes. Celia had always cried easily, but it felt wrong to be crying now and she forced herself to stop. She did not want the Colonel to think her a sobbing weakling.

"No, I'm the one who's sorry, Colonel," she said. "Your question was entirely proper, and I'm grateful for your interest. I'm afraid I haven't had many personal conversations lately and I'm out of practice." She gently blew her nose, then looked at him with dry eyes. "Unfortunately, my history is not very interesting. My family works the land. That's all."

"I envy them," he said wistfully, sitting back in his chair and nodding slowly. "What a blessing it would be if all of us could just work the land."

# Chapter 35

## New Jersey
## South Carolina
## New York
## May – September 1780

As the meeting droned slowly to its conclusion, Jonathan noticed that almost no one was paying much attention. That's the way it was in these staff meetings now. "Knitting parties" Hamilton had called them. He was perhaps the most exasperated of all. Hyperkinetic, impatient, aggressive, Hamilton was always looking for the next move, calculating possibilities, arranging things. Now the war was driving him crazy. Through all of 1779, not much had happened. A skirmish here and there, an occasional maneuver, but no general engagement with Clinton's forces. Most of Clinton's army sat in New York; most of what was left of the Continental army hid out in the Watchung mountains of New Jersey. They might as well have been three thousand miles apart as forty.

At a tavern one night a few weeks ago, Hamilton had entertained Jonathan and a few other officers with an imitation of Henry Clinton leading a staff meeting of British officers. It was a revealing moment. Everything in Hamilton's satire was exactly the same as what occurred every morning at Washington's staff meetings. Only the accents were different. The officers reported on the diseases their men were suffering in camp and how this undermined their effective strength. There was endless speculation about the capabilities and movements of the enemy. What were the French up to and would they ever really fight?  When would more troops arrive?

So it went day after day: talk, talk, talk. Hamilton, who had an intellectual streak and cared much more for history than the other officers, asked them once if there'd ever been a war in history in which so little fighting actually occurred. Jonathan didn't know the answer to that, but it was hard to imagine one. Days of rage and months of boredom. It used to be that the officers would ask each other when the war would end. More often now, they asked how it could end. It seemed to most of them that the two armies were using the same strategy: avoid the enemy; last one standing wins.

As Washington called for each of the generals to give his status report, a messenger entered and handed him a note. This caught nearly everyone's attention because it was a break from the monotonous routine. As Washington scanned the note, his brow furrowed and Jonathan saw the clenching of his jaw that always indicated trouble. Washington put the note on the table, looked up and interrupted the report from Anthony Wayne. "Gentlemen," he said, "I have a report of a mutiny in the ranks. We'll end this meeting now so that I can attend to it."

In an instant, Washington was out the door and calling for his horse. Hamilton and Jonathan followed close behind. They rode across the camp to the eastern edge where they could see a large crowd gathered and hear the shouting of the men. Minor mutinies and desertions had become a way of life in the garrisoned Continental Army. The pay was poor and the currency nearly worthless. Food and clothing were always scarce. Sickness rolled through the camps in wave after wave, claiming far more men than battle ever did. But most of all, morale was very low and there were few engagements with the enemy to sustain a fighting spirit among the men or their officers. There was simply nothing in the life of a Continental soldier to recommend it. Men got fed up and left.

But military discipline had to be maintained. So whenever men deserted, others were sent to track them down. Whenever a unit mutinied, they had to be faced down, turned around, and their leaders punished. Washington complained often about the amount of time he had to spend cajoling his troops into staying in camp. The days were long gone when he could play on their honor or devotion to the cause. Those had become terms of derision in the Continental camp. And financial incentives were not an option either, since Washington had no money to offer as bonuses to his troops, at least none that was worth anything. So the primary response to mutiny now was cajolery. If that failed, the only alternative was force.

As they approached the crowd ahead of them, Washington and his aides came upon a sight unlike any they'd ever seen. A company of Connecticut regulars was standing in formation in the middle of a circle of taunting and jeering troops from other states. Many of those around the circle had their muskets leveled at the Connecticut men who, Jonathan thought, were looking more than a little uncomfortable.

Washington approached a non-commissioned officer standing at the edge of the circle and asked, "What's going on here Sergeant?"

"Connecticut boys was headin' home, sir. But the others say they ain't got no right and threatened to gun 'em down if they left."

"Why are they leaving?" Washington demanded.

"Well, they say they got discharge papers and they're headin' home."

Washington nosed his horse through the circle toward the center. It was quieter now since his arrival, and many of the men had lowered their muskets. He stopped at the head of the column of Connecticut men. "Who's in charge here?" he asked.

"I am, sir," a captain answered.

"What are you about, Captain?"

"We're going home, sir. We've been discharged," the Captain answered, obviously uncomfortable at the spectacle of which he was now the center.

"I'm aware of no discharges," Washington said. He looked up at all the men lined up in front of him. "Let me see your discharge papers."

Most of the men laid their weapons on the ground and began searching through their packs for the sheets of gray paper which they then held in the air. Washington rode along the line and collected a few of them. He stopped and squinted at them in the morning sun. Then he turned to Hamilton, "Colonel, approach please."

Jonathan watched from the edge of the circle as Hamilton rode over slowly and ceremoniously, took the papers from Washington and scrutinized them closely. Hamilton was Washington's man for paperwork. Whenever something needed verification or recalculation or a felicitous turn of phrase, Hamilton got the call. After a moment, he handed the papers back to Washington with the single word, "Fake."

Washington rode back to the Captain at the head of the column and addressed him. "Captain, your men have forged discharge papers. I want you to turn them around and bring them back into camp."

"But, sir, they won't go. They've had it with life in this camp and they're intending to go home."

Jonathan could see the General's temper begin to engage. "Captain, we operate here under the rules of war. Men are required by

486

those rules to stay their enlistments. If they do not, then they are deserters. And in this army, we hang deserters."

The Captain stepped closer and lowered his voice so most could not hear. "But, sir, I can't make them go back. I can give the order, but they won't obey. They all voted to go home. To a man."

Washington nudged his horse backward, wanting all to hear what he was about to say. "Captain, your orders are to return to camp. If you choose not to carry out those orders, then I and my officers shall depart immediately and you can answer to your comrades."

A loud shout went up from the men in the circle as they heard what Washington said. Muskets rose again to firing position, and Washington pushed his horse back toward Jonathan at the outside of the circle. They started to ride away. Behind them the jeering and taunts rose to a crescendo, then suddenly they stopped when a frightened captain from Connecticut shouted the command, "About Face," and his equally frightened troops turned around and returned meekly to duty.

The next morning at dawn, the troops of the Continental Army were called into formation to observe the hanging of Martin Handleman, a local printer in whose pockets were stuffed dozens of forged discharge papers.

Jonathan could not get used to traveling alone. It wasn't just that it was less safe without Flint at his side. It was also a lot less fun. Washington had offered him another aide; indeed it almost seemed that the General had ordered him to take one. But Jonathan had declined, knowing how short the army was of men. He would make his way to South Carolina on his own, rather than travel with a stranger.

He and Flint had come to know each other so well that they were almost like one organism. They could communicate without talking. One would laugh before the other's joke was finished—although it was usually Jonathan laughing and Flint joking. They always knew that if one was in danger, the other would be there watching out for him. Jonathan never let on, for example, that he knew Flint had snuck into the warehouse in New York and was hiding there watching out for him the night he "solved the problem" of the American supplier. He'd ordered Flint to wait in the carriage house on Beekman Street, but he'd never really doubted where he would be. Some things you just didn't talk about.

When he'd found Flint in the church after the battle of Monmouth Court House, lying there barely conscious, his leg mangled, and his face so pale he'd thought the life had gone out of him, it was the lowest moment of his life. He'd realized then how much this rollicking, ferocious, intensely loyal, indefatigable patriot had come to mean to him. He could not hold back his tears when he saw how badly Flint was wounded.

In the days that followed, Jonathan had done nothing but supervise his care. He procured a wagon from a local gentleman, in much the same way as he'd requisitioned the carriage from the Philadelphia woman to rescue General Washington from the mud. Then he drove the wagon to Princeton where he'd learned of a reputable physician named Wigmore. The army doctors were overwhelmed after the battle and it might be days before they got to Flint. Jonathan wasn't waiting.

Dr. Wigmore cleaned up Flint's wound and found that his lower leg had been broken by grapeshot. But most of the muscles seemed to be functioning and he thought the leg could be saved, though it would be a long time healing because of the severity of the break. While the doctor engaged in the painful setting of bones and cutting of flesh, Flint bit down hard on a rag and Jonathan stood at his head and pushed with all of his weight and strength on his shoulders.

When the danger of infection had safely passed, Jonathan returned with the wagon and brought Flint back to Monmouth. But by then Washington had moved on and little remained there but the ugly detritus of battle and the somber townspeople trying to get on with lives that had been savaged by the war's brief visit to their community.

It made no sense to try to follow the army. Jonathan was sure that Flint's soldiering days were over, so he would be little more than a burden on the army's already overstressed medical capabilities. But Flint had no family and there was no easy way to get him to Boston even if he had. As they discussed what to do, Jonathan hit upon an idea which he conveyed to Flint. Why not go to Still River? There was plenty of room there. Sweetie could make you meals and tend to your other needs while you're bedridden. When the leg starts to improve, you can get up and around. And when it begins to heal, you can help out on the farm.

There are never too many men on a farm, Jonathan had joked, not even cripples. Flint hated the thought of leaving the army, especially of leaving Jonathan. But the notion of recuperating at Still River had a certain appeal. Flint worried that he would be a burden on Savannah and that she'd already spent too long nursing her mother. But Jonathan doubted she'd object, and when they arrived there two weeks later, driving up in the "borrowed" wagon, Savannah's horror at the severity of Flint's wound was mitigated by the prospect of having him around.

That was two years ago, and Jonathan had not seen Flint since. He'd had a few letters from Savannah saying that Flint was recovering, that he was walking again and riding and involved in all the work on the farm, but that he had a visible limp that would probably never disappear. Beneath the clinical reports in these letters, Jonathan detected a note of delight, and that pleased him.

But now he traveled alone, on a mission from General Washington to catch up with Benjamin Lincoln who was commanding the Continental Army in the South. The spy network in London had learned that Germain wanted Clinton to push the war into the South, and Washington needed a trustworthy observer to analyze the American defense and the state of support for the government in the southern states.

The last word that came to Washington before Jonathan was dispatched was that Clinton and the redcoats had arrived off South Carolina in February and had begun a siege of the garrison at Charleston. Jonathan was on his way there, when he stopped in late May to spend the night at the home of Richard Hutson. Hutson was a leading patriot in the state and had served two years in Congress. Washington had said he was "reliable."

The Hutson homestead was everything Jonathan had heard about these fine tidewater plantations. The massive wooden frame house with broad portico stood at the top of a small knoll facing east. Cottonwoods and willows surrounded it, providing much-needed shelter from the relentless heat. Fanning out in every direction were fields planted in tobacco and corn. Behind the house and down the knoll was a small community of slave families, parallel lines of small wooden huts surrounded by slightly larger buildings: smokehouse, tannery, forge, weaver, grist mill—all the necessary pieces for a self-contained society.

Over a fine dinner that evening, Hutson described to Jonathan what had been happening in South Carolina. "Lincoln seemed to misjudge everything at Charleston. The British got their ships in close enough so that their cannons could reach the fort. Then Clinton got enough men ashore that they surrounded the place. If Lincoln had followed his instincts, he probably would have withdrawn sooner. But he paid too much attention to our Lieutenant Governor, Gadsden, who didn't want him to abandon the city. Odd, isn't it? Southerners are always complaining that New Englanders don't pay any attention to us. We finally get one who does and it ends up in a giant defeat.

"Eventually the siege succeeded. Clinton cut off all the Continental lines of retreat and the nightly bombardment did them in. Lincoln surrendered on the twelfth of May. Fifty-five hundred good men are now British prisoners. The worst of it is that twenty-five hundred of them were crack Continentals. Some of them had even fought at Saratoga with Gates."

Jonathan listened in horror, wondering if he knew any of the men from Saratoga who now sat imprisoned in British ships. "What will this mean here in South Carolina? Is there still a will to fight?"

"Hard to say, Colonel. There's always been a lot of loyalists here, especially in the back country. They've been welcoming Clinton's men. But there's plenty of folks here, too, who don't want to live under British rule. The problem is that the fall of Charleston has thrown the whole state in turmoil. Governor Rutledge has fled the state, no one seems to know where. The legislature shut down. None of the courts is operating. The only government here now is what the British have set up. They've established a few garrisons inland from Charleston and there's some order in those places. If a band of thieves came here tonight and stole my slaves or ransacked my house, I wouldn't have any place to go for help. It's very close to anarchy here now. And it's not pretty, sir."

Jonathan leaned back in his chair and looked around the large ornate dining room where they sat. It was hard to envision anarchy in a place as sedate as this, but it reminded him how slender is the thread that holds a civilized society together, how quickly things can unravel. "What will happen now?" he asked.

"No one knows. There's a lot of fear among the patriots that North Carolina will fall. Clinton could sweep up along the inland roads. There's only a few of those and the army that controls those roads pretty much controls everything. But it's not clear he has enough troops here to do that and still hold his garrisons in South Carolina. Or he could bring more ships to the coast, maybe to Norfolk and sweep down into North Carolina that way. The political situation in North Carolina isn't very different from what we have here. Loyalists and patriots are pretty well divided. Without an army to rally around, the patriots won't be able to mount much of a fight against the British army."

Jonathan was impressed by the thoroughness of Hutson's analysis. He listened quietly as his host continued. "The militias here were never as

490

strong as the ones up north. Hard to have an effective militia with everyone so spread out. We've got a few brave men who've organized their own little armies—Colonel Sumter, Elijah Clarke, Francis Marion, the one they call the "swamp fox." None of them has more than a few hundred men, but they can attack the smaller British garrisons and troops on the march and make life miserable for the redcoats. But we can't get back control of the state with them alone. We need the Continental army here, Colonel, and we need it very soon. That's why we're all so happy to hear that Gates is on the way."

"Gates?" Jonathan asked, incredulous at the news. "Gates is coming here?"

"Yes. Congress has sent him to take over the southern department. He's gathering troops and should be here any time. Things will change when he arrives. We need a hero here and he's just the man after the beating he gave Burgoyne at Saratoga."

Jonathan's mind raced as he tried to make sense of what he'd just heard. He knew that some members of Congress were still in thrall of Horatio Gates even after the failure of his efforts with Conway to wrest control of the army away from Washington. But he was sure Washington hadn't been consulted about this appointment. The General distrusted Gates and had little respect for his military skills. He never would have approved. So Congress must have made this appointment without the acquiescence of the commander-in-chief. What a strange war this is, he thought.

"Perhaps the war will end here in South Carolina," Hutson continued. "If Gates can catch the British in a general engagement and defeat them, their southern strategy will look foolhardy. That might be all the incentive the government in London needs to withdraw from America and negotiate a peace."

He took a sip of his port. "Or, I'm afraid, it might go the other way. If Gates loses a general engagement, then the south will be lost. The British will drive into North Carolina and take control with little resistance. Georgia is already on the verge of becoming a colony again. The union jack will be flying from the Chesapeake to Florida. The United States of America won't amount to much then, I'm afraid. So it's all on Gates's shoulders now."

It took more than month for Jonathan to find Gates. He was bivouacked with an army of about three thousand near King's Mountain.

If Gates found any pleasure in Jonathan's arrival in his camp, he managed not to show it. To him, Jonathan was little more than a spy for Washington and, therefore, an irritant.

Jonathan got more information from Gates's officers than from the General, especially from Baron Johann de Kalb, a friend of Lafayette's who commanded twelve hundred seasoned Continental troops from Delaware and Maryland. Like Lafayette, de Kalb was a brave and brilliant commander. Jonathan was surprised to see these troops here. They could only have been dispatched by Washington. De Kalb explained that, while Washington distrusted Gates, he wanted him to succeed in the south and so gave him some of his best men.

The rest of Gates's army, Jonathan soon learned, was composed entirely of militia, mostly men from Virginia and North Carolina with little experience in battle. It was not, Jonathan quickly discerned, much of an army.

But Gates was undeterred by the inexperience of most of his forces or by the predominance of militia. Washington had learned from hard experience that militia are best used in reserve or as a complement to regular troops. They had nearly always been unreliable in battle, as any men would be who lacked proper training and the discipline that comes only from experienced officers.

But Gates had not absorbed that lesson and Jonathan watched in horror as he planned an assault on Cornwallis's main army at the little village of Camden a few miles away. Gates reviewed the order of battle and then asked his commanders for their comments. He asked in a way that suggested how pleased he'd be if there were none. Jonathan wanted to speak, wanted to rage against the foolish plan to put militia at the center of the battle, wanted to shout to all the fine men around the table that this plan was suicidal. But he said nothing. He had no official role there, no authority, no voice.

As soon as the staff meeting ended, Jonathan found de Kalb and said, "Baron, surely you must realize that this is a dreadful battle plan. Can't you speak to Gates. He'll listen to you."

De Kalb gave Jonathan a forlorn look of sad resignation. "I have spoken to him. He was not interested in what I thought. We are not ready for a battle like this, but he is determined to find Cornwallis and engage him. Risk be damned. It is a dangerous thing, Jonathan, when a general gets that look in his eyes, that look that says glory is about to be mine. That's when judgment is lost—and many men die."

492

"Can nothing be done to change his mind, to alter the plan?" Jonathan pleaded.

"Not with this man. Not now. He looks at the battle plan and sees not soldiers and cannon and a dangerous enemy. What he sees is destiny, his destiny, and it blinds him to everything else."

Lafayette and Houghton were both away from camp, so Hamilton alone traveled with Washington on his journey to Hartford. There they'd had a desultory meeting with the Count de Rochambeau who commanded the French forces in America. Hamilton would have preferred being anywhere else, for these were the unhappiest of times.

Washington's army had dwindled to a few thousand men. Continental currency was so worthless that it would not buy supplies for the army or induce men to stay when their enlistments ended. The French had promised to send ten thousand soldiers to America but only half that many had actually arrived. And even those seemed reluctant to engage the enemy. Washington had hoped he could convince de Rochambeau at Hartford to join him in a combined attack on New York, with the Continentals sweeping down from the north while French troops attacked by sea. But de Rochambeau had laughed it off, asking—not completely in jest—whether there was any life left at all in the American revolution.

Then Jonathan's report on the action in the south had arrived. It was typically concise and direct. Gates had led his army against Cornwallis on August 16th just outside Camden, South Carolina. The order of battle had called for the Virginian and North Carolina militias along the front with the Continental regulars holding the flanks. Cornwallis perceived his opportunity immediately, or perhaps a spy had given him the right cues, and he called for a bayonet charge on the American center. The militias had never seen anything like this, and within minutes men were throwing down their weapons and fleeing. Most never fired a shot. The regulars tried to close up ranks, but the British met so little opposition in the center that they were able to flank them. The Continentals fought heroically on, but they were overwhelmed and many were killed or wounded. Baron de Kalb was one of those who died, fighting to the last beside his men.

When Washington read Jonathan's report to the small group in his traveling party, his voice broke at the part about de Kalb. He hated the loss of any soldier, but he had a special fondness for the foreign officers who were such an important part of his army and who fought in this war not to protect their homes or their families, but because they believed so fervidly in American independence and all it symbolized.

Jonathan's report concluded with a paragraph that Hamilton, a man of no small self-esteem, thought was better than anything he could have written himself.

> *As the final shots were fired on the battleground outside Camden, General Gates was nowhere to be seen. He had made what one of his officers called a 'strategic retreat,' no doubt to save himself for some future battle after he has once again convinced his friends in Congress to give him an army for his personal pleasure. Reports a few days after the engagement at Camden indicated a sighting of the General in Charlotte, sixty miles beyond the range of the British guns.*

Washington had many reasons to be glum, and he was. Hamilton hoped their planned stop at West Point would give him some cheer. West Point was the location of one of the few important American successes of 1779 when Anthony Wayne's lightning charge saved the fort from Clinton's carefully planned assault. Now it stood on the heights overlooking the Hudson, a potent deterrent to any British ships that might attempt to venture upriver.

A few months earlier, Washington had placed Benedict Arnold in command of the garrison at West Point. It was an odd appointment, for Arnold was much too good an officer to be wasted on garrison command. He should have been leading one of the armies in the field. If he'd been in charge in South Carolina, Washington sincerely believed, a disaster would not have occurred there. He was a great commander of troops and, after Saratoga, one of the war's genuine heroes.

But Arnold was often hard to figure. After he recovered from his wounds at Saratoga, Washington placed him in charge of the military forces at Philadelphia. Arnold, however, seemed always to be bickering with members of Congress, and some of them had floated the story that he was using his command for some personal profiteering. And his marriage had raised some questions among members of Congress as well. The widowed Arnold had married a twenty-year-old Philadelphia girl named Peggy Shippen whose family included a number of well-known loyalists. When Philadelphia no longer seemed a good fit for Benedict Arnold, Washington offered him his choice of alternative posts. It came as a surprise when he chose West Point, instead of a field command, but

Washington went along. It would be good to visit West Point again and to spend some time with Benedict Arnold, a soldier whom Washington much admired, in no small part because of Jonathan's account of his extraordinary heroism at Saratoga.

But when they arrived the garrison was in a turmoil and Arnold was nowhere to be found. Washington moved into the commandant's quarters and ordered Hamilton to find someone who could tell him what was going on. Within the hour Hamilton returned with Major Benjamin Tallmadge, Washington's chief of intelligence, whose presence at West Point was utter coincidence. Washington was surprised but pleased to see him and wasted no time in peppering him with questions. "Where is General Arnold, Ben?"

"General, you're not going to believe what I've discovered. A few days ago, some militia were wandering along the river and they captured a prisoner. These militia men are a sorry lot, and it's not clear to me how they happened to take a man in civilian clothes prisoner. Maybe they intended to rob him and found something that made them think otherwise. What they found was a paper in his boot that appeared to be written by General Arnold. In it, he listed his demands for helping the British to capture West Point...."

Washington turned rigid at the words and interrupted Tallmadge, "What? Arnold was going to help the British capture West Point?"

"Yes. Exactly. The negotiation had apparently been going on for some time. The man the militia captured was in fact, John André. He's the adjutant general of the British army in North America and a person very close to Clinton..."

"The adjutant general!" Washington repeated loudly.

"Yes. He'd been negotiating with Arnold in Clinton's behalf. They finally offered Arnold more than six thousand pounds and a high rank in the British army. In exchange for that, he would give them a full accounting of the defenses of West Point, the duty schedules, and a list of its most serious vulnerabilities. André was making this last trip to conclude the negotiations when he was captured."

"How did you get all this information from André?" Washington asked.

Tallmadge pursed his lips. "We have our ways, General. Even British officers will sing if you play them the right tune."

Washington smiled slightly at the image that Tallmadge's answer conveyed. "Where is General Arnold now?" he asked.

"We don't know, but most of his important belongings are gone from his house, and so is his barge. We assume he is on his way downriver to get fitted for a new uniform in New York."

"Benedict Arnold!" Washington exclaimed aloud. He leaned back in his chair and fell into silence. Hamilton could only imagine what was going through his mind. More than two years without a major engagement with the enemy. His army shrinking almost to the vanishing point. The French turning into a fickle ally. No money. Americans everywhere restless and impatient. And now the defection of one of his best officers and a genuine hero. He'd never seen Washington look so sad, so done in.

After several minutes of silence, the General leaned forward and looked forlornly at Tallmadge and Hamilton. "Benedict Arnold," he muttered several times, shaking his head.

Hamilton and Tallmadge rose, saluted, and left. This is the way the gods test strong men, Hamilton thought, as he peered briefly back into the room at a strong man desperately searching for something, some shred of good news, to sustain his faith—but finding none.

# Chapter 36

## London
## Paris
## Winter – Spring, 1781

The King was remarkably ebullient for a man so battered. Perhaps that's why he wanted a portrait that showed him triumphantly sitting atop a large white stallion. Or at least that's what Benton had been guessing.

There's never such a thing as a commission with the royal family. A messenger arrives one day and says the King wants you to come paint the queen or one of the many princes and princesses. You make whatever arrangements are necessary and come. No one is ever too busy to paint the royal family. So it was in January that the gilt carriage pulled up in front of Carlisle's house in Bloomsbury Square and a messenger all in silk came to the door. Bartholomew, the houseman, placed the piece of folded and sealed paper on a silver tray and delivered it to Benton in the studio. Benton read it, then simply said "Yes" to the houseman who returned to the messenger and said "Mr. Carlisle will be at the castle as commanded."

Three days later, after the most frenetic preparations, Benton and Nathaniel were back in the same chamber in Windsor Castle where they'd painted Prince Frederick five years earlier. The King would not actually sit on a horse during the painting sessions, of course. He would straddle a velvet covered bench, elevated for the purpose so his shoulders sloped appropriately. The horse would be painted in later. But each morning for three days, the King appeared with his dressers who helped him into his military uniform, riding boots, sword, and the coat with the dozens of medals that all kings and princes seem to wear though few of them have ever been within the sound of a gun fired in anger.

Stories about the level of the King's anxiety and the condition of his mind were the staple now of all London soirees. Few men ever spent much time with the King, but those who did shared their observations as if they were the rarest specimens of some exotic species. Others would gather around and listen to detailed descriptions of how the King twitched or stammered, how he always avoided eye contact with conversation partners, how he'd switch topics in mid-sentence or rush out of a room for no reason at all. Nathaniel had heard one of the King's ministers describe a conversation he'd tried to have with the King during the Gordon riots in London the previous summer. Only the arrival of news of the successful siege of Charleston and Clinton's defeat of Gates seemed to quell the mass of Britons angry about the length and cost of the American war and the harm it was causing to British commerce.

Yet in the middle of all this, according to the minister, the King's principal concern was to get more musicians to the castle, to play for him and drown out the noise of the raging crowds in the streets. The British had a long history of eccentric monarchs, Benton told Nathaniel one night in the studio. They'd rather come to accept that, even to be entertained by it. But the talk now wasn't about eccentricity, but about debility. "He's gone mad," was the description Nathaniel heard most often of the King's mental state.

But even the most eccentric king was still the king, and if King George III wanted a portrait of himself looking like a triumphant military leader, he would have one. Nor was Benton unhappy that the King had chosen him to paint it. Nathaniel sensed more and more that Benton's days as a portraitist were nearing an end. Because he tended only to paint very prominent people now, most of his portraits were large. He had to stand to paint them, to reach the top of the canvas. His legs cramped often during the work and he tired easily. Nathaniel doubted he could—or would—do this much longer, and a portrait of a king seemed like the right note on which to close this part of Benton Carlisle's work as a painter.

The King was a peculiar subject, unlike any they'd painted in the years that Nathaniel had been Benton's assistant. He sat perfectly still for an hour or more at a time. Except for the talking. He talked constantly, to courtiers and messengers who came in and out, and to Benton. He never seemed to look at any of those with whom he spoke, but he had much to say to everyone.

On the last day of sittings, the King began to tell Benton the entire history of the war with America. Nathaniel listened intently, but there was little in the King's chatter of any intelligence value. It was the most contorted history one could imagine. The impudent Americans had done unspeakable things to the King's governors and soldiers. They constantly took the law into their own hands, dumping crates of fine imported tea,

498

attacking troops on routine patrol in Massachusetts, trying to set up their own governments when they already had a perfectly good government that had existed for nearly a thousand years.

The revolution, he said, practically spitting the word as he spoke it, was little more than a stage for self-promoters, for men like that "buffoon Franklin" and the cousins he called "those hothead Adams brothers" from Boston, to seek an audience for their crackpot opinions. And then he went on about the failures of his own generals to crush the rebellion years ago, how he wished he could go to America himself and lead his troops against the blackguards just as Richard I had done in the Crusades and Henry V had done at Agincourt.

"But now, we're about to put an end to this," he said with a satisfied smile. "I've finally got some generals who can fight. Cornwallis has the rebels on the run in the Carolinas. Now I'm sending him to Virginia to finish them off. And then I'll bring Clinton down from New York to help chase them out of those colonies completely. They'll have no choice but to surrender then."

Nathaniel was jolted by the words. In his cryptic code, he quickly scribbled "Virginia" and "Clinton reinforce" on the margin of his sketch pad. Then he listened in wonder as the King, utterly lucid now, repeated the details of a military strategy that must have been thoroughly discussed in his presence. Nathaniel assumed that the King's enthusiasm and confidence about these plans indicated clearly that decisions had been taken and orders sent. As the King prattled on in the background, Nathaniel was consumed with the implications of what he'd heard. He needed to dispatch this information to a contact as quickly as he could to get it to America.

But he thought as well about the military implication of a British invasion of Virginia. The Virginia peninsula was a superior starting point for an attack on the heart of America so long as the invaders controlled the sea. They could reinforce themselves without encountering resistance in their rear, and if things went badly, they could evacuate by ship and minimize their losses. The British must not be allowed to do that, Nathaniel thought, or the war could end right there. This information has to get to Franklin in France, so he can get the French admiralty to move their fleet to engage the British Navy and deny them freedom of movement in the waters off Virginia.

For the rest of the morning, while Benton painted and the King fantasized about the great victory he was about to achieve in America,

Nathaniel's mind raced. By the time he and Benton entered the carriage that afternoon for the ride back to London, he had decided how to proceed.

"Do you think he knows, Lydie?" Nathaniel asked as they sat, hand in hand, on a small grassy slope on the Ile de la Cité.

"I don't know for sure. He's never said anything to me. But I suspect he's known for some time. Benton is a man of great prudence about most things. It's very possible that he knows, but also realizes there is nothing to be gained by indicating that he knows or by discussing it with you in any way."

"It does seem peculiar. Sometimes, when I have to cook up a story, as I did in getting us here, or when I've encouraged him to go to a dinner party where some of the ministers would be, or to accept a commission for yet another politician, I've had the feeling that he was going along because he understood that I had some ulterior purpose."

"What do you mean?" Lydie asked, turning and nestling her head against Nathaniel's arm, watching the river, high now with the spring rains, rush toward the sea.

"Well, for example, when we were riding back from Windsor Castle, I told him that Beaumarchais had written to me and offered the use of one of his Paris homes for a month if I wanted to come and paint here in the spring. I told him I'd like to do it now, that I felt I really needed to concentrate on my own work for a while. It will probably mean that he'll have to complete the portrait of the King by himself with me gone, a big job. But he didn't object at all. When I told him, a look came over his face that seemed to indicate he understood that painting wasn't my real reason for coming. It seemed we were engaged in some kind of word game where things don't really mean what we say.

"Then, out of the blue, he said 'Why not take Lydie with you, since you speak so little French.' Then I had the feeling, not only that he knew, but that he believed in what I was doing and wanted to help."

"I think that's probably right," Lydie said. "He never talks much about politics or the rebellion. I think in his family, his brother was the political one and he was the artistic one. So he was never expected to express, or even to have, any opinions about politics. But he does, of course. And we know he is no lover of the monarchy and that he has great admiration for Americans. He has some of those same feelings about things in France. After you visited Versailles, he told me that he had a

500

better understanding of why he'd heard so much talk about revolution in the streets of Paris."

Lydie sat up and looked directly at Nathaniel. She was thinking hard now, trying to piece tidbits of observations into an explanation of Benton's behavior. "He thinks like an old man now, Nathaniel. He's nearing the end of his life and, like most old men, he's haunted by the things he didn't do, the contributions he never made. He talks about his brother and what he sacrificed for his beliefs—how that gave his life so much meaning. And when he does, I can see in his eyes that he wishes he'd done something so courageous, so honest himself.

"And when he thinks of the struggle in America, he may know there's no role for him in helping it along, but he's proud of you. He may not know exactly what you've been doing, but he's no fool. He probably has it pretty well pieced together. And so he's taken on those political commissions and gone to the stuffy dinner parties and helped you make this trip, feeling perhaps that it makes him part of what you're doing. Maybe he even feels like an accomplice. I know he'd love that feeling."

Nathaniel laid back, letting the sun soak his face. Lydie was right, he was sure. When he and Benton had arrived in Bloomsbury Square after returning from Windsor Castle, Nathaniel had dashed to the studio and alone there had worked out the coded message for the courier to take to the boat for America. Benton had walked in while he was working on it, but said nothing to him and did not interrupt. Of course, he knew. Then when Nathaniel used the emergency procedure and took the message directly to the pub in Fleet Street and delivered it to the dark-tressed barmaid there, Benton did not ask where he was going.

Normally, Nathaniel kept his activities for the Alliance entirely separate and distant from the studio to preserve the safety of Benton and Lydie, but also to avoid tempting Benton's suspicions. But there'd been no time then for those precautions. He was glad Benton had asked no questions. As he replayed the events in his mind, he realized they were of a piece with all of Benton's tolerance of his efforts to use their portrait work as an entreé to the high offices and homes of London decision-makers. Surely Benton knew. He must know.

The wind freshened in the early hours of the afternoon and Lydie felt chilled. So she and Nathaniel walked back along the Boulevard St. Germain to the elegant town house Beaumarchais had lent them. They had been in Paris for two weeks now and, except for the few meetings Nathaniel had had with the American delegation on the Rue de Passy,

501

they'd spent all their time together bathing in the pleasures of a Paris spring. Nathaniel had painted a few hours each day, but Lydie was always at his side when he did. They'd never had more time alone together. They'd never felt so close.

When they arrived at the house, Nathaniel proposed that he set up his easel in the garden behind the house and Lydie have tea there while he worked on a painting of yellow jonquils he'd begun two days earlier. But Lydie said she thought she would nap for a while, and she retired to her room on the second floor. She would join him later.

Nathaniel became worried when Lydie hadn't appeared by late afternoon. He put his paints away and called one of the servants to carry the canvas and the easel to the small room off the library that he was using as a studio. Then he climbed the sweeping circular stairs to the second floor and knocked on Lydie's door. "Lydie," he whispered, "are you ill?" He waited a moment, but heard nothing. He knocked again, more firmly this time, and called "Lydie, are you all right." No response.

Nathaniel turned the gilt handle and slowly pushed the door open. The curtains were drawn and the room was dark except for a plane of light that slanted in where the curtains had not quite come together in the center of the window. Nathaniel had not been in Lydie's room before now and he was not sure where the furniture was located. So he paused for a moment to adjust to the dim light. Then he spotted the large canopied bed perpendicular to the wall at his left and moved toward it. Lydie was lying there, motionless, with a blanket pulled over her head. Nathaniel walked moved carefully toward the bed and sat on the edge of it. He lightly tapped what appeared to be Lydie's shoulder. There was a slight response, then some uncertain pulling and tugging as she extricated herself from the blanket.

Suddenly an arm reached behind Nathaniel's neck and pulled him down toward the bed. Lydie's smiling face emerged from the blanket and she covered his face with small kisses. The smell of her overcame him at that moment and he slowly moved his finger along the edge of her eyes, then along her cheek bone and down to her lips. He traced the edges of her mouth, slowly, enjoying every impulse of sensation. He could feel her back arch as he explored the contours of her beautiful face.

Lydie placed her hand above his and directed it along her neck and along the line of her shoulders. Small involuntary sounds, like the song of a distant nightingale, emerged from her as he explored the soft line of her shoulders. She guided his hand under the blanket and then beneath the bodice of her nightgown. He could feel her body develop a slow deep rhythm as he moved his fingers along the tops of her breasts, then lightly around her nipples. As he probed deeper into unexplored territory, she seemed to drift out of consciousness, as if transported to some place beyond explanation.

With her other hand, Lydie slid the blanket down and away, then pulled Nathaniel down beside her. She touched his lips lightly with her tongue, then pulled him hard against her and kissed him more deeply than ever before. These were places where they'd sworn they'd never go. But when they approached, they had no power to stop the momentum of their bodies, to deny the full force of the love that had built so slowly and yet so steadily for years. It had taken so very long to arrive at this place, but none of their imagining, none of their longing had prepared them for the power of the explosion when it happened.

Soon they were deeply entwined in each other, not two rational beings trying to control a passion that filled them both with guilt, but a pair of lovers consumed by a glorious intensity that even the deepest guilt could not deter. Through the rest of the afternoon and into the evening and all through the night, they explored and thrilled and devoured each other. And when morning came and the tide of guilt rose with it, they had much to feel guilty about.

Nathaniel and Lydie were the two people Benton loved most in the world, so it surprised him that he was feeling so good in their absence. The King's portrait was finished and delivered and effusively praised. Now he could enjoy the simple pleasure of being alone, of having time and freedom to sleep late in the morning and paint by the river in the afternoon. No pressure to work on portraits, nor to make conversation, not even to dress well. Solitude has it splendors, and Benton was enjoying them immensely.

This had been a particularly lovely day, as good as London gets in the early spring with steady sun and light wind. Benton was working on a small painting of the roof tops around St. Paul's and he hoped to finish before the sun fell too low. He didn't quite make it, but there was no pressure. On the way home in a sedan chair, he thought about tomorrow, then realized that he could do tomorrow exactly as he pleased.

At the curb in Bloomsbury Square, he gave the boys carrying the chair a farthing each and asked them to carry his easel and paints around to the studio. As he was about to step through the gate, two men wearing wide-brimmed wool hats converged on him from opposite directions. Benton was startled by their sudden appearance and when they asked if he was Benton Carlisle, he could only murmur a soft "Yes."

"Then you'll have to come with us," one of them said.

"Why? Who are you?" Benton queried, regaining his composure.

"Official business, sir" was all the taller man said as both of them looped their arms through his and started to lead him along the sidewalk to a wagon waiting at the corner. Benton protested, but lacked the physical strength to resist these two large men. "What is this? I haven't done anything. I'm just a painter, for God's sake."

The men said nothing. The wagon had a windowless cab behind the seat and they placed Benton inside. One of them entered with him and shut the door. The other ascended to the seat, took the reins and urged the horses to a slow canter.

In the dark of the cab, Benton could see nothing, but could sense the heavy breathing of the man who sat to his left. "What are you doing?" he asked the man several times. But he got no answer.

After a ride that Benton judged to last about 20 minutes, the wagon stopped and Benton heard what must have been a large door creak open. Then the wagon resumed its movement and drove through. The door creaked again, probably closing behind us, Benton thought.

He could hear muffled voices a short distance away, but couldn't make out what they were saying. The man sitting next to him neither moved nor spoke. Benton thought he might have fallen asleep. The possibility of escape suddenly crossed Benton's mind, but he couldn't imagine how someone of his age on legs that could barely climb stairs would ever escape men who were much younger and stronger than he. His mind searched for an explanation of this terrifying experience but none came to him. Then the handle turned and the door to the cab opened.

When his eyes adjusted to the light, Benton could see that they were inside a large carriage house of some kind. Five men stood watching as he was led from the wagon to a stool by the only lantern in the place. It was hard to see their faces and he recognized none of them. As they forced him down on the stool he noticed a sentry by the large doors through which they'd entered. Unlike the others, the sentry was dressed in the uniform of a royal dragoon, a soldier. Now Benton was truly perplexed.

The men left him sitting there for a few minutes while they whispered among themselves. Finally one of them stepped forward and said, "You are Benton Carlisle, the artist...is that correct?"

Benton looked warily at the man and then at the others standing behind him, watching. "Yes, I am. Why am I here?"

"And you did paint a portrait of the King of England in February of this year, is that correct?"

Where was this leading, Benton wondered. Are these some of those radicals who want to get rid of the monarchy? But why would they go after someone who merely painted a picture of the King?

"Carlisle?" the man shouted.

"Yes. I painted a portrait of the King."

"And while you were painting this portrait did you have occasion to overhear conversations the King had with others?"

"Yes, I suppose so. I was at Windsor for several days and in sittings for hours each day. People came and went. The King talked with them. It's always like that when painting portraits of busy men."

"Did the King talk with you when no one else was present?"

Benton thought about the question, trying to determine what these men were after. He'd never been with the King alone; Nathaniel was always there. But no need to bring Nathaniel into this. "Yes, I suppose so. Once in a while. The King is quite garrulous."

"And did the King ever discuss with you or in your presence anything that had to do with military matters in America?"

Now Benton began to see where this was going, and a shiver of terror spiked through him. It was about spying. They thought he was passing on information he'd gotten from the King during their sittings. Then he experienced a moment of relief when he realized he'd done no such thing, that he'd never told anyone anything he'd heard in his sittings with the King.

He looked up and started to answer, but was suddenly struck by a more horrible thought: Nathaniel. Nathaniel was always there, listening, making those strange symbols on the corner of his sketchpad. Perhaps Nathaniel was listening and recording in some kind of code and passing the information on. That would fit with many of the perceptions he'd had about Nathaniel's activities. So that was it, they were trying to get information from him about Nathaniel. He wondered if they'd caught Nathaniel, and where he might be now.

"He may have, I don't recall. I'm a painter, sir. And when I'm with a subject, I'm concentrating on my painting. I can't pay attention to the substance of any conversations the subject may be having."

The man moved closer until his waist was a just a few inches from Benton's face. He reached down, cupped his hand under Benton's chin, and lifted his face. For the first time, Benton could see the man's fierce eyes. "I'll ask you again. Did you ever hear the King discuss military strategy in America? You better give me a straight answer."

Benton was afraid his quivering would give away the extent of the fear he felt. How could he save himself here? How could he save Nathaniel? "I'm sorry, sir. I can only say I don't recall hearing any such discussion. I just paint."

"I see. And did you record things the King said when you were in his presence and communicate them to anyone?"

"Of course not, sir. I did no such thing."

"Did you tell things you might have heard to anyone else? A friend? An assistant? Your wife?"

Benton's thoughts were racing. He could sense the other men, standing in the shadows, watching and judging the performance of the interrogator. These men were after a spy, and they wouldn't stop until they'd caught one.

"No," Benton said, hearing the strain in his own voice. "No one. I didn't report anything to anyone."

"Well then, perhaps you're not the man we're looking for. Perhaps it's your assistant. Might he have been passing on information he overheard?"

"No. Of course not," Benton said. "He's not interested in anything like that."

"Well, now listen to me. We caught a courier on her way to a ship that was headed to America. She was carrying a coded note. We were able to decipher the code. The message reported on information directly from the King describing military strategy in America. We know the decisions that were reported there had been made in the previous three days. We've gone through everyone who was in the King's presence in that time, and eliminated everyone except you and your assistant. If it's not you who's been spying, then it must be him. Where is he now?"

Benton looked directly at the man, seeing, even in the dim light, the intensity in his eyes. His hand continued to pull on Benton's chin, as if by physical force he could drag from Benton the answer that he wanted.

506

Then Benton reached up and pushed the man's hand away and said, "It was me. It was only me. I did hear the King say things about military activities in America and I did pass them on. I've been doing this for years. My brother was ruined by the crown of England and this is my way of getting revenge. I had hoped I could get away with this until I died. But that now appears unlikely doesn't it?" Then he forced a bogus laugh.

The men in the room seemed to exhale as one. The interrogator stepped back and Benton thought he saw a smile flash across his face. Emboldened now by his success, the interrogator said, "Not unlikely at all. You wanted to get away with this until you died, and we're going to see to it that your hope is realized. Spying is a simple crime, Mr. Carlisle. Soldiers who capture a spy are authorized to hang the man. No trial, no quibbling. You see that fine dragoon standing by the door. Well, he has just caught himself a spy, and now he's going to administer the appropriate punishment."

The interrogator signaled to the soldier, who walked toward them. He leaned his long rifle against the door to a stall, then walked around a corner, disappearing for a few seconds. He was back quickly with a large coil of heavy rope. He tied a horseshoe to one end, then tossed it smoothly over a beam about fifteen feet overhead. His practiced hands quickly made a noose of one end of the rope. Then he tied the other end to a brace at the corner of the carriage house, measuring off just the right length so that the noose hung about seven feet above the floor. Benton, possessed of an artist's eye, couldn't help admiring the skill of the man arranging his death.

The interrogator then pulled Benton up from the stool and slid it under the noose. Another man joined him and the two of them lifted Benton, standing him on the stool and placing the noose over his head. The others gathered around and the soldier moved behind Benton.

"Do you now regret that you took sides with the rebels in America, Mr. Carlisle?" the interrogator asked with a look of self-satisfaction.

Benton looked slowly at all the men lined up before him, drew in his breath, and said. "I do not, sir. I shall never regret that I cast my lot with the forces of liberty." Then he shouted, for full effect, "Long live the United States of America."

The interrogator gave a signal and the soldier kicked the stool out from under Benton. For a few seconds he dangled there, his mind flooded with the most peculiar thought. Will they remember me as an important artist, he wondered as the pain tore at his neck and his last breath stalled in his lungs, will they remember the sun-dappled landscapes and the lovingly rendered still lifes and all the handsome ministers and elegant ladies? Or will I be like that American General Arnold, remembered only as the painter who was a traitor? Then all was dark, and to Benton Carlisle the answer no longer mattered.

Lydie and Nathaniel had hardly spoken during their last few days in Paris, except to agree that they had made a terrible error in allowing their passion to overwhelm them and to pledge never again to let that happen. Now as they rode through the streets of London from the docks, they sat in silence, each wondering how it would be to see Benton again after they had betrayed him so.

Lydie had thought that perhaps she would admit their betrayal, and ask Benton's forgiveness. But that might destroy the bond between Benton and Nathaniel and she didn't want to risk that. Nathaniel had thought that he should simply pack up and leave, ending the torture of being so close to Lydie yet unable to touch her or love her in the way he wanted. But he realized that his value as a source of information would be ended by that and, with peace negotiations likely to begin soon, he was more important than ever. So without any discussion between them, they'd both concluded they would say nothing to Benton, just redouble their devotion to him and try to keep their distance from each other. Neither had great confidence in the ability to endure the second part of that conclusion.

At Bloomsbury Square, Nathaniel had intended to see Lydie to the door then go along to his own room on St. Cross Street. But Lydie persuaded him that it would be impolite to do so without at least greeting Benton after their weeks apart. So they walked to the door together. When it opened, Bartholomew was standing in his usual place, but the color was completely gone from his face and his eyes looked like they hadn't closed for days. "Good day, madam," he said quietly, then he looked at Nathaniel and nodded, "Sir."

He stepped back and held the door as they entered, then signaled to the cab driver to bring the cab around to the mews where he would fetch their baggage. "Where is Mr. Carlisle?" Lydie asked.

Bartholomew looked stricken and gave an answer that seemed practiced. "I'm sorry, madam. There has been a terrible tragedy while you were gone. I think it might be best if you looked at the papers I've left on the table in the parlor."

Lydie's hand flew to her mouth, "Is he all right?" she implored.

Bartholomew looked down and said nothing. Then he raised his head slightly and motioned toward the parlor with his hand. He seemed overcome by a terrible grief and turned to tend to the baggage.

In the parlor, Lydie and Nathaniel gripped hands, sharing a frightened anticipation. On the table by the window was a copy of a week-old newspaper and an envelope with the words "Mrs. Carlisle" written across the front in formal script. Nathaniel lifted the paper and their eyes quickly scanned the narrow columns.

It was Lydie who first spotted the headline in the center, "Artist Confesses Spying And Is Hung." She gasped loudly and felt unsteady on her feet. Nathaniel caught her waist and led her to the settee, placing a pillow behind her head and helping her to lean back. Then he read quickly through the story, relaying the important details to Lydie.

Benton had been suspected of using his portrait sittings to spy on his subjects. The authorities had intercepted a coded communication from him to an American contact and realized that it could only have come from a high official in the government—Nathaniel noticed the newspaper's delicacy in not mentioning the King as the source. Carlisle had been confronted with the evidence and admitted that he had been spying "for some time." He was hung instantly by "appropriate military authority."

Lydie's heart was beating so fast, she could barely breathe. Nathaniel stroked her forehead, but it seemed to give her no relief. "Did you know this?" she asked.

Unsure what she meant, Nathaniel said, "Know what?"

"Did you know that Benton was also spying? You must have known. Why did you never tell me."

"Lydie, darling, Benton was no spy." Nathaniel was struggling to piece the facts together. "They must have intercepted something I sent just before we left and deduced that it came from him. It says that they figured it came from information overheard during a portrait session. Naturally, they'd first suspect the artist, not the assistant. They probably confronted Benton and, rather than point to me—and he must surely have known it was me—he took the blame himself. And the punishment. To save me, he allowed himself to be hung. Oh, my God." Nathaniel sat back, unable to forestall the pounding grief that took control of him.

They sat in silence for a few minutes, too sad and contrite to speak or move. Then Lydie whispered, "The envelope."

Her words penetrated the numb haze into which Nathaniel had fallen, and he rose and retrieved the letter from the table. His hands shook and he tore at it crudely to open it. It was a single sheet on the stationery of the Royal Academy of Art. Nathaniel read the few sentences aloud:

> *By vote this day, the members of the Royal Academy took note of the death of their Fellow, Benton Carlisle. In consequence of the calumnious treason that led to his execution by official hand, the members voted to banish from their collections any and all work of Benton Carlisle, to return such work to his widow, and to prohibit any work of said Carlisle from ever again hanging in the galleries of the Royal Academy. Finally, the members voted to revoke Benton Carlisle's election to the Royal Academy, to expunge his name from the records, and to terminate any benefits of membership that might pass to his widow.*
> *God Save The King.*
>
> > *Faithfully Recorded,*
> > *Charles Everingham*
> > *Secretary*

The defiling of Benton Carlisle's legacy had begun. And the two people who loved him most could only weep in despair.

# Chapter 37

## *Still River, Delaware*
## *Summer 1781*

"You sho' got yosef a good man dere, Miz Savannah," Sweetie said as she and Savannah sat on the porch shucking peas. They watched across the yard as Quiet Jack and Flint hefted large bolts of oak onto the transport wagon, laughing and challenging each other to take on heavier and heavier logs.

"Don't I?" Savannah said. "He loves it here, doesn't he?"

"He sho' do.

"I think it's your rhubarb pie, Sweetie. He loves that more than anything in the world."

"On, no, Miz Savannah. Not more'n you."

Sweetie was right, and Savannah was warmed by her words. This unusual man loved her more than she'd ever been loved before. And she loved him with an intensity almost the equal of his. Sometimes she was sure it was a dream—the way they'd encountered each other at the barren tavern in New Jersey, his sudden appearance here as Jonathan's aide, her brother's brilliant kindness to them both in sending him to the farm to recover from his wound after Monmouth. She was afraid she'd awaken one morning and find that none of it had ever happened.

But then she placed her hands lightly on the growing curve of her belly and felt the soft twinges of movement. Surely, this couldn't be a dream. One couldn't just conjure up something this real and wonderful. All those times when she was sure that she was fated for a spinster's life, when loneliness seemed her plight, when she wondered if she'd ever know the fire of passion. Funny, she laughed, that it took a man named Flint to ignite that fire.

"When dat boy arrive here, Miss Savannah, I din' know if he was ever gone walk agin. Now you don't hardly notice da limp. You musta had some pow'ful healin' spell on him."

Savannah smiled and thought back to those first months. Poor irrepressible Flint. The pain was terrible, and it got worse every time he tried to rise from his bed, as he did almost every day, desperately seeking to make himself useful. Finally one night, she stood over him and talked to him more sternly than she'd ever spoken to anyone in her life. "I love you, Ezekial Isaac Flint," she'd said, knowing that the use of his full name would get him to listen. "And I'm intending to live the rest of my life with you. But I don't want to spend it pushing around some useless cripple. There'll be plenty of time for you to be up and about, and plenty for you to do when you are. But now you're going to stay in this bed and take your treatments or you're going to find out that we Delaware women can be the meanest old crones you've ever seen."

Flint feigned a look of deep fear, but it passed quickly and the grin returned. "Can we go back to the love part," he asked, "and the part about spendin' your life with me? That kinda' resembled a proposal of marriage."

Savannah suddenly flushed with embarrassment. She hadn't intended to say quite that, and she wasn't sure where those words came from. Except her heart.

Before she could say more, Flint spoke again. "I accept," he said. "Now let's set a date."

And that was that, Savannah recalled. Perhaps not the kind of marriage proposal little girls imagine, but another special piece of the life they were building together. At Savannah's suggestion, they decided to postpone any wedding plans until Flint's leg had healed enough that he could, as he said, walk to the altar like a man. She knew this would inspire him to be a much better convalescent, and it did. The scars healed by the end of the summer without any infection and Flint was walking the fields—limping the fields was more like it—by the time the leaves fell.

They were married on Christmas eve at the little church in Still River. Henry was there, every inch the proud father. He was relieved that Savannah would not be consigned to a life of loneliness, which was something he'd long feared. And he liked this fellow Flint. This was not the political match he'd once wanted for Savannah, back when Marinus Marshall seemed the best catch in Delaware. But the country was changing. A new generation of men was emerging: patriots, soldiers, diplomats, spies, the people who were making the revolution. When the war was over, Henry'd come to believe, they'd claim their right to lead this new society they'd done so much to build. Flint would be one of

512

those. He might not have any political interests and probably had none of the patience required to endure the squabbling of legislatures. But people would listen when he spoke. He'd laid his life on the line for this new country, this bold idea, and people would owe him that.

So, though the war dragged on and kept both Jonathan and Celia away, the wedding was a happy moment in this dark time in Still River. As Flint's leg got stronger, he took on more and more work on the farm. He'd never farmed, and there was much to learn. But he bore into it with the same joyous energy he'd brought to soldiering. Soon the timber production was up to levels it had never reached before. And Flint had a knack for finding the best stud horses in Kent County and negotiating reasonable fees with their owners. The herd grew faster than Savannah had projected.

Flint had no interest in the paperwork or record keeping. Nor was he much interested in ordering supplies or many of the other details of running a business like the one that was growing larger at Still River Bend. So Savannah tended to all that, while Flint spent his days outdoors in the fields and the woods. They were a good team, and Flint was happy to be a partner in a life that was richer and happier than anything he'd ever known.

Until his leg healed. And then the guilt began to set in. Sometimes he'd bolt awake in the middle of the night, escaping from a dream in which waves of British soldiers were pounding down upon a beleaguered force of Continentals. He could see Lafayette and Daniel Morgan and John Glover, and they were all looking for him. "Where's Captain Flint?" they would call to each other above the sounds of battle. And he could see Jonathan, off his horse, sword drawn, trying to stave off a score of redcoats charging at him with bayonets, looking over his shoulder, calling "Flint! Flint!"

The dreams were so vivid that sometimes they'd stay with him all through the morning. In the woods, riding the fields along the river, it sometimes felt like he was back at Freeman's Farm or Trenton or Monmouth. He expected to hear gunfire coming from behind the trees in the distance, to see a column of redcoats coming over the knoll to the north. And sometimes he wished for that. At least then he wouldn't feel like he was cheating by being here, living this good life, while the army, his army, was still in the field.

When Henry returned from Congress at the end of June, he

seemed more tired than Savannah had ever seen him. A few days back on the farm brightened him some, especially the afternoon he and Flint had spent on horseback looking everything over. "You've done a wonderful job of running this place," Henry said to him as the two men stopped to let their horses drink in the river. The afternoon sun was still bearing down heavily though it was now nearly six o'clock. "A lot of Delaware Houghtons built this place, Flint. They'd be proud of what a Boston boy has done to improve it."

"Hell, Henry, t'ain't me. Savannah's the one that makes the important decisions. I just do what she tells me. But it's a beautiful place. Growin' up a wharf rat in Boston, I never had much chance to get to know the country life. I gotta tell ya', I like it right fine."

"It treats a man well, if he tends to business," Henry said, squinting back up over his fields toward the tall trees at the top of the hill beyond the cemetery. "And it'll be a fine place to raise your child, especially when the war ends and things return to normal."

"Damned if it's ever gonna end," Flint said. "Ya' know, when we dug in on the hilltop in Charlestown that night in '75, most of us thought the thing would be over in a few days, maybe a coupla weeks at most. The militias from New Hampshire and Connecticut—why them fellas thought they'd just be away from their farms for a few days. Hadn't made much provision for tendin' their crops 'cause they didn't think they needed to. Now it's six years later, almost to the day, and it ain't any closer to bein' over than it was then."

Henry nodded in sad agreement, then said, "I guess we have to try to dwell on the good news. Morgan's down in North Carolina now and his boys seem to be saving the day. After the awful rout of Gates in South Carolina, it was looking pretty bleak. But Morgan gave their cavalry a thrashing in January and Greene fought Cornwallis to a draw in March, so now it seems that things have evened up again."

Some old instinct engaged and Flint sat up in his saddle, smiled broadly and said, "It ain't much of a draw when you leave a heap of your soldiers dead on the field. The British may be callin' it a draw, but old Cornwallis is a smart critter. He knows he took a beatin' and he'll be wantin' to get out of the Carolinas now. British don't like to get too far from their ships, and where they been the last couple months ain't very close to the ocean. I'm bettin' they're marchin' toward Charleston right now."

514

"In Congress, we keep asking ourselves how much longer they'll have a stomach for this war." Henry dismounted and sat on the bank while his horse drank. "It's expensive. The opposition is getting angrier and angrier. If it hadn't been for their victory at Charleston last year, the rioters in London might have driven the King off his throne. And now we hear the French and the Spaniards are sailing freely in the English Channel. The only things that seem to keep them here are pride and the King's unshakable belief that he can win."

Flint was enjoying the political conversation and was grateful for Henry's interest in his opinions. "You'd think they'd look at us governin' ourselves and realize that there ain't no turnin' back now. You get used to bein' your own boss, it's hard to go back to slavin' for someone else. Even if they could beat us in battle, how they goin' to take back the government."

Henry laughed and shook his head. "Some days I wish they would, then we'd have someone to blame. You know what you were saying about how the soldiers at Charlestown thought the war would be over quickly? I think a lot of us in Congress thought that setting up a new government would be just as simple. It took a while for some of us to come around to believing that independence was the right course, but once we agreed to that in '76, nobody thought much about what would come next. We just assumed that governing ourselves would be the most natural thing in the world.

"What a delusion that was. It took us more than a year to draft the Articles of Confederation, then we couldn't get all the states to sign on until Maryland finally did this March. Three and half years, Flint! Three and a half years just to approve the procedures for the government. Now we're trying to make them work and it's even more frustrating. We've been setting up executive departments like War and Finance and Foreign Affairs, but we argue about what their duties will be and who's going to run them.

Henry picked a up a handful of stones and tossed them one-at-a-time into the water as he poured out his frustration. "We just keep tinkering, trying one thing, then trying another. Nobody's ever tried to run a country as big as this with a democracy before. So there's no place we can look to get the plans. We just have to keep inventing things. It's like trying to figure out how to grow a new crop. Sometimes it takes years before you figure how close to plant the seeds, what fertilizer to use, how much rain you need, what kind of soil, all those things. Same with a new government. You think something will work, then you try it and it doesn't work it all. So then you have to try something else."

Flint listened closely. He'd never thought much about the difficulties of operating a legislature before. To him, as to most soldiers, the Congress failed to provide for the army because its members were blind, deaf, and dumb, not because of something as arcane as faulty processes.

"It'd be easier," Henry continued, "if some of the men had stayed who were in Congress when I first went there. That John Adams could drive a man mad, but he was about the smartest fellow I ever knew. And Ben Franklin would sit on the edge of the hall, not saying much until just the right minute. Then he'd speak a few words and it was like the sun coming out after a storm. Everything cleared up. Young Jefferson was another smart one, solid, good judgment. But now they're all gone, all off on other duties. We miss them. We even miss men like Joseph Galloway. How I admired his courage when we were arguing about independence. You never had to question Galloway's integrity. But he lost faith, now he's in New York, siding with the British.

"Too many of the men who are there now don't have the vision of the ones they've replaced. They think they owe everything to their states and they'll squabble over the pettiest details to make sure their states don't have to pay any more than any others. When the secretary read Jefferson's declaration to us in '76, it was like seeing an angel emerge from the darkness. It was one of the greatest days of my life, like the birth of a beautiful child. But those were just words. Glorious words, but just words. Trying to turn them into a government may kill us yet."

Flint joined Henry on the bank, scooped a handful of water and rinsed his sweaty face with it. He turned to Henry and smiled. "So let me see if I got this straight," he said. "We may win the war or we may lose it. But it don't make no difference. If we lose, we got the King runnin' things again. If we win, we got a government that's even worse than the King because it don't know what it's doin'?"

Henry looked hard at Flint, squinting to avoid the slanting rays of the sun. "No," he said, "it makes all the difference whether we win the war. If we don't win this war, all of the ideas we've been fighting for will become laughingstocks—revolution, liberty, independence. Many of our own countrymen will turn away in disgust. They'll never want to attempt self-government again. It'll kill the spirits of all those people in France and other countries looking to us as a beacon for their own futures. And think of all the men like you and Jonathan who've given so many years of your lives—many of them gave their lives—because they believed that good people could govern themselves better than a King could. We have to believe they're right, that they made those sacrifices in a good and just cause."

Henry looked tired now and old, a man chastened by the wisdom he'd gained. "We've learned some stern lessons about how hard it is to govern ourselves when we give everyone a say. And we'll learn a lot more before we're done. But just because something is hard doesn't mean you shouldn't keep at it.  That's where faith comes in, Flint. Believing you're doing the right thing even as you're finding out how complicated it is. None of the important things in life is easy. You always come to treasure most the things that were hardest to get."

"What are you doing with all that?" Savannah asked when she entered the room the boys had used when they were children and found Flint going through the trunk where his army gear was stored.

He looked up, surprised that she found him there. This wasn't the way he wanted to broach the subject. He drew a long breath and pointed toward the bed. "Sit here a minute," he said.

The quizzical look on her face turned to fear. It was so unusual for Flint to answer her without a smile or some bit of whimsy or caprice that she knew something was wrong. "What is it?" she asked. "What's going on?"

He came to her, cupped his hand behind her head and stroked her long hair. His words came slowly. "I been thinkin' 'bout a lot of things lately," he said. "Durin' all those  months when my leg was healin', I didn't feel no guilt or remorse 'bout bein' here. I'd a been a useless soldier and they would a rid me right out of there. So I didn't have no choice. And, besides, I was so happy here, fallin' in love with you, getting healed, workin' on the farm. All that filled me up with good feelin's.

"And there wasn't much happenin' in the war, especially with General Washington's army. So it seemed like this was the right place for me to be.

"But now I'm gettin' different feelin's. My leg is good enough now so I could be a passable soldier again…" Savannah stiffened at the words. "…And Washington's headin' south to go after Cornwallis down there. Things are heatin' up again…"

He slid his hand softly under Savannah's chin and lifted her face toward his. "I got this strong feelin', Savannah, that I should go back to the Army until the war's over. I don't think it'll be much longer. But I ought to be there. We don't want to lose this thing now. And we need every good soldier we got. And I'll tell you, even with a bum leg, I'm a pretty fair soldier."

Savannah was silent for a minute, but Flint could see tears forming at the edges of her eyes. She sniffled slightly to hold them back, then said, "Soldier? I thought chess was your game."

Flint smiled and held his wife as tightly as he ever had. "I hate this, Savannah. Ain't no one in this country wants this war over more than I do, got more to look forward to than I have. That baby's gonna' 'rive in November, and if I have any say in things, I'll be back here then to wish him a fine howdy do."

"Or her," Savannah said.

"What?"

"Or her. It might be girl."

"Jesus, then, I better get back as quick as I can. Or you'll have her runnin' the place and there won't be nothin' for me to do here."

Savannah pulled him down beside her on the bed and kissed him deeply. Then she held his face between her hands and said, "I never doubted that this moment would come. I'm only surprised it wasn't sooner. I hate this, too. More than I can ever tell you. But I know you pretty well, Ezekial Isaac Flint, and I know it couldn't be any other way. Just you remember now that you're going to be a father, that you're a husband. Win this war for us. Win it soon. Then come home as quickly as you can and we'll spend the rest of our lives on this place making it all worthwhile."

Flint smiled. "I promise," was all he said.

"And one more thing," Savannah added. "Bring that little brother of mine home too, will you?"

# Chapter 38

## Yorktown, Virginia
## Fall, 1781

Again the boats. How the soldiers hated the boats. Long days, nothing to do, cramped quarters, awful heat or bitter cold, seasickness, the wretched smells of too many men in too small a place.

Armistead knew how important the ships had been to the British. Without them, there would have been no blockade, no escape from Boston neck, no seizure of New York, no movement of troops to the south. And now as the Third Battalion sailed to the aid of Lord Cornwallis in Virginia, he knew that ships would matter once again: bringing fresh troops, providing water-borne artillery, standing by to evacuate forces under siege.

It was quiet now, a clear autumn night. The wind was light and the only sounds on deck were those of the ritual reports of the watch and the rhythmic creaking of wood against wood. Armistead stood on the lee rail, looking off toward the distant shore, a faint shadow in the moonlight. America.

His battalion was heading to Yorktown, not far from where some of the earliest settlers landed 180 years earlier. They'd come to find a better life, but not to stop being Englishmen. They'd even named their settlement after the King: Jamestown.

They expected to find nirvana in Virginia and vast riches. Legend had it that they brought more silversmiths than carpenters. It hadn't turned out that way. America was a hard country and the Jamestown colony had failed. But other Englishmen made the same treacherous journey, driven by their own dreams for wealth, for the chance to worship god in their own way, for the freedom to make whatever life their wits allowed. They never stopped coming. Probably never will, Armistead guessed.

Williamsburg is near here, named after another king. Nothing especially important about that place, but Armistead remembered the name from something he'd read just before he shipped out from London in '74. Some radical named Patrick Henry had given a speech there that stirred up the enemy. "Give me liberty or give me death" was what he said. More than a few times, he'd thought about those words as he watched the enemy do brave and dangerous things. Death had been the fate of many of them, some at his own hand. That was the choice they'd made, liberty or death.

What choice had he made? He'd certainly risked death, many times. But for what? For his King? His King, from all reports, was a mad man. For his country? A country that assigned one's fate at birth, that made no exceptions even for those of great talent or industry? For an idea perhaps: honor, loyalty, an oath, the right order of things? To be a good soldier was to avoid those questions. But more and more these days, they crept into his mind, resistant to all efforts to hold them at bay.

He'd trained in the arts of war since he was a young man. Half his life had been spent at war. But this war was so strange, so unlike the others where the professional army of one king fought the professional army of another. Americans didn't see things that way. They weren't soldiers doing a job, making a living, having a career. Hell, most of them had hardly been paid a shilling since the war started. They all had their reasons for going to war, he knew, and they weren't all the same. But never before had men gone to war for so long for themselves, for something they wanted so much they would lay down their lives to get it.

Armistead leaned against the rail and looked at the shore, trying to imagine what America might be like a hundred years into the future. There'd be more people certainly. It was a treasure-trove, this country in the wilderness. Tall virgin trees, rich soil, bays full of fish and woods overrun with game. That would draw people here, no matter who governed the place. But if the Americans won the war, people would come for another reason. Freedom. They'd come to escape. They'd come to let their children grow up without all the restrictions and threats they and their ancestors had always endured.

And even those who didn't come, the little people in other countries would look at this war and be inspired. They'd see that might doesn't always make right, that kings and tyrants are not invincible when they come up against men fighting for something more important than honor and a wage and a career. If the Americans win, who knows what will come next. A revolution in England? In Spain? In France? No one ever threw off a king before and set up a government where men made their own decisions. If that happens in America, if it works, then men everywhere will finally have a separate vision to compare with the only thing most of them have ever known. The divine right of kings. Lords and peasants. You are what you're born to be.

Why had he been thinking about all this so much? In the early years, this was just another war, just another campaign. But now he kept wondering about what it meant and whether he was on the right side. Perhaps it had been the many months in the garrison in New York, especially the times with Celia and little Godfrey. The boy was now the age of his own son when he'd perished. But if the Americans won the war and their independence, Godfrey would grow up in a country that welcomed his gifts and his energy. His own son would have grown up in a country where the prospects were far more limited, even for the son of an army officer. The pedigree was wrong, and the pedigree was all that really mattered.

He'd hated to leave New York, even with the anticipation that the war might end, one way or the other, on this peninsula in Virginia. What then? Back to England and assignment to some other war at the edge of the empire, some other effort to protect His Majesty from the depredations of yet another king or the cravings for liberty of some of his other subjects? Perhaps. Wasn't that the natural order of things?

But Celia said I should leave the army when the war ended and come back to make my home in New York. With her. With young Godfrey. If we win here, it would be a life as a British subject in America. No harsh questions to answer then. Everything quite familiar. If we lose, then it would be different, a life as an American. Would that be possible? The thought rambled shapelessly through his mind, as Colonel Armistead looked out toward Virginia and wondered about the military situation he and the Third battalion would encounter at this place called Yorktown.

"Military situation?" Jonathan responded. "You're not going to believe it." He was still a little short of breath from the surprise that struck him when the horse pulled up in front of General Washington's headquarters beyond the swamp west of Yorktown and Captain Flint reported for duty.

Jonathan hadn't seen Flint for more than three years, not since he'd driven his mangled body to the farm in the summer of 1778 and left him for Savannah to cure. She must have worked a miracle because here he was, looking bronzed and strong in his clean uniform. There was some limp when he walked, but it seemed remarkable to Jonathan that he could walk at all. The army doctor in Monmouth had wanted to amputate his leg. Only Jonathan's quick intervention had saved him from the surgeon's saw. Now he was almost whole again.

He'd saluted quite formally when he dismounted, then he and Jonathan had embraced. Flint said that he'd waited as long as he could for Jonathan to win this war, but he couldn't wait any longer, so he'd come to finish it himself. "What is the military situation?" he'd asked when they sat down to talk business.

"We're facing the kind of outlook the redcoats have usually faced. This time we've got the navy on our side and they're trapped on a peninsula. I wish you could have seen the General when we learned that the French were actually going to use their navy to help us after all those years of promises unkept. Their admiral, de Grasse, got his fleet in the Bay and scared off Graves and the British ships that were here. Cornwallis had pulled his army down to Yorktown and fortified the place, apparently thinking he'd use it as a supply depot and a base for his operations in Virginia.

"The past few months, the British have been roaming pretty freely over the countryside, up to Richmond--they burned a lot of it--and up toward Charlottesville. Mr. Jefferson's the Governor now and he was at his home, but he had to go hide in the woods when a British cavalry troop pulled up and took it over. Thing was, there was nobody much to oppose them. Nathanael Greene's been the general in charge down here since Gates got run off, but he's never had much of an army. Lafayette came down with a small force, but it wasn't until General Washington arrived that we had enough men for a real fight. He decided to gamble that he could find Cornwallis here, and he and most of the French soldiers did a hard march down here from New York. Now most of the Continental Army is right here."

Flint listened intently, then asked, "So what's Cornwallis doin'?"

"Digging in," Jonathan replied. "We guess that he thought his own fleet would be behind him, not the French, and thought it safe to fortify the place. Now we've got him under siege. Come, look."

Jonathan led the way to the top of a small knoll. He pointed to the York River and identified the masts of the dozen or so French ships patrolling there. Then he traced the line of British trenches and redoubts. "Looks like they've done some powerful diggin'," Flint noted. "They could hole up there all winter."

522

"We're not going to let them do that" Jonathan replied. Then he began to point out the American and French positions and the proximity of their trenches to the British defenses. "We've got about a hundred guns pounding them all day and all night. The French brought some of their big siege guns from Newport and we've been using them to blow the roofs off the houses. So now they've got to sleep in the rain and mosquitoes every night. And the engineers are digging all the time, moving our lines closer and closer to theirs.

"We've been in some tight places, you and me--Charlestown, Brooklyn Heights--but we've never been closed off as badly as they are here. They've got no escape and no way to re-supply. It's just a matter of time before they run out of food or cannonballs. We're going to squeeze them even tighter tomorrow night with an attack on their two forward redoubts down there, near the shore. The French are going after one; we'll go after the other."

Flint tried to take it all in but found it hard to picture a British army under one of their best generals trapped in so inescapable a position. "Who's leadin' the attack on the redoubt?" he asked as he tried to pick it out of the lines of trenches and fortifications that snaked across the landscape in front of him.

"Lafayette's light infantry, but Hamilton's commanding the attack," Jonathan replied. "I've been drilling a company from New Jersey that lost their commander to a fever and I'll be leading their line on his flank. It'll be at night. Mostly bayonets. When we secure those redoubts, we can move some of our guns up there and shoot down on them with grapeshot. That should finish them off quickly."

"Can I get in on this?" asked Flint, the familiar grin flashing brightly across his face.

"You don't think you're a little rusty?"

"Sure I am. But even rusty, even bein' a gimp, I can lick twice my weight in redcoats."

Jonathan laughed. "You're probably right. God, I've missed you here. But listen. I've saved your life a couple times already. I may be running out of miracles. Besides you're going to be a father soon. You've got to be especially careful now for my nephew."

"Or niece!"

"What? ...Oh yes, right, or niece."

"Don't worry about it, Colonel," Flint said, pushing back his hat and smiling confidently. "It's my turn now. I owe ya'."

October fourteenth, and cool. The thick cloud cover made the darkness almost impenetrable. Only the flares from exploding artillery offered an occasional glimpse of his men curling through the trenches toward their objective. Jonathan followed the scout with Flint right behind him. The wind was gentle and from the north, blowing in their faces. Good, Jonathan thought, it will be harder for them to smell us or hear us coming.

As they reached the forward trench, about two hundred yards from Redoubt Number Ten, Jonathan spread his men along the line spaced four or five feet apart. Their bayonets were fixed and each had a charge loaded and primed. Close quarters here; there would be no room for the ordered firing that Von Steuben continued to preach every day. In attacking an enemy's fortifications, the important thing is speed. Get there quickly, surprise him, get some men over the top.

It felt good to have Flint back at his side, and Flint looked like a man who'd found a long-lost prized possession. He'd cleaned his new rifle to a high gleam. His bayonet was probably the sharpest in the Continental Army. He'd gone around and met most of the younger officers and some of the men to make sure he knew who he was fighting with. Flint was a warrior, and to a warrior, nothing but war really feels like home.

Baron Viomenil was commanding the French assault on Redoubt Number Nine, and he and Hamilton had arranged a series of bird sounds to signal their simultaneous attack. Jonathan listened closely for the sounds to come down the line. Finally he heard it, the scree-scree sound of an owl. He shouted "Charge, boys," and his men pulled themselves out of their trench, quickly formed a solid line, lowered their weapons parallel to the ground and began to run forward across the open ground toward their target. Flint had forgotten how quiet several hundred men could be when a little noise might cost their lives.

They were within thirty yards of the front of the redoubt before the first shot was fired by a British sentry. Others followed shortly, but they all whistled over the heads of the charging Americans, indicating the British could hear but not really see them. Then a British gun fired a flare and suddenly there was light.

Even with his bad leg, Flint was only a few yards behind the others. He could see that Jonathan's men had stayed in line and were closing on their sector of the redoubt like a noose tightening around its neck. "Don't fire," he wanted to shout, knowing that American fire now was as likely to hit other Americans as redcoats.

The defenders leaned over their fortifications and fired, then pulled back and reloaded. But the Americans were gaining ground quickly. Within a minute of the first flare, some of the charging Continentals had begun to cross the ditch in front of the redoubt and were starting to scale its outer wall. Flint could see fear in British eyes as the inevitability of the outcome became apparent to them. He guessed they would pull back and abandon the redoubt any minute.

Flint reached the ditch and started to make his way up the steep bank. About ten yards away he could see Jonathan nearing the top, directing other men over the thick dirt wall. Flint struggled to the top and rose to his feet. Before him he could see men in hand-to-hand combat, slashing at each other in the darkness with long rifles outstretched, bayonets searching for targets. The attackers had the defenders badly outnumbered, but no one had given the British the order to retreat. Perhaps their officers had been killed, Flint thought. This should have been over by now.

He looked toward Jonathan who stood still for a moment, assessing the situation. Behind Jonathan on the top of the wall, Flint's eye detected some movement and he saw a downed British soldier rise to his knees, then to his feet. He held his bloody arm for a moment, as if testing it, then picked up his rifle, checked the bayonet, and looked down into the redoubt. Not far in front of him, he saw an American officer, standing still. He lowered his rifle, and began to lurch down the hill, bayonet pointed directly at the officer's back.

Flint watched all this in horror, and began to shout to Jonathan to watch his rear. But in the middle of this melee, his voice was just one more indistinct war sound. So he began to run toward Jonathan, calculating that he could get to him and cut off the attacker from the side before the British soldier reached his target.

But his mind was calculating on old assumptions. The old Flint would have been there in plenty of time to interrupt the attack. But the old Flint hadn't had his leg mangled at Monmouth. Flint cried out again, half in frustration, half in a final agonized attempt to warn Jonathan. He lurched forward as fast as he could, holding his rifle far in front of him to shorten the distance it needed to travel. A sharp pain shot through his shin as he tried to make the leg move faster than it had in three years.

Then one more terrible tormented bellow as Flint watched the British soldier leap forward and drive his bayonet high into Jonathan's back. The two men, attacker and victim, then fell forward together. Their bodies tangled and they rolled over each other toward the floor of the redoubt. When they came to a stop, there was no movement for a minute, then the British soldier stood up. He looked down briefly at the American officer lying face down beside him, the butt end of a British "Brown Bess" pointing toward the sky.

As the soldier grabbed the barrel of the rifle and started to pull the bayonet from Jonathan's back, Flint reached him and drove his own bayonet clean through the surprised soldier's stomach. Then he quickly withdrew it and made another violent lunge at the man's throat. A stream of blood spurted out as Flint withdrew the bayonet a second time. He pulled his arms back for a third thrust, but the soldier lay on the ground now, all life gone, his blood soaking heavily into the dark Virginia dirt.

Flint dropped to Jonathan's side and rolled him over. The front side of his uniform had only a small hole to the right of one of its brass buttons. But blood had soaked his coat, and Jonathan's eyes seemed to roll loosely in their sockets. Flint shouted to him several times, but Jonathan could not hear. He moaned softly, sounds not words, their meaning evident only at the fringes of consciousness of a dying man.

Flint looked quickly around and saw that the fighting had ended. Some of the defenders had retreated, some had been captured, several lay on the ground. The redoubt was now in American hands. The charge led by Colonel Jonathan Houghton had succeeded. The last charge he would lead. The last charge any American would lead in this long and deadly war.

In all the years in army camps, all the lonesome hours around campfires and in tents, all the nights of quiet contemplation, Flint thought he had imagined every event, every scene that might play out in this war. But he'd never imagined this one. It was an oversight he didn't understand, for surely men at war would anticipate what its end would look like.

It looked like this. No one stood guard. No one spent the morning cleaning a rifle or sharpening a bayonet or shining buttons. No one complained about the food or needing boots. Men continued to salute their officers, more or less, but there was a smile on both faces when salutes were exchanged. Campfires burned all night and men gathered around them, drank heavily and sang rowdy songs. Officers who would have once kept their distance now joined in.

The day of the surrender had been respectful enough, and so had the days that followed. When the men in the siege trenches heard the single British drummer, at first they didn't know what to make of it. They'd never heard a drum like that during the day before. Not on the line. Then a redcoat stood up, pointing a pole in the air with a white flag hanging limply at the end. The order went out and the heavy guns stopped firing. When the smoke lifted, the soldier with the flag approached the American lines and was taken off to a small building in the rear. The word quickly spread through the trenches. The British were going to surrender.

The officers negotiated for a while, the way they always do, but then it was settled. Complete surrender. All the soldiers and sailors in the British garrison—almost eight thousand of them—would be prisoners. None would be allowed to return to England. On October nineteenth, five days after the successful capture of the British redoubts, Lord Cornwallis would come to sign the surrender at Washington's tent.

But he didn't come. When the British troops lined up to march to the surrender, the general leading them was a Brigadier, Charles O'Hara, Cornwallis's second-in-command. Cornwallis was sick and couldn't attend, or so O'Hara told Washington. Washington said nothing but Flint could see his disgust at this final sign of dishonor. He refused to accept the surrender himself and called out Benjamin Lincoln, his own second-in-command, to meet with O'Hara.

In the afternoon, the entire British garrison, again without Cornwallis, formed up and marched the half mile down to the meadow along the Williamsburg Road. The French army lined one side of the road in their brilliant white uniforms. The Continentals in their blue and gold and the militias in their mixture of blue and brown and buckskin lined up on the other side of the road.

The fifes blew and the drums beat their steady cadence as the British troops marched by. Flint had seen a sight like this once before, at Saratoga. But this was different. At Saratoga, the Americans felt like David having beaten Goliath. There was a feeling of surprise to it, and there Americans had watched their British captives stack their arms, feeling like amateurs who'd had an especially good day against professionals. On that day in 1777, most men on both sides thought that the better army had lost.

527

This was different. Flint looked up and down the long rows of American and French troops, as the dejected, emaciated British marched between them. Nobody in Virginia that day thought the better army had lost. Many of these men on both sides had been fighting each other for more than six years. Everybody now understood that victory was the only true test of which was the better army. The victors knew it. And the long lines of tired men methodically stacking their weapons in the middle of the meadow knew it as well.

Then there was the other difference. At Saratoga, most of the Americans felt hopeful. The victory there meant they had a chance. The country would not be split down the middle. On a good day, they could beat a British army in the field. They had survived. There was no feeling of conclusion, only a renewed optimism that they could continue.

Here in Yorktown was something that no one had felt at Saratoga. A feeling of finality. The British could not imagine that they would fight again against this enemy. How many armies must they lose before the politicians would give up the ghost? The Americans were not going to collapse. They believed in what they were doing. They would fight forever. You knock them down, but they get back up, refresh themselves, and come back at you. This was not a European army, following ancient rules, leaving the field when the outcome was determined. The Americans would never leave the field. The sad men stacking their arms knew that now; many of them had learned the lesson long ago.

That same air of finality filled the smiles of the men in the American line. There was still the large British garrison in New York, and a few outlying posts here and there. But the outcome was no longer in doubt. After six years of fighting, after thousands of deaths, the British commanded only a few square miles of territory in their former colonies. This victory would convince most wavering Americans that their country would stand. And it would convince the European allies that they'd made the right choice in siding with the Americans. The peace negotiations about to begin would be on favorable terms now because the British had so few cards to play. The stacks of Brown Besses were testimony to that.

Flint knew that for the men along the line beside him this was the happiest day of their lives. For him, it was one of the saddest. Two days ago they'd buried Jonathan Houghton behind a small stone church on the shore of the York River. All of the officers were there and General Washington, choked with grieved affection, had given the eulogy. Few Americans had died in this long siege, and so Jonathan's death loomed especially large, a bleak reminder of the tens of thousands of brave Americans who'd lost their lives in this war. "An emblem of all we believe, of our every faith," Washington had said. "To the last minute, to the last man, he carried the battle to the army of a King who would deny us the liberties that we believe to be our birthright." Men cried, even men who barely knew Jonathan. They all knew the meaning of his death, the meaning of all those deaths over all those years.

Now these men were getting ready to go home. There was no official word that the war was over. It wasn't really over. Everyone knew that it would take months, maybe more. But there was no longer any reason for the soldiers to stay. There was no enemy to fight. The war had been won, even if the politicians hadn't yet signed all the papers that said so.

So men got their kits together and said their last affectionate good-byes. Some of them—the Pennsylvania boys, the New Jersey line, the men from New Hampshire, some of whom came first to Charlestown with John Stark—had been together for a big piece of their lives. They'd be going back to families that were strangers to them. And they wouldn't much resemble the gangly, enthusiastic boys who'd marched off to war years earlier to fight for a vague cause in which they thought they believed.

These were the survivors, the victors, the patriots. People would build statues in their honor. They'd be given places in the front of the parade on the Fourth of July and some, propelled by their courage and endurance in battle, would rise to great heights in the new country they'd made possible.

But not without cost. Even those who went home intact, with limbs and minds uncharred by the fire of war, would be different. None of them would ever be young again. None would ever again believe that anything important came easily, that any truth was simple, that good intentions were good enough. All of them, even the ones who were still boys, left youth and innocence behind. And it was a greater loss than any of them yet knew.

Flint thought about all of this, but he could not help thinking about the last few minutes of Jonathan's Houghton's life. He hadn't slept peacefully since then, even though at night now the guns were silent. Over and over, the picture replayed in his mind. Jonathan surveying the fighting in front of him, the British soldier rising to his feet, checking his bayonet, and charging downhill at Jonathan's back. Flint trying to get there first to save the friend who had saved him so many times before.

But in the picture in his mind, his lame leg looked like a giant cannonball, weighing him down, holding him back. He could still feel the sharp pain in his throat from the shouts that Jonathan couldn't hear. He could still see the rifle extended at the end of his arms in front of him but not far enough to reach its red-coated target. He could still see the British bayonet driving into the spot between Jonathan's shoulders. Still hear him moaning those final few sounds. None of the ceremonies, none of the joy spreading among the victorious soldiers here could keep those pictures out of his mind. Nothing ever would.

# Epilogue

## Still River, Delaware
## April, 1787

Nathaniel thought about what he would say, thought hard as he cantered along the muddy roads that led from Philadelphia. He was the oldest, and his sisters would expect him to give the eulogy. But it was no simple task. Not because there wasn't a great deal to say about the life of Henry Houghton, nor because he felt anything less than deep affection for his father. The difficulty was not in finding something to say, but in finding the right thing to say. How do you capture the meaning of a life, of this life especially, in a few words at a funeral?

As he had so many times over the past few years, he wished Lydie were there. She was always so good at helping him find his way. But things had never been the same with Lydie after Benton sacrificed his own life to save Nathaniel's. They'd been done in by the guilt they both felt about their betrayal of him at the very moment when he was sacrificing everything for Nathaniel—his good name, his reputation as an artist, his life. They never recovered from that, never escaped from the permanent shadow that darkened the love they'd shared.

When Nathaniel made his hasty plans to leave London, he asked Lydie to come with him. But, as always, she saw things more clearly than he and realized that this great tragedy would always haunt them, that the memory of Benton's sacrifice would always deny their love the freedom it needed to flourish. So she stayed in the house on Bloomsbury Square, though he assumed that with neither Benton nor Nathaniel around, with Benton's name so horribly besmirched, she would soon find English society utterly intolerable and make her way back to France. It had been almost six years now, but Nathaniel had never stopped missing her. And he felt her absence keenly on this day as he rode to his father's funeral.

He'd been to see his father a week after the apoplexy hit him and stayed with him for several days. It was painful to see him so suddenly changed, his vigorous father now looking very fragile, unable to move his left arm or leg, his jaw frozen. Henry could speak little, but he seemed to understand what Nathaniel was saying and so the son talked on and on about his experiences in London, describing the famous people he had seen and known—King George, Lord North, Germain, Howe, the beautiful and scandalous Duchess of Devonshire, King Louis of France and Marie Antoinette. All these names that were distant and exotic mysteries to Henry, but flesh and blood to his son. Occasionally as they talked Nathaniel would pick up his pen and draw a quick sketch of one of these people to give his father a better sense of some peculiar physical feature.

Then there came the morning when, through interpretation of Henry's hand signals, Nathaniel realized that his father wanted to hear about his work as a spy. Nathaniel had been back in America since his escape through France almost six years earlier, but he'd spoken to no one about his work in the Alliance. He assumed that he and Jonathan would talk about it some day, but Jonathan was killed at Yorktown before Nathaniel had a chance to see him.

Nathaniel was surprised at Henry's request; he hadn't known that Henry was even aware of his spying. He later learned that Flint had blurted it out one night at dinner when Savannah was saying how grateful she was that Nathaniel had stayed out of danger during the war, that she couldn't have borne the loss of both brothers. Flint had nearly choked on that and then told his wife and her father that Nathaniel Houghton had been one of the Continental Army's most important sources of information in London. He said he didn't know many details of Nathaniel's work, except the value of the information he provided, but that he imagined the danger was almost constant.

So when Henry asked, Nathaniel slowly talked his way through all the details, from the first contact, to the techniques he used to communicate, to the important secrets he'd overheard in his portrait sessions with Benton. He told Henry about the night he was chased and nearly killed, leaving out the part about killing the man who attacked him. He described the months he spent hiding in Scotland. And, in luxuriant detail, he described his kidnapping in Paris and the surprise meeting with Dr. Franklin. The sparkle in Henry's eyes indicated his great pleasure in that part of the story.

Henry's left side had been paralyzed by the apoplexy, but he could still make some awkward movements with his right hand. One afternoon, he tried to signal something to Nathaniel, but the son couldn't decipher it. After a few minutes of this ineffective communication, it finally struck Nathaniel that his father wanted to know about his painting. That brought a grateful smile to Nathaniel's face and his father understood the glow. Then for an hour, Nathaniel talked about his work, the still lifes and landscapes, the large canvas he'd done from memory of the church of Sainte Chapelle, the portraits he'd been painting in Philadelphia since he returned.

Henry knew about these, of course, because Nathaniel's reputation as a portrait artist had spread quite rapidly through Henry's circle of friends at Congress. When the war ended, many of them wanted their portraits painted to commemorate their participation in the successful revolution. Then there were all the generals and colonels who had to be painted as well so their pictures could be hung as heroes of the revolution in public buildings all over the new country. A portrait by Nathaniel Houghton had become a prized possession in America.

Father and son both knew the private irony of this. When Nathaniel took an interest in painting, Henry worried that it was distracting him from his real work on the farm. When Nathaniel left for London, Henry felt his dreams were dashed—that his first-born son would not fill the role that five generations of ancestors had filled. He'd even hoped that Nathaniel would go into politics and become a leader in Delaware. Now, of course, Nathaniel had become much more famous and admired than he ever would have as a farmer or politician. And, in the face of grave dangers, he'd proven himself a patriot and a man of courage. And he'd done it his own way, pursuing his dreams, not Henry's.

If he'd been a wiser man, Henry had often thought in later years, he would have understood all this earlier. Dreams are neither transferable nor inherited. Fathers should only hope that their children have dreams and have the freedom and the means to pursue them. They overstep when they try to impose those dreams. He should have listened to all those things he'd said at the meetings in Kent County, all the things he'd said in Philadelphia. That's what independence was about, he told his listeners then, that's what the war was about: the freedom for each of us to dream our own dreams and then to try to live them. It was as simple as that, for his own children as well as the country's.

When Nathaniel left to return to Philadelphia after that last visit a few weeks ago, Henry had lifted his weak right arm and signaled to Nathaniel to bend toward him. Then he lifted his head slightly from his pillow and kissed his son on the forehead. Nathaniel placed his hand on Henry's cheek and tried to find an expression that revealed the love he felt, the love that had always—by the ocean that separated them or the chasm of awkwardness that sometimes disconnects fathers and sons— gone unspoken. He thought he'd succeeded.

He was glad that he'd had that last visit with his father, but regretted that it had taken the catalyst of Henry's apoplexy to close the circle that bound them. Now as he thought about the words he'd say at Henry's funeral, his thoughts were not burdened by the guilt of the prodigal who hadn't returned. He was grateful for that. But still he wondered which words to choose.

Sweetie had worked night and day to make the tiny suits of velvet for the boys and the dark cotton dress for Martha. None of them had ever been to a funeral before, but Savannah thought they should all be at the graveside for their grandfather. He would live forever, she was sure, in the grateful memory of his state and country, as one of the fathers of the Revolution. They were too young to retain more than faint recollections of Henry in life, but she hoped the funeral and the words they would hear about him there would stay with them forever, one of the many stories they could pass on to their grandchildren about their grandfather.

Savannah examined Sweetie's handiwork, then stepped around the parlor table and gave her an affectionate hug. "They're just what I wanted, Sweetie. Thank you so much."

"Yo' welcome, Miz Savannah. I think they's gonna look right smart. Too bad it has to be fo' sich a sad a 'casion."

Savannah nodded in agreement and started to walk away, but Sweetie spoke up again, "Miz Savannah, kin I aks you a question?"

"Of course, what is it?"

"Yo' think it might be possible for me and Jack to come to da funeral? Mr. Henry been good to us, and now he set us free, we sho' would like to pay him our r'spects."

Savannah smiled and nodded her assent. "Of course," she said. "It never occurred to me that you wouldn't be there."

"Never been to a funeral fo' no white person befo', Miz Savannah. Didn't think it was allowed."

Savannah loved Sweetie like a sister. From the time Sweetie arrived when Savannah was seventeen, for almost twenty years, she'd spent more time with her, conversed more with her, syncopated the

534

rhythms of her days more with her than with anyone else in her life. But she realized there were many things she didn't understand about Sweetie's view of the world. And only after Henry had decided to free his two slaves, after Nathaniel returned home and convinced him to do so, had Savannah begun to think about what it had meant for Sweetie to be an owned person, not merely an employed one.

They'd never talked about this, not in any direct way. But in fragments of conversation, she'd started to see that Sweetie's had been a world of walls and strict rules and rigid constraints. It had never occurred to Savannah that Sweetie and Quiet Jack might doubt that they were welcomed at Henry's funeral.

But, of course, they felt that way. They'd never been invited to the Marshall Balls or the New Year feasts or Celia's wedding. They hadn't been on the hillside when Patience was buried, though they'd watched from a distance. And when famous men came to visit Henry after he retired from Congress, no one had ever introduced them to the visitors. So, of course, they wondered if it was proper for them to attend Henry's funeral. Savannah loved Sweetie, but she was coming to realize that there were some realities that even love didn't seem to penetrate, and some levels of faith and respect for which it was no substitute.

Savannah walked through the kitchen and out to the dooryard where she found Flint sitting alone in the warm morning sun. He was usually in the fields or the woods at this time of day, but he hadn't been to either place since Henry died. She'd been worried, though not surprised, by how deeply he'd been affected. The two men had grown very close in the few years since Henry left Congress and Flint came home from the war. She thought they filled a great need in each other—Flint for the father who'd been killed when he was very young, Henry for the son he'd lost at Yorktown, and perhaps as well for the son he'd lost to Europe years before that.

Their personalities couldn't have been more different: Henry patient, thoughtful, reserved, rarely showing his emotions; Flint never hiding a thing, irreverent, funny, hell-bent. But they shared some things that came to tie them closely to each other: an interest in practical things and solving problems, a feeling for the land and the sheer joy of working it, satisfaction in the simple pleasures of family life, pride in Savannah. In the past year, when young Jonathan, as they all called Flint and Savannah's older son, had joined them a few times in their rides along the fence line, they'd both felt something deep and special. For Henry a sense of continuance, of a new generation joining the long ancestral line that had turned this wilderness into a home. For Flint a sense of belonging, that for the first time in his life he was part of a real family, that in some mysterious but powerful way his son had joined him to that same line.

But there was one other emotional knot that tied Flint and Henry together, perhaps the strongest of all. At some level where conversation rarely reached, they shared a great sense of accomplishment for the roles they'd played in making their country.

Flint was no politician; words were not his stock-in-trade. Henry was no soldier; he'd never fired a weapon in anger at anyone and wasn't sure he could. But Flint knew there would have been no independence without brave men who could use words to serve their cause, who faced down the hangman's noose to put their names on what they believed. He was glad that a man as good as Henry Houghton had been one of them.

And Henry knew that there would have been no independence without soldiers to risk their lives—to lose their lives—to win it in the smoke and din of battle, and he was glad that a man as brave as Flint had been one of them. That was their bond, as it was the bond of so many men they knew, men who by chance had been born at a time when human history was able to crack out of the shell that had encased it for centuries, men who saw the opportunities their time presented them, men who took grave risks and changed the world. Few men have such opportunities; even fewer take them. Those who do, know a feeling, share a bond, that has no equal.

So Flint had been laid low by Henry's death and Savannah had never seen his natural ebullience so dulled as it was now. She sat beside him and put her arm around his shoulder. He turned to her and gently kissed her forehead. "I miss the old man," he said, the words squeezing hard past the knot in his throat.

"I know. We all do." She slowly rubbed her hand along his strong arm.

"I ain't a Houghton," he said, "but when Jonathan died and now with Henry dyin', I can't imagine that I'd a felt any worse if they'd been kin. I guess ya can love a person like family, even when they ain't family."

Savannah was glad to hear Flint talking again. He'd been so unusually quiet the past few days. So she just let him talk—about adventures he'd shared with Jonathan from one end of the country to the other, about the way he and Henry had built a water wagon to overcome the drought two years ago, about the day that father and grandfather had hooted and hollered when young Jonathan rode around the paddock on his own for the first time. His words were a salve, and she needed one just now. So she just listened and let her eyes rise up to follow the slope of the knoll to the spot where Quiet Jack and old Thom Mason were digging her father's grave.

It seemed funny to her that they still called it "Celia's room." She hadn't slept alone in it since December of 1770. But that first night, lying there in the dark and quiet, it almost felt like she'd never left. The feeling of safety, of serenity, of knowing that only loved ones were nearby swept back in on her after all the years in New York.

All those years, she thought, and to what did they amount? She'd loved being a city belle, attending the parties and teas with the finer women of the city, living in the big house on Beekman Street and owning so many beautiful things, seeing the new plays and dancing to the happy music. But after the soldiers came and then after Godfrey died, those things were all gone from her life. The soldiers stayed in New York until 1783. It was awful at first when they came to live in the big house. But after Aubrey started to come around, the soldiers were much more respectful. He even got them to contribute some of their wages to help her manage the house.

After the treaty, they all sailed away, and then she had no money at all. In desperation, she began to take in boarders. The big beautiful house on Beekman Street, once a center of New York society, became a common boarding house. And Celia Carter, once a society belle, became just a woman who let rooms.

But it wasn't bad. She began to realize that she didn't miss the parties and the beautiful things. Not very much. And she especially didn't miss the feeling that her life was merely decorative, that it had no practical purpose. Those years when Godfrey made the decisions, controlled the money, kept his little secrets—she never felt she was entitled to complain about any of it. She never even really thought about it all that much. Until it was gone. Now as she looked back on those years, she could only form a picture of herself standing helplessly, smothered in velvet and silk. She would never be a belle again, probably never own beautiful things again. But she would never be just an ornament in someone else's life again either.

As she lay there and let the years roll through her mind, the years that separated her from the last time she lay in this bed, she thought as well about the peculiar man she'd married and the good man who never returned. She knew she would go to her grave still wondering about Godfrey Carter. Wondering about those years when he said so little about his work, but seemed to spend so much time at it. Then, after he died, the little pieces she uncovered that didn't fit with her image of the hard-working, ambitious, and successful businessman. Why had no soldiers quartered in their house when he was alive, but then appeared almost immediately after he'd died? How did it happen that he died while helping to load a ship when he never said a word to her about being on the docks and never came home with dirt on his hands or his clothes? Why was there no money when he died? What were the mysterious "business debts" that the solicitor claimed had eaten up all his savings? Why did the warehouse sell for so little? And what was she to make of the strange woman who came to the house one night a few months after he died, the brazen woman with rouged face and stuffed bodice, demanding money and claiming that the baby in her arms was the child of Godfrey Carter? It was a puzzle, and so many of the pieces didn't fit.

But when her thoughts turned to the tall British colonel, a warm feeling replaced the anxiety that memories of Godfrey caused in her now. For two years, until his regiment shipped out to Virginia, Aubrey Armistead had been at her house almost every day. At first, he came around to see the other officers there, then he came on the pretext of seeing the other officers but spent most of his time talking with Celia.

Then, in March of 1781 when fresh troops arrived in New York from England, Aubrey had used the crowding of the officers quarters as an excuse to move into one of the rooms at Celia's house. It was the only other room, besides hers, in the old servants' quarters. And it wasn't long before the evenings of proper conversation over tea in the library became evenings of affection and passion in the rooms above the kitchen. Aubrey was so unlike Godfrey: attentive, interested, kind. How odd, she thought once after hours of love-making with Aubrey, that a soldier should be so sweet and gentle and a gentlemen so harsh and abrupt.

They'd begun to talk about their lives after the war. Celia wanted Aubrey to come back to New York. He thought that might be possible if the British won, but he doubted that a retired British colonel would be welcome in New York if the Continentals won. When he came back from Virginia, they intended to talk more.

538

But she never heard from him again. She didn't think he'd been killed in Virginia. She'd asked many officers still in New York, and to a man they assumed he'd been one of the prisoners taken when Cornwallis surrendered. Most of them had been marched off through the Shenandoah Mountains to a prison in Frederick, Maryland. She'd heard that conditions were hard there and many had died of disease before they were repatriated. Had he died? Had he gone back to England? Had he settled in the west and fallen in love with someone else? She didn't know and feared she never would.

But now, back in this familiar place, all of that seemed more distant and more bearable. The sadness she felt at her father's death consumed her now, a different sadness than the one her mother's death had caused. Then she'd felt that Patience had died before her time, that the life had been squeezed out of her unfairly by events she couldn't control or endure. There was an emptiness about her mother's death, a sense of life unfulfilled that she didn't feel now. Henry died a few weeks after the apoplexy struck, not after years of suffering. And his life had been full of everything he could have hoped—except, of course, for Jonathan's death. He carried on that rich tradition that meant so much to him, and the farm he left to his children was a better, more prosperous place than the one his father had left to him.

Had that been the entire summary of his life, he probably would have died a satisfied man. But few people outside their family would look back on the life of Henry Houghton and remark that he was a good farmer or a fine father. No, he'd done things that lifted him above the ordinary plane on which most men live their lives. His mark was on history now, not just on a patch of land by the Still River. The farm he inherited was part of the British empire. The Union Jack hung from the flagstaff on the porch on the day they'd buried Henry's father. But when everyone arrived for the funeral tomorrow a different flag would hang there, one with thirteen bars and a circle of white stars.

The land was American now and so were the people. No one knew how long the young country would survive or what it would become; it was just a few years ago that most people thought there would never be a new country. But there was. And there was because men like Henry Houghton—and Henry Houghton's sons--had done their part. That was their legacy now. Henry would be buried on the hillside among his ancestors, but he didn't belong just to them any more. He belonged to his country now. His new country. And it gladdened Celia to know that. It would be part of her son's legacy, too, that he was the descendent of patriots—his richest inheritance.

It was comfortably warm on the morning of April nineteenth and, blessedly, the showers that fell in the night seemed to have passed. The mourners started arriving more than an hour before the service scheduled for noon. The Balfour boys came in a large wagon with more than a dozen neighbors. Even old James, blind now and lame, came with them to pay his respects. Other neighbors and old friends from Kent County, some even from Dover, came on foot and horseback. They walked to the porch and said hello to Celia and Savannah and Nathaniel. All wanted to tell a story about Henry, recapture a moment in time when their lives were touched by the great man. Tears fell gently as they told their tales to his children and to each other.

John Dickinson arrived and seemed deeply honored when Savannah told him that Henry had once called him "a man with more integrity than anyone I've ever known." Robert Morris came in a handsome coach which he left at the foot of the path so as not to appear ostentatious. Flint welcomed him and took the time to remind him of the night he and Jonathan came to see him for General Washington and how he'd saved the country by raising the money to prevent the army from disintegrating.

Other members of Congress appeared as well. And as people were gathering by the dooryard to walk up the hill together behind Henry's coffin, an unexpected mourner, a handsome, light-haired man arrived alone on horseback. Celia asked Savannah who he was, but Savannah didn't know. She nudged Flint, who was still reminiscing with Morris, and asked him. Flint glanced toward the man and Savannah saw once again the smile that had disappeared days ago. "Hamilton," he said, "Alexander Hamilton."

Flint excused himself from the conversation with Morris and walked quickly toward Hamilton. He resisted the instinct to salute, but did say, "Mornin', Colonel, it's so good of you to come." Hamilton slid off his horse with the same grace he brought to all things. He and Flint embraced, old warriors, old comrades. "How'd you get here so quickly from New York?"

"Oh, I wasn't in New York. I was in Philadelphia, and Henry's death was, of course, a cause of great sadness there. Things in Philadelphia are a disgrace. The Congress can't seem to act on anything.

When I arrived there, fewer than half the states even had delegates in attendance. They've been talking about the rebellion in western Massachusetts last year, but nobody feels they have any power to do anything about it. It really worries me, Flint. I think this government is close to breaking down."

"That's what worried Henry 'fore he died. He said that some of the delegates had a conference in Annapolis last fall and decided to git together in Philadelphia next month to look at the whole scheme a government. Ya know anythin' about that?"

"That's what happened. They went to Annapolis to talk about some commerce problems, but then they realized the problem was much larger than the customs duties the states are charging each other. Who knows where the meeting in Philadelphia will end up, but almost everyone thinks we need to make some changes. I heard from John Jay the other day, and he thinks we need a king. He even wrote to General Washington asking him if he'd be the king. I think he may be right. But then there're others who hate the idea of having a king and just want to try to build some kind of strong republic. I don't know. That's never been done before, not in a country the size of ours."

Even though these two old soldiers had rarely talked politics in the old days, they slid easily into this exchange, so American they didn't even think about it. Alexander Hamilton, thinker and politician, brilliant writer and financial mastermind, and Ezekial Isaac Flint, farmer and father, sharing mutual concern and mutual grief.

"It looks like I'll be one of the delegates from New York," Hamilton continued, "but I'm not confident we can get everyone to agree on anything." He pushed his hat back and Flint could see the exasperation in his eyes. "The struggle never seems to end, Flint. The feeling of closure we had at Yorktown was an illusion, I'm afraid. When you're trying to create a government where everyone has a say, you probably never get one that everybody likes."

Flint thanked Hamilton for coming, but Hamilton raised his hand to indicate that no thanks were necessary. "Duty called me here," he said. "I knew Henry Houghton only slightly, but I came to honor Jonathan's father. Over the years we were together, Jonathan and I must have told each other everything about our lives. I barely knew my own father and Jonathan had such love and respect for his. I always envied him that, but his telling me about it always seemed an act of great generosity, like he was sharing a beneficence with me. I shall always be grateful to him for that."

Then Hamilton looked down and hesitated for a moment. "And, of course, I'll always feel guilty that he died while under my command on Redoubt Number Ten. I've relived those moments hundreds of times in my mind, hoping each time that the outcome would be different, that Jonathan would be standing there with the rest of us as we surveyed the redoubt that we'd captured, sharing the feeling we all felt that night that the end had been reached at last."

His voice cracked a little and he struggled to hold back his anguish. Flint stepped to him and put an arm around his shoulder. Nothing more needed saying. The feelings that passed between them now required no words.

Flint led Hamilton to the family and introduced him to Savannah and Nathaniel. Hamilton expressed his sympathies about Henry and added a few carefully chosen words about their father's contributions to his country. Then he complimented Savannah on her fine-looking children and told Nathaniel how honored he was to meet the famous artist. When he turned away, Flint introduced him to Celia, saying she had come down from New York just a few days before. Hamilton's mind seemed to turn rapidly at that statement, then he and Flint exchanged sad, knowing glances.

As the gathering began the procession up the hill, Henry's three children, Flint, and his grandchildren walked in front behind the coffin. The neighbors and townspeople followed, then the visiting dignitaries. One of the Balfour boys guessed it was the biggest funeral ever held in Kent County.

Henry's coffin was placed on the ground beside the stone that marked his wife's resting place and the mourners gathered in a semicircle below it. Nathaniel looked sadly at his sisters, then stepped behind the coffin.

"My name is Nathaniel Houghton," he said. "And for all of us in the Houghton family, I want to thank you for coming today." Nathaniel paused to collect his thoughts, then began the eulogy that had been forming in his mind since he left Philadelphia.

"My father loved all of this land, but he loved this spot the best. When my brother and sisters and I were young, he would bring us up here. We'd walk through the gravestones and he'd tell us stories about the

542

relatives and ancestors who rest here now. He brought them to life for us and made them real.

"Each of those people had a hand in what this land became, had a hand in what each of us has become. My father knew that more surely than anyone. He believed that men and women have obligations. Obligations to honor the good intentions and hard work of those who came before them. Obligations to create opportunities for those who come after. No one took those obligations more seriously than Henry Houghton.

"When we were children the woods beyond me were thicker than they are now. He harvested many of those trees and saw them turned into fine homes and tall ships. He planted more trees to grow where those fell. And if you look below us, you can see a thriving farm, his great pride. He will rest comfortably here, knowing that he passed it on to us a better place than his father passed to him. And he would know that he honored his father and his father's father by so doing.

"He had those same feelings about his community and his state and what came to be his country. My father never bore the illusion that anything valuable came easily. He was patient, but persistent. When one thing didn't work, he tried another. If the objective mattered, there was no end to the work and ingenuity he'd commit to it. All of you know that about him, though you saw it in different ways. The Henry Houghton who spent months tinkering with a plow to get it to cut straighter and deeper rows was the same man who spent months in Congress trying to build consensus for some improvement in the law.

"My father had dreams, dreams for himself, dreams for his children, dreams for his country. But he also had the good sense to know that other people had dreams too—even his own children—and they didn't always coincide with his. He was never a man to make fiery statements or lead bold charges. His strength was accommodation, coordination, compromise. Henry Houghton's great lesson to us was this: perfection is singular, but life is plural. He knew that we could never have exactly the country that John Adams wanted, or John Dickinson or Edward Rutledge. But he believed that if all these good men worked together, they could make a country in which all of us could take pride, imperfect though its details might seem to any of us.

"If God sheds his blessings on our new country, then my father and my brother and the other brave and wise men who made it will fill a pantheon in the minds and hearts of our posterity. Their names will endure and people will celebrate the most important of their deeds. My father would probably be amused by that because he knew these men and he admired them. But he also knew they were not gods or saints. They were good men, but like him they were just human. They had quirks and flaws, tempers and discontents. He would remember their doubts, their second guesses, their bad predictions, and their misjudgments.

"History is a powerful cleanser. It washes away the stains of doubt and removes the blight of failure. An accomplishment, an invention always looks easier and more solid after it's done. Looking backward, you don't see all the choices that were faced, all the uncertainties that had to be borne, all the false starts.

"For a long time after he went off to Philadelphia the first time, my father had doubts about independence. Many of you here today did as well. He wondered, too, whether men so untutored in the arts of government could learn quickly enough how to govern themselves. Some of you shared those doubts as well. Prudence required him and others to feel the way they did. Their doubts were legitimate. And the slow process of overcoming them was an important and healthy part of this country's birth.

"But when future generations look back at this time, they won't see those doubts, those uncertainties, those powerful disagreements that divided good men. What reasonable man would not have doubted the chances of revolting against a king when no one had ever done it before? What responsible man would not have wondered whether independent people scattered over a thousand miles could govern themselves when that had never happened before in the entire history of the world? My father suffered those uncertainties and those doubts. But like our new country, he confronted them and overcame them.

"We pass our beloved father on to history now. I hope his memory will not be clouded by simplicity and romanticism. Like so many of his colleagues in the statehouses and Congress who tried to carve a secure path from tyranny to self-government, like so many Americans who took up arms, Henry Houghton was an ordinary man who lived in extraordinary times. But it was the measure of his life, as it was the measure of so many lives in our time, that he saw the chance to make life better and he pursued it with all the wisdom and courage and energy he could muster.

"Henry Houghton is part of our history now. But let us not deify him, for that does him great injustice. Let us remember his doubts as well as his conclusions, his false starts as well as his successful finishes. If we fail to do that, then those who come after us will think that all that freedom demands, all that self-government requires, is a few great men. Henry Houghton would want us to tell them that they're wrong, that what's required for a people to be free, for them to govern themselves wisely is not great men but simply good men willing to suffer and sacrifice and work together in their pursuit of great goals. That is the lesson of Henry Houghton's life, his good life."

Nathaniel stepped back when he was done and moved to stand beside Savannah. She reached down and squeezed his hand as they watched young men slide the ropes that lowered Henry's coffin into the ground. Then his grandchildren stepped forward—Godfrey Houghton Carter who had never been here before and the three children of Savannah and Flint who had never been anywhere else—and each tossed a small handful of dirt into the hole.

Then the mourners started to move slowly back down the hill. All except Nathaniel, who lingered by the graveside to say the words that were not in his eulogy but should have been, the words he'd never spoken to his father but should have. He looked down into the grave at his father's coffin, sprinkled with dirt from the land he cherished and said softly, "I love you."

Nathaniel stood silently for a moment longer then turned and started back down the hill, toward the Houghton farm that tied him to all the souls in the ground behind him, toward the Still River that had flowed gently past them for generations, and toward the vast green land beyond where he hoped free people would always remember the debt they owed to the brother and the father, the stalwart soldier and the patient politician, who left it better than they found it.

29721641R00307

Made in the USA
Middletown, DE
29 February 2016